GIVEN BY NESFA PRESS

www.NESFA.ORG

WAR & SPACE

BY LESTER DEL REY

edited by
STEVEN H SILVER

NESFA
PRESS

Post Office Box 809, Framingham, MA 01701
www.nesfa.org/press
2009

© 2009 by The Estate of Lester Del Rey

"The Magnificent Lester" © 2009 by Frederik Pohl

Cover Art © 2009 by John Picacio

Cover Design by Alice Lewis & John Picacio

ALL RIGHTS RESERVED.
NO PART OF THIS BOOK MAY BE REPRODUCED IN ANY FORM OR BY ANY ELECTRONIC, MAGICAL OR MECHANICAL MEANS INCLUDING INFORMATION STORAGE AND RETRIEVAL WITHOUT PERMISSION IN WRITING FROM THE PUBLISHER, EXCEPT BY A REVIEWER, WHO MAY QUOTE BRIEF PASSAGES IN A REVIEW.

FIRST EDITION, August 2009

International Standard Book Number
1-886778-76-0
[978-1-886778-76-4]

First Appearances

"For I Am A Jealous People!," first printed in *Star Short Novels*, edited by Frederik Pohl, New York, NY: Ballantine, 1954.

"Return Engagement," first printed in *Galaxy*, August 1961

"Omega and the Wolf-Girl," first printed in *Out of This World Adventures*, July 1950 [reprinted as "And the Darkness"].

"Uneasy Lies the Head," first printed in *10 Story Fantasy*, Spring 1951.

"And There Was Light," first printed in *Future Combined with Science Fiction Stories*, July 1951.

"Battleground," first printed in *Fantastic Universe*, July 1954.

"Kindness," first printed in *Astounding*, October 1944.

"Wind Between the Worlds," first printed in *Galaxy*, March 1951.

"Earthbound," first printed in *Galaxy*, August 1963

"Dark Mission," first printed in *Astounding*, July 1940.

"Shadows of Empire," first printed in *Future Combined with Science Fiction Stories*, July/August 1950.

"Moon-Blind," first printed in *Space Science Fiction*, September 1952, as by Erik van Lhin.

"Thunder in Space," first printed in *Amazing*, June 1962.

"My Name Is Legion," first printed in *Astounding*, June 1942.

"The Deadliest Female," first printed in *Worlds Beyond*, February 1951.

"Helping Hand," first printed in *Star 4*, edited by Frederik Pohl, November 1958.

"No Place Like Home," first printed in *Astounding*, August 1952.

"Done Without Eagles," first printed in *Astounding*, August 1940, as by Philip St. John.

"And It Comes Out Here," first printed in *Galaxy*, February 1951.

"The Band Played On," first printed in *Infinity*, June 1957.

"The Faithful," first printed in *Astounding*, April 1938.

"The Luck of Ignatz," first printed in *Astounding*, August 1939.

"Operation Distress," first printed in *Galaxy*, August 1951.

"Fool's Errand," first printed in *Science Fiction Quarterly*, November 1951.

"The Stars Look Down," first printed in *Astounding*, August 1940.

"The Still Waters," first printed in *Fantastic Universe*, June 1955 [reprinted as "In the Still Waters"].

"The One-Eyed Man," first printed in *Astounding*, May 1945, as by Philip St. John.

"Habit," first printed in *Astounding*, November 1939.

"Nerves," first printed in *Astounding*, September 1942.

For
Robin and Melanie
and, as always,
Elaine

and with thanks to
John Alvarez, R. Alvarez, Lester del Rey, Ramon Alvarez del Rey, Cameron Hall, Marion Henry, Philip James, Wade Kaempfert, Leonard Knapp, Henry Marion, Edson McCann, John Raymond, Charles Satterfield, Philip St. John, Erik van Lihn, John Vincent, and Kenneth Wright

Contents

The Magnificent Lester (Frederik Pohl)	11
For I Am a Jealous People!	15
Return Engagement	53
Omega and the Wolf-Girl	65
Uneasy Lies the Head	81
And There Was Light	97
Battleground	107
Kindness	119
Wind Between the Worlds	133
Earthbound	169
Dark Mission	173
Shadows of Empire	189
Moon-Blind	203
Thunder in Space	229
My Name Is Legion	257
The Deadliest Female	279
Helping Hand	291
No Place Like Home	311
Done Without Eagles	321
And It Comes Out Here	337
The Band Played On	349
The Faithful	375
The Luck of Ignatz	385
Operation Distress	413
Fool's Errand	423
The Stars Look Down	429
The Still Waters	461
The One-Eyed Man	479
Habit	499
Nerves	511

War & Space

by Lester Del Rey

The Magnificent Lester

Quite a few years ago—well, eighty of them, to be exact—I was the teen-age editor of two professional science-fiction magazines for the giant pulp firm of Popular Publications. I didn't pay much for the stories that went into my magazines but I did pay something, and so most of the science-fiction writers of that era dropped by from time to time to see if I would care to relieve them of a few of their stack of *Astounding* rejects. People like hoary old Ray Cummings and bright-minted new stars like L. Sprague de Camp came by my little office at the end of 42d Street, just where it stops dead at the East River, and one day our switchboard girl, Ethel Klock, informed me that I had a new visitor named Lester del Rey. Though I'd never met the man I knew the name; I had seen it, enviously, any number of times on the *Astounding* contents page. "Shoot him right in!" I commanded, hoping that he would come bearing manuscripts, and a couple of minutes later there he was, short, angel-faced, no more than a couple of years older than myself—and, yes, with two short-story manuscripts in his hands!

There is an established procedure for such events. It doesn't allow the editor to snatch the typescripts from the author's hands, or the author to throw them in from the doorway without a word. There has to be a little chatting back and forth first, so I had to wait until Lester was back in the elevator to start reading. The stories were short. I finished them both in a quarter of an hour.

Then I rejected them both.

What was wrong with them? I don't remember. What were they about? I don't remember that, either. And not only did I bounce them, so did every other editor Lester showed them to. Years later I asked him what had become of them. He said he had no idea, didn't remember anything about them, and hoped I would never ask him such embarrassing questions again.

So that was my unpromising start to knowing Lester del Rey. Fortunately later on things got better.

Later on they did, as I say, but it took a few years. John Campbell got over his nasty habit of rejecting any of Lester's stories, so he had nothing to sell me; and then the Air Force invited me to join them for World War II so I had no magazine to buy them for, anyway. Then, postwar, we ran into each other now and then, and in 1947 we ran into the big one. That was the '47 World Science Fiction Convention in Philadelphia. We were both there. When it was over we were having a cup of coffee together somewhere when we got to thinking. We had had such a great time mingling again with our nearest and dearest (as well as some of our farthest and dislikedest) from the world of science fiction that we decided we really ought to organize some sort of local sf group so we have more of those great times. So Lester commandeered a couple of his friends and brought them to my Greenwich Village apartment, where I had collected a few of mine, and we sat down and created the Hydra Club. (Why Hydra? Because there were nine of us there, and the mythological Hydra had had nine heads.) This was a public service because for years thereafter the Hydra Club was the place where sf writers from out of town visited when they came to New York to find people they could talk to. (Out of town sometimes meant very out of town, as from England, which gave us visits from Arthur Clarke, and from Australia (that was A. Bertram Chandler) and from many points in between.)

The Hydra Club wasn't just a place to have a drink or two while trading shop talk with colleagues. Lester and I both found wives there, and we two couples made a habit of going to cons together. What made that easy is that after a while Lester and Evelyn del Rey came out to visit with Carol and me and our growing number of children in our big old house in Red Bank, New Jersey. Their intention was to spend a weekend. They wound up staying seventeen years. (They did at some point buy a house of their own down the street.) It might have been longer, but one day, driving toward a little vacation in Florida, their car got entangled in the wake of an eighteen-wheeler and was sent spinning off the road. Evelyn was thrown clear, but then the car rolled over on her and she was killed.

After that Lester could not stay in their house. He sold it for a pitiful amount—furniture, books, wine cellar and all—to the first person who thought to make him an offer, and moved back to the city.

For all those years we had been keeping busy, Lester writing, me doing some of that but also fooling around with editing and other diversions. After putting together a string of anthologies for Ian Ballantine I wound up as editor of a couple of science-fiction magazines, *Galaxy* and *If*. It was not a well-paying job but I loved it. It gave some welcome perks, including a full-time assistant. When hiring a new one I interviewed a recent Barnard graduate named Judy-Lynn Benjamin, who seemed to be bright and energetic enough but presented two problems. One was that her specialty was critical studies of the works of James Joyce and she knew nothing at all about science fiction. That I figured could be handled; I would not ask her to make any buy-or-bounce decisions, and everything else I could easily teach her. The other struck me as tougher. Judy-Lynn was an achondroplastic dwarf, not much over three feet tall, and I didn't know how she would manage to reach the top drawers of the filing cabinets. But I took a chance, and it turned out that she had dealt with far tougher problems

Introduction 13

in her life. Actually she worked out rather well. After I left the magazines Judy-Lynn went to work for Ballantine Books, winding up running the enterprise.

Lester entered the picture when my publisher, Bob Guinn, urged me to add a fantasy magazine to my group. I had nothing against fantasy, but I didn't have a great deal of interest in it, either, and anyway I didn't want to add to my work load. So I persuaded Lester, now a widower for some years, to come aboard as its editor. He did well and the three of us got along well, too, in fact better than I realized until I got a phone call from Lester to say that he and Judy-Lynn were getting married, and would I care to be his best man?

I would. They did it. And after a while he joined Judy-Lynn at Ballantine, And—no surprise to anyone who knew them—with Lester handling the fantasy side of the operation while Judy-Lynn continued with the sf they were fabulously successful, given their own imprint of Del Rey Books and leading the field in the number of their books that wound up on the *New York Times* best-seller list.

But one of the penalties of being an achondroplastic dwarf is the likelihood of a short life span. After a goodly number of very good years Judy-Lynn had a massive stroke and then died of it, and a few years later Lester followed her.

They will not be forgotten. No other husband-wife editorial team has come close to matching their record, and I don't really think anyone ever will.

Well, I've been talking about Lester del Rey as a friend and as an editor and haven't spent as much time as I should have liked in his incarnation as writer. But that's all right. Here in this volume are a couple dozen of his best stories, some of which I was lucky enough to publish myself (including the one I think close to his very best of all, "For I Am a Jealous People!"), so you can form your own opinions. Just turn the page and start reading.

–Frederik Pohl
Palatine, Illinois
September 2008

For I Am a Jealous People!

1

...the keepers of the house shall tremble, and the strong men shall bow themselves...and the doors shall be shut in the streets, when the sound of the grinding is low...they shall be afraid of that which is high, and fears shall be in the way, and the almond tree shall flourish...because man goeth to his long home, and the mourners go about the streets...

Ecclesiastes, 12:3-5
THE BOOK OF THE JEWS

There was the continuous shrieking thunder of an alien rocket overhead as the Reverend Amos Strong stepped back into the pulpit. He straightened his square, thin shoulders slightly, and the gaunt hollows in his cheeks deepened. For a moment he hesitated, while his dark eyes turned upward under bushy, grizzled brows. Then he moved forward, placing the torn envelope and telegram on the lectern with his notes. The blue-veined hand and knobby wrist that projected from the shiny black serge of his sleeve hardly trembled.

Unconsciously, his eyes turned toward the pew where his wife should be, before he remembered that Ruth would not be there this time. She had been delayed by the arrival of the message and had read it before sending it on to him. Now she could not be expected. It seemed strange to him. She hadn't missed service since Richard was born nearly thirty years ago.

The sound of the rocket hissed its way into silence over the horizon, and Amos stepped forward, gripping the dusty surface of the rickety lectern with both hands, he straightened and forced his throat into the pattern that would give his voice the resonance and calm it needed.

"I have just received final confirmation that my son was killed in the battle of the moon," he told the puzzled congregation, which had been rustling uncertainly since he was first interrupted. He lifted his voice, and the resonance in it deepened. "I had asked, if it were possible, that this cup might pass from me. Nevertheless, not as I will, Lord, but as Thou wilt."

He turned from their shocked faces, closing his ears to the sympathetic cries of others who had suffered. The Church had been built when Wesley was twice its present size, but the troubles that had hit the people had driven them into the worn old building until it was nearly filled. He pulled his notes to him, forcing his mind from his own loss to the work that had filled his life.

"The text today is drawn from Genesis," he told them. "Chapter seventeen, seventh verse; and chapter twenty-six, fourth verse. The promise which God made to Abraham and again to Isaac." He read from the Bible before him, turning to the pages unerringly at the first try. "And I will establish my covenant between me and thee, and thy seed after thee, in their generations, for an everlasting covenant, to be a God unto thee, and to thy seed after thee.

"And I will make thy seed to multiply as the stars of heaven, and will give unto thy seed all these countries: and in thy seed shall all the nations of the earth be blessed."

He had memorized most of his sermon, no longer counting on inspiration to guide him as it had once done. He began smoothly, hearing his own words in snatches as he drew the obvious and comforting answer to their uncertainty. God had promised man the earth as an everlasting covenant. Why then should men he afraid or lose faith because alien monsters had swarmed down out of the emptiness between the stars to try man's faith? As in the days of bondage in Egypt or captivity in Babylon, there would always be trials and times when the faint-hearted should waver, but the eventual outcome was clearly promised.

He had delivered a sermon from the same text in his former parish of Clyde when the government had first begun building its base on the moon, drawing heavily in that case from the reference to the stars of heaven to quiet the doubts of those who felt that man had no business in space. It was then that Richard had announced his commission in the lunar colony, using Amos' own words to defend his refusal to enter the ministry. It was the last he saw of the boy.

He had used the text one other time, over forty years before, but the reason was lost, together with the passion that had won him fame as a boy evangelist. He could remember the sermon only because of the shock on the bearded face of his father when he had misquoted a phrase. It was one of his few clear memories of the period before his voice changed and his evangelism came to an abrupt end.

He had tried to recapture his inspiration after ordination, bitterly resenting the countless intrusions of marriage and fatherhood on his spiritual forces. But at last he had recognized that God no longer intended him to be a modern Peter the Hermit, and resigned himself to the work he could do. Now he was back in the parish where he had first begun; and if he could no longer fire the souls of his flock, he could at least help somewhat with his memorized rationalizations for the horror of the alien invasion.

Another ship thundered overhead, nearly drowning his words. Six months before, the great ships had exploded out of nothing in space and had fallen carefully to the moon, to attack the forces there. In another month they had begun a few forays against Earth itself.

And now, while the world haggled and struggled to unite against them, they were establishing bases all over and apparently setting out to conquer the world mile by mile.

Amos saw the faces below him turn up, hate-filled and uncertain. He raised his voice over the thunder, and finished hastily, moving quickly through the end of the service.

He hesitated as the congregation stirred. The ritual was over and his words were said, but there had been no real service. Slowly, as if by themselves, his lips opened, and he heard his voice quoting the Twenty-seventh Psalm. "The Lord is my light and my salvation; whom shall I fear?"

His voice was soft, but he could feel the reaction of the congregation as the surprisingly timely words registered. "Though an host should encamp against me, my heart shall not fear; though war should rise against me, in this will I be confident." The air seemed to quiver, as it had done long ago when God had seemed to hold direct communion with him, and there was no sound from the pews when he finished. "Wait on the Lord: be of good courage, and he shall strengthen thine heart; wait, I say, on the Lord."

The warmth of that mystic glow lingered as he stepped quietly from the pulpit. Then there was the sound of motorcycles outside, and a pounding on the door. The feeling vanished.

Someone stood up and sudden light began pouring in from outdoors. There was a breath of the hot, droughty physical world with its warning of another dust storm, and a scattering of grasshoppers on the steps to remind the people of the earlier damage to their crops. Amos could see the bitterness flood back over them in tangible waves, even before they noticed the short, plump figure of Dr. Alan Miller.

"Amos! Did you hear?" He was wheezing as if he had been running. "Just came over the radio while you were in here gabbling."

He was cut off by the sound of more motorcycles. They swept down the single main street of Wesley, heading west. The riders were all in military uniform, carrying weapons and going at the top speed of their machines. Dust erupted behind them, and Doc began coughing and swearing. In the last few years, he had grown more and more outspoken about his atheism; when Amos had first known him, during the earlier pastorate in Wesley, the man had at least shown some respect for the religion of others.

"All right," Amos said sharply. "You're in the house of God, Doc. What came over the radio?"

Doc caught himself and choked back his coughing fit. "Sorry. But damn it, man, the aliens have landed in Clyde, only fifty miles away. They've set up a base there! That's what all those rockets going over meant."

There was a sick gasp from the people who had heard, and a buzz as the news was passed back to others. Faces grayed. Some dropped back to the hard seats, while others pressed forward, trying to reach Doc, shouting questions at him.

Amos let himself be shoved aside, hardly noticing the reaction of his flock. It was Clyde where he had served before coming here again. He was trying to picture the alien ships dropping down, scouring the town ahead of them with gas and bullets. The grocer on the corner with his nine children, the lame deacon who had served there, the two Aimes sisters with their horde of dogs and cats and their constant crusade against younger sinners. He tried to picture the green-skinned, humanoid aliens moving through the town, invading the church, desecrating the altar! And there was Anne Seyton, who had been Richard's sweetheart, though of another faith...

"What about the garrison nearby?" a heavy farmer yelled over the crowd. "I had a boy there, and he told me they could handle any ships when they were landing! Shell their tubes when they were coming down..."

Doc shook his head. "Half an hour before the landing, there was a cyclone up there. It took the roof off the main building and wrecked the whole training garrison."

"Jim!" The big man screamed out the name, and began dragging his frail wife behind him, out toward his car. "If they got Jim..."

Others started to rush after him, but another procession of motorcycles stopped them. This time they were traveling slower, and a group of tanks were rolling behind them. The rear tank drew abreast, slowed, and stopped, while a dirty-faced man in a major's untidy uniform stuck his head out.

"You folks get under cover! Ain't you heard the news? Go home and stick to your radios, before a snake plane starts potshooting the bunch of you for fun. The snakes'll be heading straight over this town if they're after Topeka, like it looks!" He jerked back down and began swearing at someone inside. The tank jerked to a start and began heading away toward Clyde. There had been enough news of the sport of the alien planes in the papers. The people melted from the church. Amos tried to stop them for at least a short prayer and to give them time to collect their thoughts, but gave up after most of the people began moving away. A minute later, he was standing alone with Doc Miller.

"Better get home, Amos," Doc suggested. "My car's half a block down. Suppose I give you a lift?"

Amos nodded wearily. His bones felt dry and brittle, and there was a dust in his mouth thicker than that in the air. He felt old, and for the first time, almost useless. He followed the doctor quietly, welcoming the chance to ride the six short blocks to the little house the parish furnished him.

A car of ancient age and worse repair rattled toward them as they reached Doc's auto. It stopped, and a man in dirty overalls leaned out, his face working jerkily. "Are you prepared, brothers? Are you saved? Armageddon has come, as the Book foretold. Get right with God, brothers! The end of the world as foretold is at hand, amen!"

"Where does the Bible foretell alien races around other suns?" Doc shot at him.

The man blinked, frowned, and yelled something about sinners burning forever in hell before he started his rickety car again. Amos sighed. Now, with the rise of their troubles, fanatics would spring up to cry doom and false gospel more than ever, to the harm of all honest religion. He had never decided whether they were somehow useful to God or whether they were inspired by the forces of Satan.

"In my Father's house are many mansions," he quoted to Doc as they started up the street. "It's quite possibly an allegorical reference to other worlds in the heavens."

Doc grimaced, and shrugged. Then he sighed and dropped one hand from the wheel onto Amos' knee. "I heard about Dick, Amos. I'm sorry. The first baby I ever delivered—and the best-looking!" He sighed again, staring toward Clyde as Amos found no words to answer. "I don't get it. Why don't we ever drop atom bombs on them? Why didn't the moon base use their missiles?"

Amos had no answer to that, either. There was a rumor that all the major powers had sent their whole supply of atomic explosives up to the moon base early in the invasion, and that a huge meteorite had buried the stockpile under tons of debris, where there had been no chance to excavate it. It matched the other cases of accidents that had beset all human resistance.

He got out at the unpainted house where he lived, taking Doc's hand silently and nodding his thanks.

He would have to organize his thoughts this afternoon. When night fell and the people could move about without the danger of being shot at by chance alien planes, the church bell would summon them, and they would need spiritual guidance. If he could help them to stop trying to understand God, and to accept Him... There had been that moment in the church when God had seemed to enfold him and the congregation in warmth—the old feeling of true fulfillment. Maybe, now in the hour of its greatest need, some measure of inspiration had returned.

He found Ruth setting the table. Her small, quiet body moved as efficiently as ever, though her face was puffy and her eyes were red. "I'm sorry I couldn't make it, Amos. But right after the telegram, Anne Seyton came. She'd heard—before we did. And..."

The television set was on, showing headlines from the Kansas City *Star*, and he saw there was no need to tell her the news. He put a hand on one of hers. "God has only taken what he gave, Ruth. We were blessed with Richard for thirty years."

"I'm all right." She pulled away and picked up a pot, turning toward the kitchen, her back frozen in a line of nut misery. "Didn't you hear what I said? Anne's here. Dick's wife! They were married before he left, secretly—right after you talked with him about the difference in religion. You'd better see her, Amos. She knows about her people in Clyde."

He watched his wife move from the room, his heart heavy with her grief, while the words penetrated. He'd never forbidden marriage, he had only warned the boy, who had been so much like Ruth. He hesitated, and finally turned toward the tiny second bedroom. There was a muffled answer to his knock, and the lock clicked rustily.

"Anne?" he said. The room was darkened, but he could see her blonde head and the thin, almost unfeminine lines of her figure. He put out a hand and felt her slim fingers in his palm. As she turned toward the weak light, he saw no sign of tears, but her hand shook with her dry shudders. "Anne, Ruth has just told me that God has given us a daughter…"

"God!" She spat the word out harshly, while the hand jerked back. "God, Reverend Strong? Whose God? The one who sends meteorites against Dick's base, plagues of insects and drought against our farms? The God who uses tornadoes to make it easy for the snakes to land? That God, Reverend Strong? Dick gave you a daughter, and he's dead! Dead! Dead!"

Amos backed out of the room. He had learned to stand the faint mockery with which Doc pronounced the name of the Lord, but this was something that set his skin into goose pimples and caught at his throat. Anne had been of a different faith, but she had always seemed religious before.

It was probably only hysteria. He turned toward the kitchen to find Ruth and send her in to the girl.

Overhead, the staccato bleating of a ramjet cut through the air in a sound he had never heard. But the radio description fitted it perfectly. It could be no Earth ship with such a noise!

Then there was another and another, until they blended together into a steady drone.

And over it came the sudden firing of a heavy gun, while a series of rapid thuds came from the garden behind the house. Rover let out two loud barks, and then screamed in animal agony!

Amos stumbled toward the back door, but Ruth was already ahead of him. "Dick's dog! Now they've got his dog!" she cried out.

Before Amos could stop her, she threw back the door and darted out. There was another burst of shots and a sick cry. Ruth was crumpling before he could get to the doorway.

2

My God, my God, why hast thou forsaken me? I am poured out like water, and all my bones are out of joint: my heart is like wax; it is melted in the midst of my bowels. My strength is dried up like a potsherd; and my tongue cleaveth to my jaws; and thou hast brought me into the dust of death.

Psalm 22:1,14,15
THE BOOK OF THE JEWS

There were no more shots as he ran to her and gathered her into his arms. The last of the alien delta planes had gone over, heading for Topeka or whatever city they were attacking.

Ruth was still alive. One of the ugly slugs had caught her in the abdomen, ripping away part of her side, and the wound was bleeding horribly. But he felt her heart still beating, and she moaned faintly when he lifted her. Then, as he put her on the couch, she opened her eyes briefly, saw him, and tried to smile. Her lips moved, and he dropped his head to hear.

"I'm sorry, Amos. Foolish. Nuisance. Sorry."

Her eyes closed, but she smiled again after he bent to kiss her lips. "Glad now. Waited so long."

Anne stood in the doorway, staring unbelievingly. But as Amos stood up, she unfroze and darted to the medicine cabinet, to come back and begin snipping away the ruined dress and trying to staunch the flow of blood.

Amos reached for the phone, unable to see it clearly. He mumbled something to the operator, and a minute later to Doc Miller. He'd been afraid that the doctor would still be out. He had a feeling that Doc had promised to come, but could remember no words.

The flow of blood outside the wound had been stopped, but Ruth was white, even to her lips. Anne forced him back to a chair, her fingers gentle on his arm.

"I'm sorry, Father Strong. I—I..." He stood up after a few minutes and went over to stand beside Ruth, letting his eyes turn toward the half-set table. There was a smell of scorching food in the air, and he went out to the old wood-burning stove to pull the pans off and drop them into the sink. Anne followed, but he hardly saw her, until he heard her begin to cry softly. There were tears this time.

"The ways of God are not the ways of man, Anne," he said, and the words released a flood of his own emotions. He sank tiredly onto a stool, his hands falling limply onto his lap. He dropped his head against the table, feeling the weakness and uncertainty of age. "We love the carnal form and our hearts are broken when it is gone. Only God can know all of any of us or count the tangled threads of our lives. It isn't good to hate God!"

She moved beside him as he rose and returned to the living room. "I don't, Father Strong. I never did." He couldn't be sure of the honesty of it, but he made no effort to question her, and she sighed. "Mother Ruth isn't dead yet!"

He was saved from any answer by the door being slammed open as Doc Miller came rushing in. The plump little man took one quick look at Ruth and was beside her, reaching for plasma and his equipment. He handed the plasma bottle to Anne, and began working carefully.

"There's a chance," he said finally. "If she were younger or stronger, I'd say there was an excellent chance. But now, since you believe in it, you'd better do some fancy praying."

"I've been praying," Amos told him, realizing that it was true. The prayers had begun inside his head before she was outside the door, and they had never ceased.

They moved her gently, couch and all, into the bedroom, where the blinds could be drawn, and where the other sounds of the house couldn't reach her. Doc gave Anne a shot of something and sent her into the other bedroom. He turned to Amos, but didn't insist when the minister shook his head.

"I'll stay here, Amos," Doc said, "with you. As long as I can until I get another emergency call. The switchboard girl knows where I am."

He went back into the bedroom without closing the door. Amos stood in the center of the living room, his head bowed, for long minutes.

It was a whining sound that finally called him back to the world around him. He went to the back door and stared out. The Scotty was still alive, pulling its little body along the dirt of the garden toward the house. The whole hind section was paralyzed, and the animal must have been in agony from the horrible wound on its back. But it saw him and whined again, struggling toward him.

He went out automatically. He had never been fond of the dog, nor it of him. But now there was an understanding between them. "Shh, Rover," he told the dog. "Quiet, boy. The mistress is all right."

Rover whined again, and a wet tongue caressed Amos' hand. He bent as gently as he could to examine the wound. Then he stood up, trying to reassure the animal.

He found Richard's hunting rifle in one of the trunks and made sure it was unrusted. He loaded it carefully, feeling his skin crawl at the touch of the gun. It seemed strange to use the weapon on Rover when the dog and Richard had both found such pleasure in hunting with this same gun. But he couldn't see the animal suffering. Rover looked up and tried to bark as he saw the gun. Amos dropped beside him, feeling that the dog knew what he meant to do. The eyes looked up at him with a curious understanding as he placed the muzzle near the animal's head. Amos stopped, wondering. The wound was a horrible thing—but Doc might be able to save the animal, even though he was no veterinarian. If it had been a wounded human, the attempt would have to be made. Rover drew back his lips, and Amos stopped, expecting a growl. He even reached out to put the gun away. But the wet tongue came out again, brushing across his hand, accepting the fate intended, and blessing him for it. He patted the dog's head, closed his eyes, and pulled the trigger. It was merciful. There wasn't even time for a cry of pain.

If the dog had fought him, if it had struggled against its fate in a final desire to live... But it had submitted to what it considered a superior being. Only man could defy a Higher Will. Rover had accepted...and Rover was dead. He buried the small body in the soft dirt of the garden.

Doc stood in the doorway when he started back for the house. "I heard the shot and thought you were trying something foolish," the doctor said. "I should have known better, I guess, with your beliefs. Then I waited here, listening for a snake plane, ready to pull you back. According to the television, they must be returning by now."

Amos nodded. He found Ruth still in a coma, with nothing he could do. Then he remembered the planes and turned to watch the television. Topeka was off the air, but another station was showing news films.

Hospitals, schools, and similar places seemed to have been the chief targets of the aliens. Gas had accounted for a number of deaths, though those could have been prevented if instructions had been followed. But the incendiaries had caused the greatest damage.

And the aliens had gotten at least as rough treatment as they had meted out. Of the forty that had been counted, twenty-nine were certainly down.

"I wonder if they're saying prayers to God for their dead?" Doc asked. "Or doesn't your God extend his mercy to races other than man?"

Amos shook his head slowly. It was a new question to him. But there could be only one answer. "God rules the entire universe, Doc. But these evil beings surely offer him no worship!"

"Are you sure? They're pretty human!" Amos looked back to the screen, where one of the alien corpses could be seen briefly. They did look almost human, though squat and heavily muscled. Their skin was green, and they wore no clothes. There was no nose, aside from two orifices under their curiously flat ears that quivered as if in breathing. But they were human enough to have passed for deformed men, if they had been worked on by good make-up men.

They were creatures of God, just as he was! And as such, could he deny them? Then his mind recoiled, remembering the atrocities they had committed, the tortures that had been reported, and the utter savageness so out of keeping with their inconceivably advanced ships. They were things of evil who had denied their birthright as part of God's domain. For evil, there could be only hatred. And from evil, how could there be worship of anything but the powers of darkness?

The thought of worship triggered his mind into an awareness of his need to prepare a sermon for the evening. It would have to be something simple; both he and his congregation were in no mood for rationalizations. Tonight he would have to serve God through their emotions. The thought frightened him. He tried to cling for strength to the brief moment of glory he had felt in the morning, but even that seemed far away.

There was the wail of a siren outside, rising to an ear-shattering crescendo, and the muffled sound of a loudspeaker with its amplifier driven to high distortion levels.

He stood up at last and moved out onto the porch with Doc as the tank came by. It was limping on treads that seemed to be about to fall apart, and the amplifier and speaker were mounted crudely on top. It pushed down the street, repeating its message over and over.

"Get out of town! Everybody clear out! This is an order to evacuate! The snakes are coming! Human forces have been forced to retreat to regroup. The snakes are heading this way, heading toward Topeka. They are looting and killing as they go. Get out of town! Everybody clear out!"

It paused, and another voice blared out, sounding like that of the major who had warned the town earlier. "Get the hell out, all of you! Get out while you've still got your skins outside of you. We've been licked. Shut up, Blake! We've had the holy living pants beat off us, and we're going back to momma. Get out, scram, vamoose! The snakes are coming! Beat it!"

It staggered down the street, rumbling its message, and now other stragglers began following it—men in trucks, piled together like cattle; men in ancient cars of every description. Then another amplifier sounded from one of the trucks.

"Stay under cover until night! Then get out! The snakes won't be here at once. Keep cool. Evacuate in order, and under cover of darkness. We're holing up ourselves when we get to a safe place. This is your last warning. Stay under cover now, and evacuate as soon as it's dark."

There was a scream from the sky, and alien planes began dipping down. Doc pulled Amos back into the house, but not before he saw men being cut to ribbons by missiles that seemed to fume and burst into fire as they hit. Some of the men on the retreat made cover. When the planes were gone, they came out and began regrouping, leaving the dead and hauling the wounded with them.

"Those men need me!" Amos protested.

"So does Ruth," Doc told him. "Besides, we're too old, Amos. We'd only get in the way. They have their own doctors and chaplains, probably. Those poor devils are risking their lives to save us, damn it. The Army must have piled all its movable wounded together and sent them to warn us and to decoy the planes away from the rest who are probably sneaking back through the woods and fields. They're heroes, Amos, and they'd hate your guts for wasting what they're trying to do. I've been listening to one of the local stations, and they've already been through hell."

He turned on his heel and went back to the bedroom. The television program tardily began issuing evacuation orders to all citizens along the road from Clyde to Topeka, together with instructions. For some reason, the aliens seemed not to spot anything smaller than a tank in movement at night, and all orders were to wait until then.

Doc came out again, and Amos looked up at him, feeling his head bursting, but with one clear idea fixed in it. "Ruth can't be moved, can she, Doc?"

"No, Amos." Doc sighed. "But it won't matter. You'd better go in to her now. She seems to be coming to. I'll wake the girl and get her ready."

Amos went into the bedroom as quietly as he could, but there was no need for silence. Ruth was conscious, as if some awareness of her approaching death had forced her to make the most of these last few minutes of her life. She put out a frail hand timidly to him. Her voice was weak, but clear.

"Amos, I know. And I don't mind now, except for you. But there's something I had to ask you. Amos, do you…?"

He dropped beside her when her voice faltered, wanting to bury his head against her, but not daring to lose the few remaining moments of her sight. He fought the words out of the depths of his mind, and then realized it would take more than words. He bent over and kissed her again, as he had first kissed her so many years ago.

"I've always loved you, Ruth," he said. "I still do love you."

She sighed and relaxed. "Then I won't be jealous of God anymore, Amos. I had to know."

Her hand reached up weakly, to find his hair and to run her fingers through it. She smiled, the worn lines of her face softening. Her voice was content and almost young. "And forsaking all others, cleave only unto thee…"

The last syllable whispered out, and the hand fell.

Amos dropped his head at last, and a single sob choked out of him. He folded her hands tenderly, with the worn, cheap wedding ring uppermost, and arose slowly with his head bowed.

"Then shall the dust return to the earth as it was; and the spirit shall return unto God who gave it. Father, I thank thee for this moment with her. Bless her, O Lord, and keep her for me."

He nodded to Doc and Anne. The girl looked sick and sat staring at him with eyes that mixed shock and pity.

"You'll need some money, Anne," he said. "I don't have much, but there's a little…"

She drew back and shook her head. "I've got enough. Reverend Strong. I'll make out. Doctor Miller has told me to take his car. But what about you?"

"There's still work to be done," he said. "I haven't even written my sermon. And the people who are giving up their homes will need comfort. In such hours as these, we all need God to sustain us."

She stumbled to her feet and into her bedroom. Amos opened his old desk and reached for pencil and paper.

3

The wicked have drawn out the sword, and have bent their bow, to cast down the poor and needy, and to slay such as be of upright conversation.
I have seen the wicked in great power, and spreading himself like a green bay tree.

Psalm 37:14, 35
THE BOOK OF THE JEWS

Darkness was just beginning to fall when they helped Anne out into the doctor's car, making sure that the tank was full. She was quiet, and had recovered herself, but she avoided Amos whenever possible. She turned at last to Doc Miller.

"What are you going to do? I should have asked before, but…"

"Don't worry about me, girl," he told her, his voice as hearty as when he was telling an old man he still had forty years to live. "I've got other ways. The switchboard girl is going to be one of the last to leave, and I'm driving her in her car. You go ahead, the way we mapped it out. And pick up anyone else you find on the way. It's safe; it's still too early for men to start turning to looting, rape, or robbery. They'll think of that after the shock of this wears off a little."

She held out a hand to him, and climbed in. At the last minute, she pressed Amos' hand briefly. Then she stepped on the accelerator and the car took off down the street at top speed.

"She hates me," Amos said. "She loves other men too much and God too little to understand."

"And maybe you love your God too much to understand that you love men,

Amos. Don't worry, she'll figure it out. The next time you see her, she'll feel different. Look, I really do have to see that Nellie gets off the switchboard and into a car. I'll see you later."

Doc swung off toward the telephone office, carrying his bag. Amos watched him, puzzled as always at anyone who could so fervently deny God and yet could live up to every commandment of the Lord except worship. They had been friends for a long time, while the parish stopped fretting about the friendship and took it for granted, yet the riddle of what they found in common was no nearer solution.

There was the distant sound of a great rocket landing, and the smaller stutterings of the peculiar alien ramjets. The ships passed directly overhead, yet there was no shooting this time.

For a moment, Amos faced the bedroom window where Ruth lay, and then he turned toward the church. He opened it, throwing the doors wide. There was no sign of the sexton, but he had rung the bell in the tower often enough before. He took off his worn coat and grabbed the rope.

It was hard work, and his hands were soft. Once it had been a pleasure, but now his blood seemed too thin to suck up the needed oxygen. The shirt stuck wetly to his back, and he felt giddy when he finished.

Almost at once, the telephone in his little office began jangling nervously. He staggered to it, panting as he lifted the receiver, to hear the voice of Nellie, shrill with fright. "Reverend, what's up? Why's the bell ringing?"

"For prayer meeting, of course," he told her. "What else?"

"Tonight? Well, I'll be—" She hung up.

He lighted a few candles and put them on the altar, where their glow could be seen from the dark street, but where no light would shine upward for alien eyes. Then he sat down to wait, wondering what was keeping the organist.

There were hushed calls from the street and nervous cries. A car started, to be followed by another. Then a group took off at once. He went to the door, partly for the slightly cooler air. All along the street, men were moving out their possessions and loading up, while others took off. They waved to him, but hurried on by. He heard telephones begin to ring, but if Nellie was passing on some urgent word, she had forgotten him.

He turned back to the altar, kneeling before it. There was no articulate prayer in his mind. He simply clasped his gnarled fingers together and rested on his knee, looking up at the outward symbol of his life. Outside, the sounds went on, blending together. It did not matter whether anyone chose to use the church tonight. It was open, as the house of God must always be in times of stress. He had long since stopped trying to force religion on those not ready for it.

And slowly, the strains of the day began to weave themselves into the pattern of his life. He had learned to accept; from the death of his baby daughter on, he had found no way to end the pain that seemed so much a part of life. But he could bury it behind the world of his devotion, and meet whatever his lot was to be without anger at the will of the Lord. Now, again, he accepted things as they were ordered.

There was a step behind him. He turned, not bothering to rise, and saw the dressmaker, Angela Anduccini, hesitating at the door. She had never entered, though she had lived in Wesley since she was eighteen. She crossed herself doubtfully, and waited.

He stood up. "Come in, Angela. This is the house of God, and all His daughters are welcome."

There was a dark, tight fear in her eyes as she glanced back to the street. "I thought—maybe the organ…"

He opened it for her and found the switch. He started to explain the controls, but the smile on her lips warned him that it was unnecessary. Her calloused fingers over the stops, and she began playing, softly as if to herself. He went back to one of the pews, listening. For two years he had blamed the organ, but now he knew that there was no fault with the instrument, but only with its player before. The music was sometimes strange for his church, but he liked it.

A couple who had moved into the old Surrey farm beyond the town came in, holding hands, as if holding each other up. And a minute later, Buzz Williams stumbled in and tried to tiptoe down the aisle to where Amos sat. Since his parents had died, he'd been the town problem. Now he was half-drunk, though without his usual boisterousness.

"I ain't got no car and I been drinking," he whispered. "Can I stay here till maybe somebody comes or something?"

Amos sighed, motioning Buzz to a seat where the boy's eyes had centered. Somewhere, there must be a car for the four waifs who had remembered God when everything else had failed them. If one of the young couple could drive, and he could locate some kind of vehicle, it was his duty to see that they were sent to safety.

Abruptly, the haven of the church and the music came to an end, leaving him back in the real world—a curiously unreal world now.

He was heading down the steps, trying to remember whether the Jameson boy had taken his rebuilt flivver when a panel truck pulled up in front of the church. Doc Miller got out, wheezing as he squeezed through the door.

He took in the situation at a glance. "Only four strays, Amos? I thought we might have to pack them in." He headed for Buzz. "I've got a car outside, Buzz. Gather up the rest of this flock and get going!"

"I been drinking," Buzz said, his face reddening hotly.

"Okay, you've been drinking. At least you know it, and there's no traffic problem. Head for Salina and hold your speed under forty and you'll be all right." Doc swept little Angela Anduccini from the organ and herded her out, while Buzz collected the couple. "Get going, all of you!"

They got, with Buzz enthroned behind the wheel and Angela beside him. The town was dead. Amos closed the organ and began shutting the doors to the church.

"I've got a farm tractor up the street for us, Amos," Doc said at last. "I almost ran out of tricks. There were more fools than you'd think who thought they could hide it out right here. At that, I probably missed some. Well, the tractor's nothing elegant, but it can take back roads no car would handle. We'd better get going. Nellie has already gone, with a full load."

Amos shook his head. He had never thought it out, but the decision had been in his mind from the beginning. Ruth still lay waiting a decent burial. He could no more leave her now than when she was alive. "You'll have to go alone, Doc."

"I figured." The doctor sighed, wiping the sweat from his forehead. "I'd remember to my dying day that believers have more courage than an atheist! Nope, we're in this together. It isn't sensible, but that's how I feel. We'd better put out the candles, I guess."

Amos snuffed them reluctantly, wondering how he could persuade the other to leave. His ears had already caught the faint sounds of shooting, indicating that the aliens were on their way.

The uncertain thumping of a laboring motor sounded from the street, then wheezed to silence. There was a shout, a pause, and the motor caught again. It seemed to run for ten seconds before it backfired, and was still. Doc opened one of the doors. In the middle of the street, a man was pushing an ancient car while his wife steered. But it refused to start again. He grabbed for tools, threw up the hood, and began a frantic search for the trouble.

"If you can drive a tractor, there's one half a block down," Doc called out

The man looked up, snapped one quick glance behind him, and pulled the woman hastily out of the car. In almost no time, the heavy roar of the tractor sounded. The man revved it up to full throttle and tore off down the road, leaving Doc and Amos stranded. The sound of the aliens was clearer now, and there was some light coming from beyond the bend of the street.

There was no place to hide, except in the church. They found a window where the paint on the imitation stained glass was loose and peeled it back enough for a peephole. The advance scouts of the aliens were already within view. They were dashing from house to house. Behind them, they left something that sent up clouds of glowing smoke that seemed to have no fire connected to its brilliance. At least, no buildings were burning.

Just as the main group of aliens came into view, the door of one house burst open. A scrawny man leaped out, with his fat wife and fatter daughter behind him. They raced up the street, tearing at their clothes and itching frantically at their reddened skin.

Shouts sounded. All three jerked, but went racing on. More shots sounded. At first, Amos thought it was incredibly bad shooting. Then he realized that it was even more unbelievably good marksmanship. The aliens were shooting at the hands first, then moving up the arms methodically, wasting no chance for torture.

For the first time in years, Amos felt fear and anger curdle solidly in his stomach. He stood up, feeling his shoulders square back and his head come up as he moved toward the door. His lips were moving in words that he only half understood. "Arise, O Lord; O God, lift up Thine hand; forget not the humble. Wherefore doth the wicked condemn God? He hath said in his heart, Thou wilt not requite it. Thou hast seen it, for Thou beholdest mischief and spite, to requite it with Thy hand: the poor commiteth himself unto Thee; Thou art the helper of the fatherless. Break Thou the arm of the wicked and the evil ones; seek out their wickedness till Thou find none..."

"Stop it, Amos!" Doc's voice rasped harshly in his ear. "Don't be a fool! And you're misquoting that last verse!"

It cut through the fog of his anger. He knew that Doc had deliberately reminded him of his father, but the trick worked, and the memory of his father's anger at misquotations replaced his cold fury. "We can't let that go on!"

Then he saw it was over. The aliens had used up their targets. But there was the sight of another wretch, unrecognizable in half of his skin...

Doc's voice was as sick as Amos felt. "We can't do anything. I can't understand a race smart enough to build star ships and still stupid enough for this. But it's good for our side, in the long run. While our armies are organizing, the snakes are wasting time on this. And it makes our resistance get tougher, too."

The aliens didn't confine their sport to humans. They worked just as busily on a huge old tomcat they found, And all the corpses were being loaded onto a big wagon pulled by twenty of the creatures.

The aliens obviously had some knowledge of human behavior. At first they had passed up all stores and had concentrated on living quarters. The scouts had passed on by the church without a second glance. But they moved into a butcher shop at once, to come out again carrying meat, which was piled on the wagon with the corpses.

Now a group was assembling before the church, pointing up toward the steeple where the bell was. Two of them shoved up a mortar of some sort. It was pointed quickly and a load was dropped in. There was a muffled explosion, and the bell rang sharply, its pieces rattling down the roof and into the yard below. Another shoved the mortar into a new position, aiming it straight for the door of the church. Doc yanked Amos down between two pews. "They don't like churches, damn it! A fine spot we picked. Watch out for splinters!"

The door smashed in and a heavy object struck the altar, ruining it. Amos groaned at the shattering sound it made.

There was no further activity when they slipped back to their peepholes. The aliens were on the march again, moving along slowly. In spite of the delta planes, they seemed to have no motorized ground vehicles, and the wagon moved on under the power of the twenty green-skinned things, coming directly in front of the church. Amos stared at it in the flickering light from the big torches burning in the hands of some of the aliens. Most of the corpses were strangers to him. A few he knew. And then his eyes picked out the twisted, distorted upper part of Ruth's body, her face empty in death's relaxation.

He stood up wearily, and this time Doc made no effort to stop him. He walked down a line of pews and around the wreck of one of the doors. Outside the church, the air was still hot and dry, but he drew a long breath into his lungs. The front of the church was in the shadows, and no aliens seemed to be watching him.

He moved down the stone steps. His legs were firm now. His heart was pounding heavily, but the clot of feelings that rested leadenly in his stomach had no fear left in it. Nor was there any anger left, nor any purpose.

He saw the aliens stop and stare at him, while a jabbering began among them.

He moved forward with the measured tread that had led him down the aisle when he married Ruth. He came in the wagon and put his hand out, lifting one of Ruth's dead-limp arms back across her body.

"This is my wife," he told the staring aliens quietly. "I am taking her home with me."

He reached up and began trying to move the other bodies away from her. Without surprise, he saw Doc's arms moving up to help him, while a steady stream of whispered profanity came from the doctor's lips.

Amos hadn't expected to succeed. He had expected nothing.

Abruptly, a dozen of the aliens leaped for the two men. Amos let them overpower him without resistance. For a second, Doc struggled; then he too relaxed while the aliens bound them and tossed them onto the wagon.

4

He hath bent his bow like an enemy: he stood with his right hand as an adversary, and slew all that were pleasant to the eye in the tabernacle of the daughter of Zion: he poured out his fury like fire.

The Lord was as an enemy: he hath swallowed up Israel, he hath swallowed up all her palaces: he hath destroyed his strong holds, and hath increased in the daughter of Judah mourning and lamentation.

The Lord hath cast off his altar, he hath abhorred his sanctuary, he hath given up into the hand of the enemy the walls of her palaces; they have made a noise in the house of the Lord, as in the day of a solemn feast.

Lamentations 2:4,5,7
THE BOOK OF THE JEWS

Amos' first reaction was one of dismay at the ruin of his only good suit. He struggled briefly on the substance under him, trying to find a better spot. A minister's suit might be old, but he could never profane the altar with such stains as these. Then some sense of the ridiculousness of his worry reached his mind, and he relaxed as best he could.

He had done what he had to do, and it was too late to regret it. He could only accept the consequences of it now, as he had learned to accept everything else God had seen fit to send him. He had never been a man of courage, but the strength of God had sustained him through as much as most men had to bear. It would sustain him further.

Doc was facing him, having flopped around to lie near him. Now the doctor's lips twisted into a crooked grin. "I guess we're in for it now. But it won't last forever, and maybe we're old enough to die fast. At least, once we're dead, we won't know it, so there's no sense being afraid of dying."

If it were meant to provoke him into argument, it failed. Amos considered it a completely hopeless philosophy, but it was better than none, probably. His own faith in the hereafter left something to be desired; he was sure of immortality and the existence of heaven and hell, but he had never been able to picture either to his own satisfaction.

The wagon had been swung around and was now being pulled up the street, back toward Clyde. Amos tried to take his mind off the physical discomforts of the ride by watching the houses, counting them to his own. They drew near it finally, but it was Doc who spotted the important fact. He groaned. "My car!"

Amos strained his eyes, staring into the shadows through the glare of the torches. Doc's car stood at the side of the house, with its left front door open! Someone must have told Anne that he hadn't left, and she'd forgotten her anger with him to swing back around the alien horde to save him!

He began a prayer that they might pass on without the car being noticed, and it seemed at first that they would. Then there was a sudden cry from the house, and he saw her face briefly at a front window. She must have seen Doc and himself lying on the wagon!

He opened his mouth to risk a warning, but it was too late. The door of the house swung back, and she was standing on the front steps, lifting Richard's rifle to her shoulder. Amos' heart seemed to hesitate with the tension of his body. The aliens still hadn't noticed. If she'd only wait...

The rifle cracked. Either by luck or some skill he hadn't suspected, one of the aliens dropped. She was running forward now, throwing another cartridge into the barrel. The gun barked again, and an alien fell to the ground, bleating horribly.

There was no attempt at torture this time, at least. The leading alien finally jerked out a tubelike affair from a scabbard at his side and a single sharp explosion sounded. Anne jerked backward as the heavy slug hit her forehead, the rifle spinning from her dead hands. The wounded alien was trying frantically to crawl away. Two of his fellows began working on him mercilessly, with as little feeling as if he had been a human. His body followed that of Anne toward the front of the wagon, just beyond Amos' limited view.

She hadn't seemed hysterical this time, Amos thought wearily. It had been her tendency to near hysteria that had led to his advising Richard to wait, not the difference in faith. Now he was sorry he'd had no chance to understand her better.

Doc sighed, and there was a peculiar pride under the thickness of his voice. "Man," he said, "has one virtue which is impossible to any omnipotent force like your God. He can be brave. He can be brave beyond sanity for another man or for an idea. Amos, I pity your God if man ever makes war on Him!"

Amos flinched, but the blasphemy aroused only a shadow of his normal reaction. His mind seemed numbed. He lay back, watching black clouds scudding across the sky almost too rapidly. It looked unnatural, and he remembered how often the accounts had mentioned a tremendous storm that had wrecked or hampered the efforts of human troops. Maybe a counterattack had begun, and this was part of the alien defense. If they had some method of weather control, it was probable. The moonlight was already blotted out by the clouds.

Half a mile farther on, there was a shout from the aliens, and a big tractor chugged into view, badly driven by one of the aliens who had obviously only partly mastered the human machine. With a great deal of trial and error, it was backed into position and coupled to the wagon. Then it began churning along at nearly thirty miles an hour, while the big wagon bucked and bounced behind. From then on, the ride was a physical hell. Even Doc groaned at some of the bumps, though his bones had three times more padding than Amos could boast.

Mercifully, they slowed when they reached Clyde. Amos wiped the blood off his bitten lip and managed to wriggle to a position where most of the bruises were on his upper side. Beyond the town there was a flood of brilliant lights where the alien rockets stood, and he could see a group of strange machines driven by nonhuman creatures busy unloading the great ships. But the drivers of the machines looked totally unlike the other aliens.

One of the alien trucks swung past them, and he had a clear view of the creature steering it. It bore no resemblance to humanity. There was a conelike torso, covered with a fine white down, ending in four thick stalks to serve as legs. From its broadest point, four sinuous limbs spread out to the truck controls. There was no head, but only eight small tentacles waving above it.

He saw a few others, always in control of machines, and no machines being handled by the green-skinned people, as they passed through the ghost city that had been Clyde. Apparently there were two races allied against humanity, which explained why such barbarians could come in space ships. The green ones must be simply the fighters, while the downy cones were the technicians. From their behavior, though, the pilots of the planes must be recruited from the fighters.

Clyde had grown since he had been there, unlike most of the towns about. There was a new supermarket just down the street from Amos' former church, and the tractor jolted to a stop in front of it. Aliens swarmed out and began carrying the dead loot from the wagon into big food lockers, while two others lifted Doc and Amos.

But they weren't destined for the comparatively merciful death of freezing in the lockers. The aliens threw them into a little cell that had once apparently been a cashier's cage, barred from floor to ceiling. It made a fairly efficient jail, and the lock that clicked shut as the door closed behind them was too heavy to be broken. There was already one occupant—a medium-built young man whom Amos finally recognized as Smithton, the Clyde dentist. His shoulders were shaking with sporadic sobs as he sat huddled in one corner. He looked at the two arrivals without seeing them. "But I surrendered," he whispered to himself. "I'm a prisoner of war. They can't do it. I surrendered..."

A fatter-than-usual alien, wearing the only clothes Amos had seen on any of them, came waddling up to the cage, staring in at them, and the dentist wailed off into silence. The alien drew up his robe about his chest and scratched his rump against a counter without taking his eyes off them. "Humans," he said in a grating voice, but without an accent, "are peculiar. No standardization."

"I'll be damned!" Doc swore. "English!"

The alien studied them with what might have been surprise, lifting his ears. "Is the gift of tongues so unusual, then? Many of the priests of the Lord God Almighty speak all the human languages. It's a common miracle, not like levitation."

"Fine. Then maybe you'll tell us what we're being held for?" Doc suggested.

The priest shrugged. "Food, of course. The grethi eat any kind of meat—even our people—but we have to examine the laws to find whether you're permitted. If you are, we'll need freshly killed specimens to sample, so we're waiting with you."

"You mean you're attacking us for *food*?"

The priest grunted harshly. "No! We're on a holy mission to exterminate you. The Lord Almighty commanded us to go down to Earth where abominations existed and to leave no living creature under your sun."

He turned and waddled out of the store, taking the single remaining torch with him, leaving only the dim light of the moon and reflections from farther away.

Amos dropped onto a stool inside the cage. "They had to lock us in a new building instead of one I know," he said. "If it had been the church, we might have had a chance."

"How?" Doc asked sharply.

Amos tried to describe the passage through the big unfinished basement under the church, reached through a trap door. Years before, a group of teenagers had built a sixty-foot tunnel into it and had used it for a private club until the passage had been discovered and bricked over from outside. The earth would be soft around the bricks, however. Beyond, the outer end of the tunnel opened in a wooded section, which led to a drainage ditch that in turn connected with the Republican River. From the church, they could move to the stream and slip down that without being seen. There was even an alley—or had been one—behind the store that would take them to the shadow of the trees around the church.

Doc's fingers were fumbling with the lock as Amos finished. He grunted and reached for his pocket, taking out a few coins. "They don't know much about us, Amos, if they expect to hold us here, where the lock is fastened from the inside. Feel those screws."

Amos fumbled over the lock surface. There were four large screws on the back of the lock, holding it to the door. The cashier's cage had been designed to keep others out, not to serve as a jail. At best, he thought, it was a poor chance. Yet was it merely chance? It seemed more like the hand of God to him.

"More like the stupidity of the aliens, to my mind," Doc objected. He was testing the screws with a quarter now. He nodded in some satisfaction, then swore. "Damn it, the quarter fits the slot, but I can't get enough leverage to turn the screw. Hey, Smithton or whatever your name is, pull out that money drawer and knock the bottom out. I need a couple of narrow slats."

Smithton had been praying miserably—a childhood prayer for laying himself down to sleep. But he succeeding in kicking out splinters from the drawer bottom.

Doc selected two and clamped them around the quarter, trying to hold them in place while he turned them. It was rough going, but the screws turned. Three came loose finally, and the lock rotated on the fourth until they could force the cage open.

Doc stopped and pulled Smithton to him. "Follow me, and do what I do. No talking, no making a separate jump, or I'll break your neck. All right!"

The back door was locked, but from the inside. They opened it to a backyard filled with garbage. The alley wasn't as dark as it should have been, since open lots beyond let some light come through. They hugged what shadows they could until they reached the church hedge. There they groped along, lining themselves up with the side office door. There was no sign of aliens.

Amos broke ahead of the others, being more familiar with the church. It wasn't until he had reached the door that he realized it could have been locked; it had been kept that way part of the time. He grabbed the handle and forced it back—to find it unlatched.

For a second, he stopped to thank the Lord for their luck. Then the others were with him, crowding into the little kitchen where social suppers were prepared. He'd always hated those functions, but now he blessed them for providing a hiding place that gave them time to find their way. There were sounds in the church, and odors, but none that seemed familiar to Amos. Something made the back hairs of his neck prickle. He took off his shoes and tied them around his neck, and the others followed suit.

The way to the trap door lay down a small hall, across in front of the altar, and into the private office on the other side.

They were safer together than separated, particularly since Smithton was with them. Amos leaned back against the kitchen wall to catch his breath. His heart seemed to have a ring of needled pain around it, and his throat was so dry that he had to fight desperately against gagging. There was water here, but he couldn't risk rummaging across the room to the sink.

He was praying for strength, less for himself than for the others. Long since, he had resigned himself to die. If God willed his death, he was ready; all he had were dead and probably mutilated, and he had succeeded only in dragging those who tried to help him into mortal danger. He was old, and his body was already treading its way to death. He could live for probably twenty more years, but aside from his work, there was nothing to live for—and even in that, he had been only a mediocre failure. But he was still responsible for Doc Miller, and even for Smithton now.

He squeezed his eyes together and squinted around the doorway. There was some light in the hall that led toward the altar, but he could see no one, and there were drapes that gave a shadow from which they could spy the rest of their way. He moved to it softly, and felt the others come up behind him.

He bent forward, parting the drapes a trifle. They were perhaps twenty feet in front of the altar, on the right side. He spotted the wreckage that had once stood as an altar. Then he frowned as he saw evidence of earth piled up into a mound of odd shape.

He threw the cloth back farther, surprised at the curiosity in him, as he had been surprised repeatedly by the changes taking place in himself. There were two elaborately robed priests kneeling in the center of the chapel. But his eye barely noticed them before it was attracted to what stood in front of the new altar.

A box of wood rested on an earthenware platform. On it were four marks, which his eyes recognized as unfamiliar, but which his mind twisted into a sequence from no alphabet he had learned; yet in them was always more than they were. And above the box was a veil, behind which Something shone brightly without light.

In his mind, a surge of power pulsed, making something that might almost have been words through his thoughts.

"I AM THAT I AM, who brought those out of bondage from Egypt and who wrote upon the wall before Belshazzar, MENE, MENE, TEKEL, UPHARSIN, as it shall be writ large upon the Earth, from this day forth. For I have said unto the seed of Mikhtchah, thou art my chosen people and I shall exalt thee above all the races under the heavens!"

5

And it was given unto him to make war with the saints, and to overcome them: and power was given him over all kindreds, and tongues, and nations.

He that leadeth into captivity shall go into captivity: he that killeth with the sword must be killed with the sword.

Revelation 13:7, 10
THE BOOK OF THE CHRISTIANS

The seed of Mikhtchah. The seed that was the aliens…

There was no time and all time, then. Amos felt his heart stop, but the blood pounded through his arteries with a vigor it had lacked for decades. He felt Ruth's hand in his, stirring with returning life, and knew she had never existed. Beside him, he saw Doc Miller's hair turn snow white and knew that it was so, though the was no way he could see Doc from his position.

He felt the wrath of the Presence rest upon him, weighing his every thought from his birth to his certain death, where he ceased completely and went on forever, and yet he knew that the Light behind the veil was unaware of him, but was receptive only to the two Mikhtchah priests who knelt unaware.

All of that was with but a portion of his mind so small that he could not locate it, though his total mind encompassed all time and space, and that which was neither; yet each part of his perceptions occupied all of his mind that had been or ever could be, save only the present, which somehow was a concept not yet solved by the One before him.

He saw a strange man on a low mountain, receiving tablets of stone that weighed only a pennyweight, engraved with a script that all could read. And he knew the man, but refused to believe it, since the garments were not those of his mental image, and the clean-cut face fitted better with the strange Egyptian headpiece than with the language being spoken.

Amos saw every prayer of his life tabulated. But nowhere was there the mantle of divine warmth which he had felt as a boy and had almost felt again the morning before. And there was a stirring of unease at his thought, mixed with wrath; yet while the thought was in his mind, nothing could touch him.

Yet each of those things was untrue, because he could find no understanding of that which was true.

It ended as abruptly as it had begun, either a microsecond or a million subjective years after. It left him numbed, but newly alive. And it left him dead as no man had ever been hopelessly dead before.

He knew only that before him was the Lord God Almighty, who had made a covenant with Abraham, with Isaac, and with Jacob, and with their seed; and that mankind had been rejected, while God now was on the side of the enemies of Abraham's seed, and all the nations of earth.

Even that was too much for a human mind no longer in touch with the Presence, and only a shadow of it remained.

Beside him, Amos heard Doc Miller begin breathing again, brushing the white hair back from his forehead wonderingly as he muttered a single word. "God!"

One of the Mikhtchah priests looked up, his eyes turning about; there was a glazed look on his face, but it was leaving.

Then Smithton screamed! His open mouth poured out a steady, unwavering screaming, while his lungs panted in and out. His eyes opened, staring horribly. Like a wooden doll on strings, the man stood up and walked forward. He avoided the draperies and headed for the Light behind the veil. Abruptly, the Light was gone, but Smithton walked toward it as steadily as before. He stopped before the falling veil, and the scream cut off sharply.

Doc had jerked silently to his feet, tugging Amos up behind him. The minister lifted himself, but he knew there was no place to go. It was up to the will of God now...Or...

Smithton turned on one heel precisely. His face was rigid and without expression, yet completely mad. He walked mechanically forward toward the two priests they sprawled aside at the last second, holding two obviously human-made automatics, but making no effort to use them. Smithton walked on toward the open door at the front of the church.

He reached the steps, with the two priests staring after him. His feet lifted from the first step to the second and then he was on the sidewalk.

The two priests fired!

Smithton jerked, halted, and suddenly cried out in a voice of normal, rational agony. His legs kicked frantically under him and he ducked out of the sight of the doorway, his faltering steps sounding farther and farther away. He was dead—the Mikhtchah marksmanship had been as good as it seemed always to be—but still moving, though slower and slower, as if some extra charge of life were draining out like a battery running down.

The priests exchanged quick glances and then darted after him, crying out as they dashed around the door into the night. Abruptly, a single head and hand appeared again, to snap a shot at the draperies from which Smithton had come. Amos forced himself to stand still, while his imagination supplied the jolt of lead in his stomach. The bullet hit the draperies, and something else.

The priest hesitated, and was gone again. Amos broke into a run across the chapel and into the hall at the other side of the altar. He heard the faint sound of Doc's feet behind him.

The trap door was still there, unintentionally concealed under carpeting. He forced it up and dropped through it into the four-foot depth of the incompleted basement, making room for Doc. They crouched together as he lowered the trap and began feeling his way through the blackness toward the other end of the basement. It had been five years since he had been down there, and then only once for a quick inspection of the work of the boys who had dug the tunnel.

He thought he had missed it at first, and began groping for the small entrance. It might have caved in, for that matter. Then, two feet away, his hand found the hole and he drew Doc after him.

It was cramped, and bits of dirt had fallen in places and had to be dug out of the way. Part of the distance was on their stomachs. They found the bricked-up wall ahead of them and began digging around it with their bare hands. It took another ten minutes, while distant sounds of wild yelling from the Mikhtchah reached them faintly. They broke through at last with bleeding hands, not bothering to check for aliens near. They reached a safer distance in the woods, caught their breaths, and went on.

The biggest danger lay in the drainage trench, which was low in several places. But luck was with them, and these spots lay in shadow.

Then the little Republican River lay in front of them, and there was a flatbottom boat nearby.

Moments later they were floating down the stream, resting their aching lungs, while the boat needed only a trifling guidance. It was still night, with only the light from the moon, and there was little danger of pursuit by alien planes. Amos could just see Doc's face as the man fumbled for a cigarette.

He lighted it and exhaled deeply. "All right, Amos—you were right, and God exists. But damn it, I don't feel any better for knowing that. I can't see how God helps me—nor even how He's doing the Mikhtchah much good. What do they get out of it, beyond a few miracles with the weather? They're just doing God's work."

"They get the Earth, I suppose—if they want it," Amos said doubtfully. He wasn't sure they did. Nor could he see how the other aliens tied into the scheme; if he had known the answers, they were gone now. "Doc, you're still an atheist, though you now know God is."

The plump man chuckled bitterly. "I'm afraid you're right. But at least I'm myself. You can't be, Amos. You've spent your whole life on the gamble that God is right and that you must serve Him—when the only way you could serve was to help mankind. What do you do now? God is automatically right—but everything you've ever believed makes Him completely wrong, and you can only serve Him by betraying your people. What kind of ethics will work for you now?"

Amos shook his head wearily, hiding his face in his hands. The same problem had been fighting its way through his own thoughts. His first reaction had been to acknowledge his allegiance to God without question; thirty years of conditioned thought lay behind that. Yet now he could not accept such a decision. As a man, he could not bow to what he believed completely evil, and the Mikhtchah were evil by every definition he knew.

Could he tell people the facts, and take away what faith they had in any purpose in life? Could he go over to the enemy, who didn't even want him except for their feeding experiments? Or could he encourage people to fight, with the old words that God was with them—when he knew the words were false? Yet their resistance might doom them to eternal hellfire for opposing God.

It hit him then that he could remember nothing clearly about the case of a hereafter—either for or against it. What happened to a people when God deserted them? Were they only deserted in their physical form, and still free to win their spiritual salvation? Or were they completely lost? Did they cease to have souls that could survive? Or were those souls automatically consigned to hell, however noble they might be?

No question had been answered for him. He knew that God existed, but he had known that before. He knew nothing now beyond that. He did not even know when God had placed the Mikhtchah before humanity. It seemed unlikely that it was as recent as his own youth. Otherwise, how could he account for the strange spiritual glow he had felt as an evangelist?

"There's only one rational answer," he said at last. "It doesn't make any difference what I decide! I'm only one man."

"So was Columbus when he swore the world was round. And he didn't have the look on his face you've had since we saw God, Amos! I know now what the Bible means when it says Moses' face shone after he came down from the mountain, until he had to cover it with a veil. If I'm right, there's little help for mankind if you decide wrong!"

Doc tossed the cigarette over the side and lit another, and Amos was shocked to see that the man's hands were shaking. The doctor shrugged, and his tone fell back to normal. "I wish we knew more. You've always thought almost exclusively in terms of the Old Testament and a few snatches of Revelation—like a lot of men who became evangelists. I've never really thought about God—I couldn't accept Him, so I dismissed Him. Maybe that's why we got the view of Him we did. I wish I knew where Jesus fits in, for instance. There's too much missing. Too many imponderables and hiatuses. We have only two facts, and we can't understand either. There is a manifestation of God which has touched both Mikhtchah and mankind; and He has stated now that He plans to wipe out mankind. We'll have to stick to that."

Amos made one more attempt to deny the problem that was facing him. "Suppose God is only testing man again, as He did so often before?"

"Testing?" Doc rolled the word on his tongue, and seemed to spit it out. The strange white hair seemed to make him older, and the absence of mockery in his voice left him almost a stranger. "Amos, the Hebrews worked like the devil to get Canaan; after forty years of wandering around a few square miles, God suddenly told them this was the land—and then they had to take it by the same methods men have always used to conquer a country. The miracles didn't really decide anything. They got out of Babylon because the old prophets were slaving night and day to hold them together as one people, and because they managed to sweat it out until they finally got a break. In our own time, they've done the same things to get Israel, and with no miracles! It seems to me God always took it away, but they had to it back by themselves. I don't think much of that kind of a test in this case."

Amos could feel all his values slipping and spinning. He realized that he was holding himself together only because of Doc; otherwise, his mind would have reached for madness, like any intelligence forced to solve the insoluble. He could no longer comprehend himself, let alone God. And the feeling crept into his thoughts that God couldn't wholly understand him, either.

"Can a creation defy anything great enough to create it, Doc? And should it, if it can?"

"Most kids have to," Doc said. He shook his head. "It's your problem. All I can do is point a few things out. And maybe it won't matter, at that. We're still a long ways inside Mikhtchah territory, and it's getting along toward daylight."

The boat drifted on, while Amos tried to straighten out his thoughts and grew more deeply tangled in a web of confusion. What could any man who worshipped God devoutly do if he found his God was opposed to all else he had ever believed to be good?

A version of Kant's categorical imperative crept into his mind; somebody had once quoted it to him—probably Doc. "So act as to treat humanity, whether in thine own person or in that of any other, in every case as an end withal, never as a means only." Was God now treating man as an end, or simply as a means to some purpose, in which man had failed? And had man ever seriously treated God as an end, rather than as a means to spiritual immortality and a quietus to the fear of death?

"We're being followed!" Doc whispered suddenly. He pointed back, and Amos could see a faint light shining around a curve in the stream. "Look—there's a building over there. When the boat touches shallow water, run for it!"

He bent to the oars, and a moment later they touched bottom and were over the side, sending the boat back into the current. The building was a hundred feet back from the bank, and they scrambled madly toward it. Even in the faint moonlight, they could see that the building was a wreck, long since abandoned. Doc went in through one of the broken windows, dragging Amos behind him.

Through a chink in a wall they could see another boat heading down the stream, lighted by a torch and carrying two Mikhtchah. One rowed, while the other sat in the prow with a gun, staring ahead. They rowed on past.

"We'll have to hole up here," Doc decided. "It'll be light in half an hour. Maybe they won't think of searching a ruin like this."

They found rickety steps, and stretched out on the bare floor of a huge upstairs closet. Amos groaned as he tried to find a position in which he could get some rest. Then, surprisingly, he was asleep.

He woke once with traces of daylight coming into the closet, to hear sounds of heavy gunfire not far away. He was just drifting back to sleep when hail began cracking furiously down on the roof. When it passed, the gunfire was stilled.

Doc woke him when it was turning dark. There was nothing to eat, and Amos' stomach was sick with hunger. His body ached in every joint, and walking was pure torture. Doc glanced up at the stars, seemed to decide on a course, and struck out. He was wheezing and groaning in a way that indicated he shared Amos' feelings.

But he found enough energy to begin the discussion again. "I keep wondering what Smithton saw, Amos. It wasn't what we saw. And what about the legends of war in heaven? Wasn't there a big battle there once, in which Lucifer almost won? Maybe Lucifer simply stands for some other race God cast off?"

"Lucifer was Satan, the spirit of evil. He tried to take over God's domain."

"Mmm. I've read somewhere that we have only the account of the victor, which is apt to be pretty biased history. How do we know the real issues? Or the true outcome? At least he thought he had a chance, and he apparently knew what he was fighting."

The effort of walking made speech difficult. Amos shrugged, and let the conversation die. But his own mind ground on.

If God was all-powerful and all-knowing, why had He let them spy upon Him? Or was He still all-powerful over a race He had dismissed? Could it make any difference to God what man might try to do, now that He had condemned him? Was the Presence they had seen the whole of God—or only one manifestation of Him? His legs moved on woodenly, numbed to fatigue and slow from hunger, while his head churned with his basic problem. Where was his duty now? With God or against Him?

They found food in a deserted house, and began preparing it by the hooded light of a lantern while they listened to the news from a small battery radio that had been left behind. It was a hopeless account of alien landings and human retreats, yet given without the tone of despair they should have expected. They were halfway through the meal before they discovered the reason.

"Flash!" the radio announced. "Word has just come through from the Denver area. Our second atomic missile has exploded successfully! The alien base has been wiped out, and every alien ship is ruined. It is now clear that the trouble with the earlier bombs we assembled lay in the detonating mechanism. This is being investigated, while more volunteers are being trained to replace this undependable part of the bomb. Both missiles carrying suicide bombers have succeeded. Captive aliens of both races are being questioned in Denver now, but the same religious fanaticism found in Portland seems to make communication difficult."

It went back to reporting alien landings, while Doc and Amos stared at each other. It was too much to absorb at once—the official admission of two races, the fact that bombs had been assembled and tried, and the casual acceptance of suicide missions. It was as if God could control weather and machines, but not the will of determined men. Free will or...

Amos groped in his mind, trying to dig out something that might tie in the success of human suicide bombers, where automatic machinery was miraculously stalled, together with the reaction of God to his own thoughts of the glow he had felt in his early days. Something about men...

"They can be beaten!" Doc said in a harsh whisper.

Amos sighed as they began to get up to continue the impossible trek. "Maybe. We know God was at Clyde. Can we be sure He was at the other places to stop the bombs by His miracles?"

They slogged on through the night, cutting across country in the dim moonlight, where every footstep was twice as hard. Amos turned it over, trying to use the new information for whatever decision he must reach. If men could overcome those opposed to them, even for a time...

It brought him no closer to an answer.

The beginnings of dawn found them in a woods. Doc managed to heave Amos up a tree, where he could survey the surrounding terrain. There was a house beyond the edge of the woods, but it would take dangerous minutes to reach it. They debated, and then headed on.

They were just emerging from the woods when the sound of an alien plane began its stuttering shriek. Doc turned and headed back to where Amos was, behind him. Then he stopped. "Too late! He's seen something. Gotta have a target!"

His arms swept out, shoving Amos violently back under the nearest tree. He swung and began racing across the clearing, his fat legs pumping furiously as he covered the ground in straining leaps. Amos tried to lift himself from where he had fallen, but it was too late.

There was the drumming of gunfire and the earth erupted around Doc. He lurched and dropped, to twitch and lie still.

The plane swept over, while Amos disentangled himself from a root. It was gone as he broke free. Doc had given it a target, and the pilot was satisfied, apparently. He was still alive as Amos dropped beside him. Two of the shots had hit, but he managed to grin as he lifted himself on one elbow. It was only a matter of minutes, however, and there was no help possible. Amos found one of Doc's cigarettes and lighted it with fumbling hands.

"Thanks," Doc wheezed after taking a heavy drag on it. He started to cough, but suppressed it, his face twisting in agony. His words came in an irregular rhythm, but he held his voice level. "I guess I'm going to hell, Amos, since I never did repent—if there is a hell! And I hope there is! I hope it's filled with the soul of every poor damned human being who died in less than perfect grace. Because I'm going to find some way—"

He straightened suddenly, coughing and fighting for breath. Then he found one final source of strength and met Amos' eyes, a trace of his old cynical smile on his face.

"—some way to urge Lucifer to join us!" he finished. He dropped back, letting all the fight go out of his body. A few seconds later, he was dead.

6

...Thou shalt have no other peoples before me...Thou shalt make unto them no covenant against me...Thou shalt not foreswear thyself to them, nor serve them...for I am a jealous people...

Exultations 12:2-4
THE BOOK OF MAN

Amos lay through the day in the house to which he had dragged Doc's body. He did not even look for food. For the first time in his life since his mother had died when he was five, he had no shield against his grief. There was no hard core of acceptance that it was God's will to hide his loss at Doc's death. And with the realization of that, all the other losses hit at him as if they had been no older than the death of Doc.

He sat with his grief and his newly sharpened hatred, staring toward Clyde. Once, during the day, he slept. He awakened to a sense of a tremendous sound and shaking of the earth, but all was quiet when he finally became conscious. It was nearly night, and time to leave.

For a moment, he hesitated. It would be easier to huddle here, beside his dead, and let whatever would happen come to him. But within him was a sense of duty that drove him on. In the back of his mind something stirred, telling him he still had work to do.

He found part of a stale loaf of bread and some hard cheese and started out, munching on them. It was still too light to move safely, but he was going through woods again, and he heard no alien planes. When it grew darker, he turned to the side roads that led in the direction of Wesley.

In his mind was the knowledge that he had to return there. His church lay there; if the human fighters had pushed the aliens back, his people might be there. If not, it was from there that he would have to follow them.

His thoughts were too deep for conscious expression, and too numbed with exhaustion. His legs moved on steadily. One of his shoes had begun to wear through, and his feet were covered with blisters, but he went grimly on. It was his duty to lead his people, now that the aliens were here, as he had led them in easier times. His thinking had progressed no further.

He holed up in a barn that morning, avoiding the house because of the mutilated things that lay on the doorstep where the aliens had apparently left them. And this time he slept with the soundness of complete fatigue, but he awoke to find one fist clenched and extended toward Clyde. He had been dreaming that he was Job, and that God had left him sitting unanswered on his boils until he died, while mutilated corpses moaned around him, asking for leadership he would not give.

It was nearly dawn before he realized that he should have found himself some kind of a car. He had seen none, but there might have been one abandoned somewhere. Doc could probably have found one. But it was too late to bother, now. He had come to the outskirts of a tiny town, and started to head beyond it, before realizing that all the towns must have been well searched by now. He turned down the small street, looking for a store where he could find food.

There was a small grocery with a door partly ajar. Amos pushed it open, to the clanging of a bell. Almost immediately a dog began barking, and a human voice came sharply from the back.

"Down, Shep! Just a minute, I'm a-coming." A door to the rear opened, and a bent old man emerged, carrying a kerosene lamp. "Darned electric's off again! Good thing I stayed. Told them I had to mind my store, but they wanted to take me with them. Had to hide out in the old well. Darned nonsense about…"

He stopped, his eyes blinking behind thick lenses, and his mouth dropped open. He swallowed, and his voice was startled and shrill. "Mister, who are you?"

"A man who just escaped from the aliens," Amos told him. He hadn't realized the shocking appearance he must present by now. "One in need of food and a chance to rest until night. But I'm afraid I have no money on me."

The old man tore his eyes away slowly, seeming to shiver. Then he nodded, and pointed to the back. "Never turned nobody away hungry yet," he said, but the words seemed automatic.

An old dog backed slowly under a couch as Amos entered. The man put the lamp down and headed into a tiny kitchen to begin preparing food. Amos reached for the lamp and blew it out. "There really are aliens—worse than you heard," he said.

The old man bristled, met his eyes, and then nodded slowly. "If you say so. Only it don't seem logical God would let things like that run around in a decent state like Kansas."

He shoved a plate of eggs onto the table, and Amos pulled it to him, swallowing a mouthful eagerly. He reached for a second, and stopped. Something was violently wrong, suddenly. His stomach heaved, the room began to spin, and his forehead was cold and wet with sweat. He gripped the edge of the table, trying to keep from falling. Then he felt himself being dragged to a cot. He tried to protest, but his body was shaking with ague, and the words that spilled out were senseless. He felt the cot under him, and waves of sick blackness spilled over him.

It was the smell of cooking food that awakened him finally, and he sat up with a feeling that too much time had passed. The old man came from the kitchen, studying him. "You sure were sick, Mister. Guess you ain't used to going without decent food and rest. Feeling okay?"

Amos nodded. He felt a little unsteady, but it was passing. He pulled on the clothes that had been somewhat cleaned for him, and found his way to the table. "What day is it?"

"Saturday, evening," the other answered. "At least the way I figure. Here, eat that and get some coffee in you." He watched until Amos began on the food, and then dropped to a stool to begin cleaning an old rifle and loading it. "You said a lot of things. They true?"

For a second, Amos hesitated. Then he nodded, unable to lie to his benefactor. "I'm afraid so."

"Yeah, I figured so, somehow, looking at you." The old man sighed. "Well, I hope you make wherever you're going."

"What about you?" Amos asked.

The old man sighed, running his hands along the rifle. "I ain't leaving my store for any bunch of aliens. And if the Lord I been doing my duty by all my life decides to put Himself on the wrong side, well, maybe He'll win. But it'll be over my dead body!"

Nothing Amos could say would change his mind. The old man sat on the front step of the store, the rifle on his lap and the dog at his side, as Amos headed down the street in the starlight.

Amos felt surprisingly better after the first half-mile. Rest and food, combined with some treatment of his sores and blisters, had helped. But the voice inside him was driving him harder now, and the picture of the old man seemed to lend it added strength. He struck out at the fastest pace he could hope to maintain, leaving the town behind and heading down the road that the old man had said led to Wesley.

It was just after midnight when he saw the lights of a group of cars or trucks moving along another road. He had no idea whether they were driven by men or aliens, but he kept steadily on. There were sounds of traffic another time, on a road that crossed the small one he followed. But he knew now that he was approaching Wesley, and he speeded up his pace.

When the first dawn light came, he made no effort to seek shelter. He stared at the land around him, stripped by grasshoppers that could have been killed off if men had worked as hard at ending the insects as they had at their bickerings and wars. He saw the dry, arid land, drifting into dust and turning a fertile country into a nightmare. Men could put a stop to that.

It had been no act of God that had caused this ruin, but man's own follies. And without help from God, man might set it right in time.

God had deserted men. But mankind hadn't halted. On his own, he'd made a path to the moon and had unlocked the atom. He'd found a means, out of his raw courage, to use hydrogen bombs against the aliens when miracles were used against him. He had done everything but conquer himself—and he could do that, if he were given time.

Amos saw a truck stop at the crossroads ahead and halted, but the driver was human. He saw the open door and quickened his step toward it. "I'm bound for Wesley!"

"Sure." The driver helped him into the seat. "I'm going back for more supplies myself. You sure look as if you need treatment at the aid station there. I thought we'd rounded up all you strays. Most of them came in right after we sent out the word on Clyde."

"You've taken it?" Amos asked.

The other nodded wearily. "We took it. Got 'em with a bomb, like sitting ducks; we've been mopping up since. Not many aliens left."

They were nearing the outskirts of Wesley, and Amos pointed to his own house. "If you'll let me off there…"

"Look, I got orders to bring all strays to the aid station," the driver began firmly. Then he swung and faced Amos. For a second, he hesitated. Finally he nodded quietly. "Sure. Glad to help you."

Amos found the water still running. He bathed slowly. Somewhere, he felt his decision had been made, though he was still unsure of what it was. He climbed from the tub at last and began dressing. There was no suit that was proper, but he found clean clothes. His face in the mirror looked back at him, haggard and bearded as he reached for the razor.

Then he stopped as he encountered the reflection of his eyes. A shock ran over him, and he backed away a step. They were eyes foreign to everything in him. He had seen a shadow of what lay in them only once before, in the eyes of a great evangelist; and this was a hundred times stronger. He tore his glance away to find himself shivering, and he avoided them all through the shaving. Oddly, though, there was a strange satisfaction in what he had seen. He was beginning to understand why the old man had believed him, and why the truck driver had obeyed.

Most of Wesley had returned, and there were soldiers on the streets. As he approached the church, he saw the first-aid station, hectic with business. And a camera crew was near it, taking shots for television of those who had managed to escape from alien territory after the bombing.

A few people called to him, but he went on until he reached the church steps. The door was still in ruins and the bell was gone. Amos stood quietly waiting, his mind focusing slowly as he stared at the people, who were just beginning to recognize him and to spread hasty words from mouth to mouth. Then he saw little Angela Anduccini, and motioned for her to come to him. She hesitated briefly, before following him inside and to the organ.

The little Hammond still functioned. Amos climbed to the pulpit, hearing the old familiar creak of the boards. He put his hands on the lectern, seeing the heavy knuckles and blue veins of age as he opened the Bible and made ready for his Sunday morning congregation. He straightened his shoulders and turned to face the pews, waiting as they came in.

There were only a few at first. Then more and more came, some from old habit, some from curiosity, and many only because they had heard that he had been captured in person, probably. The camera crew came to the back and set up their machines, flooding him with bright lights and adjusting their telelens. He smiled on them, nodding.

He knew his decision now. It had been made in pieces and tatters. It had come from Kant, who had spent his life looking for a basic ethical principle, and had boiled it down in his statement that men must be treated as ends, not as means. It had come from Rover's passive acceptance of the decision of a god who could do nothing for him, and from the one rebellious act that had won Anne his respect. It had been distilled from Doc's final challenge, and from the old man sitting in his doorway, ready to face any challenger.

There could be no words with which to give his message to those who waited. No orator had ever possessed such a command of language. But men with rude speech, and limited use of what they had, had fired the world before. Moses had come down from a mountain with a face that shone, and had overcome the objections of a stiff-necked people. Peter the Hermit had preached a thankless crusade to all of Europe, without radio or television. It was more than words or voice.

He looked down at them when the church was filled and the organ hushed.

"My text for today," he announced, and the murmurs below him hushed as his voice reached out to the pews. "Ye shall know the truth and the truth shall make men free!"

He stopped for a moment, studying them, feeling the decision in his mind, and knowing he could make no other. The need of him lay here, among those he had always tried to serve while believing he was serving God through them. He was facing them as an end, not as a means, and he found it good.

Nor could he lie to them now, or deceive them with false hopes. They would need all the facts if they were to make an end to their bickerings and to unite themselves in the final struggle for the fullness of their potential glory.

"I have come back from captivity among the aliens," he began. "I have seen the hordes who have no desire but to erase the memory of man from the dust of the earth that bore him. I have stood at the altar of their God. I have heard the voice of God proclaim that He is also our God, and that He has cast us out. I have believed Him, as I believe Him now."

He felt the strange, intangible something that was greater than words or oratory flow out of him as it had never flowed in his envied younger days. He watched the shock and the doubt arise and disappear slowly as he went on, giving them the story and the honest doubts he still had. He could never know many things, or even whether the God worshipped on the alien altar was wholly the same God who had been in the hearts of men for a hundred generations. No man could understand enough. They were entitled to all his doubts, as well as to all of which he knew.

He paused at last, in the utter stillness of the chapel. He straightened and smiled down at them, drawing the smile out of some reserve that had lain dormant since he had first tasted inspiration as a boy. He saw a few smiles answer him, and then more—uncertain, doubtful smiles that grew more sure as they spread.

He could feel himself reach them, while the television camera went on recording it all. He could feel his regained strength welding them together. He could feel them suddenly one and indivisible as he went on.

But there was something else. Over the chapel there was a glow, a feeling of deepening communion. It lifted and enshrouded him with those below him. He opened himself up to it without reserve. Once he had thought it came only from God. Now he knew it came from the men and women in front of him. Like a physical force, he could sense it emanating from them and from himself, uniting them and dedicating them.

He accepted it, as he had once accepted God. The name no longer mattered, when the thing was the same.

"God has ended the ancient covenants and declared Himself an enemy of all mankind," Amos said, and the chapel seemed to roll with his voice. "I say to you: He has found a worthy opponent."

Return Engagement

It was later than Daniel Shawn had thought when they finally came out of the little farmhouse and headed for the big car belonging to Tommy Rogers. It was almost sundown. And there had been a light rain, since the grass was wet and the air had that crystal look where every color seemed deepened and purified. He took a slow breath, almost tasting the vigor of the air.

Strange that it should be late, though. Time had seemed to go so slowly. The whole visit had been a mistake that was hard on both of them. Now it was ending as clumsily as it had begun and continued in awkwardness. Once Tommy, now Professor Rogers, had been his friend, but that was before Tommy had gone into Administration and Shawn had given it all up to come back here to the little Minnesota farm where he had been born.

"A rainbow!" Tommy exclaimed suddenly. "I haven't seen one in years."

"Nor missed it, I'll warrant," Shawn guessed, raising his eyes to see it. It lay in the gap between the locust trees, adding a jeweled light to their dark greenness.

Tommy laughed his administrator's unoffended laugh and glanced back over the little farmyard before climbing into the car. "What do you find here, Dan? Kerosene lamps, outdoor plumbing, not even a radio. I still say it's no place for you when you could take over the Chair of History if you'd be sensible."

"I was born here," Shawn replied, evading the part of the question he didn't want to answer.

"But that was forty-five years ago!"

Shawn nodded. "Yes. And sometimes, I think, so was I. Let it be, Tommy, and I'll ride into Utica with you."

Tommy couldn't let it go, of course. There was that in the man which hated any way of life he could not understand. Maybe that was why he'd once studied sociology, only to find that the science could never supply the simple answers he wanted. He repeated his question as the motor started. And this time, there was no good way to evade it.

"I don't know," Shawn said slowly, fumbling for his pipe as he tried to answer it to himself. "Something I almost saw as a child and then lost. Something maybe all of us lost once. That's why I turned to history, to find where it went. But I never found it. You used to do a lot of reading once, Tommy. You tell me. What was in Spencer, in Coleridge a little, in *Orlando*, like an echo only, but which is gone now from all our writing?"

"I never thought there was anything like that," Tommy said flatly.

Shawn sighed. He should have known the reaction that was a part of the man. Then they reached the little village, no more than a mile from the farm, and he got out, putting out a hand awkwardly.

But Tommy wasn't ready to end it yet. "If you're going to eat here, I'll join you," he suggested.

Shawn shrugged, then nodded. He was sorry that he had given in to the man's importunings over the phone and let him make the useless drive from Chicago. There should have been an end to it now. Yet Shawn had intended to dine here, since his own cooking was no better than it should be.

He picked up tobacco and the paper at the pool hall before leading the other to the little restaurant beside the gas station. They ordered and waited for the food, with nothing to say between them.

The paper, Shawn saw from the headline, had been another mistake, but he glanced at it while consuming the tasteless food. There was a dark ugliness to the news, as there always was. The lilt of life was lacking in every part of it. It was heavy and ponderous, even when it tried to be witty. And around him, the few diners were filled with a heaviness that made their laughter a deliberate effort and gave them no pleasure in the stories they told endlessly to each other.

"Why?" Shawn asked abruptly, pointing to the headlines. "You're still a sociologist, Tommy. Tell me why we're like this? Why all the dark ugliness?"

For a moment, it seemed that there was a measure of understanding in the man. He sighed. "Sociologists don't know much more about the present cultural matrix than anyone else, Dan. Too much technology, maybe, before the culture can absorb it. Or maybe this is just one of the plateaus in an evolution towards a sense of group maturity."

"Maturity?" Shawn questioned bitterly. "It could be." And now the administrator's optimism was creeping back into the face of Tommy. "Oh, I know, there's still hate and ugly conflict. But think of the earlier ages, Dan. Look at the superstitious panics, the persecutions, the witch-burnings. There was a time when anything different from what was considered human was to be killed on sight. Children ostracize or fight with anyone who differs from the group norm. Seems to me we've improved a lot in that respect. At least in this country, we're trying to understand other peoples. Why, right now, Dan, if little green men got out of a saucer, most people would be delighted to meet them. Lots of men are hoping to find alien races. Look at Project Ozma. Or look at the case of that priest who is writing about the question of redemption for nonhuman beings. If there were werewolves today, I'll bet that there'd be a lot more scientific interest in them than fear or hatred. There wouldn't be any persecution of witches, unless they went in for some form of criminal activity. All that could be considered a form of maturity."

Or maybe the human race was so unconsciously sick of its own sordidness that it would welcome even alien relief, Shawn thought. But he let the conversation die. There was as little answer to the problem in sociology as in history, and he had already been aware of that.

He went out with Tommy at last, putting out his hand awkwardly in silence as the other reached his car.

"You sure you won't come back, Dan?" Tommy asked for the last time. "You're definitely turning President Schuyler down?"

"I won't come back, Tommy," Shawn answered again.

He stepped back from the car and stood watching it drive away. Then he sighed and dismissed the whole unfortunate business from his mind.

It was already so far into dusk that the stars were shining as he turned to walk homeward. The moon was up, full and startlingly white in the dark sky. There were wisps of clouds to fleece its path, but the night was going to be one of loveliness, he saw. For a moment he was glad he had ridden in, since it gave him an excuse to travel back through the beauty of it.

The road went across the railroad tracks that fed to all the earth, and yet with rails that seemed to lead nowhere in the moonlight. It carried him on, past the school where once a teacher had touched his mind, but where now there was preparation only for bearing the dullness of eternal ugliness in the news. Then it passed the old cemetery, shaded and filled with hollows of darkness. For a moment, there was a touch of the spiritual hush he had felt long before as he moved by the quiet place. Then it was shattered by a coarse laugh, and a burst of the smut-tinged words of a juke song on a transistor radio.

Superstition was dying, as Tommy had said. At least, the older superstitious fear of things in the night. But the darkness of it was being replaced by an even darker veil of sordid ugliness.

Even the dead had no peace. A couple had found the retreat for their own use, but without even the respect of silence. And maybe these dead could never feel the lack, if they could know. Yet Shawn felt his soul rubbed in dirt as he guessed the ages of the couple. They were using the time for what should have been an opening up in them for things better reserved for later years, and better served with reverence for their bodies than with mere eagerness.

The houses thinned out and were behind him, except for a single light back from the road half a mile ahead. Here the land dipped down, carrying the road with it. It had been a graveled road once, and Shawn missed the sound of the pebbles. But the moon was the same he had known long ago, and its light was like a kiss across the fields. Even crops cultivated by great machines instead of horses could take on a difference in the silvering from above.

Where had men lost whatever they had lost? History had taught him nothing, though he had searched. And the keys in literature were too elaborately carved to fit the lock. Books were written to bury the feelings of a past generation, not to reveal what might be happening.

There had been a magic in men once. Oh, to be sure, it had been rare enough, and whole areas had missed it. Rome had been mighty in valor and function without it. Much of Greece had lost it, though it lay somewhere in the soft hint of legends older than Olympus. But there had been Persia. There had been Queen Maev and the Isle of Avalon, the sea warriors of Ys, and the dreams that misted across man's rise from a beast. No time had ever been without it before.

Yet this time was lacking whatever it was. Save for a few bits borrowed from the past in Yeats, there was no song or dream in the poetry now; and nobody even read poetry to look for such things. The art was as ugly and machine-symbolled as the thoughts of the little minds that made it. The music was cacophony. And there was no legend anywhere, save the legend of power.

A car filled with teen-agers passed him, noisy with the machine cries of boys and girls. The top was down in the car, but none of them were seeing the moonlight. One of their age now who looked for it would have been exiled from their rigid ranks.

Shawn passed the sandstone ridge beside the road that marked the edge of his farm, and his steps quickened. A few hundred feet on, he lifted a wire gate and left the road. Here the woods still stretched along the road, and they were his woods, as they had been once when he was a boy. There, along the little rutted trail through them, was the hazel bush, or one like the one he remembered. Farther away in the dark mystery of the woods, there was the bush with the musty fruit whose name he had never known. He passed it, and came to the edge where woods blended into stubble fields. The wild grapes were ripe and sweet, beaded with the rain or dew. He tasted them and went on.

There had been a lilting in a few men's thoughts once, enough to lighten the others, and to echo still faintly out of the filter of older literature and legendry. But somewhere it had gone. Maybe the industrial revolution? But that was a poor answer, since the revolution had touched only lightly on much of the world, yet the wonder had vanished just as quickly. Maybe the drive towards power? And yet, there had been power before without the death of the glamour he could sense without defining.

Something had gone out of men. In its place was only the body of man's work—the machines, the dark forces that drove him on to bombs and destiny, the rockets that could lift him towards outer space but hide the dancing of the stars. Hundreds of years before, the lilt—and there was no other word—had vanished. History had failed to show why.

Shawn had come back here, looking for the threads he had lost in childhood.

He was still seeking them, though there was little promise yet that he could pick them out of the tangled skein of his mind, even here.

He walked on through the stubble left from the harvested barley. He had bought the farm and lived on it, but the farming of it he left to the neighbors. They thought he was odd, of course, but they were glad enough of the free use of his fields.

Maybe, after all, Tommy Rogers was right, and he belonged back at the University, quieting the last vestiges of yearning left among the students. Maybe his whole search here was a mistake.

"No!"

He said it aloud, as if ordering the doubt from his mind. But he knew already that he could not give up the search. Because in the last decades after the two wars of sordidness, the dark curve of ugliness had increased. Like all unchecked trends, it rose asymptotically. With the end of the lilt, the ugliness had crept out slowly, but now it was riding unreined, rushing faster and faster. A single generation had gone further with it than all who had come before. And unless the need for something else which man seemed unable to find could be filled, there would be no end to the dark forces.

He started to turn towards the little house. But something seemed to whisper in his veins. There was the feeling in him that he should go on. He went, past the sagging barn and down the lane towards the orchard. The pump at the old well creaked and gave forth water that was reddened with rust, but cold and tingling on his palate. He stopped to pluck an apple from an unpruned tree and munched on it.

And now the tingling was stronger, and there was a faint singing of the blood in his ears, as if a horn were being blown somewhere. It became louder as he crossed a stile into the meadow.

The grass was faintly damp. There was the smell of clover in the air, and under that the faint, rich musk of the earth itself. He moved across it, listening to the bending of the grass and the soft scuttling sounds of the little creatures that lived in it. From a pond beyond the orchard lane, the croaking of frogs reached him. The eerie call of a screech owl sounded over the other noises, and the chirping of crickets was a constant threnody.

The bugling of the strange excitement in his mind was stronger now. He headed for the little dip near the centre of the meadow. As a boy, he had lain there in the sunlight out of the wind and read *Princess of Mars* and Haggard and Dunsany, or in the moonlight at times when he was too restless to sleep and too filled with unremembered plans. It was too damp now for a man of forty-five to return to the earth, but the spot drew him to itself, all the same.

And then he saw the thing, centered in the spot towards which he was headed, and his heart seemed to leap with shock and then with expectancy. He moved to it slowly, trying to tell himself it was something left behind by some wooing couple or as a practical joke by his neighbors. But he knew better.

It looked like a shell made of something milky-white. Half was almost buried in the grass, and the other half of the opened shell was resting backwards against a rock. It seemed to be lined with a softness like the packed down of a milkweed pod. And it was perhaps eight feet long.

But it was the sweep of the lines and the tightness of the form that held his eyes. There was a fluting of the milky substance that lifted something in him as he had felt it lift before at an ancient jade screen or a phrase of Mozart.

There was no mark to show how it had come there, though he knew it must have been after the rain, since the lining was dry and soft to his touch.

Inevitably, he thought of flying saucer accounts. But he threw the idea out of his mind, like a man brushing dirt from himself. The ugliness of the times was reflected in the pitiful situation where men's dreaming of better things led only to the banality of the cults; and of all the cults, the flying saucer ones were the least alive with a spark of the lilt he sought.

Yet he knew without questioning that this thing had never been shaped on Earth. And as if to confirm his idea, his eyes caught sight of a design that was revealed softly in the moonlight against the lid of the shell. He bent to se it, but it was still too dim.

Finally, as he had known he was going to do, he kicked off his wet shoes and stepped into the hollow of the padding, letting himself down gently until his eyes were near the carving.

Moonlight shone gently through the lid, making it hard to be sure of details. But somehow, his eyes filled with the figure. It was a woman—or rather, not a woman, since the features were planed as no human face could be. A strange woman, thinner than any human and more supple, from the dance in which she was frozen. The final proof of lack of humanity lay in the hair that rippled from her head and grew into a double crest on her back, spreading outwards across each of her shoulders, but standing well above her skin.

And suddenly, her hand seemed to move! Shawn blinked, but it had been no illusion. The carved fingers opened and the arm moved towards him, just as the lid began to move inward to close the shell. There was a dancing cloud of motes that sprang from her hand and spread towards him. He lifted his arm, but it was too late. The gleaming motes struck his eyes, and they closed. Gentle waves of sleep washed across his brain. He had only time to feel the shell lift somehow and ride upwards into the moonlight before the sleep claimed him completely.

There was a sense of the passage of time, eventually. His eyes would not open, but he lay somewhere that was not on Earth, and he could sense that hours had passed. Hours, he thought—not days or weeks, but only hours.

Around him, there was a stirring. He could sense that the shell was gone, and there was an alien but earthy odor in his nostrils. Now sounds came. Voices—but no voices he had ever heard. There was a silvery quality to them, like the voices of children mysteriously robbed of the harsh overtones of childish screams. These were almost liquid. Yet he could sense a frenzy and worry in them. In the background, there was a chanting, and the heart inside him seemed to be crying as it ended.

He tried to sit up and open his eyes, but his mind was still not in control of his body. Some sign must have shown, however. There was a gentle touch on his forehead, and a few words obviously meant to be soothing. The words held a hint of familiarity, but he could understand none of them.

"Where am I?" he asked.

There was a sigh near him, and another voice answered. It was a strong, masculine voice with a power of command and responsibility behind it, even though there were no really deep tones. "You would call it Mars," the words came in oddly accented English.

"Mars? In a few hours?" Yet as Shawn protested, he sensed the rightness of the answer. The weight of him was little more than a third that which he had always known.

The voice was sober and somehow withdrawn. "Our ways are not your ways, Earthling. Our science means as little to you as yours to us. We accept the way of the universe where you bend the laws of nature against themselves. Who shall say which is better? Yet for this one thing of moving beyond the distances you know, we have ways you have not."

"Yet you speak English. Where—"

"There have been others—not many, but some few we have carried here." The voice was falling, like the ending of an organ note. "So few. And now…" It died away, and then resumed more normally. "But enough. We go to confer. Use the time until we return as you will."

There were rustlings again, and then light shone weakly through Shawn's lids. Something touched his face, and he found his eyes opening. This time when he tried to sit up, his body obeyed, though the motion was awkward in the unfamiliar pull of the planet.

A dream, he told himself. A fantasy. He'd wake in the morning wet and soaked in the meadow, sneezing with a cold from exposure. But he knew better. A dream like this could be none of his making. There were elements in it, as he stared about, that could never have come from his mind.

There wasn't much to see. He was in a room that must have been carved from colored rock, and there was a sense of a great many feet of similar rock above him. The light seemed to be in the air itself, diffused and softly silver over everything. He lay on what must be a couch, but a couch with soft curves and ornaments no man could have planned. And beyond him was a fountain.

It was a tiny fountain, carved out of the wall of rock, with a thin spray of water falling over into a basin, making a soft tinkling sound. And in front of the basin was the carving of a kneeling girl. This time there was only a hint of the shoulder crests of hair, but the green of the stone made the other features easier to see. No human artist could have fashioned that, and no human model could have posed for it. The girl was beautiful, but it was as if she came from a race that had descended from some of the lighter monkeys, as man claimed descent from the greater anthropoid ancestor of himself and the gorilla.

Then, without warning, a curtain seemed to fall across the room, cutting off most of it, and leaving him with only a little space before the couch. But if the blackness was of cloth, it fell without the rustle that should have warned his ears. It was suddenly there, soundless and dark before his eyes. And behind it was the stirring of others moving into the room and finding places—strange, odd stirrings unlike any he had known.

Behind the screen, the voice he took to be that of a leader began again. "What are you called, Earthling? I am Porreos, a prince of my people."

"Danny," Shawn answered. His own response surprised him. He'd not called himself that since his childhood. But he let it stand.

"Then, Danny, we have conferred. And we feel you are better for not seeing us, since you cannot remain with us. We are sorry to have brought you here, though it is too late to alter that. But you will be returned."

Shawn puzzled over it, finding no logic to the decision. Why couldn't he remain? Why pick him up and bring him over all the distance for nothing but this? And why was the shell on Earth in the first place?

He must have spoken aloud, because Porreos sighed and began to answer. "We had hoped for a child of your race Danny. One who could learn to live with us, as you could never do here. And the call of the shell was set for the yearning of one of your children. Strange that you should have answered. As strange as the shells that have returned to us empty. It has been so long, so long…"

Again it was the fading of an organ note. And behind it came the hint of a wailing song in many voices, a snatch of group response that cut into Shawn's nerves and brought tears to his eyes, though he could understand none of it. There was a delicacy here, a lack of strength and force, that hardly matched a race able to span space.

The air around him was almost as thick as that of Earth, and there had been a fountain of water. It fitted no picture of Mars, as these voices fitted no people he had expected to find on the harshness of the little world. Suspicion grew in his mind suddenly.

"You never came from this planet, Porreos!"

This time, the wailing chant began before the prince could answer. It was a thing of beauty and tradition, but the ache in it was like the ache of a man who would reach for the stars to melt them against the palm of his hand, and then look to find them gone. And there was a laughter to it like the laughter that there would be because of the aching he felt too strong inside his breast for anything else.

Shawn learned more from the song behind the words than from the answer that Porreos made. No, they had never developed on Mars, but far away. They had been an old race ten million years before. But on their world there had been another race, stronger, younger, with all that they lacked. And for a time, the two had touched falteringly, to the benefit of both. But then had come a great change over the younger race.

Something that the old ones could not understand had taken over the total emotions of the new ones, and had built a sudden hatred. The race that had sometimes feared and sometimes loved the race of Porreos was deliberately filled with superstition and belief that all other creatures were things of ultimate evil, to be shunned, hated and mistreated. And the old race had been unable withstand it. They had never been strong. They had dwelt on only a part of the home planet at any time. But now, finally, they were forced to flee.

Mars was the best they could find. They had carved dwellings out under the surface and trapped what little air and water there was. It was a poor home to them, but all they could find.

And now they were dying slowly, gently. They each lived for a long time, but they bred slowly to make up for it. And there was no longer the heart in them to keep up their numbers. All of the race that was left was here, behind the curtain.

"All," Porreos repeated as the song came to its end like the sound of the last leaf falling in the forest of winter. "Full attendance is a respect we owe you, at least, for disturbing you."

"But you'd disturb children, Porreos. You don't mind stealing them and bringing them here?"

"Don't condemn us without understanding," the voice said, and there was dignity and hurt in it. "We're a lonely people. We need others, and even a single child we can adopt and make one of us helps. And besides, there's another need which doesn't concern you."

And there, Shawn realized, must lie the real crux of the matter. There was some need—there had to be, to send the shells across space looking for someone from Earth. "Maybe it does," he decided slowly. "You've brought me here, and the reason should concern me as much as it would concern a child."

"No!" It was almost too strong a denial. Shawn waited patiently, as an adult might put pressure on a balky child. He heard the same pressure mount behind the screen, with a rising tempo of rustlings and subdued whispers in the tantalizingly familiar alien tongue.

And abruptly, that pressure of his waiting seemed to grow too strong for them.

"Don't ask us that, Danny!" It was almost a roar of pain from the prince. "Don't ask us. A child we can adopt and make one of us and be bound to. But it is not for you to ask. We're an old and a proud people, and our traditions are stronger than the laws of nature you Earthlings fight. We cannot ask favors outside our own, we cannot beg. No, we could not even beg for a part of the world that was our own. And we shall not beg of you!"

It was a nightmare experience, with a nightmare logic of its own, Shawn decided. And his logic was in abeyance, as if some part of him had already recognized that normal logic could not be used. But it was no more a nightmare than his own culture had become to him in the last few years. Beside that ugliness, this unreason was almost childishly simple.

"You're not begging," he told the group behind the curtain. "I'm giving. Tell me what you want of me and take it."

There was a shock of silence, and a whisper that was not in the voice of the prince. "You trust us that much?"

To his own surprise, he did. Somewhere, his mind was making a pattern out of all this, and he was not afraid of them.

"As a free gift, then," Porreos said at last, and some of the fatigue seemed to lift from the voice. "We have one who is dying. And there is something in your blood which can save her—a resistance that our bodies lack. We need a few drops of your blood, Danny."

Shawn got up quietly from the couch and approached the curtain. He thrust out his bared arm experimentally, surprised when it penetrated with almost no resistance. He grinned at himself as he waited. The Army had taken enough without asking, but he hadn't been able to help that. There'd been appeals bombarding him from all sides on Earth to give blood, however, and he'd managed to deny them. He'd somehow had no desire to share his blood—the blood that was the life of him—with the dark and ugly currents of the life around him. Yet now he felt no objections.

There was the tiniest of prickings on his finger, and a brief itching. When he withdrew his hand, something like a fine mesh of cobweb lay over the end of the finger. Somehow, he was sure there would be no infection.

There were stirrings but no voices behind the screen, and he waited, staring again around the limited section of the room he could see. It was beautiful. There was a shaping of beauty no man could have rendered. But there was a weakness, a lack of the very brutal force he sensed in even the ugliness that was overtaking Earth. And there was no lilt here either.

"Danny," Porreos called at last. "Danny, there is life among us in one who was dying, and your blood is our debt. Before we return you to Earth, there is another tradition which we must keep. And it is as strong as the tradition that prevented our begging, even for life. So believe it and accept it fully."

Shawn smiled again to himself, and the pattern in his mind was taking shape at last. "I'll believe you," he promised.

"Then make one request of us, as is your right now. And if we can fulfill it, the boon is yours."

It was what Shawn had expected. It could be no other. And there was still a surprise to the discovery of it.

No, he thought, there could be no lilt here and none among his people. The dark force there and the fair lack of force here were both incomplete. And the lilt he had named and sought could only come from a true completion. No wonder the shell had come to him in answer to his yearning. No wonder that these people sought a child of Earth while his lost people overcame even their ancient xenophobia to make wish-dreams of alien contact from the stars.

"Porreos," he asked, "can you follow my thoughts?"

"A little, Danny Shawn." The voice was reluctant, as if the admission carried unknown dangers. Then it was suddenly filled with intensity. "Yes, oh yes, we can follow!"

The curtain vanished, leaving the room visible to Shawn, and he could see all of the elder race that was left before him. There were less than a hundred of them, green-clad and brown-garbed men, and women with delicate, winglike mantles of hair. Their faces were inhuman and their tiny bodies were strange. Yet they were familiar as no alien being could ever be familiar.

"Ask your boon," the prince of the fairy folk cried. But they already knew, and there was laughter rising and smiles spreading across the elfin faces that looked up towards the human.

Shawn met their laughter with his own, and there was a lilt in his voice now.

"Come home," he asked them. "Come back to Earth. We need you!"

Omega and the Wolf-Girl
[a.k.a. And the Darkness]

There was no space in the tiny cabin for nervous pacing. A scant eight feet separated the hallway entrance from the small porthole that showed the dull black of space; and across, the distance from the locked door on one sidewall to that on the other could have been spanned by the young man's arms. Only his eyes were free to roam the narrow room, and they were tired with endless repetition.

For a moment, his gaze rested idly on the porthole, and he stared outward through the cold and the darkness to the tiny point of light that was Earth; but there was no conscious recognition of what he saw. His eyes dropped back to the shelf that held his manuscript, his ink, and the purple, untouched candle. And it was only as he picked up the lump of wax with slow, reluctant fingers that he thought of the valley in the hell world that had produced it…

The man's shoulders were bowed under the grim weight on his back, and the alpine stock trembled in his grasp. But he fought upward over the last remaining feet until he was at the top of the pass and the wastelands were behind. Even then, he could not trust the weight of his burden to his shaking hands, but sank carefully to a sitting posture until it touched the ground and he could ease his arms out from the straps. Finding a reasonably portable generator to replace the one they could patch no more had been a miracle, and he had no faith in a second one.

For a time he lay quietly, breathing in ragged gasps and staring into the valley that was cut off completely from the world by the surrounding mountains, except for this one narrow pass. Dirty snow straggled down to blend with leprous, distorted scrub trees and run down to flat land. And there a few log and stone buildings stuck up uncertainly among the crumbling ruins, to mark the last failing outpost of the human race, three centuries after the Cataclysm. The man grimaced and began to pull himself to his feet.

Then an answering clatter of stones sounded from around a rock, and Gram was beside him, pulling him upright and massaging his still trembling shoulders with gentle hands. Her seamed old face broke into a brief flicker of perfect teeth, and her fingers were unsteady, but there was no emotionalism in her voice. "I saw your smoke signal last night, so I've been waiting. I guess I must have been catching a catnap, though. You've been gone a long time, Omega. Okay?"

"Okay, Gram. The generator's in there, and enough fluorobulbs to light all the huts. But I'm glad I didn't have to stretch rations another day. I had to work my way clear to old Fairbanks to find it. That wasn't pretty! They knew it was coming hours before the stuff hit them!"

"Umm. Here! I figured you'd be hungry. As for the bulbs—" She shrugged and pointed to the purplish plants that grew all around, a mutation as deadly as the hard radiations that had produced them. "I'll stick to sprayberry-wax candles. They have other uses; or at least Peter thought so."

So gentle, patient old Peter was dead, and there was only an even dozen of them now! But Omega was too tired to care much about anything except the food Gram held out. She watched him wolf it down, and her face lighted faintly as she dropped beside him.

"Eleven worn-out old people and you, now. The last dozen poor supermen," she said with a nod toward the valley; and her voice was filled with the same grim humor that had made her christen him Omega when his mother committed suicide over the rock-mangled body of his father.

But Omega knew it was more than humor. In a normal world, with a decent background and half a chance, they might almost have passed for supermen; except that no such world could have produced them. That had required an Earth left wrecked by the Cataclysm from a cold and casually unjust universe—a world where hard radiations made every birth a mutation and where every undesirable change was savagely purged from the race.

In a way, it was ironic that men had barely avoided wrecking the planet themselves with plutonium, the lithium chain reaction, or the final discovery of a modified solar-phoenix bomb. But somehow they had eliminated that danger at last—and found their triumph useless. It had been a simple communiqué from the new Lunar Observatory, at first; they had spotted a meteor having a paradoxically weak but impossibly hot level of radiation that indicated contraterrene, or "inside-out" matter. The second announcement spoke guardedly of the danger of grazing contact. And fifteen minutes later, the moon ripped apart as electrons canceled out positrons into energy and left a great flood of unattached and destructive neutrons.

Surprisingly, there were survivors of the rain of hell-fragments that fell to the earth. Near the poles, a few deep and narrow valleys were only grazed slightly, and where there were contained mines or caverns to offer some protection against the radioactive dust that fell everywhere, a measure of life went on after a fashion, and a thousand or so survived. Now three centuries had whittled down the number, and wild mutations and ruthless survival of the fit had compressed a thousand generations of evolution into one.

There was Gram, who might have saved the race, if her cell structure had appeared in time. Like the wolves and the rabbits that had inherited the Earth, her cells had finally found the mutation of totipotency that defied all but the most intense concentration of radiation to burn them or cause further mutations. When a wild new plague had wiped out her people in another valley, she had taken the boy who was to become Omega's father, a rifle, and a sled, and set out through a roaring blizzard to cross four hundred miles of hell to this place. Now, sixty years later, she could still outwork any man in the valley, except for Omega's maternal uncle Adam, on the rare occasions when he exerted himself.

For Adam had specialized in pure laziness and purer logic that seemed to leap from isolated hints of facts to full-grown knowledge without effort. He had slouched in when Omega was fumbling over calculus and his eyes had lightened with sudden interest in the books he had never troubled to read. Hours later, he had been explaining and making clear the complex mathematics which his mind had carried beyond the wildest dreams of the prechaos scientists. With the same ease, he had seized upon the French books Omega brought back from a trip. Even if there had been a grammar or dictionary, he would have regarded them as too much trouble to use.

But it required more than such wild talents to separate a group of freaks from supermen; it took background, opportunity, racial culture, and a future. And in those things, the wolves were their superiors.

Sudden light flashed from the valley, disappeared, and returned to hover beside them. Then the spot wobbled erratically across the pass and came to rest against a flat, shaded rock, danced crazily, and steadied down to business. Below, the thin, lanky hands of old Eli must have been using the big mirror on a long board to give the microscopic leverage that was all he needed. His talent lay in a coordination and control of nerves and muscles so nearly perfect that he could shape and handle the infinitesimal tools needed to manipulate individual micro-organisms within the field of a microscope. Now the spot of light fluttered, but its motions were clear enough to spell out letters.

"*Hurry, need generator,*" Gram read, and chuckled. "Sure you found one, eh? Let them—uh...*Wolf girl located!*"

A gamut of expressions washed over her face, giving place to sudden determination. "Come on, Omega! You can rest later. Here, let me help you with that pack."

"Why the hurry, and what's all this wolf-girl stuff about?" After the short rest, the pack weighed a ton, and the pass looked ten miles long. No wolf was that important, whatever it had done.

Gram slowed up a little. "Something we never meant to bother you with—Ellen's baby, your cousin. Grown up now, must be. We saw her with a wolf pack once before when you were away, but thought she'd died later. Oh, come on, before they start a search without shields. I'll tell you some other time."

"They won't start without shields," he assured her. "She was living with wolves, Gram?"

"Must have been. And they'd start, all right. Tom and Ed died out there last time, before you invented the shields! When it comes to race preservation, they'd rather all burn than see you go unmated! Will you hurry?"

He hurried; nobody disobeyed Gram. But there was a picture of what a wolf-girl must be in his mind, and the idea of such a mating sat heavier on him than the pack. And he'd thought the old fires of racial preservation were dead!

Adam met them, took the pack, kicked aside one of the shaggy, huge-eared pigs, and paced beside Gram without a trace of laziness. Its squeals gave the boy time to get over the shock of that before his uncle answered Gram's questions.

"Jenkins—off by himself as usual—went to sleep at the far end. Early morning a howling woke him, and there she was with a couple of wolves. He got a good look—seemed human, all right, a stick in her hand. Time he got there, she was gone, but he saw the direction; reckon I know where she lairs. He came in half an hour ago, fagged out. Soon as we got it out of him, we signaled."

"Umm. Wonder where she's been since we saw her the other time, Adam?"

"Off somewhere. Studied wolves when I was a kid—they wandered all over. And with your blood, so could she. Lucky she's back." They reached the powerhouse and Adam shut up, while Eli began bolting down the generator on a rough base and connecting it to the old waterwheel. There was a glow to his face that was new to Omega, and it was reflected by the faces of the rest of the group.

They were all there, except for Jenkins, whose green pigmentation and chromosomes that came in triplets instead of pairs represented the only remaining physical abnormality. With that had gone a whole host of wild extrasensory talents that made him fully aware of the unpopularity they won him. Of the others, Eli, Adam, and Simon were already harnessed into the shields. A product of Adam's mathematics, Eli's amazing workmanship, and some of Omega's ideas, they made space a nonconductor of all radiation beyond a certain energy level. They also distorted gravity slightly for some reason, but it was the only way the others could travel in the outlands.

Simon snapped the last battery in place as it finished flash-charging, while Gram made a hasty inspection. "Omega's worn out, and I don't want her to remember me as the one who caught her, if I'm to handle her, so it's up to you. Think you can do it, Adam?"

"I figured some on it. We'll get her."

"Good." She watched them start and turned back to her hut. "Let the others gaup, Omega, but we're eating, and then you're going to bed...after I tell you about Ellen and the girl."

It wasn't much of a story. Beside Omega's father, Gram's hitherto-unmentioned baby daughter had survived the plague and the trip. She'd grown up, married Simon after Omega was born, and there'd been a baby coming. Jenkins, who would know, had said it was to be a girl.

But some accident on the hellish march had twisted Ellen's mind, and she grew up as an insanely religious fanatic. Apparently the thought of her baby marrying a cousin had been a heinous sin in her eyes. Anyway, they found a wild note, but they had never been able to trace her.

"God knows, we tried." Gram's soup was untouched before her. "You never spent years praying for just one girl-child—one fertile girl in a world dying of sterility, Omega! Just one, because the hard rays couldn't trap your kind from the world anymore. My line's fertile, and the baby would have been... You're too young to understand, but the old need babies; when you're close to death, you need proof that you're physically immortal through the race—not just soul-stuff. Oblivion's close and taut around you when there's nobody left to remember... Oh, go to bed before I start blubbering!"

But Omega's mind was filled with an idiot-faced thing in human shape, making animal sounds and snapping with raised hackles. Kipling's *Jungle Books* had been only wish-dreams; those who grow up with animals must always be less than the beasts they follow.

But his emotions were less logical; under his disgust, a queer tingle mixed with an unformed picture of abstract but intensely personal posterity. One fertile female, and they could bask in the warm physical immortality of racial perpetuity; a race that had been dead and unmourned now could think in future tense again...Tearing her food with drooling tooth and savage fang, growling animal noises, pacing her cage with wild idiocy in her eyes...

"Can they catch her alive?" he asked as Gram began drawing the pig's-wool blankets up over him.

"They'll do it, somehow; we made an agreement to that. Either they come back with her alive, or they rot out there!"

She closed the door quietly behind her, and Omega was alone to wonder at the savage drive that had lain dormant and unknown so long around him. But no thoughts could keep a man awake after the grueling trek he'd just finished, and somewhere in the middle of the thought, he blanked out.

The searchers were already in sight when Gram awakened him, two of them staggering under the twisting gravity of the shields; but Adam apparently was able to predict the shifting force, and the leading figure was steady and resolute. Between the others, there was a covered figure on a long pole, and the tiny clan was gathered outside the hut in a shouting group. But by the time Omega had doused his head in water and joined them, they were silent again. The three were closer now, and their faces and the pose of their bodies could be seen, even in the gathering twilight.

They dropped their burden in the same rigid silence, and Simon, who had been Ellen's mate and father to the child, turned, motioning to his twin sister, and went off toward their hut. The others waited uncertainly, until Adam bent down to pull the blanket from the figure on the ground.

"Wrong word accented on wolf-girl, Gram, but here she is. Now what?" And he yanked the cover from the forlorn creature that lay bound by its feet to the pole.

It was a wolf; strange and odd of form though it was, there could be no shadow of doubt as to her lupine origin. The teeth that gleamed through the ropes around her jaws were wolf fangs, and the tail settled any further question.

Yet it was easy to see how Jenkins could have thought her a woman in the dim starlight, for the mutation that had somehow produced her in spite of her parental totipotency had shaped her into a mockery of human form, and she was as anthropoid as wolfish. Her rear legs were long and her short front ones ended in lengthened toes to caricature human hands. Her forehead bulged and her jaw was foreshortened, while the mane on her neck might have been mistaken for a head of hair if she stood upright. And because she was built in a woman's shape, there was something pitiful about her as she lay glaring up at them.

Jenkins felt it first, and his sigh broke their silence; he pushed forward, his shy, fearful eyes half-filled with tears. For a second, he hesitated, before his hands ripped aside the cords that bound her mouth. Her lips drew back, but she made no move to snap at him as he faced the others, his quavering, timid voice filled with bitterness and apology. "The ropes cut her lips, Gram. Her mind's all dark and swirling fog, hard to see, but she's crying. Not for herself, but for her babies back there, little ones like her. Do we have to kill her, Gram?"

Gram shook her head to clear it, and her voice was as low as his, and as uncertain. "But you saw the wolf-girl carrying a stick. Can we be sure...? Look further into her mind."

"We found the stick," Adam answered for him. "She'd need one, with her build. Couldn't run on all fours, not quite ready to go upright very long. Jenkins, what's her name?"

"Her name? I—I can't see very well. Something about hunger-pain, I think."

"*Bad-Luck*. Called that because of the way she's built, I guess. Not much of a language, unless they changed it since I was a kid. Better'n your telepathy, though. You read off what I think, while I try her."

His lips contorted out of shape, and a queer wailing whine slid eerily out. The wolf-girl's head jerked around, and her eyes shot behind him, to come back reluctantly to his as he called again. At the third try, her own lips parted in an effort, closed, and opened in sounds between a growl and a whine, yet somehow articulated and hopeless. Perhaps the sight of a man and a wolf-mutation talking was as logical an ending for the day as any other; at least, the little audience watched in unchanging dull listlessness.

Jenkins' voice droned forth, reading the meaning from Adam's mind. "Surprised at him...Not mad at us, why should she be?...Hunting's natural...Is he man or wolf?...Yes, she'll answer his questions. No, never saw any human shes outside the valley...No baby shes...When are we going to eat her?"

"Ugh! I suppose... Oh, let her go! I wish I'd never known she could talk, Adam, but now—" Gram sighed, staring about for suggestions and finding none. "Tell her we'll feed her, since we ruined her hunting, and let her go; but she's to keep out of our valley and let our stock alone. I guess that's all we can do now. Can you tell her that in her language?"

"Say it all right—they've improved it some; but for her to understand's another thing. Translate the Bible to wolfish, if I had to, but it wouldn't mean much to her. Takes semantic training to work out much with a hundred-odd words, though it can be done. Umm." He frowned, considering, and Little Jenkins, again conscious that his gifts were unwelcome among normal minds, slipped away quietly before Adam began.

It took longer this time, and there could be no doubting the surprise and slow dawn of hope on the creature's face as the meaning finally sank in. She lay quietly, her eyes riveted on his as he untied her; but it wasn't until he placed a frozen leg of pork in her oddly human hands that she believed him. Her tongue came out in a hasty licking motion against his hand. Then she was gone at a jerking run.

But she stopped, hesitantly, as a high wail broke from him, and paused long enough to answer his cries before her figure faded away into the twilight. He grinned crookedly at Gram, and shrugged. "No smell of people outside that she knows of."

"No." Gram sighed again and pushed the door open. "Come on inside, Adam, Omega. The rest of you go back to your huts. There's no good to be had from freezing out here. We had our fun, but it's over now, and we can forget the wolf-girl idea."

In that, she was wrong. It was less than three hours later when a subdued howl from outside drew Adam up from the table and out into the night. Outlined in the dim light of the open door, Bad-Luck had returned, and beside her hovered an old and grizzled wolf, with raised hackles and bared fangs, but motionless as the feared man-beast approached.

Their conversation was erratic and uncertain, with long silences, but eventually Adam nodded and the wolves melted into the darkness. He came back to the hut with a shake of his head and a strange smile, and dropped onto the stool to watch Gram's hands go on remorselessly with her Canfield.

"The old wolf is their Far-Food-Sniffer; keeps in touch with all other packs, I gather. Anyhow, no wolf on the whole planet knows the smell of men, except here…Funny! Nature seems to be cooking up replacements for us, and not wasting time. Came a long way since I studied them. Ethics! Gratitude!"

Gram nodded wearily, and dead, dull silence settled over the hut, relieved only by the monotonous slap of the cards.

It was barely past noon when Simon and his sister were found the next day, deep in the catalepsy of sprayberry poison. Within them, the incredibly slowed labor of breath and heartbeat would go on for hours longer, but it was too faint to be detected, and their bodies were already cool to the touch. Yet they could still be revived, and Omega turned automatically to get the neutralizing drug. Adam's hand stopped him.

"No use, boy. There's always more poison." He looked around the room once more, taking in the magnificent paintings the twins had done, then pulled the door shut behind them and began nailing boards over it. Wooden steps carried them back to the cold-frames where Gram and Eli were at work setting cabbage seedlings. But the hammering had carried the news before them, and no comments were made.

The only sound was a distant drone, like an early swarm of bees, and it disappeared as Omega dropped to the cold earth and began replanting. How many, he wondered, would live to eat the plants when they were grown? There were only ten now!

Then the buzzing was back, and Gram was dragging the others up to face the sky, where a roaring something grew out of emptiness, flashed over, and faded away again. "A ship! A jet plane!"

It couldn't have been, and yet it was. There was no habitable land below 60° north latitude; one colony of the original three had reported itself dying of famine; Gram's had perished in the plague; and the wolves knew of no smell of men outside the valley.

But they were already at the powerhouse, and Eli's hands flipped over the switches of the crude spark-gap transmitter the first survivors had built, and the current danced between the electrodes in code so rapid it was like a steady crackle. He waited futilely for an answer from the humming speaker, and began transmitting again. Then the roar was back, and they had only time to look out before a flash of metal screamed down, wriggled, zipped up across the pass, and was gone again. Gram lifted her fist. "The dirty spalpeens! Making fun—"

Before she could complete the gesture, a young masculine voice burbled out of the speaker. "Hi, people! Took a little time to find and match your frequency—your signal sprays all over the kilocycles. I can't understand that greased-lightning c.w., though, so give me three slow dots if you can receive modulated stuff... Fine! Sorry I couldn't land with my fuel reserves, but I'll be back. Meantime, take a look at the film I dropped. Planet Mars, signing off!"

Mars! They'd been almost ready for that, but... And his voice had been filled with a strange quality that instinct recognized as youthful enthusiasm and sure self-confidence. It must be nice—

Jenkins interrupted their reverie by laying a package on the bench. That would be the film, though he alone had seen it fall. For the first time any of them could remember, Eli's hand fumbled as he ripped at the junk wound hastily around the thing, and it was Adam who finally freed the little machine and found the light switch. He focused it carefully against the gray stone wall, located another button, and sat back to watch the moving scenes.

They were obviously conventionalized drawings at first, but they were clear enough. A man labeled Mason stood in the port of a crude rocket ship with his young wife, while a crowd cheered and drew back. They waved, shut the port, and lifted on a jet of flames. The Earth shrank behind, while the moon slid into view and went quickly past. But Mason was framed in a porthole, just as the moon broke loose in lancing hellfire. Scenes showed his wife trying to nurse his burned body and frantically fighting to bring the ship down on Mars in a crumpled landing. And thin, furry, four-armed anthropoid things came out to take them down to a strange underground primitive world.

After that, Mason was their teacher. They had been dying for lack of power, but now the ship's atomotors gave them the margin they needed to rush upward to a self-sustaining civilization that could even bake air and water out of the dead crust of the planet. Mason grew older, and six girls were born to him. But careful schematics showed that the moon-blast had rendered his male sperm cells sterile, and there were no boys. They stored his superfrozen spermatozoa and sought valiantly for a cure, but they had not succeeded when the screen portrayed his funeral procession.

The final scene showed a glorified statue of Mason, holding a book in one hand and stretching a symbolic atom upward with the other. Below, eight young and human women were grouped about a great rocket, with their faces turned to the sky and their arms lifted in mute appeal. Then the film ended.

Omega wasted no time on the others' comments. The boards on Simon's door came ripping off under his straining muscles, and he was inside and forcing black liquid down the throats of the twins. The vegetable dye they used to color their clothes and serve as their writing ink had revived poisoned pigs before and should serve equally well for men. It did. The late afternoon sun saw twelve of them again, watching as the ship settled downward on its jets a hundred yards away.

A thin, four-armed, furry figure came out, to be followed by two apparently identical others. And then, while the dozen humans waited in tense expectancy, the door closed firmly and the aliens headed toward the group—three Martians and no Earthmen! Beside him, Omega heard Gram's breath whistle out heavily, and an animal snarl from Jenkins. Only Adam seemed unruffled and unsurprised as he sauntered forward to grasp the leader's hand and make proper introductions.

Jaluir's furry face remained expressionless, but his voice was the warmly enthusiastic one that had come over the speaker. "So you really do exist? Where the deuce were you last winter? There wasn't a sign of life that we could see."

"Holed up. Snow gets twenty feet deep down here—covers everything. We seal up and hibernate in the caverns back there till after the spring floods. Explore all nonradioactive areas?"

"All seventeen. This one came last, and our plane broke down for a month, or we'd probably have found you." He shrugged, a gesture that must have come down from Mason. "After that, we gave up hope until I made a forced landing in old Fairbanks. I was pretty sure someone had been there recently, and Commander Hroth let us stay over another week. But it was a devil of a job locating your campfire sites to get a fix."

"Why bother? You didn't come just to see us—not with people of our kind on Mars!" Gram's voice was suddenly old, tired, and suspicious, and the Martian blinked in surprise.

"We needed some metals, of course—but wouldn't have crossed space yet for just that." He hesitated, and his next words were fumbling and uncertain. "The girls who saw us off—we failed, in spite of them—they are the last. We had only the Prophet's male germs... We have taboos, too, ma'am, but—well, we had to do what we could. Now, when our hopes were gone, the gods have given us life again!"

"Umm. Well, you might mean it. You and your friends had better come inside, I suppose. No use standing out here."

"If it's all the same, I'd rather see that radio transmitter of yours," he answered.

Gram nodded grudging approval, and Omega was glad of the excuse to rescue Jaluir from their frozen faces. It didn't make sense. When even a Martian crossed forty million miles to pay a neighborly visit, he deserved a little warmth in his reception. Instead, Gram was adopting the same attitude with which she'd greeted Adam's proposal to scrap English and switch to a fully semantic language of his devising. The boy fell into step with the alien, while the others followed.

The transmitter held Jaluir's attention for only a minute before his eyes began traveling over the rest of the powerhouse. The crude Millikan microscope Adam had designed from the fruits of Omega's wanderings was inspected more thoroughly, to be followed by one of the little radiation shields.

"Cuts off high energy radiation," Adam volunteered, and his eyes were speculative, in spite of his easy grin. "Take it along if you can use it."

The Martian nodded and dropped it into a pouch on his belt—his only article of clothing. "Simple after someone else discovers the principle. Thanks! We certainly can use it... We wondered how you reached Fairbanks."

Gram grunted. "Nonsense! Omega and I don't need contraptions; we're naturally immune to radiations."

"*Zot luil!* You're—!" The face that he turned to the boy now was no longer expressionless. It held a burning excitement that no alienness could conceal. He twisted on his heel and snapped out syllables in a strange tongue that sent the other two Martians toward their ship at a clumsy run. But when he faced them again, his emotions were under control, and his voice was even and friendly.

"Sorry, but I've got to go back to the ship for a few minutes. Look, let's get down to brass tacks, shall we? How soon can you leave?"

"For Mars?" Gram asked.

"For Mars. It'll be five hundred years before Earth is really habitable again, at least. And you can't go on in these little valleys. What better sanctuary than a grateful Mars? Of course, you'll need a little time—but talk it over until I get back."

And he was gone after his companions.

Gram sighed wearily, and the stiffness drained out of her body. "Sanctuary—or slave pen? He seemed nice enough, but—"

"He's a monster!" Jenkins' normal meek whisper was distorted into a savage, hate-filled wheeze. "An inhuman monster! His brain is blank—all blank. I can't even feel it."

Adam's cool voice cut into his ravings. "Take it easy! If you can't snoop in his mind, you don't know what he is. And you don't hate a man for that—or do you? Personally, I liked Jaluir."

"So did I," Gram admitted, but there was no lifting of the frown on her face. "We would! You can't catch a wolf without something attractive for bait. And maybe he is all sweetness and light. The missionaries meant to help the Aztecs, until they found gold and Cortes came. And our ancestors made slaves of the black people and tried to exterminate the Jews for not being exactly like themselves—and Mars is a lot stranger to us than anything we found here. Maybe we're gods to them, as he says; and maybe we're animals."

Their doubts were growing by a process of mutual induction, until even Omega's ideas began to veer toward them. But his words carried no conviction in either direction. "Of course, we can't be sure; we have only the evidence they designed for us. But he seemed friendly."

"Why shouldn't he be, when our planet's loaded with minerals they need? We're used to gravity that makes them uncomfortable, and we can stand the radiations, now. He liked that part—a little too much!"

Gram hesitated, and her gaze turned to the east where her native valley lay. "We always took even better care of our animals than ourselves. I know, because we had horses when I was a girl—until a careless fool left a gate open and our two stallions were killed by wolves. He tried to hide the evidence, because he knew what we'd do to him. But I saw it all, and I was young enough to carry tales. Poor devil! They turned him out to the wolves, eventually...Men will do strange things for beasts of burden, Omega."

"Or for pets," Adam added thoughtfully. "Vote?"

But no vocal poll was needed. Simon and his sister moved toward the door, and his sad, dulled eyes were quietly reproving as he looked at Omega. Gram turned from one to another, and at last she nodded quietly and went out toward the huts. In a moment, only Adam and Omega were left in the building.

Jaluir found them there, and the lilting jingle on his lips broke off in a sudden puzzled grunt. Adam chuckled wryly! "Gone! Took a vote, after a fashion. It's a lousy world, Jaluir, but we're staying. And don't ask why, because I don't know."

"But you can't—you're... *All* of you? Omega too?"

"That's up to him; he didn't vote. Rest of us stay, anyhow."

"Oh." Jaluir considered it, shrugged, and gave it up as a hopeless riddle. "I won't pretend I can understand, but if that's the way you really want it, I'll explain it to Commander Hroth somehow. Anyway, I've got to return to the main ship before it gets too dark, so I'd better shove off now. But I'll be back in the morning to pick you up, Omega."

He grasped the hand Adam held out and was gone, to take off a minute later in a flaming roar and go speeding over the mountains. Adam slumped against the door for a few seconds, then came in and began quietly buckling on a radiation shield.

"Going up to talk with the wolf-girl," he volunteered with deliberate casualness as he finished. "Curiosity. If I don't get back in time to see you off—"

"Who made up my mind I was going—Jaluir or you?"

"Fate! If they're nice people, you should; if not—well, they'll have weapons and ways. Good luck, son!" He slapped his nephew's back lightly, grinned, and went sauntering off, leaving Omega alone with his thoughts. They were not good company.

But Adam's logic was unanswerable, and Omega's packing was done in the morning when he awoke from fitful slumber to see the plane already landed and waiting beside the row of silent, boarded-up huts. He had helped Gram nail them shut during the night, and he knew that only Gram and he were left, beside Adam, still among the wolves. Even little Jenkins and his queer, twisted talents! Gram sighed, and her eyes, red with lack of sleep, followed his gaze.

"Forget them, boy. Jenkins was always a little crazy, and Eli was dying of cancer, anyhow. The rest were—useless! Sometimes I used to wonder about such things—the warped, strange ideas of isolated little communities, and the references in the psychology books to contagious suicide during times of trouble. But there's something more."

She shook her head wearily, drawing her hand across her forehead. "It's a curse, a will to death that made them sterile because they wanted to be, and made them die whenever they had an excuse—no matter how much they refused to believe it. Call it a mutation that crept in unnoticed, or say the whole race gave up and went quietly insane after the hell years. They could have built some kind of glider plane and kept contact between the valleys, if they'd had the spunk, and none of this would have happened. Anyway, there's a curse on the valleys… You'd better go now, Omega. Don't keep Jaluir waiting too long."

There were words inside him, but they wouldn't come out. Gram laid her brown old hand gently on his mouth, and the ghost of a smile appeared on her lips. "No, just go. And sometime, if you have children—not slave children, Omega, but men—tell them of the last men on Earth. I'd like that!"

The doors of the huts were all closed when he looked back from the plane, after all his gear was stowed. Jaluir motioned him to a seat beside a window away from the huts, and he sat staring at the instrument board for what seemed hours while the plane waited. Then the jets screamed out suddenly, and they were airborne after a brief run.

"Below," the Martian said softly, and pointed.

Tiny but distinct against a patch of snow, a figure stood waving up at them, surrounded by dark dots that must have been the wolves. Jaluir dropped the plane and circled as close as he could, and for a moment Adam's easy smile was visible. Then he turned and slipped into a cave with the pack, and there was only the Martian's silent grip on the boy's shoulder and the sound of the jets as they sped off across the wastelands.

…The warmth of his hands had softened the purple wax, and he sat molding it idly, while his eyes remained unfocused on the shelf before him. Now Earth was faint in the distance, with Mars looming up large and red before them, but he was less certain than before of what awaited him there. Sanctuary or slavery—he could not tell. Somewhere within the notes before him must lie the answer; but his mind went on pacing an endless circle, unable to break from the ruts it had worn, and the key eluded him.

When he began his manuscript a week before, it had seemed simple, and the ink and candle were still there to remind him of the plan. Among men, it might have worked. But even human motives were uncertain, and these strange men from Mars were of another race. He had mixed with them, supped with their quiet commander, and listened to the tales of Mars that Jaluir told so well. But he did not know them; nor could he hope to before his children were old enough to curse or bless him for the outcome; and that would be too late.

With a sudden sweep of his arm, he knocked the things from the shelf into a trash container, and swung around—just in time to see one of the side doors swing open quietly and an old and familiar figure slip from behind it.

"Gram!"

"Naturally. Who else would spend twelve days watching you through a one-way mirror to see whether she had a fool for a grandson?" But the strain in her voice ruined the attempt at humor, and she gave it up. "I found the candle in your bag, Omega, and I knew you'd find other ways if I destroyed it. So I made an agreement with Jaluir, and my stuff was on the plane when you awoke… And yet, at the end, I wouldn't have saved you. If there's any difference, I'd rather see my descendants slaves than quitters!"

Omega shook his head dully. "I wasn't planning suicide, Gram. I thought they might dump me and my notes at once if they were slavers, like the man in your story who tried to cover up and escape punishment for carelessness. Or if they were friends, they'd wait until they read my notes and found out how to revive me."

"Umm. And you'd have no responsibility either way, eh? No, boy. Men could have colonized the planets ten years before the Cataclysm; but they were too busy with their fears. Until the last minute, they were so afraid of war that all they could do was prepare for it and nothing else. The survivors could have found ways to get to all the valleys and multiply again, but they gave up and sat blubbering about the dirty trick fate played on them. We've been a race of irresponsible, sniveling brats! And now it's time we grew up out of our nightmares and accepted our responsibilities."

Gram shrugged, dismissing the subject, and turned toward the doorway to the hall. "Come on, boy. Jaluir says we're almost there, and we might as well see what it looks like."

But Omega could not dismiss the subject so readily. It was good to have her old familiar strength beside him, but in the final analysis, she could not help. The decision he had been forced to make was his responsibility, and no other could share it. Men had their faults, and they were great ones. They had come up too fast, and their cleverness outstripped their wisdom. But no single individual could deny the race one more chance for the good that was in it.

Three centuries of bitter hibernation had burned away some of their childhood, and they could start anew to learn the lessons they had neglected, if they had the courage and were given the chance. The hard radiations that had come, like the rain from heaven on Sodom and Gomorrah, had left gifts to replace the things they had burned away, and it could be a great race—almost a new one. Together with another people and another culture to temper its faults and encourage its virtues, it could develop beyond the dreams of all the poetic prophecies. But would it happen that way, or would men become only the cunning vassals of an alien lord?

"I am Alpha and Omega—the Beginning and the End," Gram quoted softly, as if reading his mind. But the words that should have been encouraging were grim and foreboding. For she had named him Omega, and he was the last of the Earth race. But there was no one to call him Alpha or to promise that he was the beginning of a new race, no longer Earthbound.

Now they reached the end of the passage, and already the red disk of Mars was pushing back the cold and the darkness of space before them. Omega sighed gently. He could only pray that it was an omen of the future—and wonder.

Perhaps he would never know.

Uneasy Lies the Head

Hudson was beautiful at night, with its great spread of lighted ways and its parks grown mysterious by moonlight. Even the ugliness of the river docks had been hazed into a shadowy glamour, and the moonswath over the ocean beyond was churned into white froth by the graceful immensity of a seagoing liner. Then, between the Parliament House and the Palace, dancing letters of fire sprang into life, proudly flaunting the weakness that underlay all its beauty.

> HUDSON, THE DIRECTOR'S CITY
> *May He Reign Forever!*

An unforgettable century had tried men's souls beyond endurance and found them wanting. Where men had once carved a great Republic out of the wilderness, their descendants swarmed the streets and gazed up at that symbol of dictatorship with gentle, contented docility. It was Jason's world, and a pleasant one. Bless the Director!

Six hundred feet above them, Jason leaned weakly against the window as his heart struggled and missed, and a suffocating constriction tightened on his chest. He shuddered, fighting back the physical hysteria of the attack, but his voice was still calm and level. "How long, then?"

"Maybe six months, if tomorrow's lab reports are favorable!"

Six months! It should have come as a relief, after seventy years of sole responsibility for a world too passive to do its own worrying, but even now he dared not accept the death sentence his body had placed upon him. He shook his head wearily, and let his eyes drop back to the streets below.

Twelve decades had seen two chemical wars, one with nuclear fission, and two more with all the incredible hell of material energy. Yet somehow, the race had survived, even though the last nineteen-year reign of fury had taken three billion lives, decayed from spheres to nations, and vented its final chaos between village and village. Sixty million had passed through all that, but its psychic trauma had left them weak and submissive. Those who had struggled were dead, and the weak had reluctantly inherited the earth and passed their psychoses on to an apathetic progeny. Men had sought power, and men had died; better a live serf than a dead crusader!

Two generations of listless anarchy had followed, before a rude paretic named Knude, driven by half-insane frenzies, had built himself up from self-claimed rule of a village to world mastery. It had taken a scant twenty years, and he had found no opposition, save his own fumbling mistakes. His queer genius had built union, and Jason's had given it form, Now…six months!

But the worst of the attack had passed, and the Director turned back to the darkness that was relieved by a single bulb, Dr. Sorgen was waiting with the mercifully silent understanding that was typical of the man. Jason mustered his strength to hold his turban-covered head erect and his face a mask of quiet firmness as he resumed his seat and moved a knight deliberately.

"Sorry, Sorgen; what about Herker's ACS work?"

"A brilliant fizzle, like Bogolometz' original." Sorgen said, and his normally placid, middle-aged face was puckered into a frown. "Napier's longevity technique should have given you a hundred and fifty years minimum, though."

"Except that I had your predecessor remove my sleep center so I could burn out twenty-four hours a day. New heart?"

"Could you stand twenty minutes of necrolepsy, even if I broke the record? Oh, damn it!…Check!" Sorgen hunched his shoulders in professional disgust, but his voice was over-brusque as he fumbled for his pipe. "Why the devil didn't you let me check up when I wanted to, instead of demanding a spot prognosis now? You must have known; you're not a complete fool, Jason!"

"Fool enough to think I could solve the insolvable. I need ten years, maybe a hundred. One I *must* have!" But he read the answer in the doctor's averted eyes, and slumped back into the leather chair, idly scratching at the heads of the two big dogs beside him. "Somebody once called benevolent dictatorship the best government short of ideal anarchy, Sorgen, and it's true for this world, though a strong people can afford democracy. But even perfect dictatorship is the most dangerous rule ever devised! When your ruler dies, his successor may be a fool, a brute, and a weakling—and there's no check on him. Not even the royal tradition of *noblesse oblige!*… Nema, what about Bill 693?"

"Passed unanimously, Excellence," a primly efficient voice answered from the communicator.

Jason grunted. "In five hours—eighty pages of legal gobbledegook! And that's the only check on my power, after fifty years of trying to create a real democracy!… In all that time, *one* man accepted his real responsibility. I had great hopes for him—until his constituents decided I might blame his 'treason' on them. They pulled him out of bed in his pajamas, and chased him out of town in midwinter to die of pneumonia! And now I have six months to find a successor!"

The weaker the people, the stronger must be their ruler. He dared not demand less than he had been forced to become, and so far there had been no other with the strength for that iron self-discipline. Probably somewhere in the world there were a thousand capable of replacing him, but the Director had no means of subjecting three hundred millions to all the tests needed to find one of them. The very benevolence of his rule had eliminated the opposition that might have developed and revealed a worthy successor.

"But aren't you forgetting history, Jason. When Knude I died—"

"History isn't always accurate, Sorgen," Jason answered wearily. "Knude died of curare on a nail designed to work through his shoe! He chose me as the world's best scientific mind, counting on a scientist's lack of political ability, and forgetting that the master of a dozen sciences could learn even that, if he had to. I had to—I knew Knude's plans! The responsibility is mine, not history's... Checkmate in four moves!"

Sorgen shook his head doubtfully. "Not if I move—Mmm! Which leads to what, aside from the fact that a robot would make a better chess partner for you?"

"Which leads, of course, to your robot. If I can't find a successor, then I have to make one!" The Director watched the confusion on the other's face, and a slow smile crept over his mouth. "Suppose robots existed? You know people—would you build metal men, Sorgen? Would you call them robots with that word's semantic connotations, even if they could think, learn and remember with genuine intelligence? Well?"

"No, not unless I wanted trouble, I suppose. I'd probably call them something like heterofiddle deedee phlumphees, and build them into switchboards, calculators, or—" Sorgen's speculative look jumped to confused awe, and then twisted into sudden certainty. "Jason! Voice-operated typewriters! What else would know I meant *too* instead of *to*?"

The Director's smile broadened. "Exactly! Your vocatype and one of my chessboards are robots, inhibited against independence... Nema, will you come in?... So are my two dogs incidentally, to give me protection against any chance insane crackpot. But are you sure you'd rule out humanoids? Bodies are easy to build, now."

"Absolutely. Men have protoplasmic habits—they giggle, follow archaic taboos, and think mostly with their endocrines, so they'd spot any imitation. And they still believe in Frankenstein's monster."

Jason grunted doubtfully. Men also saw faces in clouds, and read purely human intelligence and contrariness into their mechanical inventions. If an office clerk behaved like a machine, they called it efficiency and gave him a raise!

But a quiet, mousy little woman had come in through the door on silent feet, and he dropped the argument. "The perfect secretary—the result of fifteen months of analyzing the best human for the job, and using her as an education pattern. Suppose you show him, Nema!"

"But—but, Excellence! Dr. Sorgen—"

"Will share all my secrets," he finished for her. "From now on, if anything happens, I'll need him, so he's my shadow. Show him!"

Nema dropped reluctantly onto one knee and began a series of operations that ended with her holding the top of her skull in her hands, and her head open to view. Inside lay a three-inch sphere, enmeshed in a maze of wires, and nothing else. Jason waited while the doctor let his mouth close slowly, then motioned her to her feet and dismissed her.

"Thank you, Nema, that's all." There was no smile on his face as he moved toward a panel that lifted to reveal a small private elevator. "And now, Sorgen, if you'd like to be the first visitor in my personal laboratory, I'll show you my mechanical double, and—perhaps—your future Director!"

A stereo producer would have developed severe frustrations in the laboratory; except for a panel of controls and outlets before a desk, and a table of metal-working tools, it might have been a locker room. Yet it was home to Jason, and he dropped gratefully into a chair and motioned Sorgen to another. The slight exertion of the trip had been enough to set his heart pounding, but it quieted as he began the old routine.

From his turban came scanner and recorder reels to be replaced by new tape for later use. The old ones were slipped into receivers on the panel, and tiny cables came out to couple him directly into the recording "brains" while he was in the laboratory. The old tapes began playing on a screen before him, varying as automatic habits took over the task of controlling emotional response and annotations that would shape them into the closest possible semblance to his own personal reactions. From older records, the brains could draw on accumulated past experience to fill in the picture.

"Every minute of my life is there," he told the doctor, without looking up from his work. "Everything I could recall from my very earliest childhood has been re-enacted just as I saw it and heard it. Every decision I ever made has been remade by this. I've spent half of the last fifty years on it. As for the history and how it operates—you'll find it all in this introductory manual for students in my private commercial laboratories. It will give you the picture while I finish this... There isn't as much to it as you might think."

There wasn't much to it—in the book. Applications tend to become increasingly simplified as theory is extended. When subject to magnetic current, certain metal colloids in a silicon jelly would propagate links between affected nodes, intermittent conductivity increasing with use. After the momentary passage of current, however, the links became resistances to cut off further flow until another stimulus. It was vaguely like the response and inhibition pattern of interaction between brain cells.

Unlike the brain, however, all nodes could link, and the links propagate sub-links, in turn propagating others. Nema had five hundred nodes, and this model possessed ten thousand, to yield fifty million links, a quadrillion sub-links, and one and a half novillion sub-sub-links. There would be no danger of overloading the memory circuits! Even the crude first model that Justin Ehrlich had developed was still as flexibly open to new knowledge as ever, after over a century.

Sorgen chuckled suddenly, and the book was open to the old man's picture. "Quite a character, that grandfather of yours!"

"The stubbornest and most crotchety man that ever lived," Jason agreed, but there was affection in his voice. Justin had spent twenty years on the vocatype because of a petty fight with his typist. When the final war began, he had packed up and dug into MacQuarie Island and gone doggedly on, building up the simple little magnetronic memory tube to a thousand input model. While the war raged, he had spent fifteen hours a day pronouncing words and typing them until the machine was conditioned to the flow of words, and even the tricks of punctuation and homonyms!

And then, back in the post-war ruin, he had stubbornly begun dictating the original book that had started it all, and that no one would ever read—only to find his machine a mutineer. In the middle of a passage, it had stopped, kicked out the paper, and deliberately begun a revision. Twenty dictations and failures later, even his stubbornness had relaxed enough for him to learn that his hero's middle name had been Xavier, as typed, and not Xenophon!

He never finished the book, but he left thousands of pages to show his progress in teaching the meaning of words to the brain. Years after he died, the original Brain had finished the novel from his notes, revised to suit the new conditions, and it had been a best seller.

And it had been that Brain, working with Jason, which had finally solved the seemingly hopeless problem of the long years of labor required to educate each brain. Now modified "implanter" brains, coupled with individual erasable memory tanks, could feed the required knowledge into the new mind in a matter of hours. Behind the laboratory panels, fifty separate implanters were coordinated to hold and develop the pattern of Jason's mind, though full integration could never occur until the time when the final robot was awakened.

Jason stirred finally, and swung around to see Sorgen finished with his reading and waiting patiently. "You'll find the robot in a cradle behind Panel C," he answered the other's searching look. "But it's only a perfect mechanical duplicate of my body, with a few connecting wires that will come off after integration. A touch of this red button—a few hours—and Jason II becomes ruler! The panel's unlocked."

Sorgen shrugged and disregarded the panel. "It would only be the outside, not what interest me, Jason. I've been thinking while you worked... Oh, I'm not immune to the usual phobias about robots! I was all set to sound off on a sermon concerning your dissimilarity to God! Now I'll skip that, because I think you've already delivered it to yourself—fifty years of it. You brought me here for advice, I take it?"

"I'm not planning on turning a monster loose, Sorgen. It was Knude's discovery of this and his ideas that forced my hand to murder. Since then, fortunately, few have guessed the secret, and they're included in the tight inner clique. Curiosity seems to be another vanished human characteristic, anyhow. But—before saying the ruler must be human—remember that my successor will control this secret, too. If he's a fool..."

"I already thought of that; knowledge can't be withdrawn, once put into use. Then the question boils down to how human your robot can be—right?"

The Director nodded, deliberately letting the long responsibility fall from his shoulders for the grateful moments that another could pick it up. The Brain had stated flatly that it could not help him, and had suggested a human consultant. He should have taken its advice sooner.

"Ability to learn, to remember, to correlate, and to decide—or to be conscious of self?" Sorgen mused. "The last, I think, since it leads to social consciousness. I suppose Nema was a very limited trial balloon, and that you asked whether she had that trait? And she said she did?"

"She would have. Any imitation of a man has to have a pattern of that kind implanted, to avoid misuse of pronouns, and impersonal adjectives instead of possessives," Jason answered. He let the tone of his voice indicate the long and futile tests that had failed to establish the reality of that consciousness of self.

Sorgen fumbled with his pipe, packing and tamping the tobacco while he reshuffled his thoughts. "So it breaks into two problems: Can a robot pass as a man? And can it be trusted as a man? You've taken care of the first, now that I look back on it, by dropping all possible human traits yourself—deliberately depersonalizing yourself to the public. Want me to sum up the questions on the other angle?"

"No. They're obvious."

No mechanical education could possibly include all the details of a man's life, particularly of the early formative years. The all-important emotional color of the thoughts must be supplied from within—and with two different types of brains, could similar "experience" assure an identical response? The Brain had written the end of Justin's highly emotional novel, but who could say how coldly it had shaped those paper emotions? Pure intelligence could never be enough.

A man or a nation with no sense of humor would always be a piece of social dynamite, needing only a spark to fan out into megalomaniac barbarism. Frankenstein's monster had been a gentle, pitiful wretch at first; and a sense of humor to absorb the shock of men's reaction to him might have made the transition to his final form impossible! The old German Reich had been quiet and industrious, but a mere sense of horseplay and jollity had been too little to save it from its well-deserved oblivion.

"Damn Herker's failure and damn our mass-murdering ancestors!" Sorgen knocked his pipe against the table, watched the bowl break off and bounce on the floor, and threw the bit against a wall. Then he caught himself and grinned crookedly. "I was going to damn you for throwing this at me, but I see the pressure you're under."

"Some of it, maybe. I've had decades to study the fine art of worrying."

"Umm. And it hasn't helped your heart. If you appoint even a slightly wrong successor, his power coupled with this knowledge may go to his head. If you don't make a choice, somebody like our efficient police chief stands to take over by simply declaring himself in... With time enough, you could vitalize the robot and watch for trouble, ready to step in if needed, but... No way to check up without vitalizing, I suppose?"

"No good way, but I can check its decisions." While not fully integrated, the implanter brains were linked, and there was a circuit that permitted asking questions without affecting the memory links. "I've checked it against every problem to face me, found the reasons when its answer wasn't mine, and corrected them. Now it seldom errs—sometimes it even antecedes my decisions. But I can't be sure. In dealing with myself, practically, I may tip my hand."

The doctor frowned, and then was on his feet, moving purposefully toward the panel. And sudden relief washed over the Director as he caught the thought. Of course, Sorgen would not be dealing with a deliberate copy of his own mind. His questions would not tip his hand! And as the man followed the simple directions and slipped into the headphone and mike harness, Jason located a stale pack of cigarettes and let his mind go almost blank, while the half-forgotten feel of the smoke spread soothingly into his lungs.

The other's low mutter was meaningless, but he was uninterested in the nature of the questioning. It wasn't until the doctor finished that he snapped back to full consciousness. Sorgen swung around slowly, pushing the harness away, and his eyes were on the floor.

"Nonsense," he stated dully.

There were seventy years of discipline behind Jason, as well as seventy years of failure, and his face remained unmoved. He crushed out the cigarette and stood up. "Better get some sleep, Sorgen; there's a cot folded into the wall there."

He should never have had his sleep center removed; the time it had given him had been useless, and now the healing power of the long hours of semi-consciousness were denied him. There was nothing to keep him from remembering, and the memories were not pleasant. Futile dreams, wasted hopes, a son killed in an accident before he could assume rule, a grandson...

He had need of that iron discipline in the morning as he watched his grandson and the young man's wife move down the long length of the reception hall. There was no emotion on Jason's face, even as the boy went out without a backward look, dragging his spite-filled mate quickly after him. Sorgen came around the big desk, and dropped a sympathetic hand on his shoulder, but the Director shrugged it off and rose to move between his dogs toward the office.

"You heard the whole sordid story," he said woodenly. "Do you see now why the old problem of my successor became so suddenly acute, after lying dormant? I learned all this only yesterday, before I called you in."

The doctor dropped into the office chair with a weariness that showed how little good his sleep had done, and his voice held some of the same lack of expression. "Paul's still brilliant. At least he has the Ehrlich mind!"

"Which is why he's still Governor. I suppose his weakness is my fault. I never had time to supervise him as Grandfather Justin trained me when I was young, and he's this world's child... But he's certainly not Director material. If Bella can twist him, others can. And she doesn't twist him for his own good. Ever hear her sing?"

"Once." Sorgen's wry grin mirrored the Director's.

"Exactly. Naturally it took a lot of pulling strings and chicanery to get even with the men who wouldn't let her star in the State Opera. And since he was willing to cheapen his office for her personal pique... Sorgen, we'll have to risk a heart-graft! I need time to find a successor!"

It seemed hours as the slow minutes passed, and at first, Jason was only conscious of irritation at the long delay; then the truth seeped in slowly. The other fidgeted with his new pipe and groped for a good professional opening, but he wasn't particularly good as an actor, and he knew it. The Director's long sigh broke the silence and ended the need for a beginning.

"I see. So the report has come in already. That bad?"

"Weeks—maybe!"

Jason let the fact sink in deliberately, sitting with his hands motionless before him and without a quiver to mark his thoughts; there were no thoughts. Finally he turned to the communicator and pressed a button that brought Nema's quiet little figure into the room. "The record officials here, Nema?"

"They've been waiting, Excellence. I'll call them." She was gone for a minute, to return with the five officials and their recording machine.

Nema spread a paper on the table, and the men adjusted their apparatus. The final signed and witnessed document went into a slot, and they moved out again, but the secretary still lingered.

Jason waved dismissal. "That's all, Nema, unless you have something else... Well?"

"Excellence, with—with your permission?" She hesitated and stopped, waiting for his nod before turning uncertainly to the doctor. "Dr. Sorgen, in my outer office... Please, the Clinic Supervisor has been waiting..."

Jason cut through the other's protests with emotionless words. "Go ahead, Sorgen. You'll find me in the laboratory when you're finished. Nema has a key."

He could think better there. Not that his thinking would matter much, but the habit of decades led his feet unerringly to his retreat, with the old phrase uppermost in his mind. For the moment, he was content to let his muscles guide him.

Instinct carried him to the work-panel, where he began the automatic business of feeding in reels of used tape and reinserting fresh ones. He knew there was no point to it all, now that the robot idea must be abandoned, but it served to pass the time as well as anything else. He coupled himself to the board and went on about the usual routine of editing the tapes, while he reoriented his thoughts to the idea that there was nothing he could do.

Oddly, it was no shock. It was as if something that had lain festering in his mind had broken, releasing its poisons, and leaving only a numbness behind. Death itself would be welcome, after the long weary years and the last painful months. The responsibility remained, but he had done all he could.

The will which he had recorded was at best a desperation measure, the gesture of a man seizing at a straw. Now that he knew how short his time was though, there was little could do to improve on it. Sorgen was an able man, and a thoroughly honest and decent one; whether he would be weak in office was something only the future could decide. A man who makes no effort to attain power is seldom a good choice for its control, but it was obviously a better solution than his spiritless grandson.

The Director grinned bitterly at the emotions that insisted on flooding back. No man likes to leave an empire without seeing his own blood inheriting it; even a religious man turns without thought to the hope of physical perpetuity through his offspring. He had pinned too many hopes on that! And too many others on direct personal inheritance of his empire in a mind that was a copy of his own!

Perhaps that very vanity—his subconscious craving for a direct inheritance—had ruined his chances of finding a successor. Jason, builder of a dynasty—a sorry, power-crazed fool along with all the other stupid rulers of old!

But he knew better. The robot idea had been justified, and had been right. While he could trust himself, there could another independent mind of which he was equally sure.

And perhaps the thing had not been a failure! No mind scattered into fifty divisions could be expected to duplicate a single integrated unit. He could never know certainly until the button was pressed and the real robot came out, fully experienced and alive. Only then could he pass accurate judgment.

For a second, he reached toward the red button, to catch himself and jerk his hand away. Weeks! It was too late. He should have done it long before, when he could wait for the years needed to assure himself that it was no Frankenstein monster, no clumsy impostor who would reveal its falsity at the first crisis. Now it was too late.

Too late... The numbed, repressed emotions were crowding up now, pushing aside all the savage discipline of the years. Too late, *too late*, TOO LATE!

Reason returned suddenly, along with agony! The vise was back about his chest, choking him, and his heart was pounding with a wild increasing clamor that wrenched a scream from his lips. Heart failure should be gentle, peaceful! Why did his have to fail in so spectacularly agonizing a fashion? Why couldn't it finish the attack, before the strain burst it? With an effort that brought cold sweat trickling down his forehead, he forced his lungs to empty and fill, but the choking did not abate!

Even as he heard the click of the key in the door and saw Sorgen's surprisingly happy face twist into a knot of horror, he realized that it would never be weeks. He was dying now! Inside him, his heart pounded once more, and then seemed to explode. The pain stopped.

There was a haze over everything as he brought a thousand-ton hand up through a million miles into a gesture of salute. And then great slow waves of peace rolled over him, and turned jet black!

It was only a faint stirring, hardly to be called consciousness, at first, yet somewhere mixed into the vagueness was a feeling of existing. It went away, and a definite sense of time elapsed separated it from the first flicker that had meaning. It was only a picture of a meadow, with an old man swearing savagely at a box that kept arguing back with the same note of angry sureness.

Then there was a play of blurred, cloudy realizations, all jumbled upon one another until none made sense, and a rushing and strange whispering down all his nerves. A feeling of well-being came which he was vaguely sure did not belong to him; there was an expectation of pain and agony, but the cool, soothing comfort continued.

He tried to open his eyes, but they remained tightly closed and he could hear no sounds. Something sneaked into his mind and then tried to hide, but he chased it down relentlessly, forcing it from corner to corner until at last it gave up and came to meet him.

Death! He'd been dying. Something about his heart? Of course, his heart had been failing. But he wasn't dead. He was quite positive of that, without bothering to reject any doubts as to an afterlife; he had never doubted that death was the end, and he did not question but what he was alive. Now the mists were slowly clearing from his mind, opening up wider and wider frontiers of consciousness.

Once before there had been something like this, when his sleep center was removed, and he was regaining consciousness. Well, so he hadn't died—that meant that Sorgen must have found him in time and performed the impossible job of making the heart-graft. He groped for pain, found none, and decided it must have happened days before, and that Sorgen had kept him under drugs until the work had time to heal.

He'd forgotten, after the years of slowly increasing trouble, what it was to have a body that behaved normally, and permitted full efficiency. Just being alive was a pleasure again! He could have felt no better if his lost youth had returned.

Or had it? Sorgen's face had looked so completely free of worry before his eyes had spotted Jason's trouble. Herker must have stumbled on a line of ACS work that succeeded; maybe that was why the Clinic Supervisor had wanted Sorgen. It made sense—a new hope for rejuvenation, and a miracle by Sorgen that somehow had preserved a flicker of life in him until it could be used!

Then the tension released, and he sat up, to spin around easily and feel his feet contact the floor as his eyes opened. Good man, Sorgen! The doctor was there, waiting in front of him. But…It was still the lab, and Sorgen's face had been a dark cloud of gloom, only now changing to a sudden elation. The lab! What kind of a miracle had Herker—or someone—dug up that could perform a miracle like this with no medical equipment and no time to move a man's dying body?

"God!" Sorgen came to sudden life, and his voice was incredulous. He was across the room, even as Jason came to his feet, his arms slipping around the Director and supporting him.

For a minute, Jason had need of the support, since his feet seemed determined to work against him; but the clumsiness passed quickly, to be replaced by sure certainty. He pushed the other aside, enjoying the purely physical pleasure of moving about without paying for each step with deadening fatigue.

"What the deuce happened, Sorgen?" he wanted to know. "I'd have sworn I was dead. And now—"

"Now you're alive!"

"Obviously. But how did you do it?"

Sorgen shook his head, and a little doubt returned to his face. "That can wait, Jason. Thank God, the idea wasn't as cockeyed as I thought while waiting for you to come to. You've been—out—for hours! Now, how do you feel? Anything wrong? Any signs of some kind of shock?"

"Not a thing. I never felt better in my life. Those last few minutes before I blacked out..." Jason checked his words, shook his head. Funny! He had no memory of how he'd felt, though he could remember every sight and sound, including the last theatrical gesture, and Sorgen running toward the panel. He'd heard of pain so intense that it could burn memory of itself from the brain, but he'd never really believed it. "Anyhow, what happened? I know you did the impossible, but how?"

Sorgen shrugged, hesitated, and began reaching for his inevitable safety-valve. At last, he stuck the pipe in his mouth and fumbled for words. "I didn't do a thing, Jason—you did it yourself—except for one minor little detail. And then I thought I'd muffed it, since it took so long. Here, come over here. Look at that and draw your own conclusions!"

The sight of the naked robot's body on the floor meant nothing to the Director, except the puzzle of why it wasn't back in the cradle, but he dropped obediently to inspect it. When he arose, his face was tense, and he groped back into a chair before facing the human being in front of him. No wonder he couldn't remember what the pain had felt like nor, accurately, any feeling of pain ever, though he could remember its physical results!

But his voice was still level as he faced the impossible fact. "So you pressed the button, eh, Sorgen? Thanks for changing the clothes to this body and taking me out of the cradle... Funny, I don't feel any different. I feel like the man who was ruler of this world for seventy years, except that somehow another seventy doesn't seem to bother me any more. My mind's the same as it was."

"You wouldn't know if it weren't," Sorgen pointed out reasonably. "It doesn't matter, anyway. It's consistent, human and close enough to the original. The years of checking all decision and cross-checking until you had time to find the same solution as your original took care of that. Know what that decision of yours was—the one I called nonsense? No you were cut out of the memory circuit, of course...was to make me your successor!"

"But that wasn't nonsense. I—he—*I* did name you Director!"

"So Nema told me. Incidentally, she wanted to see me alone, and that story of a Supervisor waiting was just a trick—a robot lie—to get me away from you. She wanted to ask me how you were, because she was worried by your obvious sickness and your sudden will. She's scared sick, both for you and what will become of her!"

Jason frowned. "I never built such ideas into her."

"Naturally. But you built thought in. I'm beginning to think the brain controls the endocrines a lot more than the reverse. My guess, now, is that intelligence can't be pure—not if as carefully mechanical a mind as Nema can develop a personality. If a robot had no feeling of self, it would turn itself off and stop bothering!"

Sorgen stopped to relight his pipe and to glance at a clock on the panel. "While you were integrating, I had time for a bunch of thought, and I took a Ps.D. degree before my M.D, as you know. Put down that 'human' intelligence rot to vanity; the noun doesn't need the adjective. After all, a complete amnesiac remains pretty much the same sort of man as before—sometimes a better one. You're no amnesiac; you're lacking a lot of detail, which you'll color up and dub in eventually till you won't know it, but you have 99% of Jason's experience. He started out with almost no reactions to events, and he didn't need some outside twisting of his emotions to create his thoughts. The same goes for you. For forty years or more, you saw exactly the same, heard the same, and reacted the same as he did—so you had to think the same."

"Rather a backwards statement of cause and effect," Jason objected. "But I'm the last person to call it wrong."

Sorgen went on, paying no attention as he worked things out while they were still fresh in his mind. "Man gets the world through six senses—of which your sense of smell is crude now, and your kinesthetic sense a little different. But to the average man, those don't count too much. The 99% overrides the trivia.

"And I'm not mixing cause and effect. Psychology isn't that simple; we learned long ago that they're two names for the same thing. Start acting happy, and you soon are happy, as well as vice versa. Anyhow, as far as I'm concerned, Jason never died!"

The new Director accepted the other's hand with emotions as complicated as any purely human brain could have held. There was no use wasting words in thanks to the man who saved him, when he might have as easily taken over control of the world. Sorgen wasn't the type to violate the spirit of his Hippocratic oath, even had he wanted to rule, which he obviously didn't.

"Then suppose we put this body in the cradle until we can dispose of it and forget all this," he decided. "There was nothing in my education to make me like staring at my own corpse!"

The other chuckled, and they began clearing the laboratory, while Jason's mind opened up on the new vistas before him. Five hundred years of full activity should be enough to restore hope and independence to the world; until he would no longer be needed. And by then the planets should be open—all the planets now, since men could go forth clad in imperishable bodies suited to their environments. There would be time to lick the problem of letting the race in on this secret. He'd always wanted to see what Jupiter was really like.

They were almost at the lift when the doctor stopped and grunted.

"Just thought of something," he answered the Director's look. "I seem to have worked myself out of a job, and to be unemployed as of now. You hardly need a physician!"

Jason's grin flashed on with the ease of a man who no longer had to keep his life to a mechanical level capable of easy imitation by a functional robot. "I'll need someone to explain my miraculous life-span and perform magic cures later when the world gets enough spirit to want to assassinate me. And having spent fifty years on a decision I never made, I don't care to get along without a mind to check mine for five hundred. No, it'll take maybe ten years to build another robot, but if you'll permit a slight change in body, I think can guarantee you a rather long job!"

"Umm. Long enough to become a decent chess partner, maybe? Seems to offer reasonable security. I'll take it." Sorgen stuffed his pipe in his pocket, and the easy chuckle was back in his voice. "Now we'd better go up and comfort Nema before she turns neurotic!"

And There Was Light

Stefanie was still white and weak, but the worry on her face had nothing to do with her recent sickness as she rushed about the small, crudely furnished apartment, trying to appear normal. Johann Volcek studied his young wife, worrying more about her than the meeting for the moment.

If the child had only lived...

Then he smiled a bit ironically, before letting his mind come up with the old palliatives. There'd be other children for him and Stefanie—and for this half of the world. The other half would simply have to suffer painlessly through a generation, for the good of the whole world.

"But the Director, Johann..." Stefanie's voice was on the thinnest edge of hysteria. "Johann, to our place! If I'd known, I could have made curtains, at least. And can you be sure..."

"It isn't suspicion, *radost moya*," he assured her quickly. "I told you the Director trusts me—he has to. And he simply wants to see you. You know he's a family man himself."

But he let her work, fussing about the place, refilling his coffee, brushing an imaginary speck of dust off his coat. The doctor had told him that work was best for her—anything to get her mind off the lost child until there could be others. And the Director may have been a better distraction than any of the others, aside from the flattery of it.

Then the telephone on the wall rang sharply, and he answered it. smiling back at her. "Volcek."

"Good, Johann." It was the Director's Secretary of Science, Jean Petrecci and Volcek's sponsor. "We shall be there soon—and it's a beautiful day for the test, not so?"

Johann agreed quickly, though he had not yet had time to look through the windows even, with Stefanie's worry over the visit of the Director. But as he looked out now, he saw that it was a good day, clear, with only thin wisps of cloud in the sky.

Then, in the street below, there was a stirring, first of big cars, and then the shouts of the people. It was silenced, and the creaking elevator began to thump upwards. Stefanie made a last frantic dash into the bedroom, brushing nervously at her hair, and came out just as the knock sounded.

Johann had been right—the Director must have trusted him, since the big man had come up with only three of his guards, and now came thrusting his broad shoulders in, his greyed head not even, darting about the room, his eyes leading him toward the Volceks.

Quick admiration filled his eyes at sight of Stefanie, and his gruff voice was soft, the voice the radio brought them when he was the Father of the State, or when he was telling them of the new plans for more food and better living.

"Sit—I'm only one of you, you know. Ah, Johann, this is the little Stefanie. I've wanted to meet you, to see the one Johann has spoken of so often." His language was perfect, but with the queer stilted effect it always had when he was not reading a prepared speech.

Watching Stefanie stammer over the honor of the Director's presence, and then relax gradually as the spell of the man took over, Johann began to smile more naturally. The Director was talking of his own beginnings—in much less than this—and the moving they would soon be doing, into a newer apartment, a fine new suburb. And surprisingly, he was talking of his own wife and children, and Stefanie was answering.

Remembering stories of the Director, Johann found it hard to recognize this as reality. The man had come up from the lowest ranks, an iron hand leading him up the ladder of Centralia's autocratic bureaucracy. But now the hand was sheathed, and even Stefanie began to smile.

Then it was over, and the Director was rising. Johann kissed his wife quickly, embarrassed slightly at the Director's approving smile, and they were out in the elevator, heading toward the big, waiting cars. "Now I trust you, Johann Volcek," the Director told him. "Now I can go with you to this test. With such a wife waiting you, there can be no trickery against the State. No—don't say it! It is not you I could distrust—it is everyone I must distrust. But not now. What does the doctor say?"

"Another year." For a time they had been afraid that Stefanie could never have children again, but the new treatments had apparently been effective. Centralia's progress in all phases of gynecology had been spectacular.

The Director nodded. "Good. The State needs such children as you will have. And a man has need of little ones. But tell me—you still feel sure of this test?"

Then the talk became technical. Johann was sure. There had been smaller tests, during the two years the project had been going on, and all of them had been effective.

Then cold fingers ran over him, tingling at the ends of his nerves, as he realized the trick semantics was playing on him.

Test? It had been the name they had given it, and in time it had come to be no more than that in his mind—a test of his theories. But this was not just a test. This was the feat itself, the step that would bring an end to half the world, the culmination of the hopes of Centralia, and the final, positive proof of the ideas of Volcek.

He had been almost unaware of the power that had grown from his idea, but now it hit him. It wasn't easy to do that to half a world, even in these days. But it had to be done.

Thirty years before, there had been a sprawling group of small nations and several large powers. But with the beginning of the atomic age, that had shaken itself down until now there were actually only the two hemispheres. Centralia had most of the world's population, but the West had achieved equality by its head-start in the sciences and in industry. For thirty years, little nation had accreted to big nation, until now there were the two of them. Nominally, the little nations still existed; but it was a polite fiction, like the fiction of bland softness the Director had adopted before Stefanie.

And this was not a world where two powers could exist. They had somehow achieved it, while the accretion of control over the neighboring states went on. There had been fracas piled onto struggle, but never outright war. Now, though, things had reached a stage where each side knew that sooner or later the hydrogen-bombs must fall, and where those bombs were of a size and efficiency that might even end the world. There were even rumors of solar-phoenix bombs which could turn the world into a flaming, lesser sun.

Volcek sighed. This was better than that. Better that half the world should slow down and come to a gradual halt than that the rain of hell should descend from the heavens, perhaps igniting the world itself.

They were at the laboratories, now, and Volcek got out of the car behind the Director, vaguely conscious that taking second place was a mark of honor. Inside the building, one of the rooms had been cleared, leaving a few seats, a stand, and a single board of levers against the wall. Already, the seats were taken, and men were rising to salute the Director.

Ki Fong, Tsamatsu, Bhandaputra, Simonolov, Schwartzkopf, Jordssen—all of the big names of government and science—were there. Some were scowling intently as they tried to digest the printed formulae on the big blackboard—which gave part of the theory behind Volcek's work; others were smiling, assured only that this was the day when Centralia would come into its own. And some, as always, were estimating Volcek, wondering how his importance would conflict with their own.

The Director smiled thinly, dropping an arm over Volcek's shoulder. "After this day, Johann, you'll need bodyguards. I have seen to that. And Petrecci... well, we shall see..."

Johann caught himself before he could wince. He'd liked Petrecci, had no desire to replace him. But if the implication of the Director's words was what he thought...still, it would be good for Stefanie. She had had too much trouble, and it was time life smiled on her a little. It would be good for their children, too, to grow up with comfort, even a little luxury, tutored perhaps with the children of the Director, himself. As Secretary of Science, Johann Volcek could give his family a great deal. He caught Petrecci's eyes on him, and turned his head quickly back to the other men.

At the Director's nod, he began outlining the facts to them. Some already knew of what was being done here, but all were listening as if the Director himself were speaking.

He could only give the barest facts. He'd been experimenting with a means of controlling fission for some power application, working on the problem of getting hydrogen to fission at temperatures below the millions of degrees where it normally began, and in tiny amounts. And by sheer accident, he had stumbled on a process where nitrogen fissioned, instead—two atoms of nitrogen combining into one, straining the nucleus that now held fourteen protons and fourteen neutrons, distorting it until some of the binding force of the nucleus released energy, and it broke up into simpler atoms again—as if both fission and fusion were going on.

It had not been successful, from a commercial angle, but it had produced an unexpected result. The mice which had been kept to test out danger of radiation had not been killed—but they had been sterile, as events proved, from then on. The release of radiation was not quite normal gamma rays; it was subtler than that—some queerly polarized radiation that struck at the fertility of animals and ended it.

"But you were not sterilized," Ki Fong interrupted him.

"I was lucky—I had been using a shield that was heavy enough to turn aside the radiation—the four-foot walls of the oven where the experiment was conducted. It only leaked out through the panel we later found had a crack in it—but that was toward the mice."

Three years had been spent in testing it on mice, before the reports had found Petrecci, and brought him to the little laboratory of Johann Volcek. By then, Volcek had developed a complete control of the process, and had learned to fuse and fission oxygen as well as nitrogen, but without the production of sterilizing radiation this time.

After that, there had been no more mice. Volcek shuddered, trying to conceal it, as he remembered the prisoners who had stood before the portal of the oven, and gone away, sterile. And there had been tests in the big, deserted wastes near the Gobi, where balls of fire had leaped from his tiny little devices, and cracked themselves into flaming energy that grew and spread before vanishing. More sterility had followed.

"It requires very little apparatus," Volcek said, finally. He pulled a small tube from a drawer near the wall, and held it out to them. "This is the source. A small battery, these coils, tubes, this little crucible—nothing more. Once we knew why it started the fusion, it was easy to simplify."

And it was simple. A man could carry one of the devices with him in a small bag, and it was meaningless in appearance. It could be built into a radio, as if it were part of the tuning device. It could slip past customs, harmless in its looks, and be spread wherever wanted.

And now...

The Director took over, then, telling them what had already been done. In every city and hamlet, from coast to coast and from polar cap to polar cap, the West was covered with these tiny little devices, each equipped with a little crystal delicately attuned to one here, so that they would all function at once.

There would be no war. Centralia had labored to avoid war in spite of the hatred and lusts of the West. Now, they would be even more agreeable, even more meek. They would take the insults; they would not fight. Because, once the nitrogen of the air had done its job, there would be only a generation of patience, while no more children were born to the West. And some day, there would be only one Power—Centralia.

Schwartzkopf asked the question that was bothering the others, though he already knew the answer. "But these balls of fissioning or fusioning nitrogen—when they go off over the West, they are too much like atomic bombs. Won't the West feel it is attacked and retaliate with their genuine bombs?"

"We, too, shall be attacked!" It was Volcek's other process, of course. Simultaneously, there would be released similar "bombs" over all of the territory of Centralia. The heat and power would do a minor amount of damage, of course—but this process produced no sterilizing radiation. "Only New Zealand will be free."

New Zealand had somehow held out of the two coalitions, by its hardest efforts and with the help of its location. It was weakly allied to the West, but too remote.

The Director smiled again, the tight smile that was reserved for private meetings. "We shall, of course, accuse the West—but within the hour, when word of their trouble comes, we shall ask for a truce to find the culprit. Simple, is it not?"

The clock on the wall indicated five minutes before zero hour, and Volcek wiped his hands surreptitiously against his coat. It was simple enough, this use to which they had put his discoveries. And, he told himself again, it was better than any rain of real atomics. The West would not be hurt seriously—it would simply die out slowly, as no more children were born. It was really the most merciful solution to the politics of this world.

He could picture some of the panic, of course, when the little tubes did their work. First a tiny spark would form in the tube, with a spitting and hissing. Then it would grow, breaking out of the tube and through walls or anything in its way, growing and rising, spreading erratically horizontally, moving with a strange random motion, as it climbed upwards and grew larger and larger. It would reach the size of a normal atomic bomb, in a few minutes. And some would be killed by its heat, as some buildings would catch fire from it.

But mostly, there would be the terror as the people in the cities saw it spread its visible radiation and heard the familiar crackling thunder of its detonation. The terror would kill some of them, in their panic-flight, even while the thing itself drifted upwards until it found a layer of air too thin for it to go on, and it came to an automatic end.

But they would mostly escape, except for bad cases of "sunburn" and the results of their own panic. Dry material flamed quickly before its peculiar radiation, but men were not made of dry material, and it was almost harmless. They would simply have no children. And that was better than most of them could expect in a day when each morning marked the beginning of a new fear of hydrogen bombs or worse.

One more minute.

Volcek had expected the Director to move to the panel where the big switch would cut on the surprisingly small oscillator that would trigger the little crystals in the tube projectors. But the Director was stepping back, motioning him forward. "You, Johann—it is an honor I have reserved for you."

There was silence in the laboratory room as Volcek moved slowly toward the board. He straightened, his eyes going down to his coat, where a bit of lint clung to it. Stefanie would have spotted it at once and rushed to brush it off. Stefanie who knew nothing of what his great work was, but who was awed by having a husband who could receive a visit from the Director. Stefanie who could have other children, after all, in this world that would have ultimate peace in spite of all the war threats, because of the work her husband was now about to do.

Suddenly, he wondered how many Stefanies there might be in the West. How many women would wait for the children they wanted, and never find them? How many would curse him, when they finally realized the truth, without ever knowing that he was the man they were cursing?

He cut off the thought, savagely. There would be others in the long centuries to come, who would know his name and would then bless him, as their children grew up without the threat of war and extinction. His children would be proud of him—his and Stefanie's.

And There Was Light

He touched the switch that was to set off the harmless, fake "bombs" over their own world first. The Director was at his side, his face no longer smiling, but narrowed to that of a wolf.

Then the Director chuckled, and the edge of his lips curled up. "*Let there be light,*" he quoted, and his eyes showed that he knew the original usage of the term in the Book he was quoting.

And there was light, as Johann's finger hit the switch. A tiny, spitting, hissing thing lifted from the nearby city, going up and forward in weird, erratic movements, growing larger, and spreading out, now beginning the muttered, staccato thunder that was not unlike a plutonium bomb.

The Director reached over and pressed the other switch that would send the sterilizing bombs up over the West—but he did not depress it fully. He stopped, and nodded to Volcek, and again Johann's hand went out, pushing the lever of the switch.

He should have brought Stefanie—if only she could have known nothing of the results. She would have been proud of him then, as the Director solemnly shook the hand that had done its work, and the other men began to cluster around him.

Then they moved toward the windows, hesitantly at first, not quite sure that this fire in the heavens over the city beyond was really the safe kind. But the Director lead them, together with Volcek, and they stood gazing out.

It was a huge ball of blazing fire in the sky now, partially softened by the filters that had sprung shut over the windows automatically, and the mutter of its detonation reached them as they stood there.

There was some damage, of course, even here. Some of the older wooden buildings near where it had first appeared were bursting into flames, and the distant figures of people had gone into a panic—they had to believe it was real, just as the West must believe for a time that both powers had received the same treatment.

Stefanie? But Volcek had taken care of that, with a drug in her coffee. She would be asleep, unaware of the tumult, and not one of the mob trying frantically to escape what could never harm them.

Now the ball of fire was rising upwards more steadily, its own heat driving it up as a blast of hot air is carried up over a fire. The brightness began to fade as they watched, moving up and turning smaller, shrinking, and finally going away.

Volcek sighed, and the Director echoed it, a satisfied sigh, and a somewhat regretful one. "It is hard to see even a few of my people hurting themselves," the Director said slowly. "But it is best. And—it is done."

He turned to Volcek, and Johann straightened, reminding himself that whatever the Director said must be remembered. He would have to tell Stefanie—and someday, he could tell his children, and his grandchildren. He must remember it.

But the Director's words were never spoken. There was a shout from the windows, and they swung back, to see another tiny flame leaping up, this time nearer, growing and spitting.

There was something wrong with it. The other had grown more slowly. This raged out, savagely, growing more sure of itself as it leaped toward them, then darted sidewise.

Volcek turned suddenly to the instruments packed in the drawers. The spectrovisor and the diffractograph came out in his shaking hands, and he slapped them down onto the wooden sill of the window, already beginning to smoke faintly.

Then his hands steadied as he adjusted the instruments.

One look was enough. This was the nitrogen-fusion, not the harmless oxygen reaction.

His eyes met the Director's, and he nodded, but the nod was unnecessary. The Director had already guessed.

They moved toward him, a harsh mob sound coming from them, but the Director was before them.

"No! Stop!" The voice that had been trained to command a power greater than men had ever held before stopped them. "No, if the West has scientists too, that is no fault of Johann Volcek. Johann, you did not fail; you will not suffer."

Volcek heard him, and saw them fall back. He thought again of the lint on his coat, and looked down at it. He picked it off, while the others drew back, and the Director was assuring him that all would be well with him.

Stefanie would have no children now. There would be no grandchildren to hear the Director's senseless words, telling him he would not suffer.

You don't suffer when you've killed a race.

Battleground

Beyond the observation port of the hypercruiser *Clarion* lay the utter blackness of nothing. The ship was effectively cutting across space without going through it, spanning parsecs for every subjective day of travel.

There were neither stars, space nor time around them, and only the great detectors built into the ship could keep them from being hopelessly lost. These followed a trail of energy laid down on the way out from Earth years before, leading them homeward, solar system by solar system.

Acting Captain Lenk stood with his back to the other three, studying their sullen reflections in the port. It was better than facing them directly, somehow, even though it showed his own bald scalp, tautly hollow face and slump-shouldered body.

"All right," he said at last. "So we vote again. I'll have to remind you we're under orders to investigate all habitable planets on a line back to Earth. I vote we follow orders. Jeremy?"

The xenologist shrugged faintly. His ash-blond coloring, general slimness and refinement of features gave him a look of weakness, but his voice was a heavy, determined bass. "I stand pat. We didn't explore the last planet enough. I vote we go back and make a thorough job of it."

"Home—at once!" The roar came from the squat, black-bearded minerologist, Graves. "God never meant man to leave the world on which He put him! Take us back, I say, where…"

"Aimes?" Lenk cut in quickly.

They'd heard Graves' violently fundamentalist arguments endlessly, until the sound of his voice was enough to revive every antagonism and hatred they had ever felt. Graves had been converted to the newest and most rapidly expanding of the extreme evangelical faiths just before they had left. And unfortunately for the others, he had maintained that his covenant to go on the exploration could not be broken, even though venturing into space was a cardinal sin.

Aimes glowered at the others from under grizzled eyebrows. Of them all, the linguodynamicist took part in the fewest arguments and apparently detested the others most. He turned his heavy body now as he studied them, seemingly trying to make up his mind which he detested most at the moment. Then he grunted.

"With you, Captain," Aimes said curtly.

He swung on his heel and stalked out of the control cabin, to go back to studying the un-deciphered writing of the planets they had visited.

Graves let out a single hiss and followed, probably heading for the galley, since it was his period to cook.

Jeremy waited deliberately until the mineralogist's footsteps could no longer be heard, and then turned to leave.

Lenk hesitated for a second, then decided that monotony was worse than anything else. "How about some chess, Jeremy?" he asked.

The other stopped, and some of the sullenness left his face. Apparently the protracted arguments had wearied him until he was also feeling the relief of decisive action. "Why not?" Jeremy said. "I'll set up the board while you fiddle with your dials."

No fiddling was necessary, since Lenk had never cut them off their automatic detecting circuit, but he went through the motions for the other's benefit. Gravitic strain came faintly through hyperspace, and the ship could locate suns by it. If approach revealed planets of habitable size, it was set to snap out of hyper-space automatically near the most likely world.

Lenk had been afraid such a solar system might be found before they could resolve the argument, and his own relief from the full measure of cabin fever came from the end of that possibility.

They settled down to the game with a minimum of conversation. Since the other four members of the crew had been killed by some unknown virus, conversation had proven less than cheerful. It was better when they were on a planet and busy, but four people were too few for the monotony of hypertravel.

Then Jeremy snapped out of it. He cleared his throat tentatively while castling, grimaced, and then nodded positively. "I was right, Lenk. We never did explore those other planets properly."

"Maybe not," Lenk agreed. "But with the possibility of alien raiders headed toward Earth…"

"Bunk! No sign of raiders. Every indication was that the races on those worlds killed themselves off—no technology alien to their own culture. And there would have been with aliens invading."

"Timed that way? Coincidence can account for just so much."

"It has to account for the lowering cultural levels in the colonizing direction," Jeremy said curtly. "Better leave that sort of argument to Aimes. He's conditioned to it."

Lenk shrugged and turned back to the chess. It was over his head, anyhow.

Men had built only three other cruisers capable of exceeding the speed of light, so far. The first had gone out in a direction opposite to that of the *Clarion* and had returned to report a regular decline in culture as the distance of habitable worlds from Earth increased. The nearest was in a medieval state, the next an early bronze culture, then a stone-age one, and so on, down to the furthest explored, where the native race had barely discovered fire.

It had been either impossible coincidence or the evidence of some law nobody has been quite ready to accept, save for the newly spreading fundamentalists, who maintained it proved that Earth was the center of the universe.

The other two cruisers had not reported back when the *Clarion* took off.

And their own trip had only added to the mystery, and they had touched on four habitable systems. And on each, there had been evidence of a highly developed race and some vast struggle that had killed off that race completely.

The furthest had lain fallow for an unguessable period of time, and in each succeeding one, evidence indicated the time interval since the destruction of the culture had been less. On the world they had left, the end must have come not more than a few thousand years before.

"Suppose one race had gone along in a straight line, seeding the systems with life," Lenk guessed. "Remember, every race we found had similarities. And suppose another race of conquerors stumbled on that line and is mopping up? Maybe with some weapon that leaves no trace."

Jeremy looked at him. "Suppose Graves is right, and his God wipes out all wicked races. He keeps planting races, hoping they'll turn out right, and wiping out the old ones?" he snorted. "Only, of course he thinks Earth is the only world that counts. We're dealing with facts, Lenk, not wild theories. And why should an alien race simply wipe out another race, wait a thousand years or so, and move on—without using the planet afterwards, even for a base for the next operation? Also, why should we find plenty of weapons, but no skeletons?"

"Skeletons are pretty fragile. And if somebody had the mythical heat ray..."

"Bunk! If it would vaporize calcium in the bones, it would vaporize some of the parts of the weapons we found." Jeremy moved a rook, considered it, and pointed. "Check. And there are always some parts of skeletons that will last more than a thousand years. I've got a theory, but it's..."

Pale light cut through the viewing port, and a gong sounded in the room. Lenk jerked to his led and moved to his screens.

"Maybe we'll know now," he said. "We'll be landing on a planet in about an hour. And it looks pretty much like Earth, from here."

He cranked up the gain on the magnifiers, and studied it again, scanning the surface of the planet below them. There were clouds in the sky, but through a clear patch he made out enough evidence.

"Want me to set us down near a city?" he asked, pointing.

Jeremy nodded. Like all the other planets on this trip, the one below was either inhabited or had been inhabited until recently.

They knew before the ship landed that the habitation was strictly past tense, at least as far as any high level of culture was concerned. The cities were in ruins.

At one time, they must have reared upwards to heights as imposing as those of the free state of New York City or the commonwealth of Chicago. But now the buildings had lost their topmost towers, and the bases showed yawning holes in many places.

They landed in the center of the largest city, after a quick skim over the surface to be sure that no smaller city had escaped. A quick sampling of the air indicated it was breathable, with no poisons and only a touch of radioactivity, too low to be dangerous.

Aimes and Jeremy went out, each in a little tractor. While making explorations, they were capable of forgetting their antagonisms in their common curiosity.

Graves remained on the ship. He had decided somewhere along the line that setting foot on an alien planet was more sinful than travel through space, and refused to be shaken.

Lenk finished what observations were necessary. He fiddled around, bothered by the quiet city outside. It had been better on the other worlds, where the ruins had been softened by time and weather. Here, it was too easy to imagine things. Finally, he climbed into rough clothes, and went out on foot.

Everything was silent. Grass almost identical with that of Earth was growing through much of the torn pavement, and there were trees and bushes here and there. Vines had climbed some of the ruined walls. But there were no flowers. Much of the planet had apparently been overgrown with forest and weeds, but this city was in a temperate zone, and clear enough for easy travel.

Lenk listened to the wind, and the faint sighing of a few trees nearby. He kicked over stones and rubble where they lay on patches of damp earth. And he kept looking at the sky.

But it was no different from other worlds as far as the desolation went. There were no insects, and no animals stared warily up from the basements, and the grass showed no signs of having been grazed. It was as if the animal kingdom had never existed here.

He made his way back from the section of largest buildings, toward what might have been a park at one time. Here there was less danger of being trapped in any collapsing ruin, and he moved more confidently. The low buildings might have been public sites, but they somehow seemed more like homes.

He stumbled on something, and leaned down to pick it up. At first, the oddness of its design confused his vision. Then he made out a barrel with rifling inside, and a chamber that still contained pellets, now covered with corrosion. It would have fitted his hand oddly, but he could have used the pistol.

Beyond it lay a line of rust that might have been a sword at one time. Coiled over it was a heavy loop of thick plastic that ended in a group of wires, apparently of stainless steel. Each wire ended in a row of cutting points. It might have been a cross between a knout and a bolas. He had a vision of something alien and sinister coming at him with one of those, and shuddered.

There was a ruin of rust and corroded parts further on that might have been a variation of a machine gun. Lenk started for it, to be stopped by a shout.

"Hold it!" It was Jeremy's voice, and now the tank came around a corner, and headed toward him. "Stay put, Lenk. That thing may be booby-trapped. And we can't be sure here that there has been time enough to make it safe."

Lenk shuddered again, and climbed in hastily as Jeremy held open the door. It was tight inside, but reasonably safe, since the tank had been designed for almost anything. Jeremy must have seen him leaving the ship and followed.

But by noon they had abandoned the fear of booby-traps. Either there had never been any or time had drawn their stings.

Lenk wandered through the section already roughly surveyed, and declared safe. He felt convinced the inhabitants of this world once had been more like men than most other races. They had been two-legged, with arms and heads in a human position on their upright bodies.

Judging from the size of the furniture, they had been slightly larger than men but not enough to matter. The pictures on the walls were odd mostly for the greenish tints of the skin and the absence of outward noses or ears. With a little fixing and recoloring, they might have been *people*.

He came to a room that had been sealed off, pried open the door, and went in. It smelled stale enough to indicate that it had been reasonably air-tight. Benches and chairs ran along one wall, and a heavy wooden table occupied the middle. On that were piled bits and pieces in a curious scramble. He studied them carefully—belts, obviously, buttons, the inevitable weapons, scraps of plastic material.

A minute later, he was shouting for Jeremy over the little walkie-talkie. The xenologist appeared in less than five minutes. He stared about for a second, then grinned wryly.

"Your first, eh? I've found a lot of them. Sure, those were corpses there once." He saw Lenk's expression, and shrugged. "Oh, you were right to call me. It proves we weren't crazy. Wood and some cloth still preserved, but no bones. I've got a collection of pictures like that."

"A corrosive gas—" Lenk suggested.

Jeremy shook his head vigorously. "No dice, Captain. See that belt? It's plant fiber—something like linen. No gas strong enough to eat up a body would leave that unharmed. And they had skeletons, too—we've found models in what must have been a museum. But we can't even find the fossil skeletons that should be there. Odd, though."

He prodded about among the weapons, shaking his head. "All the weapons in places like this show evidence of one homogeneous design. And all the ornaments are in a T shape, like this one."

He lifted a stainless metal object from the floor and dropped it. "But outside in the square, there are at least two designs. For once, it almost looks as if your idea of an alien invader might be worth considering."

The radio at his side let out a squawk, and he cut it on listening to the thin whisper that came from it. Abruptly, he swung about and headed toward his tractor outside, with Lenk following.

"Aimes has found something," Jeremy said.

They found the linguodynamicist in the gutted ruins of a building into which great concrete troughs led. A rusty ruin in one of the troughs indicated something like a locomotive had once run in it, apparently on great ball bearings. The fat man was pointing excitedly toward something on one of the walls.

At first glance, it seemed to be a picture of more of the green people, apparently undergoing some violent torture. Then their eyes swept on—and they gasped.

Over the green people, three vaguely reptilian monstrosities were hovering, at least twice the size of the others, all equipped with the fanged whips Lenk had seen. One of the green men was apparently trying to defend himself with a huge T-shaped weapon, but the others were helpless. The reptilian monsters sprouted great ugly wings of glaring red from their shoulders.

"The invaders," Lenk said. They were horrible things to see. "But their weapons weren't that big…"

"A war poster!" Aimes said bitterly. "It doesn't tell a thing except that there were two groups."

Jeremy studied it, more closely. "Not necessarily even that. It's designed for some emotional effect. But at least, it's a hint that there may have been enemies unlike the ones who lived here. Lenk, can I take the scout ship out?"

"Go ahead," Lenk told him. He frowned at the poster. "Jeremy, if that means the human, race is going to have to face an alien invasion from monsters like that…"

"It means nothing!"

Jeremy went off, with Aimes apparently in agreement for a change. Lenk stood studying the poster. Finally he ripped it down, surprised to find how strong it still was, and rolled it up to carry back to the ship.

Each world had been razed more recently, and each with the same curious curse. The race had risen to a high culture, and then had seemingly been wiped out in a few brief years. The destruction had accounted for all life on the planet, other than vegetable—and had wiped out even the bones. All that had been left was a collection of weapons and relics of more doubtful use.

The pattern was the same. The direction was steadily toward Earth, leaping from planet to planet at jumps of thousands of years apart, or perhaps mere hundreds. This planet must have been attacked less than five hundred years before, though it was hard to tell without controlled study of decay here.

Even now Earth might be suffering the invasion! They had been gone nearly three years. And during that time, the monsters might have swooped down hideously out of space.

They might return to find the Earth a wasteland!

His thoughts were a turmoil that grew worse as he stared at the poster. The unknown artist had done his job well. A feeling of horror poured out of it, filling him with an insensate desire to find such monstrosities and rend and maim them, as they had tormented the unfortunate green people.

Graves came stomping up to the control room, carrying lunch, and took one look at the picture. "Serves the heathens right," he grumbled. "Look at them. In hell, suffering from the lashes of the devils of the pit. And still holding up that heathen charm."

Lenk blinked. But Graves' idea wasn't too fantastic, at that. The creatures did look like devils, and the T-shaped object might be a religious symbol. Hadn't some faith or other used the taucross in its worship? And those objects on the third world back had resembled swastikas, which were another religious symbol on Earth.

That part fitted. During periods of extreme stress or danger, man sought some home in his faith. Was it so unnatural that alien races might do the same?

"Isn't there anything hopeful in your religion, Graves?" he asked bitterly, wondering what the man had been like before his conversion to the rigidity he now possessed. He'd probably been as violent an atheist. Usually, a fanatic who switched sides became doubly fanatical.

The revival of religious devotion had begun some fifteen years before, and from what Lenk had seen, the world had been a better and more kindly place for it. But there would always be those who thought the only true devotion lay in the burning of witches. Or maybe Graves needed psychiatric treatment for his morose moods were becoming suspiciously psychotic, and his fanaticism might be only a sign of deeper trouble.

The man went off muttering something about the prophecy and the time being at hand for all to be tried in fire. Lenk went back to staring at the poster until he heard the scout come back. He found Aimes and Jeremy busy unloading what seemed to be loot enough to fill two of the scouts.

"A whole library, almost intact," Aimes spoke with elation. And plenty of it is on film, where we can correlate words and images! In two weeks, I'll speak the language like a native."

"Good!" Lenk told him. "Because in about that time, we'll be home on Earth. As long as there's any chance that our people should be warned about invaders, I'm not delaying any longer!"

"You can forget the alien invaders," Jeremy objected.

Then he exploded his thunderbolt. The horrible aliens had proved to be no more than a group of purple-skinned people on the other side of the planet with a quite divergent culture, but of the same basic stock as the green-skinned men. They also exaggerated in their drawings, and to about the same degree.

Fortunately the treasure-trove from the library would give the two men enough for years of work, and required the attention of a full group. They were eager now to take off for Earth and to begin recruiting a new expedition, taking only enough with them for the first basic steps.

Lenk headed directly for the control room. He began setting up the proper directions on the board while Jeremy finished the account.

"But *something's* hitting the planets," he objected. His hand found the main button and the *Clarion* began heading up through the atmosphere on normal gravity warp, until she could reach open space, and go into hyperdrive. "Your monsters prove to be only people—but it still doesn't explain the way disaster follows a line straight toward Earth! And until we know…"

"Maybe we'd be better off not knowing," Jeremy said. But he refused to clarify his statement.

Then the hyperdrive went on.

The homeward trip was somewhat different from the others. There were none of the petty fights this time.

Aimes and Jeremy were busy in their own way, decoding the language and collating the material they had.

Graves was with them, grumbling at being around the heathen things, but apparently morbidly fascinated by them.

Lenk could offer no help, and his duty lay with the ship. He pondered over the waves of destruction that seemed to wash toward Earth, and the diminishing cultural levels on the planets beyond. It couldn't be pure coincidence. Nor could he accept the idea that Earth was the center of the universe, and that everything else was necessarily imperfect.

Surprisingly, it was Graves who gave him his first hopeful suggestion. A week had passed, and they were well into the second when the men really caught his attention. Graves was bringing his lunch, actually smiling. He frowned.

"What gives?" he asked.

"It's all true!" Graves answered, and there was an inner glow to him. "Just as it's prophesied in *Revelations*. There were times when I had doubts, but now I know. God has set the heathens before me as proof that Armageddon will come, and I have been singled out to bring the glad tidings to His faithful!"

"I thought you didn't believe God would have anything to do with heathens!" Lenk objected. He was trying to recall whether a sudden phase of manic joy was a warning symptom or not.

"I misunderstood. I thought God had forbade space flight. But now it is proved how He loves us. He singled us out to teach us to fly through space that we could learn." Graves gathered up the dishes without noticing that Lenk hadn't touched them and went off in a cloud of ecstasy.

But his point had been made, and Lenk turned it over. Then, with a shout, he headed toward the headquarters of the two remaining scientists. He found them sitting quietly, watching a reel of some kind being projected through an alien device.

"I hear it's Armageddon we're facing," he said.

He expected grins of amusement from them—or at least from Jeremy. But none came. Aimes nodded.

"First progress in all directions. Then a period when religion seems to be in the decline. Then a revival, and a return to faith in the prophecies. All religions agree on those prophecies, Lenk. Revelations refer to the end of Armageddon, when the whole world will wipe itself out before the creation of a better world, in one planet-wide war. The old Norse legends spoke of a Fimbulwinter, when the giants and their gods would destroy the earth in war. And these green-skinned peoples had the same religious prophecies. They came true, too. Armageddon. Contagious Armageddon."

Lenk stared from one to the other, suspecting a joke. "But that still leaves coincidence—the way things move from planet to planet..."

"Not at all," Jeremy said. "These people didn't have space travel, but they had some pretty highly developed science. They found what we thought we'd disproved—an ether drift. It would carry spores from planet to planet—and in the exact direction needed to account for what we've seen. Races were more advanced back that way, less so the way we first went, simply because of the time it took the spores to drift."

"And what about the destruction?" Lenk asked woodenly. Their faces were getting him—they looked as if they believed it. "Is there another disease spore to drive races mad?"

"Nothing like that. Just the natural course of cultures when they pass a certain level," Jeremy answered. "I should have seen that myself. Every race follows the same basic pattern. The only question is how much time we've left—a week or a thousand years?"

They turned back to their projection device, but Lenk caught the xenologist by the shoulder and swung him back. "But they didn't have space travel! That doesn't fit their pattern. Even if you're right…"

Jeremy nodded. "We don't have the secret of immortality, either. And this race did. But, damn it, I'd still like to know hat happened to all those skeletons?"

Lenk went back to his control room. And perversely, his thoughts insisted on accepting their explanation. It would be like man to think that important things could only happen on his own home planet, and prophecy an end for his own race, never dreaming it could happen to others.

It would be normal for him to sense somehow out of his own nature what his inevitable end must be—and then to be completely amazed when he found the same end for other races.

But…

Space travel—travel at faster than light speeds—had to make a difference. There were the other worlds on the other side of the sun, where men were already planning to colonize. Even if a world might normally blow up in a final wild holocaust, it would have its whole racial pattern changed when it began to spread out among the stars. It would have to have a revival of the old pioneering spirit. There had been the beginnings of that when they left. And with that, such a war could be prevented forever.

He heard Graves moving about in the galley, singing something about graves opening, and grimaced.

Besides, Jeremy had admitted that they didn't have all the answers. The mystery of the vanished skeletons remained—and until that was accounted for, nothing could be considered explained.

He forgot about the skeletons as he began planning how he'd wangle his way into one of the colonies. Then, even if catastrophe did strike Earth in another thousand years or so, the race could go on. Ten more years, and man would be safe…

He was feeling almost cheerful as they finally came out of hyper-space near Earth…and landed…

The skeletons—lay scattered everywhere.

Kindness

The wind eddied idly around the corner and past the secluded park bench. It caught fitfully at the paper on the ground, turning the pages, then picked up a section and blew away with it, leaving gaudy-colored comics uppermost. Danny moved forward into the sun-light, his eyes dropping to the children's page exposed.

But it was no use; he made no effort to pick up the paper. In a world where even the children's comics needed explaining, there could be nothing of interest to the last living *homo sapiens*—the last normal man in the world. His foot kicked the paper away, under the bench where it would no longer remind him of his deficiencies. There had been a time when he had tried to reason slowly over the omitted steps of logic and find the points behind such things, sometimes successfully, more often not; but now he left it to the quick, intuitive thinking of those about him. Nothing fell flatter than a joke that had to be reasoned out slowly.

Homo sapiens! The type of man who had come out of the caves and built a world of atomic power, electronics and other old-time wonders—thinking man, as it translated from the Latin. In the dim past, when his ancestors had owned the world, they had made a joke of it, shortening it to *homo sap*, and laughing, because there had been no other species to rival them. Now it was no longer a joke.

Normal man had been only a "sap" to *homo intelligens*—intelligent man—who was now the master of the world. Danny was only a left-over, the last normal man in a world of supermen, hating the fact that he had been born, and that his mother had died at his birth to leave him only loneliness as his heritage.

He drew farther back on the bench as the steps of a young couple reached his ears, pulling his hat down to avoid recognition. But they went by, preoccupied with their own affairs, leaving only a scattered bit of conversation in his ears. He turned it over in his mind, trying senselessly to decode it.

Impossible! Even the casual talk contained too many steps of logic left out. *Homo intelligens* had a new way of thinking, above reason, where all the long, painful steps of logic could be jumped instantly. They could arrive at a correct picture of the whole from little scattered bits of information. Just as man had once invented logic to replace the trial-and-error thinking that most animals have, so *homo intelligens* had learned to use intuition. They could look at the first page of an old-time book and immediately know the whole of it, sinse the little tricks of the author would connect in their intuitive minds and at once build up all the missing links. They didn't even have to try—they just looked, and knew. It was like Newton looking at an apple falling and immediately seeing why the planets circled the sun, and realizing the laws of gravitation; but these new men did it all the time, not just at those rare intervals as it had worked for *homo sapiens* once.

Man was gone, except for Danny, and he too had to leave this world of supermen. Somehow, soon, those escape plans must be completed, before the last of his little courage was gone! He stirred restlessly, and the little coins in his pocket set up a faint jingling sound. More charity, or occupational therapy! For six hours a day, five days a week, he worked in a little office, painfully doing routine work that could probably have been done better by machinery. Oh, they assured him that his manual skill was as great as theirs and that it was needed, but he could never be sure. In their unfailing kindness, they had probably decided it was better for him to live as normally as they could let him, and then had created the job to fit what he could do.

Other footsteps came down the little path, but he did not look up, until they stopped. "Hi, Danny! You weren't at the Library, and Miss Larsen said, pay day, weather, and all, I'd find you here. How's everything?"

Outwardly, Jack Thorpe's body might have been the twin of Danny's own well-muscled one, and the smiling face above it bore no distinguishing characteristics. The mutation that changed man to superman had been within, a quicker, more complex relation of brain cell to brain cell that had no outward signs. Danny nodded at Jack, drawing over reluctantly to make room on the bench for this man who had been his playmate when they were both too young for the difference to matter much.

He did not ask the reason behind the librarian's knowledge of his whereabouts; so far as he knew, there was no particular pattern to his coming here, but to the others there must be one. He found he could even smile at their ability to foretell his plans.

"Hi, Jack! Fine. I thought you were on Mars."

Thorpe frowned, as if an effort were needed to remember that the boy beside him was different, and his words bore the careful phrasing of all those who spoke to Danny. "I finished that, for the time being; I'm supposed to report to Venus next. They're having trouble getting an even balance of boys and girls there, you know. Thought you might want to come along. You've never been Outside, and you were always bugs about those old space stories, I remember."

"I still am, Jack. But—" He knew what it meant, of course. Those who looked after him behind the scenes had detected his growing discontent, and were hoping to distract him with this chance to see the places his fathers had conquered in the heyday of his race. But he had no wish to see them as they now were, filled with the busy work of the new men; it was better to imagine them as they had once been, rather than see reality. And the ship was here; there could be no chance for escape from those other worlds.

Jack nodded quickly, with the almost telepathic understanding of his race. "Of course. Suit yourself, fellow. Going up to the Heights? Miss Larsen says she has something for you."

"Not yet, Jack. I thought I might look at—drop by the old Museum."

"Oh." Thorpe got up slowly, brushing his suit with idle fingers. "Danny!"

"Uh?"

"I probably know you better than anyone else, fellow, so—" He hesitated, shrugged, and went on. "Don't mind if I jump to conclusions; I won't talk out of turn. But best of luck—and good-by, Danny."

He was gone, almost instantly, leaving Danny's heart stuck in his throat. A few words, a facial expression, probably some childhood memories, and Danny might as well have revealed his most cherished secret hope in shouted words! How many others knew of his interest in the old ship in the Museum and his carefully-made plot to escape this kindly charity-filled torture world?

He crushed a cigarette under his heel, trying to forget the thought. Jack had played with him as a child, and the others hadn't. He'd have to base his hopes on that and be even more careful never to think of the idea around others. In the meantime, he'd stay away from the ship! Perhaps in that way Thorpe's subtle warning might work in his favor—provided the man had meant his promise of silence.

Danny forced his doubts away, grimly conscious that he dared not lose hope in this last desperate scheme for independence and self-respect; the other way offered only despair and listless hopelessness, the same empty death from an acute inferiority complex that had claimed the diminishing numbers of his own kind and left him as the last, lonely specimen. Somehow, he'd succeed, and in the meantime, he would go to the Library and leave the Museum strictly alone.

There was a throng of people leaving the Library as Danny came up the escalator, but either they did not recognize him with his hat pulled low or sensed his desire for anonymity and pretended not to know him. He slipped into one of the less used hallways and made his way toward the Historic Documents section, where Miss Larsen was putting away the reading tapes and preparing to leave.

But she tossed them aside quickly as he came in and smiled up at him, the rich, warm smile of her people. "Hello, Danny! Did your friend find you all right?"

"Mm-hmm. He said you had something for me."

"I have." There was pleasure in her face as she turned back toward the desk behind her to come up with a small wrapped parcel. For the thousandth time, he caught himself wishing she were of his race and quenching the feeling as he realized what her attitude must really be. To her, the small talk from his race's past was a subject of historic interest, no more. And he was just a dull-witted hangover from ancient days. "Guess what?"

But in spite of himself, his face lighted up, both at the game and the package. "The magazines! The lost issues of *Space Trails?*" There had been only the first installment of a story extant, and yet that single part had set his pulses throbbing as few of the other ancient stories of his ancestors' conquest of space had done. Now, with the missing sections, life would be filled with zest for a few more hours as he followed the fictional exploits of a conqueror who had known no fear of keener minds.

"Not quite, Danny, but almost. We couldn't locate even a trace of them, but I gave the first installment to Bryant Kenning last week, and he finished it for you." Her voice was apologetic. "Of course the words won't be quite identical, but Kenning swears that the story is undoubtedly exactly the same in structure as it would have been, and the style is duplicated almost perfectly!"

Like that! Kenning had taken the first pages of a novel that had meant weeks and months of thought to some ancient writer and had found in them the whole plot, clearly revealed, instantly his! A night's labor had been needed to duplicate it, probably—a disagreeable and boring piece of work, but not a difficult one! Danny did not question the accuracy of the duplication, since Kenning was their greatest historical novelist. But the pleasure went out of the game.

He took the package, noting that some illustrator had even copied the old artist's style, and that it was set up to match the original format. "Thank you, Miss Larsen. I'm sorry to put all of you to so much trouble. And it was nice of Mr. Kenning!"

Her face had fallen with his, but she pretended not to notice. "He wanted to do it—volunteered when he heard we were searching for the missing copies. And if there are any others with pieces missing, Danny, he wants you to let him know. You two are about the only ones who use this division now; why don't you drop by and see him? If you'd like to go tonight—"

"Thanks. But I'll read this tonight, instead. Tell him I'm very grateful, though, will you?" But he paused, wondering again whether he dared ask for tapes on the history of the asteroids; no, there would be too much risk of her guessing, either now or later. He dared not trust any of them with a hint of his plan.

Miss Larsen smiled again, half winking at him. "Okay, Danny, I'll tell him. 'Night!"

Outside, with the cool of evening beginning to fall, Danny found his way into the untraveled quarters and let his feet guide him. Once, as a group came toward him, he crossed the street without thinking and went on. The package under his arm grew heavy and he shifted it, torn between a desire to find what had happened to the hero and a disgust at his own *sapiens* brain for not knowing. Probably, in the long run, he'd end up by going home and reading it, but for the moment he was content to let his feet carry him along idly, holding most of his thoughts in abeyance.

Another small park was in his path, and he crossed it slowly, the babble of small children's voices only partly heard until he came up to them, two boys and a girl. The supervisor, who should have had them back at the Center, was a dim shape in the far shadows, with another, dimmer shape beside her, leaving the five-year-olds happily engaged in the ancient pastime of getting dirty and impressing each other.

Danny stopped, a slow smile creeping over his lips. At that age, their intuitive ability was just beginning to develop, and their little games and pretenses made sense, acting on him like a tonic. Vaguely, he remembered his own friends of that age beginning uncertainly to acquire the trick of seeming to know everything, and his worries at being left behind. For a time, the occasional flashes of intuition that had always blessed even *homo sapiens* gave him hope, but eventually the supervisor had been forced to tell him that he was different, and why. Now he thrust those painful memories aside and slipped quietly forward into the game.

They accepted him with the easy nonchalance of children who have no repressions, feverishly trying to build their sand-castles higher than his; but in that, his experience was greater than theirs, and his judgment of the damp stuff was surer. A perverse glow of accomplishment grew inside him as he added still another story to the towering structure and built a bridge, propped up with sticks and leaves, leading to it.

Then the lights came on, illuminating the sandbox and those inside it and dispelling the shadows of dusk. The smaller of the two boys glanced up, really seeing him for the first time. "Oh, you're Danny Black, ain't you? I seen your pi'ture. Judy, Bobby, look! It's that man—"

But their voices faded out as he ran off through the park and into the deserted byways again, clutching the package to him. Fool! To delight in beating children at a useless game, or to be surprised that they should know him! He slowed to a walk, twitching his lips at the thought that by now the supervisor would be reprimanding them for their thoughtlessness. And still his feet went on, unguided. It was inevitable, of course, that they should lead him to the Museum, where all his secret hopes centered, but he was surprised to look up and see it before him. And then he was glad. Surely they could read nothing into his visit, unpremeditated, just before the place closed. He caught his breath, forced his face into lines of mere casual interest, and went inside, down the long corridors, and to the hall of the ship.

She rested there, pointed slightly skyward, sleek and immense even in a room designed to appear like the distant reaches of space. For six hundred feet, gleaming metal formed a smooth frictionless surface that slid gracefully from the blunt bow back toward the narrow stern with its blackened ion jets.

This, Danny knew, was the last and greatest of the space liners his people had built at the height of their glory. And even before her, the mutations that made the new race of men had been caused by the radiations of deep space, and the results were spreading. For a time, as the log book indicated, this ship had sailed out to Mars, to Venus, and to the other points of man's empire, while the tension slowly mounted at home. There had never been another wholly sapient-designed ship, for the new race was spreading, making its greater intelligence felt, with the invert-matter rocket replacing this older, less efficient ion rocket which the ship carried. Eventually, unable to compete with the new models, she had been retired from service and junked, while the War between the new and old race passed by her and buried her under tons of rubble, leaving no memory of her existence. And now, carefully excavated from the old ruins of the drydock where she had lain so long, she had been enthroned in state for the last year, here in the Museum of Sapient History, while all Danny's hopes and prayers had centered around her. There was still a feeling of awe in him as he started slowly across the carpeted floor toward the open lock and the lighted interior.

"Danny!" The sudden word interrupted him, bringing him about with a guilty start, but it was only Professor Kirk, and he relaxed again. The old archaeologist came toward him, his smile barely visible in the half-light of the immense dome. "I'd about given you up, boy, and started out. But I happened to look back and see you. Thought you might be interested in some information I just came onto today."

"Information about the ship?"

"What else? Here, come on inside her and into the lounge—I have a few privileges here, and we might as well be comfortable. You know, as I grow older, I find myself appreciating your ancestors' ideas of comfort, Danny. Sort of a pity our own culture is too new for much luxuriousness yet." Of all the new race, Kirk seemed the most completely at ease before Danny, partly because of his age, and partly because they had shared the same enthusiasm for the great ship when it had first arrived.

Now he settled back into one of the old divans, using his immunity to ordinary rules to light a cigarette and pass one to the younger man. "You know all the supplies and things in the ship have puzzled us both, and we couldn't find any record of them? The log ends when they put the old ship up for junking, you remember, and we couldn't figure out why all this had been restored and restocked, ready for some long voyage to somewhere. Well, it came to light in some further excavations they've completed. Danny, your people did that, during the War; or really, after they'd lost the War to us!"

Danny's back straightened. The War was a period of history he'd avoided thinking about, though he knew the outlines of it. With *homo intelligens* increasing and pressing the older race aside by the laws of survival, his people had made a final desperate bid for supremacy. And while the new race had not wanted the War, they had been forced finally to fight back with as little mercy as had been shown them; and since they had the tremendous advantage of the new intuitive thinking, there had been only thousands left of the original billions of the old race when its brief course was finished. It had been inevitable probably, from the first mutation, but it was not something Danny cared to think of. Now he nodded, and let the other continue.

"Your ancestors, Danny, were beaten then, but they weren't completely crushed, and they put about the last bit of energy they had into rebuilding this ship—the only navigable one left them—and restocking it. They were going to go out somewhere, they didn't know quite where, even to another solar system, and take some of the old race for a new start, away from us. It was their last bid for survival, and it failed when my people learned of it and blasted the docks down over the ship, but it was a glorious failure, boy! I thought you'd want to know."

Danny's thoughts focused slowly. "You mean everything on the ship is of my people? But surely the provisions wouldn't have remained usable after all this time?"

"They did, though; the tests we made proved that conclusively. Your people knew how to preserve things as well as we do, and they expected to be drifting in the ship for half a century, maybe. They'll be usable a thousand years from now." He chucked his cigarette across the room and chuckled in pleased surprise when it fell accurately into a snuffer. "I stuck around, really, to tell you, and I've kept the papers over at the school for you to see. Why not come over with me now?"

"Not tonight, sir. I'd rather stay here a little longer." Professor Kirk nodded, pulling himself up reluctantly. "As you wish...I know how you feel, and I'm sorry about their moving the ship, too. We'll miss her, Danny!"

"Moving the ship?"

"Hadn't you heard? I thought that's why you came around at this hour. They want her over in London, and they're bringing one of the old Lunar ships here to replace her. Too bad!" He touched the walls thoughtfully, drawing his hands down and across the rich nap on the seat. "Well, don't stay too long, and turn her lights out before you leave. Place'll be closed in half an hour. 'Night, Danny."

"'Night, Professor." Danny sat frozen on the soft seat, listening to the slow tread of the old man and the beating of his own heart. They were moving the ship, ripping his plans to shreds, leaving him stranded in this world of a new race, where even the children were sorry for him.

It had meant so much, even to feel that somehow he would escape some day! Impatiently, he snapped off the lights, feeling closer to the ship in the privacy of the dark, where no watchman could see his emotion. For a year now he had built his life around the idea of taking this ship out and away, to leave the new race far behind. Long, carefully casual months of work had been spent in learning her structure, finding all her stores, assuring himself bit by bit from a hundred old books that he could operate her.

She had been almost designed for the job, built to be operated by one man, even a cripple, in an emergency, and nearly everything was automatic. Only the problem of a destination had remained, since the planets were all swarming with the others, but the ship's log had suggested the answer even to that.

Once there had been rich men among his people who sought novelty and seclusion, and found them among the larger asteroids; money and science had built them artificial gravities and given them atmospheres, powered by atomic-energy plants that should last forever. Now the rich men were undoubtedly dead, and the new race had abandoned such useless things. Surely, somewhere among the asteroids, there should have been a haven for him, made safe by the very numbers of the little worlds that could discourage almost any search.

Danny heard a guard go by, and slowly got to his feet, to go out again into a world that would no longer hold even that hope. It had been a lovely plan to dream on, a necessary dream. Then the sound of the great doors came to his ears, closing! The Professor had forgotten to tell them of his presence! And—!

All right, so he didn't know the history of all those little worlds; perhaps he would have to hunt through them, one by one, to find a suitable home. Did it matter? In every other way, he could never be more ready. For a moment only, he hesitated; then his hands fumbled with the great lock's control switch, and it swung shut quietly in the dark, shutting the sound of his running feet from outside ears.

The lights came on silently as he found the navigation chair and sank into it. Little lights that spelled out the readiness of the ship. "Ship sealed…Air Okay…Power, Automatic…Engine, Automatic…" Half a hundred little lights and dials that told the story of a ship waiting for his hand. He moved the course plotter slowly along the tiny atmospheric map until it reached the top of the stratosphere; the big star map moved slowly out, with the pointer in his fingers tracing an irregular, jagged line that would lead him somewhere toward the asteroids, well away from the present position of Mars, and yet could offer no clue. Later, he could set the analyzers to finding the present location of some chosen asteroid and determine his course more accurately, but all that mattered now was to get away, beyond all tracing, before his loss could be reported.

Seconds later his fingers pressed down savagely on the main power switch, and there was a lurch of starting, followed by another slight one as the walls of the Museum crumpled before the savage force of the great ion rockets. On the map, a tiny spot of light appeared, marking the ship's changing position. The world was behind him now, and there was no one to look at his efforts in kindly pity or remind him of his weakness. Only blind fate was against him, and his ancestors had met and conquered that long before.

A bell rang, indicating the end of the atmosphere, and the big automatic pilot began clucking contentedly, emitting a louder cluck now and then as it found the irregularities in the unorthodox course he had charted and swung the ship to follow. Danny watched it, satisfied that it was working. His ancestors may have been capable of reason only, but they had built machines that were almost intuitive, as the ship about him testified. His head was higher as he turned back to the kitchen, and there was a bit of a swagger to his walk.

The food was still good. He wolfed it down, remembering that supper had been forgotten, and leafing slowly through the big log book which recorded the long voyages made by the ship, searching through it for each casual reference to the asteroids. Ceres, Pallas, Vesta, some of the ones referred to by nicknames or numbers? Which ones?

But he had decided by the time he stood once again in the navigation room watching the aloof immensity of space; out here it was relieved only by the tiny hot pinpoints that must be stars, colored small and intense as no stars could be through an atmosphere. It would be one of the numbered planetoids, referred to also as "The Dane's" in the log. The word was meaningless, but it seemed to have been one of the newer and more completely terranized, though not the very newest where any search would surely start.

He set the automatic analyzer to running from the key numbers in the manual and watched it for a time, but it ground on slowly, tracing through all the years that had passed. For a time, he fiddled with the radio, before he remembered that it operated on a wave form no longer used. It was just as well; his severance from the new race would be all the more final.

Still the analyzer ground on. Space lost its novelty, and the operation of the pilot ceased to interest him. He wandered back through the ship toward the lounge, to spy the parcel where he had dropped and forgotten it. There was nothing else to do.

And once begun he forgot his doubts at the fact that it was Kenning's story, not the original; there was the same sweep to the tale, the same warm and human characters, the same drive of a race that had felt the mastership of destiny so long ago. Small wonder the readers of that time had named it the greatest epic of space to be written!

Once he stopped, as the analyzer reached its conclusion and bonged softly, to set the controls on the automatic for the little world that might be his home, with luck. And then the ship moved on, no longer veering, but making the slightly curved path its selectors found most suitable, while Danny read further, huddled over the story in the navigator's chair feeling a new and greater kinship with the characters of the story. He was no longer a poor Earth-bound charity case but a man and an adventurer with them!

His nerves were tingling when the tale came to its end, and he let it drop onto the floor from tired fingers. Under his hand, a light had sprung up, but he was oblivious to it, until a crashing gong sounded over him, jerking him from the chair. There had been such a gong described in the story...

And the meaning was the same. His eyes made out the red letters that glared accusingly from the control panel: RADIATION AT TEN O'CLOCK HORIZ—SHIP INDICATED!

Danny's fingers were on the master switch and cutting off all life except pseudogravity from the ship as the thought penetrated. The other ship was not hard to find from the observation window; the great streak of an invert-matter rocket glowed hotly out there, pointed apparently back to Earth—probably the *Callisto*!

For a second he was sure they had spotted him, but the flicker must have been only a minor correction to adjust for the trail continued. He had no knowledge of the new ships and whether they carried warning signals or not, but apparently they must have dispensed with such things. The streak vanished into the distance, and the letters on the panel that had marked its changing position went dead. Danny waited until the fullest amplification showed no response before throwing power on again. The small glow of the ion rocket would be invisible at the distance, surely.

Nothing further seemed to occur; there was a contented purr from the pilot and the faint sleepy hum of raw power from the rear, but no bells or sudden sounds. Slowly, his head fell forward over the navigator's table, and his heavy breathing mixed with the low sounds of the room. The ship went on about its business as it had been designed to do. Its course was charted, even to the old landing sweep, and it needed no further attention.

That was proved when the slow ringing of a bell woke Danny, while the board blinked in time to it: Destination! Destination! Destination Reached!

He shut off everything, rubbing the sleep from his eyes, and looked out. Above, there was weak but warm sunlight streaming down from a bluish sky that held a few small clouds suspended close to the ground. Beyond the ship, where it lay on a neglected sandy landing field, was the green of grass and the wild profusion of a forest. The horizon dropped off sharply, reminding him that it was only a tiny world, but otherwise it might have been Earth. He spotted an unkempt hangar ahead and applied weak power to the underjets, testing until they moved the ship slowly forward and inside, out of the view of any above!

Then he was at the lock, fumbling with the switch. As it opened, he could smell the clean fragrance of growing things, and there was the sound of birds nearby. A rabbit hopped leisurely out from underfoot as he stumbled eagerly out to the sunlight, and weeds and underbrush had already spread to cover the buildings about him. For a moment, he sighed; it had been too easy, this discovery of a heaven on the first wild try.

But the sight of the buildings drove back the doubt. Once, surrounded by a pretentious formal garden, this had been a great stone mansion, now falling into ruins. Beside it and further from him, a smaller house had been built, seemingly from the wreckage. That was still whole, though ivy had grown over it and half covered the door that came open at the touch of his fingers.

There was still a faint glow to the heaters that drew power from the great atomic plant that gave this little world a perpetual semblance of Earthliness, but a coating of dust was everywhere. The furnishings, though, were in good condition. He scanned them, recognizing some as similar to the pieces in the Museum, and the products of his race. One by one he studied them—his fortune, and now his home!

On the table, a book was dropped casually, and there was a sheet of paper propped against it, with what looked like a girl's rough handwriting on it. Curiosity carried him closer, until he could make it out, through the dust that clung even after he shook it.

Dad:

Charley Summers found a wrecked ship of those things and came for me. We'll be living high on 13. Come on over, if your jets will make it, and meet your son-in-law.

There was no date, nothing to indicate whether "Dad" had returned, or what had happened to them. But Danny dropped it reverently back on the table, looking out across the landing strip as if to see a worn old ship crawl in through the brief twilight that was falling over the tiny world. "Those things" could only be the new race, after the War; and that meant that here was the final outpost of his people. The note might be ten years or half a dozen centuries old—but his people had been here, fighting on and managing to live, after Earth had been lost to them. If they could, so could he!

And unlikely though it seemed, there might possibly be more of them out there somewhere. Perhaps the race was still surviving in spite of time and trouble and even *homo intelligens*.

Danny's eyes were moist as he stepped back from the door and the darkness outside to begin cleaning his new home. If any were there, he'd find them. And if not—

Well, he was still a member of a great and daring race that could never know defeat so long as a single man might live. He would never forget that.

Back on Earth, Bryant Kenning nodded slowly to the small group as he put the communicator back, and his eyes were a bit sad in spite of the smile that lighted his face. "The Director's scout is back, and he did choose 'The Dane's.' Poor kid. I'd begun to think we waited too long, and that he never would make it. Another six months—and he'd have died like a flower out of the sun! Yet I was sure it would work when Miss Larsen showed me that story, with its mythical planetoid-paradises. A rather clever story, if you like pseudohistory. I hope the one I prepared was its equal."

"For historical inaccuracy, fully its equal." But the amusement in old Professor Kirk's voice did not reach his lips. "Well, he swallowed our lies and ran off with the ship we built him. I hope he's happy, for a while at least."

Miss Larsen folded her things together and prepared to "Poor kid! He was sweet, in a pathetic sort of way. I wish that girl we were working on had turned out better; maybe this wouldn't have been necessary then. See me home, Jack?"

The two older men watched Larsen and Thorpe leave, and silence and tobacco smoke filled the room. Finally Kenning shrugged and turned to face the professor.

"By now he's found the note. I wonder if it was a good idea after all? When I first came across it in that old story, I was thinking of Jack's preliminary report on Number 67, but now I don't know; she's an unknown quantity, at best. Anyhow, I meant it for kindness."

"Kindness! Kindness to repay with a few million credits and a few thousands of hours of work—plus a lie here and there—for all that we owe the boy's race!" The professors voice was tired, as he dumped the contents of his pipe into a snuffer, and strode over slowly toward the great window that looked out on the night sky. "I wonder sometimes, Bryant what kindness Neanderthaler found when the last one came to die. Or whether the race that will follow us when the darkness falls on us will have something better than such kindness."

The novelist shook his head doubtfully, and there was silence again as they looked out across the world and toward the stars.

Wind Between the Worlds

I

It was hot in the dome of the Bennington matter transmitter building. The metal shielding walls seemed to catch the rays of the sun and bring them to a focus there. Even the fan that was plugged in nearby didn't seem to help much. Vic Peters shook his head, knocking the mop of yellow hair out of his eyes. He twisted his lanky, angular figure about, so the fan could reach fresh territory, and cursed under his breath.

Heat he could take. As a roving troubleshooter for Teleport Interstellar, he'd worked from Rangoon to Nairobi—but always with men. Pat Trevor was the first of the few women superintendents he'd met. And while he had no illusions of masculine supremacy, he'd have felt a lot better in shorts or nothing right now.

Besides, a figure like Pat's couldn't be forgotten, even though denim coveralls were hardly supposed to be flattering. Cloth stretched tight across a woman's hips had never helped a man concentrate on his work.

She looked down at him, grinning easily. Her arm came up to toss her hair back, leaving a smudge on her forehead to match one on her nose. She wasn't exactly pretty; her face had too much honest intelligence for that. But the smile seemed to illumine her gray eyes, and even the metal shavings in her brown hair couldn't hide the red highlights.

"One more bolt, Vic," she told him. "Pheooh! I'm melting… So what happened to your wife?"

He shrugged. "Married a lawyer right after the divorce. Last I knew, they were doing fine. Why not? It wasn't her fault. Between hopping all over the world and spending my spare time trying to get on the moon rocket they were building, I wasn't much of a husband. Funny, they gave up the idea of going to the moon the same day she got the divorce."

Unconsciously, his lips twisted. He'd grown up before DuQuesne discovered the matter transmitter, when reaching the other planets of the Solar System had been the dream of most boys. Somehow, that no longer seemed important to people, now the world was linked through Teleport Interstellar with races all across the galaxy.

Man had always been a topsy-turvy race. He'd discovered gunpowder before chemistry, and battled his way up to the atom bomb in a scant few thousand years of civilization, before he had a worldwide government. Most races, apparently, developed space travel thousands of years before the matter transmitter and long after they'd achieved a genuine science of sociology.

DuQuesne had started it by investigating some obscure extensions of Dirac's esoteric mathematics. To check up on his work, he'd built a machine, only to find that it produced results beyond his expectations; matter in it simply seemed to disappear, releasing energy that was much less than it should have been, but still enough to destroy the machine.

DuQuesne and two students had analyzed the results, checked the math again, and come up with an answer they didn't believe. But when they built two such machines, carefully made as nearly identical as possible, their wild idea had proved true; when the machines were turned on, anything in them simply changed places—even though the machines were miles apart.

One of the students gave the secret away, and DuQuesne was forced to give a public demonstration. Before the eyes of a number of world-famous scientists and half a hundred reporters, a full ton of coal changed places with a ton of bricks in no visible time. Then, while the reporters were dutifully taking down DuQuesne's explanation of electron waves that covered the universe and identity shifts, something new was added. Before their eyes, in the machine beside them, a round ball appeared, suspended in midair. It had turned around twice, disappeared for a few seconds, and popped back, darting down to shut off the machines.

For a week, the papers had been filled with the attempts to move the sphere from the machine, crack it open, or at least distract it long enough to cut the machines on again. By the end of that time, it was obvious that more than Earth science was involved. Poor DuQuesne was going crazy with a combination of frustration and crackpot publicity.

Vic's mind had been filled with Martians then, and he'd managed to be on the outskirts of the crowd that was present when the sphere came to life, rose up, cut on the machine, and disappeared again. He'd been staring at where it had been when the Envoy had appeared. After that, he'd barely had time to notice that the Envoy seemed to be a normal human before the police had begun chasing the crowd away.

The weeks that followed had been filled with the garbled hints that were enough to drive all science fiction fans delirious, though most of the world seemed to regard it as akin to the old flying saucer scare. The Envoy saw the President and the Cabinet. The Envoy met with the United Nations. The Envoy was admittedly a robot! India walked out; India came back. Congress protested secret treaties. General Autos held a secret meeting with United Analine. The Envoy would address the world in English, French, German, Spanish, Russian, and Chinese.

There were hundreds of books on that period now, and most schoolboys knew the speech by heart. The Galactic Council had detected the matter transmittal radiation. By Galactic Law, Earth had thus earned the rights to provisional status in the Council through discovery of the basic principle. The Council would now send Betzian engineers to build transports to six planets scattered over the galaxy, chosen as roughly comparable to Earth's culture. The transmitters used for such purposes would be owned by the Galactic Council, as a nonprofit business, to be manned by Earth people who would be trained at a school set up under DuQuesne.

In return, nothing was demanded. And no further knowledge would be forthcoming. Primitive though we were by the standards of most worlds, we had earned our place on the Council—but we could swim up the rest of the way by ourselves.

Surprisingly, the first reaction had been one of wild enthusiasm. It wasn't until later that the troubles began. Vic had barely made his way into the first engineering class out of a hundred thousand applicants. Now, twelve years after graduation...

Pat's voice cut in on his thoughts. "All tightened up here, Vic. Wipe the scowl off and let's go down to check."

She collected her tools, wrapped her legs around a smooth pole, and went sliding down. He yanked the fan and followed her. Below, the crew was on standby. Pat lifted an eyebrow at the grizzled, cadaverous head operator. "Okay, Amos. Plathgol standing by?"

Amos pulled his six-foot-two up from his slump and indicated the yellow standby light. Inside the twin poles of the huge transmitter that was tuned to one on Plathgol a big, twelve-foot diameter plastic cylinder held a single rabbit. Matter transmitting was always a two-way affair, requiring that the same volume be exchanged. And between the worlds, where different atmospheres and pressures were involved, all sending was done in the big capsules. One-way handling was possible, of course—the advanced worlds could do it safely—but it involved the danger of something materializing to occupy the same space as something else—even air molecules; when space cracked open under that strain, the results were catastrophic.

Amos whistled into the transport-wave interworld phone in the code that was universal between worlds where many races could not vocalize, got an answering whistle, and pressed a lever. The rabbit was gone, and the new capsule was faintly pink, with something resembling a giant worm inside.

Amos chuckled in satisfaction. "*Tsiuna*. Good eating. I got friends on Plathgol that like rabbit. Want some of this, Pat?"

Vic felt his stomach jerk at the colors that crawled over the *tsiuna*. The hot antiseptic spray was running over the capsule, to be followed by supersonics and ultraviolets to complete sterilization. Amos waited a moment and pulled out the creature.

Pat hefted it. "Big one. Bring it over to my place and I'll fry it for you and Vic. How's the Dirac meter read, Vic?"

"On the button." The 7 percent power loss was gone now, after a week of hard work locating it. "Guess you were right—the reflector was off angle. Should have tried it first, but it never happened before. How'd you figure it out?"

She indicated the interworld phone. "I started out in anthropology, Vic. Got interested in other races, and then found I couldn't talk to the teleport engineers without being one, so I got sidetracked to this job. But I still talk a lot on anything Galactic policy won't forbid. When everything else failed, I complained to one Ecthinbal operator that the Betz II boys installed us wrong. When I got sympathy instead of indignation, I figured it could happen. Simple, wasn't it?"

He snorted and waited while she gave orders to start business. Then, as the loading cars began to hum, she fell behind him, moving out toward the office. "I suppose you'll be leaving tonight, Vic? I'll miss you—you're the only troubleshooter I've met who did more than make passes."

"When I make passes at your kind of girl, it won't be a one-night stand," he told her. "And in my business, it's no life for a wife."

But he stopped to look at the building, admiring it for the last time. It was the standard Betz II design, but designed to handle the farm crops around, and bigger than any earlier models on Earth. The Betz II engineers knew their stuff, even if they did look like big slugs with tentacles and with no sense of sight. The transmitters were in the circular center, surrounded by a shield wall, a wide hall all around, another shield, a circular hall again, and finally the big outside shield. The two opposite entranceways spiraled through the three shields, each rotated thirty degrees clockwise from the entrance portal through the next shield. Those shields were of inerted matter that could be damaged by nothing less violent than a hydrogen bomb directly on them—they refused to soften at less than ten million degrees Kelvin. How the Betzians managed to form them in the first place, nobody knew.

Beyond the transmitter building, however, the usual offices and local transmitters across Earth had not yet been built; that would be strictly of Earth construction, and would have to wait for an off season. They were using the nearest building, an abandoned store a quarter mile away, as a temporary office. Pat threw the door open and then stopped suddenly.

"Ptheela!"

A Plathgolian native sat on a chair with a bundle of personal belongings around her, her three arms making little marks on something that looked like a used pancake. The Plathgolians had been meat-eating plants once. They still smelled high to Earth noses, and their constantly shedding skin resembled shaggy bark, while their heads were vaguely flowerlike.

Ptheela wriggled one of her three arms. "The hotel found it had to decorate my room," she whistled in Galactic Code. Many of the other races could not vocalize, but the whistling Code could be used by all, either naturally or with simple artificial devices. "No other room—and all the hotels say they're full up. Plathgolians stink, I guess. So I'll go home when the transmitter is fixed."

"With your trade studies half done? Don't be silly, Ptheela. I've got a room for you in my apartment. How are the studies, anyhow?"

For answer, the plant woman passed over a newspaper, folded to one item. "What trade? Your House of Representatives just passed a tariff on all traffic through Teleport!"

Pat scanned the news, scowling. "Damn them. A tariff! They can't tax interstellar traffic. The Galactic Council won't stand for it; we're still only on approval. The Senate will never okay it!"

Ptheela whistled doubtfully, and Vic nodded. "They will. I've been expecting this. A lot of people are sick of Teleport."

"But we're geared to Teleport now. The old factories are torn down, the new ones are useless to us without interstellar supplies. We can't get by without the catalysts from Ecthinbal, the cancer-preventative from Plathgol. And who'll buy all our sugar? We're producing fifty times what we need, just because most planets don't have plants that separate the levo from the dextro forms. All Hades will pop!"

Ptheela wiggled her arms again. "You came too early. Your culture is unbalanced. All physics, no sociology—all eat well, little think well."

All emotion, little reason, Vic added to himself. It had been the same when the industrial revolution came along. Old crafts were uprooted and some people were hurt. There were more jobs, but they weren't the same familiar ones. Now Plathgol was willing to deliver a perfect Earth automobile, semi-assembled and just advanced enough to bypass Earth patent laws, for half a ton of sugar. The Earth auto industry was gone. And the motorists were mad because Plathgol wasn't permitted to supply the improved, ever-powered models they made for themselves.

Banks had crashed, industries had folded, men had been out of work. The government had cushioned the shock, and Teleport had been accepted while it was still bringing new wonders. Now there was a higher standard of living than ever, but not for the groups who had controlled the monopolies. And too many remembered the wrenching and changing they'd had forced on them.

Also, it hadn't proved easy to accept the idea of races superior to Man. What was the use of making discoveries when others already knew the answers? A feeling of inferiority had turned to resentment, and misunderstandings between races had bred contempt here. Ptheela was kicked out of her hotel room—and a group had tried to poison the "hideous" Betz II engineers last year.

In an off-election year, politics could drop to the lowest level.

"Maybe we can get jobs on Plathgol," he suggested bitterly.

Ptheela whistled doubtfully. "Pat could, if she had three husbands—engineers must meet minimum standards. You could be a husband, maybe."

Vic kept forgetting that Plathgol was backward enough to have taboos and odd customs, even though Galactically higher than Earth, having had nearly a million years of history behind her to develop peace and amity.

The televisor connecting them with the transmitter building buzzed, and Amos' dour face came on. "Screwball delivery with top priority, Pat. Professor named Douglas wants to ship a capsule of lunar vacuum for a capsule of Ecthinbal deep-space vacuum. Common sense says we don't make much shipping vacuums by the pound!"

"Public service, no charge," Vic suggested, and Pat nodded. Douglas was a top man at Caltech and his goodwill testimony might be useful sometime. "Leave it on, Amos—I want to watch this. Douglas has some idea that space fluctuates, somehow, and he can figure out where Ecthinbal is from a sample. Then he can figure how fast an exchange force works, whether it's instantaneous or not. We've got the biggest Earth transmitters, so he uses us."

As he watched, a big capsule was put in place by loading machines and the light changed from yellow to red. A slightly greenish capsule replaced the other. Amos signaled the disinfection crew and hot spray hit it, to be followed by the ultrasonics. Something crackled suddenly, and Amos made a wild lunge across the screen.

The big capsule popped, crashing inward and scattering glass shards in a thousand directions. Pressure glass! It should have carried a standard code warning for cold sterilization and no supersonics. Vic started toward the transmitter building.

Pat's cry brought him back. There were sudden shrieks coming from the televisor. Men in the building were clinging frantically to anything they could hold, but men and bundles ready for loading were being picked up violently and sucked toward the transmitter. As Vic watched, a man hit the edge of the field and seemed to be sliced into nothingness, his screams cut off, half formed. Death was inevitable to anything caught in the edge of the field.

A big shard of glass had hit the control wiring, forcing together and shorting two bus bars, holding them together by its weight. It was wedged in firmly and the transmitter was locked into continuous transmit. And air, with a pressure of fifteen pounds per square inch, was running in and being shipped to Ecthinbal, where the pressure was barely an ounce per square inch! With that difference, pressure on a single square foot of surface could lift over a ton. The poor devils in the transmitter building didn't have a chance.

He snapped off the televisor as Pat turned away, gagging. "When was the accumulator charged?"

"It wasn't an accumulator in that installation," she told him weakly. "The whole plant uses an electron-pulse atomotor—good for twenty years of continuous operation."

Vic swore and made for the door, with Pat and Ptheela after him. The transmitter opening took up about two hundred square feet—which meant somewhere between fifty and five hundred thousand cubic feet of air a second were being lost. Maybe worse.

Ptheela nodded as she kept pace with him. "I think the tariff won't matter much now," she whistled.

II

Vic's action in charging out had been pure instinct to get where the trouble lay. His legs churned over the ground, while a wind at his back made the going easier.

Then his brain clicked over, and he dug his heels into the ground, trying to stop. Pat crashed into him, but Ptheela's arms lashed out, keeping him from falling. As he turned to face them, the wind struck at his face, whipping up grit and dust from the dry ground. Getting to the transmitter building would be easy—but with the wind already rising, they'd never be able to fight their way back.

It had already reached this far, losing its force with the distance, but still carrying a wallop. It was beginning to form a pattern, marked by the clouds of dust and debris it was picking up. The arrangement of the shields and entrances in the building formed a perfect suction device to set the air circling around it counterclockwise, twisting into a tornado that funneled down to the portals. Men and women near the building were struggling frantically away from the center of the fury. As he watched, a woman was picked up bodily, whirled around, and gulped down one of the yawning entrances. The wind covered her cries.

Vic motioned Pat and Ptheela and began moving back, fast. Killing himself would do no good. He found one of the little hauling tractors and pulled them onto it with him, heading back until they were out of the worst of the rising wind. Then he swung to face Ptheela.

"All right, now what? Galactic rules be damned, this is an emergency, and I need help!"

The shaggy Plathgolian made an awkward gesture with all three arms, and a slit opened in her chest. "Unprecedented." The word came out in English surprisingly, and Pat's look mirrored his; they weren't supposed to be able to talk. "You're right. If I speak, I shall be banished by our council from Plathgol for breaking security. But we can communicate more fully this way, so ask. I may know more—we've had the Teleport longer—but remember that your strange race has a higher ingenuity quotient."

"Thanks." Vic knew what the five husbands back on her home planet meant to her; they were not only a mark of status, but a chance to have stronger and more capable offspring. But he'd worry about that after he could stop worrying about his own world. "What happens next?"

She dropped back to the faster, if less precise, Galactic Code for that. As he knew, the accidental turning on of the transmitter had keyed in the one on Ecthinbal automatically to receive, but not to transmit; the air was moving between Earth and Ecthinbal in one-way traffic. The receiving circuit, which would have keyed in the Ecthinbal transmit circuit had not been shorted. Continuous transmittal had never been used, to her knowledge; there was no certainty about what would happen. Once started, no outside force could stop a transmitter; the send and stop controls were synchronous, both tapped from a single crystal, and only that proper complex wave form could cut it off. It now existed as a space-strain, and the Plathgolians believed that this would spread, since the outer edges transmitted before matter could reach the center, setting up an unbalanced resonance that would make the field grow larger and larger. Eventually, it might spread far beyond the whole building. And, of course, since the metal used by the Betz II engineers could not be cut or damaged, there was no way of tunneling in.

"What about Ecthinbal?" Pat asked.

Ptheela spread her arms. "The same, in reverse. The air rashes in, builds up pressure to break the capsule, and then rushes out—in a balanced stream, fortunately, so there's no danger of crowding two units of matter in one unit of space."

"Then I guess we'd better call the Galactic Envoy," Vic decided. "All he's ever done is to sit in an office and look smug. Now—"

"He won't come to help. He is simply an observeer. Galactic Law says you must solve your own problem or die."

"Yeah." Vic looked at the cloud of dust being whirled into the transmitter building. "And all I need is something that weighs a couple dozen tons per cubic foot—with a good crane attached."

Pat looked up suddenly. "Impossible. But how about one of the small atom-powered army tanks—the streamlined ones? Flavin could probably get you one."

Vic stamped on the pedal, swinging the little tractor around sharply toward the office. The wind was stronger already, but still endurable. He clicked the televisor on, noticing that the dust seemed to disappear just beyond the normal field of the transmitter. It must be starting to spread out.

"How about it?" he asked Ptheela. "If it spreads, won't it start etching into the transmitter and the station?"

"No. Betz II construction. Everything they built in has some way of grounding out the effect. We don't know how it works, but the field won't touch anything put in by the Betzians."

"What about the hunk of glass that's causing the trouble?"

For a moment she looked as if she were trying to appear hopeful. Then the flowerlike head seemed to wilt. "It's inside the casing-protected from the field."

Pat had been working on the private wire to Chicago, used for emergencies. She was obviously having trouble getting put through to Flavin. The man was a sore spot in Teleport Interstellar. He was one of the few political appointees; nominally, he was a go-between for the government and the Teleport group, but actually he was simply a sop to bureaucratic conventions. Finally Pat had him on the screen.

He was jovial enough, as usual, with a red spot on each cheek which indicated too many luncheon drinks. A bottle stood on the desk in front of him. But his voice was clear enough. "Hi, Pat. What's up?"

Pat disregarded the frown Vic threw her and began outlining the situation. The panic in her voice didn't require much feigning, Vic guessed. Flavin blustered at first, then pressed the hold button for long minutes. Finally, his face reappeared.

"Peters, you'll have full authority, of course. And I'll get a few tanks for you, somehow; I have to work indirectly." Then he shrugged and went rueful. "I always knew this sinecure would end. I've got some red slips here that make it look as if you had a national disaster there."

His hand reached for the bottle, just as his eyes met Vic's accusing look. He shook his head, grinned ruefully again, and put the bottle away in a drawer, untouched. "I'm not a fool entirely, Peters. I can do a little more than drink and chase girls. Probably be no use to you, but the only reason I drink is boredom, and I'm not bored now. I'll be out shortly."

In his own field, Flavin was apparently good. The tank arrived by intercity teleport just before he did. They were heavy, squat affairs, super-armored to stand up under a fairly close atomic bomb hit, but small enough to plunge through the portals of the transmitter building. Flavin came up as Vic and Pat were studying them. His suit was designed to hide most of his waistline, but the fat of his jowls shook as he hurried up, and there was sweat on his forehead, trickling down from under his toupee.

"Two, eh? Figured that's what I'd get if I yelled for a dozen. Think you can get in—and what'll you do then?"

Vic shrugged. He'd been wondering the same thing. Still, if they could somehow ram the huge shard of glass and crack it where it was wedged into the wiring inside the shielding, it might release the shorted wires. That should effect an automatic cutoff. "That's why I'm with the driver. I can extemporize if we get in."

"Right," Pat agreed quickly. She caught a hitch in her coveralls and headed for the other tank. "And that's why I'm going with the other."

"Pat!" Vic swung toward her. But it wasn't a time for stupid chivalry. The man or woman who could do the job should do it. He gave her a hand into the compact little tank. "Luck, then. We'll need it."

He climbed into his own vehicle, crowding past the driver and wriggling into the tiny observer's seat. The driver glanced back, then reached for the controls. The motor hummed quietly under them, making itself felt by the vibration of the metal around them. They began moving forward, advancing in low gear. The driver didn't like it, as he stared through his telescreen, and Vic liked it even less from the direct view through the gun slit. Beside them, the other tank got into motion, roughly paralleling them.

At first it wasn't too bad. They headed toward the north portal, traveling cautiously, and the tank seemed snug and secure. Beside him, Vic saw a tree suddenly come up by its roots and head toward the transmitter. It struck the front of the tank, but the machine went on, barely passing the shock through to the two men.

Then the going got rough. The driver swore at the controls, finding the machine hard to handle. It wanted to drift, and he set up a fixed correction, only to revise it a moment later. The tank began to list and pitch. The force of the wind increased by the square inversely as they cut the distance. At fifty feet, the driver's wrists were white from the tiny motions needed to overcome each tilt of the wind.

Vic swallowed, wondering at the nerve of the man driving, until he saw blood running from a bitten lip. His own stomach was pitching wildly. "Try another ten feet?" the driver asked.

"Have to."

"Not bad guts for a civilian, fellow. Okay, here we go."

They crawled by inches now. Every tiny bump threatened to let the force of the wind hit under them and pitch them over. They had to work by feeling, praying against the freak chance that might overcome all their caution. Vic wiped his forehead and wiped it again before he noticed that the palm of his hand was as damp as his brow.

He wondered about Pat, and looked for her. There was no sight of the other machine. Thank God, she'd turned back. But there was bitterness in his relief; he'd figured Pat was one human he could count on completely. Then he looked at the driver's wider view from the screen, and sick shock hit him.

The other tank had turned turtle and was rolling over and over, straight toward the portal! As he looked, a freak accident bounced it up, and it landed on its treads. The driver must have been conscious; only consummate skill accounted for the juggling that kept it upright then. But its forward momentum was still too strong, and it lurched straight toward the portal.

Vic jerked his mouth against the driver's ear, pointing frantically. "Hit it!"

The driver tensed, but nodded. The shriek of the insane wind was too strong for even the sound of the motor, but the tank leaped forward, pushing Vic down in his webbed and padded seat. The chances they were taking now with complete disregard seemed surely fatal, but the driver moved more smoothly with a definite goal. The man let the wind help him pick up speed, jockeying sidewise toward the other tank. They almost turned turtle as they swung, bucking and rocking frantically, but the treads hit the ground firmly again. They were drifting across the wind now, straight toward the nose of the other tank.

Vic was strained forward, and the shock of sudden contact knocked his head against the gun slit. He hardly felt it as he stared out. The two tanks struggled, forcing against each other, while the portal gaped almost straight ahead. "Hit the west edge and we have a chance," Vic yelled in the driver's ear. The man nodded weakly, and his foot pressed down harder on the throttle. Against each other, the two tanks showed little tendency to turn over, but they seemed to be lifted off the ground half the time.

Inch by slow inch, they were making it. Pat's tank was well beyond the portal, but Vic's driver was sweating it out, barely on the edge. He bumped an inch forward, reversed with no care for gears, and hitched forward and back again. They seemed to make little progress, but finally Vic could see the edge move past, and they were out of the direct jet that was being sucked into the portal.

A new screen had lighted beside the driver, and Pat's face was on it, along with the other driver. The scouring of the wind made speech impossible over the speakers, but the man motioned. Vic shook his head, and indicated a spiral counterclockwise and outward, to avoid bucking against the wind, with the two tanks supporting each other.

They passed the south portal somehow, though there were moments when it seemed they must be swung in, and managed to gain ten feet outward on the turn. The next time around, they had doubled that, and it began to be smoother going. The battered tanks lumbered up to their starting point eventually—and a little beyond, since the rising wind had forced everyone farther back.

Vic crawled from the seat, surprised to find his legs stiff and weak; the ground seemed to reel under him. It was some comfort to see that the driver was in no better shape. The man leaned against the tank, letting the raw wind dry the perspiration on his uniform. "Brother! Miracles! You're okay, mister, but I wouldn't go in there again with the angel Michael."

Vic looked at the wind maelstrom. Nobody else would go in there, either. Getting within ten feet of the portal was begging for death, even in the tank—and it would get worse. Then he spotted Pat opening the tank hatch and moved over to help her out. She was bruised and more shaky than he, but the webbing over the seat had saved her from broken bones. He lifted her out in his arms, surprised at how light she was. His mind flickered over the picture of her tank twisting over, and his arms tightened around her. She seemed to snuggle into them, seeking comfort.

Her eyes came up, just as he looked at her. She lifted her face, and he met her lips in a firm, brief contact. "You scared hell out of me, Pat."

"Me, too." She was regaining some color, and motioned him to put her down. "I guess you know how I feel about what you did in there."

Flavin cut off any answer Vic could have made, waddling up with his handkerchief out, mopping his face. He stared at them, gulped, and shook his head. "Lazarus twins," he growled. "Better get in the car—there's a drink in the right door pocket."

Vic lifted an eyebrow and Pat nodded. They could use it. They found the car and chauffeur waiting farther back. He poured her a small jigger and took one for himself before putting the bottle back. But the moment's relaxation over cigarettes was better than the drink.

Flavin was talking to the tank drivers, and a small roll changed hands, bringing grins to their faces. For a political opportunist, he seemed a lot more of a man than Vic had expected. Now he came back and climbed in beside them. "I've had the office moved back to Bennington—the intercity teleport manager offered us space." The locally owned world branches of intercity teleport were independent of Teleport Interstellar, but usually granted courtesy exchanges with the latter. "They'll be evacuating the city next, if I know the Governor. Just got a cease-and-desist order—came while you were trying to commit suicide. We're to stop transmitting at once!"

He grunted at Vic's grimace and motioned the chauffeur on, just as a call reached them. Vic shook his head at the driver and looked out to see Ptheela ploughing along against the wind, calling to them. The plant woman's skin was peeling worse than ever.

Flavin followed Vic's eyes. "You aiming to have that ride with us? The way Plathies stink? Damned plants, you can't trust 'em. Probably mixed up in this trouble. I heard…"

"Plathgol rates higher in civilization than we do," Pat stated flatly.

"Yeah. A million years stealing culture we had to scratch up for ourselves in a thousand. So the Galactic Council tells us we've got to rub our noses to a superior race. Superior plants! Nuts!"

Vic opened the door and reached for Pat's hand. Flavin frowned, fidgeted, then reached out to pull them back. "Okay, okay. I told you that you were in charge here. If you want to ride around smelling Plathies—well, you're running things. But don't blame me if people start throwing mud." He had the grace to redden faintly as Ptheela came up finally, and changed the subject hastily. "Why can't we just snap a big hunk of metal over the entrances, to seal them up?"

"Too late," Ptheela answered, sliding down beside Pat, her English drawing a surprised start from Flavin. "I was inspecting those two tanks, and they're field-etched where they touched. That means the field is already outside the building, though it will spread more slowly without the metal to resonate it. Anyhow, how could you get metal plates up?"

"How long will the air last?" Pat asked.

Vic shrugged. "If it keeps increasing, a month at breathing level, maybe. Fortunately the field doesn't spread downward much, with the Betzian design, so it won't start working on the earth itself. Flavin, how about getting the experts here? I need help."

"Already sent for them," Flavin stated. They were heading toward the main part of Bennington now, ten miles from the station. His face was gray, and he no longer seemed to notice the somewhat pervasive odor of Ptheela. They drew up to a converted warehouse finally, and he got out, starting up the steps just as the excited cries of a newsboy reached his ears. He flipped a coin and spread the extra before them.

Word had spread quickly. It was all over the front page, with alarming statements from the scientists first interviewed and soothing statements from later ones. No Teleport Interstellar man had spoken, but an interview with one of the local teleport engineers had given the basic facts, along with some surprisingly keen guesses as to what would happen next.

But above everything was the black headline:

BOMB TRANSMITTER SAYS PAN-ASIA!

The ultimatum issued by Pan-Asia was filled with high-sounding phrases and noble justification, but its basic message was clear enough. Unless the loss of air—air that belonged to everyone—was stopped and all future transmitting of all types halted, together with all dealings with "alien antiterrestrials," Pan-Asia would be forced to bomb the transmitters, together with all other resistance.

"Maybe..." Flavin began doubtfully, but Vic cut him off. His faith in mankind's right to its accidental niche in the Galactic Council wasn't increasing much.

"No dice. The field is a space-strain that is permanent, unless canceled by just the right wave form. The canceling crystal is in the transmitter. Destroy that, and the field never can be stopped. It'll keep growing until the whole Earth is gone. Flavin, you'd better get those experts here fast!"

III

Vic sat in the car the next morning, watching the black cloud that swirled around the station, reaching well beyond the old office. His eyes were red, his face was gray with fatigue, and his lanky body was slumped onto the seat. Pat looked almost as tired, though she had gotten some sleep. Now she took the empty coffee cup and thermos from him. She ran a hand through his hair, straightening it, then pulled his head down to her shoulder and began rubbing the back of his neck gently.

Ptheela purred approvingly from the other side, and Pat snorted. "Get your mind off romance, Ptheela! Vic's practically out on his feet. If he weren't so darned stubborn, this should make him go to sleep."

"Romance!" Ptheela chewed the idea and spat it out. "I've read the stories. All spring budding and no seed. A female should have pride from strong husbands and proven seeding."

Vic let them argue. At the moment, Pat's attention was soothing, but only superficially. His head went on fighting for some usable angle and finding none. The men who were supposed to be experts knew no more than he did. He'd swiped all the knowledge he could from Ptheela, without an answer. Plathgol was more advanced than Earth, but far below the Betz II engineers, who were mere servants of the top creatures of the Council.

No wonder man had resented the traffic with other worlds. For centuries he had been the center of his universe. Now, like the Tasmanians, he found himself only an isolated island of savages in a universe that was united in a culture far beyond his understanding. He'd never even conquered his own planets; all he'd done was to build better ways of killing himself.

Now he was reacting typically enough, in urgent need of someone even lower, to put him on middle ground, at least. He was substituting hatred for his lost confidence in himself. Why learn more about matter transmitting when other races knew the answers and were too selfish to share them?

Vic grumbled to himself, remembering the experts. He'd wasted hours with them, to find that they were useless for anything but argument. The names that had been towers of strength had proved no more than handles for men as baffled as he was. With even the limited knowledge he'd pried from Ptheela, he was far ahead of them—and still farther behind the needs of the problem.

The gun Flavin had insisted he wear was uncomfortable, and he pulled himself up, staring at the crew of men who were working as close to the center of wind as they could get. He hadn't been able to convince them that tunneling was hopeless. All they needed was a one-millimeter hole through the flooring, up which blasting powder could be forced to knock aside the glass shard. They refused to accept the fact that the Betz II shielding could resist the best diamond drills under full power for centuries. He shrugged. At least it helped the general morale to see something being done; he'd given in finally and let them have their way.

"We might as well go back," he decided. He'd hoped that the morning air and sight of the station might clear his head, but the weight of responsibility had ruined that. It was ridiculous, but he was still in charge of things.

Flavin reached back and cut on the little television set. With no real understanding, he was trying to learn tolerance of Ptheela, but he felt more comfortable in front, beside the chauffeur.

Pat caught her breath, and Vic looked at the screen, where a newscast was showing a crowd in Denver tearing down one of the Earth-designed intercity teleports. Men were striking back at the menace blindly. A man stood up from his seat in Congress to demand an end to alien intercourse; Vic remembered the fortune in interstellar trading of levo-rotary crystals that had bought the man his seat—and the transmitter-brought drugs that had saved him from death by cancer. He'd spouted gratitude, once!

There were riots in California, the crackpot Knights of Terra were recruiting madly, and murder was on the increase. Rain had fallen in Nevada, and there were severe weather disturbances throughout the country, caused by the unprecedented and disastrously severe low over Bennington. People were complaining of the air, already claiming that they could feel it growing thinner, though that was sheer hysterical nonsense. The Galactic Envoy was missing.

The editorial of the *Bennington Times* came on last, pointing a finger at Vic for changing the circuits, but blaming it on the aliens who hoarded their knowledge so callously. There was just enough truth to be dangerous. Bennington was close enough to the transmitter to explain the undertone of lynch law that permeated the editorial.

"I'll put a stop to that," Flavin told Vic angrily. "I've got enough muscle to make them pull a complete retraction. But it won't undo all of it."

Vic felt the automatic, and it seemed less of a nuisance now. "I notice no news on Pan-Asia's ultimatum."

"Yeah. I hear the story was killed by Presidential emergency orders, and Pan-Asia has agreed to a three-day stay—no more. My information isn't the best, but I gather we'll bomb it with our own bombs if it isn't cleared up by then."

Vic climbed out at the local station office, with the others trailing. In the waiting room, a vaguely catlike male from Sardax waited, clutching a few broken ornaments and a thin sheaf of Galactic credits. One of his four arms was obviously broken and yellow blood oozed from a score of wounds.

But he only shrugged at Vic's whistled questions, and his answer in Code was unperturbed. "No matter. In a few moments, I ship to Chicago and then home. My attackers smelled strongly of hate, but I escaped. Waste no time on me, please."

Then his whistle stopped at a signal from the routing office, and he hurried off, with a final sentence. "My attackers will live, I am told."

Remembering the talons on the male's hands, Vic grinned wryly. The Sardaxians were a peaceful race, but they were pragmatic enough to see no advantage in being killed. The mob had jumped on the wrong alien this time. But the others races...

He threw the door to his little office open, and the four went in. It wasn't until he started toward his desk that he noticed his visitor.

The Galactic Envoy might have been the robot he claimed to be, but there was no sign of it. He was dressed casually in expensive tweeds, lounging gracefully in a chair, with a touch of a smile on his face. Now he got up, holding out a hand to Vic.

"I heard you were running things, Peters. Haven't seen you since I helped pick you for the first-year class, but I keep informed. Thought I'd drop by to tell you the Council has given official approval to your full authority over the Earth branch of Teleport Interstellar, and I've filed the information with the U.N. and your President."

Vic shook his head. Nice of them to throw it all on his shoulders. "Why me?"

"Why not? You've learned all the theory Earth has, you've had more practical experience with more stations than anyone else, and you've picked Ptheela's brains dry by now. Oh, yes, we know about that; it's permissible in an emergency for her to decide to help. You're the obvious man."

"I'd rather see one of your high and mighty Galactic experts take over!"

The Envoy shook his head gently. "No doubt. But we've found that the race causing the trouble usually is the race best fitted to solve it. The same ingenuity that maneuvered this sabotage—it was sabotage, by the way—will help you solve it, perhaps. The Council may not care much for your grab-first rule in economics and politics, but it never doubted that you represent one of the most ingenious races we have met. You see, there really are no inferior races."

"Sabotage?" Pat shook her head, apparently trying to grasp it. "Who'd be that stupid?"

The Envoy smiled faintly. "The Knights of Terra are flowing with money, and they are having a very successful recruiting drive. Of course, those responsible had no idea of what risks they were taking for your planet. I've turned the details over, of course."

There was no mistaking his meaning. The Knights of Terra had been a mere rabble of crackpots, without any financial power. But most of the industries forced from competition by the transmitters had been the largest ones, since they tended to lack flexibility. Some of their leaders had taken it in good grace, but many had fought tooth and nail, and were still fighting. There were enough men who had lost jobs, patent royalties, or other valuables due to the transmitters. Even though the standard of living had risen and employment was at a peak now, the period of transition had left bitter hatreds, and recruits for the hate groups should be easy enough to find for a well-heeled propaganda drive.

"Earth for Earth, and down with the transmitters," Vic summed it up. The Envoy nodded.

"They're stupid, of course. They forget that the transmitters can't be removed without Council workers," he said. "And when the Council revokes approval, it destroys all equipment and most books, while seeing that three generations are brought up without knowledge. You'd revert to semi-savagery and have to make a fresh start-up. Well, I'll see you, Vic. Good luck."

He left, still smiling. Flavin had been eyeing him with repressed dislike that came out now. "A helluva lot of nerve for guys who claim they don't interfere!"

"It happened to us twice," Ptheela observed. "We were better for it, eventually. The Council's rules are from half a billion years of experience, with tremendous knowledge. We must submit."

"Not without a fight!"

Vic cut in. "Without a fight. We wouldn't have a chance. We're babes in arms to them. Anyhow, who cares? All the Congressional babble in Hades won't save us if we lose our atmosphere. But the so-called leaders can't see it."

The old idea—something would turn up. Maybe they couldn't turn off the transmitter from outside, and had no way of getting past the wind to the inside. But something would turn up!

He'd heard rumors of the Army taking over, and almost wished they would. As it stood, he had full responsibility—and nothing more. Flavin and the Council had turned things over to him, but the local cop on the beat had more power. It would be a relief to have someone around to shout even stupid orders and get some of the weight off his shoulders.

Sabotage! It couldn't even be an accident; the cockeyed race to which he belonged had to try to commit suicide and then expect him to save it. He shook his head, vaguely conscious of someone banging on the door, and reached for the knob. "Amos!"

The sour face never changed expression as the corpselike figure of the man slouched in. But Amos was dead! He'd been in the transmitter. They all realized it at once and swung toward the man.

Amos shook off their remarks. "Nothing surprising, just common sense. When I saw the capsule start cracking, I jumped for one headed for Plathgol, set the delay, and tripped the switch. Saw some glass shooting at me, but I was in Plathgol next. Went out and got me a mess of *tsiuna*—they cook fair to middling, seeing they never tried it before they met us. Then I showed 'em my pass, came back through Chicago, took the local here, and went home; I figured the old woman would be worried. Nobody told me about the extent of the mess till I saw the papers. Common sense to report in to you, then. So here I am."

"How much did you see of the explosion?" Pat asked.

"Not much. Just saw it was cracking—trick glass, no temperature tolerance. Looked like Earth color."

It didn't matter. It added to Vic's disgust to believe it was sabotage, but didn't change the picture otherwise. The Council wouldn't change its decision. They treated a race as a unit, making no exception for the behavior of a few individuals, whether good or bad.

Another knock on the door cut off the vicious cycle of hopelessness. "Old home week, evidently. *Come in!*"

The uniformed man who entered was the rare example of a fat man in the pink of physical condition, with no sign of softness. He shoved his bulk through the doorway as if he expected the two stars on his shoulders to light the way and awe all beholders. "Who is Victor Peters?"

Vic wiggled a finger at himself, and the general came over. He drew out an envelope and dropped it on the desk, showing clearly that acting as a messenger was far beneath his dignity. "An official communication from the President of the United States!" he said mechanically, and turned to make his exit back to the intercity transmitters.

It was a plain envelope, without benefit of wax or seals. Vic ripped it open, looked at the signature and the simple letterhead, and checked the signature again. He read it aloud to the others:

"'To Mr.'—dammit, officially I've got a doctor's degree!—'to Mr. Victor Peters, nominally'—oof!—'in charge of the Bennington branch of Teleport Interstellar'—I guess they didn't tell him it's *nominally* in charge of all Earth branches. Umm…'You are hereby instructed to remove all personnel from a radius of five miles minimum of your Teleport branch not later than noon, August 21, unless matters shall be satisfactorily culminated prior to that time. Signed, Homer Wilkes, President of the United States of America.'"

"Bombs!" Pat shuddered, while Vic let the message fall to the floor, kicking it toward the wastebasket. "That's what it has to mean. The fools—the damned fools! Couldn't they tell him what would happen? Couldn't they make him see that it'll only make turning the transmitter off impossible—forever?"

Flavin shrugged, unconsciously dropping onto the couch beside Ptheela. "Maybe he had no choice—either he does it or some other power does it."

Then he came to his feet, staring at Vic. "My God, that's *tomorrow* noon!"

IV

Vic looked at the clock later and was surprised to see that it was already well into the afternoon. The others had left him, Ptheela last when she found there was no more knowledge she could contribute. He had one of the electronic calculators plugged in beside him and a table of the so-called Dirac functions propped up on it; since the press had discovered that Dirac had predicted some of the characteristics that made teleportation possible, they'd named everything for him.

The wastebasket was filled, and the result was further futility. He shoved the last sheet into it, and sat there, pondering, There had to be a solution! Man's whole philosophy was built on that idea.

But it was a philosophy that included sabotage and suicide. What did it matter any…

Vic jerked his head up, shaking it savagely, forcing the fatigue back by sheer will. There was a solution. All he had to do was find it—before the stupidity of war politics in a world connected to a Galaxy-wide union could prevent it.

He pulled the calculator back, just as Flavin came into the room. The man was losing weight, or else fatigue was creating that illusion. He dropped into a chair as Vic looked up.

"The men evacuated from around the station?" Vic asked.

Flavin nodded. "Yeah. Some of the bright boys finally convinced them that they were just wasting time, anyhow. Besides, the thing is still spreading and getting too close for them. Vic, the news gets worse all the time. Can you take it?"

"Now what? Don't tell me they've changed it to tomorrow morning?"

"Tomorrow hell! In *two hours* they're sending over straight blockbusters, radar controlled all the way. No atomics—yet—but they're jumping the gun, anyhow. Some nut convinced Wilkes that an ordinary eight-ton job might just shake things enough to fracture the glass that's holding the short. And Pan-Asia is going completely wild. I've been talking to Wilkes. The Generalissimo over there probably only wanted to make a big fuss, but the people are scared silly, and they're preparing for quick war."

Vic nodded reluctantly and reached for the Benzedrine he'd hoped to save for the last possible moment, when it might carry him all the way through. What difference did it make? Even if he had an idea, he'd be unable to use it because a bunch of hopheads were busy picking themselves the station as a site for target practice.

"And yet…" He considered it more carefully, trying to figure percentages. There wasn't a chance in a million, but they had to take even that one chance. It was better than nothing.

"It might just work—if they hit the right spot. I know where the glass is, and the layout of the station. But I'll need authority to direct the bomb. Flavin, can you get me President Wilkes?"

Flavin shrugged and reached for the televisor. He managed to get quite a ways up by some form of code, but then it began to be a game of nerves and brass. Along his own lines, he apparently knew his business. In less than five minutes, Vic was talking to the President. For a further few minutes, the screen remained blank. Then another face came on, this time in military uniform, asking quick questions, while Vic pointed out the proper target.

Finally the officer nodded. "Good enough, Peters. We'll try it. If you care to watch, you can join the observers—Mr. Flavin already knows where they will be. How are the chances?"

"Not good. Worth trying."

The screen darkened again and Flavin got up. The thing was a wild gamble, but it was better to jar the building than to melt its almost impregnable walls. Even Betz II metal couldn't take a series of hydrogen bombs without melting, though nothing else could hurt it. And with that fury, the whole station would go.

They picked up Pat and moved out to Flavin's car. Vic knew better than to try to bring Ptheela along. As an alien, she was definitely taboo around military affairs. The storm had reached the city now, and dense clouds were pouring down thick gouts of rain, leaving the day as black as night. The car slogged through it, until Flavin opened the door and motioned them out into a temporary metal shelter.

Things were already started. Remote scanners were watching the guided missiles come down, and mechanical eyes were operating in the bombs, working on infrared that cut through the rain and darkness. It seemed to move slowly on the screen at first, but picked up apparent speed as it drew near the transmitter building. The shielding grew close, and Pat drew back with an involuntary jerk as it hit and the screen went blank. Dead center.

But the remote scanners showed no change. The abrupt break in the airmotion where the transmitter field began, outside the shielding, still showed. Another bomb came down, and others, each spaced so as to hit in time for others to be turned back if it worked. Even through the impossible tornado of rotating fury, it was super-precision bombing.

But the field went on working, far beyond the shielding, pulling an impossible number of cubic feet of air from Earth every second. They stopped watching the screen shown by the bomb-eyes at last, and even the Army gave up.

"Funny," one observer commented. "No sound, no flash when it hits. I've been watching the remote scanners every time instead of the eye, and nothing happens. The bomb just disappears."

Pat shook herself. "The field—they *can't* hit it. They go right through the field, before they can hit. Vic, it won't matter if we do atom-bomb the station. It can't be reached."

But he was already ahead of her. "Fine. Ecthinbal will love that. The Ecthindar wake up to find exploding atomic bombs coming at them through the transmitter. They've already been dosed with our chemical bombs. Now guess what they'll have to do."

"Simple." It was the observer who got that. "Start feeding atom bombs into their transmitters to us. We get keyed in to receive automatically, right? And we receive enough to turn the whole planet radioactive."

Then he shouted hoarsely, pointing through a window. From the direction of the station, a dazzle of light had lanced out sharply, and was now fading down. Vic snapped back to the remote scanner and scowled. The field was still working, and there was no sign of damage to the transmitter. If the Ecthindar had somehow snapped a bomb into the station, it must have been retransmitted before full damage.

The Army man stared sickly at the station, but Vic was already moving toward the door. Pat grabbed his arm, and Flavin was with them by the time they reached the waiting car. "The Bennington office," Vic told the driver. "And fast! Somebody has to see the Ecthindar in a hurry, if it'll do any good."

"I'm going too, Vic," Pat announced. But he shook his head. Her lips firmed. "I'm going. Nobody knows much about Ecthinbal or the Ecthindar. You call in Code messages, get routine Code back. We can't go there without fancy pressure suits, because we can't breathe their air. And they never leave. But I told you I was interested in races, and I have been trying to chitchat with them. I know some things—and you'll need me."

He shook his head again. "They'll probably welcome us with open arms— firearms! It's enough for one of us to get killed. If I fail, Amos can try—or Flavin. If he fails—well, suit yourself. It won't matter whether they kill me there or send through bombs to kill me here. But if one of us can get a chance to explain, it may make some difference. I dunno. But it may."

Her eyes were hurt, but she gave in, going with him silently as he stepped into the local Bennington unit and stepped out in Chicago, heading toward the Chicago Interstellar branch. She waited patiently while the controlmen scouted out a pressure suit for him. Then she began helping him fasten it and checking his oxygen equipment. "Come on back, Vic," she said finally.

He chucked a fist under her chin lightly and kissed her quickly, keeping it casual with a sureness he couldn't feel. "You're a good kid, Pat. I'll sure try."

He pulled the helmet down and clicked it shut before stepping into the capsule and letting the seal shut. He could see her swing to the interstellar phone, her lips pursed in whistled code. The sound was muffled, but the lights changed abruptly, and her hand hit the switch.

There was no noticeable time involved. He was simply on Ecthinbal, looking at a faintly greenish atmosphere, observable only because of the sudden change, and fifty pounds seemed to have been added to his weight. The transmitter was the usual Betz II design, and everything else was familiar except for the creature standing beside the capsule.

The Ecthindar might have been a creation out of green glass, coated with a soft fur, and blown by a bottle-maker who enjoyed novelty. There were two thin, long legs, multijointed, and something that faintly resembled the pelvis of a skeleton. Above that, two other thin rods ran up, with a double bulb where lungs might have been, and shoulders like the collar pads of a football player, joined together and topped by four hard knobs, each with a single eye and orifice. Double arms ran from each shoulder, almost to the ground.

He expected to hear a tinkle when the creature moved, and was surprised when he did hear it, until he realized the sound was carried through the metal floor, not through the thin air.

The creature swung open the capsule door after some incomprehensible process that probably served to sterilize it. Its Galactic Code whistle came from a device on its feet and through Vic's shoes from the floor. The air was too thin to transmit sound normally. "We greet you, Earthman. Our mansions are poor, but yours. Our lives are at your disposal." Then the formal speech ended in a sharp whistle. "Literally, it would seem. We die."

It didn't fit with Vic's expectations, but he tried to take his cue from it. "That's why I'm here. Do you have some kind of a ruler? Umm, good. How do I get to see this ruler?" He had few hopes of getting to see the ruler, but it never did any harm to try.

The Ecthindar seemed unsurprised. "Of course, I shall take you at once. For what other purpose is a ruler but to serve those who wish to see it. But—I trespass on your kindness in the delay—but may I question whether a strange light came forth from your defective transmitter?"

Vic snapped a look at it and nodded slowly. "It did."

Now the ax would fall. He braced himself for it, but the creature ceremoniously repeated his nod.

"I was one who believed it might. It is most comforting to know my science was true. When the bombs came through from you, we held them in an instant shield, since we had expected some such effort on your part to correct your transmitter. But in our error, we believed them radioactive. We tried a new negative aspect of space to counteract them. Of course, it failed, since they were only chemical. But I had postulated that some might have escaped from receiver to transmitter, being negative. You are kind. You confirm my belief. And now, if you will honor my shoulder with the touch of your hand, so that my portable unit will transport us both..."

Vic reached out and the scene shifted at once. There was no apparent transmitter, and the trick beat anything he had heard from other planets. Perhaps it was totally unrelated to the teleport machine. But he had no time to ask.

A door in the little room where they were now opened, and another creature came in, this time single from pelvis to shoulders, but otherwise the same. "The ruler has been requested," it whistled. "That which the ruler is shall be yours, and that which the ruler has is nothing. May the ruler serve?"

It was either the most cockeyed bit of naiveté or the fanciest run-around Vic had found, but totally unlike anything he'd been prepared for. He gulped and began whistling out the general situation on Earth.

The Ecthindar interrupted politely. "That we know. And the converse is true—we too are dying. We are a planet of thin air, and that little is chlorine. Now from a matter transmitter comes a great rush of oxygen, which we consider poison. Our homes around are burned in it, our plant life is dying of it, and we are forced to remain inside and seal ourselves off. Like you, we can do nothing—the wind from your world is beyond our strength."

"But your science..."

"Is beyond yours, true. As is our *average* intelligence. We run from an arbitrary lowest of one to a highest of two relatively, however, while you run from perhaps a low of an eighth to a high of nearly three, as we figure. We lack both your very lows and your genius level—some of you are more intelligent than any of us, though very few. But you are all adaptable, and we are too leisurely a race for that virtue."

Vic shook his head, but perhaps it made good sense. "But the bombs..."

A series of graceful gestures took place between the two creatures, and the Ruler turned back to Vic.

"The ruler had not known, of course. It was not important. We lost a few thousand people whom we love. But we understood. There is no anger, though it pleases us to see that your courtesy extends across space to us in commiseration. May your dead pass well."

That was at least one good break in the situation. Vic felt some of his worry slide aside to make room for the rest. "Then I don't suppose...Well, then, have you any ideas on how we can take care of this mess..."

There was a shocked moment, with abrupt movements from the two creatures. Then something came up in the Ruler's hands, vibrating sharply. Vic jumped back—and froze in mid-stride, to fall awkwardly onto the floor. A chunk of ice seemed to form in his backbone and creep along his spine, until it touched his brain. Death or paralysis? It was all the same—he had air for only an hour more. The two creatures were fluttering at each other and moving toward him when he blacked out.

V

His first feeling was the familiar, deadening pull of fatigue as his senses began to come back. Then he saw that he was in a tiny room—and that Pat lay stretched out beside him!

He threw himself up to a sitting position, surprised to find that there were no aftereffects to whatever the Ruler had used. The darned fool, coming through after him! And now they had her, too.

Surprisingly, her eyes snapped open, and she sat up beside him. "Darn it, I almost fell asleep waiting for you to revive. It's a good thing I brought extra oxygen flasks. Your hour is about up. How'd you insult them?"

He puzzled over it while she changed his oxygen flask and he did the same for her. "I didn't. I just asked whether there wasn't some way we could take care of this trouble."

"Which meant to them that you suspected they weren't giving all the help they could—after their formal offer when you came over. I convinced them it was just that you were still learning Code, whatever you said. They're nice, Vic. I never really believed other races were better than we are, but I do now and it doesn't bother me at all."

"It'd bother Flavin. He'd have to prove they were sissies or something. How do we get out?"

She pushed the door open, and they stepped back into the room of the Ruler, who was waiting for him. It made no reference to the misunderstanding, but inspected him, whistled approval of his condition, and plunged straight to business.

"We have found part of a solution, Earthman. We die—but it will be two weeks before our end. First, we shall set up a transmitter in permanent transmit, equipped with a precipitator to remove our chlorine, and key it to another of your transmitters—whichever one you wish. Ecthinbal is heavy but small, and a balance will be struck between the air going from you and the air returning. The winds between stations may disturb your weather, but not seriously, we hope. That which the Ruler is, is yours. A lovely passing."

It touched their shoulders, and they were back briefly in the transmitter, to be almost instantly back in the Chicago branch. Vic was still shaking his head.

"It won't work—the Ruler didn't allow for the way our gravity falls off and our air thins out a few miles higher up. We'd end up with maybe four pounds pressure, which isn't enough. So we both die—two worlds on my shoulders instead of one. Hell, we couldn't take that offer from them, anyhow. Pat, how'd you convince them to let me go?"

She had shucked out of the pressure suit and stood combing her hair. "Common sense, as Amos says. I figured engineers consider each other engineers first and aliens second, so I went to the head engineer instead of the Ruler. He fixed it up somehow. I guess I must have sounded pretty desperate, at that, knowing your air would give out after an hour."

They went through the local intercity to Bennington, and on into Vic's office, where Flavin met them with open relief and a load of questions. Vic let Pat answer, while he mulled over her words. Somewhere, there was an idea—let the rulers alone and go to the engineers. Some obvious solution that the administrators would try to understand, run into their preconceptions, and be unable to use? He shoved it around in his floating memory, but it refused to trigger an idea.

Pat was finishing the account of the Ecthindar offer, but Flavin was not impressed. Ptheela came in, and it had to be repeated for her, with much more enthusiastic response.

"So what?" Flavin asked. "They have to die, anyhow. Sure, it's a shame, but we have our own problems. Hey—wait. Maybe there's something to it. It'd take some guts and a little risk, but it might work."

Flavin considered it while Vic waited, willing to listen to any scheme. The man took a cigar out and lit it carefully, his first since the accident; he'd felt smoking used up the air. "Look, if they work their transmitter, we end up with a quarter of what we need. But suppose we had four sources. We connect with several oxygen-atmosphere worlds. Okay, we load our transmitters with delayed-action atom bombs and send one sample capsule to each world. After that, they either open a transmitter to us with air, or we really let them have it. They can live—a little poorer, maybe, but still live. And we're fixed for good. Congress and the President would jump at it."

"That all?" Vic asked.

Flavin nodded, just as Vic's fist caught him in the mouth, spilling him onto the floor. The man lay there, feeling his jaw and staring up at Vic. Then the anger was gone, and Vic reached down to help him up.

"You're half a decent guy and half a louse," he told Flavin. "You had that coming, but I should have used it on some of the real lice around. Besides, maybe you have part of an idea."

"'Sall right, no teeth lost—just the first cigar I've enjoyed in days." Flavin rubbed his jaw gingerly, then grinned ruefully. "I should have known how you feel. But I believe in Earth first. What's this big idea of yours?"

"Getting our air through other planets. *Our* air. It's a routing job. If we can set up a chain so the air going out of one transmitter in a station is balanced by air coming in another in the same station, there'd be a terrific draft; but most of it would be confined in the station, and there wouldn't be the outside whirlwind to keep us from getting near. Instead of a mad rush of air in or out of the building, there'd be only eddy currents outside of the inner chamber. We'd keep our air, and maybe have time to figure out some way of getting at that hunk of glass."

"Vic! You honey!" Pat's shoulders straightened. But Flavin shook his head.

"Won't work. Suppose Wilkes was asked to permit us to route through like that for another planet—he'd have to turn it down. Too much risk, and he has to consider our safely first."

"That's where Pat gave me the tip. Engineers get used to thinking of each other as engineers instead of competing races—they have to work together. They have the same problems and develop the same working habits. If I were running a station and the idea was put to me, I'd hate to turn it down, and I might not think of the political end. I've always wanted to see what happened in continuous transmittal; I'll be tickled pink to get at the instrument rolls in the station. And a lot of other engineers will feel the same."

"We're already keyed to Plathgol on a second transmitter in there," Pat added. "They could send to us, though the other four transmitters were out of duty. And the Ecthindar indicated they had full operation when it happened, so they're keyed to five other planets that could trigger them to transmit. But they don't connect to Plathgol, as I remember the charts."

"Bomb dropping starts in about four hours," Flavin commented. "Atomic, this time. After that, what?"

"No chance. They'll go straight through, and the Ecthindar can neutralize them—but one is pretty sure to start blasting here and carry through in full action. Then there'll be no other transmitter in their station. Just a big field on permanent receive."

"Then we'd better find a route from Ecthinbal to Plathgol—and get a lot of permissions—pronto!" Flavin decided. "And we need all the charts we can find."

The engineers at the Chicago branch were busy shooting dice when the four came through the intercity transmitter. Ptheela had asked to accompany the three humans, and her offer was welcome. More precisely, two engineers were playing. There was no one else in the place, and no sign of activity. Word of the proposed bombing had leaked out and the engineers had figured that answering bombs would come blasting back through all Earth teleports. They knew what Earth governments would have done and didn't know of the Ecthindar philosophy. The engineers had passed the word to other employees, and only these two were left, finishing a feud of long standing in the time left.

"Know anything about routing?" Vic asked. He'd already looked in the big barnlike building just outside the main shell, now empty of its normal crew. When they indicated no knowledge, he chased them out on his Teleport Interstellar authority and took over. He had no need of more engineers, and they were cynical enough about the eventual chances there to leave gladly. Vic had never had any use for Chicago's manager and the brash young crew he'd built up; word shouldn't have gone beyond the top level. If it leaked out to the general public, there'd be panic for miles around.

But Chicago's routing setup was the best in the country, and he needed it. Now how did he go about getting a staff trained to use it?

"Know how to find things here?" Flavin asked Pat. He accepted her nod, and looked surprised at Ptheela's equally quick assent. Then he grinned at Vic and began shucking off his coat. "Okay, you see before you one of the best traffic managers that ever helped pull a two-bit railroad out of the red, before I got better offers in politics. I'm good. You get me the dope, Vic can haggle on the transmitter phones, and I'll route it."

He was good. His mind could look at the complicated interlocking block of transmitter groups and jump to the next step without apparent thought—and he had to have information only once before engraving it on his mind. It was a tough nut, since the stations housed six transmitters, keyed to six planets each—but in highly varied combinations; each world had its own group of tie-ins with planets. Routing was the most complicated job in the work.

Plathgol was handled by Ptheela, who was still in good standing until her council was informed of her breaking the Law by talking to Vic. There was no trouble there. But trouble soon developed. The Ecthinbal station had been keyed to only two other planets when the accident happened, it turned out. Vromatchk was completely cold on the idea and flatly refused. Ee, the other, seemed difficult.

It surprised Vic, because it didn't fit with Pat's theories of engineers at all. He scowled at the phone, then whistled again. "All right, no matter. Your zeal is commendable. Now put an engineer on!"

The answering whistle carried a fumbling uncertainty of obvious surprise. "I—how'd you know? I gave all the right answers."

"Sure. Right off the Engineer Rule Sheet posted over the transmitter. No real engineer worries that much about them—he has more things to think of. Put the engineer on."

The answer was obstinate. "My father's asleep. He's tired. Call later."

The connection went dead at once. Vic called Ecthinbal while clambering into the big pressure suit. He threw the delay switch and climbed into the right capsule. A moment later, an Ecthindar was moving the capsule on a delicate-looking machine to another transmitter. Something that looked like a small tyrannosaurus with about twenty tentacles instead of forelegs was staring at him a second later, and he knew he was on Ee.

"Take me to the engineer!" he ordered. "At once."

The great ridges of horny substance over the eyes came down in a surprisingly human scowl. But the stubbornness was less certain in person. The creature turned and led Vic out to a huge shack outside. In answer to a whooping cry, a head the size of a medium-large car came out of the door, to be followed by a titanic body. The full-grown adult was covered with a thick coat of ropy hair.

"Where from?" the Ee engineer whistled. "Wait—I saw a picture. Earth? Come in. I hear you have quite a problem down there."

Vic nodded. It came as a shock to him that the creature could probably handle the whole station by itself, as it obviously did, and quite efficiently, with that size and set of tentacles. He stated the problem quickly.

The Looech, as it called itself, scratched its stomach with a row of tentacles and pondered. "I'd like to help you. Oh, the empress would have fits, but I could call it an accident. We engineers aren't really responsible to governments, after all, are we? But it's the busy season. I'm already behind, since my other engineer got in a duel. That's why the pup was tending while I slept. You say the field spreads out on continuous transmit?"

"It does, but it wouldn't much, if there isn't too long a period of operation."

"Strange. I've thought of continuous transmittal, of course, but I didn't suspect that. Why, I wonder?"

Vic started to give Ptheela's explanation of unbalanced resonance between the vacuum of the center and the edges in contact with matter, but dropped it quickly. "I'll probably know better when I can read the results from the instruments."

The Looech grumbled to itself. "I suppose you wouldn't send me the readings—we're about on a Galactic level, so it wouldn't strain the law too much."

Vic shook his head. "If I can't complete the chain, there won't be any readings. I imagine you could install remote cutoffs fairly easily."

"No trouble, though nobody ever seemed to think of them. I suppose it could be covered under our emergency powers, if we stretch them a little. Oh, blast you. Now I won't sleep for worrying about why it spreads. When will you begin?"

Vic grinned tightly as they arranged the approximate time and let the Looech carry him back to the capsule. He flashed through Ecthinbal and climbed out of the Chicago transmitter to find Pat looking worriedly at the capsule, summoned by the untended call announcer.

"You're right, Pat," he told her. "Engineers run pretty much to form. Tell Flavin we've got Ee."

But there were a lot of steps to be taken still. He ran into a stumbling block at Noral, and had to wait for a change of shifts, before a sympathetic engineer cut the red tape to clear him. And negative decisions here and there kept Flavin jumping to find new routes.

They almost made it, to find a decision had been reversed on them by some authority who had gotten word of the deal. That meant that other authorities would probably be called in, with more reverses, in time. Once operating, the engineer could laugh at authority, since the remote cutoff could be easily hidden. But time was running out. There were only twenty-seven minutes left before the bombs would be finally ordered dropped, and it would take fifteen to countermand their being dropped.

"Give me that," Flavin ordered, grabbing the phone. "There are times when it takes executives instead of engineers. We're broken at Seloo. Okay, we don't know where Seloo ships." His Galactic Code was halting, but fairly effective. The mechanical chirps from the Seloo operator leaped to sudden haste. A short pause was followed by an argument Vic was too tired to catch until the final sentence of assent. Then Pat took over, to report shortly to Flavin. "Enad to Brjd to Teeni clear."

"Never heard of Brjd," Vic commented.

Flavin managed a ghost of a swagger. "Figured our lists were only partial and we could stir up another link. Here's the final list. I'll get in touch with President Wilkes—now that we've got it, he'll hold off until we see how it works."

It was a maze, but the list was complete; from Earth to Ecthinbal, Ee, Petzby, Noral, Szpendrknopalavotschel, Seloo, Brjd, Teeni, and finally through Plathgol to Earth. Vic whistled the given signal and the acknowledgments came through. It was in operation. And Flavin's nod indicated Wilkes had confirmed it and held off the bombs.

Nothing was certain, still; it might or might not do the trick. But the tension dropped somewhat. Flavin was completely beaten. He hadn't had decent exercise for years, and running from communications to routing had been almost continual. He flopped over on a shipping table. Ptheela bent over him and began massaging him with deft strokes of her arms. He grumbled, but gave in, then sighed gratefully.

"Where'd you learn that?"

She managed an Earth giggle. "Instinct. My ancestors were plants that caught animals for food. We had all manner of ways to entice them—not just odor and looks. I can feel exactly how your body feels in the back of my head. Umm, delicious!"

He struggled at that picture, his face changing color. Her arms moved slowly, and he relaxed. Finally he reached for a cigar. "I'll have nightmares, I'll bet—but it's worth it. Oh-oh, some of the rulers are catching on, and don't like it!"

The minimum staff left in Bennington was reporting by normal televisor contact, but while things seemed to be improving, they couldn't get near enough to be sure. The tornado around the city was abating, they thought, but Earth's weather patterns were slow to change, once thoroughly upset. The field was apparently collapsing as the air was fed inside it, but very slowly.

Ptheela needed no sleep, but Flavin was already snoring. Pat shook her head as Vic started to pull himself up on a table. She led him outside to the back of one of the sheds, where a blanket lay on a cot, apparently used by one of the supervisors. She pushed him toward it. As he started to struggle at the idea of using the only soft bed, she dropped onto it herself and pulled him down.

"Don't be silly, Vic. It's big enough for both, and it's better than those tables."

It felt like pure heaven, narrow through it was. But his body was too tired to respond properly. The tension remained, reminding him that nothing was sure yet. Beside him, Pat stirred restlessly. He rolled over, pulling himself closer to her, off the hard edge of the cot, his arm over and around her.

For a moment, he thought she was protesting, but she merely turned over to face him, settling his arm back. In the half-light, her eyes met his, wide and serious. Her lips trembled briefly under his, then clung firmly. Her body slid against him, drawing tighter, and his own responded, reaching for the comfort and end of tension hers could bring.

It was automatic, almost unconscious, and yet somehow warm and personal, with an edge of tenderness all the cloudiness of it could not dull. Then she lay relaxed in his arms while his own muscles released themselves to the soft comfort of the cot. She smiled faintly, pushing his hair back.

"I'm glad it's you, Vic," she said softly. Then her eyes closed as he started to answer, and his own words disappeared into a soft fog of sleep.

The harsh rasp of a buzzer woke him, while a light blinked on and off near his head. He shook some of the sleep confusion out of his thoughts and made out an intercom box. Flavin's voice came over it sharply as he nipped the switch.

"Vic—where the hell are you? Never mind. Wilkes just woke me with his call. Vic, it's helped—but not enough. The field is about even with the building now. But it's stopped shrinking, and we're still losing air. There's too much loss at Ecthinbal, and at Ee—the engineer there didn't get the portals capped right, and Ecthinbal can't do anything. We're getting about two thirds of our air back. And Wilkes can't hold the pressure for bombing much longer! Get in here!"

VI

"Where's Ptheela?" Vic asked as he came into the communication and transmitter room. She needed no sleep and should have been taking care of things.

"Gone—back to Plathgol, I guess. Said something about an appeal. She was flicking out by the time I really woke up. Rats deserting the sinking ship, seems to me—though I had her figured different. It just shows you can't trust a plant."

Vic swept his attention to the communicator panel. The phones were still busy. They were still patient—even the doubtful ones were now accepting things; but it couldn't last forever. Even without the risk, the transmitter banks were needed for regular use. Many did not have inexhaustible power sources, either.

A new note cut in over the whistling now, and he turned to the Plathgol phone, wondering what Ptheela wanted. The words were English. But the voice was different.

"Plathgol calling. This is Thlegaa, Wife of Twelve Husbands, Supreme Plathgol Teleport Engineer, Ruler of the Council of United Plathgol, and Hereditary Goddess, if you want the whole routine. Ptheela just gave me the bad news. Why didn't you call on us before—or isn't our air good enough for you?"

"Hell, do you all speak English?" Vic asked, too surprised to care whether he censored his thoughts. "Your air always smelled good to me. Are you serious?"

The chuckle this time wasn't a mere imitation. Thlegaa had her intonation down exactly. "Sonny, up here we speak whatever our cultural neighbors do. You should hear my French nasals and Hebrew rough-breathings. Now that you know we can speak, there's no point in keeping the law against free communication. And I'm absolutely on the level. We're pulling the stops off the transmitter housing. We run a trifle higher pressure than you, so we'll probably make up your whole loss. But I'm not an absolute ruler, so it might be a good idea to speed things up. You can thank me later. Oh—since she broke the law before it was repealed, Ptheela's been exiled. So when you get your Bennington plant working, she'll probably be your first load from us. She's packing now."

Flavin's face held too much relief. Vic hated to disillusion him as the man babbled happily about knowing deep down all along that the Plathgolians were swell people. But he knew the job was a long ways from solved. With Plathgol supplying extra air, the field would collapse back to the inside of the single transmitter housing, and there should be an even balance of ingoing and outcoming air, which would end the rush of air into the station and make the circular halls passable, except for eddy currents. But getting into the inner chamber, where the air formed a gale between the two transmitters, was another matter.

Flavin's chauffeur was asleep at the wheel of the car as they came out of the Bennington local office, but instinct seemed to rouse him, and the car cut off wildly for the Interstellar station. Vic had noticed that the cloud around it was gone, and a mass of people were grouped nearby. The wind that had been sucked in and around it to prevent even a tank getting through was gone now, though the atmosphere would probably show signs of it in freak weather reports for weeks after.

Pat had obviously figured out the trouble remaining, and didn't look too surprised at the gloomy faces of the transmitter crew who were grouped near the north entrance. But she began swearing under her breath, as methodically and levelly as a man. Vic was ripping his shirt off as they drew up.

"This time you stay out," he told her. "It's strictly a matter of muscle power against wind resistance—and a man has a woman beat there."

"Why do you think I was cursing?" she asked. "Take it easy, though."

The men opened a way for him. He stripped to his briefs and let them smear him with oil to cut down air resistance a final fraction. Eddy currents caught at him before he went in, but not too strongly. Getting past the first shielding wasn't too bad. He found the second entrance port through the middle shield and snapped a chain around his waist.

Then the full picture of what must have happened on Plathgol hit him. Chains wouldn't have helped when they pulled off the coverings from the entrances—the sudden rush of air must have crushed their lungs and broken their bones—or whatever supported them—no matter what was done. Imagine volunteering for sure death to help another world! He had to make good on his part.

He got to the inner portal, but the eddies there were too strong to go farther. Even sticking his head beyond the edge almost sucked him into the blast between the two transmitters. Then he was crawling out again.

Amos met him, shaking a gloomy head. "Never make it, Vic. Common sense. I've been partway in there three times with no luck. And the way that draft blows, it'd knock even a tractor plumb out of the way before it could reach that glass."

Vic nodded. The tanks would take too long, anyhow, though it would be a good idea to have them called. He yelled to Flavin, who came over at a run, while Vic was making sure that the little regular office building still stood.

"Order the tanks, if we need them," he suggested. "And get them to ship in a rifle, some hard-nosed bullets, an all-angle vise big enough to clamp on a three-inch edge, and two of those midget telesets for use between house and field—quick."

Amos stared at him, puzzled, but Flavin's car was already roaring toward Bennington, with a couple of cops leading the way with open sirens. He was back with everything in twenty minutes.

Vic motioned to Amos questioningly and received an answering nod. The man was old, but he must be tough to have made three tries inside. Pat was setting the midget pickup in front of the still-operating televisor between the transmitter chamber and the little office. Vic picked up the receiver and handed the rest of the equipment to Amos.

It was sheer torture fighting back to the inner entrance port, but they made it, and Amos helped to brace him with the chain while Vic clamped the vise to the edge of the portal and locked the rifle into it, somehow fighting it into place. In the rather ill-defined picture on the tiny set's screen, he could see the shard of glass, out of line from either entrance, between two covering uprights. He could just see the rifle barrel, also. The picture lost detail in being transmitted to the little office and picked up from the screen for retransmittal back to him, but it would have to do.

The rifle was loaded to capacity with fourteen cartridges. He lined it up as best he could and tightened the vise, before pulling the trigger. The bullet ricocheted from the inner shield and headed toward the glass—but it missed by a good three feet.

He was close on the fifth try—not over four inches off. But clinging to the edge while he reset the vise each time before he pulled the trigger was getting harder, and the wind velocity inside was tossing the bullets off course.

He left the setting and fired four more shots in succession before he had to stop to rest. They were all close, but scattered. That could keep up all day, seemingly.

"Better let me try, Vic," Amos shouted over the roar of the wind inside. "Been playing pool, making bank shots, more than thirty years. And I had a rifle in my hands long before that."

He pulled himself into place, made a trifling adjustment on the vise setting, and squeezed the trigger. Then he leaned against the rifle stock slightly, took a deep breath, let it out, and fired again. There was no sound over the roar of the wind—and then there was a sound, as if the gale in there had stopped to cough.

A blast of air struck them, picking them up and tossing them against the wall. Vic had forgotten the lag before the incoming air could be cut! And it could be as fatal as the inrush alone.

But it was dying as he struck. His flesh was bruised from the shock, but it wasn't serious. Plathgol had managed to make their remote control cut out almost to the microsecond of the time when the flow to them had stopped, or the first pressure released—and transmitter waves were supposed to be instantaneous.

He tasted the feeling of triumph as he crawled painfully back. With this transmitter off and the others remotely controlled, the whole business was over. Ecthinbal had keyed out automatically when Earth stopped sending. And from now on, every transmitter would have a full set of remote controls, so the trouble could never happen again.

He staggered out, unhooking the chain, while workmen went rushing in. Pat came through the crowd with a towel and a pair of pants, to begin wiping the oil off him while he tried to dress. Her grin was a bit shaky, and he knew it must have looked bad when the final counterblast whipped out.

Amos was busy cleaning himself off, and Vic grinned at him. "Good shooting, Amos. I guess it's all solved."

The old man nodded. "Sure. Took a little common sense, that's all."

From the crowd, the Galactic Envoy shoved through, holding out his hands to them and smiling. "Co-operative sense, you mean, and that's not as common as it should be on any world. And, Amos, you'll be glad to know you're not under suspicion any longer. I have been able to furnish your government with a list of the real saboteurs, and they're all in custody. As I told you, I'm only an observer—but a very good observer of all that goes on!"

"Figured I'd be on the list. Common sense when I was closest to the accident and got away," Amos said. He shrugged. "You going to let the guys who did it get regular Earth trials?"

"Certainly," the Envoy answered. "It looks better. Nice work, Pat, Vic, Amos—you, too, Flavin. I wasn't sure you had it in you. You solved it—by finding you could co-operate with other worlds, which is the most mature way you could have solved it. So I consider that Plathgol and Earth have passed the final test, and are now full members, under Ecthinbal's tutelage. We're a little easier at lending a hand and passing information to proven planets. Congratulations! But you'll hear all about it in the news when I make the full announcement. See you around—I'm sure of that."

He was gone, barely in time for Ptheela to come trooping up with six thin, wispy versions of herself in tow. She chuckled. "They promoted me before they banished me, Pat. Meet my six strong husbands. Now I'll have the strongest seed on all Earth. Oh, I almost forgot. A present for you and Vic."

Then she also was gone, leading her husbands toward Flavin's car while Vic stared down at a particularly ugly *tsiuna* in Pat's hands. He grinned a bit ruefully.

"All right. I'll learn to eat the stuff," he told her. "I suppose I'll have to get used to it. Pat, will you marry me?"

She dropped the *tsiuna* into Amos' hands us she came to him, her lips reaching up for his. It wasn't until a month later that he found *tsiuna* tasted slightly better than chicken.

Earthbound

It was hours after the last official ceremony before Clifton could escape the crowd of planetlubbers with their babblings, their eligible daughters, and their stupid self-admiration. They'd paid through the nose to get him here, and they meant to get their money's worth. The exit led only to a little balcony, but it seemed to be deserted. He took a deep breath of the night air and his eyes moved unconsciously toward the stars.

Coming back to Earth had been a mistake, but he'd needed the money. Space Products Unlimited wanted a real deepspace hero to help celebrate its hundredth anniversary, and he'd just finished the Regulation of Rigel, so he'd been picked. Damn them and their silly speeches and awards—and damn Earth! What was one planet when there were a billion up there among the stars?

From the other side of a potted plant there was a soft, quavering sigh. Clifton swung his head, then relaxed as he saw the other man was not looking at him. The eyes behind the dark glasses were directed toward the sky.

"Aldebaran, Sirius, Deneb, Centaurus," the voice whispered. It was a high-pitched voice with an odd accent, but there was the poetry of ancient yearning in it.

He was a small, shriveled old man. His shoulders were bent. A long beard and dark glasses covered most of his face, but could not entirely conceal the deep wrinkles, even in the moonlight.

Clifton felt a sudden touch of pity and moved closer, without quite knowing why. "Didn't I see you on the platform?"

"Your memory is very good, Captain. I was awarded publicly for fifty years of faithful service making space boots. Well, I was always a good cobbler, and perhaps my boots helped some men out there." The old man's hand swept toward the stars, then fell back to grip the railing tightly. "They gave me a gold watch, though time means nothing to me. And a cheap world cruise ticket, as if there were any spot on this world I could still want to see." He laughed harshly. "Forgive me if I sound bitter. But, you see, I've never been off Earth!"

Clifton stared at him incredulously. "But everyone—"

"Everyone but me," the old man said. "Oh, I tried. I was utterly weary of Earth and I looked at the stars and dreamed. But I failed the early rigid physicals. Then, when things were easier, I tried again. A strange plague grounded the ship. A strike delayed another. Then one exploded on the pad and only a few on board were saved. It was then I realized I was meant to wait here—here on Earth, and nowhere else. So I stayed, making space boots."

Pity and impulse forced unexpected words to Clifton's lips. "I'm taking off for Rigel again in four hours, and there's a spare cabin on the *Maryloo*. You're coming with me."

The old hand that gripped his arm was oddly gentle. "Bless you, Captain. But it would never work. I'm under orders to remain here."

"Nobody can order a man grounded forever. You're coming with me if I have to drag you, Mr.—"

"Ahasuerus." The old man hesitated, as if expecting the name to mean something. Then he sighed and lifted his dark glasses.

Clifton met the other's gaze for less than a second. Then his own eyes dropped, though the memory of what he had seen was already fading. He vaulted over the balcony railing and began running away from Ahasuerus, toward his ship and the unconfined reaches of space.

Behind him, the Wandering Jew tarried and waited.

Dark Mission

The rays of the sun lanced down over the tops of the trees and into the clearing, revealing a scene of chaos and havoc. Yesterday there had been a wooden frame house there, but now only pieces of it remained. One wall had been broken away, as by an explosion, and lay on the ground in fragments; the roof was crushed in, as if some giant had stepped on it and passed on.

But the cause of the damage was still there, lying on the ruins of the house. A tangled mass of buckled girders and metal plates lay mixed with a litter of laboratory equipment that had been neatly arranged in one room of the house, and parts of a strange engine lay at one side. Beyond was a tube that might have been a rocket. The great metal object that lay across the broken roof now only hinted at the sleek cylinder it had once been, but a trained observer might have guessed that it was the wreck of a rocketship. From the former laboratory, flames were licking up at the metal hull, and slowly spreading towards the rest of the house.

In the clearing, two figures lay outstretched, of similar size and build, but otherwise unlike. One was a dark man of middle age, completely naked, with a face cut and battered beyond all recognition. The odd angle of the head was unmistakable proof that his neck was broken. The other man might have been a brawny sea Viking of earlier days, both from his size and appearance, but his face revealed something finer and of a higher culture. He was fully clothed, and the slow movement of his chest showed that there was still life in him. Beside him, there was a broken beam from the roof, a few spots of blood on it. There was more blood on the man's head, but the cut was minor, and he was only stunned.

Now he stirred uneasily and groped uncertainly to his feet, shaking his head and fingering the cut on his scalp. His eyes traveled slowly across the clearing and to the ruins that were burning merrily. The corpse claimed his next attention, and he turned it over to examine the neck. He knit his brows and shook his head savagely, trying to call back the memories that eluded him.

They would not come. He recognized what his eyes saw, but his mind produced no words to describe them, and the past was missing. His first memory was of wakening to find his head pounding with an ache that was almost unbearable. Without surprise, he studied the rocket and saw that it had come down on the house, out of control, but it evoked no pictures in his mind, and he gave up. He might have been in the rocket or the house at the time; he had no way of telling which. Probably the naked man had been asleep at the time in the house.

Something prickled gently in the back of his mind, growing stronger and urging him to do something. He must not waste time here, but must fulfill some vital mission. What mission? For a second, he almost had it, and then it was gone again, leaving only the compelling urge that must be obeyed. He shrugged and started away from the ruins toward the little trail that showed through the trees.

Then another impulse called him back to the corpse, and he obeyed it because he knew of nothing else to do. Acting without conscious volition, he tugged at the corpse, found it strangely heavy, and dragged it toward the house. The flames were everywhere now, but he found a place where the heat was not too great and pulled the corpse over a pile of combustibles.

With the secondary impulse satisfied, the first urge returned, and he set off down the trail moving slowly. The shoes hurt his feet, and his legs were leaden, but he kept on grimly, while a series of questions went around his head in circles. Who was he, where, and why?

Whoever had lived in the house, himself or the corpse, had obviously chosen the spot for privacy; the trail seemed to go on through the woods endlessly, and he saw no signs of houses along it. He clumped on mechanically, wondering if there was no end, until a row of crossed poles bearing wires caught his eye. Ahead, he made out a broad highway, with vehicles speeding along it in both directions, and hastened forward, hoping to meet someone.

Luck was with him. Pulled up at the side of the road was one of the vehicles, and a man was doing something at the front end of the car. Rough words carried back to him suggesting anger. He grinned suddenly and hastened toward the car, his eyes riveted on the man's head. A tense feeling shot through his brain and left, just as he reached the machine.

"Need help?" The words slipped out unconsciously, and now other words came pouring into his head, along with ideas and knowledge, and that seemed wrong somehow. The driving impulse he felt was still unexplained.

The man had looked up at his words, and relief shot over the sweating face. "Help's the one thing I need," he replied gratefully. "I been fussing with this blasted contraption darned near an hour, and nobody's even stopped to ask, so far. Know anything about it?"

"Ummm." The stranger, as he was calling himself for want of a better name, tested the wires himself, vaguely troubled at the simplicity of the engine. He gave up and went around to the other side, lifting the hood and inspecting the design. Then sureness came to him as he reached for the tool kit. "Probably the...umm...timing pins," he said.

It was. A few minutes later, the engine purred softly and the driver turned to the stranger. "Okay now, I guess. Good thing you came along; worst part of the road, and not a repair shop for miles. Where you going?"

"I—" The stranger caught himself. "The big city," he said, for want of a better destination.

"Hop in, then. I'm going to Elizabeth, right on your way. Glad to have you along; gets so a man talks to himself on these long drives, unless he has something to do. Smoke?"

"Thank you, no. I never do." He watched the other light up, feeling uncomfortable about it. The smell of the smoke, when it reached him, was nauseous, as were the odor of gasoline and the man's own personal effluvium, but he pushed them out of his mind as much as possible. "Have you heard or read anything about a rocketship of some kind?"

"Sure. Oglethorpe's, you mean? I been reading what the papers had to say about it." The drummer took his eyes off the road for a second, and his beady little eyes gleamed. "I been wondering a long time why some of these big-shot financiers don't back up the rockets, and finally Oglethorpe does. Boy, now maybe we'll find out something about this Mars business."

The stranger grinned mechanically. "What does his ship look like?"

"Picture of it in the *Scoop*, front page. Find it back of the seat, there. Yeah, that's it. Wonder what the Martians look like?"

"Hard to guess," the stranger answered. Even rough half-tones of the picture showed that it was not the ship that had crashed, but radically different. "No word of other rockets?"

"Nope, not that I know of, except the Army's test things. You know, I kinda feel maybe the Martians might look like us. Sure." He took the other's skepticism for granted without looking around. "Wrote a story about that once, for one of these science-fiction magazines, but they sent it back. I figured out maybe a long time ago there was a civilization on Earth—Atlantis, maybe—and they went over and settled on Mars. Only Atlantis sunk on them and there they were, stranded. I figured maybe one day they came back, sort of lost out for a while, but popped up again and started civilization humming. Not bad, eh?"

"Clever," the stranger admitted. "But it sounds vaguely familiar. Suppose we said instead there was a war between the mother world and Mars that wrecked both civilizations, instead of your Atlantis sinking. Wouldn't that be more logical?"

"Maybe, I dunno. Might try it, though mostly they seem to want freaks—Darned fool, passing on a hill!" He leaned out to shake a pudgy fist, then came back to his rambling account. "Read one the other day with two races, one like octopuses, the other twenty feet tall and all blue."

Memory pricked tantalizingly and came almost to the surface. Blue—Then it was gone again, leaving only a troubled feeling. The stranger frowned and settled down the seat, answering in monosyllables to the other's monologue, and watching the patchwork of country and cities slip by.

"There's Elizabeth. Any particular place you want me to drop you?"

The stranger stirred from the half-coma induced by the cutting ache in his head, and looked about. "Any place," he answered. Then the surge in the back of his mind grabbed at him again, and he changed it. "Some doctor's office."

That made sense, of course. Perhaps the impulse had been only the logical desire to seek medical aid, all along. But it was still there, clamoring for expression, and he doubted the logic of anything connected with it. The call for aid could not explain the sense of disaster that accompanied it. As the car stopped before a house with a doctor's shingle, his pulse was hammering with frenzied urgency.

"Here we are." The drummer reached out toward the door handle, almost brushing one of the other's hands. The stranger jerked it back savagely, avoiding contact by a narrow margin, and a cold chill ran up his back and quivered its way down again. If that hand had touched him—The half-opened door closed again, but left one fact impressed on him. Under no conditions must he suffer another to make direct contact with his body, lest something horrible should happen! Another crazy angle, unconnected with the others, but too strong for disobedience. He climbed out, muttering his thanks, and made his way up the walk toward the office of Dr. Lanahan, hours 12:00 to 4:00.

The doctor was an old man, with the seamed and rugged good-nature of the general practitioner, and his office fitted him. There was a row of medical books along one wall, a glass-doored cabinet containing various medicaments, and a clutter of medical instruments. He listened to the stranger's account quietly, smiling encouragement at times, and tapping the desk with his pencil.

"Amnesia, of course," he agreed, finally. "Rather peculiar in some respects, but most cases of that are individual. When the brain is injured, its actions are usually unpredictable. Have you considered the possibility of hallucinations in connection with those impulses you mention?"

"Yes." He had considered it from all angles, and rejected the solutions as too feeble. "If they were ordinary impulses, I'd agree with you. But they're far deeper than that, and there's a good reason for them, somewhere. I'm sure of that."

"Hmm." The doctor tapped his pencil again and considered. The stranger sat staring at the base of his neck, and the tense feeling in his head returned, as it had been when he first met the drummer. Something rolled around in his mind and quieted. "And you have nothing on you in the way of identification?"

"Uh!" The stranger grunted, feeling foolish, and reached into his pockets.

"I hadn't thought of that." He brought out a package of cigarettes, a stained handkerchief, glasses, odds and ends, that meant nothing to him, and finally a wallet stuffed with bills. The doctor seized on that and ran through its contents quickly.

"Evidently you had money... Ummm, no identification card, except for the letters L. H. Ah, there we are; a calling card." He passed it over, along with the wallet, and smiled in self-satisfaction. "Evidently you're a fellow physician, Dr. Lurton Haines. Does that recall anything?"

"Nothing." It was good to have a name, in a way, but that was his only response to the sight of the card. And why was he carrying glasses and cigarettes for which he had no earthly use?

The doctor was hunting through his pile of books and finally came up with a dirty red volume. "*Who's Who*," he explained. "Let's see. Umm. Here we are. 'Lurton R. Haines, M.D.' Odd, I thought you were younger than that. Work along cancer research. No relatives mentioned. The address is evidently that of the house you remember first—'Surrey Road, Danesville.' Want to see it?"

He passed the volume over, and the stranger—or Haines—scanned it carefully, but got no more out of it than the other's summary, except for the fact that he was forty-two years old. He put the book back on the desk, and reached for his wallet, laying a bill on the pad where the other could reach it.

"Thank you, Dr. Lanahan." There was obviously nothing more the doctor could do for him, and the odor of the little room and the doctor was stifling him; apparently he was allergic to the smell of other men. "Never mind the cut on the head—it's purely superficial."

"But—"

Haines shrugged and mustered a smile, reached for the door, and made for the outside again. The urge was gone now, replaced by a vast sense of gloom, and he knew that his mission had ended in failure.

They knew so little about healing, though they tried so hard. The entire field of medicine ran through Haines' mind now, with all its startling successes and hopeless failures, and he knew that even his own problem was beyond their ability. And the knowledge, like the sudden return of speech, was a mystery; it had come rushing into his mind while he stared at the doctor, at the end of the sudden tenseness, and a numbing sense of failure had accompanied it. Strangely, it was not the knowledge of a specialist in cancer research, but such common methods as a general practitioner might use.

One solution suggested itself, but it was too fantastic for belief. The existence of telepaths was suspected, but not ones who could steal whole pages of knowledge from the mind of another, merely by looking at him. No, that was more illogical than the sudden wakening of isolated fields of memory by the sight of the two men.

He stopped at a corner, weary under the load of despondency he was carrying, and mulled it over dully. A newsboy approached hopefully. "*Time* a' *News* out!" the boy sing-songed his wares. "*Scoop* 'n' *Juhnal* ! Read awl about the big train wreck! Paper, mister?"

Haines shrugged dully. "No paper!"

"Blonde found muidehed in bath-tub," the boy insinuated. "Mahs rocket account!" The man must have an Achilles' heel somewhere.

But the garbled jargon only half registered on Haines' ears. He started across the street, rubbing his temples, before the second driving impulse caught at him and sent him back remorselessly to the paper boy. He found some small change in his pocket, dropped a nickel on the pile of papers, disregarding the boy's hand, and picked up a copy of the *Scoop*. "Screwball," the boy decided aloud, and dived for the nickel.

The picture was no longer on the front page of the tabloid, but Haines located the account with some effort. "Mars Rocket Take-Off Wednesday," said the headline in conservative twenty-four-point type, and there was three-quarters of a column under it. "Man's first flight to Mars will not be delayed, James Oglethorpe told reporters here today. Undismayed by the skepticism of the scientists, the financier is going ahead with his plans, and expects his men to take off for Mars Wednesday, June 8, as scheduled. Construction has been completed, and the rocket machine is now undergoing tests."

Haines scanned down the page, noting the salient facts. The writer had kept his tongue in his cheek, but under the faintly mocking words there was the information he wanted. The rocket might work; man was at last on his way toward the conquests of the planets. There was no mention of another rocket; obviously, then, that one must have been built in secret in a futile effort to beat Oglethorpe's model.

But that was unimportant. The important thing was that he must stop the flight! Above all else, man must not make that trip! There was no sanity to it, and yet somehow it was beyond mere sanity. It was his duty to prevent any such voyage, and that duty was not to be questioned.

He returned quickly to the newsboy, reached out to touch his shoulder, and felt his hand jerk back to avoid the touch. The boy seemed to sense it, though, for he mined quickly. "Paper?" he began brightly before recognizing the stranger. "Oh, it's you. Watcha want?"

"Where can I find a train to New York?" Haines pulled a quarter from his pocket and tossed it on the pile of papers.

The boy's eyes brightened again. "Four blocks down, tuihn right, and keep goin' till you come to the station. Can't miss it. Thanks, mister!"

The discovery of the telephone book as a source of information was Haines' single major triumph, and the fact that the first Oglethorpe he tried was a colored street cleaner failed to take the edge off it. Now he trudged uptown, counting the numbers that made no sense to him; apparently the only system was one of arithmetical progression, irrespective of streets.

His shoulders were drooping, and the lines of pain around his eyes had finally succeeded in drawing his brows together. A coughing spell hit him, torturing his lungs for long minutes, and then passed. That was a new development, as was the pressure around his heart. And everywhere was the irritating aroma of men, gasoline, and tobacco, a stale mixture that he could not escape. He thrust his hands deeper into his pockets to avoid chance contact with someone on the street, and crossed over toward the building that bore the number for which he was searching.

Another man was entering the elevator, and he followed mechanically, relieved that he would not have to plod up the stairs. "Oglethorpe?" he asked the operator uncertainly.

"Fourth floor, Room 405." The boy slid the gate open, pointing, and Haines stepped out and into the chromium-trimmed reception room. There were half a dozen doors leading from it, but he spotted the one marked "James H. Oglethorpe, Private," and slouched forward.

"Were you expected, sir?" The girl popped up in his face, one hand on the gate that barred his way. Her face was a study in frustration, which probably explained the sharpness of her tone. She delivered an Horatio-guarding-the-bridge formula. "Mr. Oglethorpe is busy now."

"Lunch," Haines answered curtly. He had already noticed that men talked more freely over food.

She flipped a little book in her hand and stared at it. "There is no record here of a luncheon engagement, Mr.—"

"Haines. Dr. Lurton Haines." He grinned wryly, wriggling a twenty-dollar bill casually in one hand. Money was apparently the one disease to which nobody was immune. Her eyes dropped to it, and hesitation entered her voice as she consulted her book.

"Of course, Mr. Oglethorpe might have made it some time ago and forgotten to tell me—" She caught his slight nod, and followed the bill to the corner of the desk. "Just have a seat, and I'll speak to Mr. Oglethorpe."

She came out of the office a few minutes later, and winked quickly. "He'd forgotten," she told Haines, "but it's all right now. He'll be right out, Dr. Haines. It's lucky he's having lunch late today."

James Oglethorpe was a younger man than Haines had expected, though his interest in rocketry might have been some clue to that. He came out of his office, pushing a Homburg down on curly black hair, and raked the other with his eyes. "Dr. Haines?" he asked, thrusting out a large hand. "Seems we have a luncheon engagement."

Haines rose quickly and bowed before the other had a chance to grasp his hand. Apparently Oglethorpe did not notice, for he went on smoothly. "Easy to forget these telephone engagements, sometimes. Aren't you the cancer man? One of your friends was in a few months ago for a contribution to your work."

They were in the elevator then, and Haines waited until it opened and they headed for the lunchroon in the building before answering. "I'm not looking for money this time, however. It's the rocket you're financing that interests me. I think it may work."

"It will, though you're one of the few who believes it." Caution, doubt, and interest were mingled on Oglethorpe's face. He ordered before turning back to Haines. "Want to go along? If you do, there's still room for a physician in the crew."

"No, nothing like that. Toast and milk only, please—" Haines had no idea of how to broach the subject, with nothing concrete to back up his statements. Looking at the set of the other's jaw and the general bulldog attitude of the man, he gave up hope and only continued because he had to. He fell back on imagination, wondering how much of it was true.

"Another rocket made that trip, Mr. Oglethorpe, and returned. But the pilot was dying before he landed. I can show you the wreck of his machine, though there's not much left after the fire—perhaps not enough to prove it was a rocketship. Somewhere out on Mars there's something man should never find. It's—"

"Ghosts?" suggested Oglethorpe, brusquely.

"Death! I'm asking you—"

Again Oglethorpe interrupted. "Don't. There was a man in to see me yesterday who claimed he'd been there—offered to show me the wreck of his machine. A letter this morning explained that the Martians had visited the writer and threatened all manner of things. I'm not calling you a liar, Dr. Haines, but I've heard too many of those stories; whoever told you this one was either a crank or a horror-monger. I can show you a stack of letters that range from astrology to zombies, all explaining why I can't go, and some offer photographs for proof."

"Suppose I said I'd made the trip in that rocket?" The card in the wallet said he was Haines, and the wallet had been in the suit he was wearing, but there had also been the glasses and cigarettes for which he had no use.

Oglethorpe twisted his lips, either in disgust or amazement. "You're an intelligent man, Dr. Haines; let's assume I am, also. It may sound ridiculous to you, but the only reason I had for making the fortune I'm credited with was to build that ship, and it's taken more work and time than the layman would believe. If a green ant, seven feet high, walked into my office and threatened Armageddon, I'd still go."

Even the impossible impulse recognized the equally impossible. Oglethorpe was a man who did things first and worried about them when the mood hit him—and there was nothing moody about him. The conversation turned to everyday matters and Haines let it drift as it would, finally dragging out into silence.

At least, he was wiser by one thing; he knew the location of the rocket ground and the set-up of guards around it—something even the newspapermen had failed to learn, since all pictures and information had come through Oglethorpe. There could no longer be any question of his ability to gain desired information by some hazy telepathic process. Either he was a mental freak, or the accident had done things to him that should have been surprising but weren't.

Haines had taken a cab from the airport, giving instructions that caused the driver to lift his eyebrows; but money was still all-powerful. Now they were slipping through country even more desolate than the woods around Haines' house, and the end of the road came into view, with a rutted muddy trail leading off, marked by the tires of the trucks Oglethorpe had used for his freighting. The cab stopped there.

"This the place?" the driver asked uncertainly.

"It is." Haines added a bill to what had already been paid and dismissed him. Then he dragged his way out to the dirt road and followed it, stopping for rest frequently. His ears were humming loudly now, and each separate little vertebra of his back protested at his going on. But there was no turning back; he had tried that, at the airport, and found the urge strong enough to combat his weakening will.

"Only a little rest!" he muttered thickly, but the force in his head lifted his leaden feet and sent them marching toward the rocket camp. Above him the gray clouds passed over the moon, and he looked up at Mars shining in the sky. Words from the lower part of the drummer's vocabulary came into his throat, but the effort of saying them was more than the red planet merited. He plowed on in silence.

Mars had moved over several degrees in the sky when he first sighted the camp, lying in a long, narrow valley. At one end were the shacks of the workmen, at the other a big structure that housed the rocket from chance prying eyes. Haines stopped to cough out part of his lungs, and his breath was husky and labored as he worked his way down.

The guards should be strung out along the edge of the valley. Oglethorpe was taking no chances with the cranks who had written him letters and denounced him as a godless fool leading his men to death. Rockets at best were fragile things, and only a few men would be needed to ruin the machine once it was discovered. Haines ran over the guards' positions, and skirted through the underbrush, watching for periods when the moon was darkened. Once he almost tripped an alarm, but missed it in time.

Beyond, there was no shrubbery, but his suit was almost the shade of the ground in the moonlight, and by lying still between dark spells, he crawled forward toward the rocket shed, undetected. He noticed the distance of the houses and the outlying guards and nodded to himself; they should be safe from any explosion.

The coast looked clear. Then, in the shadow of the building, a tiny red spark gleamed and subsided slowly; a man was there, smoking a cigarette. By straining his eyes, Haines made out the long barrel of a rifle against the building. This guard must be an added precaution, unknown to Oglethorpe.

A sudden rift in the thickening clouds came, and Haines slid himself flat against the ground, puzzling over the new complication. For a second he considered turning back, but realized that he could not—his path now was clearly defined, and he had no choice but to follow it. As the moon slid out of sight again, he came to his feet quietly and moved toward the figure waiting there.

"Hello!" His voice was soft, designed to reach the man at the building but not the guards behind in the outskirts. "Hello, there. Can I come forward? Special inspector from Oglethorpe."

A beam of light lanced out from the shadow, blinding him, and he walked forward, at the best pace he could muster. The light might reveal him to the other guards, but he doubted it; their attention was directed outward, away from the buildings.

"Come ahead," the answer came finally. "How'd you get past the others?" The voice was suspicious, but not unusually so. The rifle, Haines saw, was directed at his midsection, and he stopped a few feet away, where the other could watch him.

"Jimmy Durham knew I was coming," he told the guard. According to the information he had stolen from Oslethorpe's mind, Durham was in charge of the guards. "He told me he hadn't had time to notify you, but I took a chance."

"Hmmm. Guess it's all right, since they let you through; but you can't leave here until somebody identifies you. Keep your hands up." The guard came forward cautiously to feel for concealed weapons. Haines held his hands up out of the other's reach, where there was no danger of a direct skin to skin contact. "Okay, seems all right. What's your business here?"

"General inspection. The boss got word there might be a little trouble brewing and sent me here to make sure ward was being kept, and to warn you. All locked up here?"

"None. A lock wouldn't do much good on this shack; that's why I'm here. Want I should signal Jimmy to come and identify you so you can go?"

"Don't bother." Conditions were apparently ideal, except for one thing. But he would not murder the guard! There must be some other way, without adding that to the work he was forced to do. "I'm in no hurry, now that I've seen everything. Have a smoke?"

"Just threw one away. 'Smatter, no matches? Here."

Haines rubbed one against the friction surface of the box and lit the cigarette gingerly. The raw smoke stung against his burning throat, but he controlled the cough, and blew it out again; in the dark, the guard could not see his eyes watering, nor the grimaces he made. He was waging a bitter fight with himself against the impulse that had ordered the smoke to distract the guard's attention, and he knew he was failing. "Thanks!"

One of the guard's hands met his, reaching for the box. The next second the man's throat was between the stranger's hands, and he was staggering back, struggling to tear away and cry for help. Surprise confused his efforts for the split second necessary, and one of Haines' hands came free and out, then chopped down sharply to strike the guard's neck with the edge of the palm. A low grunt gurgled out, and the figure went limp.

Impulse had conquered again! The guard was dead, his neck broken by the sharp blow. Haines leaned against the building, catching his breath and fighting back the desire to lose his stomach's contents. When some control came back, he picked up the guard's flashlight, and turned into the building. In the darkness, the outlines of the great rocketship were barely visible.

With fumbling fingers, Haines groped forward to the hull, then struck a match and shaded it in his hands until he could make out the port, standing open. Too much light might show through a window and attract attention.

Inside, he threw the low power of the flashlight on and moved forward, down the catwalk and toward the rear where the power machinery would be housed. It had been simple, after all, and only the quick work of destruction still remained.

He traced the control valves easily, running an eye over the uncovered walls and searching out the pipes that led from them. From the little apparatus he saw, this ship was obviously inferior to the one that had crashed, yet it had taken years to build and drained Oglethorpe's money almost to the limit. Once destroyed, it might take men ten more years to replace it; two was the minimum, and in those two years—

The thought slipped from him, but some memories were coming back. He saw himself in a small metal room, fighting against the inexorable exhaustion of fuel, and losing. Then there had been a final burst from the rockets, and the ship had dropped sickeningly through the atmosphere. He had barely had time to get to the air locks before the crash. Miraculously, as the ship's fall was cushioned by the house, he had been thrown free into the lower branches of a tree, to catch, and lose momentum before striking earth.

The man who had been in the house had fared worse; he had been thrown out with the wrecked wall, already dead. Roughly, the stranger remembered a hasty transfer of clothing from the corpse, and then the beam had dropped on him, shutting out his memory in blackness. So he was not Haines, after all, but someone from the rocket, and his story to Oglethorpe had been basically true.

Haines—he still thought of himself under that name—caught himself as his knees gave under him, and hauled himself up by the aid of a protruding bar. There was work to be done; after that, what happened to his own failing body was another matter. It seemed now that from his awakening he had expected to meet death before another day, and had been careless of the fact.

He ran his eyes around the rocket room again, until he came to a tool kit that lay invitingly open with a large wrench sticking up from it. That would serve to open the valves. The flashlight lay on the floor where he had dropped it, and he kicked it around with his foot to point at the wall, groping out for the wrench. His fingers were stiff as they clasped around the handle.

And, in the beam of light, he noticed his hand for the first time in hours. Dark-blue veins rose high on flesh that was marked with a faint pale-blue. He considered it dully, thrusting out his other hand and examining it; there, too, was the blue flush, and on his palms, as he turned them upward, the same color showed. Blue!

The last of his memory flashed back through his brain in a roaring wave, bringing a slow tide of pictures with it. With one part of his mind, he was working on the valves with the wrench, while the other considered the knowledge that had returned to him. He saw the streets of a delicate, fairy city, half deserted, and as he seemed to watch, a man staggered out of a doorway, clutching at his throat with blue hands, to fall writhing to the ground! The people passed on quickly, avoiding contact with the corpse, fearful even to touch each other.

Everywhere, death reached out to claim the people. The planet was riddled with it. It lay on the skin of an infected person, to be picked up by the touch of another, and passed on to still more. In the air, a few seconds sufficed to kill the germs, but new ones were being sent out from the pores of the skin, so that there were always a few active ones lurking there. On contact, the disease began an insidious conquest, until, after months without sign, it suddenly attacked the body housing it, turned it blue, and brought death in a few painful hours.

Some claimed that it was the result of an experiment that had gone beyond control, others that it had dropped as a spore from space. Whatever it was, there was no cure for it on Mars. Only the legends that spoke of a race of their people on the mother world of Earth offered any faint hope, and to that they had turned when there was no other chance.

He saw himself undergoing examinations that finally resulted in his being chosen to go in the rocket they were building feverishly. He had been picked because his powers of telepathy were unusual, even to the mental science of Mars; the few remaining weeks had been used in developing that power systematically, and implanting in his head the duties that he must perform so long as a vestige of life remained to him.

Haines watched the first of the liquid from the fuel pipes splash out, and dropped the wrench. Old Leán Dagh had doubted his ability to draw knowledge by telepathy from a race of a different culture, he reflected. Too bad the old man had died without knowing of the success his methods had met, even though the mission had been a failure, due to man's feeble knowledge of the curative sciences. Now his one task was to prevent the race of this world from dying in the same manner.

He pulled himself to his feet again and went staggering down the catwalk, muttering disconnected sentences. The blue of his skin was darker now, and he had to force himself across the space from the ship to the door of the building, grimly commanding his failing muscles, to the guard's body that still lay where he had left it.

Most of the strength left him was useless against the pull of this heavier planet and the torture movement had become. He tried to drag the corpse behind him, then fell on hands and knees and backed toward the ship, using one arm and his teeth on the collar to pull it after him. He was swimming in a world that was bordering on unconsciousness, now, and once darkness claimed him; he came out of it to find himself inside the rocket, still dragging his burden, the implanted impulses stronger than his will.

Bit by bit, he dragged his burden behind him down the catwalk, until the engine room was reached, and he could drop it on the floor, where the liquid fuel had made a thin film. The air was heavy with vapors, and chilled by the evaporation, but he was only partly conscious of that. Only a spark was needed now, and his last duty would be finished.

Inevitably, a few of the dead on Mars would be left unburned, where men might find the last of that unfortunate race, and the germs would still live within them. Earthmen must not face that. Until such a time as the last Martian had crumbled to dust and released the plague into the air to be destroyed, the race of Earth must remain within the confines of its own atmosphere, and safe.

There was only himself and the corpse he had touched left here to carry possible germs, and the ship to carry the men to other sources of infection; all that was easily remedied.

The stranger from Mars groped in his pocket for the guard's matches, smiling faintly, darkness swept over him, he drew one of them from the box and scraped it across the friction surface. Flame danced from the point and outward—

Shadows of Empire

We slipped out of the post while Mars's sky was still harsh and black, and the morning was bitter with cold. Under us was the swish of the treads slapping the worn old sands, and from the lorries came the muttered grumbling of the men, still nursing their hangovers. The post was lost in the grayness behind us, and the town was just beginning to stir with life as we left it. But it was better that way; the Fifth had its orders back to Earth after ten generations outside, and the General wanted no civilian fuss over our going.

It had been enough, just hearing the click at the gate, and seeing the few pinch-faced, scared people along the streets as we passed. Most of us had been there well over ten years, and you can't keep men segregated from the townspeople in the outposts. Well, they'd had their leave the night before, and now we were on our way; the less time spent thinking about going, the less chance for thoughts of desertion to ripen.

At that, two of the men had sneaked off into the wastelands with a sandtractor and lorry. I'd have liked to find them; after twenty years with the Service, things like that get under your skin. But we couldn't wait for a week hunting them, when the Emperor had his seal on our orders.

Now a twist in the road showed the town in the dim dawn-light, with the mayor running up tardily and tripping over a scrap of a flag. And old Jake, the tavern-keeper, still stood among the empty boxes from which he'd tossed cartons of cigarettes to us as we went by. Lord knows how much we still owed him, but he'd been Service once himself, and I don't think that was on his mind. Yeah, it was a good town, and we'd never forget it; but I was glad when the road twisted back and the rolling dunes cut it off from view. I'm just plain people myself, not one of your steel-and-ice nobility like the General.

And that was why I was still only a Sergeant Major, even though I had to take second command nowadays. In the old times, of course, they'd have sent out young nobles to take over, with proper title, but I guess they liked it better back on Earth now. For that matter, we'd had few enough replacements in my time, except those we'd recruited ourselves from the town and country around. But what the hell—we managed. The Fifth lacked a few men and some fancy brass, but I never heard a marauding Torrakh laugh over it, even after bad fuel grounded our last helicopter.

Now the little red sun came up to a point where we could turn the heaters off our aspirators. We were passing through a pleasant enough country, little farms and canal-berry orchards. The farm folk must have figured we were out on a raid again, because they only waved at us and went on with their work; the thick-wooled sheep went on bleating at themselves with no interest in us. Behind me, someone struck up a halfhearted marching song on an old lectrozith, and the men picked it up.

That was better. I sighed to myself, found one of my legs had gone to sleep, and nursed the prickles out of it while the miles slipped behind, and the hamlets and farms began to thin out. In a little while we were reaching the outskirts of the northern desert, and the caterpillar tracks settled down to a steady sifting slap that's music to a man's ears. We ate lunch out of our packs while the red dunes rolled on endlessly in front of us.

It was a couple hours later when the General's tractor dropped abreast of me and his so-called adjutant vaulted to my seat, his usually saturnine face pinched into a wry grin. Then the radio buzzed and he lifted it to my ear with a finger across his lips.

The General's precise voice clipped out. "Close up ranks, Sergeant; we've spotted a band of Torrakhi moving in the direction of the town. Probably heard we're leaving, and they're already moving up; but they'd be happy to stop for a straggler, so keep together."

"Right, sir," I answered out of habit, and added the words on the slip of paper Stanislaus was shaking under my nose. "But couldn't we take a swipe at them first?"

"No time. This looks like the rear guard, and the main body is probably already infiltrating through the wastelands. The town will have to shift for itself."

"Right, sir," I said again, and the radio clicked off, while the Slav went on grinning to himself. There wasn't a Torrakh within miles, and I knew it, but the General usually knew what he was doing; I wasn't so dumb I couldn't guess at it.

Stanislaus stretched his lank frame on the seat and nodded slowly. "Yeah, he's crazy, too—which is why he's a good General, Major. A few like him in higher places, and we'd be on Mars for another generation or so. Though it wouldn't make much difference in the long run... *Vanitas vanitatis! There is no remembrance of former generations; neither shall there be any remembrance of the latter generations that are to come, among those that shall come after!*... That's Ecclesiastes, and worth more than the whole Book of Revelation."

"Or a dozen gloomy Slavs! There was talk of replacing the Fifth back when I was still a buck private. You should be a preacher."

"And in a way, I was, Major—*lest evil days come and the years draw nigh when thou shall say, I have no pleasure in them.* But a prophet's without honor; and as you say, I'm a gloomy Slav, even though they usually send replacements before they withdraw the Service. Well, lay on, MacDuff, for the greater glory of the Empire!"

I wasn't going to admit he had me, but I couldn't think of anything to say to that, so I shut up. The gloom-birds were probably around before that stuff was written, but civilization was still going on, though there were rumors about things back on Earth. But somehow, he always managed to make me start smelling old attics piled high with rubbish and beginning to mold. I turned and looked sideways, just as the first outskirts of an old canal swung into view.

They still call them canals, at least, though even the old-time astronomers knew they weren't, before Mars was ever reached. But they must have been quite something, ten or fifteen thousand years ago, when the V'nothi built the big earthenware pipelines thousands of miles across the planet to section it and break up the sand-shifts that were ruining it. The big osmotic pumps were still working after a fashion, and there was a trickle of moisture flowing even yet, leaking out into the bleeder lines and keeping the degenerate scrub trees going in fifty-mile swaths around them.

The V'nothi had disappeared before the Pyramids were put up, leaving only pictures of themselves in the ruins, looking like big, good-natured Vikings, complete to brawn and winged helmets. Their women folk must have been really something, even with fur all over them. Archaeologists were still swearing every time they looked at those pictures and wondered what men on horseback were doing on Mars, and why no bones had ever been found! Some of them were even guessing that the V'nothi were Earthmen, maybe from an early peak of civilization we remembered in the Atlantis myths. But even if they were, there was a lot about them to drive a man nuts without worrying about their origins. If you ask me, they were just plain domesticated animals for some other race. Still, whoever the real boss was, it must have been quite a world in their time.

Even the canal-trees weren't natural; no other plants on Mars had bellows growing out of them to supercharge themselves with air, ozone, and traces of water vapor. Even over the drone of the tractor motors, I could hear the dull mutter of their breathing. And at sun down, when they all got together in one long, wild groan...well, when I first heard that, I began to have dreams about what the master race was, though I'm not exactly imaginative. Now I'm older, and just don't know—nor much care.

But the air was drier and thinner here, where they desiccated it, and Stanislaus was breathing it with a sort of moral rectitude about him, and nodding as if he liked it. "Dust of Babylon, eh, Major? They went up a long way once, farther in some ways than we've climbed yet. In a thousand years or less they pulled themselves up to our sciences, dropped them, and began working on what we'd call sheer magic. Sometimes, just thinking of what the records hint at scares me.

They built themselves up to heaven, before the curse of bigness struck them down; and being extremists, it wasn't just a retreat, but a final rout."

"Meaning we're due for the same, 'Laus?" I always did like the way he pronounced his name, to rhyme with house.

"No, Major; we're not the same—we retreat. Nineveh, Troy, Rome—they've gone, but the periphery always stays to hibernate and come out into another springtime. An empire decays, but it takes a long time dying, and so far there's always been a certain amount passed on to the next surge of youthfulness. We've developed a racial phoenix complex. But of course you don't believe the grumblings of a gloomy Slav who's just bitter that his old empire is one of the later dust heaps?"

"No," I told him. "I don't."

He got up, knocking ashes off his parka with long, flickering fingers, and his voice held an irritating chuckle. "Stout fella, pride of the Empire, and all that! I congratulate you, Major, and dammit, I envy you." And he was over the treads and running toward where the General's tractor had stopped, like a long-drawn-out cat. If he hadn't had the grace of a devil, his tongue would have gotten him spitted on a rapier years before.

I didn't dwell on even such pleasant thoughts. The men had stopped singing, and the first reaction of forced cheer was over. They were good joes, all in all, but after the long years at the post among the townspeople, they couldn't help being human. So I dropped back to the end of the line and kept my eyes peeled for any that might suddenly decide to develop engine trouble and lag behind. It's always the first day and night that are the hardest.

Their grumbling sounded normal enough when we pulled off the trail away from the tree-mutterings, well after sundown, and I felt better; it's when they stop grousing that you have to watch them. All the same, I made them dig in a lot deeper than we needed, though it gets cold enough to freeze a man solid at night. They were sweating and stepping up the power in their aspirators before I was satisfied, and the berylite tent tops barely stuck up over the sand.

That would give them something trivial to beef about, and work their muscles down to good condition for sleeping. A good meal and a double ration of grog would finish the trick nicely, and I'd already given orders for that—which left me nothing to do but go in where Stanislaus was sprawled out on a cot, dabbling with his food and nodding in time to the tent aspirator's variations.

"Nice gadget, that—efficient," he commented, and the pinched grin was on his face. "Of course, the air's thick enough to breathe when a man's not working, but it's still a nice thing to have."

I knew what he meant, of course. The old-timers had done a lot of foolish things, like baking out enough oxygen to keep the air pressure up almost to

Earth normal. But it wasn't economical, and we were modern enough to get along without such nonsense. While I ate, I told him so, along with some good advice about how to get on well with Emperors. Besides, it was a damn-sight better aspirator than they'd had in the pioneer days.

I might as well have saved my breath. He waited until I ran down, and nodded amiably. "Absolutely, absolutely. And very well put, Major. As the Romans said when Theodoric's Goths gave them orders, we're modern and up-to-date. Being of the present time, we're automatically modern. As for the Emperor, I wouldn't think of blaming him for what's inevitable, though I'd like a chance to argue the point with him, if I didn't have a certain fondness for my neck. Meantime, Mars rebuilds the seals in its houses and puts in little wind machines. *And behold, all was vanity and a striving after wind!* You really should read Ecclesiastes. Well, sleep tight, Major!"

He ducked under a blanket and was snoring in less than five minutes. I never could sleep well under a tin tent with a man who snores; and it was worse this time, somehow, though I finally did drop off.

We were dug out and ready to march in the morning when the General's scheme bore fruit; our deserters showed up over the dunes, hot-footing it down on us. They must have spotted my tractor, because they didn't waste any time in coming up to me. The damned fools! Naturally, they had to bring the two women along with them, instead of dumping them near town. They must have been stinko drunk when they started, though the all-night drive had sobered them up—the drive plus half freezing to death and imagining Torrakhi behind every bush.

I'd never seen those two brig-birds salute with quite such gusto, though, as they hopped down, and Stanislaus' amused snort echoed my sentiments. But the big guy started the ball rolling, with only a dirty look at the Slav. "Sir, we couldn't help being AWOL, we…"

"Were caught by Torrakhi, of course," the General's smooth voice filled in behind me, and I stepped out of the picture on the double. "Very clever of you to escape, tractors and all! Unfortunately, there were no Torrakhi; the message your receiver was designed to unscramble was a trap, based on the assumption that you'd rather take your chances with us than with a marauding band of nomads infiltering around you. I suppose I could have you shot; and if I hear one sniveling word from you, I will. Or I could take you back to Earth in chains."

His lips pressed out into a thin, white line, and his eyes flicked over to Stanislaus for a bare second. "You wouldn't like that. There's a new Emperor, not the soft one we had before. I served under him once…and I rather suspect he'd reward me for bringing you back with us, after the proper modern Imperial fashion of gratitude. However, for the good of the Fifth, you're already listed as fatalities. Sergeant, do you know these women?"

"Their names are on our books, sir."

"Quite so. And they knew what they were mixed up in. Very well, leave them their side arms, but fill the tractor and lorry they returned with some of your men, and prepare to break camp. You've already forgotten all this; and that goes for the men, as well!" He swung on his heel and mounted his tractor without another look at the deserters, who were just beginning to realize what he'd meant.

Stanislaus elected to ride with me as we swung back toward the canal road, watching the four until the dunes swallowed them. Then he shrugged and lit his cigarette. "Not orthodox, Major, but effective; you can stop worrying about desertions. And take it from me, it was the right thing to do; I happen to know—rather well, in fact—why our precise and correct leader thought it wise to fake the books. But I won't bore you with it. As to those four—well, some of the pioneers were up against worse odds, but *de mortuis nil nisi bonum*. Nice morning, don't you think?"

It was, as a matter of fact, and we were making good time. The trail swung out, heading due south now, and away from the canal, and the sands were no longer cluttered with the queer pits always found around the canal-trees. By noon, we'd put a hundred more miles behind us, and the men were hardening into the swing of things, though they still weren't doing the singing I like to hear on the march—the good, clean filth that's somehow the backbone of Service morale. I sent a couple of tractors out to scout, just to break the monotony, though there wouldn't be anything to see so near the end of the desert.

Surprisingly, however, they hadn't been gone ten minutes when the report came back: Torrakhi to the left flank! A moment later, we were snapping into a tight phalanx and hitting up a rise where we could see; but by then we knew that there was no danger. They were just a small band, half a mile away, jolting along on their llama-mounts at an easy lope. Then they spotted us and beat back behind the dunes and out of sight. A small marauding band, turning back north from sacking some fool outlier's farm, probably.

But it was unusual to see them so far south. We'd never been able to eliminate them entirely, any more than the V'nothi before us had, but we'd kept the wild quasi-human barbarians in line, pretty much. And now we were swinging back to the trail again, leaving them unchecked to grow bold in raiding; there wasn't anything else we could do, since they hadn't attacked and we were under Imperial seal. Well, maybe the Second Command would get them for us sometime. I hoped so.

Stanislaus might say what he would, but he was still Service, and it had hit him, too. "Notice the long rifle they pulled? What make would you say?"

"Renegade pirates on Callisto, it looked like, at a guess. But the exiles couldn't get past the Out Fleet to trade with Torrakhi!"

He flipped his cigarette away and turned to face me, dead serious and quiet about it. "The Out Fleet's just a propaganda myth, Major! They pulled it back before I—uh, left Earth."

He couldn't know that, and I had no business believing him; yet somehow, I was sure he did know, and whatever else he was, he was not a liar. But that would mean that the Earth-Mars trade…

"Exactly," he said, as if he'd read the thought. "And now we're going back to help put down a minor little uprising in the Empire, so I hear. Write your own ticket!"

But even if it were true, it didn't prove anything. Sure, it looked bad, but I've learned you can't judge from half-knowledge. A lot of times when I've gone out swearing at the orders, I've come back alive because they weren't the kind I'd have given. Heck, even if the mesotron rifle was Callistan, there was no telling how old it was; maybe they'd pulled the Out Fleet back for the sound reason that it wasn't needed. But it did look odd, their keeping up the pretense.

We camped that night at an old abandoned fort dating back to pioneer days, and then shoved on in the morning through little hamlets and the beginning of settled land. The people looked fairly hard and efficient, but it was pleasant, after the desert, and the men seemed more cheerful. Here the road was kept surfaced and the engines went all out. A little later, we took the grousers off, and by the time another night had passed, we were in well-settled country. From then on, it was all soft going and the miles dropped away as regular as clockwork, though I missed the swish of the sand under the treads.

As we went on, the land and the people got softer, with that comfortable look I'd missed up where Torrakhi are more than things to scare children with. And the farms were bigger and better kept. For that matter, I couldn't see a man working with a rifle beside him. The Service had done that. When we first hit Mars, in the pioneer days, there hadn't been a spot on its face where a man could close both eyes. Now even the kids went running along the road alone. Oh, sure, there were some abandoned villas, here and there, but I don't think the nobles were too much missed.

And that was civilization and progress, whatever Stanislaus thought about it. Let them pull the Out Fleet back and call in the Fifth. As long as Mars had spots on it like this, it didn't look too bad for the Empire. I wanted to throw it in the Slav's face, but I knew it wouldn't do any good. He'd have some kind of answer. Better let sleeping dogs lie.

And besides, he was riding with the General again, and even at night he was busy writing in some big book and not paying attention to anything else. In a way, it was all to the good. Still, I dunno. At least, when he was spouting out his dogma, I had a chance to figure up some kind of answer to myself. There wasn't much I could do about the look on his face.

But I noticed that we always seemed to make camp about the time we were well away from the towns, and it was something to think over, along with the guff that had begun among the men. It looked as if the General meant to keep us away from any rumors going around among the ciss, and that was odd; ordinarily, civilian scuttlebutt means nothing to the Service.

And now that the novelty had worn off, there was something wrong about the number of farms we'd pass that were abandoned and that had been for a long time. There were little boarded-up stores in some of the villages, and once we went by a massive atomic by-products plant, dead and forgotten. And the softness on the people's faces began to look less pretty; one good-sized band of Torrakhi could raise hob with a whole county, even without mesotron rifles from Callisto.

The one time I did speak to a native, I had no business doing it. We'd been rolling along, with me at the rear for the moment, and there was this fine-looking boy of about twelve walking along the road. What got me was the song he was singing and the way he came to a Service salute at the sight of us. Well, the General wasn't in sight, and the kid took my slowing up as a hint to hop onto the lug rail.

"Fifth, isn't it, sir?"

"Right. But where the deuce did you learn that ditty and the proper way to address a noncom?"

He grinned the way healthy kids know how, before they grow old enough to forget. "Gramps was in the Fifth when they raised the siege of Bharene, sir, and he told me all about it before he died. Gee, it must have been great when he was young!"

"And now?"

"Aw, now they say you're going back to Earth, and Gramps wouldn't have liked that. He was a Martian, like me...Look, I live up there, so I gotta go. Thanks for the lift, Sergeant!"

So even the kids knew we were going back, and now we were just another Service Command, instead of the backbone of Mars. Strange, I hadn't thought of what it would mean, going back where people had never heard of us before. But I could see where the General was right in not letting us mix with people here. Dammit, we were still the Fifth, and nothing could change that, Mars or Earth, Emperor or Torrakhi!

We didn't spend too much time looking at the country after that, though it grew even prettier as we went on. The tractors were beginning to carbon up under the fuel we had to requisition, and we were busy nursing them along and watching for trouble. At the post, we'd had our own purifying plant to get the gum out of the vegetable fuels, but here we had to take potluck. And it was a lot worse than I'd expected. But then, a man tends to gloss over his childhood and think things were better then. I dunno. Maybe it had always been that bad.

Anyhow, we made it, in spite of a few breakdowns. It was dusk when the lights of Marsport showed up, and we went limping through the outskirts. When we hit the main drag, a motorcop ran ahead of us with his siren open, though there wasn't any need. I couldn't help wondering where the cars were, and how they managed to dig up so many bicycles. We must have looked like the devil, since we'd pushed too fast to bother much with shining up, but there were some cheers from the crowds that assembled, and a few women's faces with the look of not having seen uniforms in years. The men woke up at that, yelling the usual things, but I could feel their disappointment in the city.

Then we halted, and Stanislaus came back, while a fat and stuffy little man in noble's regalia strode up to the General's tractor, fairly sniffing the dirt on our gear as he came. Well, he could have used a better shave himself, and a little less hootch would have improved his dignity. The Slav chuckled. "Methinks this should be good, unless the O.M. has lost his touch. Flip the switch, Major; I left the radio turned on."

But no sound came out of it except a surprised grunt from the fat official as he looked at the odd-patterned ring on the General's finger. I never knew what it stood for, but all the air went out of the big shot's sails, and he couldn't hand over the official message fast enough after that. He was mopping sweat from his face when the crowd swallowed him. I've seen a bust corporal act that way when he suddenly remembered he was pulling rank he no longer had.

"Don't bother cutting off yet, Sergeant," the radio said quietly, and it was my turn to grin. Stanislaus should have known better than to try putting anything over on the General. "Ummm, I'm going to be tied up with official business at the Governor's, so you'll have to go ahead. Know where the auxiliary port is? Good. Bivouac there, and put the men to policing themselves and the hangars. No passes. That's all."

He moved to a waiting car, leaving the tractor to his driver, and we went on again, out through the outskirts and past the main spaceport; that was dark, and I couldn't tell much about it, but I remembered the mess of the old auxiliary field. They'd built it thirty miles out in barren land to handle the overflow during the old colonizing period, and it had been deserted and weed-grown for years, with hangars falling apart. It was worse than I'd remembered, though there were some lights on and a group of Blue Guards to let us in and direct us to the left side of the field.

Some clearing had been done, but there was work enough to keep us all busy as beavers, and there would be for days, if we stayed that long. At least it gave me a good excuse for announcing confinement to grounds, though they took it easier than I'd expected. It seemed they already knew in some way. And at last I was finished with giving orders and had a chance to join the Slav in inspecting the ships I'd already noticed down at the end of the field.

I'd seen the like of the double-turret cruiser before, but the two big ones were different, even in the dim lights of the field. They were something out of the history books, and no book could give any idea of their size. The rocket crews about them, busy with their own affairs, were like ants running around a skyscraper by comparison. Either could have held the whole Command and left room for cargo besides.

"So we're waiting for the Second Command to go back with us, 'Laus?"

He jerked his head back from a reverent inspection of the big hulks and nodded at me slowly. "You improve, Major, though you forgot to comment on the need of a cruiser between Mars and Earth…Two hundred years! And those ships are still sounder than the hunk of junk sent out to protect them. There was a time when men knew how to build ships—and how to use them. Now there are only four left out of all that were built. Any idea where the other two are?"

"Yeah." I'd failed to recognize them because of their size, but it hadn't been quite dark enough to conceal them completely. "Back at the other port we passed, picking up the South Commands. Dammit, 'Laus, did you have to infect me with your pessimism?"

"You're going back to Earth, Major," he answered, as if that were explanation enough. "The optimist sees the doughnut, the pessimist the hole; but you get a better view of things through a hole than through a hunk of sweetened dough. And, as Havelock Ellis put it, the place where optimism most flourished was the lunatic asylum. Come on back and I'll lend you Ecclesiastes while I finish my book."

And I was just dumb enough to read it. But I might have had the same nightmare anyway. I'd gotten a good look at the faces of the rocket gang.

In the morning, I was too busy bossing the stowing of our gear to do much thinking, though. Even with maps of the corridors, I'd have been lost in the ship without the help of one of the pilots, a bitter-faced young man who seemed glad to fill his time, but who refused to talk beyond the bare necessities. When the General came back at noon, the men were all quartered inside, except for those who were detailed to help load the collection of boxes that began to come out from Marsport.

He nodded curt approval and went to the radio in his cabin. And about an hour later, I looked up to see the Second Command come in and go straight to the second ship, a mile away. They could have saved themselves the trouble of avoiding us, as far as I was concerned. I had no desire to compare notes with them. But I guess it was better for the men, and it was a lot easier than posting guards overnight to see they didn't mix. A hell of a way to run the Service, I thought; but of course it wasn't the Service anymore—just the Second and Fifth Commands, soon to be spread around Earth!

It was after taps when they brought the civilians aboard, but I was still enjoying the freedom of second in command, and I was close enough to get a good look at them and the collection of special tools they were bringing along with the rest of their luggage. I'd always figured the technical crafts came out from automated Earth to the outlands where their skills were still needed. But that seemed to be just another sign that the old order was changing. I turned to make talk with the pilot who was beside me, and then thought better of it.

But for once, he was willing to break his silence, though he never took his eyes off the little group that was filing in. "They're needed, Sergeant! Atomic technicians are in demand again, along with plutonium for the Earth reactors—or…I suppose you guessed that's what the rear trucks are carrying, and they'll be loading it between hulls tonight—all that can be stowed safely. Of course, I'm not supposed to talk—but I was born here, and it's not like the last job we had, ferrying back the Venus Commands. Care to join me in getting drunk?"

It was an idea. Plutonium is particularly valuable for bombs, for which it's still the best material. And atom bombs are the messiest, lousiest, and most inefficient weapons any fighting man ever swore at. They're only good for ruining the land until you can't finish a decent mopping up, and poisoning the atmosphere until your own people begin dying. Not a single one had been dropped in the five centuries since we came up with the superior energy weapons. So now we were carrying the stuff from Mars's reactors back to Earth, where they already had the accumulated stuff from all their piles.

But I caught a signal from the car the General was using as I turned, and I changed my mind. I was in the mood for Stanislaus now, and whiskey's a pretty poor mental cathartic, anyway. This time I could see that the information I poured out at him wasn't something he already knew.

"*So. Even so are the sons of men snared in an evil time, when it falleth suddenly upon them.*" He let it sink in slowly, then shrugged. "Well, maybe it'll be faster that way. But it won't matter to me. I'm due in Marsport to attend my funeral—a lovely casket, I understand, though it's a pity we're so pressed for time I can't have military honors. Only the simple dignity of civilian rites. Thought you might like to bid me fond adieu, for old times' sake."

"Yeah, sure. And bring me back a bottle of the same." He shook his head gently, and the damned fool's voice was serious. "I wish I could, Major. I'd like nothing better than having you along to listen to my theories on our racial phoenix complex. But I've done the next best thing in leaving the book that's my labor of love in your cabin. All right, I was ribbing you, let's say, and I'm being transferred out to the Governor's service by special orders. Does that make sense to you?"

It did, put that way. It meant that after all the years of wishing he'd clam up, I was going to miss him plenty, now that I'd been converted, and I'd probably sit alone biting my tongue to keep from spouting the same brand of pessimism. But I wasn't much good at saying it, and he cut me off in the middle.

"Then bite it off! That stuff won't go, back there, though you're better off for having found out in advance. Trust the General to see you through. He made a mistake once, but he's wiser now. Forget Ecclesiastes and remember a jingle of Kipling's instead: *Now these are the Laws of the Jungle, and many and mighty are they; but the head and the hoof of the Law, and the haunch and the hump is—Obey!* Betray rhymes as well—but it takes a lot more background and practice. Now beat it, before I really start preaching."

I didn't need to hunt up the pilot; I had a bottle of Martian canal juice of my own in the cabin. But I'd consumed more of the book than the bottle when morning came and a knock sounded outside. The General came in when I grunted, his face pinched with fatigue, and his eyes red with lack of sleep. He nodded at the book, dropped onto my cot, and poured himself a generous slug before he looked up at me.

"A remarkable book, Bill, by a remarkable man. But you know that by now. Dynamite, of course, but something we'll have to smuggle in to save for a possible posterity. And stop looking so damned surprised! Any man Stanislaus trusted with that book is my equal or better, as far as I'm concerned. After we land, I have ways of seeing you get knighthood and a Colonel's rank, so you're practically an officer, anyhow. And I'm not acting as either General or Duke—just a messenger boy for the late deceased Stanislaus Korzynski. He died of canal fever day before yesterday, you know."

It was coming too thick and fast, and I didn't answer that. I reached for the bottle and poured a shot down my throat without bothering with a glass. The General held out his glass, watched me fill it, and downed the shot before going on again. "Not much of a Serviceman, am I, Bill? But it has to be that way. Nobody knows the name he used, but there are plenty on Earth who remember his face. Or haven't you figured out yet who he was from the book?"

"I've had my suspicions," I admitted. "Only I dunno whether I'm crazy or he was."

"Neither. You're right, he's the supposedly assassinated Prince Stellius Asiaticus, rightful ruler of the Empire! Here's a note he sent you."

There wasn't much to it:

> Friend Major—
> It was over the hill for me, after all. If you have children, as I intend to, pass on my new name to them, and someday our offspring may get together and discuss the phoenix bird.
>
> Elmer C. Clesiastes

"The phoenix," the General muttered over my shoulder while he reached for the bottle. "Now what the deuce did he mean by that?"

"What is it, anyway?"

"A legendary bird of Grecian mythology—the only one of its kind. It lived for a few hundred years, then built itself a funeral pyre and sat fanning the flames with its wings until it was consumed. After that, a new bird hatched out of the ashes and started all over again. That's why they used it for the symbol of immortality."

Below us, the rockets rumbled tentatively and then bellowed out, while the force of the jets crushed us back against the wall. Beyond the porthole, Mars dropped away from us, as the Empire turned back to its nest. But I wasn't thinking much of that, impressive though it was.

Somehow, I was going to have the children Stanislaus had mentioned, and I'd live long enough to see that they remembered the new name he'd chosen, atom bombs or no bombs. Because I knew him at last, and the pessimist was a prince, all right—the Prince of Optimists.

The General and I sat toasting him and discussing the phoenix legend and civilization's ups and downs while Mars changed from a world to a round ball in the background of space. It wasn't military or proper, but we felt much better by the time we found and confiscated the second bottle.

Moon-Blind
[as by Erik van Lhin]

After four years, the clouds looked good. From up there, they had been blurs on the white and blue ball that hung in the sky to mock him. Now, as they seemed to rush up towards him they spelled home—or death. There were worse things than death.

For the moment, the sight of the Earth swelling below him brought a lump in Bill Soames' throat. He'd hated it, cursed it, and screamed at it during the long Lunar days. He'd loathed the smug fools on it who had deserted him after calling him a hero and had left him to die or get back by himself. But now the call of his kind washed all that out. A thousand miles below were people, life, and home. It didn't matter what they'd done to him, or why they had done it; he'd lived through it somehow, and now he was almost there.

He shivered in the wash of emotions. His gaunt, almost skeletal body jerked under the flood of adrenalin, and his scarred, claw-like hands gripped the edge of the control board savagely. The starved hollows in his cheeks deepened, and the wisps of white hair on his head were beaded with drops of cold perspiration.

Behind him, the uneven roar of the rocket had been making the little ship quiver with subsonic vibrations. These halted suddenly, began again, and then were gone. The last of his bitterly acquired fuel was exhausted.

Weightlessness caught his tortured body, sending anguished cramps through him and threatening to end his hard-held hold on consciousness. He mastered himself after a moment of retching, and reached for the tiny crank that would spin the gyroscopes. He turned it madly, to the limit of his strength. Imperceptibly, the view of Earth in the plate that showed the ship's rear began to twist.

It took time to turn the ship that way, and he had little time left. The atmosphere was rushing up. He'd been luckier than he had expected; the rocket had killed most of his speed. But now he had to strike that two-hundred mile layer of air head foremost. The crank seemed to fight against him, but the ship was swinging. Here in space, Newton's third law worked perfectly. For every action, an equal and opposite reaction. A few thousand turns of the little wheel geared to the crank would turn the ship half a revolution in the other direction.

Four years before, when he had turned over to brake down to the Moon, it had been easy. He'd been strong, then, full of energy. He'd been the conquering hero. Months of conditioning and training had gone by, and he had walked up the ramp to the ship entrance with perfect health and complete confidence. He'd grinned at the generals and the reporters gathered to see the first manned flight to the Moon, and he'd known he would come back.

Well, he was coming back—through no help from them. The ship had been a gem, and the landing on the Moon had been almost routine. He'd sent back his radar message, located the single unmanned supply ship they'd sent ahead, and settled down to getting ready for the other ones still to arrive.

They never came, and there was no message back from Earth!

When he landed, July 5, 1948, he had had enough food to last him nearly four months, counting the supplies in the unmanned ship. He hadn't worried too much, at first. Air was renewed by the pumpkin vines and tomatoes that filled one chamber of the ship, and the water he used was recovered automatically. Something had held up his supply ships, but they'd be along shortly with the water that served as fuel for the big atomic-powered rocket; as for the message, probably something was wrong with his receiver.

In August, he began worrying, after he'd caught bits of some conversation on his microwave set and found it worked perfectly. There was still no message directed at him. He tried to reason it out, and decided that they must have somehow decided he was dead. He began cutting down on his eating, and planting more tomatoes and pumpkins frantically. There would be another ship up, to try it again, but it was going to take longer, probably. He'd have to survive until it landed, and then prove he wasn't dead by reaching it. He couldn't understand why they didn't hear his calls, since the radar seemed to transmit okay. But he could find out all about it when the next ship landed.

By the beginning of 1949, he was sick of pumpkins and tomatoes, and beginning to wonder. That was when he started looking up at Earth and cursing it. It wasn't until almost 1950, though, that he gave up all hope, along with attempts to understand.

It nearly broke him. But Bill Soames had been picked carefully, and he wasn't the type to give up. It took him over two years to build a solar oven out of the supply ship parts and begin baking water out of the gypsum he finally located. Then only a trickle seemed to come from his crude pipes. He hoarded it painfully, beginning to fill his fuel tanks.

He had to stop to find minerals to enrich the hydroponic tanks. He wasted days and weeks lying sick and near death from exposure, exhaustion, and near-starvation. He developed deficiency troubles, and he refused to give in to them. He never thought of failure. They'd abandoned him, and he cursed Earth with every weakened breath. But he was going back.

Finally, he stripped the ship of every drop of water he could spare, leaving himself almost none. He had already moved most of the plants into a crude hot-house outside. Now he drained their tanks, and decided that with that, added to what he had got from the gypsum, he had fuel enough.

In the spells of sickness, he had lost track of time. But he was fairly sure it was near the end of April, 1952, when he finally blasted off and headed back for Earth.

The ship was pointing ahead towards the cloud-filled atmosphere now. Soames dropped his hand from the crank, shaking with exhaustion, and waited for the first sign of air outside. He was falling fast, but that couldn't be helped.

He let the weakness grip him for a moment longer, while cold sweat stood out on his forehead, and time seemed to hang still in his frozen mind. Then he reached for the controls that would guide the ship down on its, stubby wings.

The controls resisted faintly when he touched them. The refrigerator inside the ship was whining, and he knew the hull must be hot already. This was familiar ground—he'd piloted experimental rocket planes enough to have the feel of supersonic flight. It was a matter of keeping the ship up in the superthin air until it began to lose speed, then letting it glide down to a landing.

He should hit somewhere inside the Atlantic Coast, from his rough calculations. He might do damage there—but the chances were against it. Anyhow, they hadn't thought of him for four long years—they'd have to take their chances now.

The ship was getting hot inside. He fought against the controls, trying to hold it just inside the atmosphere until its speed came down enough. The clouds below were lost from his sight. He stole a quick glance at the thin section of hull he could see. It wasn't glowing yet.

He fought mechanically, with his mind buried somewhere down in its deepest sections, trying not to think. The ship groaned, and the stubby wings seemed about to fall off. Somewhere to the rear, something gave with the sound of an express rifle. The ship grew hotter. The thin, worn coveralls were wet with his sweat, and the wristwatch seemed to burn his skin.

Then the speed was dropping, and he was going into his glide.

He came down through the clouds, finally, just as he left the darkness behind. His eyes darted to the little port that would show the surface below. He should be nearing the coast.

Soames' gasp was a hoarse choke. The line that separated sea and land was directly below him! He'd overshot. He drew back on the control, trying to steepen the glide, but it was already too late. The ship went plunging down through the air, heading out to sea. He cursed to himself, but there was nothing to be done, in the time left. He began a slow turn, but he knew it would fail.

He was miles from land when the first sound of the water slapping against the ship reached his ears. She was coming down smoothly enough. Spray leaped up, and the ship lurched as the braking force of the sea hit it while it still was making better than 200 miles per hour. But he managed to avoid being thrown forward. Then she was skipping a bit, with the sound of rifle-like popping coming from the rear again. A moment later, the ship was coasting smoothly over the fairly calm sea.

He was down—home—back to Earth—and alive!

And brother, would the brass hats have some explaining to do now!

Wetness touched his bare feet. He jerked his eyes down, to see an inch of water on the "floor" of the ship—and it was rising as he looked. The ship had sprung a leak during the battle through the air and the pounding of the landing. Now it would sink almost at once.

Bill threw the straps of the seat off and was on his feet, jumping for the airlock as he saw it. With a leak, this thing would sink like a piece of lead. He grabbed down his good-luck charm as he went. The sheaf of hundred dollar bills—eight in all—had been left from the going-away present his mother had sent him, and he'd forgotten them until half way out from Earth. Somehow, they had always been a symbol that he'd get back—but now, if he lived; they'd be of more immediate use. He reached for the packet of exposed film, but the water was coming up too fast; it touched the control-board and the films slid along the wet surface and vanished. There was no time to grope for them.

Soames struggled through the water as the little lock finally opened. He pulled himself out. The land was lost from view, and the sea was all around him.

But there was no time to wait. He jumped into the water and began paddling frantically. It was icy cold, and it shocked his body, driving the breath from his lungs. In his emaciated condition, keeping afloat was going to be hard work. Eight miles...

It never really occurred to him that he couldn't make it. He was heading toward the land when the suction of the ship's sinking caught him, and he didn't look back. He settled down to the best compromise between endurance and speed he could make and drove on. He was back on Earth, and they couldn't defeat him now.

Fifteen minutes later, the boat appeared. It was a Coast Guard cutter, he saw. It circled, and a line was tossed to him. On the rail, he could see the figures of men. All the loneliness of the Moon hit at him, then. He pulled on the line, dragging forward; it wasn't the thought of rescue, but the sound of human voices that drove him now.

"I'm Bill Soames," he began shouting, over and over.

They pulled him up, crying something to him—something about luck that had let them see his plane going down on their radar screen. But he hardly heard the words.

"I'm Soames," he repeated. "Major William Soames. Goddman it, can't you understand? That was a rocket ship—the *Lunatic*. I've come back from the Moon. Four years—four damned long years—but I've come back."

"Shock," one of the men said. "Okay, Bill, take it easy. You'll—be all right."

He shrugged off their hands. "I *am* all right. Damn it, don't you even remember me? I took off for the Moon in 1948—July 1, 1948! Now I'm back!"

He saw consternation on their faces and pity mixed with it. He shook his head. After all the publicity there had been, it hardly seemed that a man on Earth could help knowing about the trip. Yet maybe these men hadn't heard. Maybe they didn't care about rockets and the Moon.

"Didn't get a rocket out of the atmosphere until February, 1949," the Coast Guardsman said slowly. "That was when they shot the Wac Corporal up, using the V-2 to carry her. Got up about 250 miles, as I remember it. Brother, this is 1952—not 1975. You've been seeing too much fantasy on the television. Come on, we'll fix up a bunk."

A fine welcome for a hero, Bill thought. He'd expected his name to be enough to stop them cold. Now something was stopping him…tired…everything getting black…so tired, so dead…He felt himself falling, but was too far gone into unconsciousness to care.

They held him two weeks in the hospital. The semi-starvation and the exhaustion had added to the shock of the cold swim. But he hadn't been delirious as they claimed. He'd recovered the first night. Maybe he had raved a little—surely among all those doctors and nurses, one should have known about the take-off of the Moon ship, or should have known his name. They'd pretended to, after a while; but he knew they had been lying. They really believed all that guff about Man still being unready for Space!

He finished his lunch and reached for the dessert. Then he shuddered violently, and shoved it away. Pumpkin pie! His stomach seemed to turn over at the sight of it, and he pushed it as far from him as he could, tomatoes and pumpkins were no longer fit to eat, as far as he was concerned.

He reached for the book on the table again. *Rockets, Missiles, and Space Travel*, by Willy Ley. He'd read the original version of it in 1947. This edition bore the date of 1951. It had a good deal of new material and all the charm and sound thinking he expected of Ley. But it didn't fit with his memory of a big, black-haired man who had boomed out farewells to him while he climbed the ramp for the take-off. Ley wasn't just an expert—he was an enthusiast, and nobody wanted space-travel more than he did. Yet the book contained no mention of Bill's flight. It didn't list the method of turning water to monatomic hydrogen and ozone for rocket fuel discovered in 1946; there was nothing on the first compact atomic motor to provide power built late in 1947. Both had been highly secret at the time, but they had been announced publicly before his flight.

He'd expected to find proof of his facts in the book. Instead, he found only confusion for his mind. They couldn't have covered up that thoroughly. Yet the date of February 24, 1949 was listed for man's first step beyond the atmosphere—the same 250 mile flight the Coast Guardsman had mentioned.

Soames sighed, and dropped the book as the nurse came for his tray, the eternal mechanical smile on her lips. "Dr. Willoughby will see you soon," she told him.

He'd tried to talk to her, but he knew it was useless. These people really didn't know about his trip. It should have been on the front pages of every newspaper in the world, and there shouldn't be a literate person alive who didn't know of it. Instead, they had treated his facts as the ravings of a man suffering from shock.

What could account for something big enough to suppress such news—not only to suppress it, but to kill what had already gone before?

Even his former commanders had failed him. He'd been refused the right to send a telegram, but the Coast Guardsman who had visited him had promised to mail his letters to the men of Operation Space. General Bartley should have come tearing in, threatening to rip the place apart unless he was released at once. But the letters had vanished, if they had ever been mailed, without an answer.

Dr. Willoughby came in quietly. "Well, young man, how do you feel today? Still think you're chasing girls on the moon, heh?"

Soames wanted to push the smiling face back into the man's adenoids, but he managed to grin. In hospitals, you had to grin. He'd learned already that patients had to humor doctors and nurses and agree to anything they suggested.

"No more of that," he answered. "I still can't remember, but I'm sane enough. When do I get out of here?"

The doctor seemed to consider it weightily. "Well, now, I guess we can let you go. You did some fearful things to that body of yours—just what I can't tell; but you're well enough now. A little amnesia, of course, but that will wear off. Such cases happen from shock. You sure you want to leave?"

"I certainly am. I can get a job…"

The doctor wasn't listening. He nodded without waiting to hear the answer. "The nurse will bring you clothes, and then lead you to my office. I'll have some papers there. And there's a Colonel Hadley to see you."

He was gone before Soames' shout could get from his throat. So the Army had his letters! The hospital must have been holding him until Hadley could get there. They'd been stalling, but not for the reason he had expected. Now his troubles would soon be over.

He signed for the clothes they had bought at his order and the property they held for him. The clothes were picked without taste, as if some store had packaged them at random. He looked more human when he finished shaving. His face was still gaunt and tense, and his hair was thin and white, as it had grown in after a long bout of illness. But he felt almost himself again as he followed the girl to the doctor's office.

Willoughby introduced him and withdrew discreetly. Colonel Hadley was a plump, youngish man, with the rocky face and false pleasantness that could carry a man to his position but would never let him advance much beyond it. He obviously had no imagination, and couldn't trust it in others.

He got down to business at once. "These your letters? Umm. I've been talking to Dr. Willoughby. Understand you were pretty sick. So we won't discuss this nonsense about the moon. In fact, under the circumstances, perhaps we can forget…"

"Did you ever hear of Major William Soames?" Bill asked. "Before this, I mean?"

"Certainly. That's what made Bartley send me up here, instead of routine procedure. Naturally, Soames was on Bartley's flight over Berlin when the Nazis got him. Brave man. Saved Bartley's life. Got a posthumous Congressional Medal, you know. A hero."

"He—he *died*!"

"Right. May 23, 1943. Sad business. Had a brother—Lieutenant Roger Soames—on the same flight. Both got it."

Bill Soames let his legs lower him carefully into a chair, studying the Colonel's face. It wasn't the face of a man who could lie. It was the face of a man reporting hard fact that he knew to be true. Yet it was the sheerest nonsense. Bill had started on that flight—but his plane had developed motor trouble half an hour out from England and he'd put back. He'd always felt he was somehow to blame for Roger's death. He tried to say something, but no words would come.

"Very sad," Hadley added. "Never knew Major Soames, but I got on well with his brother. Saw the whole business myself. Felt sick for a whole day afterwards—first Roger, then the Major." He cleared his throat. "You can guess what we thought when we heard you were impersonating him. Naturally, we had to investigate. Crank letters come often enough, but not like that. Deuce of it was that Bartley swore it was like the Major's handwriting. And you know, you do look a little like the pictures I saw… Know what happens to anyone who impersonates an Army officer, young man? Bad. But—well, Dr. Willoughby tells me it was just shock. What about that?"

"I'm—I'm Bill Soames," Soames answered, while his head went around in crazy circles. He tried to pretend it was a gag to himself, but it wasn't. He fell back on the lying that had finally convinced the staff of his sanity. "I—I guess I must have been kind of a hero worshipper; when I got the shock, I thought I was the other William Soames—and went all the way on the hero stuff. If I caused you any trouble…"

"You did. You certainly did. Two days up here, checking your fingerprints, doing everything. Prints don't match, of course. Took me a whole day in Washington just getting Soames' prints, too, you know. Funny, you'd think they'd be careful with the records of a hero; almost lost! Heh! Well, anyhow, I guess we can close the case. No sign of fraud. Hope you get your full memory back."

He stood up to go, and Bill got to his feet. He took the other's perfunctory handshake and watched him leave. He saw Willoughby come in, beaming. There must have been some exchange of words, though he couldn't remember them. Then the papers were signed, and he was going out of the hospital. The sun was shining brightly as he came down the steps, mechanically counting out the four hundred odd dollars he had left.

It had, to be hypnotism. Hadley had thought he was telling the truth. But they had hypnotic drugs now. They might use them, If they wanted to pretend a man who'd flown to the Moon had been dead years before. If General Bartley had meant to send Soames a warning that the subject was top secret, and to go slow…if he'd been unable to come himself…

It still didn't make sense. It hadn't made sense when they had abandoned him on the Moon, and it made less now. What national danger could possibly be averted by lying about this—particularly when they were still talking about the fact that the first nation to get a base on the Moon would rule Earth?

There was only one answer. He had to see Bartley in person. He was due in Washington, it seemed—overdue by some four years.

Seeing Bartley proved to be more trouble than he'd thought. The Pentagon wasn't open to casual visitors—not the part he wanted. He couldn't use his own name, either. But even Generals are human beings. They eat, and they have to have places to sleep. Soames gave up direct efforts, and waited patiently.

He was lucky. He spotted Bartley getting into a car alone on the third day, just as he was driving up to park his own rented car. He could tell the way the gears ground that the man was bound for the old familiar place. Bartley was short and plump, a little Santa Claus of a man with fierce black hair and a totally unconvincing bristle of a moustache. When he was angry, he looked more jovial than ever—which was probably why he had his favorite bar well out Bethesda, away from the usual run of other officers.

Soames kept a casual eye on the car, but he was sure of himself when Bartley headed out Wisconsin Avenue. He drove into the little parking lot, just as Bartley disappeared into the pleasant bar across the way. Then he took his time. The General would need a beer by himself before he could be approached. When Bill finally went in, he found the place almost unchanged. He ordered his own beer and moved back to the jukebox. Bartley was sitting beside it. He set his beer on the table, and began feeding nickels into the machine. None of the new tunes meant anything to him, but luck was still with him. There was one of the old platters there—"A Long Long Trail." He let it start, and saw Bartley glance up.

Soames had worn a hat to cover his hair, but he had carefully turned his face to the light. Now he saw Bartley's eyes slip to his own, and hesitate. He smiled faintly, drew an answering doubtful smile, and slipped into the booth. The other man offered no objections.

"Beer here is worth coming a long ways for," Bill said casually. "Worth a quarter million miles."

The General smiled doubtfully, then frowned as if the joke escaped him. It was a good act, Bill had to admit. "Good beer," he finally admitted. "Like the stuff the Germans had for their officers—almost."

"Honigsbrau," Bill agreed. "A couple cases of it. They'd just started to crack it and drink when we strafed 'em. It was warm by the time we reached the shack, but it was worth all the trouble we had."

The General nodded. "Good. Dark and heavy stuff. I can still taste it. Used to…"

His mouth fell open, making him look more than ever like a comic cherub. "Good God! Man, you couldn't be! You…Bill Soames!"

Bill nodded, and the fears washed away. "In the flesh, Tom. I had a helluva time getting back—I'm still mad about being left there. But I knew you'd be glad to see me!"

"Glad! You sunovagun! We knew you were dead. You couldn't have lived in that smash-up, Bill!" He was pumping Bill's hands, his own arm jerking spasmodically. "Man, wait'll they hear about this!"

"They don't seem to want to hear about it," Bill told him.

"They will, boy, they will! We didn't go through the war together for nothing!"

"Or Operation Space? Remember how we used to dream about that, when I found you were human enough to read those stories. Rockets—space… We didn't think then…"

Hartley sighed. "Yeah. And when the V-2's fell into our hands, I did a lot more dreaming, Bill. It was tough, not getting assigned to White Sands. I really wanted to work on the rockets. But I guess they knew what they were doing when they turned me down."

"They turned you down?" Hell, Tom Bartley had been the one to get him in, after his first application was turned down. Bartley had been the first officer picked for the job.

"They did. I guess I forgot about your being somewhere in Germany— Say, when did you get back? And how? Come on, give."

Bill sat back, staring at him. It was his turn to sit with his mouth open. He glanced up to see if anyone else could have come near to cut off the honesty he'd found here before. They were alone. The bartender was at the other end, and all the booths were deserted.

"Okay," he said. "I guess you had some reason for the game, but not between us, Tom. Leaving me up on the Moon without answering my signals was a dirty trick. It took me four years to get back, and then I cracked your precious ship into the ocean, where the salt water can eat its magnesium to bits. But it's time to stop the, pussy-footing. You know damned well I never cracked up on the Moon. I've left my signature up there. Now I'm back. And I want some explanations."

Bartley's face had gone white, and now was turning fiery red. His hand around the beer glass tautened until the glass snapped. Blood seeped out on his fingers, but he didn't look at it. Finally he took a deep breath.

"For a minute you fooled me," he began in a deadly quiet voice. "For a minute. I was fool enough to think Bill Soames had managed to live somehow, when I knew he'd burned up in the plane. But I should have remembered those damned letters. You fooled Hadley—he thought you were sick, not crazy. But you can't fool me. You damned rotten…"

The fist that landed in Bill's face hardly traveled six inches, backed by sheathes of muscles that only looked like fat. Bill's head snapped back against the rear of the booth, while hot pain lanced through him. He slid down, barely holding onto his consciousness. He heard Bartley get up and dash to the phone. He heard the crisp orders to come for him.

For a second, he wanted to lie there and let them get him. There was nothing left. The others could be fooled or try to fool him—but Tom Bartley wouldn't do that. That blow had been based on real feelings. Bartley had believed he'd never worked at White Sands. And generals weren't hypnotized, even for security.

Then the stubbornness that had carried him through four years of desertion on the Moon and brought him back alive came to the surface. He shook the blackness away from his head, sending up lancing pains, and got to his feet. The beer bottle was under his hand. He lifted it, and threw it, four feet behind Bartley. As the man turned toward it, his legs drove him forward. He was out of the bar, and across the street. He threw a bill at the parking attendant, and gunned his rented car to life. Then he began twisting crazily through side streets. Washington wouldn't be healthy for him after this.

He had no time to think, but his mind had already been made up. There was one place and only one where he could go. And he'd better get started there fast.

The key that had been with his wallet—the stuff he'd forgotten to leave behind when he took off—still fitted the lock. He opened the door of the quiet apartment when no one answered his knock. The furniture was mostly the same, and there were pictures of himself and Roger on the piano. He called, but there was no answer. Then he moved back toward the windows that opened on Central Park South.

It was hard to believe; after the war, the tests, and the Moon, that he'd grown up here, in the quiet luxury of the money his father had left them. But he found his old room still as it had been the last day before he left. He closed the door on it quickly; it brought back too much that he'd forgotten.

He found a chair near the door and settled down to wait. The rest of the world might deceive him. Even Tom Bartley might lie—he'd left Bill on the Moon, and he probably had enough guilt feelings from that to account for anything. But Bill knew that his mother wouldn't lie to the craziest stranger. Surely he'd find the truth here. She had never understood his craving for adventure beyond Earth, and she wouldn't know too much about advances in the world. But she'd accept him. All their lies about his having died over Berlin wouldn't mean anything to her, after they'd spent so many week-ends here when the war was over. She'd remember the ring on his finger that had been her idea, to help him cut his way out of a Nazi prison if he were captured; she'd thought that diamonds were somehow safe and that they could cut steel bars as well as glass. She'd remember the thousand dollars that had been meant to give him a grand party with the men, since he insisted on being fool enough to try to reach the Moon. She'd been tearful then, but she'd seen something of his drive, and had seemed proud of him, at the end.

He sat there, soaking up peace and quiet from the room around him. The sunlight disappeared from the windows at the far end, and there was a bit of gloom that finally ended when the street-lights went on. They left the room thick with shadows, and rich with the fancies he'd woven around them when he was only a kid, playing with Roger.

He made no effort to turn on the light, but waited quietly.

Then he heard the elevator stop, and her feet on the floor of the hall. He was still sitting as the key turned in the lock, and a beam of light struck him. She closed the door quietly, looking older and frailer than he remembered, but still upright and carrying herself with the ordered pride of good breeding.

She snapped on the lights and turned to face him. For a moment, surprise struck her. Then she mastered herself. "Good evening, young man. How did you get in here?" Her voice was firm, but calm enough, as if this were a minor upset in some fond routine.

He stood up, moving toward the light. She watched him, then smiled doubtfully. "If you're a burglar, you're quite welcome to what money I have here. Only don't make any commotion, please. I can't stand vulgarity." She was trying to make a joke of it, he knew. Then her voice caught. "But you…you look like…"

"Hi, Mom," he said, nodding.

She stood there, suddenly old and shrunken, though her back was straighter than ever. Her perfectly applied make-up was ghastly on her white face. She backed against the door slowly, hand went to her throat.

"You look like Bill—like Bill—like Bill. Just like Bill." It was a soft moan, unconscious. "Bill was a nice boy. He died in the war—the same time Roger died. It wasn't fair. He died—they told me he died horribly. And they sent me his papers, what was left—and half a letter he'd begun—and they gave him a medal. He was such a nice boy. I saved them all…I…"

She began to fall, still stiffly. Bill caught her in his arms, and eased her onto a couch. He'd never seen her faint before. He knew she hadn't fainted when she heard that Roger had been killed. He stood helpless. Finally he lowered her head and raised her feet, waiting for her to come to. His eyes moved to the drawer where she'd stared, the drawer under the two smaller pictures from their childhood.

He found them all there—the notice, with its accusing date, half of a letter he actually had written—but completely—his papers, and some knick-knacks that seemed to have been in a fire!

He pawed through them quickly, and then went back to the couch. He knew what he had to do, and began rummaging into his few belongings. He was rubbing her forehead when she came to. She looked at him, but he was holding his face as taut as he could, to build up the lines that the hard years had put on it. She shook her head slowly.

"You're—not…"

"No, ma'am. I guess I forgot, calling you 'Mom' the way Bill always did. He was my buddy, you knew. Used to laugh at how we looked alike. A great guy. We were in prison over there together. That's why I came back, to bring you this—all he had left when he died. But he didn't die in the plane, ma'am. They shot him trying to escape, and it was quick and painless. That's why I came here, why I had his key…"

He'd rehearsed it in his mind, but hadn't known whether it would work. Now he saw life come back into her. She drew herself up, and straightened her hair. Her voice was calm again. "Silly of me, of course. I—I'm glad you came. I never did believe Bill died in the plane. He was so much at home in any kind of machinery. Thank you for bringing my picture back to me. And now, can't I get you a drink, before I apologize for being so weak?"

He shook his head. "I'll have to rush, ma'am. I waited too long. Bill wanted you to have the picture—it was what he valued most. But—well, I *have* got to rush."

She let him go. She was not the sort to hold any nervous man against his will. She saw him to the door, and her fingers rested briefly on his arm. The smile she gave him would have been reward enough, if his story had been true.

Then he went down the stairs and out into the night on this world which had erased him and which refused to admit he had ever left it.

There had been another picture in his wallet, but he'd been a fool to look at it. He'd looked at it often enough that first year up there, wondering whether she'd wait for him, but somehow the memory of Sherry had grown weak with time. He'd been a bigger fool to spend the night making phone calls to locate her.

He knew it now as he sat on the too-lavish couch. He'd heard a faint gasp when she first saw him, but she'd never thought he was Bill Soames, and he hadn't tried to tell her he was. He'd used the same line on her as he'd finally used on his mother, with a change in the picture. It sat on the table near her now, its water-stained younger image of her face staring up.

She slid a trifle sideways, exposing one knee from under her negligee, and reached across him for her drink. She'd always had a nice bosom, and she'd always known it. She sipped the drink and put it back. "Poor Bill," she said throatily. "He was such a kid—but I guess I was too, then. I suppose he really expected me to wait for him?"

"I don't know—maybe not," Bill answered her. "Things were pretty tough in the prison."

"I meant to wait for him. But it was so long. I guess it wasn't very nice, marrying Bob Stanton just six months after Bill went overseas, but you know how it is. And then we heard Bill had died, but I was just having Junior…"

"Junior?" Bill jerked at that, his eyes flickering over the slightly too-decorated room. She couldn't have had a child in 1943—she *had* waited for him; she'd promised to wait again when he left for the rocket in 1947. And imagination wouldn't supply a child…

She laughed and pointed to a picture of a boy of about eight. "He's away at school now, of course. You know how important it is give them the *best* education." She sighed, and reached for the drink. "But it's terribly hard on a boy's mother, having him away. The place gets so lonely, now that Bob's away in Washington so much of the time. I think I'll go mad…"

She wasn't even subtle about it. For a moment, it worked. Bill had spent too long away from women. Then the ease of her passion was too much for him; it told him too strongly what a fool he'd been ever to believe her accounts of the missing dates that had always come between them. He pushed her away, pulled her negligee shut firmly, and added insult to the injury by making no attempt to turn his eyes away.

She was just switching from surprise to querulous hurt as his feet carried him across the living room to the foyer. Her voice was rising to a shriek of outraged anger as he closed the door behind him. This time the night air felt good. There were worse things than being marooned on the Moon. He might have come back and married her!

Then he frowned. It wasn't night, anymore, after all. The lights were still on, but day was breaking in the east.

He grimaced. Well, he'd gotten things out of the night. He'd found that his mother knew he was dead, and had been dead years before he took off for the Moon; he'd found the papers that had the authentic appearance of age to prove it. He'd found that the girl who'd been single and willing to wait for him in 1947 had not only been married, but had had a child in 1943 or 1944. That would take some explaining! He couldn't swear to some things about her, but he knew damned well there had been no marriage or child in the past from which he came.

It hit him, then—the stories he'd read once had been filled with the idea that time is a matter of multiple choice, and that the future is a fan-shaped thing, with many branches. If he'd gone to the Moon from one such probability world and somehow gotten switched over to another on the return—a world where he had never left…

He shrugged. It was fine for speculation, but there was no way to account for such a switch. Anyhow, that stuff was based on the need for a good story-gimmick, and not on facts. There was a lot more sense in a universe where there was an absolute relation between cause and effect. This was the same world he'd left—however much deceit was involved, and whatever the tricks they used to deny him. It might be a crazy world, but not one of those improbable ones.

He considered that. A crazy world—or one person who was crazy. Then he grinned savagely. He didn't feel crazy. It was no solution, anyhow. If he were crazy, he wouldn't know it. The same stubbornness that had let him survive for four years on the Moon made him reject the idea at once. There had been times when the whole world was wrong and only one man was right; as far as he was concerned, this was another such case.

He came up to a newsstand and stood staring at the magazines. There were more dealing in the fantastic than he remembered, but they looked familiar. Space-ships and weird landscapes vied with half-nude girls and bug-eyed monsters. He started to buy one, and then gave up the idea; after being up there, he didn't want someone else's guess. As for alien life-forms...

He thought about it for a second, but little more. Maybe some alien civilization that wanted to keep man Earthbound might suppress knowledge and even change memories; but it didn't fit the case. It would have been easier for such a race to eliminate him, or to prevent the ship ever having taken off. There was no answer there.

He bought a newspaper and went into a coffee shop for breakfast. He still enjoyed eating real food. The sight of two eggs, over light, surrounded by crisp bacon, together with toast and coffee was better than any scene off Earth. He took his plate to a little table and began glancing through the paper as he ate. Most of the news meant nothing to him—the war beginning in Asia now so soon after the last war was something he preferred to ignore. Most of the rest of the paper was filled with things that he couldn't understand or didn't care to read. Even the comics were dull, without the continuity of regular reading.

Then he stopped, and looked back at a picture. Professor Arnold Rosenblum had delivered a lecture on the need for a space station outside Earth's atmosphere. When interviewed later at the Weldon Arms Hotel, he had stated...

Rosenblum had been the man who had invented the method of using water as the propellant! He'd been part of Operation Space from the beginning. If Bill could see him...

He knew the result. Rosenblum wouldn't remember. Yet the man was a scientist, and science isn't something that deals with belief. It sticks to facts. Bill turned it over, considering. The man might not believe a word he would have to say—yet he couldn't argue against provable facts. And to a real scientist, there were facts that could be proved!

The phone booth was in the back, and there was no trouble in getting his message put through to the scientist. Apparently men of science still didn't have to be suspicious of callers, as did movie stars. The voice at the other end was sleepy, but not hostile. "Yes?"

"Dr. Rosenblum? I'm James Cross, former student—class of '44. I was wondering whether you—about the space stations? I—" He halted his story about being a reporter, considering what he knew of the man. Then he hesitated deliberately. "I—I don't have any reason to bother you, but I missed your lecture, and I couldn't get much out of the newspaper articles. For breakfast, perhaps?"

"Cross?" Rosenblum seemed to turn it over and decide names didn't matter. "Well, why not? I don't wonder you couldn't understand the newspaper account. Ten minutes—wait, where are you?"

"Ten minutes will be fine," Bill said, "And thanks."

"Pleasure. Always glad to find someone still curious. Usually they forget after college." The phone clicked down, covering the last of a yawn. Bill went outside quickly to flag a cab.

It took fifteen minutes, but he managed to beat the professor to the lobby. Rosenblum was tall and thin, with a face like that of Lincoln, and eyes that managed to be both sharp and friendly, even with traces of sleep in them. He made no comment at not recognizing Bill.

Soames had given up expecting recognition. He ordered breakfast again, and grinned at Rosenblum's order—the scientist obviously believed in enjoying life. Then he plunged into it.

"I've been thinking that problem of fuels over, Dr. Rosenblum. You mentioned flourine and beryllium as a theoretical ideal. What about ozone and monatomic hydrogen? Wouldn't they have a higher exhaust velocity? Maybe enough to avoid the need for a step rocket?"

"Very fine," Rosenblum admitted with a grin, around a thick slice of ham. "Excellent—if you'll tell me how to get them and store them."

"Don't. Make them out of water. Like this." Bill pulled out a pad and began scribbling on it, mixing it with comments as he gave all that he could remember of what Rosenblum had originally discovered. He was watching for signs of suspicion, but there were none. The professor showed interest, but no indication that this was some highly secret discovery of his own.

He studied it. "You'd need power for this, of course, Mr. Cross. But I suppose the work being done on submarine atomic motors might provide that, for a large ship. Still…"

Bill relaxed at the interest on the other's face. Facts—science had to deal with facts. And no casual interviewer could know enough about both fuels and atomics to reveal such information—Rosenblum would have to believe him. "I've been thinking about it. If we use a heavy-water moderated pile, but design it…"

He plunged into that. It was hard work, trying to remember it all, but he was sure he'd covered most of the points. Rosenblum sat back, his breakfast forgotten, nodding. Bill looked up with a final nod of his own at the scrawls on the paper. "Well?"

"Interesting. Unfortunately, it won't work. I tried to do exactly that with water for a fuel back in 1946—and it failed. The theory looks good—but it takes too much power. I had some students working on it, too, but we had to abandon the idea. As for your atomic motor…" He shook his head sadly. "Well, that's out of my field, but some of the material they've just released covers such an idea. I understand it isn't controllable."

"But—"

Rosenblum shook his head and began attacking his breakfast again. "Oh, I think you've done a lot of clear thinking, and I'm not calling you a fool, young man. I only wish I had a few more students like you. But you have to remember that there are hundreds of men working on these things today, and they've had these ideas, too. It's a beautiful piece of logic—but unfortunately, logic isn't everything; it won't work."

"It did work!" Bill told him grimly. "It worked when you tried it in 1946! Security be damned! I know it. I was the guy who rode the rocket using it to the Moon and back! I tell you, I *know!*"

A change crept over Rosenblum's face. He studied Bill for a moment, then shook his head, making clucking sounds.

"Another one, eh? Last week it was my colleague, Dr. Dickson, who had invented a variation of this, late in 1949. Now *I* invented it in 1947. And of course, the man who told him about it had been to the Moon personally, too. You don't fit the description, or I might think you were the same man. Mr. Cross, in spite of what the papers say, college professors are neither credulous idiots nor crazy."

He picked up his check, and put down change for the tip. "I have no intention of reporting you to the establishment. But I think you'd be wise to leave, at once! Good day."

Rosenblum walked toward the cashier, leaving Bill to stare down at the working diagrams that had taken him to the Moon, but had been proven not to work. Sure, science dealt in facts! It had been a beautiful theory.

The library had a complete file of the *New York Times* back through 1947. Bill had half expected to find missing issues, but they were all there. He riffled back to June, thumbing through. The advance feelers put out by the Army were there—meaningless by themselves, of course, but leading up to what was to come. He came to July, and tensed.

There were no missing headlines—but there was nothing on the flight of a rocket to the Moon. He combed July thoroughly. There was no mention of him. He went back to July 2nd, when the news should have been broken. On the front page, one of the men who had covered the take-off had a by-line story; it dealt with ordinary news, though, and would have required that the man be in New York the day before. Bill turned to the science columns—and again, a name that had been among those covering the take-off hit his eye. But the story dealt with something totally unrelated to the flight, and again would have had to be written by a man nowhere near the take-off spot!

It took him four hours to complete his search, and netted him only one item. That stopped him when he came to it. It was in the same month; this time it was a more sensational paper, and the account was buried under a miscellaneous collection of scandals. *Ham Claims Contact With Man In Moon!* It seemed that a radio amateur had picked up a signal from someone who claimed to be marooned on the Moon, asking for supply ships. It must have been *his* signal!

He took it to be photostated, amazed at his violent reaction to even this bit of evidence. His hands were trembling as he held it up and pointed out the piece. But the man who came to help him only glanced at it with amusement.

"Fortean, eh? Well, I get a kick out of such things, too. But you'll find a lot of things like this printed in the summer. That's why reporters call it the silly season, I guess." He read through it, grinning again. "Mm-hm. They ran almost the same story in 1950—I remember it, because my father was visiting us... You know, I had a man here a couple weeks ago who told me he sent the message. Never cracked a grin... Hey, mister, don't you want your stat?"

Bill went down the street slowly. He'd have to get a room, of course. And a job. His money wouldn't last forever—even if he hocked the diamond ring and his watch. Time for lunch. Hell, he wasn't hungry. He glanced at a television store, noticing that the screens looked immense, though the prices were lower than he'd thought they would ever be. But men could make progress in amusement, even if their leading scientists insisted they'd failed at work that might have sent man to the planets, given time.

He bought a paper and skimmed it. He found the first of the "silly season" accounts on Page 7, though it wasn't summer yet. It dealt with the flying saucers, of course, since they were still the current fad. He turned on. Maybe it was a lean day, and news was scarce. Three pages further he found a brief mention of a 97-year-old woman who could recite the Bible in Hebrew, though she'd never spoken a word of it in her life. Telepathy, she claimed; thought communication with a scholar who had lived two thousand years before.

He threw the paper in the disposal can, and stared up at the sign moving across the Times Building.

They'd covered up perfectly. There wasn't any real evidence left. A ship had disappeared on the Moon, but nobody had missed it. A man who waited for help was tagged as dead years before, his own mother could remember how he had died. Science had proved that he couldn't make the trip with the equipment he had. The papers were complete—and spurious.

It was the stuff of madness. Yet he knew inside himself he wasn't mad. Somehow, reality had been altered for everyone. A thousand men who had seen the ship take-off now probably all knew that they had been doing something else. Papers had been changed.

Men had invented the steamboat long before Fulton. Their attempts had been buried, though some of them had worked. Leif Ericson had crossed the Atlantic and discovered America before Columbus—and the account had been lost, until the evidence was found. Had the facts been altered then? Had Ericson come home to find that everyone knew he had been in Iceland all along? And then, when the evidence was finally found, centuries later after America had been discovered again, had things been doctored up the opposite way, so that people thought the evidence had been there all along?

What about the hot-air engine? It was known before the gasoline motor, and it had been just as good. Yet it had lain unused for decades, until after gasoline was powering every car on the road; then it had been rediscovered, and someone had scratched his head and wondered how it had been overlooked. Prontosil was developed during World War I, but the sulfa part wasn't used to kill germs until twenty years later. Penicillin had appeared and proved its germ killing power before 1930, but no one got around to using it until World War II.

Why was everything so significant overlooked? And would some man, a hundred years from now, stand on the Moon and stare down at his crude solar still, to recognize he'd been there first? Would they mysteriously find the accounts in old papers then, and wonder why they hadn't known about it before?

Or would this ultimate step of mankind be buried for good, while the race went on warring its way to destruction? A base on the Moon could spell enforced peace, if they got it in time.

Bill walked on, without purpose. He was finished. There was no use fighting now. Maybe he really wasn't Bill Soames. Maybe he'd been James Cross all along—maybe a nephew of old Robert Cross, who'd inherited a small fortune when the old man died. Gone on a hunting trip by airplane, gotten lost, half starved before he could find the plane, then landed in the ocean. Three children, one a girl with amazing dark red hair and the deepest blue eyes that could smile at a man. A vision of a pleasant apartment swam into his mind. He'd better call home...

He cut it off savagely. He was Major William Soames, back to a crazy Earth after four years on the Moon. Neither his own mind nor any outside force was going to change his knowledge of that.

For a second, he was tempted to call the phone number that had been in his mind. Maybe there was such a number under the name of James Cross, and such a family. Maybe they had a convenient slot for him to fit into, just as they'd destroyed his own slot. But he couldn't fool with it. Giving in might be just what they wanted—whoever or whatever *they* were.

He shook his head. It was too late to change his mind. The doubtful number had disappeared, along with the fantasms that went with it. He was no longer uncertain about himself, at least. Yet he knew that he had to find some kind of proof, if he didn't want the fantasy thoughts to come back.

Where could he go for specific information? How could he locate the news from all the papers, dealing with a specific subject, instead of having to plow through edition after edition, requiring a life-time of effort?

Then he had it. There were clipping bureaus that did that for one. They could cull out everything except articles dealing with rockets, space-flight, and so on. He had no idea of the cost, but he could find out. He studied the signs along the street, and began pulling off the ring. He'd never get what it was worth—but even at a discount, five carats should be worth a considerable sum. Then he could investigate the clipping bureaus.

Again, luck changed capriciously. The ring had brought more than he'd expected—at least half of what it was worth—and he found the bureaus listed in the classified section of the book. Most of them obviously specialized in names, rather than subjects. Some agreed that they could get him clippings. And one stated doubtfully that they had some. But the seventeenth one seemed pleasantly surprised when he broached the idea.

"How about photostats? They do you as well?"

Bill could see no reason to object to that. The voice at the end of the line became even more pleasant. "Fine. We've been making up a file on that subject. Another day, and you'd have been too late. But we can run off a copy for you tonight, and have it ready at nine tomorrow. It'll save you a lot of expense, too. We've had to get extra copies of some of the papers from back years; and that runs into money, not counting the overtime work. This way, that's all paid for, and we can be pretty reasonable."

"Nine o'clock tomorrow," Bill agreed. "I suppose you'll want some money in advance?"

The voice brightened again. They made arrangements for a messenger to pick up the money in the lobby of a near-by hotel. Bill registered at the desk while taking, using the same fictitious name he had given the agency. He was tired in a way that he'd never been during all the grueling effort to get back to Earth. It would be easy to relax and pretend the world was right—it was hard to keep fighting it. But something in his head refused to surrender. Somehow, he was going to collect the recognition they owed him, if it took him his whole remaining life time to get it!

He should have felt better after a night's sleep, but bitterness was apparently getting to be a habit again. Nine o'clock found him outside the clipping bureau. He saw tired, lackluster women entering and punching their cards into the time clock; they began gathering up newspapers and filing towards desks, where the routine job of marking, cutting, and pasting the items began. They'd probably throw away a thousand hints of new ideas and inventions that would be buried for years or decades, and never know what they had missed—if the news was even there. They'd go on collecting the names of men who liked to see those names in print. And at night they'd go home too tired and dreary to look up at the sky. Would it really make any difference if they knew that somewhere up there parts of a supply rocket had been turned into a solar still, so that a starved, crazy fool could come back here to bring them news nobody would believe?

"Mr. Foster?" a voice behind him said for the third time, and he suddenly remembered that he'd chosen that as his name the day before. "Ah, good morning. Everything's ready—and quite a file, too. I was looking it over last night. Strange material here—enough for a book, at least. People hear messages from the Moon, people see big ships land, people announce they've built a rocket to go to Mars. A Coast Guard yeoman even reported picking a man out of the sea who claimed he'd just come from the Moon. Something about living up there four years without air or water. People! Are you a writer?"

"Sort of." Bill evaded his question. He picked up the file with a shudder at realizing he had made the news, even if it hadn't been quite the way he'd intended.

The clerk was busy making a flourish of computing the sales tax, then counting the money. Bill picked up the bulky envelope and started to leave, just as a big, blond man entered. The clerk nodded toward him. "The man who ordered this originally," he started, as if to introduce them. But Bill didn't wait. He'd seen a quiet little bar on the corner, and he headed for it. It was nearly empty, and he found a booth off by himself, where he could go through the photostats.

Most of it was what he had expected, and it had been padded out with flying saucer stories, of course. He began weeding out the junk, keeping everything that seemed to have the faintest use. There was an account on July 1 of a kid who'd run away—it made no sense until a July 8 follow-up pasted to it showed that the kid had been found, safe enough, but swearing he'd gone to see the big rocket go up. Bill checked the date again. It was 1948, and the location had been about right. The kid could have run off to see him leave, if word had leaked. But it was no proof by itself.

"Hi," a soft voice said. The big blond man was sliding down across from him. "Hear you got a bargain. Not that I care—nothing exclusive. Interested in space flight?"

Bill frowned, and then decided he could use a little chance to talk socially. "You might say so," he admitted. "Mostly about the Moon. I got interested in Professor Rosenblum's lecture. It gets to be a bit expensive as a hobby, though."

"Pays off, if you know how. That's my angle. I make process shots for the movies, now that they've gone in for this stuff. Do it cheaper and better than they can. I figured some of this might give me some ideas." The man's voice was friendly, but he seemed vaguely disappointed, as if he had expected something else from Bill.

For his own part, Bill was wondering about leaving. It had seemed to offer some possibility interest when he'd realized that the other was sinking money into finding all he could about such things. But Bill wasn't interested in process shots. The films that had been lost on his ship were the real thing—and they showed it. No trick of photography could give the same effect.

He started to gather up the mess of photostats, but the other had signaled for more beer. "I'm Brad Wollen."

"Bill Soames," he answered automatically, and then cursed himself as the other's eyebrows lifted. "A cousin of the fellow who got the Medal of Honor, if that's what you were thinking."

Wollen nodded. "Funny. And I'm the cousin of the Army test pilot who cracked up in that new supersonic job back in '49. Quite a coincidence, isn't it? Hey, wait a minute…didn't I see something about a guy who claimed he was your cousin in one of these…"

He began searching through the clippings busily. Bill swore hotly to himself. He'd thought his name had escaped publication—they usually left out names, in such cases. He shoved back his beer, and began framing an excuse to leave.

Then he stopped—Lying on the table was an eight-by-ten glossy picture.

And it was no process shot. The lighting couldn't be duplicated. That was a shot of the Moon—the real Moon!

His hands fumbled with it as he tried to pick it up. No tricks could do that! And the rocket ship in the background was too detailed for any of the stuff they were doing now. It was different from his—but it might have been another model of the same ship, just as this picture was like the crater he'd known, though not quite the same.

"It's real!" he said slowly. "The way the light bounces, the way those rocks look eroded, yet aren't rounded off! Damn it, you *can't* fake that."

He realized he was being a fool as he said it, but the words piled out before he could stop them. It wasn't the stupidity that brought him to a halt, though. It was the sudden blanched shock on the other man's face. Wollen had heaved himself half out of his seat and was staring at him as if he'd just come out of hell, complete with brimstone.

"Mister, how do you know how those rocks look?" The man's voice was a hoarse whisper.

Bill sighed wearily. "Because I was the fool that took off in the first ship—in 1948, for the record. The blind fool who wouldn't die, but managed to live up there four years until I could come back here to be shown what a real fool is. Now go ahead and laugh. Tell me you never heard of a rocket then, and that Bill Soames died over Berlin. Tell me I'm a liar now!"

"I never heard of a '48 rocket, and I did hear you died." Wollen was sinking back slowly. "But it fits—Oh, God, how well it fits. Then—you did crash in the sea!"

He didn't wait for Bill's tensed, unbelieving nod. "I was luckier. I came down in a swamp, not sixty miles from here. Make way for the hero, home from the Moon! Did they abandon you without supplies, too? Yeah. It isn't fun, baking out water, if you did it the way I did. And it isn't fun when you find you're dead—were dead before you took off, and your wife swears your kids belong to the man she married the same day she married... But I had the films. When the guys I showed them to told me they were nice process work, I caught on fast. I came closer to starving here than up there, at first. Now—well, I'm doing all right, that way. They like my process work! Almost looks real, they tell me. The blind fools! They won't even look at the ship—they call it clever of me to make such a big mock-up for my shots!"

His voice quieted suddenly. "I've been back three months. Sometimes I begin to think I never took off from Earth at all. I get funny ideas. But all the same, I took off in 1950, and I was up there seventeen months, on food enough for less than six."

They sat staring at each other, while Bill cursed himself. It had been thrown at him—the man who had approached Rosenblum's colleague, Dr. Dickson, must have been Wollen. Rosenblum had discovered the fuel method in 1946; Dickson had found it in 1949...

His eyes dropped to the clippings, but Wollen was gathering them up. "It's a nice ship, still," he said. "It needs raising upright, and a little work. But you'll like it."

It *was* a nice ship—a better model in some ways than Bill's had been. But they'd discussed that, and agreed it was natural. While the fuel trick had been buried technology in other lines had advanced a little. If there was another, later ship, it would probably be better, though still not good enough.

And there was going to be another. The clippings had proved that. All the signs that Bill and Wollen could remember from their pasts were out again, obvious to those who could read the meaning. Somewhere, someone else had discovered how to use water in an atomic power plant for fuel, and they were building a ship. In another year, it would be winging up towards the Moon. And the whole story would start over again; the fuel supply rockets would not arrive, and somehow the headlines and memories on Earth would change.

Bill had a picture of thousands and millions of people scuttling about, destroying that "ridiculous" bit of evidence, or "correcting" some mistake, to hold man down from his great leap. It had been easy to keep him fooled once. The Greeks had invented a toy steam-engine twenty-five hundred years ago, and the idea had somehow been glossed over until Watt came along. It was harder now—it must take more work each time.

Whatever was causing it was losing. But that *whatever* might still win. Man was getting close to destruction now. He had bombs that could annihilate great masses. He had a thousand new toys of war. And he was blundering along, closer and closer to using them all.

Bill helped Wollen unload the new batch of supplies off the little truck into the shed beside the rocket. Around them, the swamp was a perfect camouflage, and the hollow into which the rocket had settled in its landing glide concealed it almost completely.

The blond man wiped his hands, and stopped for a breather, picking up the conversation where he'd dropped it. "You can't give them—or it—a name, Bill. Maybe it's caused by aliens, in spite of what we believe. Maybe it's caused by a group right here on Earth who can control men's thoughts on any one limited subject at a time. Maybe it's some supernatural drive. I've even thought about the old idea of the mass-mind, capable of taking over individual humanity; that would be a pretty basic, conservative force, and it wouldn't want newfangled ideas. The thing has been operating for a good many thousand years, fighting a constant delaying action. But this is its last stand. Once we spread out, we can't be controlled—one planet will discover what the next one doesn't. It has to win now. And that means we have to win."

"We'll win," Bill answered him, and began unloading the truck again. "We've got to win, so we will."

Unconsciously, they both looked up to the sky, where the Moon would be. There was time enough for them to get the big ship righted and ready to take off. The repairs needed were minor, and the fuel for the rocket was all around them, while the atomic motors were good for at least one more trip. They'd make the Moon, and still have some leeway to maneuver about, or to jump from one crater to another.

Men had struggled with electricity and tamed it before they knew what it was. They'd been fighting gravity for millennia, whenever they did work, and still knew nothing about it, really. They knew nothing about their own minds and the minds of the larger groups being studied in mob psychology, beyond a hint and a suggestion. Men somehow always had to beat down the opposing forces and only learn what they were after the battle was won.

It didn't matter what had been doing it. Maybe they'd never know. Or maybe they'd learn as soon as it was finally overcome. All they had to do was fix it so they couldn't lose.

In another year, the third rocket would go up. This time two men would be watching for it from the Moon—men in a worn space-ship, who'd spent months baking out supplies of water from gypsum for fuel. Bill and Wollen would be ready. They'd ferry the fuel to wherever the next ship landed, the new ship could head back for Earth less than a day after it touched the Moon.

That wouldn't leave time enough for the records to changed and old memories replaced with false ones.

Bill grinned to himself. So he'd be a hero, after all, with his supposed death probably explained as a cover-up for initial flight. They'd find some way to explain it all, of course.

He shouldered another load of hydroponic tanks to replace those Wollen had left on the Moon, and his face sobered. It would take more than heroism. It would take men too stubborn to have good sense.

"Pumpkins!" he said with a new depth of feeling, "Tomatoes!"

He carried the tanks into the ship and began bolting them down, ready for an early planting.

Thunder in Space

I

In the little formal garden in Geneva, the guards had withdrawn discreetly, out of sight and hearing of the two men who sat on a carved marble bench in the center of the enclosure.

The president of the United States was too old for the days of strained public and private meetings and the constant badgering of his advisers that had preceded this final, seemingly foredoomed effort. His hands trembled as he lifted them to light a cigarette. Only his voice still held its accustomed calm.

"Then it's stalemate, Feodor Stepanovich. I can make no more concessions without risking impeachment."

The dark, massive head of the Russian Premier nodded. "Nor can I, without committing political suicide." His English was better than the rural dialect of Russian he still retained. "Call it a double checkmate. Our predecessors sowed their seeds too deep for our spades. Or should I say, too high?"

Both heads turned to the north, where a bright spot was climbing above the horizon. The space station sparkled in sunlight far above Earth, sliding with Olympian deliberation past a few visible stars until it was directly overhead. Without a timetable or a telescope, there was no way of knowing whether it was the Russian *Tsiolkovsky* or the American *Goddard*, nor did either man care. Half the world lived in almost hysterical fear of one or the other, with the rest of the human race existing in terror of both.

The Premier muttered something from the ugliness of his childhood experiences, but the President only sighed unhappily, as if sorry that his own background gave him no such expressions.

A few minutes later, the leaders separated. As they moved across the garden, their escorts surrounded them, clearing the way toward the cars that would take them to the airport. Behind them, professional diplomats stopped puzzling over the delay and began spinning obfuscations to cynical reporters. The phrases had long since lost all meaning, but the traditions of propaganda had to be maintained.

In the UN, the Israeli delegate crumpled a news dispatch and began speaking without notes, demanding that space be internationalized. It was the greatest speech of his career, and even the delegate from Egypt applauded. But national survival could not be trusted to the shaky impartiality of the UN. The resolution was vetoed by both the United States and Russia.

The Fourteenth Space Disarmament Conference was ended.

II

A month later, a thousand miles above Earth and exactly 180° behind the *Tsiolkovsky*, the *Goddard* swung steadily around the globe in a two-hour circumpolar orbit. Outwardly, it looked like the great metal doughnut that space artists had pictured for decades. On the inside, however, the evidence of hasty, crash-planned work was everywhere. The air fans whined and vibrated, the halls creaked and groaned, and the water needed to maintain balance gurgled and banged through ill-conceived piping. It was cramped and totally inadequate for the needs of the nation that had put it into space eight years before in a rush attempt to match the Russian "*Sulky*."

Jerry Blane should have been used to such conditions. He'd been one of the original space-struck men who'd helped to build it and then had been lucky enough to get a permanent assignment. Now he drifted in the weightless hub, watching the loading of a ship bound back for the home planet, wondering what hell's brew the boxes contained. The project that had usurped the cryogenic labs had involved its own crew of scientists, who were already on board the ship, taking their secret with them.

He shrugged, trying to dismiss the problem. The motion twitched him about, and he corrected automatically. His tall, thin body was accustomed to weightlessness.

Beside him, the head of the science corps on the station also floated in midair. The big body of Dr. Austin Peal was revealed in the single pair of shorts customary on the *Goddard*, and its darkness contrasted sharply with the blond hair and pale skin of Blane. Only the frowns matched.

The short, intense figure of General Devlin popped into the hub from the tube elevator ahead of the pilot, Edwards. In spite of the weightlessness, the station commandant managed to pull himself to rigid attention at sight of Blane. He scowled, but held out his hand with formal correctness.

"All right, Blane. You're in charge officially until I get back," he admitted grudgingly. He obviously resented the order that left a civilian in charge while he went down to testify for the station appropriations and receive new orders. "You'll find detailed notes on my desk. I suggest you follow them to the letter."

He grabbed a handhold and began pulling himself into the airlock to the ship without waiting for a reply.

Edwards had lingered. Now he also held out his hand. "Wish me luck, Jerry," he said. "I may need it."

***

Because of the contents of the boxes and the presence of Devlin, Edwards had been ordered to make his landing at Canaveral, under military security. Most space work was done from Johnston Island in the Pacific; the inadequate facilities at the Cape were supposed to be used only by smaller rockets. But lately the rules were shot in a lot of ways. Ever since the last meeting at Geneva, nothing seemed normal.

"You'll make out," Drake told him. "Our predictions give you perfect landing weather, at least."

"Yeah. Clear weather and thunder below." In the station slang, thunder stood for heavy trouble. The weather forecast didn't matter; there was always thunder below.

Edwards moved through the airlock and into his ship. A moment later, fire bloomed from the rocket tubes and the ship began moving away. In the station, motors began whining, restoring the hub's spin to match that of the rest of the *Goddard*.

From the viewing ports, Earth filled almost the entire field of vision, like a giant opal set in black velvet. More than half was covered by bright cloud masses, but the rest showed swirls and patterns of blue water, green forest and reddish brown barren patches. Over everything lay the almost fluorescent blue of atmosphere, forming a brilliant violet halo at the horizon. It looked incredibly beautiful. So, Blane thought, does a Portuguese man-of-war-until one sees the slime underneath or touches the poisoned stings.

"Why can't they leave us alone?" Peal asked, as if reading Blane's mind. "Why can't they blow themselves up quietly without ruining our chances here?" Blane chuckled bitterly. He'd been on vacation down there a month before, and Earth was fresher in his memory than it was to Peal. "They don't see it that way. To them, we're the danger, the biggest sword of Damocles ever invented. They look up and see us going overhead, loaded with enough megaton bombs to blast life off Earth. Every time we orbit over them, they see Armageddon right over their heads, waiting some fool's itching finger. They could risk the holocaust when everything was halfway around the world, but not when it's where they can look up and see it. Most of the thunder down there is caused by the chained lightning we're carrying up here."

It wasn't an original idea. The panic on Earth had been increasing since the building of the Russian station. Now panic bred false moves, and errors bred more panic. Sooner or later, that panic could get out of hand and bring about the very ruin they feared.

"Besides," he added, "there's the expense of keeping us up here. They think the billions needed to maintain us are pauperizing them."

"We're paying three to one on every cent we get! Even forgetting the work in astronomy, biochemistry, cryogenics and high-vacuum research, our weather predictions are worth billions a year in crop returns."

Blane shrugged. "Most of our work is for the government without payment, so Congress still has to appropriate billions for us yearly. That's all the people see. We're poison down there. They'd vote to ditch us if they weren't so scared of the bombs on the *Sulky*."

"That's what comes of putting scientific tools under government control," Peal grumbled. "The stations should have been private enterprises from the beginning."

Blane nodded automatically. It was an old argument, and it made sense. But there was no chance of the government ever letting go now. They took the clanking elevator down toward the rim, while weight built up to the normal one-third Earth gravity that was produced by the spin at the outer edge of the *Goddard*. Then they moved along the hallway that circled the rim, through the recreation hall, past the vacuum labs that were busy with some kind of military development, and past the cryogenic section, where men were busy getting ready to resume normal work. Beyond that lay the weather study section. It should have been located in the hub, but there had been too little room, and the pickups were remotely controlled, flashing their pictures of Earth onto big screens here. Now the screens showed Madagascar to the west of them as they swung northward. Men were busy plotting the final details for next month's weather predictions.

Peal followed Blane through the side door into the little office of Devlin. The General was something of a martinet, but his discipline extended to himself. Everything was in order, and the list of instructions lay in a folder in the center of the desk. Blane glanced at it, then at the basket of communications from Earth. He grimaced, and passed some of the flimsies over to Peal. "There's more evidence, if you want to prove the profit we could show."

There were requests for projects to be done here, complaints—often angry—at projects already okayed but delayed by high-priority military research. There were applications from names already famous below. Five foundations were demanding that the lunar ships be rushed to completion.

The intercom came to life with a rasping parody of the voice of Devlin's secretary. "Mr. Blane, Captain Manners insists on seeing you. He's been waiting nearly an hour."

Blane flipped through Devlin's instructions. There was an entry on Manners there: *Troublemaker, possibly paranoid. Add his figures to HQ report as routine only.*

"Send him in," Blane ordered. The red-headed young captain had been assigned here only six months ago, but Blane had met him often enough to like him.

Almost at once, the connecting office door opened and Manners shoved in. He was obviously angry, but his voice didn't show it. "Thanks for seeing me, Blane. I'd just about decided you wouldn't." He slapped a piece of film down on the desk. "Here. Look at that!"

The film was slightly darkened. Blane turned it over, recognized it as one of the strips worn by the men who worked in the bomb section to warn of any accidental exposure to radiation. But it was well under any dangerous levels of exposure. He passed it to Peal, who studied it curiously.

"That's in five hours of routine work in the bomb bay," Manners said. "Routine work! And I checked the films before issuing them, so I know they weren't pre-exposed." He pulled out a sheet of paper covered with figures and dropped it on the desk. "The radiation's up in there again. Check it yourself if you won't accept my readings."

Peal had grabbed up the figures which listed the radiation count in various sections of the bomb bay. They meant nothing to Blane, but the scientist tensed visibly as he studied them.

"I gather you showed your figures to Devlin," Blane said. "What did he say about them?"

Bitterness washed over Manner's face. "He told me to forget it, that readings were higher here than what I'd learned handling warheads below because we got so many cosmic rays. Three months ago, they were a lot higher, and he said there was an increase in cosmic radiation. But he okayed my getting the air pumped out of the bay so nothing hot would be sucked into the rest of the station. Last month, the figures went up to about half what they are now, and he mumbled something about a cosmic ray storm. I haven't been able to see him since then."

"There's no such thing as a cosmic ray storm," Peal said, flatly. "Why wasn't this reported to me? It's partly my province."

"General Devlin ordered me not to discuss it with anyone!"

"Thunder?" Blane asked the scientist.

"If it keeps doubling every month, it's disaster! The thin walls here are no protection from radiation. Even now, we'd better evacuate the bio labs beside the bay. Captain Manners, we'll have to check you on this. I'm not exactly doubting your word, but these results are impossible according to anything I know." He swung to Blane. "I think you'd better come, too, Jerry. This may be something for the authorities, and you carry the weight here now."

It was a lousy beginning to his temporary command, Blane thought. But seeing Peal's face, he simply nodded and followed the other two out into the hall. They were heading toward the bomb section when a shout went up from some of the men watching the viewing screen.

Blane swore to himself, but turned back.

He saw at once that the screens were set for top magnification, showing a section of Earth at the extreme limits of resolution. A glance at the projected coordinates showed that they were over southern Russia. His eyes were untrained at grasping details, but he saw enough to recognize that they must be viewing the great Russian rocket base that supplied the *Sulky*.

Scarfield had taken over from his subordinate and began picking out details with a moving spot of light. "Rocket—see its shadow? And there—there—there. Jerry, they've got every ship they own assembled together. And it looks as if they've been running supplies to them all. Something big's due."

"Attack?" Blane asked. One of the jobs of the station was to spot any clustering of military rockets that might presage a ground-based attack.

Scarfield shook his head. "Not a chance. Those are space rockets, not war missiles. This is like the massed flight they sent up about two years ago, remember? We never did figure out why they had to take the whole fleet out. But with what's going on below, this must mean something important. Think we should alert HQ?"

They obviously should, as soon as they were over one of their own stations. The rule was clear on that—when in doubt, shout! But meantime, they'd have to watched while still in view.

There was a faint spot of light, and Scarfield grunted. "They're blasting off! Maybe we can plot orbits and—"

The bright spot split into lances of fire, exploding savagely outwards! Every drop of monopropellant in the tanks must have let go at once to make such a flare. Then, before Blane could catch his breath, there was another flare and another. Suddenly the whole field was a great spread of flame as the other rockets were exploded by the savage blast of the first.

Before the *Goddard* had passed beyond view, they knew that every Russian ship on the field was totally demolished—which meant, according to Scarfield's estimate, every ship that could make the trip up to the *Sulky*.

They stared at the screen in shocked silence while Blane slowly began to realize the implications. It had happened while they were directly overhead. What would that mean to the ever-suspicious people of Russia who were already conditioned to think of the *Goddard* as their greatest enemy? What could be made of that in a world already close to the edge of panic?

III

By the time the *Goddard* was over the North Pole where she could make radio contact with Alaska, the news was already out. For once, Tass had released the news of a catastrophe without delay. The ground radio confirmed the fact that every supply ship for the *Sulky* had been wiped out, and that the detonation had been so great that even ships being assembled nearby had been wrecked hopelessly. It would be three months before Russia could again reach her station.

Later news filtered in slowly. Most of it had to be picked up from the regular FM news broadcasts that filtered through the ionosphere. A couple of the scientists who had learned Russian interpreted the news from Radio Moscow on their next trip over.

Surprisingly, there were no claims of American sabotage. Then Blane wondered whether it was so surprising. With the level of fear in Russia as high as elsewhere, it would probably have been a grave mistake for the leaders to suggest that any American sabotage of territory so far inside Russia was possible. The people had to count on the invulnerability of their station for what little hope they had; how that worked when the supply ships were already ruined was more than he could guess, but he had long since given up trying to understand the devious game of propaganda being played on Earth.

At least for the moment, the disaster was not being turned into another excuse to push the seemingly inevitable war another millimeter closer to the brink. Maybe the whole affair might result in some decline of tension. Once the American ships were sent up to supply the *Sulky* on an emergency basis, there might be a little good will from Russia and self-satisfaction at a good deed in America. That could give a breathing spell.

Blane had almost forgotten Manners and the worry over the strange increase in radioactivity. He had sent Manners' latest figures down with a query for instructions at the first chance to do so by tight-beam radio that would not leak security, and then had let the matter drop from his mind. It was several hours later when his secretary announced that Peal and Manners were in the outer office.

Manners looked both more worried and strangely satisfied, as if he were bursting to cry his I-told-you-so. But Peal's face was drained of any emotion except surprise.

The scientist nodded. "Captain Manners' figures were quite accurate. We've got to evacuate nearby sections of the station. In a way, we're lucky—radiation travels in straight lines, and the hull curves away from it here. There is about three hundred times normal radiation in there, and it's coming from inside the warheads. It isn't lethal yet—men can work there for a few hours at a time; but at the rate it's increasing, it soon will be. Any word from Earth?"

Blane dug through his in basket, and finally located a blue slip. It was in code, but Devlin's instructions included the location of the code book. He riffled through it for phrases each decagraph covered. *Situation within normal expectations—results being studied here—continue as at present—will apprise if new procedure advisable—regard as utmost top secret—invoke maximum security measures over affected personnel.*

"No word," he said bitterly. Probably he wasn't even supposed to say that much, or to discuss it with the other two. But he chose to interpret the part about continuing as at present to permit the discussion to continue. He tried to focus his mind on what facts he knew. "I thought the radiation rate of the stuff in the warheads was constant, and that the casings were adequate shielding."

Peal nodded. "That's what's driving me out of my mind at the moment, Jerry. Except when it reaches critical mass, uranium-235 is supposed to have an absolutely fixed half life; it shouldn't increase under any circumstances, and the mass of each section in those bombs can't increase to become nearer critical, either. It simply can't happen, according to any physics I ever learned. But it's doing so."

"What about the effects of cosmic rays?" Blane asked. Devlin might have learned more from Earth, and even if his story to Manners had been patently untrue, it might still offer some clue.

Peal shook his head, but somewhat doubtfully. "On Earth, they're mostly only mesons from strikes by cosmic radiation. Out here, we get only the extremely hard radiation—the shielding of the ship is too thin to affect them. Maybe they might speed up the half-life a little—but they shouldn't make it increase. I've been thinking about them, too. Meteorites show a much greater decay of uranium to lead than the ores on Earth, which might indicate some effect from cosmic radiation. But unless they somehow produce another isotope from uranium that's raising the activity, I can't figure it out. We need a top level nuclear physicist for this, and we don't have one here."

They discussed it at greater length, but without adding anything to their speculations. Blane felt the hairs on the back of his neck prickling, and was conscious of a vague picture in his mind of the warheads ticking away and getting set to blast spontaneously. But he put the idea aside. Earth might be a little careless of their welfare under the pressure of emergency, but right now Earth would never risk losing the station. It was only his overactive imagination.

He finally assigned Peal and Manners back to the task of studying the matter as best they could, and tried to dismiss it from his mind. There were more than enough other worries about the station. The cryogenics lab was in trouble—the group from Earth who had used the labs had badly depleted supplies and been careless about equipment that was common enough below but difficult to obtain here. The evacuation of the laboratories near the bomb bay threw severe strains on research, and Earth was demanding that some of it be speeded up. And the weather study was being crippled by the need to waste too much attention on detailed studies of every section of Russia. The whole station was on emergency orders to do twice as much as could possibly be done.

He waited for news that supplies were being sent from Johnston Island to the *Sulky*, but no such news appeared. Instead, the news carried details that were only rumors of some effort of the United States to force Russia to disarm the *Sulky* unilaterally in return for the loan of eight rocket ships and launching facilities. If such an offer had been made, it must have been turned down flatly. The next day there was not even a mention of it.

When Edwards came up again, Blane sent for him at once. The pilot had made a superb landing of his ship at Canaveral, and had then been jetted back to the Island. Normally he would have taken a long layover there before making another trip up, though he had senior pilot's right to select or refuse any flight he chose. Blane was curious about his reason for choosing the first trip he could make.

Edwards lost no time in reporting. He hadn't stopped to remove his emergency space suit, though he'd left the helmet and the oxygen tank somewhere. He clumped in, accepted coffee, and began talking even as he shucked off the suit.

"It's a wonder they even let me fly up supplies to you," ho grumbled. "Jerry, it's rough down there. They've got everything everthing sewed up under controls. I'm surprised they didn't suspect me of plotting an orbit for the *Sulky* instead of here. Damn all governments that have to mess into space affairs!"

Some of the details came out slowly, with more color than clarity. But Blane gathered that they had reacted violently to the news that the government was trying to use the emergency as a means of forcing disarmament on the Russian station.

"You mean they actually did refuse help without such an agreement?" Blane asked. He hadn't wanted to believe the rumors.

Edwards nodded angrily. "They issued a ban against any efforts to help without such agreement. They most certainly did! And you can guess how that set with us. Maybe the *Sulky*'s full of Russians, but they're Russian spacemen! Hell, when we were building this wheel here and one worker got thrown out into space, three of their pilots came up in ships to help find him—and one did find him. Remember? Sure you do. They hated our building here, but they wouldn't let a man die in space if they could help. So we owe them a few trips."

Two of the pilots had tried to steal one of the ships fueled and supplied for the *Goddard*, but had been caught before they could take off. Now they were under guard, and the ships were being watched carefully. Edwards had been permitted to make the run only after a session in which it was pointed out that landing rights would be denied any ship contacting the *Sulky*. And the other pilots were almost in a state of revolt, with nearly all of the old-time ground force supporting them.

"The government can't stick to such a policy," Blane said doubtfully. "They can't gain anything. The *Sulky* must have enough supplies for existence until at least one ship can be assembled and sent up. All we'll do by holding them up is to increase the danger. They must be bluffing for a while, hoping Russia will crack, but ready to send supplies in a few days."

Edwards stared at him in surprise. "You mean you don't know?" Then he slapped his thigh in disgust. "No, of course you don't. I keep forgetting you couldn't. The *Sulky* couldn't reach you by radio with the Earth in between. Jerry, we got a beamed message on the Island from her when she went over one time. SOS. She's in trouble right now. Can't get help from her base, and can't wait for negotiations, so she tried calling us direct. Security clamped down on the message at once, but the radio operator's as much space as we are, so he made a dupe copy for the pilots. The day after the blowup at the base, the *Sulky* ran into a meteoroid big enough to rip out part of her solar boiler. She lost most of the mercury into space, and the rest isn't enough, even when she's patched. She has to operate on batteries right now, and that won't last more than another day or so."

Blane winced at the picture. A station was dependent on power for its existence. Lights, air circulation, water for balance, heat regulation, and even the growing of plants to keep the air breathable depended upon a steady supply of power. Like the *Goddard*, the *Tsiolkovsky* used a reflecting trough on top that directed the intense solar radiation onto a pipe filled with mercury which was heated to gaseous form and operated the boiler and generator. It was far cheaper and safer than atomic power.

"The government knew of that when it refused help?" he asked incredulously.

Edwards grunted. "Didn't start their extortion plans until they knew!" Then he grinned slowly. "Funny thing, Jerry, when I checked over the supplies I brought up for you, I found some of the boxes of equipment got mixed up in shipment. They're full of cans of mercury! I left them aboard the ship, figuring you wouldn't need them here."

Blane found his face muscles were trying to frown and smile at the same time, and he caught himself before he could laugh. He went to the door to make sure it was locked, and came back to his desk slowly.

In theory, it was entirely possible to reach the *Sulky* from the *Goddard*, and every pilot knew the general orbit. The *Sulky* and the *Goddard* each took two hours to circle Earth, with one an hour behind the other. If a ship took off outward with a reasonable use of power it could get into an ellipse around Earth that would take three hours to bring it back to its starting point—and by then, the opposite station would be at that point. The maneuver could be made both ways with the fuel a final stage carry easily enough.

"You don't have fuel enough," he decided.

"Nope. But you do—out in the blasted lunar ships that are still waiting appropriations."

Blane hadn't had time to think of the lunar ships during the hectic days of commanding the station. But Edwards' statement was true enough. The ships had been nearing completion for the long-desired American exploration of the Moon a year ago when Congress had eliminated appropriations for everything not connected with the current emergency. They still trailed the station a few miles in space. The workers had all returned to Earth, but the fuel still lay in the plastic balloons. The little ferry ship used between the ships and the station was still here, too. It could be used to bring the fuel back easily, since it had been equipped with tanks for moving fuel between supply rockets and the balloons.

"It wouldn't work," he said at last. "They'd spot your ship from Earth if you took off for the *Sulky*. They'd even guess where you'd gone when you didn't return on schedule. They might even refuse to let you land, and they'd probably make things impossible up here, too."

"I'll take my chances—and so will you," Edwards protested.

"Not unless it's necessary. Sure, somebody's got to make the trip. But it doesn't have to be your ship. The ferry's a lot smaller, but it can handle that much cargo and fuel on such an orbit." He grinned at Edwards' stubborn expression. "Look, you know I ran it for a year while we built the station. I can still pilot it, and Austin Peal can handle the math in computing the orbit. I'll get it over to you and you can transship the mercury, then take off on schedule. Then let Earth guess what happens."

"And what will they do to you if they find out?"

"Nothing—officially. Nobody has told me officially that the policy is against offering help, so I'll proceed in terms of the older tradition. When you let slip the trouble on the *Sulky* and I found cans of mercury stored in the ferry, what could I do but assume the station was expected to get them to the other station?" Blane grinned, feeling sudden relief from his other worries. "Besides, I don't give a darn what they do to me. I'm only temporary boss here."

Edwards nodded. "I'll take your last reason, Jerry. Only don't bother moving the ferry. I can work it over beside my ship, and it'll make your explanation sound better. Good luck. And if you do get in a jam—all the guys will be on your side."

He went out while Blane started off to find Peal. He had doubts about involving the scientist now. The man had never been part of a real space team. Yet someone had to do the preliminary computing. He had more doubts as he tried to explain things to Peal; the man listened quietly, making no comment, and with no visible approval or disapproval.

When Blane finished, Peal stood up, nodding. "Thanks for letting me in on it, Jerry. You get the fuel and I'll have the computations off the calculator by the time you get back here."

IV

The ferry was a sausage-shaped structure of thin metal and plastic with an airlock at the front and a small reaction motor at the rear. It had been modified to hold either solid or liquid cargo and to operate off the monopropellant fuel instead of the lox and kerosene used when the station was built. There was even a plastic pipe between the cargo tank and its fuel tank to save separate filling, and no further modification was needed. Blane took it out after checking the stowage of the mercury cans. He was slightly rusty, but he steadied down as he jockeyed into position beside one of the three lunar ships. He'd picked a balloon on the sunward side, and the warm fuel was soon flowing into his tank, forced through a long tube by a tiny, built-in pump. When he took off again, the ferry was overloaded and sluggish, but it showed no evidence of weakness. Of course, if they ran into a meteoroid of any size, they'd be ruined—but the chances of that were very slight.

Peal was already outside the hub, dressed in space suit and clinging to a convenient handhold. He came through the lock, carrying his computations, a small telescope, and an extra spacesuit for Blane. "May need this," he suggested. "Our front end probably won't fit the seal on their hub."

Blane nodded. He should have thought of it. But his chief interest was in the orbit. It had been figured so that they would accelerate away from the station and up from Earth at low thrust, well within the limits of his power. There was a table of times and star angles to locate his correct course. Peal had done an excellent job, far better than Blane had expected.

"I spent two years on the Island," the scientist explained. "I learned a little about astrogation, though I'm no navigator. But this is a simple problem."

Essentially, it was; to make it simpler, it was always possible to make minor corrections, since they had more than enough fuel.

"If the stations were run properly, there'd be a regular service between them," Peal suggested when they were coasting along in their orbit. "It would be cheaper to exchange supplies than to rush up a sudden emergency shipment from Earth. In fact, if a private company had built the first one, there would probably be a dozen stations by now all connected. And we'd take over the television relay business, too."

At times, Peal sounded like the editorials from a business magazine, but Blane could find no fault with his logic. The fact was that the stations were basically service companies, delivering useful services for which they could collect enormous fees without complaints. But they were forced to render most of their service to a military struggle no one wanted and for which no one wanted to be forced to pay.

Peal went on, warming to his theme. "History proves my point, Jerry. The stations have to be too complicated in function and too flexible in purpose to be run properly by men who have to think in terms of Earth politics. Every nation that ever tried controlling a major industrial set-up has found it won't work. They tried socializing railroads, airlines and factories—not to mention farming—and the experiment failed. Every Russian industry today is run independently by its own board who share in the profits, no matter how much theoretical ownership rests with the government. And China is now nothing but a system of state capitalism, whatever they call it there."

"Fine," Blane admitted. "Why didn't private industry build the stations, then?"

Peal grimaced, then grinned. "That's the weak point, of course. You can't sell shares to fund a venture until the public sees the need—and they couldn't see the need of space until military pressure put the stations up and proved they had other values. But now the stations have proved themselves. The government should turn them back to private hands under long term loans, the same as they turned back factories after the war."

"They won't, though. And it's not just that no power is ever voluntarily given up," Blane pointed out. "They won't sell the stations because they're up here where no government on Earth could tax them. They might eventually, otherwise, but no government is going to lose its profit without getting taxes in return." For a second, Peal started to argue. Then an expression of surprise crept onto his face. He sat silently through most of the trip. Like most scientists, he'd probably considered himself a fair amateur economist, but he'd overlooked one of the most basic aspects of economy—the fact that governments also had to operate on enough of a profit to pay their executives and bond-holders.

At the end of the wide-looping three hour orbit, Blane was surprised and pleased to see that he could locate the Russian station through the telescope. They had made corrections according to Peal's figures, and the scientist had proved to be a better astrogator than could have been expected. Only a tiny corrective blast was needed to bring them into line with the Sulky.

As they drew near, Blane stared in amazement. He'd seen pictures, but they had never conveyed the true feeling of the station. Russia had a tradition of building massively for space. Her early ships had been heavy and unsophisticated, relying on strength, size and power. The station was the same. It resembled the *Goddard* superficially, but it was three times as large, and must contain more than twenty times the total volume. It had a solid, substantial look that was indefinable.

The ferry contained a tiny radio, but Blane had not expected it to be useful, since it was adjusted for the frequencies that had been used by the work forces who built the *Goddard*. He reached out and turned it on, expecting nothing. Yet there was a voice coming from it, speaking excellent English. It was a female voice, and a pleasant one.

"Ahoy, space taxi! *Tsiolkovsky* calling taxi. Oh, for Pete's sake, don't you Americans have two-way radio? Wiggle your tail or something so I'll know you're receiving, and I'll give you landing instructions!"

Peal grinned and picked up the microphone. "Ahoy, *Sulky*."

"Ah. So you can answer. Then if you can match our orbit, come beneath the hub. The smallest landing net will fit the nose of your taxi, if our records are correct. You did bring the mercury, didn't you?"

"We brought it," Peal assured her.

"Then in the name of science and humanity, I thank you. And—and I'm so glad to see you, I'll be there to kiss you welcome!"

"There are two of us," Peal started to answer, but she had clicked off. He watched as Blane began jockeying into position, cranking furiously at the little weighted wheel that controlled the angle of the ferry. "Pretty sure we'd come wasn't she?"

"Edwards had a beam antenna on his ship. He could have tipped the *Sulky* off on his way down," Blane said. The little ship was finally lined up and he blasted forward gently against the small landing net. The nose settled firmly into a silicone doughnut that formed a perfect airtight seal. They wouldn't even need to wear spacesuits.

***

There were three girls and four men waiting for them inside the enormous hub. Six moved forward promptly to begin transferring the cans of mercury, but one girl, shorter, darker and prettier than the others, stepped forward. She kissed both of them solemnly on both cheeks after the Russian formal fashion. Then she held out her hand.

"I'm Dr. Sonya Vartanian."

Peal introduced Blane and himself. After the handshaking, Blane gestured toward the main station, eager to see it and looking for an excuse. "I'm delighted to know you. But I think I'd better see your commanding officer."

"I'm in command." She said it quite simply. Then at their surprise she chuckled. "We don't have the male chauvinism of America. Besides, all the military officers were below when—when everything was destroyed. But perhaps you'd like to see our station?"

There was a great deal that seemed to be handmade where American products were smoothly machine made. But generally, it was something to arouse envy in Blane. Obviously, there had been no effort made to save on costs here, and the great Russian boosters had lifted fantastic weights where American engineers had been limited to what ships of lesser thrust would carry. With no restrictions on cost or size, the Russian engineers had simply designed for what they felt desirable, rather than what was possible. The command suite was even equipped with a bar that contained a private refrigerator, though that was now off, due to the need to save power.

The quarters of the staff were spacious, and many showed signs of never having been occupied. The laboratories were beautifully equipped, and again less than a third had ever been used.

"We had great plans—but now we are limited. The threat of war makes even our leaders hesitate to begin so many long-range plans," she explained.

Peal nodded. "You see, Jerry? It's the same here. Waste and inefficiency. This place could make ten times the profit of any other comparable investment, but it's wasted under government control."

Sonya darted him a sudden piercing gaze and stopped in her tracks. Then she laughed uncertainly. "You'll forgive me, Dr. Peal. But those words—they were just what I was going to say."

"You?" Blane stared at her doubtfully. "Isn't capitalistic talk deviationist, at least?"

"Not to an American, and sometimes now not at all." She said, as if relaxing from some strain. "We study American economics in our schools, just as we learn your language. Sometimes capitalism seems romantic to us—selling stocks, floating loans, such things. But sometimes I think about what could be done if this were all to be a separate nation, free for all time."

They crossed a great empty section of the station, and Blane recognized that they had already been through there twice before. He saw that Sonya was staring at him intently again as he glanced about more carefully. He moved closer to her, his eyes moving from her face to scratches on the floor and back. She shook her head faintly, and he let the question die unasked.

They ended the grand tour in her office. The power was already on, and the refrigerator was humming. There was no ice, but there was cold water for the drinks she offered them. "You might stay for dinner," she suggested.

Peal seemed embarrassed. "You'll need your supplies…" he began.

"Supplies?" She laughed at that. "Dr. Peal, here we have supplies to last twice our number for a year, even without a ship. You will stay?"

Blane shook his head. They'd spent too much time already. She accepted the refusal and accompanied them to the waiting taxi, holding out her hand in farewell.

"Sometime, when you need help, remember we are here," she told them. "If there should be any danger or trouble, we are anxious to offer you what we can give."

It was delivered in an almost formal tone, as if now she were rephrasing from her own language.

The trip back was simpler than the first trip, since the ferry now carried no cargo and only half as much fuel. It responded more readily. Peal was silent until they were well away from the *Sulky*. Then he shook his head as if coming out of a brown study.

"Jerry, where do they keep their bombs? We covered every single inch of that station—we went into every room and cranny. I watched to make sure she wasn't just doubling back. She did, sometimes, but she showed us the whole thing, all the same. And there were no bombs or missiles big enough to dump warheads on Earth. There was one place where they should have been, with what could have been outside release chutes. But it was empty, though there were scratches on the floor where missiles might have stood."

Blane nodded, remembering the place they'd been led across three times. "I know, I saw it. They don't have bombs. They had them, but they're gone. And Sonya Vartanian meant us to see it, too. She didn't quit leading us across the place until she knew I'd guessed."

Why let us know? So we could report that they've been pulling a colossal bluff at those disarmament meetings? That doesn't make sense."

"No." Blane had been doing his own thinking. "Nobody would believe us—it's incredible, and they'd be sure we'd been duped neatly. They wouldn't dare believe us. And it isn't because Russia is too civilized to use bombs, either; that station was better designed for war than ours, and policies don't change that fast. My guess is that they've been gone from the station two years now."

Peal considered it. "That would be when we spotted the first mass of all their ships together-probably carrying the missiles back to Earth in emergency action. Then that flight that blew up must have been set to carry new missiles up, right?"

Blane nodded. It wasn't a happy idea. It would have taken some very good reason for Russia to remove her missiles during a period of rising tension and hold off for two years before further pressures forced her to resume the idea of stockpiling weapons in space.

He studied the distant *Goddard* through his telescope as they began to draw near. "Maybe I'm wrong, Austin. But they first put warheads out in space a couple of years before we could. And maybe those warheads began to go through a rapid increase in radioactivity a couple of years before Manners noticed that ours were doing the same. If so, it must have been a pretty serious warning to make the officials disarm the station secretly."

"The girl wanted us to see that the bombs were gone, and she couldn't talk about it. Then she put too much emphasis on that business of offering help if we were in danger." Peal grimaced. "It all adds up."

"How much longer will we have?" Blane asked.

The scientist shook his head. "I don't know, Jerry, and I'm not good enough a physicist to find out."

V

The return was a letdown, the tension they had been building between them. Blane put the ferry away, leaving no traces of the trip in it, and slipped quietly back into the hub. Things looked miserable now, cramped and forced together, after the spaciousness and richness of equipment on the other station. But he forced that bitterness from his mind.

A Congressman had stated the official policy years before. "Sure, they got something bigger and stronger. But we got the old American spirit. Didn't our boys conquer the whole British navy with nothing but little wooden sailing ships once?" And hence, of course, it didn't matter how badly matched the stations might be. Nobody bothered to comment that the American fleet had grown strong by freebooting, that both sides were using little wooden ships, and that there was never more than a small fraction of the British navy along the American coast. Facts merely got in the way of good sentiment. The Congressman had been elected three times since then and still fought hard to keep any money from getting into space, though he yelled loud and often for the need of teaching the enemy a good lesson.

Blane went to his little room, to bathe in water that was at least hot and clean, and to change into fresh shorts. He had been gone for nearly nine hours, and fatigue had made him look older, but it wasn't too much different from his looks after a sound sleep. He went into the office, yawning. The secretary glanced up, shoved a new mountain of complaints and thunder-scripts at him, and went on answering the phone. Apparently, he hadn't been too much missed. It wasn't flattering, but he'd expected it.

Routine held him for hours, while he listened to the news from Earth. The Russians were announcing that they had never asked for help from the American supply ships, that the *Tsiolkovsky* was quite safe, and that under no conditions would any political deals be made under threats and pressure. It was done with a nastiness that lent a ring of sincerity to it.

And somewhere, the rumors seemed to indicate, America had modified her stand, and was now making overtures toward helpfulness, which were brusquely refused. There had been an obvious loss of support from some of the smaller nations in the UN, and that must have hurt.

Peal came in, looking more haggard than Blane. The scientist shook his head wearily. "The count is up in the bomb bay. I've been trying to sound some of the chemists out about ways to test, but I don't think we can do it. We don't know what to do or to look for. But I'm convinced now that something is going on inside those casings. It must be some new isotope being created from the uranium by the action of cosmic radiation. Those energies are high enough to cause transmutation. Whatever isotope it is, it must be a neutron emitter, and it's stirring up the uranium, just as increasing the mass does. The temperature around the casings is rising."

"Still no idea of how much margin we have?"

"Not exactly. But I can get some idea from watching how the temperature rises. Maybe a few days, maybe a couple of months." Peal dropped to a couch, rubbing his eyes. "It's getting too hot in there to work without a protective screen, so we can only make short tests. But Manners and I will take turns."

Headquarters was not greatly impressed by the rise in temperature that had been noted, though the reply was longer in coming this time. It simply suggested he stand by for later orders.

That night, a large meteorite fell in Arkansas. It was metallic, and big enough so that several hundred pounds managed to survive the burning friction of Earth's atmosphere. A large area saw the bright streak across the sky and traced it to where it fell. There it's impact had knocked over trees, destroyed a house and the inhabitants, and killed a cow. There was a large hole in the ground where it had hit, and still a trace of metallic fragments around the cup.

Blane picked up the news accounts almost at once on the radio in his office. He switched the circuits around to connect all the speakers in the station and threw the master switch, giving everyone a chance to hear.

It took almost no time for the first reports to come babbling in hysterically, claiming an atomic missile had been sent down from the *Tsiolkovsky*.

The official signal from Headquarters flashed out at Blane, and he listened. They were declaring a general alert, but it wasn't red and there was still a delay. Once it went red, it would mean putting one of the plans already prepared into operation, demanding that he send his few men down into the bomb bay to set the automatic chutes into operation. Then missiles would rain down on Russian cities and bases.

Peal and Manners came in. Manners would have to carry out the orders. Blane glanced at him, and saw doubt and worry etched across the forehead. Could any man start the holocaust going? Or, believing that the *Sulky* would be throwing bombs, as Manners must still believe, could any man refuse such an order?

Blane shook his head faintly as he met Peal's look. There were no bombs on the *Sulky*. And no bombs must fall from the *Goddard*. But in the long run, would it maike any difference. There were more than enough land-based missiles to wipe out both countries. And if Blane saw them on his screens, getting set to wipe out his nation, could he refuse to order the bombs here into operation?

He threw the side door of the office open and heard the mad action going on outside as men were beaming down the full power of their radio signals, giving the true nature and path of the meteorite, trying to override the frantic chaos already filling the atmosphere.

Then the light winked out. A voice that was weak and shaken came from all the speakers. "Attention. This is official! The object that fell from space has been determined to be a natural meteorite. No attack has been initiated. There is no cause for alarm…"

Blane cut off his speakers and went back into his cabin, shaking with reaction.

This time, there had been no holocaust. This time the alert had never gone red, and sane minds had somehow prevailed. But how long would sanity hold sway in a world where every unnatural accident was a potential trigger for a rain of bombs, a storm that might destroy most of the life on Earth and would certainly end man's adventure into space. It wouldn't really matter whether the stations managed to get off without retaliatory missiles from Earth; once the ships and supply bases were gone, there would be no possibility of continuing life here. The men who fired the missiles from these floating arsenals would be committing a long and horrible suicide. Yet he might have to order it—might reach a stage where he would even want to order it!

Peal was waiting for him with the report on the temperature of the casings when he came into the office the next day. There had been an increase of nearly two degrees, and it began to look as if the rise were an asymptotic one, that might get out of hand so quickly that there would be little warning.

"It's not much of a secret, either," the scientist stated. "I don't think Manners said anything, and I've kept it as tight as I could. But there are indirect ways of noting things going on, and the temperature gages in the hull show signs already. The men who service the bomb bay aren't all fools, either. They can guess there's trouble when they're sent in for only minutes at a time. So rumors are spreading."

Blane nodded. If the rumors got out of hand, things would go to pot in ways that might make it impossible for them to meet an emergency later. He threw the master switch for general summons again, and began speaking slowly, choosing his words with care. He wasn't going to lie, but he couldn't give them full information. He was already violating security to an extent that could bring full official wrath on him.

He told them that there was evidence that radioactivity was leaking from the warheads, though not in any measure to endanger the station at present. He said simply that there had been some related increase in temperature noted, and that the situation was being studied and reported to Earth, where fuller analysis was possible. It was all true, so far as it went-and the impression was as false as he could make it.

By the time the station was over Denver, where he could contact headquarters on his tightest beam, most of the rumors had died, and the men were discussing the situation without much excitement.

Surprisingly, headquarters took his report and switched him directly to a human, instead of the tape receiver he usually had to deal with. He gave the basic facts, and reported precisely on the fact that he had been forced to inform the crew of the station.

The voice from below sighed wearily across the thousand miles of space. "Quite right, Blane. Panic would be the worst thing you could have. Forget about the violation—we all have to cut that at times. Now, in regard to your basic situation, I'm going to do the best I can for you. But I wouldn't worry about your boiler trouble yet. It will be at least three days before repairs are really necessary, and before then Devlin will be back with you. He has a full grasp of what must be done. And good luck."

The voice cut off.

Blane sat staring at the wall. Three days—it could only mean that there were three days still to go before the runaway radiation inside the casings built up too high for something to be done—whether to dump the bombs or what, he couldn't guess. But that was shaving it pretty thin.

And how sure could he be that they knew what was going on? They had only his coded figures to go by. Yet he had to trust them. For once, he'd be glad when Devlin was back.

He called Manners and Peal in. "Seal off the bomb bay," he told them. "Just stick up a sign making it off limits and spread the word that nobody's to go in until Devlin gets back here—which will be in a couple of days." He grinned at their protests, and shook his head. "And that means off limits to you, too. Earth says we're safe until Devlin gets here, and he'll have orders. Until then, we can't do anything, so forget the warheads."

It would be a lot easier for the crew of the station to accept than would the sight of Peal and Manners going in and out in constant efforts to check. And there was nothing that their tests could show, anyhow; nobody here knew enough to interpret what the readings meant.

For a change, a sort of lucky accident helped him. One of the pipes in the circulating system got clogged with something that should never have reached the water and burst. It made a mess of most of one deck, and took a full day's cleaning and repairing. That type of misfortune was something the *Goddard* had long since grown used to, and the sight of great scientists working with cooks and power men was always a relief from the routine. Maybe stations should be built to fail in minor ways. If ever a ship was built to cross the vast gulf to another star, it should be as imperfect as safety permitted.

On the surface, everything was routine by the time Devlin's ship came up the next day. Devlin must have more pull on Earth, Blane decided; something had boosted his stock. The ship had taken off from Cape Canaveral—the same ship that had taken him down—in a tricky but successful maneuver. Edwards, of course, had been called in for the job.

Blane had only a few words with the pilot, but he gathered the ship would be standing by to take Devlin off again at some undecided later time.

General Devlin came into the office with brisk, precise steps, and stood looking at Blane with a perfect picture of a military man regarding an inferior. His short body was as straight as a rod, and his head was at precisely the right posture. But his face looked grey, and a muscle under one eye twitched. He motioned sharply as Blane stood up to relinquish the seat behind the desk.

"At ease. Stay where you are. I've been cramped in a hammock for hours, I prefer to stand. I'm not taking over your command this time, anyhow; I'm merely here to execute one order before I have to report back down there. How's the trouble here?"

He listened to Blane's report, but hardly seemed to hear it. He was apparently fully aware of everything that Blane could tell him. When it was done, he nodded. "I was told to fill you in. I'll make it brief. Dr. Peal's theory that ultra hard radiation has caused the transmutation of some of the uranium to a more dangerous isotope is correct. This effects the same results as raising the mass of each segment of the uranium trigger to critical level eventually. But there is still time to save the station, and the level of radiation will not make it dangerous for the squad to handle the missiles; they will be exposed too short a time. I would appreciate it if you would instruct Captain Manners and his men to assemble in the hub in fifteen minutes. I'll join you there."

It wasn't a lot to work on, Blane decided. But he nodded as Devlin went out, pacing toward the coffee in the rec hall. He put through the orders and shortly moved out to join the eight men and Manners. In the hub were stacked a number of boxes. He counted them, and nodded. There was one for each of the missiles.

"Looks like we dump the missiles," Manners suggested, relief heavy in his voice. "Those must be program tapes for the guidance computers on the missiles."

Devlin's voice sounded sharply behind them, bringing them to attention. If he had heard Manners, he gave no sign of it.

"In those boxes are tapes for the missiles. You are all familiar with their installation and the operation of loading the missiles into the outer chutes. Each of you will take one pile of the tapes and repair to the bomb bay. You are to enter there at precisely nine hundred. The bay is hot, but not dangerous for the length of time required to complete this operation. Captain, how long should the operation of moving all bombs into chutes require?"

"About twenty minutes, sir." There were motorized winches that did the work, and the chutes were one of the few pieces of mechanism on the *Goddard* that had not been made shoddily.

"Very good. Then at nine twenty, I shall expect you to emerge from the bomb bay and seal it again. You will then report to Mr. Blane for further instructions."

***

The orders could have been given just as easily outside the bomb bay, or to Manners alone, Blane realized. The whole affair was too precise, too much by the book. He frowned as he watched Manners and the men pick up the little boxes and move toward the elevators. They were in no great hurry, since they still had fifteen minutes before they were to enter the bomb bay. Then they were gone. And Devlin shuddered faintly and began wiping his face with a kerchief. Something cold shot up from Blane's throat to the roof of his mouth.

"What's the destination on the tapes?" he asked sharply.

Devlin stared at him or through him. Then the stiff body bent a trifle in a faint bow. "I suspect you've guessed it, Blane. They are all set to take an elliptical orbit that will bring them against the *Tsiolkovsky* in mid-Pacific."

"They can't!" But Blane knew that they could be set for just that—they had to be set for such an orbit. With their bomb stock about to become useless in a matter of a few days, and with too little time to replace them after the realization of what was happening, the military mind could decide that the only hope was to eliminate the danger from the other station. It would mean a stalemate in space, and might possibly still leave Russia doubtful enough about the striking power left on the *Goddard* to intimidate her out of retaliating.

"It would wipe men out of space!" he protested. "You've got to cancel the order."

Again Devlin gave the faint bow. "Unfortunately, I have no authority to cancel that order, Mr. Blane. I cannot do so."

Blane felt his fist move from his hip before he realized what he planned. It was an awkward blow, as all activity in nearly zero gravity must be, but it connected. Devlin was lifted from his weak contact with the floor and his head banged savagely against the roof. He drifted back toward the deck, unconscious. Blane caught himself and dashed for the elevator. There was still time to broadcast the facts to the station and to stop the men from entering the bomb bay. After that, he no longer cared what happened to him.

VI

The meeting Blane had called in the rec hall had been brief. Men and women had stared incredulously at him as he told them the facts—all the facts this time. There hadn't even been a vote, since none was needed. Now they were scurrying about, hastily following the orders he had given. Manners was destroying the tapes, the weather men were collecting the reports of future weather that should have been filed within the next few days, and others were gathering what bits of scientific material and notes they could. Edwards had somehow joined them and was already out in the little ferry, heading for the big lunar ship that was fueled and almost completed.

Devlin sat in the hub still. He was conscious now, but the blood on his head ruined what would otherwise have been a fine military posture. He made his slight bow, smiling bitterly in recognition of his helplessness.

"I'm oddly grateful to you, Blane," he said. "But I don't expect you to believe me. And I find I regret what will happen to you and the men here when this catches up with you. What are your plans for me?"

Blane hadn't thought of that. He watched through the port as the ugly, clumsy lunar ship moved toward the ship, to a distance where the ferry could be used to carry them all out to it.

"You can pilot a ship, I remember. Take Edwards' ship and go back to the Island," he decided at last.

Devlin smiled. "I thought of that, too. But with your permission, I'd rather come with you. I'm curious. And I give you my word I shall not interfere in any way. Your case is hopeless, of course—but so is mine."

Blane shrugged. "Come along, then."

Loading everyone into the lunar ship was a horrible period of chaos. It had never been meant to hold such a cargo of goods and people. But somehow room was found, and Edwards began moving out and away from the *Goddard*—the station that was now empty, except for the warheads that were growing hotter with each hour.

"I've called the Island," he said to Blane. "If the message got to anyone except some lumphead, I think they'll be waiting for us." Blane nodded, but he found little reaction to any news now. He had made his plans in some split moment between striking Devlin and reaching the office. There was nothing now to add to them. There was only a grim determination and the hope that all spacemen must share it—the determination that somehow, men had to stay out here and find an honest destiny in space.

Three hours later, when their long ellipse brought them within sight of the *Tsiolkovsky*, he saw that there were ships around the station. There were no more than half a dozen now, but he could see others approaching. It was impossible for all to leave at once, but the men there had elected to join him, and they had found enough sympathy among the staff of the Island to gain control long enough to accomplish their decision.

The awkward lunar ship came to a reluctant stop less than half a mile from the station, and Blane began picking those who were to go with him aboard the little ferry that was in tow. Manners and Peal and two others. He was looking for a sixth when Devlin moved into the group. Blane started to order him aside, and then shrugged.

They were almost as crowded in the taxi that Edwards piloted as they had been on the lunar ship. But there was no thought of that. The others were taking their cue from Blane, and Blane was simply waiting, frozen in his determination until events could shape his moves.

The landing net snapped around them, and they settled into the silicone ring, and then began moving into the huge hub of the *Sulky*.

At least a dozen people were waiting there—too many, Blane realized. He hadn't bothered to consider the size of the group he must meet. But he disregarded that.

Sonya Vartanian moved forward to greet him with the double kiss and handshake. Her eyes were unreadable, but her voice was warm. "Welcome, gentlemen. I am delighted that you remembered our offer of aid in time of trouble. You have our assurance that—"

Blane cut her off with a hasty gesture. He wanted no speeches from her. It had to be done at once, or forgotten, as he had planned it. His mind had no second line of action. He began to speak authoritatively;

"In the name of the free territory of space, I seize this ship and all that is on it," he continued coldly, "I sever all ties any may have with Earth herewith. I ban all military operations from space. I declare that no nation may own property in space, but may only trade according to the just laws and practices that shall be henceforth established for space. I—"

He was wound up to the point where he could not stop, though there was nothing more to say at the moment.

But a sudden sound choked off his words. It was a shout from those who had come to meet the crew from the *Goddard*. It was a long, surprised crescendo that slowly became a cheer.

Sonya leaned forward, grasping his hands "Thank God," she cried in his ear. "Oh thank God. I was so afraid you wouldn't see it."

He blinked, beginning to feel foolish. "You mean that you agree? Without resistance?"

"We've been trying to find some way to make it happen for two years—ever since our commander refused to permit our decaying missiles to be used against your station," she told him. "But we never really believed it could happen."

Blane knew that he had never believed it, either.

He pulled her closer, beginning to smile again. "In the name of the free territory of space!" he said, and kissed her.

VII

The blaze in the heavens that had signalled the end of the *Goddard* was less than twelve hours old. It had been a magnificent funeral pyre to an epoch, but it had not yet ended the methods of diplomacy. It had merely forced faster action.

The Premier of Russia and the President of the United States sat together, trying to keep their voices down and yet hear each other over the noise and confusion of the assembly hall in the UN building. They were surrounded by guards, as usual, and the television cameras were focused on them. But they had so far been unable either to agree or disagree. They could only wait until the time announced had arrived, as most of the world was now waiting.

Then the great system of amplifiers and speakers went into operation, and quiet began to descend over the hall.

There must have been a greeting of some formal kind, but few heard it. Jerry Blane's tired voice was already setting forth his written statement of demands when the quiet was sufficient for him to be heard. He read with the voice of a man not used to making a written speech sound natural, but nobody noticed.

The announcement of the facts was obvious, but it took on added power from the brevity that compressed everything into a single focus. America had lost a station and Russia had no supply ships. There was a supply base on Johnston Island, but the ships were all in space. Earth was completely cut off from contact with space for months to come.

And Earth could no longer exist without that contact. Her next weather reports were needed within the week, and without them the damage to crops grown dependent on them might result in famine for much of Earth. Certain drugs had to be made in space. There were hundreds of needs, without which the economy of Earth would collapse. Today, in a real sense, Earth could exist only by the use of a station in space.

But the station could exist for a longer time without Earth. There was food and supplies for more than a year. They were prepared to wait, if need be.

"You cannot use force," Blane's voice stated flatly. "For the first time, the governments of Earth cannot fall back on destruction when everything else fails. To destroy us would make your economic collapse inevitable now. You cannot go back to your past or the savage rules of your past. You can only meet us honestly and concede the just demands we propose."

Many were surprised at the proposals—the joint work of two years of thought on the *Tsiolkovsky* and a final flash of insight on the part of Blane. They wanted recognition from the UN that they were an independent territory. They wanted to incorporate as an independent stock company on Earth, under direct

UN charter. For that, they were willing to pay reasonable taxes on operations done within any country. They were willing to pay a reasonable price, to be settled by a committee of neutral nations, for the two stations, for ships—and even for the Russian ships that were destroyed—and for complete sovereignty over Johnston Island, which would now be worthless to Earth, They would pay for this by the selling of stock, which could be redeemed in time through the profits that were easily provable as more than adequate to meet their debts. And they were to have full control of further ventures and services to be transacted on the station. Weather predictions would be on a subscription basis, research on the station would be by lease, and other services could be adjusted to a fair market value.

There was more, but much of it was only repetition to make sure all was understood. It finished with a simple request for a quick decision, since no more business could be done with Earth until the agreements had been reached.

The President nodded. "You'll agree?" he asked.

"What else can we do?" the Premier asked in return. "He's right. We can't continue today without the services we're used to from space. A series of accidents has left us no choice."

The President settled back, apparently satisfied. But he was less sure. Had there been accidents involved? Some man must have hated war in space enough to sabotage a fleet of ships. Other men had hated that same war enough to break all discipline and strike out against a whole planet. And men and women on two separate stations had so detested the thought of being crushed in a surface struggle that they had independently schemed for this proposal.

He let his eyes rest on the delegate from Israel who was yielding to the delegate from Saudi Arabia. It didn't matter who made the resolution to accept the proposal of Blane on a tentative basis. There would be no veto possible now.

And on Earth, the tension was relaxing already. Perhaps now, even the surface enmities could be settled in time.

The Fifteenth Space Disarmament Conference was ending.

My Name Is Legion

Bresseldorf lay quiet under the late-morning sun—too quiet. In the streets there was no sign of activity, though a few faint banners of smoke spread upward from the chimneys, and the dropped tools of agriculture lay all about, scattered as if from sudden flight. A thin pig wandered slowly and suspiciously down Friedrichstrasse, turned into an open door cautiously, grunted in grudging satisfaction, and disappeared within. But there were no cries of children, no bustle of men in the surrounding fields, nor women gossiping or making preparations for the noon meal. The few shops, apparently gutted of foodstuffs, were bare, their doors flopping open. Even the dogs were gone.

Major King dropped the binoculars to his side, tight lines about his eyes that contrasted in suspicion with his ruddy British face. "Something funny here, Wolfe. Think it's an ambush?"

Wolfe studied the scene. "Doesn't smell like it, Major," he answered. "In the Colonials, we developed something of a sixth sense for that, and I don't get a hunch here. Looks more like a sudden and complete retreat to me, sir."

"We'd have had reports from the observation planes if even a dozen men were on the roads. I don't like this." The major put the binoculars up again. But the scene was unchanged, save that the solitary pig had come out again and was rooting his way down the street in lazy assurance that nothing now menaced him. King shrugged, flipped his hand forward in a quick jerk, and his command moved ahead again, light tanks in front, troop cars and equipment at a safe distance behind, but ready to move forward instantly to hold what ground the tanks might gain. In the village, nothing stirred.

Major King found himself holding his breath as the tanks reached antitank-fire distance, but as prearranged, half of them lumbered forward at a deceptive speed, maneuvered to two abreast to shuttle across Friedrichstrasse toward the village square, and halted. Still, there was no sign of resistance. Wolfe looked at the quiet houses along the street and grinned sourly.

"If it's an ambush, Major, they've got sense. They're waiting until we send in our men in the trucks to pick them off then, and letting the tanks alone. But I still don't believe it; not with such an army as he could throw together."

"Hm-m-m." King scowled, and again gave the advance signal.

The trucks moved ahead this time, traveling over the rough road at a clip that threatened to jar the teeth out of the men's heads, and the remaining tanks swung in briskly as a rear guard. The pig stuck his head out of a door as the major's car swept past, squealed, and slipped back inside in haste. Then all were in the little square, barely big enough to hold them, and the tanks were arranged facing out, their thirty-seven millimeters raking across the houses that bordered, ready for an instant's notice. Smoke continued to rise peacefully, and the town slumbered on, unmindful of this strange invasion.

"Hell!" King's neck felt tense, as if the hair were standing on end. He swung to the men, moved his hands outward. "Out and search! And remember—take him alive if you can! If you can't, plug his guts and save his face—we'll have to bring back proof!"

They broke into units and stalked out of the square toward the houses with grim efficiency and rifles ready, expecting guerrilla fire at any second; none came. The small advance guard of the Army of Occupation kicked open such doors as were closed and went in and sidewise, their comrades covering them. No shots came, and the only sound was the cries of the men as they reported "Empty!"

Then, as they continued around the square, one of the doors opened quietly and a single man came out, glanced at the rifles centered on him, and threw up his hands, a slight smile on his face. "*Kamerad!*" he shouted toward the major; then in English with only the faintest of accents: "There is no other here, in the whole village."

Holding onto the door, he moved aside slightly to let a search detail go in, waited for them to come out. "You see? I am alone in Bresseldorf; the Leader you seek is gone, and his troops with him."

Judging by the man's facial expression that he was in no condition to come forward, King advanced; Wolfe was at his side, automatic at ready. "I'm Major King, Army of Occupation. We received intelligence from some of the peasants who fled from here yesterday that your returned Führer was hiding here. You say—"

"That he is quite gone, yes; and that you will never find him, though you comb the earth until eternity, Major King. I am Karl Meyers, once of Heidelberg."

"When did he leave?"

"A matter of half an hour or so—what matter? I assure you, sir, he is too far now to trace. Much too far!"

"In half an hour?" King grimaced. "You underestimate the covering power of a modern battalion. Which direction?"

"Yesterday," Meyers answered, and his drawn face lighted slightly. "But tell me, did the peasants report but one Führer?"

King stared at the man in surprise, taking in the basically pleasant face, intelligent eyes, and the pride that lay, somehow, in the bent figure; this was no ordinary villager, but a man of obvious breeding. Nor did he seem anything but completely frank and honest. "No," the major conceded, "there were stories.

But when a band of peasants reports a thousand Führers heading fifty thousand troops, we'd be a little slow in believing it, after all."

"Quite so, Major. Peasant minds exaggerate." Again there was the sudden lighting of expression. "Yes, so they did—the troops. And in other ways, rather than exaggerating, they minimized. But come inside, sirs, and I'll explain over a bottle of the rather poor wine I've found here. I'll show you the body of the Leader, and even explain why he's gone—and where."

"But you said—" King shrugged. Let the man be as mysterious as he chose, if his claim of the body was correct. He motioned Wolfe forward with him and followed Meyers into a room that had once been kitchen and dining room, but was now in wild disarray, its normal holdings crammed into the corners to make room for a small of mechanism in the center and a sheeted bundle at one side. The machine was apparently in the process of being disassembled.

Meyers lifted the sheet. "*Der Führer,*" he said simply, and King stopped with a gasp to examine the dead figure revealed. There were no shoes, and the calluses on the feet said quite plainly that it was customary; such few clothes as remained had apparently been pieced together from odds and ends of peasant clothing, sewed crudely. Yet on them, pinned over the breast, were the two medals that the Leader alone bore. One side of the head had been blown away by one of the new-issue German explosive bullets, and what remained was incredibly filthy, matted hair falling below the shoulders, scraggy, tangled beard covering all but the eye and nose. On the left cheek, however, the irregular reversed question-mark scar from the recent attempt at assassination showed plainly, but faded and blended with the normal skin where it should have been still sharp after only two months' healing.

"An old, old man, wild as the wind and dirty as a hog wallow," King thought, "yet, somehow, clearly the man I was after."

Wolfe nodded slowly at his superior's glance. "Sure, why not? I'll cut his hair and give him a shave and a wash. When we're about finished here, we can fire a shot from the gun on the table, if it's still loaded...good! Report that Meyers caught him and held him for us; then, while we were questioning him, he went crazy and Meyers took a shot at him."

"Hm-m-m." King's idea had been about the same. "Men might suspect something, but I can trust them. He'd never stand a careful inspection, of course, without a lot of questions about such things as those feet, but the way things are, no really competent medical inspection will be made. It'll be a little hard to explain those rags, though."

Meyers nodded to a bag against the wall. "You'll find sufficient of his clothes there, Major; we couldn't pack out much luggage, but that much we brought." He sank back into a rough chair slowly, the hollow in his cheeks deepening, but a grim humor in his eyes. "Now, you'll want to know how it happened, no doubt? How he died? Suicide—murder; they're one and the same here. He died insane."

The car was long and low. European by its somewhat unrounded lines and engine housing, muddy with the muck that sprayed up from its wheels and made the road almost impassable. Likewise, it was stolen, though that had no bearing on the matter at hand. Now, as it rounded an ill-banked curve, the driver cursed softly, jerked at the wheel, and somehow managed to keep all four wheels on the road and the whole pointed forward. His foot came down on the gas again, and it churned forward through the muck, then miraculously maneuvered another turn, and they were on a passable road and he could relax.

"Germany, my Leader," he said simply, his large hands gripping at the wheel with now needless ferocity. "Here, of all places, they will least suspect you."

The Leader sat hunched forward, paying little attention to the road or the risks they had taken previously. Whatever his enemies might say of his lack of bravery in the first war, there was no cowardice about him now; power, in unlimited quantity, had made him unaware of personal fear. He shrugged faintly, turning his face to the driver, so that the reversed question-mark scar showed up, running from his left eye down toward the almost comic little moustache. But there was nothing comic about him, somehow; certainly not to Karl Meyers.

"Germany," he said tonelessly. "Good. I was a fool, Meyers, ever to leave it. Those accursed British—the loutish Russians—ungrateful French—troublemaking Americans—bombs, retreats, uprisings, betrayals—and the two I thought were my friends advising me to flee to Switzerland before my people—Bah, I was a fool— Now those two friends would have me murdered in my bed, as this letter you brought testifies. And the curs stalk the Reich, such as remains of it, and think they have beaten me. Bonaparte was beaten once, and in a hundred days, except for the stupidity of fools and the tricks of weather, even he might have regained his empire... Where?"

"Bresseldorf. My home is near there, and the equipment, also. Besides, when we have the—the legion with us, Bresseldorf will feed us, and the clods of peasants will offer little resistance. Also, it is well removed from the areas policed by the Army of Occupation. Thank God, I finished the machine in time."

Meyers swung the car into another little-used but passable road, and opened it up, knowing it would soon be over. This mad chase had taken more out of him than he'd expected. Slipping across into Switzerland, tracking, playing hunches, finally locating the place where the Leader was hidden had used almost too much time, and the growth within him that would not wait was killing him day by day. Even after finding the place, he'd been forced to slip past the guards who were half protecting, half imprisoning the Leader and used half a hundred tricks to see him. Convincing him of the conspiracy of his "friends" to have him shot was not hard; the Leader knew something of the duplicity of men in power, or fearful of their lives. Convincing him of the rest of the plan had been harder, but on the coldly logical argument that there was nothing else, the Leader had come. Somehow, they'd escaped—he still could give no details on that—and stolen this car, to run out into the rain and the night over the mountain roads, through the back ways, and somehow out unnoticed and into Germany again.

The Leader settled more comfortably into the seat with an automatic motion, his mind far from body comforts. "Bresseldorf? And near it—yes, I remember that clearly now—within fifteen miles of there. There's a small military depot those damned British won't have found yet. There was a new plan—but that doesn't matter now; what matters are the tanks, and better, the ammunition. This machine—will it duplicate tanks, also? And ammunition?"

Meyers nodded. "Tanks, cars, equipment, all of them. But not ammunition or petrol, since once used, they're not on the chain any longer to be taken."

"No matter. God be praised, there's petrol and ammunition enough there, until we can reach the others; and a few men, surely, who are still loyal. I was beginning to doubt loyalty, but tonight you've shown that it does exist. Someday, Karl Meyers, you'll find I'm not ungrateful."

"Enough that I serve you," Meyers muttered. "Ah, here we are; good time made, too, since it's but ten in the morning. That house is one I've rented; inside you'll find wine and food, while I dispose of this car in the little lake yonder. Fortunately, the air is still thick here, even though it's not raining. There'll be none to witness."

The Leader had made no move to touch the food when Meyers returned. He was pacing the floor, muttering to himself, working himself up as Meyers had seen him do often before on the great stands in front of the crowds, and the mumbled words had a hysterical drive to them that bordered on insanity. In his eyes, though, there was only the insanity that drives men remorselessly to rule, though the ruling may be under a grimmer sword than that of Damocles. He stopped as he saw Meyers, and one of his rare and sudden smiles flashed out, unexpectedly warm and human, like a small, bewildered boy peering out from the chinks of the man's armor. This was the man who had cried when he saw his soldiers dying, then sent them on again, sure they should honor him for the right to die; and like all those most loved or hated by their fellowmen, he was a paradox of conflictions, unpredictable.

"The machine, Karl," he reminded the other gently. "As I remember, the Jew

Christ cast a thousand devils out of one man; well, let's see you cast ten thousand out of me—and devils they'll be to those who fetter the Reich! This time I think we'll make no words of secret weapons, but annihilate them first, eh? After that—there'll be a day of atonement for those who failed me, and a new and greater Germany—master of a world!"

"Yes, my Leader."

Meyers turned and slipped through the low door, back into a part of the building that had once been a stable, but was now converted into a workshop, filled with a few pieces of fine machinery and half a hundred makeshifts, held together, it seemed, with hope and prayer. He stopped before a small affair, slightly larger than a suitcase, only a few dials and control knobs showing on the panel, the rest covered with a black housing. From it, two small wires led to a single storage battery.

"This?" The Leader looked at it doubtfully.

"This, Leader. This is one case where brute power has little to do, and the proper use everything. A few tubes, coils, condensers, two little things of my own, and perhaps five watts of power feeding in—no more. Just as the cap that explodes the bomb may be small and weak, yet release forces that bring down the very mountains. Simple in design, yet there's no danger of them finding it."

"So? And it works in what way?"

Meyers scowled, thinking. "Unless you can think in a plenum, my Leader, I can't explain," he began diffidently. "Oh, mathematicians believe they can—but they think in symbols and terms, not in the reality. Only by thinking in the plenum itself can this be understood, and with due modesty, I alone in the long years since I gave up work at Heidelberg have devoted the time and effort—with untold pure luck—to master such thought. It isn't encompassed in mere symbols on paper."

"What," the Leader wanted to know, "is a plenum?"

"A complete universe, stretching up and forward and sidewise—and durationally; the last being the difficulty. The plenum is—well, the composite whole of all that is and was and will be—it is everything and everywhen, all existing together as a unit, in which time does not move, but simply is, like length or thickness. As an example, years ago in one of those American magazines, there was a story of a man who saw himself. He came through a woods somewhere and stumbled on a machine, got in, and it took him three days back in time. Then, he lived forward again, saw himself get in the machine and go back. Therefore, the time machine was never made, since he always took it back, let it stay three days, and took it back again. It was a closed circle, uncreated, but existent in the plenum. By normal nonplenar thought, impossible."

"Someone had to make it." The Leader's eyes clouded suspiciously. Meyers shook his head. "Not so. See, I draw this line upon the paper, calling the paper now a plenum. It starts here, follows here, ends here. That is like life, machines, and so forth. We begin, we continue, we end. Now, I draw a circle—where does it begin or end? Yes, followed by a two-dimensional creature, it would be utter madness, continuing forever without reason or beginning—to us, simply a circle. Or, here I have a pebble—do you see at one side the energy, then the molecules, then the compounds, then the stone, followed by breakdown products? No, simply a stone. And in a plenum, that time machine is simply a pebble—complete, needing no justification. since it was."

The Leader nodded doubtfully, vaguely aware that he seemed to understand, but did not. If the machine worked, though, what matter the reason? "And—"

"And, by looking into the plenum as a unit, I obtain miracles, seemingly. I pull an object back from its future to stand beside its present. I multiply it in the present. As you might take a straight string and bend it into a series of waves or loops, so that it met itself repeatedly. For that, I need some power, yet not much. When I cause the bending from the future to the present, I cause nothing—since, in a plenum, all that is, was and will be. When I bring you back, the mere fact that you are back means that you always have existed and always will exist in that manner. Seemingly, then, if I did nothing, you would still multiply, but since my attempt to create such a condition is fixed in the plenum beside your multiplying at this time, therefore I must do so. The little energy I use, really, has only the purpose of not bringing you exactly within yourself, but separating individuals. Simple, is it not?"

"When I see an example, Meyers, I'll believe my eyes," the Leader answered. Meyers grinned, and put a small coin on the ground, making quick adjustments of the dials. "I'll cause it to multiply from each two minutes," he said. "From each two minutes in the future, I'll bring it back to now. See!"

He depressed a switch, a watch in his hand. Instantly, there was a spreading out and multiplying, instantaneous or too rapid to be followed. As he released the switch, the Leader stumbled back from the hulking pile of coins. Meyers glanced at him, consulted his watch, and moved another lever at the top. The machine clicked off. After a second or so, the pile disappeared, as quietly and quickly as it had come into being. There was a glint of triumph or something akin to it in the scientist's eyes as he turned back to the Leader.

"I've tried it on myself for one turn, so it's safe to living things," he answered the unasked question.

The Leader nodded impatiently and stepped to the place where the coins had been piled. "Get on with it, then. The sooner the accursed enemies and traitors are driven out, the better it will be."

Meyers hesitated. "There's one other thing," he said doubtfully. "When the—others—are here, there might be a question of leadership, which would go ill with us. I mean no offense, my Leader, but—well, sometimes a man looks at things differently at different ages, and any disagreement would delay us. Fortunately, though, there's a curious by-product of the use of the machine; apparently, its action has sonic relation to thought, and I've found in my experiments that any strong thought on the part of the original will be duplicated in the others; I don't fully understand it myself, but it seems to work that way. The compulsion dissipates slowly and is gone in a day or so, but—"

"So?"

"So, if you'll think to yourself while you're standing there: 'I must obey my original implicitly; I must not cause trouble for my original or Karl Meyers,' then the problem will be cared for automatically. Concentrate on that, my Leader, and perhaps it would be wise to concentrate also on the thought that there should be no talking by our legion, except as we demand."

"Good. There'll be time for talk when the action is finished. Now, begin!"

The Leader motioned toward the machine and Meyers breathed a sigh of relief as the scarred face crinkled in concentration. From a table at the side, the scientist picked up a rifle and automatic, put them into the other's hands, and went to his machine.

"The weapon will be duplicated also," he said, setting the controls carefully. "Now, it should be enough if I take you back from each twenty-four hours in the future. And since there isn't room here, I'll make the duplicates in rows outside. So."

He depressed the switch and a red bulb on the control panel lighted. In the room, nothing happened for a few minutes; then the bulb went out, and Meyers released the controls. "It's over. The machine has traced ahead and brought back until there was no further extension of yourself; living, that is, since I set it for life only."

"But I felt nothing." The Leader glanced at the machine with a slight scowl, then stepped quickly to the door for a hasty look. Momentarily, superstitious awe flicked across his face, to give place to sharp triumph. "Excellent, Meyers, most excellent. For this day, we'll have the world at our feet, and that soon!"

In the field outside, a curious company was lined up in rows. Meyers ran his eyes down the ranks, smiling faintly as he traced forward. Near, in almost exact duplication of the man at his side, were several hundred; then, as his eyes moved backward, the resemblance was still strong, but differences began to creep in. And farthest from him, a group of old men stood, their clothes faded and tattered, their faces hidden under mangled beards. Rifles and automatics were cupped in the hands of all the legion. There were also other details, and

Meyers nodded slowly to himself, but he made no mention of them to the Leader, who seemed not to notice.

The Leader was looking ahead, a hard glow in his eyes, his face contorted with some triumphant vision. Then, slowly and softly at first, he began to speak and to pace back and forth in front of the doorway, moving his arms. Meyers only half listened, busy with his own thoughts, but he could have guessed the words as they came forth with mounting fury, worked up to a climax and broke, to repeat it all again. Probably it was a great speech the Leader was making, one that would have swept a mob from their seats in crazy exultation in other days and set them screaming with savage applause. But the strange Legion of Later Leaders stood quietly, faces betraying varying emotions, mostly unreadable. Finally the speaker seemed to sense the difference and paused in the middle of one of his rising climaxes; he half turned to Meyers, then suddenly swung back decisively.

"But I speak to myselves," he addressed the legion again in a level, reasonable voice. "You who come after me know what is to be this day and in the days to come, so why should I tell you? And you know that my cause is just. The Jews, the Jew-lovers, the Pluto-democracies, the Bolsheviks, the treasonous cowards within and without the Reich must be put down! They shall be! Now, they are sure of victory, but tomorrow they'll be trembling in their beds and begging for peace. And soon, like a tide, irresistible and without end, from the few we can trust many shall be made, and they shall sweep forward to victory. Not victory in a decade, nor a year, but in a month! We shall go north and south and east and west! We shall show them that our fangs are not pulled; that those which we lost were but our milk teeth, now replaced by a second and harder growth!

"And for those who would have betrayed us, or bound us down in chains to feed the gold lust of the mad democracies, or denied us the room to live which is rightfully ours—for those, we shall find a proper place. This time, for once and for all, there shall be an end to the evils that corrupt the earth—the Jews and the Bolsheviks, and their friends, and friends' friends. Germany shall emerge, purged and cleansed, a new and greater Reich, whose domain shall not be Europe, not this hemisphere, but the world!

"Many of you have seen all this in the future from which you come, and all of you must be ready to reassure yourselves of it today, that the glory of it may fill your tomorrow. Now, we march against a few peasants. Tomorrow, after quartering in Bresseldorf, we shall be in the secret depot, where those who remain loyal shall be privileged to multiply and join us, and where we shall multiply all our armament ten-thousandfold! Into Bresseldorf, then, and if any of the peasants are disloyal, be merciless in removing them! Forward!"

One of the men in the front—the nearest—was crying openly, his face white, his hands clenched savagely around the rifle he held, and the Leader smiled at the display of fervor and started forward. Meyers touched his shoulder.

"My Leader, there is no need that you should walk, though these must. I have a small auto here, into which we can put the machine. Send the legion ahead, and we'll follow later; they'll have little trouble clearing Bresseldorf for us. Then, when we've packed our duplicator and I've assembled spare parts for an emergency, we can join them."

"By all means, yes. The machine must be well handled." The Leader nodded and turned back to the men. "Proceed to Bresseldorf, then, and we follow. Secure quarters for yourself and food, and a place for me and for Meyers; we stop there until I can send word to the depot during the night and extend my plans. To Bresseldorf!"

Silently, without apparent organization, but with only small confusion, the legion turned and moved off, rifles in hands. There were no orders, no beating of drums to announce to the world that the Leader was on the march again, but the movement of that body of men, all gradations of the same man, was impressive enough without fanfare as it turned into the road that led to Bresseldorf, only a mile away. Meyers saw a small cart coming toward them, watched it halt while the driver stared dumbly at the company approaching. Then, with a shriek that cut thinly over the distance, he was whipping his animal about and heading in wild flight toward the village.

"I think the peasants will cause no trouble, my Leader," the scientist guessed, turning back to the shop. "No, the legion will be quartered by the time we reach them."

And when the little car drove up into the village square half an hour later and the two men got out, the legion was quartered well enough to satisfy all prophets. There was no sign of the peasants, but the men from the future were moving back and forth into the houses and shops along the street, carrying foodstuffs to be cooked. Cellars in the stores had been well gutted, and a few pigs were already killed and being cut up—not skillfully, perhaps, but well enough for practical purposes.

The Leader motioned toward one of the amateur butchers, a copy of himself who seemed perhaps two or three years older, and the man approached with frozen face. His knuckles, Meyers noted, were white where his fingers clasped around the butcher knife he had been using.

"The peasants—what happened?"

The legionnaire's face set tighter, and he opened his mouth to say something; apparently he changed his mind after a second, shut his mouth, and shrugged. "Nothing," he answered finally. "We met a farmer on the road who went ahead shouting about a million troops, all the Leader. When we got here, there were a few children and women running off, and two men trying to drag away one of the pigs. They left it behind and ran off. Nothing happened."

"Stupid dolts! Superstition, no loyalty!" The Leader twisted his lips, frowning at the man before him, apparently no longer conscious that it was merely a later edition of himself. "Well, show us to the quarters you've picked for us. And have someone send us food and wine. Has a messenger been sent to the men at the tank depot?"

"You did not order it."

"What—No, so I didn't. Well, go yourself, then, if you…but, of course, you know where it is. Naturally. Tell Hauptmann Immenhoff to expect me tomorrow and not to be surprised at anything. You'll have to go on foot, since we need the car for the machine."

The legionnaire nodded, indicating one of the houses on the square. "You quarter here. I go on foot, as I knew I would." He turned expressionlessly and plodded off to the north, grabbing up a half-cooked leg of pork as he passed the fire burning in the middle of the square.

The Leader and Meyers did not waste time following him with their eyes, but went into the house indicated, where wine and food were sent in to them shortly. With the help of one of the duplicates, space was quickly cleared for the machine, and a crude plank table drawn up for the map that came from the Leader's bag. But Meyers had little appetite for the food or wine, less for the dry task of watching while the other made marks on the paper or stared off into space in some rapt dream of conquest. The hellish tumor inside him was giving him no rest now, and he turned to his machine, puttering over its insides as a release from the pain. Outside, the legion was comparatively silent, only the occasional sound of a man walking past breaking the monotony. Darkness fell just as more food was brought in to them, and the scientist looked out to see the square deserted; apparently the men had moved as silently as ever to the beds selected for the night. And still, the Leader worked over his plans, hardly touching the food at his side.

Finally he stirred. "Done," he stated. "See, Meyers, it is simple now. Tomorrow, probably from the peasants who ran off, the enemy will know we are here. With full speed, possibly they can arrive by noon, and though we start early, fifteen miles is a long march for untrained men; possibly they could catch us on the road. Therefore, we do not march. We remain here."

"Like rats in a trap? Remember, my Leader, while we have possibly ten thousand men with rifles, ammunition can be used but once—so that our apparently large supply actually consists of about fifty rounds at most."

"Even so, we remain, not like rats, but like cheese in a trap. If we move, they can strafe us from the air; if we remain, they send light tanks and trucks of men against us, since they travel fastest. In the morning, therefore, we'll send out the auto with a couple of older men—less danger of their being recognized—to the depot to order Immenhoff here with one medium tank, a crew, and trucks of ammunition and petrol. We allow an hour for the auto to reach Immenhoff and for his return here. Here, they are duplicated to a thousand tanks, perhaps, with crews, and fueled and made ready. Then, when the enemy arrives, we wipe them out, move on to the depot, clean out our supplies there, and strike north to the next. After that—"

He went on, talking now more to himself than to Meyers, and the scientist only pieced together parts of the plan. As might have been expected, it was unexpected, audacious, and would probably work. Meyers was no military genius, had only a rough working idea of military operations, but he was reasonably sure that the Leader could play the cards he was dealing himself and come out on top, barring the unforeseen in large quantities. But now, having conquered Europe, the Leader's voice was lower, and what little was audible no longer made sense to the scientist, who drew out a cheap blanket and threw himself down, his eyes closed.

Still the papers and maps rustled, and the voice droned on in soft snatches, gradually falling to a whisper and then ceasing. There was a final rattling of the map, followed by complete silence, and Meyers could feel the other's eyes on his back. He made no move, and the Leader must have been satisfied by the regular breathing that the scientist was asleep, for he muttered to himself again as he threw another blanket on the floor and blew out the light.

"A useful man, Meyers, now. But after victory, perhaps his machine would be a menace. Well, that can wait."

Meyers smiled slightly in the darkness, then went back to trying to force himself to sleep. As the Leader had said, such things could wait. At the moment, his major worry was that the Army of Occupation might come an hour too soon—but that also was nonsense; obviously, from the ranks of the legion, that could not be any part of the order of things. That which was would be, and he had nothing left to fear.

The Leader was already gone from the house when Meyers awoke, For a few minutes the scientist stood staring at the blanket of the other, then shrugged, looked at his watch, and made a hasty breakfast of wine and morphine; with cancer gnawing at their vitals, men have small fear of drug addiction, and the opiate would make seeming normality easier for a time. There were still threads to be tied in to his own satisfaction, and little time left in which to do it.

Outside, the heavy dew of the night was long since gone, and the air was fully warmed by the sun. Most of the legion were gathered in the square, some preparing breakfast, others eating, but all in the same stiff silence that had marked their goings and comings since the first. Meyers walked out among them slowly, and their eyes followed him broodingly, but they made no other sign. One of the earlier ones who had been shaving with a straight razor stopped, fingering the blade, his eyes on the scientist's neck.

Meyers stopped before him, half smiling. "Well, why not say it? What are you thinking?"

"Why bother? You know." The legionnaire's fingers clenched around the handle, then relaxed, and he went on with his shaving, muttering as his unsteady hand made the razor nick his skin. "In God's will, if I could draw this once across your throat, Meyers, I'd cut my own for the right."

Meyers nodded. "I expected so. But you can't. Remember? You must obey your original implicitly; you must not cause trouble for your original or Karl Meyers; you must not speak to us or to others except as we demand. Of course, in a couple of days, the compulsion would wear away slowly, but by that time we'll both be out of reach of each other... No, back! Stay where you are and continue shaving; from the looks of the others, you'll stop worrying about your hair shortly, but why hurry it?"

"Someday, somehow, I'll beat it! And then, a word to the original—or I'll track you down myself. God!" But the threatening scowl lessened, and the man went reluctantly back to his shaving, in the grip of the compulsion still. Meyers chuckled dryly.

"What was and has been—will be."

He passed down the line again, in and out among the mingled men who were scattered about without order, studying them carefully, noting how they ranged from trim copies of the Leader in field coat and well kept to what might have been demented scavengers picking from the garbage cans of the alleys and back streets. And yet, even the oldest and filthiest of the group was still the same man who had come closer to conquering the known world than anyone since Alexander. Satisfied at last, he turned back toward the house where his quarters were.

A cackling, tittering quaver at his right brought him around abruptly to face something that had once been a man, but now looked more like some animated scarecrow.

"You're Meyers," the old one accused him. "*Shh*! I know it. I remember. Hee-yee, I remember again. Oh, this is wonderful, wonderful, wonderful! Do you wonder how I can speak? Wonderful, wonderful, wonderful!"

Meyers backed a step and the creature advanced again, leering, half dancing in excitement. "Well, how can you speak? The compulsion shouldn't have worn off so soon!"

"Hee! Hee-yee-yee! Wonderful!" The wreck of a man was dancing more frantically now, rubbing his hands together. Then he sobered sharply, laughter bubbling out of a straight mouth and tapering off, like the drippings from a closed faucet. "*Shh!* I'll tell you. Yes, tell you all about it, but you mustn't tell *him*. He makes me come here every day where I can eat, and I like to eat. If *he* knew, *he* might not let me come. This is my last day; did you know it? Yes, my last day. I'm the oldest. Wonderful, don't you think it's wonderful? I do."

"You're crazy!" Meyers had expected it, yet the realization of the fact was still a shock to him and to his Continental background of fear of mental unbalance.

The scarecrow figure bobbed its head in agreement. "I'm crazy, yes—crazy. I've been crazy almost a year now—isn't it wonderful? But don't tell *him*. It's nice to be crazy. I can talk now; I couldn't talk before—*he* wouldn't let me. And some of the others are crazy, too, and they talk to me; we talk quietly, and *he* doesn't know… You're Meyers, I remember now. I've been watching you, wondering, and now I remember. There's something else I should remember—something I should do; I planned it all once, and it was so clever, but now I can't remember— You're Meyers. Don't I hate you?"

"No, No, Leader, I'm your friend." In spite of himself, Meyers was shuddering, wondering how to break away from the maniac. He was painfully aware that for some reason the compulsion on which he had counted no longer worked; insanity had thrown the normal rules overboard. If this person should remember fully—Again Meyers shuddered, not from personal fear, but the fear that certain things still undone might not be completed. "No, great Leader, I'm your real friend. Your best friend. I'm the one who told him to bring you here to eat."

"Yes? Oh, wonderful—I like to eat. But I'm not the Leader; *he* is…and *he* told me…what did *he* tell me? Hee! I remember again, *he* told me to find you; *he* wants you. And I'm the last. Oh, it's wonderful, wonderful, wonderful! Now I'll remember it all, I will. Hee-yee-yee! Wonderful. You'd better go now, Meyers. *He* wants you. Isn't it wonderful?"

Meyers lost no time in leaving, glad for any excuse, but wondering why the Leader had sent for him, and how much the lunatic had told. He glanced at his watch again, and at the sun, checking mentally, and felt surer as he entered the quarters. Then he saw there was no reason to fear, for the Leader had his maps out again, and was nervously tapping his foot against the floor; but there was no personal anger in his glance.

"Meyers? Where were you?"

"Out among the legion, my Leader, making sure they were ready to begin operations. All is prepared."

"Good." The Leader accepted his version without doubt. "I, too, have been busy. The car was sent off almost an hour ago—more than an hour ago—to the depot, and Immenhoff should be here at any moment. No sign of the enemy yet; we'll have time enough. Then, let them come!"

He fell back to the chair beside the table, nervous fingers tapping against the map, feet still rubbing at the floor, keyed to the highest tension, like a cat about to leap at its prey. "What time is it? Hm-m-m. No sound of the tank yet. What's delaying the fool? He should be here now. Hadn't we best get the machine outside?"

"It won't be necessary," Meyers assured him. "I'll simply run out a wire from the receiver to the tank when it arrives; the machine will work at a considerable distance, just as long as the subject is under some part of it."

"Good. What's delaying Immenhoff? He should have made it long ago. And where's the courier I sent last night? Why didn't he report back? I—"

"Hee-yee! He's smart, Leader, just as I once was." The tittering voice came from the door of their quarters, and both men looked up to see the old lunatic standing there, running his fingers through his beard. "Oh, it was wonderful! Why walk all that long way back when he knew it made no difference where he was—the machine will bring him back, anyhow. Wonderful, don't you think it was wonderful? You didn't tell him to walk back."

The Leader scowled, nodded. "Yes, I suppose it made no difference whether he came back or not. He could return with Immenhoff."

"Not he, not he! Not with Immenhoff."

"Fool! Why not? And get out of here!"

But the lunatic was in no hurry to leave. He leaned against the doorway, snickering. "Immenhoff's dead—Immenhoff's dead. Wonderful! He's been dead a long time now. The Army of Occupation found him and he got killed. I remember it all now, how I found him all dead when I was the courier. So I didn't come back, because I was smart, and then I was back without walking. Wonderful, wonderful, wonderful! I remember everything now, don't I?"

"Immenhoff dead? Impossible!" The Leader was out of the chair, stalking toward the man, black rage on his face. "You're insane!"

"Hee! Isn't it wonderful? They always said I was and now I am. But Immenhoff's dead, and he won't come here, and there'll be no tanks. Oh, how wonderful, never to march at all, but just come here every day to eat. I like to eat...No, don't touch me. I'll shoot, I will. I remember this is a gun, and I'll shoot, and the bullet will explode with noice, lots of noise. Don't come near me." He centered the automatic squarely on the Leader's stomach, smirking gleefully as he watched his original retreat cautiously back toward the table.

"You're mad at me because I'm crazy—" A sudden effort of concentration sent the smirk away to be replaced by cunning. "You know I'm crazy now! I didn't want you to know, but I told you. How sad, how sad, isn't it sad? No, it isn't sad, it's wonderful still, and I'm going to kill you. That's what I wanted to remember. I'm going to kill you, Leader. Now isn't that nice that I'm going to kill you?"

Meyers sat back in another chair, watching the scene as he might have a stage play, wondering what the next move might be, but calmly aware that he had no part to play in the next few moments. Then he noticed the Leader's hand drop behind him and grope back on the table for the automatic there, and his curiosity was satisfied. Obviously, the lunatic couldn't have killed the original.

The lunatic babbled on. "I remember my plan, Leader. I'll kill you, and then there won't be any you. And without you, there won't be me. I'll never have to hunt for clothes, or keep from talking, or go crazy. I won't be at all, and it'll be wonderful. No more twenty years. Wonderful, isn't it wonderful? Hee-yee-yee! Oh, wonderful. But I like to eat, and dead men don't eat, do they? Do they? Too bad, too bad, but I had breakfast this morning, anyhow. I'm going to kill you the next time I say 'wonderful,' Leader. I'm going to shoot and there'll be noise, and you'll be dead. Wonder—"

His lips went on with the motion, even as the Leader's hand whipped out from behind him and the bullet exploded in his head with a sudden crash that split his skull like a melon and threw mangled bits of flesh out through the door, leaving half a face and a tattered old body to slump slowly toward the floor with a last spasmodic kick. With a wry face, the Leader tossed the gun back on the table and rolled the dead figure outside the door with his foot.

Meyers collected the gun quietly, substituting his watch, face up where he could watch the minute hand. "That was yourself you shot, my Leader," he stated as the other turned back to the table.

"Not myself, a duplicate. What matter, he was useless, obviously, with his insane babble of Immenhoff's death. Or— The tank should have been here long before this! But Immenhoff couldn't have been discovered!"

Meyers nodded. "He was—all the 'secret' depots were; I knew of it. And the body you just tossed outside wasn't merely a duplicate—it was yourself as you will inevitably be."

"You—Treason!" Ugly horror and the beginnings of personal fear spread across the Leader's face, twisting the scar and turning it livid. "For that—"

Meyers covered him with the automatic. "For that," he finished, "you'll remain seated, Leader, with your hands on the table in clear view. Oh, I have no intention of killing you, but I could stun you quite easily; I assure you, I'm an excellent shot."

"What do you want? The reward of the invaders?"

"Only the inevitable, Leader, only what will be because it has already been.

Here!" Meyers tossed a small leather wallet onto the table with his left hand, flipping it open to the picture of a woman perhaps thirty-five years old. "What do you see there?"

"A damned Jewess!" The Leader's eyes had flicked to the picture and away, darting about the room and back to it

"Quite so. Now, to you, a damned Jewess, Leader." Meyers replaced the wallet gently, his eyes cold. "Once though, to me, a lovely and understanding woman, interested in my work, busy about our home, a good mother to my children; there were two of them, a boy and a girl—more damned Jews to you, probably. We were happy then. I was about to become a full professor at Heidelberg, we had our friends, our life, our home. Some, of course, even then were filled with hatred toward the Jewish people, but we could stand all that. Can you guess what happened? Not hard, is it?

"Some of your Youths. She'd gone to her father to stay with him, hoping it would all blow over and she could come back to me without her presence hurting me. They raided the shop one night, beat up her father, tossed her out of a third-story window, and made the children jump after her—mere sport, and patriotic sport! When I found her at the home of some friends, the children were dead and she was dying."

The Leader stirred again. "What did you expect? That we should coddle every Jew to our bosom and let them bespoil the Reich again? You were a traitor to your fatherland when you married her."

"So I found out. Two years in a concentration camp, my Leader, taught me that, well indeed. And it gave me time to think. No matter how much you beat a man down and make him grovel and live in filth, he still may be able to think, and his thoughts may still find you out—you should have thought of that. For two years, I thought about a certain field of mathematics, and at last I began to think about the thing instead of the symbols. And at last, when I'd groveled and humbled myself, sworn a thousandfold that I'd seen the light, and made myself something a decent man would spurn aside, they let me out again, ten years older for the two years there, and a hundred times wiser.

"So, I came finally to the little farm near Bresseldorf, and I worked as I could, hoping that, somehow, a just God would so shape things that I could use my discovery. About the time I'd finished, you fled, and I almost gave up hope; then I saw that in your escape lay my chances. I found you, persuaded you to return, and here you are. It sounds simple enough now, but I wasn't sure until I saw the legion. What would happen if I had turned you over to the Army of Occupation?"

"Eh?" The Leader had been watching the door, hoping for some distracting event, but his eyes now swung back to Meyers. "I don't know. Is that what you plan?"

"Napoleon was exiled; Wilhelm died in bed at Dorn. Are the leaders who cause the trouble ever punished, my Leader? I think not. Exile may not be pleasant, but normally is not too hard a punishment—normal exile to another land. I have devised a slightly altered exile, and now I shall do nothing to you. What was—will be—and I'll be content to know that eventually you kill yourself, after you've gone insane." Meyers glanced at the watch on the table, and his eyes gleamed savagely for a second before the cool, impersonal manner returned.

"The time is almost up, my Leader. I was fair to you; I explained to the best of my ability the workings of my invention. But instead of science, you wanted magic; you expected me to create some pseudo-duplicate of yourself, yet leave the real self unaltered. You absorbed the word 'plenum' as an incantation, but gave no heed to the reality. Remember the example I gave—a piece of string looped back on itself? In front of you is a string from some peasant's dress; now, conceive that piece of string—it loops back, starts out again, and is again drawn back—it does not put forth new feelers that do the returning to base for it, but must come back by itself, and never gets beyond a certain distance from itself. The coins that you saw in the pile disappeared—not because I depressed a switch, but because the two-minute interval was finished, and they were forced to return again to the previous two minutes."

Escape thoughts were obviously abandoned in the mind of the Leader now, and he was staring fixedly at Meyers while his hands played with the raveling from a peasant's garment, looping and un-looping it. "No," he said at last, and there was a tinge of awe and pleading in his voice, the beginning of tears in his eyes. "That is insane. Karl Meyers, you are a fool! Release me from this and even now, with all that has happened, you'll still find me a man who can reward his friends; release me, and still I'll reconquer the world, half of which shall be yours. Don't be a fool, Meyers."

Meyers grinned. "There's no release, Leader. How often must I tell you that what is now will surely be; you have already been on the wheel—you must continue. And—the time is almost here!"

He watched the tensing of the Leader's muscles with complete calm, dropping the automatic back onto his lap. Even as the Leader leaped from his chair in a frenzied effort and dashed toward him, he made no move. There was no need. The minute hand of the watch reached a mark on the face, and the leaping figure of the world's most feared man was no longer there. Meyers was alone in the house, and alone in Bresseldorf.

He tossed the gun onto the table, patting the pocket containing his wallet, and moved toward the dead figure outside the door. Soon, if the Leader had been right, the Army of Occupation would be here. Before then, he must destroy his machine.

One second he was dashing across the room toward the neck of Karl Meyers, the next, without any feeling of change, he was standing in the yard of the house of Meyers, near Bresseldorf, and ranging from him and behind him were rows of others. In his hands, which had been empty a second before, he clutched a rifle. At his side was belted one of the new-issue automatics. And before him, through the door of the house that had been Karl Meyers', he could see himself coming forward, Meyers a few paces behind.

For the moment there were no thoughts in his head, only an endless refrain that went: "I must obey my original implicitly; I must not cause trouble for my original or Karl Meyers; I must not speak to anyone unless one of those two commands. I must obey my original implicitly; I must not cause trouble—" By an effort, he stopped the march of the words in his head, but the force of them went on, an undercurrent to all his thinking, an endless and inescapable order that must be obeyed.

Beside him, those strange others who were himself waited expressionlessly while the original came out into the doorway and began to speak to them. "Soldiers of the Greater Reich that is to be… Let us be merciless in avenging… The fruits of victory…" Victory! Yes, for Karl Meyers. For the man who stood there beside the original, a faint smile on his face, looking out slowly over the ranks of the legion.

"But I speak to myselves. You who come after me know what is to be this day and in the days to come, so why should I tell you? And you know that my cause is just. The Jews, the Jew-lovers—" The words of the original went maddeningly on, words that were still fresh in his memory, words that he had spoken only twenty-four hours before.

And now, three dead Jews and a Jew-lover had brought him to this. Somehow, he must stop this mad farce, cry out to the original that it was treason and madness, that it was far better to turn back to the guards in Switzerland, or to march forth toward the invaders. But the words were only a faint whisper, even to himself, and the all-powerful compulsion choked even the whisper off before he could finish it. He must not speak to anyone unless one of those two commanded.

Still the words went on. "Not victory in a decade, nor a year, but in a month! We shall go north and south and east and west! We shall show them that our fangs are not pulled; that those which we lost were but our milk teeth, now replaced by a second and harder growth!

"And for those who would have betrayed us, or bound us down in chains to feed the gold lust of the mad democracies, or denied us the room to live which is rightfully ours—for those, we shall find a proper place. This time, for once and for all, there shall be an end to the evils that corrupt the earth—the Jews and the Bolsheviks, and their friends, and friends' friends. Germany shall emerge, purged and cleansed, a new and greater Reich, whose domain shall not be Europe, nor this hemisphere, but the world!

"Many of you have seen all this in the future from which you come, and all of you must be ready to reassure yourselves of it today, that the glory of it may fill your tomorrow. Now, we march against a few peasants. Tomorrow, after quartering in Bresseldorf, we shall be in the secret depot, where those who remain loyal shall be privileged to multiply and join us, and where we shall multiply all our armament ten-thousandfold! Into Bresseldorf, then, and if any of the peasants are disloyal, be merciless in removing the scum! Forward!"

His blood was pounding with the mockery of it, and his hands were clutching on the rifle. Only one shot from the gun, and Karl Meyers would die. One quick move, too sudden to defeat, and he would be avenged. Yet, as he made the first effort toward lifting the rifle, the compulsion surged upward, drowning out all other orders of his mind. He must not cause trouble for his original or Karl Meyers!

He could feel the futile tears on his face as he stood there, and the mere knowledge of their futility was the hardest blow of all. Before him, his original was smiling at him and starting forward, to be checked by Meyers, and to swing back after a few words.

"Proceed to Bresseldorf, then, and we follow. Secure quarters for yourself and food, and a place for me and for Meyers; we stop there until I can send word to the depot during the night and extend my plans. To Bresseldorf!"

Against his will, his feet turned then with the others, out across the yard and into the road, and he was headed toward Bresseldorf. His eyes swept over the group, estimating them to be six or seven thousand in number; and that would mean twenty years, at one a day—twenty years of marching to Bresseldorf, eating, sleeping, eating again, being back at the farm, hearing the original's speech, and marching to Bresseldorf. Finally—from far down the line, a titter from the oldest and filthiest reached him—finally that; madness and death at the hands of himself, while Karl Meyers stood by, watching and gloating. He no longer doubted the truth of the scientist's statements; what had been, would be.

For twenty years! For more than seven thousand days, each the same day, each one step nearer madness. God!

The Deadliest Female

Mark Tayowa groaned as the jeep went over a bump in the road across the spaceport, and his eyes lanced upward to the lanky bulk of the driver. The man chuckled, and Mark turned away, nursing his aching head in silence. Damn the smugness of these Normals!

All right, so he was a freak. He'd come into the world without tonsils, adenoids, sinuses or appendix; he weighed a hundred pounds even, and barely topped four feet of stocky, heavy-boned height. He had a nerve current speed of thirty-two hundred feet a second instead of eleven hundred, and he could take eight gravities of pressure, upright. But none of that made his hangover more pleasant.

"Wipe it off!" he told the driver, infuriated by the man's grin.

The grin widened. "You're *cute*!" the driver said, in a reedy falsetto. "I know Maisie! Some mouse. And that's some mouse you got on the eye."

For a second, Mark's arm tautened with sheer hunger to drive a fist into the other's soft-muscled belly. Then he collapsed into a sick slump on the seat. Yeah, Maisie. He'd picked her up somewhere along the line, celebrating his graduation from Spaceman special flight training and his simultaneous assignment to his first ship—in only nine months out from the crèche, too. She'd gotten him drunk, calmly picked his pocket, and then yelled for help. Naturally, the Normals stuck together against a freak. He fingered his blackened eye, then cupped his thin, strong hands around his head and groaned.

Women! It was bad enough to be brought up in the hothouse atmosphere of a crèche, raised with a few other Spacemen by Normals who were entirely too blasted "understanding," without even seeing a girl; but then to get out into the world and find the females of your own species were as flat-chested as men, and the Normal girls either wanted to pet you like a dog or roll you!

The driver nudged him. "We're here, Peewee. All out. End of the line."

Mark climbed out, lifting his thin bag of possessions. The *Venture* was an old ship, he saw, but a sound one. And it was obviously near blast-off. He should have been there an hour before, but he'd slept through the alarm. Then he saw the big Normal on the ramp, carrying triple stars on his shoulder, and snapped into salute. "Mark Tayowa, lieutenant assigned to *Venture*, sir."

The man turned and shouted inside. "Hey, Lee—it's here. Blast at three-oh-seven." Then he nodded toward Mark, and jerked a thumb inward. "Okay, you and Lee Tanming have it. And you'd better report in—you're graduated now; you don't have to stand here saluting all day."

Mark went up the little ramp, and a muffled voice came down the tiny communication shaft from control. "Seal up, Tayowa. We blast in one minute!"

He triggered the seals, watched the ramp come up and sink into place, and went through the inner lock, checking to make sure it also sealed properly. Then he hesitated, while a rumbling came from below, and the sudden punch of acceleration hit him. They were lifting at five gravities, headed out for nine months to Pluto, and he was on his first actual trip into space—the work for which he'd been destined through eight generations. He sampled it, while he began climbing up to the control room, and even the hangover was no longer important.

Starting now, he was free of the Normals, out where he belonged—where his body was no freak, but something tailored ideally for its purpose.

Then he stopped. The figure stooped over the controls was unmistakable. Stringy hair was caught back in double braids, and the shoulders had a female slope to them, while the rest of the three-foot-eight figure showed the stringy, neuter angularity of the females of his race. As he looked, Lee Tanming turned, her narrow body jerking about with a total lack of grace. For nine months he had to be cooped up with a female!

She gave him one disgusted glance before she swung back to reset the controls. "My last trip before they ground me for good," she said bitterly, "and they give me a green kid who hasn't got the brains to stay away from those grinning spaceport tramps. Where's your luggage, Romeo?"

He doubled his fists, then shrugged wearily. "Okay. Okay, I guess the whole field knew about it. Maisie got my supply money. Go ahead, laugh."

"You'll have to get funnier than that, Bobo. I don't give a damn how dumb you are ashore. But since you have one suit to your name, you'll wash it every night, or I'll throw it in the incinerator." She turned for another quick glance at him. "We'll have to live together, sonny—and I don't like it any better than you. Get some aspirin from the galley stock, toss your duffle in cabin two—mine's number one, with the lock—and then get below. Takes someone in the engine-room eventually."

He looked at her insignia, knowing Spacewomen were never promoted higher than lieutenants—his own rank—since they were automatically retired at thirty-five. That was about to happen to Tanming, evidently, and she was sore about it. "Yessir, *Captain*!"

"Seniority, sonny," she said. "I've been running the Pluto jump eleven years. *And* the fact I can stand three more gravs than you can, from practice. Get below!"

To demonstrate, she began jockeying the controls, increasing and decreasing the acceleration pressure. He stood it a few seconds, until his stomach gave in. Then he lurched away, hunting for the latrine. He found it barely in time.

It was going to be a great trip.

There was the smell of coffee when he came to, and he was surprised to find himself in a hammock. Some of the ache was gone, and his stomach felt better. He eased to the deck, dreading what he'd see when he picked up his suit; but it had been cleaned. Then Lee's fist banged on the door, and her voice reached him. "Come and get it, sonny. And better grab that aspirin on the way."

Mark shook his head, and regretted it. But maybe he'd misjudged her. He owed her an apology for not tending ship, at least; he knew she must have had hell until speed built up, running both control and engines. He'd been cross-grained from the Normals, and it must have been tough on her, nearing thirty-five and about to be grounded…whereas he was good for fifty years' service, and they both knew it.

He climbed to the galley, where a plastube of coffee waited, and headed for the medicine kit on the wall, his hands shaking. From above, an alarm sounded, and then there was a muttered damn from Lee. The ship leaped suddenly—and the medicine chest came down under his clutching fingers, bottles and supplies breaking under heavy acceleration as they hit the floor.

Moments later, she was at the door. "Nice work, sonny. Well, no medical supplies, not even a fever thermometer now. If you get space chills, all I can do for you is stuff you out the airlock. We're running a library and supplies to Pluto, not a nursery, but I guess the brass on Earth can't tell the difference. Normal administrators!"

"There must be medical supplies in the cargo—" he began.

Her laughter cut him off. "When Pluto's supercold hi-vac labs are the source of our top medicals, systemwide? We're shipping out plutonium, sonny—pure energy, practically. Scared?"

He knew what she meant. With plutonium in its insulating wraps as cargo, they'd need just one good pea-sized meteorite through the hull to blast them into nothingness. But he shook his head.

"Liar," she remarked coldly. "Incidentally, I cleaned up this time for you. Don't mention it. From now on, you do all the cooking and washing aboard. I'm turning in. Take over, sonny. And when you get me up, I'll expect these clothes clean, my eggs scrambled lightly, and no damn-fool nonsense with the controls."

She swung down to Cabin 1, and the lock clicked. Mark picked up his coffee—which was lousy, saccharine-sweet—and apologized to himself for any good ideas of her he'd had. It looked as if she'd spent her life building up resentment at being female and not a Normal, and now meant to take it all out on him. She'd probably get worse.

She did. Lee had imagination enough to vary the beat; she went from synthetic sympathy to biting arrogance, and followed it by long lectures on what would happen if she wrote up his default on takeoff. She told him the rumors about him and Maisie among the port attendants before takeoff. And she refused to lend him even one of her books.

That was the worst of all. Once blast-off is made, most of the trip is pure monotony, and the microcard books are almost a psychological necessity. He should have brought his own—but Maisie's theft had ruled that out. Mark fought it out past Mars and well towards Jupiter, and at times even welcomed the menial duties of cooking and cleaning. But there was still too much time left over.

He broke half a day's silence, finally. "What sort of a library do we ship, and where's it stowed?"

Lee looked up from a book she was too obviously enjoying and shook her hair, filling the air with the perfume she'd found he couldn't stand. "Technical. The hold marked with the big 'Entry Illegal' sign. And that sign means you."

He'd already noticed it and wondered. Well, technical books were better than nothing, and nobody needed to know he'd borrowed them. Of course, the hold was sealed with the official tape and slug, but he knew how to work them well enough to stand all but the most careful inspection. He'd learned that trick in flight training, where the older boys passed the trick down to the younger.

For the next few watches, he noticed her frequent sudden appearance when he was near the hold. He grinned, carefully avoiding any further examination of the seal, until it seemed finally that she'd given up and decided he wasn't going to try it. He waited out two more watches, and then moved suddenly, hastily stripping away the seal and throwing the hatch back.

"I could shoot you, you know."

He jerked around to find her standing casually on the landing above him, with a gun in one thin hand. "You know the rule against breaking into the room of a suspended Normal; this is worse."

He'd already seen the gelatin with which the room was filled, and guessed the answer. Apparently, it took less room to ship out a full Eidetic who could remember everything on a page forever from a tenth-of-a-second glance. Eidetics were rarer than Spacemen, and breaking one out of suspended animation, where he could stand the acceleration, would more than justify shooting.

Mark began resealing with hands that were sweating. "You could have told me," he muttered.

"More fun this way, sonny. If I enter this on the log—along with the picture I just took—well, you figure what happens when we land! Better think it over."

She bent over, running her hand around the rim of the landing. "Filthy. See that it's clean when I wake up."

Mark tried unsuccessfully to retain some dignity as he climbed down to the engine room, but his hands were shaking. Blackmail now—and she could make it stick, apparently. He brooded over a picture in his mind of her neck between his hands, mentally listening to the snap of her vertebrae. Then he got out his chem-cleaning set and began scrubbing the shaft walls and landings.

But there's a limit to anything. He reached it just beyond Jupiter, when Lee objected to lack of seasoning in the soup. He took the bulb silently back to the galley, located the red pepper and used it—generously, together with a bit of mustard and some dehydrated horseradish to make sure. Maybe she'd grown too confident; she squeezed the bulb for a generous sip.

When she came up, yelling, her gun was still clipped to the back of the chair, and Mark was on it in a single pounce. He tossed it into the shaft, put a hand on her shoulder and shoved her down again. "Eat it, you witch. I want to see you eat every damned drop of it. After that, you do the cooking and cleaning around here—and while I'm at it, I'll take that camera of yours."

"Sure of yourself, sonny?"

"Dead sure. Start eating!"

"You wouldn't strike a woman," she suggested, but she was beginning to glance about, and a worried line appeared on her forehead.

"No," he agreed. "Not a woman. But if you don't eat every drop of that soup, I'll shove your nose through the—"

Something that might have been a cross between lightning and a battering ram came up from the chair and knocked him crossways. And then she was free of the little table-shelf, and moving in, a sudden grin on her face.

"Big mistake, sonny." A fist came out, changed to a hard-edged palm, and chopped down on the bridge of his nose. "Never hit a woman—" She was lifting him then, over one shoulder, and in a twist that brought him slamming down against the deck. "—who has lived in hi-grav acceleration fourteen years." One foot was on the small of his back, and her arms were dragging his arms backwards, until he could feel the vertebrae begin to snap. "Better scream."

He held out for a moment longer, and she upped the pull. "I can hold it for an hour," she mentioned, hardly breathing harder. "It's worse than space chills. Better scream."

But the advice was needless. She'd increased the tension again, and the scream ripped out of his throat. She kicked him with casual efficiency, hoisted him over her shoulder, and carried him down to his cabin.

"You'll be all right in an hour, sonny. Only, when you come out, stick a sir after anything you say to me—or *madam*, I'm not particular. And smile, damn you…um-hmm. I think I'm going to like this trip!"

Then she located a slip of cloth in a pocket and held it out. " 'S all right, sonny. Go right ahead and cry it out. A good cry is good for you. Here."

Maybe it was the power of suggestion; Mark felt tears running hotly into his eyes, and all his determination couldn't hold them back.

He had stopped feeling sorry for himself a few minutes later, and something in the back of his mind had recognized that things could get no worse. With that decision, even the pain couldn't keep his thoughts back. He was remembering everything he knew of space chills, and grimly checking over the details of the ship in his head. The fever thermometer was broken, and the only other temperature gauge was on the thermostat.

His head reeled as he slipped out of the room and down to the engine room. There he worked quickly and surely, assembling what he needed. And he was back in the cabin when she knocked.

"Your watch. Hit the deck."

He plastered a smile on his face, and came out. "Yes. ma'am. I relieve you, ma'am."

After her door clicked, he lost no time. It was easy to clip the bearing on the thermometer needle, and to solder it onto the figure 72°. His watch gave him a timer, and the other little contacts went into place, one by one. Finally, he nodded in satisfaction. He'd have to readjust it every so often, beginning gently and working up. But it was a good job.

And the sleeping tablets hadn't been among the bottles broken, fortunately. He'd slipped them out and had been using them to help sleep away what time he could, but there were still almost a thousand in the bottle.

It should be plenty.

At that, she held out better than he expected. It was two weeks before she mentioned it, though that might have been because the beginning was so gradual. But space chills, a violent reaction of the body to radiation that couldn't all be shielded out from space, were the worst thing that could happen to any space-voyager—even a Spaceman.

They were near Saturn when it finally happened, the final stage he'd been waiting for. He'd left her coffee half an hour before, spiked with a sleeping pill, and the temperature cycle had gone into high. Now he stopped to wipe his face and hands carefully with astringent, and stepped into the control room.

She shook her head groggily, and ran sweating fingers over her forehead. And this time, finally, she got up from the chair and motioned him down. "Mark—I got 'em again. The fever, this time. Here, feel."

She'd dropped the feud a week before, and he'd let it seem to die. Now he put his hand—still cool from astringent—to her head, and shook his own. "If we only had some medicine...How long since you thought you were freezing? Two hours, wasn't it?"

She nodded unhappily. She'd stopped studying the thermometer, convinced that the fault was her own, since he seemed to feel no change in the temperature.

"Mark, I'm scared. We can't go on—I can't. There's medicine for it down there—down on Titan. Mark, you've got to set down at Gilead!"

He debated it, his face carefully showing doubt—some of which was real. Making a landing on a crude port without two fully competent Spacemen was tricky. But her hand clutched at his arm. "Mark, I'll help all I can. And—I'll do all the cooking, every bit of washing. I'll say sir all the way to Pluto and back. I've got to finish this trip—it's my last. And I need the medicine."

Finally he nodded, and reached out for the controls, refiguring the course. She looked her gratitude, and was gone, wiping perspiration from her forehead. He pulled out his astringent, and made sure his face still seemed cool, in spite of the heat of the air. He was fresh again when she came back, bringing him coffee and a bottle of cognac—the only liquor aboard the ship.

It was a long, weary business, fighting down the velocity they'd built up all the way from Earth and jockeying the ship down to Titan; but he was proud of his landing, and she was full of praise. It hadn't been bad for a first major landing, at that. He accepted the double slug of cognac she poured, and let her refill the glass before he got up.

"The doctor's house is up there, just over the hill," she said. He nodded, buckled on a jacket, and headed out.

Sure, he'd get the doctor. He grinned as he saw the distant figures of two Spacemen coming across the field toward the ship. She could take care of explanations, until he got back with the doc. And while they had the right to go aboard, he knew the Spacemen here wouldn't—there was still enough fear that space chills were contagious. When the doctor was working on her, he could remove the tricks on the thermostat.

And then let her yelp when the medico said she had nothing but blue funk from plain fear of carrying plutonium to Pluto. They'd pull her back Earthside, and he'd get someone else to carry on the rest of the trip with him—someone junior to him!

Then, as he crossed to the other side of the hill, it hit him: drowsiness, like a numbing drug poured into his veins...He was getting groggier by the minute as he fought down toward the doctor's little dome. He felt someone helping him inside the dome, and then he collapsed.

"Drunk," he heard a man's heavy voice say. But he couldn't protest.

It seemed only moments later when the voice came again, repeating, "Drunk."

"Yeah." It was a woman's voice. "Yeah, scared of the Pluto hop. Lee had a lot of trouble with him. How's he now?"

"About ready to come to. I shot enough stimulant into him."

A door opened and shut then, and Mark opened his eyes, with an effort. But his head was clearing rapidly now. And it was a Space woman who stood there.

She looked at him in disgusted silence as he staggered to a wash basin and began ducking his head. When he was finished and fully clothed, he started out the nearest door, but she motioned to another. It was a back exit, and he noticed that she stuck to dimly lighted ways, still moving in silence. Finally she swung around.

"All right, I suppose I'll have to get used to you. I'm Pat Runyon. I run the satellite freight here—and from now on, brother, you're my helper. It's tough—you'll wish you were back on the Pluto hop—but you'll run it with me. And you won't go running to a doctor before I can open the port whenever we land, either. Give me those lieutenant bars!"

"Eh?"

"You heard me. Message from Earth to demote you when Lee got authority to replace you with my helper—a nice guy, he was, too. Then they stick me with you for the rest of his contract. Well, stop staring at me, you'll get to know me in three years. But, brother, don't get cold feet on me. I'm not soft-hearted like Lee. I can't stand a yellow Spaceman! Here, she told me to give you this."

It was a little bundle of wires and relays, with his watch in the middle of it. He looked at it slowly. Then he looked up at the sky where Pluto should be, thinking of three long, back-breaking years ahead of him...three years, to give Lee Tanming plenty of time to laugh about the way she'd ground a raw kid's face into the dust—time to tell the story of that kid's clumsy trick with a thermostat, and her own cleverness with the cognac, until it grew stale—time enough even to forget the thing had ever happened.

But Mark knew that he wouldn't forget.

The same slow, bitter surge of hatred was in Mark Tayowa three years later as he dropped the freighter down, unconscious of the dozen gravities that were hitting her deck. It burned in his eyes as he passed from Spaceman's bar to hotel and on to another city. Nobody laughed at him now—long. He had chain-lightning reactions now, and muscle sheaths that almost rang when hit; he also had his lieutenant's bars back and the right to name his own next job, but those were unimportant. What counted was that he had three months' free time coming.

It took him just three weeks to track her down. She wasn't Lee Tanming, any more; she was Mrs. Ivan Aiello. Interestingly enough, Aiello was the man she'd picked up from Titan to replace him—and he was currently off to Mercury, which left things nicely uncomplicated. Mark smiled thinly and ran his tongue over his lips.

He was vaguely grateful to the builders of his race, who'd put no nonsense about chivalry into his makeup. As it was, he could beat hell out of her and enjoy every minute of it.

He punched the bell, noting that this community system for the Spacemen beat the old crèche and community halls in every way. The houses were neat, the yards attractive, and here and there the skinny, big-eyed children seemed happier and healthier.

Then someone threw open the door, and he looked up to Spacewoman standing there. He blinked, and changed the words in his head. Not a Spacewoman... a Space angel. She was unmistakably of his race—her height, just under his own; the hint of the Oriental in her black eyes and ivory skin; her slender frame. But there was nothing angular about her. She glowed. She was utterly, disarmingly beautiful.

She frowned at his stare, and then suddenly laughed. "Mark!" she said. "Mark Tayowa. And how wonderful you're looking! Pat must have done you good. Come in, let me get you some coffee." She paused, stricken by a sudden thought. "You're not mad any more, are you? Here, Herbie, get that top out of your mouth. And you, Hank, stop pulling Fido's tail. Meet the twin brats, Mark."

Mark followed her in, still dazed. It *couldn't* be Lee. He remembered the scrawny, neuter figure as well as if he'd had her picture pasted into his helmet these long three years. He started forward, then stopped as she came out of the kitchen, carrying cups and a pot of coffee, and looking completely domestic.

For want of anything else to do, he sat down and tried awkwardly to look interested in the twins. But they were normal enough Spaceman children. And she still had that glow that drew his eyes to her.

"You're beautiful," he said finally, and his voice was harsh. "I didn't recognize you."

"Oh, that!" She laughed at him. "You, Herbie. Stop it! Just wait'll your father comes back from Mercury. He'll give it to you. Mark—you didn't expect me to stay neuter after the change, did you? Silly kid! I'll bet you never saw a Spacewoman over thirty-five before, did you? Though Pat Runyon must be about thirty-four, come to think of it. We—well, we develop."

It was too magnificent an understatement; Mark couldn't think of any way to handle it. He stood up slowly, awkwardly, feeling like a fool.

"Oh, come on, you're not mad? I've thought about it lots of times. (*Her-bie!*) I was so damn mad at having to quit space to be some Spaceman's wife. I used to have the craziest ideas—I actually hated the idea of going through puberty, at my age...And you were an awful infant. I've often wondered what happened to you, you know. Ivan and I've had more fun guessing about that."

He nodded. "Yeah. I had fun, too. I guess maybe I'm still a little green around the ears."

"No-o." She considered him, smiling. "No, Mark. You've grown up. Mm-hmm. (Hank, let the dog *alone!*) But sit down, Mark, have some coffee. For old time's sake. We've got a lot to talk over, haven't we? (*Herbie!*) And I'm awfully lonesome—Ivan won't be home for another week."

Mark put his hands in his pockets slowly, and turned to the door. He took them out again, looked at Lee thoughtfully. Then he stared down at the two children. His shoulders drooped as he thrust his fists deep into his pockets.

She could never stand three gravities now, judging by the soft femininity of her.

"Sorry," he mumbled. "Like to, but I've got to report back. Just thought I'd drop in, say hello."

"Oh, but Mark... (Hank, if you don't stop that!) Mark..."

But he was already down the steps, moving toward the waiting cab, letting her voice die out behind him.

Three years of sweating, driving his body until it ached every night, goading Pat Runyon to throw the book at him, picking a fight with every Spaceman he ran into...and now a soft, female form and a couple of kids had made it all useless. He doubled up a fist, trying to imagine Lee's neck inside his grasp. But it wouldn't come as a picture now—the old straight neck with its boyish tendons was gone, and the softly rounded throat he'd seen wouldn't replace it.

He cursed. "Take me to the nearest bar," he ordered the driver curtly.

Then slowly he reconsidered. "Make it the spaceport. And step on it."

He saw the driver throw him an odd look, but he didn't care what Normals thought now. There was still time to ask for his old job back, out on Titan, freighting around the satellites. He took a deep, slow breath and leaned back against the cushions.

In another year, Pat Runyon would be thirty-five-and the change would begin. Pat wasn't a bad person, come to think of it. Not bad at all. A good person to know...

Helping Hand

I

Mankind's first contact with an intelligent alien race didn't come on some shuddersome foreign planet around a distant star, long after men had built a galactic empire.

Nor did it take place in the backyard of a flying-saucer initiate. No hordes of alien fighting ships plunged into Earth's skies for plunder and slaves. No primitive Venusians or Martians were discovered ready to worship us. No telepathic monsters took over our minds. There wasn't even a hassle of misunderstanding while the aliens tried to get through the blue ribbon and red tape of our governments. They made no such attempts.

The event took place on the least likely place for races to meet in the whole galaxy—the lifeless surface of the Moon.

Sam Osheola had no doubt about its being lifeless, and he wasn't expecting any surprises. The first manned Moon expedition had proved that the satellite was dead and always had been. Sam's only doubts concerned his being there at all, rubbing elbows with the hundred or so scientists important enough to be included this time. But mostly, he was too busy to think about that. After some of the places he'd worked, even the Moon didn't seem too strange.

He was inside the garage dome, swearing a blue streak in the nineteen languages he knew fluently and improvising in a dozen others. In the eighteen hours since landing, the schedule stated, they should have had the tractor tanks out and rolling. But somehow the labor crew had smuggled in a load of rotgut, and now they were locked up in one of the ships, with his two best mechanics passed out too cold for even pure oxygen to revive. That meant he'd have to correct their half-done work and finish it, with whatever help little Commander Larsen could dig up among the ships' crews and the scientists.

Larsen came back then, snapping off his bowl helmet as he passed through the lock. He stopped to listen admiringly as his labor boss finally ran down into a muttering of Seminole and English.

"I've got a bunch of volunteers waiting in the main dome. You can brief 'em over coffee," Larsen announced. Then he grinned. "I always thought you Indians were an unemotional race, Sam. Where's your heap big stone face?"

"Lay off the plains pidgin!" Sam snapped back. Then he caught a glimpse of his face reflected in one of the tractor bubble-tops and chuckled. Any stone in that face must have been cracked in shipment. His nose was broken from the football he had played to earn his M.E., there was a scar across his forehead from an Arab bullet while he'd been laying oil pipe in Israel, and a network of broken veins from the time his helmet had cracked while working on the first space station.

"Yeah," he admitted. "We Seminoles don't have emotions at all, Bill. We're so unemotional we refused to sign a treaty. And we go around to this day bragging that we're still technically at war with the United States. Let's get that coffee!"

They were just coming out of the garage when they saw the alien ship.

Sam stared at it unbelievingly through the polarized plastic of his helmet. His mind jumped back ten years to fears that should have been long gone. *Russians—coming to blow us off the Moon!* His hand was pawing for a gun he hadn't carried for a decade, before he checked the motion. It was a long time since that mess of politics had been cleared up; for that matter, there were a dozen Russian scientists with this expedition.

But it certainly was no ship that he'd ever seen. It was neither a winged transatmosphere rocket, a cylindrical ferry, nor one of the piles of girders and tanks used to reach the Moon. Instead, it seemed to be simply a huge sphere, maybe a hundred feet in diameter, and gleaming a bright blue all over. It was coming down in a great curve, slowing steadily, but there was no sign of atomic or even chemical exhaust.

It passed over his head and slowed to a stop over the expedition ships—hovering a hundred feet off the ground! Then, as if making up its mind, it began to settle gently beside the largest of the five ships.

There was a babble of voices in Sam's headphones; others had seen it. But the words made no sense. It certainly wasn't one of their scheduled supply ships, and the nonsense about flying saucers had been finally disposed of before the station was built.

Sam heard Larsen ordering somebody back. He glanced around toward the main dome, to see a few men in space-suits moving reluctantly back inside. It made good sense to wait until they saw what developed. But the commander was moving forward himself.

Sam fell in step with him, the hair on the back of his neck prickling faintly. "Martians?" he asked. It was a fool question, and he expected to be told so.

But Larsen shook his head. "Don't ask me, Sam! Mars didn't produce any advanced technology with her atmosphere—I think. But that thing never came from Earth. Wrong orbit, for one thing. See anything like weapons?"

"I don't see a thing," Sam told him. "What'll you do if they turn up with ray guns?"

Larsen snarled: "If they turn up with bows and arrows I'll surrender. This expedition has a total armament of one .38 automatic with seven bullets—in case someone falls into a crater where we can't rescue him. Wait a minute!" Larsen came to a stop, pointing.

A crack had appeared in the side of the blue sphere. Now it widened and a section peeled downward, to form a curved ramp to the surface. Under it was a gray substance of some kind, from which something that looked like a flight of folding steps shot out. The final step had barely appeared when the gray stuff seemed to give way. A figure emerged from it. Whatever it was looked human.

Sam grunted in surprise. He was ready for anything except that. A winged octopus wouldn't have bothered him. But a man? If any place on Earth had a ship like that and let the Moon expedition take off with the old atomic style rockets, something rotten was really going on! Better a monster than some types of human beings!

Then he wondered. The figure was in a glaring white space-suit of too slim a build—more like a man in tights than in one of the heavy suits he knew. And there was something wrong about the way it walked. Something almost rubbery, as if the legs bent all over instead of at fixed joints.

Larsen and Sam moved forward again. Another figure came from the strange ship, carrying something. This one gestured toward the two men, but it turned toward the expedition ship, following the first figure. It was running as it neared the ship, holding out whatever gadget it was using.

There was a ten second conference between the two. Then both turned and headed back toward Sam and Larsen.

"*Wallah!*" Sam's harsh voice seemed to echo in his helmet, and he felt Larsen tense beside him. But he had eyes only for the face in the other helmet nearest him.

II

The creature's head looked as if someone had managed to cross a man and a frog; a smooth, hairless skull, almost no nose, a wide mouth now partly open in a straight line, eyes that seemed to have independent motion, and a smooth, hairless skin that was so purple it seemed almost black.

The incredible part of it was that the thing was beautiful. Grotesque as it seemed in its blend of human and non-human, it had a certain innate rightness of good design about it, as a racehorse or a cat has.

Abruptly, fifteen feet away, it spread its arms straight out, with hands seeming to droop. The hands, he saw now, had only three fingers, set at even intervals around the palms, all more or less opposed.

"Peace," Sam guessed. He'd seen various human races use signs that were all different for the same idea, but all with some of the same idea behind them. "Better do the same, Bill—and pray it means what I think."

The two men moved forward to the two aliens. Sam stopped three feet away from his opposite, but the creature came on until their helmets touched.

"*Ssatah!*" it said.

"Hello yourself!" Sam answered. It hadn't been an unpleasant voice, from what he could tell by sound that had traveled through two helmet shells. It seemed to match the velvety quality of the skin he could see. He tapped his chest, then his head. "Sam!"

The straight slit of the mouth narrowed and opened. "Sam." The alien motioned toward the commander. At Sam's introduction, the same mouth gesture was repeated. "*Birr. Va. Sam t' Birr.*" One finger tapped its chest. "*Ato. Ato t' Mu'an.*" A gesture indicated that the second name applied to the other alien.

Then finally Ato stepped back, and motioned to the ship. A lithe leg moved over the ground, drawing circles into a haze around a central point. Beside it, another picture that could only be a crude schematic of a rocket appeared. Ato waited, as if expecting a reaction, then made a gesture curiously like a shrug. He put his hands together, began lifting them and spreading them out, sketching a slim upright with a big circle at the top.

"VvvvPWOOMB!"

Sam jumped, feeling cold dulls run up his back. He had been so busy watching the hands that he hadn't seen the other alien bend forward to touch helmets with him. Then the meaning of it all suddenly registered, and his pulse quieted down again.

But Larsen was ahead of him. He could have heard the sound only faintly, but he'd decoded the symbols. "He's figured out the ship rockets are atom powered!" His voice came over Sam's phones. "That gadget they're carrying must be some kind of radiation detector."

Abruptly, his voice sobered. "Sam, maybe I shouldn't have agreed. Damn it, *that was an atom bomb explosion he was signaling.* They must have used atomics for weapons."

"Might as well concede what the other side already knows," Sam told him. Down inside him, the amazement was just beginning to register. *Aliens!* Martians, Venusians—starmen—here! Alien friends to lead them across space—or alien enemies to attack from God knew where. Aliens—and Sam Osheola, a quarter million miles from the swamps where he'd been born—a billion cultures, perhaps, farther apart than he'd been from any human race he'd met!

And over his mind, the old defense mechanism was dropping down. This didn't matter, any more than football had. It was all a game—a play he was acting in—he had to go through the motions, say the right lines, but it couldn't really affect him, because things like this didn't really happen to Sam Osheola.

Other men in spacesuits were coming out now, clustering around them, and other figures from the blue ship, all in the same white, slim suits. Larsen swung around to direct the men of his command, as Ato seemed to be doing to his.

Nothing escaped the alien. One eye swiveled slightly toward the commander, and Sam was sure what passed over the purple face was surprise. Ato was guilty of picking the wrong horse, and he was just realizing it as he saw Larsen giving commands instead of Sam. At least that meant the things weren't telepaths.

This time Ato made no mistake. He headed for Larsen, motioning to his own ship. With one hand beside his mouth, he made opening and closing signs, then used his other hand to repeat the gesture beside the commander's face. With hands facing each other, he pantomimed a conversation, and again pointed to the ship. Larsen's gesture toward the main dome brought a complicated set of signs that were probably refusal and explanation of some sort, then another motion toward the blue ship.

Finally, Ato swung on his "heels" and headed toward it alone. His fellows watched him, making no move to follow. When the alien reached whatever served as an airlock, he stopped and stood waiting patiently.

"Maybe he's got some kind of educating machine there, Bill," Sam offered. "He's pretty insistent. We could use one—it took me three months to learn Arabic, and that's a human language!"

The back of his mind was warning him that he was stepping over the line. Leave the guesses and suggestions to the brass, it told him, just as it had ordered him to stay on the ground when the space station began, or to stay clear of the girl who could teach him to read Arabic—or the little crook in Burma...Some day his curiosity would get him killed.

Larsen took the bait, probably deliberately. "All right, Sam. I'm no linguist. If you're willing to volunteer, see what he wants."

Ato still waited as Sam started across the pumice and dust toward the blue ship. If the alien was surprised at the switch, there was no sign of it. But that was only good dickering. "Don't let 'em get your signals," Sam muttered to himself.

Then he wondered what equivalent of that could exist in Ato's language. A speech was more than semantic noises—it was a whole history of culture, and you couldn't know a thing about anyone until you knew how he thought in his own tongue.

Disappointingly, the steps and what showed of the hull section looked no different from the normal alloys Earth used. The gray stuff was some flexible plastic. Earth had been experimenting on flexible locks that would let a man go through without losing air or taking up much space, but so far none had worked. Still, the principle was familiar enough.

Sam nodded as Ato touched his shoulder and backed through. Sam followed. The gray stuff molded to him without too much resistance, and then he was inside a metal-walled, featureless passageway and the alien was shedding his suit.

Underneath, it was plain that Sam's first impression had been right The purple man's bony structure hadn't fully ossified; the joints seemed to be sections where a flexible cartilage permitted bending. It would make for neater spacesuit design, of course. His nude, purple body was that of a slim, graceful watersprite, but there was an air of strength and endurance to it.

From a cabinet, Ato took out a mess of equipment. He studied Sam's suit for a moment, then located the escape valve for exhaled air and got a sample. Things moved, changed color, and precipitated, until a series of dials began registering. The alien studied them silently, then wiggled his mouth. "*Va!*"

At his gesture, Sam reached for his helmet snaps. He was consciously brave. Look at the way his ancestors had faced danger and torture without a whimper...no, damn it, those were the Sioux and the Apache! And besides, he was no dratted savage...

He suddenly realized that he was holding his breath. He let it out with a *whoosh*. When he breathed in, there was an odd odor, somewhat pungent, a trifle sweet, that seemed to come from the alien. But his lungs accepted the atmosphere gratefully. It was a bit heavier than that used in the domes and suits, and it felt good.

They went down hallways and up some kind of elevator, to reach a room that obviously had something to do with the control of the ship. There were indicators in panels along the walls, television screens showing the outside in color but with too much emphasis on blue for human eyes, and instruments that only vaguely made sense to Sam. Two other purple-skinned men were working in obvious haste on a complicated maze of wiring, with tiny bumps that might have been transistor, coils and other parts. It was obviously electronic, and they were changing the circuits.

One of them stopped to rattle off a string of high-pitched words to Ato, indicating a device on a table.

Ato nodded. He motioned to a three-legged chair that proved surprisingly comfortable, then took a seat across the table. He moved a button connected to a wire between them, then drew a switchboard from the machine within easy reach. His other hand picked up a slim shaft and made hasty marks on a writing surface with it. Apparently his palm was flexible enough to let any two fingers oppose a third. He held up the shaft.

"*Ssompa*," he said carefully. He made marks again. "*Pir*," he said. Then he pointed to a cluster of marks at a time, repeating: "*Edomi*."

It wasn't even well-organized speech instruction, much less anything as wonderful as a mechanical educator! Sam felt the disappointment thicken in him as he drew out his own pen and wrote down a group of words. "*Va*—yes. *Va*—yes. *Ssompa pir edomi*. Pen write word. *Va*. And you'd better let someone who knows how take over, Ato, or we'll be here until hell freezes over finding out how to tell each other useless sentences. Now, *one*!"

Ato shrugged and let the control pass to Sam. They went through the numbers and common operating words of arithmetic, the simplest nouns and verbs, and a negative—Ato apparently picked one from several.

Sam had already decided that grammar could go out of the window. He elected pidgin English as the simplest, most consistent language he knew. The vocabulary was limited, the rules were simple, and anything they needed to say could be conveyed by it. Anyhow, it gave him an ace up his sleeve—Ato would have a deuce of a time figuring out Sam's cultural pattern from it, no matter how clever he was.

Then he began to suspect that Ato was doing something of the same nature.

But when he finished his basic list of words and began going through applications of them to fix them indelibly in their memories, Ato would have none of it. "*No!*" he said firmly. "Make word." He was stubborn about it.

Sam frowned, but went on. If the aliens had memories that would let them master a vocabulary from a single hearing, they had him beaten. He hunched forward, sweating a little as he tried to force his mind to memorize every word and phrase. But it couldn't be done! The harder he tried, the more he lost.

Sometime during the long hours, one of the technicians sweating over the electronic panel went out and came back with a package for Sam and a bowl for Ato. Larsen must have sent the food over. Sam wolfed it down, stalling as long as he could while he went over what he could remember. Then the exchange of words resumed. At least by now they had a few basic expressions they could use to clear up doubtful points, and things moved faster.

Sometime during the session he began smoking.

Ato went into a dither until the smoke had been analyzed with the aid of a quick glittering little machine, then paid no more attention to it. He seemed to understand the coffee that was sent over, though, and began drinking a reddish liquid himself. But even with the coffee, Sam was almost dead with fatigue when Ato carefully and experimentally stretched his wide lips into what must have been meant for a human smile and leaned back. "Good," he said. He patted the machine in front of him, touched a button, and listened as Sam's voice came out of it.

"*Va*—yes. *Ssompa pir edomi*. Pen write word. One, two, three, four…"

Sam watched a technician remove one of the two spools inside the machine and thread the thin plastic into a duplicate machine, showing how it worked with a few simple gestures. He'd been a fool! Of course the aliens had perfect memories—so did men, since the invention of the tape recorder!

He was still cursing to himself as he threw the machine they gave him onto a bench and began shucking off his clothes in his little private cubicle. While he was working on his shoes Larsen came in, bringing glasses and a small bottle. The commander looked worried, but he was grinning.

"I know it's illegal to give whiskey to an Indian, Sam," he said. "But maybe the law won't reach this far."

"It's illegal to give anything to an Indian, Bill. You're supposed to take things away from them. Luck!" The liquor seemed to cut through his stomach and into his nerves at once, reminding him he hadn't picked up supper. He needed this more, though. He took a second glass, then reported briefly what had happened, playing a bit of the "tape" back. "What gives here?"

Larsen shook his head. "I wish I knew. Sam, even with this it'll take a week to get on real speaking terms, won't it? Umm. Why are they willing to spend all that time and effort? What do they want from us?"

"Why do they have to want anything?"

"They must," said Larsen patiently. "Look, suppose we'd found a strange ship already on the Moon? Would we have dropped down beside them, or would we have cased the layout first? Dropping in like that doesn't make sense, unless they needed something from us enough to take chances on our being armed—or unless they're completely invulnerable." He paused, tasting that thought. "But if so, why this desperate urge to get into communication with us? Did you see anything on the ship—their power plant, say?"

"I didn't try."

Larsen sighed. "No, naturally. But they've seen about everything we have. Their men paired up with some of ours; and I couldn't risk saying no, so they've been everywhere. And they're *good*, Sam. Too damned good. They spotted our trouble with the tractors, and they pitched in at once. You know how those things come for assembly—and how much it takes to see they're put together right? But these creatures—Perui, or whatever you call them—were hep to it all in ten minutes, and doing twice as much as our emergency crewmen could do. What's more, they didn't make any mistakes. They know machinery. What do they want?"

"You tell me," Sam suggested.

"I wish I could. But for one idea, maybe they want to know what weapons we have back on Earth."

Sam grunted. "You've been in touch with the station, Bill," he guessed. The other nodded, "Of course I have. That's my duty. And once the station scope spotted their ship, all hell was to pay down on Earth. How do we know this isn't just a scout for an invasion? They're certainly not from one of our planets. We've picked up a mess of high-frequency radiation they use in communicating from ship to men here, and we'd spot that stuff from any planet in the system that had it developed to that degree. Besides, from what you say of their air, they must come from a planet like Earth, and we know that doesn't fit any other planet here. How come we get a call from God knows just what star the minute our expedition touches the Moon?"

"Earth's seeing bogey men again," Sam said in disgust. "Either we're getting set to take someone over or someone's after us. Can't two equals simply get together?"

"Two equals, maybe. But we're not their equals." Larsen got up to leave, scowling at his own thoughts. "What has always happened when a superior culture meets an inferior one? You know the answer. See what you can learn tomorrow."

Sam muttered to himself. Well, what had happened when the whites met his people? War, of course. But it hadn't been all bad. Then he amended that; it hadn't been all bad, but it would have been if both sides had had atomic weapons. He reached for the tape recorder and turned it on, trying to concentrate on mastering more of the vocabulary. But before half an hour had passed he was sound asleep, dreaming he was playing Hermes in some tragedy.

And no matter how he read his lines or went up on them, he couldn't get it to move, and he knew the author had messed up the ending beyond all repair.

III

In the morning Ato was waiting for him outside the dome, with a smile on his purple face that now seemed almost natural to him, rather than a learned trick.

Sam saw that the other purple men were scattered about the field, mixing with the humans. Some crude measure of sign language seemed to have been worked out already, but it would be no good for abstractions. The labor gang had recovered from their binge and were out, looking somewhat chastened. Most of them were Andean Indians—a hangover from the building of the station, when it was thought they'd have a certain margin of safety in an accident. Most of them were avoiding the Perui, and he saw them making signs to ward off evil whenever a purple creature came near them. They were driving tractors on the Moon, but carrying their primitive superstition with them.

And maybe the whole Earth was doing the same about the aliens.

Inside the control room of the blue ship, the big electronic gadget seemed to be finished, and the technicians were gone. Ato dropped onto his seat, pointing to a queer glass of some liquid. "Drink it, Sam. We tested some of your drink, and this won't hurt you."

Sam gasped. It had been in pidgin, of course, but the words had been completely fluent. Yet he could have sworn Ato was saying something in Peruta at the same time. For a second, ideas of telepathy that needed initial word symbols before it could work raced through his mind. He reached for the drink, his nose telling him it was mildly alcoholic; at the moment he didn't care what else was in it, and it seemed palatable enough, though too sweet.

Then sober thought replaced the fantasy, and he turned to the electronic panel.

Ato's voice came, but there was a lag this time. Then the machine spoke—and now Sam could recognize his own voice behind the words.

"It's a putting from language to language machine," it announced. "The word, please?"

"Translating," Sam said automatically. That pause had come when the machine found no word for Ato's expression, and had to hunt for another way to say it—and found one! Maybe a human technician could have taken one of the huge plotting computers used to plan their orbits and adapted it into a translating machine in a few months; such machines had been used long enough on Earth to speed the exchange of scientific knowledge. But to make one that could overcome its own ignorance was another matter.

Bill Larsen had been right; these boys were *good*!

Then he shrugged. There was still Larsen's job to do. "All right," he said, while the machine clucked out words in Peruta. "In that case, Ato, what do you want?"

The smile came quickly this time. "A chance to talk, Sam—to talk until the machine won't make mistakes or have to hunt for words. About history, perhaps. Shall I talk, or will you?"

"Go ahead."

The purple head nodded—the first use of the motion Sam had seen.

His soft voice picked up the story of the beginnings of life from the primal seas—almost the same as the one Sam had learned. The machine spent a lot of time at first in hunting for ways to carry across the meaning, but it grew more fluent as its vocabulary increased. Sometimes it missed in its use of words, but it never made the same mistake twice.

Sam listened, fascinated in spite of himself. This was no wild story, no monstrously different way of life. It was Earth all over again, with names and events, orders of discoveries, and intervals of time changed. But it was a history he could understand as readily as his own. Fire, weapons, domestic animals, agriculture. Cities and then cruel empires. Writing and metal. Race and culture against race and culture, war, slavery…

He broke in abruptly, forgetting his resolve to give away as little about Earth as he could. "Our culture probably started on a little part of our mainland, too. We called it Greece. About twenty-five hundred years ago."

Ato listened, then drew something of a parallel, though with no Alexander, and with some strange ethical religion that sounded like a cross between Buddhism and Christianity. There had even been something like the crusades, and a discovery, much later, of four small continents occupied by savages.

Sam took over again. They alternated until they were through the current stage of Earth.

"We were earlier," Ato said. "All that came for us about two hundred of your years ago. We reached our planets—barely useful enough to encourage us to go on. We had one major atomic war, but fortunately the peace screen was discovered just in time."

The peace screen, thought Sam, filing the words.

"Then the two great powers had to get together. And we found the star ship secret. How to travel at thousands of times the speed of light—in theory; though we can't do better than hundreds yet. After that, we've been spreading, trading, growing. We've found three very primitive forms of intelligence, but too low for speech.

"And now, for the first time, another race and culture."

Sam sat back suddenly, the spell broken. Yeah, Earth would have gone through it all—but they'd missed it by two hundred years. In America, the Indians would have gone through Europe's progress in time; they'd found some measure of metal-working, the beginnings of writing, agriculture, and a lot of other things. They were moving ahead—not just the Mayans, but the Five Nations up north. The Seminoles hadn't done too badly, all things considered. But they'd missed by a couple thousand years or so, and the higher-cultured whites from Europe had found them.

Now those same whites at their planet-leaping stage had been found by a race a couple hundred years ahead.

And in a technical civilization, a couple of centuries were the same as millennia to barbarians. Earth had missed it by two hundred years—but she'd missed it. The Perui had the techniques, the star ships, and the empire. They'd crossed the galactic Atlantic, looking for trade routes—and found primitive mankind.

And the worst part of it, as he listened somberly to Ato, was that it hadn't even been deliberately planned as a voyage of discovery.

Ato ran a trading ship. He had been going from a new solar system to an older one when detectors on his ship had registered certain radiation that looked like space flight. He'd spun around and backtracked—to find the trail of the Moon ships and follow them down to their base.

"You took an awful chance, landing like that," Sam said quickly, hoping that it would at least worry the other.

But Ato seemed unconcerned. "Not at all. We saw the Moon was airless, so we knew there was no life. Why should a race able to cross space take weapons—when weight means so much in those little ships?"

"Why?"

"Why?" the purple man hesitated, then shrugged. "Wouldn't you be curious if you'd found another race? We expected to some day. Of course, we hoped it might be at our own level. But I guess we're lucky you weren't ahead of our progress…though I wonder. Our social scientists worked out the steps to be taken for any contingency, of course."

Sam leaned forward. "I suppose you know those steps then?"

He'd expected a denial, but Ato seemed perfectly willing to talk about it. And it seemed like a reasonable plan, all things considered, as Sam listened to it. A lot better than the Aztecs had got from Spain. Maybe as good as India and Egypt had managed with England. There'd be other ships here, of course—and the Perui would even supply Earth with engines to drive her ships to the planets and the nearer stars—the ones around here had not yet been taken over by the Perui. Some Earth scholars would probably be sent to Perui schools to learn more about the techniques, such as faster-than-light drive, than could be given directly to Earth technicians. There'd be little interfering with Earth rule, and a chance for Earth to lift herself up to complete independence as a part of the Peruvui empire. It would take time, of course, but…

"All this for nothing?" Sam asked doubtfully.

Ato shook his head. "Of course not, Sam. We're a practical people, like you. We're back in the trading stage—on a larger scale. We'll get things from you. There are a lot of things you can afford to do cheaper than we can, since your standard of living is so much lower for workers. You can do a lot of our smaller machining, produce certain special plants we need…after all, it's cheaper now to ship across space than across an ocean, though there's still a little more time involved. Oh, you'll earn your way."

One of the Perui came in then, snapping quick words to Ato.

To his surprise, Sam found he could understand most of them—the constant hearing of the two languages at once was wearing connections in his brain. Larsen wanted Sam.

Sam stood up as the machine began, and for the first time saw surprise register clearly on Ato's face. "All right, I'd better go," he said quickly. "Be back as soon as I can."

One of the men outside pointed to the big flagship.

Sam hurried to it and up to the control room. It was practically stripped by now, but the radio was still there, and Larsen sat before it. He listened to Sam's report, frowning heavily.

"No weapons on the ship?" he asked at last.

"How would I know, Bill? I don't suppose so, on a trading ship between friendly suns. But they could have. They must have had some dillies in that last war of theirs. What's up?"

Larsen grimaced. "All hell. Earth tried to contact the Perui. They found the right frequency, apparently, but they got no answer. Then reports came in from some amateur comet watchers—reports of stars suddenly being displaced along a line—and they've figured the Perui came in at a hundred or more times light speed and literally buckled space in doing it. Now they're scared sick down there that this is the spy for an invasion. They're dying to find what makes the ship tick. So am I, for that matter. But they want the ship held until Donahue can get here on the supply ship…"

"Donahue?" Sam repeated. He was the President's own troubleshooter—and in his case, there had been plenty of signs that the word meant a man who solved troubles by shooting them. There'd been a near riot in Burma over some of his methods, and diplomatic relations with Poland were still messed up from his last visit there. He'd had excellent reasons for his actions, of course, but…

"Donahue!" Larsen repeated. "He'll be here in three days. And I gather from something else that he's equipped."

"Equipped?"

Larsen nodded. "With a missile containing an H-warhead—to make sure the ship doesn't pull out after he gets here. But that's just a guess."

It would have to be true. There'd be no point in trying to hold the alien ship without some form of force. "So what do I do?" Sam asked.

"Hold Ato until Donahue gets here. Then pray to every manitou you know," Larsen told him. "And don't give away any secrets of ours, of course."

He started to swing back to the radio, then stopped. "Oh yeah. And find out whether their home world knows about us yet. And how far away it is, and any other little military secret you can think of. That's all, Sam!"

Sam went out sickly. And the Aztec governor sent word to the men who'd sighted the big ship of Cortez, saying to hold him and to get his military secrets. And the king sent the governor out, armed with a specially powerful obsidian sword and a mantle of the choicest feathers. All he had to do was threaten Cortez enough to hold him until the king could find a way to steal the ship. It was all simple.

But it probably wouldn't matter, he realized. It hadn't really mattered in Mexico.

In the long run, up north, where the settlers came in peacefully to trade and steal a little, the results had been the same. The white man had taken on the White Man's Burden, as he'd done in India and in Africa—except for a few tribes like the Zulus, who'd refused it with some success.

Now the Perui would take on the Spaceman's Burden, and Earth could like it or not. She'd get the castoff culture of the Perui, she'd be given a helping hand up to "independence"—and to a second-rate Perui culture. They'd have a chance to forget about being themselves and try to be something they never were. They'd be rich, in a way—just as some of the plains Indians had grown rich on oil and decay.

Thank God, Sam's ancestors had refused to suck up to the whites! They'd pulled into their swamps instead, after some bitter fighting. And today, the funny thing was, they'd somehow got into the present civilization without losing their respect for themselves or the white men's respect for them. Their war had become a good-natured joke he and Larsen could kid about.

They'd made it without being the White Man's Burden. He looked at some of the labor crew, still crossing their fingers to ward off evil spirits. Sure, they had television back home and cars—and they were here on the Moon now, with him—doing the work the scientists didn't have time for, and still only halfway to being men.

It was a great future that lay ahead of them all, because of a two hundred year lag in technology.

And Donahue was coming out with his little bomb to make it merrier. He'd insult the superior race and provoke them to force, maybe even kill this group. Then there'd be a quick retaliation, a few lessons that would end Earth's final vestige of pride, and a somewhat harsher version of the same program of Spaceman's Burden.

Running feet jarred the ground behind him, and sounded through his shoes. He turned to see Larsen, holding out a small object. "Take it and hide it," the commander said bitterly. "Orders!"

He was gone, as Sam shoved the only revolver on the Moon into his pocket and headed into the alien ship.

IV

Ato looked up, smiling. "Your government wants to talk in me, I hear," he greeted Sam. "Don't they know I'm only a trader? I can't make any arrangements with them, and I don't have time to waste on politicians. I've got to get off here tomorrow, your time, to keep on schedule. Besides, I want to report all this as soon as I can."

"You haven't reported it yet?" Sam asked, trying to control his voice.

The other nodded. "By radio on tight beam, of course. But it will take forty years for word to reach the settlement there—radio won't beat light speed. That's just a formality."

He let it drop.

Sam pondered it, his brain prickling slowly. "Suppose something happened to ground you here, Ato? What then? You'd have to stay here until the radio signal reached them, wouldn't you?"

"It's happened," the alien admitted. "That's the real reason for the signal—to locate me. Then, of course, once it reached a settlement, plans for a rescue would take a few days, and the ship would need a month more to get here. Of course, if I had bad luck, and the settlement wasn't visited for a few years, there'd be a longer wait. Now, about those plans my people have worked out, if you want more details—"

Sam shook his head. He'd gone upstage on his lines as much as the script would let him, but there came a time when it had to be torn up and an adlibbed ending was better than none. When the signals failed, and the game was in the final minutes, and the score was 7-0 against you, you got the ball if you could and put it up to your legs and your guts.

He pulled out the revolver. "Know what this is, Ato?"

The other studied it slowly. "I can guess. We had them. Fatal, of course?"

"Quite fatal. Better call your men in, but keep them out of here. And get ready to lift ship, Ato. I'm not making a joke. I'll shoot—in fact, my government would want me to shoot rather than let you leave tomorrow."

"You can't hold the weapon forever—and if I lift ship, you'll be beyond help," Ato pointed out. "Why?"

It took some fifteen seconds to tell him what Sam thought of the Spaceman's Burden business for Earth. He'd already figured out what would happen to himself. If those were the lines, and that was the game, he'd have to prove that a Seminole was as good as an Apache any day.

But he couldn't tell that to the alien. They hadn't exchanged enough cultural history for that.

"Ten seconds, Ato," he said. "If you don't obey by then, I'll shoot."

The purple head nodded slowly, and a finger reached out for a button; Ato began giving orders. The screens showed the Perui drifting back to the ship.

By the time the men began to notice, they were all aboard. "Lift ship," Sam ordered. "Take it up at less than light speed, and head for our space station, if you know where that is."

Sam had expected difficulty at this stage, but the alien only shrugged and moved slowly toward the big control panel, dragging the translating machine microphone with him. Sam followed, moving along the wall where he could keep an eye on the door. In a moment, without any feeling of motion, the big ship was lifting; the screens showed the Moon dropping below. One, set for greater magnification, showed Larsen looking up, but it was too far to read his face.

Maybe he'd understand. If not, maybe his kids might, some day—if this worked.

"There's a ship heading for the Moon, somewhere between us and the station," Sam said. "I want you to locate it, Ato. Then I want you to set up a stable circular orbit around Earth that will intersect the path of that ship. Got it?"

"As you say," Ato said quietly.

There was something strange on the alien's face, but Sam couldn't read it. He tightened his grip on the gun, keeping his eyes firmly on the face of Ato. He was counting on luck and Ato's ignorance of the fact that the supply ship was carrying a hydrogen-fusion bomb. And the fact that nothing could be much worse than it would be anyhow, so it wouldn't matter if he failed.

If Earth thought the aliens were enemies and expected a follow-up attack, she wouldn't sit still and wait for it. History told him that much about his planet, at least. She was often wrong, but rarely cowardly. She'd do her best to get ready to repel any attack—and that best was pretty phenomenal. Men had compressed twenty years of progress into five often enough before in wartime, and they could do it again, if they had to.

They'd have forty years, until that radio message reached some place or other. Then, maybe with luck, they'd only have a rescue ship to deal with, and a little more time before all the Perui realized it was war. If Earth could recover even a little of the technology of the Perui ship and blend it with her own, she'd be able to hold them off. She'd be operating from the strength of a planet base, and they'd have to carry the war to her.

It would be a period of intolerable hell. But no profitless war goes on forever, and there would be an end.

With luck—and with her own determination—Earth could at least hold her own.

History had proved what happened to the races that bowed to their superiors and accepted the help offered them so often in good faith; the history of Ato's people and his own agreed on that. And they agreed on something else—that sometimes the best way to make sure another race respected you was to fight it. One side couldn't fight a hard battle over long years against an enemy without gaining some respect. And when wars were finished, alliances could be worked out. There was England and America—and Japan. Germany and New France. Even, to some extent, Jordan and Israel. There was the respect his own people had won among the whites of their swamplands.

Enemies could become friends. But the distance between inferiors and superiors only widened, until the lesser was swallowed up in the greater. It was better this way. And yet...

Ato looked around. "We're going to cross the little ship's orbit soon, Sam. I suppose you want me to threaten it—and then wait for the bomb it must carry?"

Sam stared at the purple man, without anything to say. It was exactly his plan. And if the other could guess it so easily...

"I have nearly fifty other men aboard, Sam," Ato said quietly. "Some are my friends, and I'm responsible for all of them. There's a life raft large enough to get them to the planet you call Mars. No farther, Sam. They can manage to live there. Let them go and I'll call your ship."

It could be a trick, Sam knew. And with all the lives already at stake, a few more shouldn't matter. But he nodded.

"Send them off."

A minute later, almost as soon as Ato finished speaking, there was a lurch, and one of the screens showed a part of the blue ship apparently dropping away and picking up speed away from the sun.

Ato reached for the dials on his board and began fiddling until a barrage of words spilled in through the speaker. They were obviously coming from the supply ship.

"I have the power high enough to reach Earth with this," Ato said. He pulled the translator over and began speaking harshly into the microphone. "Earth ship, you are my prisoner! Earth ship, you are my prisoner! Surrender at once and prepare to let my men aboard. Or I shall destroy you!"

Then he cut the switch and swung back to face Sam again.

Sam stared at him unbelievingly. If the Perui were as easily cowed as this, or as willing to sell their race short—but they couldn't be: not if any part of their history was true.

"*Why?*" he asked savagely.

Ato shrugged. "Shoot me and find out, Sam. Go ahead. Or no, I'll tell you. It would do you no good to shoot, because there is the peace shield we found between you and me. There has been since you walked in with what my detectors said was a weapon. And there's one around the ship, too. No weapon you now have could wreck it."

Sam fired—coldly and deliberately. A moment later, the useless gun hung empty in his hands, and there were seven blobs of melted lead on the floor. Ato stood unharmed.

"All right," Sam said finally. "I suppose I should have saved the final one for myself. Now what?"

"Who knows what comes after death?" Ato asked softly. "Sam, do you think we want what you call the Spaceman's Burden? Don't you realize that our history shows us the results, too? It's no kinder to the superior than the inferior—it rots him inside. Doesn't your history show—as mine shows—that no true peace and progress can come until it comes among equals?"

He made a sound curiously like a sigh. "I don't like your solution either, Sam. I don't like it at all. But I like ours less. And if you can die for it, can one of the Perui do less?" He threw down a small red lever.

"You can come here now, Sam. That breaks the screen between us. But now, if there is to be anything of this ship and its library left for your people, I'll need your help. It takes two to maintain part of a shield while canceling the other part. There—that button—and this lever—so…"

I told you so, something in the back of Sam's head said. *You WOULD go to the Moon. Now you'll die.*

And another part of his mind was playing the game, fumbling for the ball to boot over the posts. He stood quietly beside Ato, watching the screens and holding down the lever while the missile headed toward them from the supply ship. It was bad to die, he through. But if death had to be, it was good that it was shared…with a friend.

No Place Like Home

Sid Mallon didn't quite believe it, still. He never would be able to believe all that had happened. But now the ship was there, raising its tip high among the stars, with the full moon washing it with light, and a few spotlights picking out the details of the big power tube and the fins that would guide it through the air.

Seeing it, Sid drew his small figure more nearly erect, and his narrow shoulders squared a little. The hints of grey in his ash-colored hair and the lines of strain around his vague blue eyes might be due to the ship—but she was worth every bit of it. Tonight, the whole human race had a finger pointing at the stars—and one knuckle of the finger was his!

"Feels good, doesn't it, Sid?" The big, brunette bulk of Doug Swanson had come up, silently as always, to join him. His eternally expressionless face lifted, rising along the ship to its nose, and then to the stars in the Arizona sky above it. Doug hadn't changed in the past five years, except that the hint of weariness was gone from him now, and the faint tinge of what might have been a Scandinavian accent had been worn from his voice.

"Yeah, Doug. Plenty good."

Five years. Sid shook his head, trying to remember that it had been no longer than that, though it seemed half his lifetime. He'd been promoting the careers of two of the hottest rising stars in Hollywood. Then he'd picked Doug up; Sid didn't pick up hitchhikers, but somehow he hadn't been able to refuse the tired, awkward giant that time.

It had taken Doug about forty miles to warm up, maybe fifty more to sell Sid on the idea. How, he'd never quite known. But the big guy could talk of rockets and his dreams and his designs until a brass monkey could feel the pumice of the moon under his feet. Sid was pretty good at talking; but he'd only dug up the angles, while Doug did the selling. Nobody else could have convinced Max Westman to sink a fortune in a real ship instead of process shots for his next space picture; only Doug could have sold the same idea to a group of twenty producers, and got them out hustling for more money.

Even when they found they'd been rooked, and that it would take three years to build the moon ship, they'd gone right on putting up funds. Doug had convinced them he could somehow beat the whole government to space. After the first ship, when Doug did reach the moon and came back, it had been easier. Then Sid had been able to take over the promoting, while Doug turned his energies to building the *Centaurian*, leaving the moon ship for the Air Force men to use as a nucleus of their moon fleet in place of their now-obsolete boosters and capsules.

"Five years," Sid said aloud. Five years to do everything Doug had promised, and give them a ship that could reach Mars—even the stars, maybe, if anyone wanted to be a damned fool by trying.

Doug shook his big head. "Twelve for me, Sid. Seven of them fighting my way up until I could meet and sell someone like you. I'm—well, a little older than I look."

Sid glanced at him, wondering. But he'd learned before not to ask Doug Swanson for details. Others had tried to pump the man on his degrees and how he developed the mass of ideas that poured out of his head, or get something of his personal background. But while Doug could speak endlessly of the ship when required to, he froze up on everything else. Sid knew little more than he'd learned that first day. He no longer cared. What was right for Doug Swanson was right with Sid Mallon.

They stood quietly for minutes more, leaning against the guard fence and looking at the ship. A single guard was on duty in his little hut, with the electric eyes to warn him of any fool curiosity-driven intruder. But the ship was actually its own best guardian. The crowd that had collected during the day had vanished now, though it would increase as the day of take-off grew near. The workmen were paid off and sent on their way. And the *Centaurian* sat there on her tripod fins, stocked with an unbelievable mass of supplies, waiting.

"Doug!" Sid said, finally. The big guy looked down silently, and Sid cleared his throat, trying to remember the rules of promoting that had normally become sheer instinct. They weren't working now. The words wouldn't come right, and he gave them up, blurting out what was in his mind. "Doug, you call her *our* ship. She's your idea, sure—but I've got half my guts in her, too. I didn't kick when you hiked off to the moon alone. But this is different. Oh, damn it, I want to go!"

Doug looked down again, slowly shaking his head. "I'd like to take you, Sid. It's going to be lonely out there, and I'm not the glory-hog I may seem. But I'm going alone. I have to."

There was a bitterness in Sid's mouth as he swallowed that. He knew how inflexible Doug could be; he'd seen the top brass of the Air Force trying to threaten and cajole Doug into giving advance plans on this big ship, and he'd seen them fail—and accept their failure. Now he shrugged. "If you change your mind, Doug—well, it's a week to take-off."

"Take-off's tonight!" Doug's arms had come down off the fence, and his big figure seemed straighter. "Sorry, Sid—I had to keep it from everyone. I'm going off without fanfare. The other date was just a cover-up. So—I guess it's so long."

"Now?" Sid digested it as the other nodded. His shoulders dropped, and his eyes went back to the ship and the big entrance port down near the base, open and inviting, with the little ladder running up to it.

He should have guessed. It was logical enough, while there were no crowds to catch the backwash of fire from the tube, or get in the way. He shrugged again, and stuck out his hand. "Then, so long—and good luck!"

Doug's hand met his, the other big paw dropping on his shoulder for a second's pressure. Then the man vaulted over the fence in a smooth flow of muscle power and was walking quietly towards the ship. He went up the ladder and into the blackness of the airlock without looking back. Across the distance, Sid could hear his feet clumping up the tiny stairs to the control room. The tread was steady, measured, as final as Gabriel's trumpet.

The guard would be safe in his hut, but Sid knew he should be running back, before the blast from the tube struck down, washing across the ground in great waves. Instead, he was at the top of the fence. Doug must have reached the control room. There was a sigh from the valves, and the big outer door of the airlock began to inch inward.

Then Sid was off the fence, running harder than he'd forced his legs for years. The door was half shut, then even closer. He could almost feel it catching him in the middle, gradually cutting through him. But he did not draw back; instead, he forced his way up the little ladder, throwing himself through. He barely made it, feeling both shoulders scrape against metal, but he was inside, and ducking through the inner lock before it began closing. Behind him, the outer seal clicked shut.

Blast-off would come almost at once, and he knew something of the frightful pressures of that. He ducked around stanchions and through the engine-hatch room, then up a little stairway to the hydroponic room. Here the plants that would keep the air fresh and provide food enough for several men for years were compactly grouped under intense ultraviolet lamps. At least he wouldn't be imperiling Doug's life, even if they crashed on Mars. Both could live on the supplies, until they were rescued or died as old men.

Below, a preliminary rumble came from the tube, a mere hiss as it was warmed for later blasts. But it sent sweat bursting from Sid's forehead, and made him redouble his speed. He had to be set as best he could, and there were only fractions of minutes left. He couldn't take the blast without some preparation.

He was in one of the storerooms off the hydroponic cell, yanking out materials. He was lucky; he'd helped supervise some of the stockpiling of this section. Then he had the rubber mat that was to be used when lying under the tanks, draining and cleaning them. He had no time to locate the little pump. He forced the valve back with a broken match and began blowing into it. It wasn't too good, but it filled slowly, and it would help. He yanked out the match, tossed the mat on to the floor, and threw himself out on it, his body horizontal against blast direction.

He was barely in time. There was a roar from the tube that rose to a screaming fury of insane sound waves, and the weight of the universe seemed to clamp down on him. He could feel his flesh run like hot butter, the muscles straining back from his legs, his mouth slipping towards his ears, and his eyeballs seeming to drive back into his head. The blood beat wildly. The mat gave under him, until his hips and shoulders were against the floor.

Doug was using full power—more than they'd ever talked of using! Prone, on tests, Sid had felt five gravities hit him, and had taken it. This was worse. The blood began washing back from his mind, forced by sheer pressure-weight towards the back of his head and his bursting hips. Blackness began to rush at him. He tried to cry out, but his lungs wouldn't work. Only the most shallow movement was possible.

Outside, they must have either exceeded the speed of sound or leaped beyond the atmosphere. The sound of the tube went dead, with only a dull mutter coming through the metal of the hull. Doug was crazy. Even in an acceleration harness, no man could stay conscious under that force. And if he passed out, without cutting it, they'd go roaring on until they were dead!

The thought brought no emotional response. It was too dull; his mind was losing control of itself, a grey fog of pain and weight creeping over him. It got darker, then was black. For a second, the pain remained. Then even that was gone, and Sid was completely unconscious.

He came out of it slowly, with a vague feeling that long hours had passed. His mouth was dry and hot, his stomach sick with fatigue and emptiness. But the pressure was gone from his lungs and heart. He'd always known he was tough—his thin wiriness had stood the test, somehow. Every muscle ached, and all were stiff as he tried to use them. But it was a stiffness that spoke of a long time to recuperate from the pressure of that initial acceleration.

He looked at his watch, but it had stopped. The pressure had been too much for it. He had only his mouth to go by, and that cried for water with more than a day's thirst.

Slowly he worked his way to his feet, stumbling and staggering as his muscles shrieked and his head threatened to burst from the pain. Only blind luck had prevented a burst blood vessel in his brain, probably. His back was one solid bruise, and he could feel the soreness of broken capillaries near the skin of his shoulders. But the mat had made the difference.

He staggered forward, falling from one foot to the other and somehow catching himself before he fell completely. He weighed more than normal still—about a quarter more, which would indicate they were still pressing on at a greater acceleration than one gravity. He tried to figure distance, at an average acceleration of two gravities. He'd done enough of that to learn the basic physics. D equals $\frac{1}{2}gt^2$—distance figures half the acceleration used times the square of the time; feet and seconds, convert to hours, change to miles—he couldn't do it, but he knew that ten hours would put them nearly eight million miles out; twenty hours, four times as far; thirty, nine times. And it felt more like thirty.

But that was ridiculous! They couldn't have blasted that long. Then he had it—of course, they were blasting down against Mars. They'd be landing soon.

He found a valve that supplied water to the plants, and quenched his thirst. A little of the stiffness was going, though he felt even sorer as he moved. But it was worth it. One of the first two men to reach another major planet—a chance to find what the canals were, to walk across plants that had never known Earth, maybe even to find some measure of alien intelligence!

He straightened from the water, biting his lips at the pain in his shoulder. The gun he'd worn around the construction site, in keeping with everyone else against some chance psycho, was still there, and had pressed against him during all that killing acceleration. He fingered it, and nodded. It might be handy on Mars. Who knew?

But he had to get up to the control room. He wanted to see this time, and to be able to tell his children, if he ever had any, of this landing! He found the little stairway and began crawling up it, past the various hatches and controls. Walking was bad, and climbing was worse, but nothing mattered.

The three hundred foot climb was still too much for him against the extra weight of the drive. He stopped about midway up, meaning to sink down and catch his breath. Then he remembered that one of the storerooms carried an escape port for emergencies—with a section of thick glass from which he could look. He located it one more flight up, and moved to it. He'd see Mars first, with luck. Then he could finish the climb.

He hadn't really hoped to find the planet, though; if it were dead astern as they braked down, it would be out of sight. But it was worth the chance. He noticed that they were rotating very slowly on their axis, since the hot edge of the sun was just swinging out of view. He watched the stars wheel slowly past.

Mars came into view, far down at the edge of the glass. He lifted himself on tiptoe, staring out; there was no mistaking the red disc with its tantalizing hints of canals and its dull red and faintly greenish markings. Two million miles, maybe, judging by the views he'd had from telescopes and the pictures he'd studied.

It wouldn't be long now…

Realization hit him suddenly. The location of the sun and of Mars abruptly registered, together with the course of the ship. He had a good visual imagination, and he couldn't be wrong. They had already passed beyond Mars—well to the side. They must be a million and a half miles out and a half a million or more beyond Mars' orbit! They'd missed junction!

And their acceleration was carrying them on, farther and farther away from it.

A thousand fantasies went through his mind, rooted out of all the stories he'd read; he'd never believed a planet could be missed in a ship with enough power to maintain continual push. But they'd done it. Doug! Doug was a bear for punishment, and he'd had the shock cushions to held him, but it only took one little bursting blood vessel to kill a man.

Maybe Doug was still alive. He might have revived just enough to cut the acceleration down a little—or perhaps that had happened when a dead arm hit a control. Sid shook his head, and managed a weak stumbling run towards the stairway. He had to get there. He wouldn't make much of a pilot—but he could at least stop their drive and somehow reverse, until he could revive Doug if the man still lived. If not...

He preferred not to think of that. He'd have to make a landing, then. He'd probably be killed. But that was a minor matter. Doug was Doug—and the big guy couldn't be dead!

He forced his feet up the steps, hating each one that held him back. He wasn't stopping for rests now. He whipped his mind along, hardly feeling the grinding ache as his bruised hips and shoulders touched against the walls of the tiny stairway. He called once, but his voice echoed back without an answer. Up here, there were doors on the various landings, designed to isolate the sections from each other in case a meteorite hit. His voice couldn't reach Doug, even if the other could hear.

He opened them, one by one, letting them close automatically. Then there was only one ahead of him, and he'd be in the bigger control room. The *Centaurian* was unlike the little preliminary moon ship; there was room enough to turn around in her main quarters. There had to be, if a man was to live on her while exploring another planet.

He threw the last door open, giving a narrow view of the control panel and the big pilot seat. The tiny galley was off it, together with the little sleeping quarters. But he didn't bother with them. He called again, softly this time. There was no answer. He moved forward, hating what he might find, fearing the worst, but driven forward towards whatever lay in the pilot's seat.

The big padded back cut off his view until he was beside it. Then his eyes went down.

There was no sign of Doug. A thin series of lines of some kind of doodling were on a pad before the seat, and the ship was set on automatic. All the big lights were green. It looked as if the man had had time to operate them. But he was missing.

Sid swung towards the sleeping quarters, tossing the tiny door aside.

A shoe on the floor caught his eye first, then a leg. Doug's body lay sprawled out under the hammock, on the floor, sagging and unnatural in shape, as if every bone in his body had been broken. He couldn't be alive!

Sid dropped to the floor with a low moan, reaching for the mangled heap. His hand went out. He drew it back, staring, to drag out the stuff that he had thought was Doug. The head was a rubbery mask, and there was a strange assortment of plastic shell and metallic stiffeners under the clothing. And there was a smell to the inside, where a zipper had exposed it. It wasn't unpleasant, but totally unlike anything Sid had smelled before.

He squatted there, picturing the thing that had been inside this human shell, but getting no clear image. This was Doug—all the Doug the world had ever seen. But it is only a hollow casing for something else. With sickness heavy in his stomach, Sid came to his feet, his hand going to the automatic and pulling it out. The seven years Doug had spent before Sid had found him were meaningful now. Seven years of making this shell, of learning to mix with men.

When you're shipwrecked on a savage island, you paint your skin dark and get the natives to build you a dug-out.

"Only a raft, Sid," the voice of Doug said from behind him, and he swung to see a thin, wiry creature coming from the galley. It was vaguely manlike, but jointless, without visible features on the face. The voice was still the same, though. And Sid realized he'd been muttering his thoughts to himself, loud enough to be heard.

"Only a raft," the voice repeated. "One that takes eleven hard years to paddle home… And it's a shock to find a native stowed away. But you can't go back, or they'd confiscate even your raft. You've got to go home!"

Sid lifted the automatic, sighting it carefully. The thing that had been Doug jerked straighter upright, but no other sign showed the surprise. The featureless head nodded slowly, and the creature stood waiting.

Sid looked at the gun, and across to the target. Then, very slowly, he put the automatic back in the holster. His eyes went to Mars, falling farther behind, and towards the stars ahead. He looked at the empty shell that he had thought was Doug Swanson, and then at the real Doug Swanson.

He was wondering what a backward native would think of civilization when the raft came paddling up the harbor. He probably wouldn't like it—but it would be interesting.

He chunked the automatic down solidly, snapped the clasp on the holster, and reached out a hand for the thin, wire-like hand of the friend who'd earned his right to go home.

Done Without Eagles
[as by Philip St. John]

The triangulator registered eight thousand miles up from Earth, though naturally we couldn't see the old ball behind us. When they built the *Kickapoo*, they left out all windows and covered her with a new laboratory product to bounce back hard radiations, which is why I have a couple of normal kids instead of half-monsters; cosmic rays just love to play around with a man's genes and cause mutations if they get a chance. Anyway, the spy instruments we used were worth a whole factory of portholes.

Captain Lee Rogers ran his eyes over the raised indicators when I signaled that we'd made one diameter, and found them all grooved where they should be. He pushed back his shoulders and tapped down for normal space acceleration before swinging around to face me. "They all come back, Sammy," he said, for no good reason I could see. "Once a man's been outside the atmosphere, you can't keep him grounded. Remember Court Perry?"

How could I help it, with some of the records he'd made still unbeaten? He'd won his eagles back in the old quartz-window days. Then, when they built the *Kickapoo* as the first blind ship and made him captain, he'd made history and legends for six years, until even the die-hards admitted spy instruments worked, and every student in navigation school with marrying ideas darned near worshiped him. After that, his landings and takeoffs began to go sour, and got worse for months. They seemed to be improving again at the last, but it was too late then; the officials called him in and yanked his eagles, offering him an office job instead, which he turned down. That had been five years before and nobody had heard a word of the captain since.

"Sure," I told Lee. "It was before I got my copilot ticket on the *Kickapoo*, but they gave us his life for inspirational reading in navigation school. Why?"

He handed me over a hen-scratched paper giving the passenger listings. "Take a look at the angel roll. The steward sent it up for my okay on the use of the superdeck cabin."

"Inspector eyeing our flare?" The superdeck cabin is reserved for officials, usually, and lies right down the hall from the dugout-navigation room—next to the captain and pilot's quarters.

Lee shook his head. "Free-wing angels. We're carrying a full load this trip, and they came aboard with 'any consideration will be appreciated' passes, so I had to okay it. You might read it, you know."

It was an idea, though I was beginning to catch on. All the same, my eyes popped when I saw the names after Cabin Q-A. "Captain Courtney R. Perry,

Ret., and Stanley N. Perry, M.A., M.M., Ph.D., F.R.P.S., F.R.S.," I read. "Mmm. So he's come out of the hole. Who's the alphabet?"

"Court Perry's son, and that's only part of his degrees and such. One of the hard-radiation mutes." Mutation, he meant, not speechless. "Born while the captain was on the old ships, so don't be surprised when you see him. Claims he's a superman, and maybe he is— Get ready for trouble, Sammy."

"I don't get it." I'd been wanting to meet Court Perry for years, and this looked like a first-class opportunity to me.

Lee grimaced. "Naturally, not knowing him. I was his pilot before they sacked him, though, and I know what he'll think of another man pushing his ship. Inside of an hour, you'll hear a knock on the door there, and won't have to guess who it is."

Lee was wrong, partly. It wasn't more than half an hour before the knock came, and the door opened to show the hugest body I'd seen on a man six feet tall and not fat. It was topped by a head that was simply magnificent; beautiful describes it better than handsome. And below that—well, the man had four arms, all fully developed, and muscled like a gorilla's, with long hands that ended in six tapering fingers apiece. Apparently the double shoulder system left no room for a waist, but ran in a straight line from hips up. I must have gasped, but the mute took no notice of it. "Hi, Lee. How's tricks?"

Lee gave him a rather troubled grin and came to his feet to grab one of the arms. "Not bad, Stan, though the two of you might have written once in a while. You're looking good. How's Court?"

"All right, I guess." He swung a couple of hands in an uncertain gesture that gave me the heebies. "He wants to join you here for a while, if you don't mind."

"Afraid I can't. The rules forbid passengers—"

"What's that?" The voice rapped out from the hall and swung me around to face a little, thin man with a ramrod down his back and a neat Vandyke on his face. He looked like the sort who'd hit heaven and been routed through hell on the return ticket, but come through it. Pride, authority, and indignation were all mixed, and another expression I couldn't quite place. Something about him made me pull my stomach in and come to attention, even though he wasn't wearing twin eagles on his old space cap.

"What's that, Lee?" he rapped out again, pushing forward to the dugout. "When have I ever been an angel, eh? Don't be an ass!"

Lee's arm barred his way. "Sorry, sir, but technically you're an angel now. The rule clearly states that no passengers are to be admitted to navigation or engine rooms under any circumstances. You taught me those rules were to be obeyed!"

"I taught you not to be a blamed fool! Out of my way, Lee. I'm coming in. I want to find out what's happened to my ship while you've been running it. Stan, make way for me!"

Stan started forward, and I didn't like the look of those bulking shoulders, but Lee waved him back with a sharp gesture. There were little creases torturing his forehead, and the muscles along his jaw stood out sharply. "Sorry, Captain Perry. I'm wearing the eagles on this ship. Return to your quarters!"

For only a fraction of a second, Court Perry winced, and then his face froze into a blank. "Very good, Captain Rogers," he said precisely, coming to salute. He executed a right-about-turn with a snap and marched down the hall, fingering the place where the eagles should have been, Stan following.

I swung to Lee. "Good Lord, man, did you have to—"

"I had to." The cigarette in his hands was mashed to a pulp, and he tossed it away savagely, fiddling with the controls, while the air machine clicked out the only noises in the room and I made myself busy with charts. Finally he shrugged and reached for another cigarette.

"Court Perry dug me out of an orphanage, Sammy, put me through navigation school, and taught me all he knew about running the *Kickapoo*. He's—" Lee stopped and looked to see how I was taking it. "All right, I suppose it does make me seem an ungrateful pup. But if I'd broken that rule or let him override my authority, he'd have hated me for a weakling and himself for having failed with me. Now let's forget it and wait for his next move. He won't give up on the first try."

He didn't. Almost as Lee finished speaking, the etherphone *ikked* from behind the controls and I jumped to answer it. " 'Lee Rogers,' " I read as it came over, " 'Captain, *Kickapoo*: Captain Courtney Perry and son are to have full freedom of ship. Signed, Redman, president—' How'd they get word through without sending on our transmitter?"

"Probably Stan built a sender from the pile of gadgets he always carries along."

"In fifteen minutes?"

"Mm-hmm. He does those things when he wants to. I've seen him take a computator apart and reassemble it in ten." Lee glanced at the clock and slid off the throne. "Take over. So Court still has pull in the office, it seems. Redman had no business interfering; we're in space and my word is supposed to be final. Nothing I can do about it, though. Come in!"

The door snapped open to show Court Perry standing with his feet exactly on the imaginary line of the dugout, Stan behind him. He came to rigid attention and saluted stiffly. Lee returned it. "The freedom of the ship is yours, Captain Perry," he acknowledged. "Sammy, see that Captain Perry is provided with a set of master keys to the lower decks."

"Thank you, Captain Rogers." Court's square shoulders were perhaps a trifle farther back as he stepped over the line and approached the control seat. He reached out as I slid up to let him take it, then hesitated. "With your permission, sir."

"Permission granted." It was the first time I'd seen formality in space, and I felt awkward as a two-tailed comet between them. Lee disappeared around the panel to the etherphone cubbyhole with a handful of miscellaneous and unrelated charts in his hands.

As Court took the seat I had vacated, the huge bulk of Stan moved in front of me, cutting off my view. He was almost too big for the little room. But I could hear the faint sounds of the old man's fingers on the panel, as he tested it bit by bit. He grunted once or twice, and Stan seemed to mutter something, then twitched his arms slightly and looked around. Court got up.

"Copilot—Sammy's the name, isn't it? Good." He nodded faintly at that. "Sammy, where are the testing instruments? I used to keep them under the panel, but apparently they're no longer there."

"We don't have testers, sir; at least, I've never seen any."

"No testers, eh?" He swallowed it carefully, then tossed his voice over the instrument panel. "Captain Rogers, your copilot informs me there are no instrument testers. Is that correct?"

Lee's voice bounced back at him. "It is, Captain Perry. Under the new regulations, we're checked over at both ends, and no tests are made in space. That system has proved entirely satisfactory."

"Hmm. I distinctly remember explaining to you the reasons for space tests. Takeoff accelerations sometimes jar loose a delicate control, and furthermore, ground men are sometimes careless; they're not trained in actual flight conditions, and their lives aren't involved. I advise an immediate test of your instruments. Hull Indicator C responds slowly, and the meteor repeller itself may be at fault instead of the indicator."

"Sorry, sir, that's impossible. We have no testers."

Court grimaced at that. "Your engine-room testers can be adapted. I believe I also taught you how that was done."

"Sorry, Captain Perry," Lee decided positively. "I don't consider such measures necessary under the present regulations."

Seeing the uselessness of arguing, Court shrugged. "Take over, Sammy," he said, relinquishing the controls. "And if he'll listen, you might remind Captain Rogers that Mars lies in the region of the Little Swarm now. Meteors—even peanut-sized ones—aren't pleasant company when the hull repellers are out of order. Now, if I could have those keys—"

When the door closed again, Lee came out of the hole. "Easier than I thought...Mmm. Nothing wrong with Indicator C that I can see. It answers to a change in the hull charge perfectly. Wonder what happens next."

Nothing really happened for a while, except that Stan and Court were poking over the ship in a methodless hunt for inefficiency. It was just that something was in the air, an unpleasantness that traveled from the control room down to the crew deck, and finally hit the passengers. But any little thing in space does that, and the old customers of the line shrugged and forgot it, as much as they could. Court wandered about the ship with Stan at his heels, but I could see no particular point to his activities.

I was off duty on a prowl when the first trouble came. Down from the cook's galley came a caterwauling and sounds of some sort of scrap, with the shrill yelps of the little cook predominating. As I bounced around a corner, I saw Tony leave the deck in a flying leap and plunge toward the entrance of his domain.

Then one of Stan's big arms came out carelessly and caught him in midair. "Naughty boy," the mute said softly. "You'll hurt yourself trying that. Lucky I was here to catch you." He held the cook easily, while the little man squirmed and fumed helplessly.

"What's going on here?" I wanted to know. Tony swung away at the sound of my voice and bounced up and down before me.

"Mr. Noyes, you gotta help me, you gotta! They steal my galley; they snoop all over; they won't let me work. How can I cook without I get in? Get 'em out, Mr. Noyes, kill 'em, lock 'em in irons. Oh, *Santa Maria*, I'll kill 'em so dead! Alla my help's in there and I ain't telling 'em what to do! They'll spoil the dinner. Get away from my galley, you bums, or I'll make soup outa you both! Spoil my dinner, I feed you to pigs! Mr. Noyes, you gotta get 'em out."

Stan grinned at me and winked, which was my first indication that he had a sense of humor of some kind. "Tony's a little overenthusiastic, Sammy. Don't mind him." He caught one of the little man's flailing fists and drew him close, patting his head. "Sh, Tony. Dad decided to investigate the galley, so we dropped down. Tony came in just as we were looking over his pans, and set up a squawk. When he grabbed a butcher knife and came at us, I had to put him out. Finished in there, Dad?"

"All finished." Court appeared in the door. "Tony!"

The tone of voice cut through Tony's indignation and left the cook at limp attention.

"Yes—sir?"

"Tony, you use too much grease, and you don't clean your pans often enough! Look at that!" He held out a frying pan with a thin coat of oil on the bottom.

"That carries one meal's flavor over to the next food. I've found grease on your griddles, too, thick enough to come off on my finger and half stale. Anything to say about it?"

"That new helper," Tony suggested weakly. "Musta been the new helper."

"Then teach that new helper to keep clean pans. I don't like indigestion. All right, back to your work! Hello, Sammy. Any objections from headquarters?"

"Not this time, sir." I suppose Lee would have objected, but Lee didn't need to know. After all, there had been a slightly off taste to the food this voyage, and I didn't have much use for Tony's treatment of his assistants, anyway.

Court smiled, apparently in the best of spirits after his conquest of the galley. "Fine. I don't suppose Captain Lee has followed my advice, eh?... No, I thought not. Thinks I'm a meddling old fool who had no business going over his head. Pigheaded—made him that way, I guess. Needs an accident to teach him good sense—and he'll get it, or I'm mistaken. Damn!"

He caught his foot against a swabber's kit and lurched forward, rubbing at a handrail to regain his balance. "Who left that…that bucket in the middle of a man's way? Rollins still bossing the middle decks? A fine way to run a ship! You go on with Sammy, Stan. I'm seeing Rollins."

"Don't want me to go with you, Dad?"

"No, I don't need you. Rollins knows me well enough to behave himself. Swab pails in the middle of the deck!" He went muttering off toward the stairs that led to the crew quarters, carrying himself on parade dress. Stan and I turned up to the superdeck. He began filling his pipe with three hands, while I watched in fascinated silence until it was finished, and he turned back to me.

"Dad's quite a remarkable man, Sammy," he said. "You're not getting a very good slant on him, I suppose, but if you knew him better you'd find it isn't prejudice on my part—I have no prejudices."

"I've seen one thing," I agreed. "He's the only man I ever knew who could be thoroughly provoked with the captain and not take it out on the copilot as well. It's a pity he and Lee can't get together." The mute threw open the door of his cabin and motioned me in. "Make yourself comfortable. I wouldn't worry about Lee and Dad, fellow. They both put a ship's command above Heaven and Earth, but that'll be finished the minute we dock. Anyway, it's sort of a farewell fling for Dad, so he's making the most of it."

"How do you mean, farewell trip? Thanks, yes." The wine he brought out of some little gadget was cold and delicious. He sampled his own before replying.

"Heart trouble, they told him. When he found out, he decided to make one more trip in the *Kickapoo* and settle down on Mars. No dying on Earth for him. Keep this under your hat—Lee's not to know—but the chances are all against his living another year. So I left the wife and kids behind and came along."

"The wife and kids?" It had caught me off guard, and I blurted out the question like a darned fool.

There was a grin on his face then. "Sure, I'm married, and there are four children back in Dad's old house—all like me. I'm a true mutation, you know; pass on my differences to any children. It's my duty to continue my strain; otherwise the human race may have to wait a few thousand more years for another superman."

There was certainly no false modesty about him; neither was his tone boasting. About all I could say to that was a grunt.

He grinned again. "It's the truth, Sammy, so why should I deny it? I look strange to you; but you must admit I have advantages physically; among others, I'm practically immune to all diseases. I finished high school and college in the absolute minimum time. I got the 'F.R.P.S.' after my name for working out a process for grinding lenses in a true parabola to an accuracy of one molecule's thickness—using a colloidal abrasive suspended in air, and controlled by the irregularities themselves; that was something they said couldn't be done. Want more proof?"

Something suddenly brought me up out of the seat and toward him, and I could feel a flood of anger running through me at his egotism. I hated the man with a red blood lust that made me crouch in grim determination to clutch and mangle and bite. Then, as quickly as it had come, it was gone, and I found him laughing at me. "Telepathic control, Sammy, so don't feel foolish. Convinced of my right to call myself super now?"

It was as good an explanation of his ability as anything else, but there were still angles on it. "Okay, you're a superman. But why aren't you out turning the world over? I've never read of a superman in a story where the fellow minded his own business like the average man."

"You won't—it isn't interesting that way. But one superman in a world of normal men isn't enough to do much. His best bet is to raise children and pass it on until only the supermen are left—that's the way nature did it. I learned early to speak and act like a normal man, whatever differences there are in our way of thinking. Anyway, I was brought up by normal men, and I'm somewhat limited by that—my children won't be. More wine?"

I nodded, my head spinning. I'd felt about the same way in training school when I got my first whiff of butyl mercaptan in the chemistry class and was told a living animal could make and use a similar odor. It was a good thing Court came in then.

"Rollins knows better now," he said, satisfaction heavy in his voice. "Sammy, your name's sounding on the caller; captain wants you." And as I slipped out of the cabin toward the dugout, I caught a less-welcome sentence from him.

"Think I'll look over the engine room tomorrow, Stan."

All I could do was pray!

Apparently my prayers weren't much good, though. Near the end of Captain Lee's shift the next day, while I was waiting around to take over, the engine phone buzzed and McAllister's voice rattled through it. Lee winced and held it out so we could both hear.

McAllister was in fine fettle. "Captain, there's an old fool down here making trouble, with a freak to help him! Three of my best men have their arms broken and a couple are out. 'Twas a lovely fight, while it lasted, but I've work to be done and no more time for play. What'll I do with 'em?"

"What happened? Where are they now?"

"They're backed in a corner a-waiting for more competition right now, and the old man's using highly uncomplimentary language, so they'll get it. He came down to fiddle around, you might say, over the shininess of my turbines and the dripping of my oil, and I let him have his way with only a word or two dropped about his nose being a bit long. But when the freak found where one of the black gang had hidden some liquor and the old man broke the bottle, the bugger lumped him, and the freak joined the play. Naturally, the others didn't stand by helpless, and I had a bit of a time quieting things down... Shall I shoot them or use a club?"

Lee swore into the phone and then quieted down to make sense. "McAllister, put the fellow with the liquor in the brig! I'll settle with you later. Keep the gang of cutthroats in line and send up the other two—they'll come if you tell them I ordered it. Did any outside the engine crew hear the fight?"

"No, just a little private party that your dainty little angels won't know about. I hated to break it up, but I needed a few sound men to run the engines, and I thought you might have some slight objection... Okay, I've told 'em, and they're on the way up."

"McAllister would!" Lee slapped the phone back onto its cradle and expounded further on the beauties of a captain's life and the virtue of sundry individuals. "If he weren't the best engineer out, I'd sack him—and if there's any more drinking or fighting aboard, I will anyway. He does enough brawling in port—come in!"

I don't know what I'd expected; probably some pieces of man and mute, from the nature of McAllister's black gang. Anyway, I was wrong. Court was highly undirty and unscratched, which could only mean Stan had done the actual fighting. The mute's shirt would have made lint, and his general color was that of stale oil; but, except for a few slight scratches, he was untouched. I had a vision of those gorilla arms swinging all together, and began to see why McAllister had called Lee before the fight was completely finished.

"Discipline," said Court, while Lee was still swallowing enough ire to clear speaking space in his throat, "is terrible aboard, sir. Since you will probably insist on retaining the creature that passes for your engineer, I have asked Stan to accept his invitation and meet him after we dock; I hope you'll show better judgment in choosing the new engineer you'll need."

Lee was practically gagging by that time. "Captain Perry, you forget yourself! Only your age prevents me from confining you to the brig, sir! Keep out of my mind, Stan! That goes for you, too. If I suspect you of trying to control me, I'll brig you before I break. Angels running my ship! You will return to your quarters and remain there until we dock. During that time, you may leave to dine, only, and you will refrain from all comments to the other passengers or any members of the crew. And you, Captain Perry, will remove the uniform you wear by courtesy, and dress in civilians!"

"That exceeds your authority, Lee," Stan pointed out softly. Court was radiating a cold white anger that needed no speech. "It's true that there was some trouble below, but we were not unauthorized in our search, and the fight was not of my making; I had no choice, unless I preferred to have my father and myself mutilated. There's no need to strip Dad!"

"Except that he's been scaring the angels with wild tales while his clothes give his words weight! He's ruining my crew and destroying morale—generally making a nuisance or a laughingstock of himself. I won't have the uniform disgraced. To quarters!"

There was a click of heels from Court and the sound of feet slapping down the hall before his door shut. Stan stood a moment longer, spreading his hands at odd angles, then followed. With a glance at the clock, Lee clapped his hands down on the panel and jerked from the throne.

"Seven hours from Mars. Take over! Don't call me unless there's an emergency."

That left me alone at the controls, and the peace should have been welcome, but wasn't. I could still hear echoes bouncing from the walls, and the face of Court Perry kept getting in front of the controls. I never took sides in a ruction in a family or ship, but I'd have given half an eye to see the answer to this one. Grown men, I figured, are no worse than kids, and you can't spank them as easily. And when they're hurt, I reckon the sting lasts longer.

If I hadn't been darned fool enough to worry about something that wasn't my business, I might have taken more notice of the slight quiver that touched the ship a couple of hours later, but I put it down to temporary lag in one tube, corrected it automatically, and went on roiling around mentally. In the back of my mind, I heard the door open softly and close, and was glad Lee had returned instead of getting drunk as I feared, but didn't bother to look around. A hand slid across my back and gripped my shoulder before I swung to see Court Perry.

He'd put off his uniform and most of himself with it, and now only a small, beaten old man stood there looking at me uncertainly. There's a certain kind of hell in the back of the best minds, and Court had found it. The fact that there was no pain or bitterness on his face only made it worse, somehow. I slid out of the copilot stool.

"Sit down, sir. Lee's turned authority over to me and won't be back for hours." His look toward the chair was hesitant and I motioned toward it again. "I'm commanding now, and if I choose to request your presence here as an adviser, nobody can do anything about it."

"Don't counter your captain too much, Sammy." But he took the stool, sinking down into it like a half-pricked balloon. "Sometime you may be running your own tick. I felt the ship lurch back there. Know what it was?"

"Tube lag. I've corrected."

"I thought so. You'd naturally make that mistake. It wasn't tube lag. That lurch came from Hull Section C, or everything I've learned about the feeling of a ship is wrong—and I don't think so. That means a peanut from the Little Swarm clipped up too close before the repellers functioned, and it was soaked up too quickly for recoil compensation. That's dangerous business, and I couldn't stay berthed with it going on."

"Indicator's registering." I tapped out more current to the hull repeller and watched the pointer. It fluttered a second, and wabbled slowly over—but kept on going instead of stopping at the mark. "Hm-mm!"

"Exactly."

Right then I began to see meteors swarming up as thick as peas in a can. I grabbed the phone, yelled down for the repair crew to jury-rig whatever was wrong. Court tapped me.

"Make an overroll. They strike from the starboard side, and if we turn the weak section to port, it'll help." As he saw me grab for the calculator to figure my thrusts, he brushed my hands aside and laid his on the controls, feeling over the raised indicators with fingers that seemed jointless, then pulled on the firing pins. Spirit ran back over him.

The *Kickapoo*'s thwart tubes muttered obediently, and I could feel the faint press of overroll acceleration. While she was just starting, those long flickering fingers went back to the steering panel and made another lightning reset, twisted the delayed-fire dials, and punched the pins again to check when half-over was reached. I'd heard men claim ships could be handled by conditioned reflexes, but I'd never seen it tried before.

Court leaned back, his hands still playing over the indicators. "Not much chance of two meteors hitting the same spot for hours, anyway, but there's no sense—"

SSSping-awgh-ooOOM! Something burst in front of us, white-hot and flaming hotter as it struck through the etherphone and threw hot metal splattering over the dugout. One of us grabbed the other—which, it wasn't clear—and we lurched toward the door, just as the last sounds subsided. There was a series of rolling slams, and the automatic air gates whammed shut, one, two, three, cutting the dugout in two just behind the panel. The local danger lights went off and we stopped our scramble for the door.

Then the thwart tubes burbled again, stopping the roll of the ship after the damage was done. From below came faint sounds of excitement that meant the angels were milling around with their fear on their arms, like a pack of sheep. Court snapped up and dived for the angel communicator while I began bellowing down for the checking gang to patch the holes in the outer and inner sheaths.

His voice was brisk and confident. "The small meteor you just felt drove into the control room from which I'm speaking," he announced. "No serious damage was done, and there is absolutely no danger. Passengers are requested to continue as before. The slight inconvenience caused will in no way affect them, nor the arrival time at our destination. I assure you, there is no cause for worry."

As they began quieting down under his words and I turned to inspect the panels, Lee came bursting in and thrust himself in front of me. "What happened?"

I told him quickly, and he grunted. "Etherphone gone, of course. All instruments are dead! It must have hit the relay chamber and burned out the connections. We're flying completely blind, without spy instruments! No way of contacting Earth, where the repair ships are; none on Mars at present. Even if we could get a message out, our momentum would carry us to Jupiter by the time they could reach us."

"The controls are all right, though." It was Court's voice, breaking in on the gloom. "The overroll counterset worked. They're not connected with the spy instruments, anyway."

"What good are controls without indicators? You! I thought I gave orders you were to stay berthed! Is this accident more of your work, Captain Perry?"

"Easy, Lee." I caught him just as Stan slid through the doorway, arms and all, and completely filled what was left of the dugout. "Court was helping me, at my request, and he almost succeeded in preventing this. He might still help if you'll calm down and use your head. What next?"

"What can be next? Get Stan to signal Mars with the etherphone he used before and have them contact Earth, I guess—and then wait. There's no chance of fixing the fused mess the meteor would make of the relays."

Court shook his head. "We can't wait. I promised the passengers they'd reach Mars on time, and I mean to see they do. I'll fly it if you can't."

"Without instruments? Captain Perry, return to your quarters and keep this to yourself."

"Without instruments!" Court's voice was flat and positive.

"For the last time, will you get out?"

"No. I'm flying the *Kickapoo* to Mars Junction!"

That was a little strong, even for me. "You can't do it, sir. That would be mutiny." I grabbed for one arm as Lee caught the other, but the old man braced himself and refused to move.

"It is mutiny," he said. Then, as Lee let go and grabbed for the phone to summon help: "Stan!"

Stan stood there for a second, then moved toward us, a slow frown creeping up on his face. A flurry of arms came at us—they must have been arms, at least—and I felt myself leave the floor, twist and turn in the air, and hit something. Blackout!

Lee's voice, raging furiously and almost incoherently, was the first thing I knew later, except for the ringing that went on in my head, "—behind bars till the devil catches pneumonia! I'll—"

Stan turned from some problem he was working on, and little furrows of concentration set on his brow. "Shut up, Lee! You'll not say another word until we reach Mars. Understand?"

Lee opened his mouth and worked furiously, but nothing came out of it. Finally, he slumped back and gave up. The mute turned to me. "Sorry, Sammy, but I had to do it. Here, I'll fix that headache for you." Again there was a second of concentration, and the ringing was suddenly gone, though the lump on the back of my head was still there.

"Where are we now?"

"Half an hour from Mars; you've been out quite a while," Court answered me. "Stan plotted a course from the co-ordinates I remembered were on the panel before the crash, and we're using dead reckoning. Of course, there may be a slight error of a few hundred miles, but that isn't much."

Slight error! Technically, it was; but that wouldn't help if we crashed square into the planet or missed completely. Lee writhed in the corner and managed a hissing sound. Well, there was nothing I could do now. Court had the ship and there was no chance of outside help. All I could do was ride along and pray—fervently if not hopefully.

"Get a reading yet?" Court asked. "And better signal Mars to clear the field—I may wobble a little."

Stan picked up a little box with a few loops of wire sticking from it and began twisting a dial; it wasn't big enough to be an etherphone, as I knew one, but a faint whisper from the headset reached me, after a brief pause.

"They say all clear down there, Dad; I told them we were having a little trouble. From the directional angle I get with the loop here, we're about two seconds of an arc too high. Better correct."

"Already done. Now if I can hit into the atmosphere right, and get the feel of the air currents so I can recognize the territory I'm in, we'll be all set." He hunched himself over the panel and sat waiting a few aeons longer. Finally: "Ah, there's the first layer of thin air—we're still a little too fast! There, that should fix it. We're getting down where the air currents have character now."

"Junction on a line from us, almost," Stan reported. "Correct to port one degree five and a half seconds…two minutes…eight seconds. Good!"

"Updraft. That puts us over—mmm…"

Magic may have its place, but I wasn't used to it aboard the *Kickapoo*. "Good Lord, Stan," I begged, "do something about it! No man can fly a rocket by air currents and the feel of her! I can't even tell an updraft from a hurricane in this heavy shell."

"He can." The calm in his voice was infuriating. "Dad's memorized every square inch and reaction of the whole *Kickapoo*, until he knew every quiver of her hull and pull of her controls. Flew her for a year without using the vision plate. Dad's been blind six years, Sammy!"

"But—" That was too much for even Stan's control, and Lee squeezed the one word out hoarsely.

"This time, I've been his eyes. Telepathy, you know. Dad didn't want people to guess. When his eyesight began failing—probably from the radiation he used to have to take—he put those raised indicators in at his own expense and went ahead. And for your mental comfort, he made his last two landings with eyesight completely gone and without a hitch. If the officers' board hadn't caught on, he'd still be running a regular tick, and Lee would be copiloting without guessing the truth."

Maybe so, but the mental comfort he'd mentioned wasn't there. Those raised indicators weren't helping this trip, and Court hadn't touched a control for five years. He'd been hunched over them while Stan was speaking, but now he broke in again.

"There's Junction, by the feel of it. Test her, Stan; that should be the field."

"I think it was."

"Good! We're high, from the sound of the backblast." The *Kickapoo* veered around in a huge circle, Court fighting the controls to hold her on a level without indicators. Stan apparently was capable of nothing but confidence, which wasn't shared entirely by his father. Sweat began popping out on the old man's face. "Can't make it this time, either!"

"Steady, Dad!"

"I'm steady enough." Again the ship made a tight circle, her vanes shrieking against the air; her speed was low now, and she wobbled uncertainly. Court's hands bleached white, and his face blanched suddenly. One fist jerked away spasmodically, slapped back, and the grim fight with the controls went on. I was cooking in my own sweat.

Then something slithered under us, the rockets died, and silence reigned. From the outside came a rattle, and we went into motion again in a way that meant the field tractors were dragging us in. Safe! Stan was untying Lee and myself, and then Lee was muttering something I didn't try to understand and moving toward Court.

The old captain watched his approach with a tired smile and came slowly to his feet. "It's your throne again, Lee. It's—"

Hell splashed over his face at that moment! Stan barely managed to catch him as the legs buckled and failed him. But the salute he had started continued, and the voice went on faintly. "A very nice landing you made, Lee—you made, understand?...My cap!...Where's my cap?"

Lee caught himself and jerked his own cap up out of the corner where it had lain, making gulping motions in his throat. "Here, Captain," he said, putting it on the old man's head. "Here's your cap."

Some of the agony left Court's mouth as his fingers felt it and groped up the visor. "Eagles!" The smile that suffused his face might almost have been a prayer. "My eagles!"

Then Stan was laying the body down and clutching tight at Lee's shaking shoulders. "Not your fault," he was saying gently. "Not your fault, Lee. His heart—"

I turned and stumbled out of the dugout to oversee the passengers who were landing after another uneventful trip to Mars.

And It Comes Out Here

No, you're wrong. I'm not your father's ghost, even if I do look a bit like him. But it's a longish story, and you might as well let me in. You will, you know, so why quibble about it? At least, you always have…or do…or will. I don't know, words get all mixed up. We don't have the right attitude toward tense for a situation like this.

Anyhow, you'll let me in. I did.

Thanks. You think you're crazy, of course, but you'll find out you aren't. It's just that things are a bit confused. And don't look at the machine out there too long—until you get used to it, you'll find it's hard on the eyes, trying to follow where the vanes go. You'll get used to it, of course, but it will take about thirty years.

You're wondering whether to give me a drink, as I remember it. Why not? And naturally, since we have the same tastes, you can make the same for me as you're having. Of course we have the same tastes—we're the same person. I'm you thirty years from now—or you're me. I remember just how you feel—I felt the same way when he came back to tell me about it, thirty years ago.

Here, have one of these cigarettes. You'll get to like them in a couple more years. And you can look at the revenue stamp date, if you still doubt my story. You'll believe it eventually, though, so it doesn't matter.

Right now, you're shocked—it's a bit rugged when a man meets himself for the first time. Some kind of telepathy seems to work between two of the same people—you sense things. So I'll simply go ahead talking for half an hour or so, until you get over it. After that, you'll come along with me. You know, I could try to change things around by telling what happened to me; but he told me what I was going to do, so I might as well do the same. I probably couldn't help telling you the same thing in the same words, even if I tried—and I don't intend to try. I've gotten past that stage in worrying about things.

So let's begin when you get up in half an hour and come out with me. You'll take a closer look at the machine, then. Yeah, it'll be pretty obvious it must be a time machine—you'll sense that, too. You've seen it—just a small little cage with two seats, a luggage compartment, and a few buttons on a dash. You'll be puzzling over what I'll tell you, and you'll be getting used to the idea that you are the guy who makes atomic power practical. Jerome Boell, just plain engineer, the man who put atomic power in every home. You won't exactly believe it, but you'll want to go along.

I'll be tired of talking by then, and in a hurry to get going. So I cut off your questions, and get you inside. I snap on a green button, and everything seems to cut off around us—you can see a sort of foggy nothing surrounding the cockpit; it is probably the field that prevents passage through time from affecting us. The luggage section isn't protected, though.

You start to say something, but by then I'm pressing a black button, and everything outside will disappear. You look for your house, but it isn't there. There is exactly nothing there—in fact, there is no there. You are completely outside of time and space, as best you can guess how things are.

You can't feel any motion, of course. You try to reach a hand out through the field into the nothing around you—and your hand goes out, all right, but nothing happens. Where the screen ends, your hand just turns over and pokes back at you. Doesn't hurt, and when you pull your arm back, you're still sound and uninjured. But it looks odd, and you don't try it again.

Then it comes to you slowly that you're actually traveling in time. You turn to me, getting used to the idea. "So this is the fourth dimension?"

Then you feel silly, because you'll remember that I said you'd ask that. Well, I asked it after I was told, then I came back and told it to you, and I still can't help answering when you speak.

"Not exactly," I try to explain. "Maybe it's no dimension—or it might be the fifth; if you're going to skip over the so-called fourth without traveling along it, you'd need a fifth. Don't ask me. I didn't invent the machine, and I don't understand it."

"But..."

I let it go, and so do you. That's a good way of going crazy. You'll see why I couldn't have invented the machine later. Of course, there may have been a start for all this once. There may have been a time when you did invent the machine—the atomic motor first, then the time machine. And when you closed the loop by going back and saving yourself the trouble, it got all tangled up. I figured out once that such a universe would need some seven or eight time and space dimensions. It's simpler just to figure that this is the way time got kinked on itself. Maybe there is no machine, and it's just easier for us to imagine it. When you spend thirty years thinking about it, as I did—and you will—you get further and further from an answer.

Anyhow, you sit there, watching nothing all around you—and no time, apparently, though there is a time effect back in the luggage space. You look at your watch, and it's still running. That means you either carry a small time field with you, or you are catching a small increment of time from the main field. I don't know, and you won't think about that then, either.

I'm smoking, and so are you, and the air in the machine is getting a bit stale. You suddenly realize that everything in the machine was wide open, yet you haven't seen any effects of air loss.

"Where are we getting our air?" you ask. "Or why don't we lose it?"

"No place for it to go," I explain. There isn't—out there is neither time nor space, apparently. How could the air leak out? You still feel gravity, but I can't explain that, either. Maybe the machine has a gravity field built in—or maybe the time that makes your watch run is responsible for gravity. In spite of Einstein, you have always had the idea that time is an effect of gravity, and I sort of agree, still.

Then the machine stops—at least, the field around us cuts off. You feel a dankish sort of air replace the stale air, and you breathe easier, though we're in complete darkness, except for the weak light in the machine, which always burns, and a few feet of rough dirty cement floor around. You take another cigarette from me and you get out of the machine, just as I do.

I've got a bundle of clothes, and I start changing. It's a sort of simple, short-limbed, one-piece affair I put on, but it looks comfortable.

"I'm staying here," I tell you. "This is like the things they wear in this century, as near as I can remember it, and I should be able to pass fairly well. I've had all my fortune—the one you make on that atomic generator—invested in such a way I can get it on using some identification I've got with me, so I'll do all right. I know they still use some kind of money—you'll see evidence of that. And it's a pretty easy-going civilization, from what I could see. We'll go up, and I'll leave you. I like the looks of things here, and I won't be coming back with you."

You nod, remembering I've told you about it. "What century is this, anyway?"

I'd told you that, too, but you've forgotten. "As near as I can guess, it's about 2150. He told me, just as I'm telling you, that it's an interstellar civilization."

You take another cigarette from me, and follow me. I've got a small flashlight, and we grope through a pile of rubbish, and out into a corridor. This is a sub-sub-subbasement. We have to walk up a flight of stairs, and there is an elevator waiting, fortunately with the door open.

"What about the time machine?" you ask.

"Since nobody ever stole it, it's safe."

We get in the elevator, and I say "first" to it. It gives out a coughing noise, and the basement openings begin to click by us. There's no feeling of acceleration—some kind of false gravity they use in the future. Then the door opens, and the elevator says "first" back at us.

It's obviously a service elevator, and we're in a dim corridor, with nobody around. I grab your hand and shake it. "You go that way. Don't worry about getting lost; you never did, so you can't. Find the museum, grab the motor, and get out. And good luck to you."

You act as if you're dreaming, though you can't believe it's a dream. You nod at me, and I move out into the main corridor. A second later, you see me going by, mixed into a crowd that is loafing along toward a restaurant, or something like it, that is just opening. I'm asking questions of a man, who points, and I turn and move off.

You come out of the side corridor, and go down a hall, away from the restaurant. There are quiet little signs along the hall. You look at them, realizing that things have changed.

Steifj:Neri, Faunten, Z:rgot Dispenseri. The signs are very quiet and dignified. Some of them can be decoded to stationery shops, fountains, and the like. What a z:rgot is, you don't know. You stop at a sign that announces: *Trav:l Biwrou—F:rst-Clas Twrz—Marz and x: Trouj:n Planets. Spej:l reits to aol s:nz wixin 60 lyt iirz!* But there is only a single picture of a dull-looking metal sphere, with passengers moving up a ramp, and the office is closed. You begin to get the hang of the spelling they use, though.

Now there are people around you, but nobody pays much attention to you. Why should they? You wouldn't care if you saw a man in a leopard-skin suit—you'd figure it was some part in a play, and let it go. Well, people don't change much.

You get up your courage and go up to a boy selling something that might be papers on tapes. "Where can I find the Museum of Science?"

"Downayer rien turn lefa the sign. Stoo bloss," he tells you. Around you, you hear some pretty normal English, but there are others using stuff as garbled as his. You go right until you find a big sign built into the rubbery surface of the walk: *Miuzi:m :v Syens.* There's an arrow pointing, and you turn left. Ahead of you, two blocks on, you can see a pink building, with faint aqua trimming, bigger than most of the others. They are building lower than they used to, apparently. Twenty floors up seems about the maximum. You head for it, and find the sidewalk is marked with the information that it is the museum.

You go up the steps, but you see that it seems to be closed. You hesitate for a moment, then. You're beginning to think the whole affair is a bunch of nonsense, and you should get back to the time machine and go home. But then a guard comes to the gate—except for the short legs in his suit, and the grin on his face, he looks like any other guard.

What's more, he speaks pretty clearly. Everyone says things in a sort of drawl, with softer vowels, and slurred consonants, but it's rather pleasant. "Help you, sir? Oh, of course. You must be playing in 'Atoms and Axioms.' The museum's closed, but I'll be glad to let you study whatever you need for color in your role. Nice show. I saw it twice."

"Thanks," you mutter, wondering what kind of a civilization can produce guards as polite as that. "I—I'm told I should investigate your display of atomic generators."

    He beams at that. "Of course." The gate is swung to behind you, but obviously he isn't locking it—in fact, there doesn't seem to be a lock. "Must be a new part. You go down that corridor, up one flight of stairs, and left. Finest display in the worlds. We've got the original of the first thirteen models. Professor Jonas was using them to check his latest theory of how they work. Too bad he couldn't explain the principle, either. Someone will, some day, though. Lord, the genius of that twentieth century inventor! It's quite a hobby with me, sir. I've read everything I could get on the period. Oh—congratulations on your pronunciation. Sounds just like some of our oldest tapes."

    You get away from him, finally, after some polite thanks. The building seems deserted, and you wander up the stairs. There's a room on your right filled with something that proclaims itself the first truly plastic diamond former, and you go up to it. As you come near, it goes through a crazy wiggle inside, stops turning out a continual row of what seem to be bearings, and slips a hunk of something about the size of a penny toward you. "Souvenir," it announces in a well-modulated voice. "This is a typical gemstone of the twentieth century, properly cut to fifty-eight facets, known technically as a Jaegger diamond, and approximately twenty carats in size. You can have it made into a ring on the third floor during morning hours for one-tenth credit. If you have more than one child, press the red button for the number of stones you desire."

    You put it in your pocket, gulping a little, and get back to the corridor. You turn left, and go past a big room in which models of space ships—from the original thing that looks like a V-2, and is labeled first lunar rocket, to a ten-foot globe, complete with miniature manikins—are sailing about in some kind of orbits. Then there is one labeled *Wep:nz*, filled with everything from a crossbow to a tiny little rod four inches long and half the size of a pencil, marked *Fyn:l Hand-Arm*. Beyond is the end of the corridor, and a big place that bears a sign, *Mod:lz :v Atomic Pau:r Sorsez*.

    By that time, you're almost convinced. And you've been doing a lot of thinking about what you can do. The story I'm telling has been sinking in, but you aren't completely willing to accept it.

    You notice that the models are all mounted on tables, and that they're a lot smaller than you thought. They seem to be in chronological order, and the latest one, marked 2147—*Rincs Dyn:pot*, is about the size of a desk telephone. The earlier ones are larger, of course, but with variations, probably depending on the power output. A big sign on the ceiling gives a lot of dope on atomic generators, explaining that this is the first invention which sprang full blown into basically final form.

    You study it, but it mentions casually the inventor, without giving his name—

either they don't know it, or they take it for granted that everyone does, which seems more probable. They call attention to the fact that they have the original model of the first atomic generator built, complete with design drawings, original manuscript on operation, and full patent application. They state that it has all major refinements, operating on any fuel, producing electricity at any desired voltage up to five million, any chosen cyclic rate from direct current to one thousand megacycles, and any amperage up to one thousand, its maximum power output being fifty kilowatts, limited by the current-carrying capacity of the outputs. They also mention that the operating principle is still being investigated, and that only such refinements as better alloys and the addition of magnetric and nucleatric current outlets have been added since the original.

So you go to the end and look over the thing. It's simply a square box with a huge plug on each side, and a set of vernier controls on top, plus a little hole marked in old-style spelling, *Drop BBs or wire here.* Apparently that's the way it's fueled. It's about one foot on a side.

"Nice," the guard says over your shoulder. "It finally wore out one of the cathogrids, and we had to replace that, but otherwise it's exactly as the great inventor made it. And it still operates as well as ever. Like to have me tell you about it?"

"Not particularly," you begin, and then realize bad manners seem to be out up here. While you're searching for an answer, the guard pulls something out of his pocket and stares at it

"Fine, fine. The mayor of Altasecarba—Centaurian, you know—is arriving, but I'll be back in about ten minutes. He wants to examine some of the weapons for a monograph on Centaurian primitives compared to nineteenth-century man. You'll pardon me?"

You pardon him all over the place, and he wanders off happily. You go up to the head of the line, to that Rinks Dynapot, or whatever it transliterates to. That's small, and you can carry it. But the darned thing is absolutely fixed. You can't see any bolts, but you can't budge it, either.

You work down the line—it'd be foolish to take the early model if you can get one with built-in magnetic current terminals—Ehrenhaft or some other principle?—and nuclear binding-force energy terminals. But they're all held down by the same whatchamaycallem effect.

And finally, you're right back beside the original first model. It's probably bolted down, too—but you try it tentatively, and you find it moves. There's a little sign under it, indicating you shouldn't touch it, since the gravostatic plate is being renewed.

Well, you won't be able to change the time cycle by doing anything I haven't told you, but a working model such as that is a handy thing. You lift it—and it weighs about fifty pounds! But it can be carried.

You expect a warning bell, but nothing happens. As a matter of fact, if you'd stop drinking so much of that Scotch and staring at the time machine out there now, you'd hear what I'm saying, and know what will happen to you. But of course, just as I did, you're going to miss a lot of what I say from now on, and have to find out for yourself. But maybe some of it helps—I've tried to remember how much I remembered, after he told me, but I can't be sure. So I'll keep on talking. I probably can't help it, anyhow.

Well, you stagger down the corridor, looking for the guard, but all seems clear. Then you hear his voice from the weapons room. You bend down and try to scurry past, but you know you're in full view. Nothing happens, though.

You stumble down the stairs, feeling all the futuristic rays in the world on your back, and still nothing happens. Ahead of you, the gate is closed. You reach it, and it opens obligingly by itself. You breathe a quick sigh of relief, and start out onto the street.

Then there's a yell behind you. You don't wait. You put one leg in front of the other, and you begin moving down the walk, ducking past people, who stare at you with expressions you haven't time to see. There's another yell behind you.

Something goes over your head and drops on the sidewalk just in front of your feet, with a sudden ringing sound. You don't wait to find out about that, either. Somebody reaches out a hand to catch you, and you dart past.

The street is pretty clear now, and you jolt along, with your arms seeming to come out of the sockets, and that atomic generator getting heavier at every step.

Out of nowhere, something in a blue uniform about six feet tall and on the beefy side appears—and the star hasn't changed any. The cop catches your arm, and you know you're not going to get away. So you stop.

"You can't exert yourself that hard in this heat, fellow," the cop says. "There are laws against that, without a yellow sticker. Here, let me grab you a taxi."

Reaction sets in a bit, and your knees begin to buckle, but you shake your head, and come up for air.

"I—I left my money home," you begin.

The cop nods. "Oh, that explains it. Fine, I won't have to give you an appearance schedule. But you should have come to me." He reaches out and taps a pedestrian lightly on the shoulder. "Sir, emergency request. Would you help this gentleman?"

The pedestrian grins, looks at his watch, and nods, "How far?"

You did notice the name of the building from which you came, and you mutter it. The stranger nods again, reaches out, and picks up the other side of the generator, blowing a little whistle the cop hands him. Pedestrians begin to move aside, and you and the stranger jog down the street at a trot, with a nice clear path, while the cop stands beaming at you both.

That way, it isn't so bad. And you begin to see why I decided I might like to stay up here in the future. But all the same, the organized cooperation here doesn't look too good. The guard can get the same, and be there before you.

And he is. He stands just inside the door of the building as you reach it. The stranger lifts an eyebrow, and goes off at once when you nod at him, not waiting for thanks. And the guard comes up, holding some dinkus in his hand, about the size of a big folding camera, and not too dissimilar in other ways. He snaps it open, and you get set to duck.

"You forgot the prints, monograph, and patent applications," he says. "They go with the generator—we don't like to have them separated. A good thing I knew the production offices of 'Atoms and Axioms' were in this building. Just let us know when you're finished with the model, and we'll pick it up. What's it for—repro for a new skit in a hurry?"

You swallow several sets of tonsils you had removed years before, and take the bundle of papers he hands you out of the little case. He pumps you for some more information, which you give him at random. But it seems to satisfy your amiable guard friend. He finally smiles in satisfaction, and heads back to the museum. You still don't believe it, but you pick up the atomic generator and the information sheets, and you head down toward the service elevator. There is no button on it. In fact, there's no door there.

You start looking for other doors or corridors, but you know this is right—the signs along the halls are the same as they were.

Then there's a sort of cough, and something dilates in the wall. It forms a perfect door, and the elevator stands there waiting. You get in, gulping out something about going all the way down, and then wondering how a machine geared for voice operation can make anything of that. What the deuce would that lowest basement be called? But the elevator has closed, and is moving downward in a hurry. It coughs again, and you're at the original level. You get out—and realize you don't have a light.

You'll never know what you stumbled over, but somehow, you move back in the direction of the time machine, bumping against boxes, staggering here and here, and trying to find the right place by sheer feel. Then a shred of dim light appears—it's the weak light in the time machine, and you've located it.

You put the atomic generator in the luggage space, throw the papers down beside it, and climb into the cockpit, sweating and mumbling. You reach forward toward the green button, and hesitate—but there's a red one beside it, and you finally decide on that.

Suddenly, there's a confused yell from the direction of the elevator, and a

And It Comes Out Here

beam of light strikes against your eyes, with a shout punctuating it. Your finger touches the red button.

You'll never know what the shouting was about—whether they finally doped out the fact they'd been robbed, or whether they were trying to help you. You don't care then. The field springs up around you, and the next button you touch—the one on the board that hasn't been used so far—sends you off into the nothingness. There is no beam of light, you can't hear a thing, and you're safe.

It isn't much of a trip back. You sit there smoking and letting your nerves settle back to normal. You notice a third set of buttons, with some pencil marks over them—*Press these to return to yourself thirty years*—and you begin waiting for the air to get stale. It doesn't because there is only one of you this time.

Instead, everything flashes off, and you're sitting in the machine in your own back yard.

You'll figure out the cycle in more details later. You get into the machine in front of your house, go to the future in the subbasement, land in your backyard, and then hop back thirty years to pick up yourself, landing in front of your house. Just that. But right then, you don't care. You jump out and start pulling out that atomic generator and taking it inside.

It isn't hard to disassemble—but you don't learn a thing; just some plates of metal, some spiral coils, and a few odds and ends—all things that can be made easily enough, all obviously of common metals. But when you put it together again, about an hour later, you notice something—everything in it is brand new, and there's one set of copper wires missing! It won't work. You put some #12 house wire in, exactly like the set on the other side, drop in some iron filings, and try it again.

And with the controls set at 120 volts, 60 cycles, and 15 amperes, you get just that. You don't need the power company any more. And you feel a little happier when you realize that the luggage space wasn't insulated from time effects by a field, so the motor has moved backward in time, somehow, and is back to its original youth—minus the replaced wires the guard mentioned—which probably wore out because of the makeshift job you've just done.

But you begin getting more of a jolt when you find that the papers are all in your own writing, that your name is down as the inventor, and that the date of the patent application is 1991.

Yeah. It will begin to soak in, then. You pick up an atomic generator in the future and bring it back to the past—your present—so that it can be put in the museum with you as the inventor so you can steal it to be the inventor. And you do it in a time machine which you bring back to yourself to take yourself into the future to return to take back to yourself.

Who invented anything? And who built them?

While your riches from the generator are piling in, and little kids from school are coming around to stare at the man who changed history and made atomic power so common that no nation could hope to be anything but a democracy and a peaceful one—after some of the worst times in history for a few years—while your name becomes as common as Ampere, or Faraday, or any other spelled without a capital letter, you're thinking of that.

And one day, you come across an old poem—something about some folks calling it evolution and others calling it God. You go out, make a few provisions for the future, and come back to climb into the time machine that's waiting in the building you had put around it. Then you'll be knocking on your own door, thirty years back—or right now, from your view-telling yourself all these things I'm telling you.

But now...

Well, the drinks are finished, you're woozy enough to go along with me without protest, and I want to find out just why those people up there came looking for you and shouting, before the time machine left.

Come on, let's go.

The Band Played On

I

Inside the rocket grounds, the band was playing the inevitable *Heroes' March* while the cadets snapped through the final maneuvers of their drill. Captain Thomas Murdock stopped at the gate near the visitors' section, waiting until the final blatant notes blared out and were followed by the usual applause from the town kids in the stands. The cadets broke ranks and headed for their study halls, still stepping as if the band played on inside their heads.

Maybe it did, Murdock thought. There had been little parade drill and less music back on Johnston Island when his group won their rocket emblems fifteen years before; yet somehow there had been a sense of destiny, like a drum beating in their brains, to give them the same spring to their stride. It had sent most of them to their deaths and a few to command positions on the moon, long before the base was transferred here to the Florida coast.

Murdock shrugged and glanced upwards. The threatening clouds were closing in, scudding across the sky in dark blobs and streaks, and the wind velocity was rising. It was going to be lousy weather for a takeoff, even if things got no worse.

Behind him, a boy's voice called out. "Hey, pilot!"

He glanced about, but there was no other pilot near. He hesitated, frowning. Then, as the call was repeated, he turned doubtfully toward the stands. Surprisingly, a boy of about twelve was leaning over the railing, motioning toward him and waving a notebook emphatically.

"Autograph, pilot?"

Murdock took the book and signed the blank page automatically, while fifty pairs of eyes watched. No other books were held out, and there was complete silence from the audience. He handed the pencil and notebook back, trying to force a friendly smile onto his face. For a moment, there was a faint ghost of the old pride as he turned back across the deserted parade ground.

It didn't last. Behind him, an older voice broke the silence in disgusted tones. "Why'd you do that, Shorty? He ain't no pilot!"

"He is, too. I guess. I know a pilot's uniform," Shorty protested.

"So what? I already told you about him. He's the garbage man!"

There was no vocal answer to that—only the ripping sound of paper being torn from the notebook.

Murdock refused to look back as the boys left the stands. He went across the field, past the school buildings, on toward the main sections of the base—the business part, where the life-line to the space station and the moon was maintained. A job, he told himself, was a job. It was a word he would never have used six ships and fifteen years before.

The storm flag was up on the control tower, he saw. Worse, the guy cables were all tight, anchoring the three-stage ships firmly down in their blast deflection pits. There were no tractors or tankers on the rocket field to service the big ships. He stared through the thickening gloom toward the bay, but there was no activity there, either. The stage recovery boats were all in port, with their handling cranes folded down. Obviously, no flight was scheduled.

It didn't fit with predictions. Hurricane Greta was hustling northward out to sea, and the low ceiling and high winds were supposed to be the tag end of that disturbance, due to clear by mid-day. This didn't look that way; it looked more as if the weather men on the station had goofed for the first time in ten years.

Murdock stared down the line toward his own ship, set apart from the others, swaying slightly as the wind hit it. Getting it up through the weather was going to be hell, even if he got clearance, but he couldn't wait much longer. Greta had already put him four days behind his normal schedule, and he'd been counting on making the trip today.

There was a flash bulletin posted outside the weather shack, surrounded by a group of young majors and colonels from the pilot squad. Murdock stepped around them and into the building. He was glad to see that the man on duty was Collins, one of the few technicians left over from the old days on the Island.

Collins looked up from his scowling study of the maps and saluted casually without rising. "Hi, Tommy. How's the hog business?"

"Lousy," Murdock told him. "I'm going to have a hungry bunch of pigs if I don't get another load down. What gives with the storm signals? I thought Greta blew over."

Collins pawed the last cigarette out of a pack and shook his head as he lighted up. "This is Hulda, they tell me. Our geniuses on the station missed it—claimed Hulda was covered by Greta until she grew bigger. We're just beginning to feel her. No flights for maybe five days more."

"Hell!" It was worse than Murdock had feared. He twisted the weather maps to study them, unbelievingly. Unlike the newer pilots, he'd spent enough time in the weather shack to be able to read a map or a radar screen almost as well as Collins. "The station couldn't have goofed that much, Bill!"

"Did, though. Something's funny up there. Bailey and the other brass are holding some pow-wow about it now, over at Communications. It's boiling up to a first-class mess."

One of the teletypes began chattering, and Collins turned to it. Murdock moved outside where a thin rain was beginning to fall, whipping about in the gusts of wind. He headed for the control tower, knowing it was probably useless. In that, he was right; no clearances for flight could be given without General Bailey's okay, and Bailey was still tied up in conference, apparently.

He borrowed a raincape and went out across the field toward his ship. The rain was getting heavier, and the *Mollyann* was grunting and creaking in her pit as he neared her. The guying had been well enough done, however, and she was in no danger that he could see. He checked the pit gauges and records. She'd been loaded with a cargo of heavy machinery, and her stage tanks were fully fueled. At least, if he could get clearance, she was ready to go. She was the oldest ship on the field, but her friction-burned skin covered sound construction and he had supervised her last overhaul himself.

Then he felt the wind picking up again, and his stomach knotted. He moved around to the more sheltered side of the ship, cursing the meteorologists on the station. If they'd predicted this correctly, he could have arranged to take off during the comparative lull between storms. Even that would have been bad enough, but now…

Abruptly, a ragged klaxon shrieked through the air in a series of short bursts, sounding assembly for the pilots. Murdock hesitated, then shrugged and headed out into the rain. He could ignore the signal if he chose, since he'd been on detached duty for years, except when actually scheduled for flight; yet it was probably his best chance to see Bailey. He slogged along while the other pilots trotted across the field toward Briefing on the double. Even now, covered with slickers and tramping through mud, they seemed to be on parade drill, as if a drum were beating out the time for them.

Murdock found a seat at the rear, separate from the others, out of old habit. Up front, an improvised crap game was going on; elsewhere, they were huddled in little groups, their young faces too bright and confident. Nobody noticed him until Colonel Lawrence Hennings glanced up from the crap game. "Hi, Tommy. Want in?"

Murdock shook his head, smiling briefly. "Can't afford it this week," he explained.

A cat could look at royalty; and royalty was free to look at or speak to anyone—even a man who ferried garbage for the station. At the moment, Hennings was king, even in this crowd of self-determined heroes. There was always one man who was the top dog. Hennings' current position seemed as inevitable as Murdock's own had become.

Damn it, someone had to carry the waste down from the station. The men up there couldn't just shove it out into space to have it follow their orbit and pile up around them; shooting it back to burn up in Earth's atmosphere had been suggested, but that took more fuel in the long run than bringing it down by ship. With nearly eight hundred men in the doubly expanded station, there was a lot of garbage, too. The job was as important as carrying the supplies up, and took just as much piloting skill. Only there was no band playing when the garbage ship took off, and there could never be a hero's mantle over the garbage man.

It had simply been his bad luck that he was pilot for the first load back. The heat of landing leaked through the red-hot skin of the cargo section, and the wastes boiled and steamed through the whole ship and plated themselves against the hull when it began to cool, until no amount of washing could clean it completely; after that, the ship was considered good for nothing but the carrying of garbage down and lifting such things as machine parts, where the smell wouldn't matter. He'd gone on detached duty at once, exiled from the pilot shack; it was probably only imagination, but the other men swore they couldn't sleep in the same room with him.

He'd made something of a joke of it at first, while he waited for his transfer at the end of the year. He'd finally consented to a second year when they couldn't get anyone else for the job. And by the end of five years of it, he knew he was stuck; even a transfer wouldn't erase his reputation as the garbage man, or give him the promotions and chances for leadership the others got. Oh, there were advantages in freedom, but if there had been anything outside of the service he could do...

The side door opened suddenly and General Bailey came in. He looked older than his forty years, and the expression on his face sobered the pilots almost at once. He took his time in dropping to the chair behind the table, giving them a chance to come to order. Murdock braced himself, watching as the man took out a cigarette. Then, as it was tapped sharply on the table to pack the end, he nodded. It was going to be a call for volunteers! The picture of the weather outside raced through his mind, twisting at his stomach, but he slid forward on his seat, ready to stand at once.

"At ease, men." Bailey took his time lighting the cigarette, and then plunged into things. "A lot of you have been cursing the station for their forecast. Well, you can forget that—we're damned lucky they could spot Hulda at all. They're in bad shape. Know what acrolein is? You've all had courses in atmospherics. How about it?"

The answer came out in pieces from several of the pilots. Acrolein was one of the thirty-odd poisons that had to be filtered from the air in the station, though it presented no problem in the huge atmosphere of Earth. It could get into the air from the overcooking of an egg or the burning of several proteins.

"You can get it from some of the plastics, too," one of the men added.

Bailey nodded. "You can. And that's the way they got it, from an accident in the shops. They got enough to overload their filters, and the replacements aren't enough to handle it. They're all being poisoned up there—just enough to muddle their thinking at first, but getting worse all the time. They can't wait for Hulda to pass. They've got to have new filters at once. And that means—"

"Sir!" Hennings was on his feet, standing like a lance in a saddle boot. "Speaking for my crew, I ask permission to deliver whatever the station needs."

Murdock had been caught short by Hennings' sudden move, but now he was up, protesting. His voice sounded as hollow as he felt after the ringing tones of the younger man. "I'm overdue already on schedule, and by all rights—"

Bailey cut him off, nodding to Hennings. "Thank you, Colonel. We'll begin loading at once, while Control works out your tapes. All right, dismissed!" Then finally he turned to Murdock. "Thanks, Tom. I'll record your offer, but there's no time for us to unload your ship first. Afraid you're grounded for the storm."

He went out quickly, with Hennings following jauntily at his heels.

The others were beginning to leave, grumbling with a certain admiration at Hennings' jumping the gun on them. Murdock trailed along, since there was no chance for him to change the orders now. He wondered what excuse would have been used if he'd been first to volunteer and if his ship had been empty. The choice of pilot had probably been made before the token request for volunteers, and he was certain that his name hadn't been considered.

The storm seemed to have let up when he started across the field, but it was only a lull. Before he could reach the shelter of the weather shack, it began pelting down again, harder than ever. He stopped inside the door to shake off some of the wetness. Collins was intently studying one of the radar screens where a remote pickup was showing conditions, alternately working a calculator and yelling into a phone. He looked up, made a desperate motion with his fingers for a cigarette, and went back to the phone.

Murdock shoved a lighted smoke toward him, then pulled a stool up to the window where he could watch the field. By rights, he should be heading back to his farm, to do what he could there; but he had no intention of leaving before the take-off. Lifting a ship in this weather was mostly theory. It had been done once on the Island, but the big ships were still too unstable to make it anything but a desperate emergency measure. He'd discussed it with the pilot after that trip, and he'd spent a lot of time trying to work out a method in case he had to try it, but Hennings had his sympathy now. It took more than courage and confidence to handle this situation.

He studied the storm, trying to get the feel of it. During his first two years back here, he'd spent a lot of his free time flying a light plane, and some of the weather had been fairly bad. It gave him some idea of what Hennings had to face; he wondered whether the younger pilot realized what was coming.

Sodium lights were blazing on the field, he saw, clustered about Hennings' *Jennilee*, and men were slipping and sliding around in the mud, getting her ready and loading the filter packs. Two men were being run up on a lift to the crew entrance; Hennings carried both a co-pilot and a radio man, though many of the pilots now used only a single crewman.

Collins looked up from the phone. "Fifteen minutes to zero," he reported.

Murdock grunted in surprise. He'd expected the take-off to be two hours later, on the next swing of the station. It must mean that orders for loading the ship had been given before Bailey came into Briefing. It confirmed his suspicion that the pilot had been picked in advance.

A few minutes later, Hennings appeared, marching across the field toward the lift in the middle of a small group. Several of them rode up with him. As the lift began creaking backward, the pilot stood poised in the lock, grinning for the photographers. Naturally, the press had been tipped off; the service had learned long before that maximum publicity helped in getting the fattest possible appropriations.

When the lock was finally sealed and the field cleared, Murdock bent over the counter to study the radar screens. The storm was apparently erratic, from the hazy configurations he could see. Zero would be a poor choice for the take-off, though, from what he could estimate. Hennings would be smarter to delay and make manual corrections on his tape.

Then the klaxon went on, signalling the take-off. The last man on the field was darting for cover. From the blast pit, a dull, sickly red began to shine as the rockets were started. Murdock swore. The fool was taking off on schedule, trusting to his tapes!

The smoky red exhaust ran up the spectrum to blue, and the ship began to tremble faintly. The sound rose to crescendo. Now the *Jennilee* started to lift. Wind hit it, throwing it toward the side of the pit. The wings of the top stage caught most of the force, and the whole ship was tilting—the worst thing that could happen. They should have swiveled the ship around to put the wings parallel to most of the storm, instead of bucking it.

Murdock heard Collins' breath catch harshly, but suddenly the worst danger was over. A lull for a second or so gave Hennings his chance. He was at least riding his controls over the automatics. The blast deflection vanes shot the blue flame sidewise, and the ship shifted its bottom, righting itself. It was beginning to make its real climb now. The wings near the top literally vibrated like the arms of a tuning fork, and the blast trail was ragged.

Yet she rose, her blast roar rising and falling as the wind altered, blowing some of the sound away from the watchers.

Now the Doppler effect began to be noticeable, and the sound dropped in pitch as the *Jennilee* fought her way up. The overcast of scudding clouds hid all but the bright anger of the exhaust.

Murdock turned with the technician to another radar screen. Unlike those in Control, it wasn't set properly to catch the ship, but a hazy figure showed in one edge. "Right into some of the nastiest stuff blowing!" Collins swore.

II

He was right. The timing had been as bad as possible. The blob of light on the screen was obviously being buffeted about. Something seemed to hit the top and jerk it.

The screen went blank, then lighted again. Collins had shifted his connections, to patch into the signal Control was watching. The blip of the *Jennilee* was now dead center, trying to tilt into a normal synergy curve. "Take it up. Damn it!" Murdock swore hotly. This was no time to swing around the Earth until after the ship was above the storm. The tape for the automatic pilot should have been cut for a high first ascension. If Hennings was panicking and overriding it back to the familiar orbit…

As if the pilot heard him, the blip began rising again. It twisted and bucked. Something seemed to separate from it. There was a scattering of tiny white dots on the screen, drifting behind the ship. Murdock couldn't figure them. Then he forgot them as the first stage let go and began falling backward from the ship, heading on its great arc toward the ocean. Recovery would be rough. Now the second stage blasted out. And finally, the ship was above the storm and could begin to track toward its goal.

Abruptly the speaker in the corner snapped into life, and Hennings' voice sounded from it. "*Jennilee* to Base. Cancel the harps and haloes! We're in the clear!"

Collins snapped his hand down against a switch, killing the speaker. "Hotshot!" he said thickly, and yet there was a touch of admiration in his voice. "Ten years ago, they couldn't build ships to take what he gave it. So that makes him a tin god on wheels. Got a cigarette, Tommy?"

Murdock handed him the package and picked up the slicker again. He'd seen enough. The ship should have no further trouble, except for minor orbital corrections, well within the pilot's ability. For that matter, while Collins' statement was true enough, Hennings deserved a lot of the credit. And if he had to boast a little—well, maybe he deserved credit for the ability to snap back to normal after the pounding his body and nerves must have taken.

In the recreation hall, some of the pilots were busy exaggerating the dangers of the take-off for the newsmen, making it sound as if no parallel feat had been performed in all history. Murdock found a phone where he had some privacy and put through a call to let Pete and Sheila know when he'd be back—and that he was returning without a load. They'd already heard the news, however. He cut the call short and went out across the soggy field, cursing as his shoes filled with water. From the auditorium of the school, he could hear the band practicing; he wondered for a moment whether the drumbeat could make the cadets feel like heroes as they moved through mud with shoes that squished at every step. It had no such lifting effect on him.

The parking lot beyond the drill grounds was almost deserted, and his big truck seemed to huddle into the wind like a lonely old bull buffalo. He started the turbine and opened the cab heater, kicking off his sodden shoes. The dampness in the air brought out the smell of refuse and pigs from the rear, but he was used to it; anyhow, it was better than the machine-human-chemical stench of the space station.

Driving took most of his attention. The truck showed little wind-sway and the roads were nearly deserted, but vision was limited and the windshield kept steaming up, in spite of the silicone coating. He crawled along, grumbling to himself at the allocation of money for tourist superhighways at the expense of the back roads.

A little ways beyond the base, he was in farm country. It was totally unlike the picture of things he'd had originally. He'd expected only palm trees and citrus groves in Florida, though he'd known vaguely that it was one of the major cattle-producing states. This part wasn't exactly like the Iowa section where he'd grown up, but it wasn't so different, either.

Pete Crane had introduced him to it. At the time, Pete was retiring after twenty years of service and looking for something to do. He'd found a small farm twenty miles from Base and had approached Murdock with the hope of getting the station garbage for food for the hogs he planned to buy. The contractor who took care of the Base garbage wouldn't touch the dehydrated, slightly scorched refuse, and disposal had always been a problem.

They ended up as partners, with permanent rights to all the station wastes. Pete's sister, Sheila, joined them to keep house for them. It beat living in holds and offered the first hope for the future Murdock had. Unless his application for Moon service was accepted—which seemed unlikely, since he was already at the age limit of thirty-five—he had no other plans for his own compulsory twenty-year retirement. The plan also gave some purpose to his job as garbage collector for the station.

For two years, everything went well. Maybe they grew over-confident then. They sank everything into new buildings and more livestock. When the neighboring farm suddenly became available, they used all their credit in swinging the mortgage, leaving no margin for trouble. And trouble came when Pete was caught in front of a tractor that somehow slipped into gear; he was hospitalized for five weeks, and his medical insurance was only enough for a fraction of the cost. Now, with Hulda canceling the critically necessary trip to the station…

The truck bumped over the last half mile and into the farmyard. Murdock parked it near the front door and jumped out. He let out a yell and made a beeline for the kerosene heater, trying to get his feet warm on the floor near it. The house was better built than many in Florida, but that wasn't saying much. Even with the heater going, it was probably warmer in their new pig sty.

Sheila came through the dining room from the kitchen, spotted his wet feet, and darted for his bedroom. In a second she was back with dry clothes. "Change in here where it's warm. I'll have lunch ready in a couple of minutes," she told him, holding her face up for a kiss.

Sheila wasn't a beautiful woman and apparently didn't care. Murdock's mother would probably have called her plain good looks "wholesome," and referred to her slightly overweight body as "healthy." He only knew that she looked good to him, enough shorter to be comfortable, eyes pleasantly blue, and hair some shade of brown that seemed to fit her.

He pulled her to him snugly, but she wriggled away after a brief kiss. "Pete's in town, trying to get help. He'll be back any minute," she warned him.

He grinned and let her go. They'd gone through the romantic binge of discovering each other long enough ago to be comfortable with each other now, except for the occasional arguments when she didn't want to wait. Mostly, though, she had accepted their agreement. In eight more months he'd be thirty-six and too old for assignment on the Moon; if he didn't make that, they'd get married. But he had no intention of leaving her tied to him if he did leave, since the chance of taking her along was almost nil. Pete had backed him up on his decision, too.

He slipped into coveralls and dry boots and went out to the dining room, where a hot meal was waiting. At least their credit was good at the local grocery between paydays. He filled her in on what had happened while they ate. At the hour mark, he switched on the television to the news. It was filled with the station emergency and rescue, of course. Most of it seemed to be devoted to pictures of Hennings entering the ship and a highly colored account of the flight. But at least he learned that the flight had been completed. It made good publicity for the service. A sound track of a band playing *The Heroes' March* had been spliced into the movies. Maybe that was good publicity, too. He had to admit that Hennings fitted the music better than he could have done.

For a moment, the racket of the wind outside died, and another sound reached his ears. The hogs knew it was past feeding time and were kicking up a fuss. Murdock grimaced. He shoved away from the table, feeling almost guilty at having stuffed himself, and dug rain clothes out of the back closet. He hated going out in the weather again, but the animals had to be pacified.

They heard him coming and set up more of a racket. He bent against the wind and made a dash for it, getting his feet wet again in a puddle. But the inside of the building was warmer than the house, as he had expected. He lifted the cover of the mash cooker and began ladling out the food into the troughs. His pail was scraping the bottom of the cooker, while the sleek Poland China hogs fought and shoved toward the spot where he was emptying it. They'd been on half rations since yesterday, and they were obviously hungry.

He stopped when he had used half of what was in the cooker and headed for the next building. On the way, he paused for a futile look in the big storage shed, but he knew the answer. Pete had used the last bag of grain in cooking the day's food. They'd exhausted the last of the waste from the station earlier and had to fall back on the precious commercial feed usually only used as a supplement. Damn Greta and double damn Hulda! If the weekly predictions had been right, he could have wangled clearance for a flight ahead of schedule, before the storms, and they wouldn't be in this mess.

It was worse in the brooder house. The sows seemed to know that milk for their sucklings depended on their feeding. They received a somewhat larger portion, but it disappeared from the troughs as he watched. The animals fought for the last scraps and then began rushing about looking for more. They were smart enough to know he was the source of it, and they stared at him, expressing their demands in eloquent hog language. They weren't like other animals. Cows were too stupid to realize they'd been gypped, sheep were always yelling even when things went well. But hogs could pretty nearly swear in English when they felt robbed, as these did. Even the sucklings were squealing unhappily in sympathy with their mothers.

Murdock heard the door open behind him and turned to see Pete coming in, drenched to the skin. He looked worn out, and his back was still stiff from the accident, though he'd made a fine recovery. "Hi, Tom. Sis told me what happened at the field. Good thing, too. This stuff's no good for flights. How long till it clears?"

"Five days!" Murdock told him, and saw the older man flinch. The hogs might not starve to death in that time, but they'd suffer, as well as losing weight that would be hard to put back. He had no idea of how it would affect the milk supply for the little pigs, and he didn't want to guess.

They left the squealing hogs and slogged back to the house to change before Pete would report on his luck in town. It seemed to be all bad. They could get a loan against the mature hogs or they could sell some, but with the week-end coming up they would have to wait for money until they would no longer need it. Their credit at the only feed and grain store was used up.

Murdock frowned at that. "You mean Barr wouldn't let us have enough to carry us over in an emergency like this? After all out business with him?"

"Barr's gone north on some business," Pete reported. "His brother-in-law's running things. Claims he can't take the responsibility. Offered to lend me twenty bucks himself if I needed it, but no credit from the store. And he can't locate Barr. Darn it, if I hadn't had to get in front of that tractor —"

"If!" Sheila snorted. "If I hadn't insisted you two pay the hospital in full, or if I hadn't splurged on spring clothes… How much can we get for my car?"

Pete shrugged. "About half enough, but not till maybe Tuesday or Wednesday, after title transfer. I already asked at Circle Chevy. How about getting the weather reports, Sheila? With luck, the center of Hulda might pass right here!"

There seemed no immediate danger of that, though. Hulda following Greta, due to swing out to sea, and they'd miss the worst of her. Anyhow, Murdock knew that Bill Collins would call them if the farm was in danger. But with predictions gone sour from the station, they couldn't be sure. The new buildings were supposed to be hurricane proof, but…

They spent the afternoon trying to play canasta and listening to the rain and wind, until Pete slapped the cards back in the drawer in disgust. They ate early, dawdling over the food to kill time. Finally, the two men went out reluctantly. This time they scraped the bottom of the cookers dry. There was no sense in trying to spread the little food further and thinner.

How would a hero feel when a hog looked at him with hungry eyes? Or would the band playing destiny in his head drown out the frantic squealing of the animals? Murdock sighed and turned sickly back toward the house, with Pete at his heels.

Sheila met them at the door, motioning for silence and pointing to the television set. More news was finally coming through on the rescue flight by Hennings. And there was a picture on the screen showing the little third-stage rocket as seen from the station. It was obvious without the announcer's comment that the wings had been nearly wrenched from it and that it was in no condition for the return flight. Murdock's respect for Hennings' courage went up another notch. After a buffeting like that, it was a wonder he'd been able to make the effort of speaking to Base at all.

Then the rest of the news began to penetrate, and even the carefully chosen words couldn't make it sound too good. "…loss of filters when the airlock was sprung open on take-off was considerable, but it is believed that the replacements will be adequate until another flight can be made. Dr. Shapiro on the station reports that the men seem to be bearing up well, except for the two children. Plans are being made to isolate them in a special room, with extra filtration…"

Commander Phillips' kids, Murdock thought. The man had no business keeping them up there, anyhow. But the business about the sprung airlock…

Then he remembered the smaller blips on the radar screen that had separated from the *Jennilee*, before the first stage broke away. He frowned, trying to figure things more carefully. Just a few filters couldn't have made that much trace on the radar! But with the hasty packing, as he'd seen it, and the ship beginning to turn so the airlock was down, enough could have spilled to account for the trace—nearly the whole cargo, in fact!

He started for the phone, then shook his head. This would be better in person. He grabbed for the zipper on his coveralls and headed for his bedroom, while Pete frowned in slow comprehension.

"Tom, you can't do it!"

"I can try," he called back. "Warm up the truck, Sheila."

The zipper stuck. He swore at it, then forgot it. He wasn't dressing for parade drill. He dragged on his uniform cap, slipped into boots that might give some protection from the mud on the field, and stuffed his necessary papers and cards into the pockets of the coveralls. The service slicker was dry now, and he used it to hide most of his appearance.

"Any word of another flight planned?" he called out. It would be a sorry mess to reach the field just as some young pilot was taking off, ending any chance he had.

"None." Pete had the door open, and one of his big hands slapped against Murdock's shoulder. "Luck, you idiot!"

III

Murdock jumped out and into the open door of the truck. He started to shove Sheila out of the driver's seat, but she shook her head and began gunning the turbine. "I can handle this as well as you can, Tom. I won't have you starting that after wearing yourself out driving in. And stop looking at me like that! I'm not going to say what I'm thinking about this!"

He settled back in the passenger seat, reaching one hand out to touch her briefly. "Thanks, Hon," he said, as the truck swung out of the driveway and picked up speed on the road. She'd never been the kind to talk about worrying over his life, as some of the wives of the pilots did. She took it as part of him and accepted it, however she felt. Now she was pushing the big truck to the maximum safe speed, as if sharing his eagerness.

After a second, she caught his hand in hers and smiled, without taking her eyes from the road. He relaxed on the seat, letting the swish of the wipers and the muffled storm sounds lull him into a half trance, resting as much as he could. He should be thinking of what he'd say to Bailey, but the relaxation was more important.

He was half asleep when the truck slopped at the guard house. He began fumbling for his papers, but the guard swung back after flashing his face and called out something. A corporal darted out of the shack and into the truck, reaching for the wheel. "General Bailey's expecting you and the young lady, sir," he said. "I'll take care of your truck."

Murdock grunted in surprise. Pete must have managed to get through to Bailey. It might make things more difficult, but it would at least save time; that could be important, if he were to take off while the station was in optimum position.

Bailey's aide met them at GHQ, escorting them directly to the general's private office, and closing the door behind them. Bailey glanced at Murdock's appearance, frowned, and motioned them to chairs. His own collar was unbuttoned and his cap lay on the desk, indicating that formality was out the window. He lifted a bottle toward three waiting glasses. "Tom? Miss Crane?"

He seemed to need the drink more than they did. His face was gray with fatigue and his hand was unsteady. But his voice was normal enough as he put down the empty glass, "All right, Tom, I know what you're here for. What makes you think I'm crazy enough to send another ship up in this weather?"

"A couple of kids who may be dying up there," Murdock answered. He saw the general flinch and knew he'd guessed right; the service wouldn't want the publicity of their deaths without further effort to save them, and the pressure on Bailey must be terrific by now. "How many filters got through?"

"Two bundles—out of thirty! But losing a man and ship won't help anything. I've turned down about every pilot here already. I'd need at least three good reasons why you're a better choice before I'd even consider you, in spite of the hell Washington's raising. Got them?"

He should have been thinking of them on the ride here, Murdock realized. "Experience, for one thing. I've made almost a thousand flights on the run I was assigned," he said, making no effort to conceal the bitterness that crept into his voice. "Has any of your hotshots made a hundred yet?"

Bailey shook his head. "No."

"How about ability to operate solo without help from the automatic pilot? You can't trust machinery in unpredictable situations, and there's no time for help from a crew." The combination of improved ships and the difficulty of getting a crew for the garbage run had resulted in Murdock's operating solo most of the time for nearly five years now. He saw two of Bailey's fingers go up, and groped for something that would finish his case. Again, he heard the bitterness in his voice. "Third, expendability. What's a garbage man and an old ship against your bright hopes for tomorrow?"

"I've thought of the first two already. They're valid. The third isn't." Bailey filled a second glass halfway, his eyes on the liquor. "I can get plenty of pilots, Tom. So far, I haven't been able to find one other reliable garbage man, as you call it—after fifteen years! You'll have to do better than that."

Sheila's heels tapped down on the floor sharply. "After fifteen years of doing a job nobody else will take, don't you think Tom has any right to a favor from you? Isn't that good enough a reason?"

Bailey swung his gaze to her, surprise on his face. He studied her for half a minute, nodding slowly. "My God, you're actually willing to have him go!" he said at last. "I thought... Never mind. If you're willing to trust his ability, it's no reason I should. Or maybe it is. Maybe I want to be convinced. All right, Tom, we'll unload your ship and get the filters in. Want me to pick a volunteer crew for you?"

"I'll take it solo," Murdock told him. The fewer lives he was responsible for, the better; anyhow, there would be no time for help through the critical first few miles. "And leave the machinery in. Your filters are all bulk and no weight. She'll pitch less with a full load, from what I saw today. I'll be better off with the ballast.

Bailey reached for the phone and began snapping orders while Murdock turned to say good-bye to Sheila. She made it easier than he'd expected.

"I'll wait here," she told him. "You'll need the truck when you come down." She kissed him again quickly, then shoved him away. "Go on, you don't have time for me now."

She as right in that, he knew. He started for Control at a run, surprised when a covered jeep swing beside him. Lights came up abruptly, showing the *Mollyann* dimly through the murk, with men and trucks pouring toward her. He sent the driver of the jeep after them with orders to see about turning the base so the wings of the third stage would be edge on to the wind. In Control, he found everything disorganized, with men still dazed from sleep staring at him unbelievingly. But they agreed to set up the circuit that would give him connection through his viewing screen to the weather radar. Over the phone, Collins' language was foul and his voice worried, but he caught onto what was wanted almost at once.

The *Mollyann* was shaking against her guy cables as the jeep took him out to her; removal of the cables would be the last thing before take-off. Half a dozen tractors were idling nearby, and Bailey came running toward him, waving toward the top and yelling something about turning her.

Murdock shrugged. He hadn't expected things to be smooth in this last-minute rush; if he had to take her up wrong, he had to. "Okay, forget it," he said. "So you can't turn her. I'll manage."

"Take a look," Bailey told him, pointing up again, a tired grin on his face. "The way the wind is now, she's perfect. We finally checked, after getting all set, and there she was."

It was true, and Murdock swore hotly at his own stupidity in not checking first. The big wings were parallel to the wind already, saving them precious minutes. It still left the steering vanes on the upper stage at the mercy of the wind, but they were stubbier, and hence considerably sturdier.

The portable lift was running up the filter packs. He climbed on as a flashbulb went off near him and began going up. He heard some sort of cry from the photographer, but there was no time for posing now, and he couldn't have looked less suitable for pictures, anyhow. There'd be time for that on his return, he hoped.

He checked the stowing of the packs and made sure that they were lashed down well enough to ride up, even if his airlock broke open. The technician in charge pointed out the extra dogs they were installing on the lock, swearing it would hold through anything. It looked right. The ship was swaying and bobbing noticeably up here, and he could hear the creak of the cables. He tried to close his ears as he crawled up the little ladder to the control cabin and began the final check-out. There was a yell from the speaker as he cut on connections to Control, but he paid little attention to it. After fifteen years, he had little need of them to tell him the exact second of ideal take-off. He found the picture of the weather on the screen as he settled into the acceleration couch under the manual control panel, designed to swivel as a unit under changing acceleration.

The weather image was his biggest hope. Here, his study could pay off and give him the advantage he needed. It might look showy to take off on the split second and fight whatever the weather handed out; he preferred to pick his own time, if possible. With luck, he could spot a chance to ride up without being tipped for the first few seconds.

He glanced at the chronometer and began strapping himself down, while trying to absorb the data on the storm Collins was sending into his earphones. The weatherman had several screens to work from, and could give a better general picture than the single one Murdock was able to watch.

He began to get the feel of it. The wind, this far from the center of the hurricane, was erratic; there were moments of comparative quiet, and some measure of prediction was possible from the pattern on the screen. The real trick of taking off was to take advantage of every break. Once he began ascension, he'd have to trust to the automatic reflexes he'd developed and the general plan he'd worked out over the years as pure theory, with little help from reasoned thought. But until then, he could use his brains to make it as easy as it could possibly be.

He had no desire to take what was coming as a personal challenge. The kids in the station and the pigs on the farm were interested in results, not in his show of bravery.

Collins' voice cut off as Control interrupted to notify him that loading was complete and that the lifts, trucks and men were all clear.

He put one hand on the switch that would unlock the guy cables simultaneously. With the other, he started the peroxide pump for the fuel and threw the switch to ignite the rockets. He could hear the whine of the pump and feel the beginnings of power rumble through the ship, but he kept it at minimum. His eyes were glued to the weather picture on the screen that indicated his best chance coming up. Control was going crazy. With their count-off already finished, they wanted him off! Let them stew! A few seconds' difference in take-off was something he could correct for later.

Then his hand depressed the main blast lever all the way, a split second before he released the cable grapples. The *Mollyann* jumped free and began to walk upstairs on stilts, teetering and yawing in the wind. But his choice of take-off time had been correct. For the first hundred feet, she behaved herself, though the wind was driving him away from the blast deflection pit.

Then hell began. Acceleration mauled him backwards until only muscles toughened by a thousand previous flights could stand the power he was using. His fingers and arms could barely move against it. Yet they had to dance across the controls. The ship twisted and tilted, with every plate of her screaming in agony from the torsion and distortion of the pressures. Somehow, automatically, his fingers found a combination that righted her. His ears were clogged with the heavy pounding of his blood, his sense of balance was frozen, and his eyes could barely manage to focus on the dials in front of him.

He had stopped normal thinking and become a machine. The ship spun crazily in the twisting chaos of pressure differences. Unaccountably, she stayed upright as his hands moved with an unwilling life of their own, while fuel poured out at a rate that should have blacked him out from the acceleration. It was wasteful, but his only chance was to get through the storm in the shortest possible time and hang the consequences. If he could make the station at all, there would be fuel there for his return kick-off.

He was making no effort to tilt into a normal curve. A red light on the controls sprang into hazy existence before his eyes. The ship was going too fast for the height, heating the hull. He had to risk that, though.

Then surprisingly, the ship began to steady. He'd climbed over the storm.

He cut power back to normal, feeling a return of thought and hearing, and began tilting slowly to swing around the Earth toward his destination on the other side and a thousand miles up. It would make a rotten imitation of a synergy curve, but he'd survived! He felt the big first stage let go, followed by a brief moment with no pressure, until the second stage roared out. Only a little over a minute had passed in the storm, in spite of the hours of torture he had felt.

A voice started shouting in his phones, but he paid no attention to it. Now was his chance to say something heroic, to make the jest that was the ultimate in braggadocio!

"Shut up, damn it! I'm all right!" he screamed into the microphone. How could he figure out a proper saying for the papers when they wouldn't let him alone? Then slowly he realized he'd already answered, and it was too late for pretty phrases.

The second stage kicked off finally, and the third stage went on alone. He set up the rough corrections for his atypical takeoff, hoping he hadn't missed too much, while the second hand swept around until he could cut off all power and just drift. Then he lay back, welcoming weightlessness. He was trembling now, and his whole body seemed to be a mass of bruises he couldn't remember getting. Sweat poured from his forehead and goose pimples rose on his arms. He barely made it to the little cabinet in time to be sick without splattering the whole cabin.

He made a lousy hero. The only music in his head was the ringing in his ears and the drumming in his heart!

Yet the trip up was by far the easier part of his job. He still had to bring his cargo down in its unpowered glide through a storm that would be closer to its worst, or the whole trip would be useless for him, no matter how many lives it saved.

He was feeling almost himself again, though, when he finally matched orbits with the station. As far as he could determine, his wings and stabilizers were still sound, and air pressure in the cargo space indicated nothing had sprung there. He even had a few drops of fuel left after making his final corrections. At least he'd done an adequate job of piloting on the ascension.

With luck, he'd get the *Mollyann* down again intact. But he'd need that luck!

IV

The big multi-tube affair into which the station had grown looked normal enough in the sunlight. But the men who came out in the little space ferry showed the hell of slow poisoning they'd been through, even over their jubilation at the sight of the filters. When they made seal-to-seal contact and he released the lock, the smell of their air was positively foul. They must have been reporting their plight as a lot better than it really was.

Commander Phillips came through first, almost crying as he grabbed Murdock's hand. He seemed at a complete loss for words.

"Hello, Red," Murdock greeted him Phillips had been part of his own class, fifteen years before. "How are the kids?"

"Shapiro says they'll be okay, once we get some filters that aren't plated with contaminants.. Tommy, I'd invite you over for champagne right now, but our air would ruin it. Just figure that anything I've got…"

Murdock cut him off. "I'll call it quits if you'll get this cargo out and my usual load in here on the double, along with some fuel. And you might have one of your engineers look over my wings for signs of strain. I've got to ride the next orbit back, two hours from now."

"Go back into that! You're crazy!" Phillips' shock drove everything else from, the man's face. "You can't do it! I won't clear you!"

"I thought you were just offering me anything you had," Murdock pointed out.

It took five minutes more of heavy arguing to arrange it, and he might not have succeeded even then if he'd waited until the commander had recovered from his first burst of gratitude, or if the man hadn't been worn down by the poisons in the air and the fatigue of their desperate fight for survival. Phillips was hoarse and sick when he finally gave in and stumbled back to the. loaded ferry. He croaked something about idiocy and grateful humanity and took off. Murdock tried, idly, to untangle it in his mind, but at the moment he was again more concerned with hungry pigs.

It was too busy a stretch for him to have time to worry. The square magnesium cans of dehydrated garbage began to come out, along with fuel. Sick men were somehow driving themselves to a final burst of energy as they stowed things carefully to preserve the trim of the ship. From outside, there was a steady tapping and hammering as others went over the skin of the controls with their instruments.

At the end, there was another visit from Phillips, with more arguing. But finally the man gave in again. "All right, damn it. Maybe you can make it. I certainly hope so. But you're not going it alone. You'll take Hennings along as co-pilot. He volunteered."

"Send him over, then," Murdock said wearily. He should have expected something like that. Hennings apparently reacted to the smell of glory like a warhorse to gunpowder.

He took a final look at the cargo, nodding in satisfaction. There was enough waste there to keep the farm going until they were over the hump. If Barr got back and they could enrich it with commercial food on temporary credit, Pete and he would be in clover. He pulled himself about and up to the control cabin, to see the ferry coming out on its last trip.

A minute later, Hennings came through the connecting seal and dogged it closed. "Hi, Tommy," he called out. "Ah, air again. How about letting me run her down for you? You look beat."

"The automatic pilot's disconnected," Murdock told him curtly. It had begun misfunctioning some twenty trips back, and he'd simply cut it out of the circuits, since he seldom used it.

Some of the starch seemed to run out of the younger man. He halted his march toward the controls and stared down at them doubtfully. Actually, little automatic piloting could be done on the down leg of a flight, but pilots were conditioned into thinking of the automatics almost reverently, ahead of anything else on the ship. It dated from the days when the ascension would have been physically impossible without such aid, and Murdock had felt the same for the first five years of piloting.

"Better strap in," he suggested.

Hennings dropped into the co-pilot couch while Murdock ran through the final check. The ship began swinging slowly about as the gyroscope's hummed, lining up for the return blast. "Ten seconds," Murdock announced. He ran a count in his head, then hit the blast lever gently. They began losing speed and dropping back toward Earth, while the station sailed on and away.

Then, with power off, there was nothing to do but stare at what was coming. It would still be night at Base, and even the sodium flares and radar beacons wouldn't be as much help as they should be in the storm. This time, they'd have to depend on lift, like a normal plane landing. It would be tough for any plane, for that matter, though possible enough in fully powered flight. But they had to come down like a glider. If there were any undetected strains in the wings…

"You came up *without* a tape?" Hennings asked suddenly.

Murdock grimaced, resenting the interruption to his brooding. He liked Hennings better as a cocky hero than as a worried young man. "A tape's no good for unpredictable conditions."

"Okay, if you say so," the younger man said doubtfully at last. He sat staring at the controls with an odd look on his face. Then surprisingly, he laughed and settled back loosely in his seat. "I guess maybe you don't need me, then."

He was snoring five minutes later. Murdock scowled at him, suspecting it was an act at first. Finally he shrugged and turned back to his worrying. He knew there'd been a good measure of luck to his take-off, in spite of all his careful efforts. He couldn't count on luck for the landing.

He could still put in an emergency call and ask to land at some large airfield out of the storm, in theory. But it would do no good. Hulda was blanketing too great an area—any other field would be so far from the farm that trucking the garbage back would be out of the question. He might as well have remained at the station. Besides, he was already on a braking orbit that would bring him near Base, and changes now would involve risks of their own.

He watched the thin haze of the upper atmospheric levels approach, trying to force his muscles to relax and his nerves to steady. The worst part of the return was the chance for nervousness to build up. Hennings went on snoring quietly, floating in the co-pilot's couch. His relaxation didn't help Murdock any.

It was almost a relief when they finally hit the first layers of detectable air, where the controls became effective again, and where he could take over. The ship had to be guided steadily now, its dip into atmosphere coordinated with its speed to avoid the dangers of skipping out or of going low enough to overheat. Murdock eased her down, watching his instruments but depending more on the feel of the *Mollyann*. A feeling of weight began to return along with noise from outside, while the hull pyrometer rose to indicate that friction was working on them, turning their speed into heat. This part of the descent was almost a conditioned reflex to him by now. Outside, he knew, the skin of the ship would be rising slowly to red heat, until they could lose enough speed to drop into the lower layers of air where they could cool off.

The heat in the cabin rose slowly. The *Mollyann* was an old model among the ships; her cabin was less completely insulated and airtight than most of the others. But for the brief period of high heat, she was safe enough. Slowly the air picked up a faint odor, that grew stronger as the hot hull radiated into the cargo space. He hardly noticed it, until Hennings woke up sniffing.

"Garbage," Murdock told him. "There's still enough water in it to boil off some. You get used to it."

They were dropping to denser air now, and he could feel perspiration on his palms. He dried them hastily. His head felt thick, and his stomach began to knot inside him. "Contact Control and have them shoot me the weather," he told Hennings.

When the pattern of it snapped onto the screen, he felt sicker. There was going to be no area of relative calm this time, and he couldn't wait for one to appear. He tried to get the weather pattern fixed in his mind while their descent flattened and they came closer to the storm area. He'd have to turn and follow the course set by the wind, heading into it; it meant coming down on a twisting curve, since there was some local disturbance near the field.

Then the first bumpiness registered. The ship seemed to sink and skid. There was no pressure of acceleration now, but his fingers felt weighted with lead, almost too slow to adjust the controls. The *Mollyann* dipped and tilted, and his stomach came up in his throat. He heard Hennings gasp, but he had no time to look at the other. The top of the storm was a boiling riot of pockets.

Things were getting worse by the second now. The last few miles were going to be hell. Lift wasn't steady, and eddies in the driving storm shook and twisted the ship. Her wing-loading wasn't bad, but she lacked the self-correcting design of the light planes he'd flown. The wings groaned and strained, and the controls seemed frozen. He was on the weather map now, a white blip that scudded along the edge. It gave him orientation, not the sight of his course offered little reassurance.

They hit a larger pocket and seemed to drop a hundred feet. The wings creaked sickeningly, and something whined from the rear controls. The elevators abruptly bucked back at him, catching him unaware and he had to brace himself and fight against them, putting his muscles into it. Obviously, the servo assist had conked out. Probably something had happened during take-off. He was left with only his own strength to buck the currents now, operating on the mechanical cable. If that couldn't hold…!

He was sweating as he fought the buffeting. In spite of his best efforts, they were pitching more now. Another violent swoop came, and was followed by a thump and scraping from the cargo section. The ship lost trim. Some of the cans had come loose from their fastenings and were skidding about!

He saw Hennings jerk from his couch and fight his way to the hatch. He yelled angrily, knowing the fool could get killed by something grinding into him down there. Then he had no time to worry as the heavy odor told him the boy had already gone through the hatch. He fought to hold the ship steady, but there was no predicting its behavior. His muscles were overworked and unable to handle the controls as smoothly as they should. Now the field was only a few miles away, and he had to buck and twist his way through the wind to arrive within the limits of the landing strip. To make things worse, the wind velocity must have been higher than he had estimated, and he had lost more speed than he could afford. It was going to be close, if he made it at all.

Then the ship began steadying as he could feel the trim restored. He had only time for a single sigh of relief before Hennings was up, dripping with sweat and garbage odor as he groped his way back to the couch. Murdock tried to call his thanks, knowing the courage it had taken to risk the cargo hold. But Hennings' whole attention was focused sickly on the weather map.

The field was coming at them, but not soon enough. Too much speed had been lost to the wind resistance. Murdock tried to flatten the glide, but gave up at once. They were already as near a stall as he dared risk in this stuff, and they'd still miss the field by a mile! They'd land and go crashing into trees, rocks and maybe even houses down there!

Murdock swore and grabbed for the blast lever. There was no time to warm up properly, but he had to have more speed.

He heard Hennings' voice yell a single shocked word before his hand moved the lever. Behind them, sound roared out for a split second and the ship lurched forward. Power such as that wasn't meant for minor corrections in speed, and there was no way to meter it out properly, yet it was the only possible answer. He cut the blast, then threw it on again for a split second. Then he had to snap his hand back to the elevator controls, fighting against them to regain stability.

He couldn't risk more speed. If they undershot, they were lost. And if their speed were too high, there would be no second chance to try a landing. They couldn't turn and circle in the storm. They were only getting through by heading straight into the wind, jockeying to avoid cross currents. Beyond the field was the ocean, and these modern ships weren't designed for water landings—particularly in the seas they'd find running now.

A glint of yellow caught his eye. The field markers! And he was too high. He threw his weight against the sloppy controls and felt the ship beginning to go down. He'd picked up too much speed in the brief burst of power, but he had to land somehow at once.

He could make out some of the flares now, and he had to aim between them. He kicked out the landing wheels and fought her down savagely. He was already past the near edge of the field. Too far!

Suddenly the wheels hit. The ship bounced as the wind caught it from below and began slewing it around. Then it hit again, while he fought with brakes and controls to right it. It staggered, skidded, and went tearing down the runway. Ahead of them, the crash fence loomed up in the yellow light. Ten feet—another ten—

Murdock felt the ship hit and bounce. He was just feeling his relief that their

The Band Played On

speed was too low to crash through when his head struck against the control panel, and his mind exploded in a shower of hot sparks that slowly turned black.

He had a vague period of semi-consciousness after that when he realized Hennings was carrying him out of the ship, with rain pelting on him and the sound of the gale in his ears. Something bright went off, and he had a vision of the photo they must have taken: Hennings carrying a body from the *Mollyann*—Hennings, immune to alll accidents, standing poised and braced against the storm, marching straight toward the photographers, smiling...

There was another vague period when he seemed to hear the voices of Sheila and Bailey. The prick of a needle...

He swam up from a cloud of dark fuzz at last. There was a dull ache in his head and a bump on his scalp The light hurt his eyes when he opened them, and he clamped them shut again, but not before he saw he was on a couch in the recreation hall. At least that must mean no concussion; it had been just an ordinary bump, on top of the strain and nervous fatigue.

From outside, there was a confused mixture of sounds and a hammering that seemed to be against the building. He started to pull himself up to look for the cause, but it was too much effort for the moment. He started to drift off into a half doze, until he heard steps, and Hennings' voice.

"...absolutely magnificent, Miss Crane! I'll never forget it. He didn't even try to kid around to keep his spirits up. He just sat there without a sign of worry, as if he was doing a regular milk run. He didn't bat an eyelash when he had to decide to use power. So help me, he was like one of the heroes out of the kids' serials I used to watch. And that lousy reporter writing that I brought the ship down. If I find him—"

"Forget it, Larry," Sheila's voice said quietly.

"I won't forget it! It was bad enough they try to cut him down to a quarter column on the take-off and had to call it a lull in the storm! But this time, I'm going to see they print the facts!"

"That should give them another column on how you're modestly trying to give credit to someone else," Sheila answered quietly. "Let them print what they want. It won't change the facts that we all know. And Tom won't mind too much. He's used to the way things are."

Murdock opened his eyes again and sat up, cutting off their conversation. He still felt groggy, but after a second his vision cleared. He smiled at Sheila and pulled her down beside him.

"She's right, Hennings. Let them print what they like. It's good publicity for the service the way they probably have it. Besides, you did your share." He reached out a hand for the younger man's arm, conscious that he couldn't even do that with the right flourish. "It took guts, trimming the cargo when you did. I meant to thank you for that."

Hennings muttered something awkwardly, and then straightened into his old self as he marched out the door to leave them alone. Sheila smiled after him with a mixture of fondness and amusement.

"What happened to the *Mollyann* and her cargo? And how's the farm making out?" Murdock asked her a moment later.

"The farm's safe enough, from the latest reports," she told him. "And the ship's a little banged up, but nothing serious. General Bailey sent the cadets out to load the cargo into our truck. He said a little garbage smell should be good for them." She smiled again, then glanced at her watch. "He should be back now, for that matter."

Murdock grinned wryly. It was a shame the hogs would never know the attention their food was getting. It must have been something to see the cadets practicing being heroes while unloading the smelly cans. He glanced out the window, but the storm was still too thick for clear vision. Someone scurried past, just outside, and there was more banging and a flurry of activity beyond the door, but apparently it had nothing to do with Bailey's return.

It was five minutes more before the general came in, walking over to stare at Murdock. "Your truck's outside, Tom. And don't bring it through the gates again until you're wearing a proper uniform!" He chuckled. "With eagles on the collar. I've been trying to wrangle them for you a long time now. Congratulations, Colonel! You earned them!"

Murdock pulled Sheila closer as he accepted Bailey's hand, feeling the strength of her against him. There were other strengths, too—the words he'd heard Hennings saying, the recognition and security the new rank offered, the awareness that he hadn't failed his job. But he still found himself awkward and unable to rise to the occasion. He didn't try, but silently let Bailey guide them toward the door.

Then he turned. "There's one other thing. That application for Moon service—"

He felt Sheila stiffen briefly and relax against him again, but his words brought the general to a complete standstill.

Bailey's head nodded, reluctantly. "All right," he said at last. "I hate to let you go, Tom, but I'll put it through with a recommendation."

"Don't!" Murdock told him. "Tear it up! I've got a lot of hogs depending on the garbage run."

He threw the door open and saw the loaded truck waiting outside. He started toward it, drawing Sheila with him. Then he stopped, his mouth open in surprise, seeing what had caused all the banging he had heard.

There was a wide, clumsy plywood canopy built over the doorway now, running out to the truck. Lined up under it were all the pilots, with Hennings at the front, moving forward to open the door of the truck with a flourish. Precisely as Murdock's foot touched the ground, the band struck up the notes of *Heroes' March*.

Feeling like a fool, Murdock stumbled forward, awkwardly helping Sheila in and getting into the driver's set, while fifty pairs of eyes remained zeroed in on him. Hennings shut the door with another flourish and stepped back into the ranks.

And suddenly Murdock knew what to do. He leaned from the window of the truck as Sheila settled into position beside him. He grinned at the pilots, raised his hand, placed his thumb against his nose and wriggled his fingers at them.

Hennings' face split into a wide grin and his arm lifted in the same salute, with fifty others following him in the gesture by a split second.

Murdock rolled up the window, and the big truck began moving across the field, heading toward home and the hogs.

Behind him, the band played on, but he wasn't listening.

The Faithful

Today, in a green and lovely world, here in the mightiest of human cities, the last of the human race is dying. And we of Man's creation are left to mourn his passing, and to worship the memory of Man, who controlled all that he knew save only himself.

I am old, as my people go, yet my blood is still young and my life may go on for untold ages yet, if what this last of Men has told me is true. And that also is Man's work, even as we and the Ape-People are his work in the last analysis. We of the Dog-People are old, and have lived a long time with Man. And yet, but for Roger Stren, we might still be baying at the moon and scratching the fleas from our hides, or lying at the ruins of Man's empire in dull wonder at his passing.

There are earlier records of dogs who mouthed clumsily a few Man words, but Hungor was the pet of Roger Stren, and in the labored efforts at speech, he saw an ideal and a life work. The operation on Hungor's throat and mouth, which made Man-speech more nearly possible, was comparatively simple. The search for other "talking" dogs was harder.

But he found five besides Hungor, and with this small start he began. Selection and breeding, surgery and training, gland implantation and X-ray mutation were his methods, and he made steady progress. At first money was a problem, but his pets soon drew attention and commanded high prices.

When he died, the original six had become thousands, and he had watched over the raising of twenty generations of dogs. A generation of my kind then took only three years. He had seen his small backyard pen develop into a huge institution, with a hundred followers and students, and had found the world eager for his success. Above all, he had seen tail-wagging give place to limited speech in that short time.

The movement he had started continued. At the end of two thousand years, we had a place beside Man in his work that would have been inconceivable to Roger Stren himself. We had our schools, our houses, our work with Man, and a society of our own. Even our independence, when we wanted it. And our life-span was not fourteen, but fifty years or more.

Man, too, had traveled a long way. The stars were almost within his grasp. The barren moon had been his for centuries. Mars and Venus lay beckoning, and he had reached them twice, but not to return. That lay close at hand. Almost, Man had conquered the universe.

But he had not conquered himself. There had been many setbacks to his progress because he had to go out and kill others of his kind. And now, the memory of his past called again, and he went out in battle against himself. Cities crumbled to dust, the plains to the south became barren deserts again, Chicago lay covered in a green mist. That death killed slowly, so that Man fled from the city and died, leaving it an empty place. The mist hung there, clinging days, months, years—after Man had ceased to be.

I, too, went out to war, driving a plane built for my people, over the cities of the Rising Star Empire. The tiny atomic bombs fell from my ship on houses, on farms, on all that was Man's, who had made my race what it was. For my Men had told me I must fight.

Somehow, I was not killed. And after the last Great Drive, when half of Man was already dead, I gathered my people about me, and we followed to the North, where some of my Men had turned to find a sanctuary from the war. Of Man's work, three cities still stood—wrapped in the green mist, and useless. And Man huddled around little fires and hid himself in the forest, hunting his food in small clans. Yet hardly a year of the war had passed.

For a time, the Men and my people lived in peace, planning to rebuild what had been, once the war finally ceased. Then came the Plague. The anti-toxin which had been developed was ineffective as the Plague increased in its virulency. It spread over land and sea, gripped Man who had invented it, and killed him. It was like a strong dose of strychnine, leaving Man to die in violent cramps and retchings.

For a brief time, Man united against it, but there was no control. Remorselessly it spread, even into the little settlement they had founded in the north. And I watched in sorrow as my Men around me were seized with its agony. Then we of the Dog-People were left alone in a shattered world from whence Man had vanished. For weeks we labored at the little radio we could operate, but there was no answer; and we knew that Man was dead.

There was little we could do. We had to forage our food as of old, and cultivate our crops in such small way as our somewhat modified forepaws permitted. And the barren north country was not suited to us.

I gathered my scattered tribes about me, and we began the long trek south. We moved from season to season, stopping to plant our food in the spring, hunting in the fall. As our sleds grew old and broke down, we could not replace them, and our travel became even slower. Sometimes we came upon our kind in smaller packs. Most of them had gone back to savagery, and these we had to mold to us by force. But little by little, growing in size, we drew south. We sought Men; for fifty thousand years we of the Dog-People had lived with and for Man, and we knew no other life. In the wilds of what had once been Washington State we came upon another group who had not fallen back to the law of tooth and fang. They had horses to work for them, even crude harnesses and machines which they could operate. There we stayed for some ten years, setting up a government and building ourselves a crude city. Where Man had his hands, we had to invent what could be used with our poor feet and our teeth. But we had found a sort of security, and had even acquired some of Man's books by which we could teach our young.

Then into our valley came a clan of our people, moving west, who told us they had heard that one of our tribes sought refuge and provender in a mighty city of great houses lying by a lake in the east. I could only guess that it was Chicago. Of the green mist they had not heard—only that life was possible there.

Around our fires that night we decided that if the city were habitable, there would be homes and machines designed for us. And it might be there were Men, and the chance to bring up our young in the heritage which was their birthright. For weeks we labored in preparing ourselves for the long march to Chicago. We loaded our supplies in our crude carts, hitched our animals to them, and began the eastward trip.

It was nearing winter when we camped outside the city, still mighty and imposing. In the sixty years of the desertion, nothing had perished that we could see; the fountains to the west were still playing, run by automatic engines.

We advanced upon the others in the dark, quietly. They were living in a great square, littered with filth, and we noted that they had not even fire left from civilization. It was a savage fight, while it lasted, with no quarter given nor asked. But they had sunk too far, in the lazy shelter of Man's city, and the clan was not as large as we had heard. By the time the sun rose there was not one of them but had been killed or imprisoned until we could train them in our ways. The ancient city was ours, the green mist gone after all those years.

Around us were abundant provisions, the food factories which I knew how to run, the machines that Man had made to fit our needs, the houses in which we could dwell, power drawn from the bursting core of the atom, which needed only the flick of a switch to start. Even without hands, we could live here in peace and security for ages. Perhaps here my dreams of adapting our feet to handle Man's tools and doing his work were possible, even if no Men were found. We cleared the muck from the city and moved into Greater South Chicago, where our people had had their section of the city. I, and a few of the elders who had been taught by their fathers in the ways of Man, set up the old regime, and started the great water and light machines. We had returned to a life of certainty.

And four weeks later, one of my lieutenants brought Paul Kenyon before me. Man! Real and alive, after all this time! He smiled, and I motioned my eager people away.

"I saw your lights," he explained. "I thought at first some men had come back, but that is not to be; but civilization still has its followers, evidently, so I asked one of you to take me to the leaders. Greetings from all that is left of Man!"

"Greetings," I gasped. It was like seeing the return of the gods. My breath was choked; a great peace and fulfillment surged over me. "Greetings, and the blessings of your God. I had no hope of seeing Man again."

He shook his head. "I am the last. For fifty years I have been searching for Men—but there are none. Well, you have done well. I should like to live among you, work with you—when I can. I survived the Plague somehow, but it comes on me yet, more often now, and I can't move nor care for myself then. That is why I have come to you.

"Funny." He paused. "I seem to recognize you. Hungor Beowulf XIV? I am Paul Kenyon. Perhaps you remember me? No? Well, it was a long time, and you were young. Perhaps my smell has changed with the disease. But that white streak under the eye still shows, and I remember you."

I needed no more to complete my satisfaction at his homecoming.

Now one had come among us with hands, and he was of great help. But most of all, he was of the old Men, and gave point to our working. But often, as he had said, the old sickness came over him, and he lay in violent convulsions, from which he was weak for days. We learned to care for him, and help him when he needed it, even as we learned to fit our society to his presence. And at last, he came to me with a suggestion.

"Hungor," he said, "if you had one wish, what would it be?"

"The return of Man. The old order, where we could work together. You know as well as I how much we need Man."

He grinned crookedly. "Now, it seems, Man needs you more. But if that were denied, what next?"

"Hands," I said. "I dream of them at night and plan for them by day, but I will never see them."

"Maybe you will, Hungor. Haven't you ever wondered why you go on living, twice normal age, in the prime of your life? Have you never wondered how I have withstood the Plague which still runs in my blood, and how I still seem only in my thirties, though nearly seventy years have passed since a Man has been born?"

"Sometimes," I answered. "I have no time for wonder, now, and when I do—Man is the only answer I know."

"A good answer," he said. "Yes, Hungor, Man is the answer. That is why I remember you. Three years before the war, when you were just reaching maturity, you came into my laboratory. Do you remember now?"

"The experiment," I said. "That is why you remembered me?"

"Yes, the experiment. I altered your glands somewhat, implanted certain tissues into your body, as I had done to myself. I was seeking the secret of immortality. Though there was no reaction at the time, it worked, and I don't know how much longer we may live—or you may; it helped me resist the Plague, but did not overcome it."

So that was the answer. He stood staring at me a long time. "Yes, unknowingly, I saved you to carry on Man's future for him. But we were talking of hands.

"As you know, there is a great continent to the east of the Americas, called Africa. But did you know Man was working there on the great apes, as he was working here on your people? We never made as much progress with them as with you. We started too late. Yet they spoke a simple language and served for common work. And we changed their hands so the thumb and fingers opposed, as do mine. There, Hungor, are your hands."

Now Paul Kenyon and I laid plans carefully. Out in the hangars of the city there were aircraft designed for my people's use; heretofore, I had seen no need of using them. The planes were in good condition, we found on examination, and my early training came back to me as I took the first ship up. They carried fuel to circle the globe ten times, and out in the lake the big fuel tanks could be drawn on when needed.

Together, though he did most of the mechanical work between spells of sickness, we stripped the planes of all their war equipment. Of the six hundred planes, only two were useless, and the rest would serve to carry some two thousand passengers in addition to the pilots. If the apes had reverted to complete savagery, we were equipped with tanks of anesthetic gas by which we could overcome them and strap them in the planes for the return. In the houses around us, we built accommodations for them strong enough to hold them by force, but designed for their comfort if they were peaceable.

At first, I had planned to lead the expedition. But Paul Kenyon pointed out that they would be less likely to respond to us than to him. "After all," he said, "Men educated them and cared for them, and they probably remember us dimly. But your people they know only as the wild dogs who are their enemies. I can go out and contact their leaders, guarded, of course, by your people. But otherwise, it might mean battle."

Each day I took up a few of our younger ones in the planes and taught them to handle the controls. As they were taught, they began the instruction of others. It was a task which took months to finish, but my people knew the need of hands as well as I; any faint hope was well worth trying.

It was late spring when the expedition set out. I could follow their progress by means of television, but could work the controls only with difficulty. Kenyon, of course, was working the controls at the other end, when he was able.

They met with a storm over the Atlantic Ocean, and three of the ships went down. But under the direction of my lieutenant and Kenyon, the rest weathered the storm. They landed near the ruins of Capetown, but found no trace of the Ape-People. Then began weeks of scouting over the jungles and plains. They saw apes, but on capturing a few they found them only the primitive creatures which nature had developed.

It was by accident they finally met with success. Camp had been made for the night, and fires had been lit to guard against the savage beasts which roamed the land. Kenyon was in one of his rare moments of good health. The telecaster had been set up in a tent near the outskirts of the camp, and he was broadcasting a complete account of the day. Then, abruptly, over the head of the Man was raised a rough and shaggy face.

He must have seen the shadow, for he started to turn sharply, then caught himself and moved slowly around. Facing him was one of the apes. He stood there silently, watching the ape, not knowing whether it was savage or well disposed. It, too, hesitated; then it advanced.

"Man—Man," it mouthed. "You came back. Where were you? I am Tolemy, and I saw you, and I came."

"Tolemy," said Kenyon, smiling. "It is good to see you, Tolemy. Sit down; let us talk. I am glad to see you. Ah, Tolemy, you look old; were your father and mother raised by Man?"

"I am eighty years, I think. It is hard to know. I was raised by Man long ago. And now I am old; my people say I grow too old to lead. They do not want me to come to you, but I know Man. He was good to me. And he had coffee and cigarettes."

"I have coffee and cigarettes, Tolemy." Kenyon smiled. "Wait, I will get them. And your people, is not life hard among them in the jungle? Would you like to go back with me?"

"Yes, hard among us. I want to go back with you. Are you many?"

"No, Tolemy." He set the coffee and cigarettes before the ape, who drank eagerly and lit the smoke gingerly from a fire. "No, but I have friends with me. You must bring your people here, and let us get to be friends. Are there many of you?"

"Yes. Ten times we make ten tens—a thousand of us, almost. We are all that was left in the city of Man after the great fight. A Man freed us, and I led my people away, and we lived here in the jungle. They wanted to be in small tribes, but I made them one, and we are safe. Food is hard to find."

"We have much food in a big city, Tolemy, and friends who will help you, if you work for them. You remember the Dog-People, don't you? And you would work with them as with Man if they treated you as Man treated you, and fed you, and taught your people?"

"Dogs? I remember the Man-Dogs. They were good. But here the dogs are bad. I smelled dog here; it was not like the dog we smell each day, and my nose was not sure. I will work with Man-Dogs, but my people will be slow to learn them."

Later telecasts showed rapid progress. I saw the apes come in by twos and threes and meet Paul Kenyon, who gave them food, and introduced my people to them. This was slow, but as some began to lose their fear of us, others were easier to train. Only a few broke away and would not come.

Cigarettes that Man was fond of—but which my people never used —were a help, since they learned to smoke with great readiness.

It was months before they returned. When they came, there were over nine hundred of the Ape-People with them, and Paul and Tolemy had begun their education. Our first job was a careful medical examination of Tolemy, but it showed him in good health, and with much of the vigor of a younger ape. Man had been lengthening the ages of his kind, as it had ours, and he was evidently a complete success.

Now they have been among us three years, and during that time we have taught them to use their hands at our instructions. Overhead, the great monorail cars are running, and the factories have started to work again. They are quick to learn, with a curiosity that makes them eager for new knowledge. And they are thriving and multiplying here. We need no longer bewail the lack of hands; perhaps in time to come, with their help, we can change our forepaws further, and learn to walk on two legs, as did Man.

Today, I have come back from the bed of Paul Kenyon. We are often together now—perhaps I should include the faithful Tolemy—when he can talk, and among us there has grown a great friendship. I laid certain plans before him today for adapting the apes mentally and physically until they are Men. Nature did it with an apelike brute once; why can we not do it with the Ape-People now? The Earth would be peopled again, science would rediscover the stars, and Man would have a foster child in his own likeness.

And—we of the Dog-People have followed Man for fifty thousand years. That is too long to change. Of all Earth's creatures, the Dog-People alone have followed Man thus. My people cannot lead now. No dog was ever complete without the companionship of Man. The Ape-People will be Man.

It is a pleasant dream, surely not an impossible one.

Kenyon smiled as I spoke to him, and cautioned me in the jesting way he uses when most serious, not to make them too much like Man, lest another Plague destroy them. Well, we can guard against that. I think he, too, had a dream of Man reborn, for there was a hint of tears in his eyes, and he seemed pleased with me.

There is but little to please him now, alone among us, wracked by pain, waiting the slow death he knows must come. The old trouble has grown worse, and the Plague has settled harder on him.

All we can do is give him sedatives to ease the pain now, though Tolemy and I have isolated the Plague we found in his blood. It seems a form of cholera, and with that information, we have done some work. The old Plague serum offers a clue, too. Some of our serums have seemed to ease the spells a little, but they have not stopped them.

It is a faint chance. I have not told him of our work, for only a stroke of luck will give us success before he dies.

Man is dying. Here in our laboratory, Tolemy keeps repeating something; a prayer, I think it is. Well, maybe the God whom he has learned from Man will be merciful, and grant us success.

Paul Kenyon is all that is left of the old world which Tolemy and I loved. He lies in the ward, moaning in agony, and dying. Sometimes he looks from his windows and sees the birds flying south; he gazes at them as if he would never see them again. Well, will he? Something he muttered once comes back to me:

"For no man knoweth—"

The Luck of Ignatz

Maybe it was superstition, but Ignatz knew it was all his fault. For the last three days, Jerry Lord had sat in that same chair, his eyes conjuring up a vision of red hair and a dimple on the wall, and there was nothing Ignatz could do about it.

He grunted and grumbled his unhappiness, dug his tail into the carpet, and shoved forward on his belly plate until his antennae touched the Master's ankle. For the hundredth time he tried to mumble human words, and failed. But Jerry sensed his meaning and reached down absently to rub the horn on his snout.

"Ignatz," the Master muttered, "did I tell you Anne star-hops on the *Burgundy* tonight? Bound for South Venus." He sucked on his cold pipe, then tossed it aside in disgust. "Pete Durnall's to guide her through Hellonfire swamps."

It was no news to Ignatz, who'd heard nothing else for the last three days, but he rumbled sympathetically in his foghorn voice. In the rotten inferno north of Hellas, any man who knew the swamps could be a hero to a mudsucker. Even veteran spacemen were usually mudsuckers on Venus, and Anne was earthbound, up to now.

Ignatz knew those swamps—none better. He'd lived there some hundred odd years until the Master caught him for a mascot. Oh, the swamp animals were harmless enough, most of them, but Anne wouldn't think so when she saw them. She'd screamed the first time she saw him—even a Venusian *zloaht*, or snail-lizard was horrible to an Earthman; the other fauna were worse.

But the memory of the swamps suggested heat to Ignatz. He crawled up the portable stove and plunked down into a pan of boiling water; after a few minutes, when the warmth took full effect, he relaxed comfortably on the bottom to sleep. Jerry'd have to solve his own problems, since he couldn't learn zloaht language. What was the sense of solving problems if he couldn't boast about it?

There was a thud and clank outside, and a chorus of shrieks rent the air. By the time Ignatz was fully awake, a man was pounding on the door, grumbling loudly. Jerry threw it open, and the hotel manager plunked in, face red and temper worse.

"Know what that was?" he shrieked. "Number two elevator broke the cable—brand-new it was, too. Stuck between floors, and we've got to cut through with a blow torch. Now!"

"So what? I didn't do it." The old weariness in Jerry's voice was all too familiar to Ignatz. He knew what was coming.

"No, you didn't do it; you didn't *do* it. But you were here." The red face turned livid, and the fat chest heaved convulsively. He threshed his fist in front of

Jerry's face, and shrilled out in a quavering falsetto: "Don't think I haven't heard of you! I felt sorry for you, took you in for only double rates, and look what happens. Well, I'm through. Out you go—hear me? Out, now, at once."

Jerry shrugged. "Okay." He watched with detached interest as Ignatz climbed out of the pan and dropped over onto the manager's leg. With a wild shriek of confused profanity, the man jerked free and out. He went scurrying down the hall, his fat hands rubbing at the burned flesh.

"You shouldn't have done that, Ignatz," Jerry remarked mildly. "He'll probably have blisters where you touched him. But it's done now, so go cool off and help me pack." He put a pan of cold water on the floor and began opening closets and dragging out clothes. Ignatz climbed into the water and let his temperature drop down to a safe limit, considering this latest incident ruefully.

Not that there was anything novel about it; the only wonder was that they had been in the hotel almost a week before it happened. And it was all his fault; he never did anything, but he was there, and trouble followed blissfully after. Of course, Jerry Lord should have known better than to catch a snail-lizard, but he did it, and things started.

The luckiest man in the star fleet, the Master had been head tester for the new rocket models until the O. M. decided he needed a rest and sent him to Venus. Any normal man would have been killed when the ship cracked up over the swamps, but Jerry came walking into Hellas with two hundred ounces of gold under one arm and Ignatz under the other.

Naturally, the Venusians had warned him. They knew, and had known for generations, that it was good luck to have a zloaht around in the swamps, but horribly bad outside. The members of Ignatz's tribe were plain Jonahs, back to the beginning. Ignatz knew it, too, and tried to get away; but by the time they were well out of the swamps, he liked the Master too well to leave.

To any other man, Ignatz would have spelled personal bad luck, with general misfortune left over. But Jerry's personal luck held out; instead of getting trouble himself, others around him were swamped with it. The test ships cracked up, one after another, while Jerry got away without a scratch. Too many cracked up, and the O. M. gave Jerry another vacation, this time a permanent one.

His reputation waxed great, and doors closed silently but firmly before him. "Sorry, Mr. Lord, we're not taking on new men this year." They weren't to be blamed; hadn't something gone wrong by the time he left the office—not just something, but everything? Nowadays, an ambulance followed casually wherever he went walking with Ignatz, and some innocent bystander usually needed it.

Then Jerry met Anne Barclay, and the inevitable happened. Anne was the O.

M.'s daughter, and as cute a yard engine as ever strode down the training field of the Six World Spaceport. Jerry took one look at her, said "Ah," and developed a fever. He still had some of his money left, and he could dance, even if the orchestra always missed their cues when he was on the floor. By the time he'd known her three weeks she was willing to say yes; that is, she was until the O. M. put her wise. Then she remembered that she'd lost the ring her mother had given her, had tooth trouble, sinus trouble, and a boil on her left shoulder, all since she met Jerry. With the O. M. helping her imagination along, she did a little thinking about what married life might lead to; they decided that a little trip to Venus, with Pete Durnall, the Old Man's favorite, was just the answer, and that Jerry could cool his heels and rot.

Not that they were superstitious, any more than all star jumpers and their daughters were; Ignatz understood that. But when too many coincidences happen, it begins to look a bit shady. Now she was gone, or at least going, and Jerry was going out on his ear, from her life and from the hotel. Ignatz swore lustily in lizard language and crawled out of the pan. He rolled over in a towel, then began helping Jerry pack—a simple thing, since most of Jerry's wardrobe rested comfortably in old Ike's pawnshop.

"We'll go to the dock," Jerry decided. "I'm practically broke, fellow, so we'll sleep in a shed or an outbuilding if we can slip past the watch. Tomorrow, I'll look for work again."

He'd been looking for work for months, any work, but the only job he knew was handling the star-jumpers, or spaceships; and they had enough natural bad luck without adding Luckless Jerry to the crew. Ignatz wondered what the chances of finding open garbage pails around the dock were, but he followed meekly enough.

A raw steam pipe led around the shed with the loose lock at the rear. It happened to be super-hot steam, so Ignatz's sleep was heavy and dreamless, and daylight came and went unknown. The first thing he knew was when Jerry knocked him down and dipped him in a cold puddle to wake him up. At least, it smelled like Jerry, though the face and clothes were all wrong.

The Master grinned down at Ignatz as the water fizzed and boiled. Over night, apparently, he had grown a beard, and his straight hair was a mass of ringlets. Over one eye a scar ran down to his mouth, and pulled his lips up into a rough caricature of a smile; and the face was rough and brown, while his clothes might have been pulled off a refuse truck.

"Pretty slick, eh, Ignatz?" he asked. "Old Ike fixed me up for my watch and ring." He picked the zloaht up and chucked him into a traveling bag. "We can't let them see you now, so you'll have to stay under cover till we hit berth."

Ignatz hooted questioningly, and Jerry chuckled. "Sure, we've got a job—keeping the bearings oiled on a space-hopper. Remember that old tramp who was sleeping here last night? Well, he'd been a star-jumper till the weed hit him, and his papers were still clear. I got them for practically nothing, had Ike fix me up, and went calling today. Our luck's changed again. We're riding out tonight, bound for Venus!"

Ignatz grunted again. He might have known where they were bound for.

"Sure," Jerry was cocky again, banking on his luck. "Not another grunt from you, fellow. I can't take any chances on this trip."

The zloaht settled down on the clothes in the bag and chewed slowly on a piece of leather he'd found outside. Anything might happen now, but he had ideas of what that anything might be. The bag jerked and twisted as the Master slipped past the guards and out onto the rocket field where the hiss of rockets told Ignatz some ship was warming up, testing her exhaust. He stuck his eye to a crack in the bag and peered out.

It was an old freighter, but large and evidently well kept. They were moving the derricks back and battening down the hatches, so the cargo was all aboard. From the smell, he decided they were carrying raisins, peanuts and chocolate, all highly prized by the spore prospectors on Venus. Venus grew little that equaled old Earth foods, and only the most concentrated rations could be carried by those wandering adventurers.

As he watched, Ignatz saw a big tanker run out on the tracks and the hose tossed over to fill the tanks with hydrogen peroxide to be burned into fuming exhaust gases by the atomic converters; the isotope plates were already in, apparently. Mechanics were scurrying around, inspecting the long blast tubes, and the field was swarming with airscrew tugs ready to pull the big freighter up where her blast could shoot out harmlessly and her air fins get a grip on the air.

These big freighters were different from the sleek craft that carried the passengers; the triangles were always neatly balanced on their jets, but the freighter was helpless in the grip of a planet unless buoyed up by the tugs until she reached a speed where the stubby fins supported her.

Evidently the Master had made it barely in time, for the crew plank was being unhitched. He ran up to it, presented his papers, and was ordered to his berth. As he turned to leave, there was a halloo from below, and the plank was dropped again. Blane, the freighter's captain, leaned over, swearing.

"Supercargo! Why can't he take a liner? All right, we'll wait for him twenty minutes." He stumped up the stairs to the conning turret, and words drifted down sulfurously. "Every damned thing has gone wrong on this trip. I'm beginning to think there's a Jonah in the crew."

Jerry waited to hear no more, but moved to his berth—a little tin hole in the wall, with a hard bunk, a pan of water, and a rod for his clothes. He tested the oxygen helmet carefully, nodded his satisfaction, and stretched out on the bunk.

"You stay there, Ignatz," he ordered, "and keep quiet. There might be an inspection. I'll let you out when I go on second shift. Anyway, there isn't a steam pipe in the hole, so it wouldn't do you any good."

The port above was closing with a heavy bang. "Supercargo must have come up early. Wonder who he was? Must have been somebody important to hold Blane waiting for him—friend of the O. M.'s, I guess." He grinned comfortably, then wiped it off his face as a shout came down the stairwell.

"Hey, down there! Bring up some tools, and make it snappy. The crew port's stuck, and we're taking off in five minutes."

Jerry swore, and Ignatz turned over with a disgruntled snort. "Well," the Master reflected, "at least I won't get the blame for it this time. But it's funny, all the same. Darned funny!"

Ignatz agreed. This promised to be an interesting voyage, if they ever reached Venus at all. If the Master had to keep a zloaht for a pet, he might have stayed on the ground where their necks would have been safe, instead of running off on this crazy chase after a girl. For once he was glad that Venus knew no sex—unless the incubator cows were called females.

Jerry let Ignatz out when he came back from shift. He was tired and grouchy, but nothing had gone wrong in particular. There had been two minor accidents, and one of the tenders had his foot smashed by a loose coupling, but a certain amount of that had to be expected. At least no one had accused him of causing trouble.

"I found out who the supercargo is," he told the zloaht. "Nobody but the Old Man himself. So you lie low and I'll keep out of his way. The old buzzard has eyes like a hawk, and nobody ever called his memory bad."

The works of Robert Burns were unknown to Ignatz, but he did know the gist of the part that goes: "The best laid schemes o' mice and men gang aft agley." He waited results with foreboding, and they came when Jerry's next shift was half through.

It was the O. M. himself who opened the door and turned to a pair of brawny wipers. "All right, bring him in here, and lock the door. I don't know who he is, and I don't care. We can find that out later; but I do know he isn't the man his card says. That fellow has been rotten with weed for ten years."

"And Captain Blane," he addressed the officer as they tossed Jerry on the bunk, "in the future inspect your men more carefully. I can't make a tour of inspection on every freighter, you know. Maybe there's no harm in him, but I don't want men working for me on fake cards."

As they locked the door and went down the hall, the captain's voice was placating, the O. M. raving in soft words that fooled nobody by their mildness. Ignatz crawled out from under the bunk, climbed up the rail, and nuzzled Jerry soothingly.

Jerry spat with disgust. "Oh, he came down, pottered around the generator room and wanted to see my card; said he didn't know any oiler with a scar. Then Hades broke loose, and he yelled for Blane. Anyway, he didn't recognize me. Thank the Lord Harry, you had enough sense to duck, or my goose would have been cooked."

Ignatz rooted around and rubbbed the horn on his snout lightly against the Master's chest. Jerry grinned sourly.

"Sure, I know. We haven't sunk yet, and we're not going to. Go on away, fellow, and let me think. There must be some way of getting off this thing after we reach Venus."

Ignatz changed the "after" to "if" in his mind, but he crawled back dutifully and tried to sleep; it was useless. In half an hour, Captain Blane rattled on the door and stalked in, his face pointing to cold and stormy. There was an unpleasant suggestion in the way he studied Jerry.

"Young fellow," he barked, "if the Old Man didn't have plans for you, I'd rip you in three pieces and strew you all over this cabin. Call that damned zloaht of yours out and take off those whiskers, Jerry Lord."

The Master grunted, as a man does after a blow to the stomach. "What makes you think I'm Lord?"

"Think? There's only one Jonah that big in the star fleet. Since you came aboard, every blamed thing's been one big mess. The O. M. comes on board as supercargo, the port sticks, three men get hurt fitting a new injector, I find Martian sand worms in the chocolate, and the O. M. threatens to yank my stars. Don't tell me you're anyone else!" He poked under the bunk. "Come out of there, you blasted zloaht!"

Ignatz came, with a rueful honk at Jerry, who pulled his false beard anxiously. "Well, captain, what if I am? Does the O. M. know?"

"Of course not, and he better hadn't. If he found I'd shipped you with the crew, I'd never draw berth again. When we hit Venus, I'll try to let you out in a 'chute at the mile limit. Or would you rather stay and let the Old Man figure out ways and means?"

Jerry shook his head. "Let me out on your 'chute," he agreed hastily. "I don't care how, as long as I get free to Venus."

Blane nodded. "I'll catch hell anyway, but I'd rather not have you around when we land. I never did trust my luck when a ship breaks up." He pointed at Ignatz. "Keep that under cover. If the O. M. finds out who you are, I'll put you off in a lead suit, *without* a 'chute, Savvy, mister?"

Jerry savvied plenty. He motioned Ignatz back under the bunk and moved over to the shelf where his grub lay. Blane turned to go. And then raw Hades broke loose.

There was a sick jarring, and a demon's siren seemed to go off in their ears. The shelf jumped across the room; Jerry hit the captain with his head. For half a second, there was complete silence, followed by bedlam, while the ship jerked drazily under their feet. Acting on instinct, both the captain and Master dashed for the oxygen helmet, and a private war started before either realized what had happened.

Jerry straightened up first. "That was the control engine," he yelled in Blane's ear. The man couldn't hear, but he caught the idea. "Get out of here and find out what happened."

There was no thought of prisoners. Jerry pounded along at the captain's heels, and Ignatz had only time to make a convulsive leap and slide down Jerry's neck under his jacket. Men were swarming down the stairwell and up from the main rocket rooms. A babble of voices blended with a shrilling of alarms and a thud of feet on cuproberyl decks.

The Old Man was in the engine room before them. "Blane! Blane—Hey, somebody find that lunkhead before these fools wreck the whole ship!"

Blane saluted roughly, his mouth open, his eyes darting about the wreck of the steering engine. "Hu-whu-what happened?"

One quick glance had told Jerry. "Which one of you oilers let the main bearings run dry?"

A wiper pointed silently to a shapeless lump of bones and assorted cold cuts. While eyes turned that way, Ignatz slipped out and pushed from sight between a post and wall that were still partly whole.

Jerry Lord's mouth was set as he swung to Blane. "Got a spare engine? No. Well, dismantle one of your gyro-stablizer engines and hook it up. Send men to inspect what damage was done the controls. Get the doctor up here to look over these men who are still in one piece. Wake up, man!"

Blane shut his mouth slowly, wheeled back to the men and began shouting instructions, until some order came out of the milling mass of men. In the confusion, the O. M. hadn't noticed Jerry, but he swung to him now.

"Who let you out? Never mind; you're here. It's a good thing somebody has some sense, or that yellow-belly'd still be dreaming! Captain Blane, get that wreck out of here, put this prisoner to work. We can't waste time or men now.

I'm going back to the control co-ordinators to inspect the damage."

Now that the shock of his first major accident was over, Blane snapped briskly into it. He glared at Jerry, but postponed it for later; Ignatz knew this was to be held against the Master, as all the other troubles were, and he mumbled uncomfortably.

With the engine in scattered parts, little dismantling was necessary. The men were cleaning the parts away, cutting such few bolts as were left in the base, and preparing the space for the new engine. The stabilizer motor came in, one part at a time, and Jerry oversaw its placement and assembly, set its governor, and hooked the controls to it as rapidly as the crew could cut away the bent rods and weld new ones in their place. In an emergency, no group of men on Earth can do the work that a space-crew can turn out in a scant half-hour, and these were all seasoned star-jumpers; to them the lack of gravity was as help rather than a hindrance in the swift completion of the work.

By the time the O. M. was back, the walls were being welded over, the new engine was timed, the controls hitched, and the captain was sweating and swearing, but satisfied that the work had been well done. Jerry came back from the stabilizer hold to report the motors retimed and set for the added load given by the loss of one of the five engines, with the juice feeding in evenly.

The Old Man motioned silently, his face blank and expressionless, and Blane gulped as he turned to follow. Jerry strung along without invitation, tucking Ignatz carefully out of sight under his clothes.

Back in the nerve center of the ship the control integrators were a hopeless mess. The main thrust rods that coupled the control turret to the engine were still intact, but the cables and complex units of gears and eveners that formed the nearly human brain of the ship were ruined beyond possibility of repair.

The O. M.'s voice was almost purring, but his eyelids twitched. "Have you repairs, captain?"

"Some. We might be able to jury-rig part of it, but not enough to couple the major rockets to the control panel. That looks to me like a one-way ticket to hell." Under the stress of danger, the man had relapsed into a numb hopelessness.

"How many hours to Venus, and where's the danger point?"

"Sixty hours, and we either get control in ten, or we fall straight into the sun. We're in orbit C-3 now, and we'll miss Venus entirely."

"Not a chance to get repairs sent out in time," the O. M. muttered. "Well, I guess that's that."

Jerry pushed past the captain, saluted the O. M. quietly. "Beg pardon, sir, but it might be possibly to control the ship manually from here, with observations relayed from the control turret."

Momentarily their eyes brightened, but only for a split second. "Not one man in a thousand knows the layout of the cables here, and the job would be physically impossible. I don't know whether this rod should be forced back or that one forward. When the old manual controls were still in, we had them arranged logically in banks, but this is uncharted confusion."

"I know the layout," Jerry offered evenly. "It's simply a question of being able to move around fast enough to coordinate the thrust rods." Yet he looked at the mass of rods, levers, and cables with doubt large in his heart. It meant covering an eight-foot wall, and keeping the tangle of eveners clear in his mind every second of the time, though it might be done.

There was a snort from Blane, but the O. M. silenced it. "We have to believe in miracles now. It's our only chance. Are you sure you can do it, mister?"

"Fairly sure, sir."

"How many helpers?"

Jerry grinned sourly. "None; it's easier and surer doing it than telling others how to do it, and maybe having them mess things up. Has to be a one-man job."

"Right." There was grudging approval on the scowling face. "Blane, you take orders from him; get the wrecked parts out, uncouple the remaining automatics. You and the navigators will take turns relaying the chart data to this room—and it'd better be right. Get a phone hooked up at once, and put this man to work. If we get to Venus, he's free, no questions asked, and a good job waiting for him. If we don't, he won't need the job."

When the O. M. was gone, the captain shook his fist under Jerry's nose. "Jonah! If you hadn't been along, this wouldn't have happened. You'd better be good, Mr. Lord." He stopped suddenly, a new thought hitting him. "Do you realize that means sixty hours of steady, solid work down here?"

"Naturally, since your navigators never learned more than they had to." Jerry shrugged with an entirely false optimism. "And you'll remember that hereafter every man on this ship will take orders from me, sir? I must insist on absolute cooperation."

"You'll get it, Jonah or not." Blane stuck out a hand. "I don't like your reputation, Lord, but I do like your guts. Good luck!"

In making an impressive exit, the captain forgot the oil on the floor; he executed a jerky half twist before his back hit the deck. Ignatz backed further out of sight and prepared for the worst.

"Jonah!" said Blane, and it covered everything with no wasted syllables.

With the wreck carted out, the communications man came in, hooked up a phone and coupled it by a spring reel of wire to sponge-covered earphones. He handed over a chart of present position and estimated orbit, then cleared out.

Jerry cut in on the phone. "All clear?"

"Waiting for orders, sir. Stern rocket seven has a point-oh-six underblast you'll have to counteract, and the stabilizers only work three-five. Venus now in position—" The navigator rattled off his co-ordinates, and Jerry set them up in his head as he reached for the main blast rods.

"Okay. Leave orders I'm not to be bothered by anyone but the mess boy." He pulled Ignatz out, patted his back, and grinned. "The room's yours, fellow—Stand to blast!"

"Clear to blast, sir. All-ll positions set! Trim-mm and stow all-ll!" The time-honored call rang down the stairwell as Jerry threw the manuals and braced himself for gravity-on.

The freighter shook like a cat coming out of a bathtub, groaned and bucked sullenly, as the controls were thrown one at a time; reluctantly she settled down to business. For a bottom-blaster, she was a sweet old bus, put out with the craftsmanship of men who longed for the stars and took out that longing in building ships to carry others. Even with the overworked stabilizers and slight underblast she answered her helm better than some of the new triangles. Jerry bit into her levers savagely at first, then gently as she became part of him, hard to reach, yet sweet and honest.

The navigator was shouting down co-ordinates, drift ratios, and unnecessary pep talk, and the O. M.'s voice came through occasionally, sounding almost pleasant. The crusty old scallawag had what it took, Jerry conceded; no hysteria or nonsense about him. Under such an example, the captain and first navigator took heart, and the second navigator was jaunty with hope when he came on. Faith was dirt cheap in the conning turret at the moment; Jerry could have used more of it himself, but was careful not to show it in his voice.

The first ten hours were no worse than steady attention and driving work could make them, and he began to get the feel of the ship. His mind timed in on the creaking of her girders, the sway of her deck, and the strange harmony that couples flesh to well-built metal. The pattern of the controls etched itself indelibly into his brain, short cuts came, and ways of throwing his combinations in less time and with less effort, until he became a machine integral with the parts he handled.

When food was brought down, he grinned confidently at the mess boy and snatched it in mouthfuls as the coordinates were sent down and the movement felt sent him dancing across the room. Watching him, the boy grinned back, and snapped his fingers gleefully. Hop to Venus with ruined controls? A cinch!

Ignatz waited doubtfully, but nothing more seemed likely to happen. He honked hopefully—and an answering bark came out of the vent tubes. The exhaust blower went on noisily, but the current of cool air stopped.

Jerry cut in on the phone. "What happened?"

"Dust explosion in the filter chamber, sir. I'm afraid it'll take some time to fix it."

It did. While the hours passed, heat leaked in from the engine and refused to go out. Normal perspiration gave way to rivulets of sweat that tried to get in the Master's eyes and made his hands wet and slippery.

Ice and water, brought down at hourly intervals, helped, but did not alleviate the temperature. Men were working on the air ducts, but it promised to be a long job. Ignatz had secretly crawled up the maze of vent pipes to find the obstruction, nearly got lost, and came down without success.

When the twenty-hour period was up, Jerry was rocking on his heels, cursing the heat with every labored breath. He wore ice packs on every safe place, and still couldn't keep cool. The blowers were working again, keeping a steady current of air moving, but it was hot. Under the Master's shoes were heavy pads of rubberoid, and he wore stiff space mittens on his hands, but still the heat came through from the hot floor and control rods. A few more degrees would spell the limit.

Then the temperature reached a mark and held it. The heat seeping in and the air going out balanced, and Jerry settled down to a regular routine of ice packs and heat; even the air he breathed was filtered through an ice mask.

The phone buzzed and the O. M.'s voice came over. "One of the refrigerators overheated and burned a bearing. You'll have to cut down to half rations of ice."

"Okay." The Master stared thoughtfully at Ignatz, then caught him up and draped him over his shoulders. "Not enough ice, fellow. You like heat, but you'll have to cool me off. Come on, pal, show your stuff."

Ignatz did his best. He had the finest heat-regulating system on nine planets, and he put it to work, soaking up the heat from Jerry's sweaty body, dissipating it out into the air. Jerry never understood how it was done, but he knew Ignatz could absorb heat or radiate it off at high efficiency; now the zloaht was absorbing on his flexible belly-plate and radiating from his back.

Jerry sighed with relief. "Ah, fine, fellow. You've got the ice packs beat three ways from Sunday." His eyes pulled shut and he relaxed against the control bars. Ignatz prodded him with the sharp end of his tail, waking him to his duties. "Regular two-man crew we've got, fellow," the Master muttered. "You'll make me win this thing through yet, maybe." His beard was peeling off in the humid heat, and he pulled it away, along with the scar. The brown pigment had gone hours before.

But now things were letting up a little. The freighter had settled into the groove of her orbit, was balanced nicely, and required little more attention until they reached Venus. Jerry had an insulated chair rigged up and dropped into it when the pressure of the work would let him, while Ignatz listened for the opening buzz of the phone or watched gravely for a flash from the extension feed indicators. Fifteen minutes here, twenty there, once even a whole hour; Jerry's over-worked system grabbed greedily at each minute, sucking up relief and rest like a dry sponge. If only the drugging, tiring heat would lift.

And then, miraculously, a shot of cold air whooshed out of the vent ports, and Jerry jerked up from his stupor. "They've got it, Ignatz; it's fixed!" He shivered gratefully under the draft, drew back from it while his body begged for coolness, afraid of too sudden a drop in temperature. "Now you can forget the heat, fellow; just wake me when I need it."

The air was dropping down smoothly, a degree every five minutes, and life seemed to flow back into the Master. Ignatz muttered softly and relaxed. The two-way heat control had been a heavy nervous strain on him, requiring hard mental discipline; he was thankful to fall back to normal.

The three-quarters mark came and went, with only fifteen hours ahead—and the hardest part of the job was still to do. Under his breath, Jerry was talking to himself, ordering his muscles as he might a crew of men, trying to forget the dull ache that found every muscle of his body, the hot acid pain in his head, the feeling of an expanding balloon against his brain. Another five hours, and they'd be teetering down through the heavy gravity zone, where every tube would have to be balanced until the tugs came to take over.

Old Man Barclay came down in place of the mess boy, a serious, worried O. M., but with a smile on his lips—until he saw Ignatz and Jerry's normal face. Then something hard shot into his eyes. He whistled.

"I had a hunch," he said softly. But his voice was even, his face relaxed. "You always were a fool, Jerry, even if you happen to be the best man that ever rode a star-hopper. This, and our cursed luck, should have told me. What is it—Anne?"

Jerry nodded, patted Ignatz back into place as the zloaht moved to avoid the O. M.'s look. "Anne," he agreed. He thrust back into the machinery as the navigator sent down fresh data, backed out, and faced the other quietly. "Well?"

"Of course." The old face never moved a muscle. "What I can't understand is how your luck can reach out ten million miles and hit another ship, though. Never mind, I'll tell you later—maybe."

Jerry dropped limply back into his chair, and the other moved over with a drink. Noting the trembling hands that lifted the glass, the Old Man's face softened. "Too much work for one man, son. I used to be pretty much up on the layout here. Maybe I can spell you."

"Maybe. It's routine stuff now, Mr. Barclay. All you need are the feed controls and gyro-eveners banked together there." The Master pointed them out, one by one, while the O. M. nodded. "I'll have to take over in four, five hours though. Sure you can do it till then?"

"That much, yes." The O.M. tossed a blanket over the younger man and then moved over by the projecting feed bars. "Ever strike you as funny I came on this trip?"

"Didn't have time to think," said the Master. Barclay squatted down on a beam, his eyes on the controls.

"I don't do things without a purpose, Lord. Venus needs radium—needs it bad. They offer double price for three million dollars' worth, Earth price, when delivered at Hellas. But they want it quick, so it has to be sent in one load. You can't get insurance on that for one a one-shipment cargo: too much risk. And no private company will ship it without insurance."

"So?"

"So I bought the radium on the market, had it stowed secretly with the chocolate—mutiny never happened, but it might—and came along to watch it. That represents my entire personal fortune. If it reaches Venus, I double my money; otherwise, I won't be there to worry about it."

He stopped, then went on in the same even voice. "That's why I could cheerfully kill you for putting a jinx on this voyage. But I won't. I have reasons for reaching Venus in a hurry. Put this ship down in one piece on the surface of Venus, and one-third of the profit is yours—one million dollars, cold cash, in any bank you want it."

Ignatz honked softly—for him—and Jerry blinked. He swung off at a tangent. "You spoke of my luck hitting another ship across ten million miles; and now you've got reasons for reaching Hellas quickly. Anne?"

The O. M. repeated Jerry's earlier answer. "Anne. Saw it from the conning turret. The *Burgundy* broke a steering tube bank, had to make a forced landing. We got the start of an SOS, but it faded off—must have ruined the radio as they hit."

"Where?"

"Latitude 78° 43' 28" south, longitude 24° 18' 27" west. SOS started with something about twin mountains. Know where it is?"

"Minerva's Breasts, in the middle of Despondency. I camped near the north breast. Worst spot on Venus that isn't too hot for life."

"Exactly. We radioed Hellas, but in that jungle it may take weeks to find them. So there's a million in it for you—*and* my place in New Hampshire where your darned luck won't bother anyone but yourself—but not Anne, definitely not!"

But Jerry was dead to the world, and Ignatz, curled up in his lap, was deciding to sleep while he could, now that everything was settled.

They were only eight hours from Hellas when Ignatz stirred and looked up. The Old Man was a frenzy of action, a scowl of concentration etched across his forehead, but he was still doggedly at the controls. Again the zloaht prodded his Master awake, and Jerry sat up, some of the bleariness gone from his eyes. He reached out for a caffeine and strychnine capsule, to help him stay awake, and tapped Barclay's shoulder.

"You should have dug me up hours ago, sir. I'll take over now; fresh as a daisy." That was a lie and the other knew it. "You've done a beautiful job, but I know the controls better."

The O.M. mustered a smile and looked up casually enough—even patted Ignatz—but he relinquished the job gratefully. "I couldn't have held on much longer," he agreed. "These controls are beyond me. Have to extend the navigator's knowledge in the future."

Jerry looked his thanks. "I didn't expect the relief, you know. But don't think what you said about Anne means anything to me!"

"So you did hear that? Look, son, I don't hold anything against you, personally—always liked you. But unless you give up that animal and get rid of your hoodoo—"

Jerry's backbone stiffened visibly. "Ignatz stays."

"I thought so. In that case, I don't want you around. Nothing personal, you understand, but I'm not taking chances."

"Nothing personal, of course, sir." The door closed softly as the O. M. slipped out, and Jerry chuckled. For a second there was a sparkle in his eyes before the ache in his body cut it off. "Imagine the old boy taking over that way. Some father-in-law, eh, fellow?"

They hadn't landed yet, Ignatz thought, and Anne might have something to say. There was heavy doubt in his grunt, which Jerry interpreted correctly. But the Master was busy with his own thoughts.

Now that the fingers of Venus' gravity were reaching out harder for them, the lack of full efficiency from the stabilizers made itself felt. The long, cigar-like shape put the center of gravity above the rockets and the old ship suggested that it would be so much nicer to turn over and let gravity do its work; the suggestion was mild at first, but the freighter grew more positive with each mile, shimmying sidewise toward the planet like a girl edging toward her first crush.

"Easy, old girl," Jerry pleaded. "We've got to swing you in line with Venus' rotation and let you ride down with her." He babied the ship along, coaxed her into the new path, and performed mathematical magic in his head as the plot of the new orbit came down with corrections. The navigators were taking half-hour turns now, with the captain overseeing their work. Fast talk and absolute accuracy would have to be continuous until the tugs took over.

But she came down smoothly, arcing in toward the south pole, held up by sheer nerve and stimulants. A thousand miles up, relative speed was nine miles a second, fall-rate three. Five hundred up, frontal speed checked to coasting, fall-rate down to normal landing curve. And then they hit the mythical cushion height, where the air was thick enough to support her on her fins, and the stabilizers purred pleasantly again. From there on they would coast into Hellas and let the tugs snag her.

"Your damned luck!" The O. M. cut in crisply. "Just got a radio that tugs are on strike at Hellas. You'll have to coast to Perdition on North Venus instead of Hellas. Can you hold her up?"

"I'll ride her. Navigator, I want co-ordinates for latitude 78° 43' 28" south, longitude 24° 18' 27" west."

"But Perdition—" The navigator was cut short by a burst of language from Barclay.

Jerry barked wearily. "Shut up! We're not going to Perdition—nor Hellas! Navigator, you heard my orders. Give me data, and see that it's right. Get scared and blunder, and you'll never know what happened."

"But the tugs are in Perdition."

"To hell with the tugs! I'll set her down on her tail!" Gulps came over the phone, and Ignatz could hear the teeth of the navigator chattering. The O. M. was yelling about insanity, but he checked his raging and there was a muttered consultation too low to hear. Then Barclay's voice cleared.

"You're all in the hands of a lunatic, but your only chance is to give him his data. We'd be dead by the time we could dig him out. Take orders from Lord!" He spoke directly into the phone. "Jerry, I'll break you like a dry stick if I live. Not one tail landing out of three works with whole controls. Listen to reason, man! We can't help her if we're dead."

The junior navigator seized the phone, his nerves steady with desperation, his voice crisp and raw. Slowly the ship settled down, driving forward through the heavy air. Finally the navigator reported destination, and Jerry tipped the ship up cautiously. She protested at such unorthodox treatment, but reluctantly answered her controls.

"Eighteen thousand feet, directly over your destination. Weather quiet, no wind—thank God, sir! Fourteen thousand. You'll have to slow up!"

Ignatz prayed fervently to his forest and swamp gods, but they seemed far away. And the ground was rushing up while the ship swayed first to one side, then the other. Jerry was dancing a war jig in front of the balance jet bars; his eyes were glassy, his hands shook on the controls, but he fought her down, foot by foot, while the sickening speed slackened.

"Four hundred feet, level ground. Now the blast strikes, we can't see. Instrument at 300—200! Slower!"

She slowed grudgingly, but listed sidewise sharply; Jerry cut power for free fall, and she righted. Power boomed out again.

"Forty feet—God help us!"

That loss of power, short as it was, had been too much. She was all out now, but falling too fast. No, she was checking it. But another sway came. Ignatz groaned, saw that Jerry had deliberately swung her sidewise to land horizontal—at forty feet! There wasn't power enough in the laterals to hold her up. The speed picked up as she wabbled on her axis, slowed, and she righted. Jerry cut controls, grabbed a girder, and slumped. Ignatz went flaccid.

It sounded like a heavy scrunch, with attendant yells. She bounced slightly before settling. And then there was silence, and they were down. Jerry picked himself up, felt Ignatz carefully. "You're tough, fellow, not even scratched. If I hadn't been limp with exhaustion, that ten-foot free fall probably would have messed me up a little; but the others should be all right. This section took most of the shock."

Half a minute later there were groans and shouts over the ship. The Master scooped Ignatz up. "Come on, fellow, we've got to go down and stock up on provisions."

The after hold was crowded with miscellaneous items for the comfort and safety of the spore-hunters, and he located a ready-packed kit of provisions, ample for three months' trek if the bearer could carry the load. He adjusted it carefully, felt to make sure of the feverin bottle, and took down three pairs of mud hooks, like skis crossed with canoes; the light beryllium frames would support a man's weight on slimy mud or water and let him shuffle forward through the ooze of the swamps without sinking.

"Durnall's fool enough to go off in the mud," the Master told Ignatz. "That guy never did have good sense, so I've got to take three sets." He swung out to the emergency port, opened the inner seal, and pulled it shut. The outer one gave slowly, and opened—on the flat, sandy expanse of the Hellas landing field!

The old freighter had berthed neatly in the center of the rocket dock, and crowds, who'd heard or seen the landing, were streaming out. Mechanics were working on the crew port, which seemed to be giving trouble again.

Heavy hands reached up suddenly and dragged Jerry out onto the ground. "This way, fellow." Three dock flunkies held him securely, grinning as they felt him over for a concealed weapon. Then the leader motioned the others to lead him toward a waiting spinner.

"Smart guy, eh?" He looked at Jerry appraisingly. "You gotta be up early to catch old Barclay. We got a radio you'd be coming out of the emergency, so we waited for you. Got a nice little reception hall fixed up for you."

Jerry stopped swearing long enough to ask the obvious. "Where to?" They grinned again, the three of them holding him firmly as they seated him in the spinner. At the motion of the leader, the pilot cut the motor in, and they rose and headed toward the outskirts of Hellas—but in the opposite direction from the jail.

"You'll be nice and comfortable, you and your pet," the headman volunteered. "The Old Man's putting you in one of the private suites belonging to Herndon, our branch manager. Says you're to have a nice long rest, where nobody'll bother you—or t'other way around."

No use questioning these dock flunkies, who probably knew less about it all than he did. Jerry slumped back silently, and Ignatz curled up to wait for the spinner to meet with an accident; but even misfortune refused to smile on them. They landed smoothly on the roof of one of the company's apartment buildings, and the men dragged the Master down through the roof entrance, across a hall, and into a well-fitted apartment.

"Make yourself to home," the big husky invited generously. "Herndon probably won't come here, so it's all yours. You'll find the walls and doors made of steel, the windows transplon, and locks that stay locked." He pulled the visiphone plug out and picked up the instrument. "Anything you'd like?"

The Master shrugged, estimating his chances. But they were all strong, young, and alert. He gave up any foolish ideas. "You might send up a diamond mine, or a dozen chorus girls."

"That's Herndon's specialty—chorines. See him about it." The flunkies grinned and began backing out. "The Old Man says he'll be down tomorrow, probably." The door closed and the key in the lock made a positive and unpleasant click.

Jerry turned in disgust toward the bedroom. "Sometimes, Ignatz," he muttered, "I begin to think—" He cut it as he saw the zloaht's expression. "Never mind, fellow. I'll turn the heat on low in the oven, and you can sleep there tonight. We both need shut-eye."

Sunlight was streaking through the translucent transplon windows when Ignatz awoke. His investigation showed that the Master was still sleeping, and he had no desire to awaken him. Muttering in disgust at the world in general, he turned to the library in search of information on the peculiar disease with which humans seemed afflicted.

The dictionary defined love, and the encyclopedia gave an excellent medical and psychological version of it; but none of the sober, rational phrases gave any key to the idiocies Ignatz associated with that emotion. Other books bore gaudy titles that hinted at possibilities. He selected three at random, waded through pages here and there, honking and snorting loudly. They only served to confirm his preconceptions on the subject, without making things any clearer. Compared with the men in the books, Jerry was a rational being.

Still, books had their uses. Ignatz sniffed them over thoughtfully and found the usual strong glue had been used in binding them. Since the dictionary and encyclopedia were useful, he put them back with some difficulty. Then he tipped down half a dozen other books whose titles indicated they were on the same subject and began ripping the covers off methodically. A most excellent glue, well-flavored and potent; of course, the paper insisted on coming off with it, but that could always be spit out. What was left, he pushed into the incinerator closet.

With his stomach filled and the sleep out of his system, there was nothing left to do but explore. Sometimes these human habitations proved most interesting. He sampled a jar of vaseline, examined the workings of an electric mixer with some interest, and decided to satisfy his curiosity on another matter which had bothered him for months.

Jerry Lord awoke with Ignatz's doleful bellow in his ears, mixed with sundry threshings and bumpings, and the jangling of an uncertain bell. He rubbed the sleep out of his eyes with hands that were sure and steady again, and looked down, to grin suddenly. "I told you to let those spring alarm clocks alone, fellow. Suppose they do go *tick-tick* instead of purring like the electrics—do you have to see why?"

Ignatz had found out why—with details. Jerry untangled the zloaht's tail from the main spring and various brass wheels, and unwrapped the alarm spring from his inky body. Once that was done, they both prowled around until satisfied that escape from the apartment was completely impossible.

Jerry tried the stereovisor while eating breakfast, but there was no news; only the usual morning serials and music came over. He dug out a book on rocket motors to kill time, while Ignatz succeeded in turning on the hot water in the bathroom and crawling into the tub. If the O. M. ran true to form, he'd show up when it suited his own convenience.

It was noon when Barclay unlocked the door and came in, leaving a couple of guards outside. "Crazy young fool!"

Jerry grinned ruefully. "A nice trick, your fake data; I actually thought I was landing at Minerva's Breasts. Well, I didn't ruin your darned freighter."

"Didn't even wreck the radio. Sweetest tail landing I ever saw, and I made a couple myself." He chuckled as the Master stared. "Sure, I used to pilot them, back when it took men. But I never tried a horizontal, though I've heard of it."

He fished out an envelope. "Here, I keep my word. Deposit book, Prospector's Commercial, one million dollars. And the deed to the house in New Hampshire, if you ever get back there—which you won't on any of my ships. You can save your thanks."

Jerry took it calmly. "I didn't intend to thank you; I earned it." He stuffed the envelope in the prospector's kit he'd brought with him. "What word from Anne? And when do I get out of here?"

"I've made arrangements to have you leave today." Seeing Jerry's look, he shook his head. "Not to jail, exactly—just to the new detention house they've erected since you were here last; they use it for drunks and weed-chewers. I've booked you as a stowaway to be held for convenient deportation, and I'll make the charge stick. Judging from last night, I don't want you in any of my employees' quarters; they get hit by sudden bad luck."

"Well?"

"Herndon got married and left me in the lurch last night—when I most need him."

"That looks like your bad luck, not his," Jerry pointed out. "Though I suppose you fired him."

"He quit—to lead the glamorous life." The O. M. smiled wryly. "His bad luck was that he married that woman who dances at the casino with a Martian sand-eel."

Jerry nodded; he'd seen her act, and there was no answer. Instead, he steered the conversation back to Anne. "You know I could locate the *Burgundy* in a couple of hours if you'd let me out of here. I didn't spend two months in Despondency for nothing. And Ignatz is supposed to bring good luck out there."

Barclay shrugged. "Good luck for you; that's what I'm afraid of. It so happens we've located the *Burgundy* already, without your help. Now we've been sending out searching parties on mud hooks for Anne and Pete; the captain had to take orders from her and let them go." His face was momentarily bitter. "I thought Durnall had better sense than to go lugging her around the swamps where even the compass is cockeyed."

"I was afraid of that. You made a mistake, sir, in making me land at Hellas instead of the Breasts."

Barclay grunted, and let it pass. They all knew there was about as much chance of one man finding her in the steaming swamp jungle as the proverbial needle. "If I thought you could find her, I'd probably be fool enough to let you go. Better pack up your luggage. These men will take you over to detention house."

***

The detention ward was comfortable enough, and Barclay had arranged for all the Master's ordinary wants. But it was no nearer Anne. He paced the room endlessly until Slim, the flunky, brought his supper. Bribery had failed before, but he tried it again.

The guard grinned. "Here's your supper, such as it is. We found the food's mostly turned sour since you moved in this noon. And your check's no good; Prospector's Commercial closed its doors until a new shipment of gold can come through from Earth."

Ignatz grunted, but the Master refused to give up. "But the check will be good when it opens."

Slim hunched his shoulders. "Not with your money in it; it won't open."

"You don't believe that superstition, do you?" Jerry's voice was not particularly convincing.

"Huh? Look, mister, since you come here, I got word my wife just had triplets—and me a poor man! I don't want nothing to do with you or yourn." He shoved the food in and swung on his heel.

Jerry swore, then called after the jailer. "Hey, wait! Can you get a message to Manager Barclay? Tell him I know how he can find his daughter. Tell him I want to see him tomorrow morning!"

Slim nodded glumly and went on. Jerry turned to his meal, refusing to answer Ignatz's inquiring grunts. The zloaht watched his Master finish and begin the endless pacing again, smoking incessantly on the pungent Venusian cigarettes. He picked up a butt and honked curiously.

"Nerves, fellow," Jerry answered. "They're supposed to calm you when something bothers you—like my pipe that I left back on Earth. Want to try one?" He placed one between Ignatz's sharp lips, and lit it. "Now, you puff in, take the smoke into your lungs, then blow it out. Sure, like that."

Ignatz coughed the smoke out and bellowed hoarsely, swearing heatedly at the Master. An odd sensation stirred in him somewhere, however, and he regarded the cigarette thoughtfully; sometimes a thing was better after a time or two. Dubiously, he picked it up with his antennae and tried again, with slightly better success. It didn't taste so nauseous that time. And the third try was still better.

"Better go easy on it, fellow," Jerry advised. "I don't know how it'll affect your metabolism; alcohol had no results with you, but this might."

Ignatz heard vaguely, but didn't trouble his head about it. There was a nice warm feeling stealing along his nerves and down toward his tail. He'd been a fool to think life was hard—it was ducky—that's what. And this room was beautiful, when it stood still. Just now, it was running around in circles; he pursued the walls in their crazy rotation, but gave up—they were too fast for him.

Jerry giggled for no reason Ignatz could see. "Ignatz, you're acting drunk. And that butt's going to burn you if you don't spit it out."

"*Hwoonk!*" said Ignatz. Still, it was a little warm; laboriously he removed the burning thing and tossed it away. "*Hwulp!*" Now why did his tail insist on jerking him up like that? "*Hwupp!*" If it insisted, he'd be the last one to stop it. He gazed up at the moon that had mysteriously sailed away from Earth and was gliding across the ceiling of the room. Such a lovely night. Must make a song about the lovely night. Lovely song.

His fog-horn voice creaked out in a quavering bellow, rose to a crescendo wail, and popped out with a sound like a starting rocket. Lovely song—lovely! Jerry stuffed him in a pillow and tried to silence him, but without immediate success. If the men in detention wanted to sleep, what of it? Anyway, they were making too much noise themselves.

Who wanted to sleep? Too nice a night to sleep. He executed a remarkable imitation of a steam buzz saw. Jerry gave up and crawled in beside him, growling unhappily. Ignatz honked reproachfully at the Master, rolled over and snored loudly.

The next morning he awoke to see the guard let the O. M. in, and tried to climb down from the bunk. Something lanced through his head, and he fell back with a mournful bellow. He hadn't felt like that last night.

Jerry grinned at him. "Hangover—what'd you expect?" He turned back to Barclay. "The flunky delivered my message, then?"

"He did." The O. M. hadn't been doing much sleeping, from the look on his face. "If your plan involves letting you out, don't bother telling me."

"It doesn't. I've found from experience there's no use trying to change your mind." He jerked back the package of cigarettes as Ignatz dived for it. "But the semi-annual mud run is due any day now, and Despondency is hell then. You've got to get her out."

The O. M. nodded; he'd been thinking the same. Jerry went on. "All right. A man can't locate anything smaller than a rocketship up there. But a zloaht can. Well, thirty miles north of Minerva's Breasts—the compass points south by southeast, in that neighborhood—there's a village, of Ignatz's people built out in a little lake. They've dammed up Forlorn River there, and built their houses on rafts, working with their antennae and practically no raw materials. They grow food, along the shores, and they've got a mill of sorts to grind it with. Of course, they're not human, but they'll be up alongside us yet, if we don't kill them off first. Highly civilized now."

The O. M. snorted, glanced at Ignatz hunting for butts. "Civilized! Sounds more like beavers to me."

"Okay, have it your way." Jerry was used to man's eternal sense of divine descent—or maybe the word was ascent. "Anyway, they've developed an alphabet of sorts and have tame animals. What's more important, I taught them some English, and they'll do almost anything for chocolate and peanuts."

Barclay caught the idea. "You mean, I'm to send up there, get in touch with them, and have them look for Anne? Sounds pretty far-fetched, but I'm willing to try anything once."

Jerry began sketching a crude map. "They can't talk to you, but when one of them comes for the chocolates, you'll know he's found her—they're honest about bargains. Then all you have to do is follow."

The O. M. took the note and started toward the door. "I'll let you know how it works," he promised. "If they find her, I'll even risk shipping you back to Earth." Jerry grunted and turned back to Ignatz, who was rumbling unhappily on the cot, his foot-and-a-quarter body a bundle of raw nerves.

It was three slow, dull days later when Slim brought another note in. "Mr. Barclay sent this down to you," he said briefly. Slim had as little to do with the Master as possible.

Jerry opened it eagerly, to find the wording terse and to the point:

> *Three spinners, trying to make your lake, broke down. Rescue crews out for them now. I'll have nothing more to do with any of your fool plans.*

He passed it to Ignatz, who read it glumly, then watched hopefully as Jerry shook out a cigarette. Seeing the pack returned to its place, beyond his reach, he snorted his disgust and retired to the corner in sulky silence.

The silence was broken by a reverberating boom that rocked the detention house like a straw in the wind. The floor twisted crazily and the transplon window fell out with a brittle snap. Then the noise quieted and Jerry picked himself up from the floor, grabbed Ignatz and the prospector pack. He wasted no words, but dived toward the open window.

Slim came racing down the corridor. "Air conditioner motor exploded right below," he yelled. "You all right, Lord?" As he saw the two climbing out the window, he grabbed for his needle gun, then rammed it back. "I ain't taking chances with this thing; it'd explode in my hands with you around. The farther you two get, the happier I'll be!"

Sometimes a bad reputation had its uses. Jerry dropped ten feet to the ground, spotted a spinner standing empty and unlocked to the rear of the building, and set out for it. He dived through the door, yanked it shut, and cut in the motor as the guards began streaming out. Ignatz looked at the fuel gauge and was surprised to see it full.

Before the gun on the roof could be lined up, the spinner was rising smoothly and speeding away. Jerry swung in a half circle and headed north, with the rheostat clear over, and the little ship cut through the air with a whistling rush. Hellas dropped behind, five miles, ten, then fifteen. Ten miles ahead lay the muck of Hellonfire, beyond that Despondency.

"Only let me reach the swamps, fellow," Jerry begged. "Don't get us in any funny business now." Ignatz had his antennae curled up in a tight knot, trying by mental concentration to oblige.

Two miles short of the swamps, the engine began to stutter, starting and stopping erratically. Jerry fussed with the controls, but the ship slowed, moving along at an uncertain speed. The first line of the Hellonfire verdure rose through the thin mists as the motor stopped. Jerry's teeth were clenched as he tried to hold the spinner in a flat curve that would carry them clear. But the ground came up steadily as the ship crawled toward the swamp.

By a hair-thick margin they cleared the tangled swamp growth, and were over Hellonfire. And the little motor caught, purred softly, and drove the vanes steadily against the air, lifting them up easily. Ignatz relaxed and Jerry reached over to pat him softly. Now, according to the legend, luck should be good.

It was. They glided along across Hellonfire smoothly, passed over the wreck of the first spinner sent out by the O. M., and headed on. The compass began to waver and twist without good reason, and Jerry was forced to rely on Ignatz's sense of direction. The zloaht held his antennae out as a pointer toward his home village, and the Master followed his direction confidently.

Hellonfire drifted by under them, and gave place to the heavy tangle of Despondency. Looking down, they could see the slow crawl of the mud-run that made the swamp even more impassable twice a year, and Jerry shook his head. If Anne were out in that, unless she stayed on a high hummock, there was little hope of finding her. They swept between the Breasts and saw the temporary camp, established as a base for searchers, being dismantled; the men would leave before the mud crept higher.

And then Ignatz hooted, and Jerry looked down to see the little lake glistening below them. Floating rafts covered it, neatly laid out in rows, and thatched over with fine craftsmanship. Zloahts like Ignatz were busily engaged in the huts and canals between them. On the shores of the lake, others were driving their tame *zihis*, twenty times as large as they were, about in the fields. Now and again, a fog-horn yelp across the lake was answered from the largest raft.

Jerry let down the pontoons and dropped the spinner lightly on the lake. Ignatz ducked out and across the water to the chief's building, dragging a waterproof package of chocolate with him. He was back inside of ten minutes, hooting shrilly, a small bundle in his mouth.

The Master took it. On the coarse papyrus he made out a roughly executed picture of a man and woman, pulled on a narrow raft by two of the zihis. Under it, there were two black squares with one white sandwiched between them, and inside the drawing was a bar of chocolate of a different brand from that which Jerry had sent them.

The Master snapped the rheostat over. "So she left a day and two nights ago, with Durnall. Traded her chocolate for zihis and raft. Know what direction she went?"

Ignatz hooted and pointed south and east, along a sluggish stream that fed into Forlorn River. Jerry turned the spinner and headed that way, searching for signs of them. Zihi travel should average twenty or more miles a day, which would place them some seventy miles out. He slowed up after fifty, noting that the stream was narrowing. If it ended before he reached Anne, it meant hours of scouting, probably hopelessly, in search of her. There were a hundred different courses she could take once she left the Little Hades.

But he sighted her before the stream ended in its twisted little feeders. She had stopped, probably picking her course and he could see her look up at the sound of his motor and begin signaling frantically. He set the spinner down sharply jerking it to a short stop within a few feet of the raft and opened the door as she headed the zihis toward him. Durnall was lying on the raft, covered by a poncho.

"Jerry Lord!" Her voice was shrill, tired, her eyes red and sleepless. "Thank heaven! Pete's got the fever—red fever—and we had no feverin in our packs." She grabbed the bottle he handed her, poured three tablets down Durnall's throat. "Help me load him in and the duffel—and take us to the hospital, pronto!"

Jerry grabbed Durnall and loaded him in the back as quickly as he could. Ignatz was giving orders to the zihis to return to the village with the raft, while Anne gathered the duffel, and climbed in back. She sank beside the sick man, whose face had the dull brick-red of an advanced case of swamp fever.

"Your father's been worried sick—so have I."

"Have you?" Her voice was flat. "Jerry, how soon can we reach the hospital?"

He shrugged. "Three hours, I guess." Ignatz glanced up at the Master's face and grunted as softly as he could. Of course, Anne had been gone for days, alone with Durnell, and sick men had a way of working on a woman's sympathies. He brushed his antennae lightly against the Master's ankles.

"How'd you find the village?" Jerry asked. "I've been trying to get a chance to help you, but I was afraid you'd be lost in the mud-run."

She looked up, but went on fussing over Durnall. "When we couldn't find the *Burgundy*, I remembered your story about getting lost yourself, and how you found the village. We headed the way you said the compass pointed, and holed up there, till I found they understood me. Then I bartered some supplies for their raft and animals. With what you'd told me helping us, we'd have made out all right if Pete hadn't come down with the fever; I was lucky, myself, and didn't catch it."

Durnall was groaning and tossing uneasily, and she turned her attention back to him. Jerry bent over his controls, and drove silently south toward Hellas, watching Despondency change to Hellonfire. Then they were out of the swamps, and he turned back to assure Anne they were almost there.

But his head jerked back sharply. The rotor, which had been circling sweetly overhead, now twanged harshly and dragged back on the motor. Ignatz ducked back to avoid the Master's look and groaned. One of the rotor vanes had cracked off, and the others were unbalanced and moving sluggishly. The ship was coming down much too fast. Jerry cut the motor off, tried to flatten the fall, and failed. He yanked the shock-cushion lever out, and a rubber mattress zipped out behind him, designed to save the passengers from a nose collision in the fog. Before he could reach the pilot's cushion lever, the ship's nose hit the ground and buckled in.

Ignatz saw the Master slump forward over the controls, and then something tore sharply at the zloaht's snout horn, and little lights streaked out. Blackness shot over him hotly.

He swam up through a gray haze, tried to snort, and failed. When he opened his eyes, he saw yards of gauze covering his snout, and Jerry was propped up in bed watching him.

"Major operation, fellow. The doc says he had to cut out half your horn because of something that splintered it. You had me beat by half a day, and the doc says I was out for forty-eight hours." He wiggled in the bed. "I'm still solid enough, though, except for a couple of bones, and a bump on the head."

Ignatz looked around slowly, conscious from his sluggish reactions that they must have given him drugs. He was in a small room, and his bed was a miniature replica of Jerry's. But it wasn't a hospital.

Jerry grinned. "They were afraid you'd be a jinx in the city, and I kept yelling for you, so they put us both up here in a house the O. M. owns just inside Hellonfire. I've been waiting for them to bring you to before we entertained visitors." He raised his voice. "Hey, nurse, tell them all clear here."

With his words, the door burst open and the Old Man hurried in. "Well, it's about time. Look fit as ever."

"Yeah, fit to go back to your lousy detention house."

The O. M. was pleased with himself. "Not this time. I figured out something else. Got the deed to the New Hampshire house still? Good. Well, I'm taking it back, and putting this deed to the swamp house in its place. That pet of yours should be harmless here. And I'm advising you to invest your money in our stock."

"So you won't ship me back to Earth, eh? Afraid I'd get your ship smashed?"

Barclay shook his head. "I'm not worried about the ship. What I'm worried about is a branch manager, and you're it—if you want the job."

Jerry took it calmly. "What's the catch?"

"None. Bad luck or not, you get things done, and you know rockets. That's what I need, you impudent young puppy. Just keep your pet out here and things should go swimmingly." He got up brusquely. "You've got another visitor."

"Don't forget what I said about—" Jerry started to shout, and then she was framed in the door.

"Hi, Jerry. You both four-oh again?"

Ignatz grunted, while Jerry stared. "Durnall?"

"He's doing all right." Anne took a seat beside him, held out her hands. "Now that he's safe, let's forget him. Pete isn't a bad guy, but I don't like darn fools who get me into messes like the last one, even when it's half my fault."

Jerry digested it slowly, and Ignatz cursed his bandages. Now was the time for him to slip back into the swamps, where Jerry could never make the mistake of taking him out again. He could see where the Master was going to need decent breaks with all the responsibility coming up. But the bandages held him securely.

Anne hauled the little bed closer, ran warm fingers over Ignatz's back. "You'll have to live out here and commute by spinner, of course, but I'll take care of Ignatz while you're gone. He owes us a lot of good fortune, and we're going to collect it."

"I— " Jerry glanced at Ignatz. "You know how your father feels about him."

She smiled impishly. "Dad figured it all out. You see, I brought back something with me in my duffel, and when he found I meant to keep it, he gave up." She reached into a little bag and hauled out the snooty head of another zloaht. "Meet Ichabod."

Jerry gulped, "Well, I'll be—" And suddenly he had a great deal of urgent business.

Ignatz longed for a cigarette, but he snorted softly and turned away.

Operation Distress

Bill Adams was halfway back from Mars when he noticed the red rash on his hands. He'd been reaching for one of the few remaining tissues to cover a sneeze, while scratching vigorously at the base of his neck. Then he saw the red spot, and his hand halted, while all desire to sneeze gasped out of him.

He sat there, five feet seven inches of lean muscle and bronzed skin, sweating and staring, while the blond hair on the back of his neck seemed to stand on end. Finally he dropped his hand and pulled himself carefully erect. The cabin in the spaceship was big enough to permit turning around, but not much more, and with the ship cruising without power, there was almost no gravity to keep him from overshooting his goal.

He found the polished plate that served as a mirror and studied himself. His eyes were puffy, his nose was red, and there were other red splotches and marks on his face.

Whatever it was, he had it bad!

Pictures went through his head, all unpleasant. He'd been only a kid when the men came back from the South Pacific in the last war; but an uncle had spent years dying of some weird disease that the doctors couldn't identify. That had been from something caught on Earth. What would happen when the disease was from another planet?

It was ridiculous. Mars had no animal life, and even the thin lichenlike plants were sparse and tiny. A man couldn't catch a disease from a plant. Even horses didn't communicate their ills to men. Then Bill remembered gangrene and cancer, which could attack any life, apparently.

He went back to the tiny Geiger-Muller counter, but there was no sign of radiation from the big atomic motor that powered the ship. He stripped his clothes off, spotting more of the red marks breaking out, but finding no sign of parasites. He hadn't really believed it, anyhow. That wouldn't account for the sneezing and sniffles, or the puffed eyes and burning inside his nose and throat.

Dust, maybe? Mars had been dusty, a waste of reddish sand and desert silt that made the Sahara seem like paradise, and it had settled on his spacesuit, to come in through the airlocks with him. But if it contained some irritant, it should have been worse on Mars than now. He could remember nothing annoying, and he'd turned on the tiny, compact little static dust traps, in any case, before leaving, to clear the air.

He went back to one of the traps now, and ripped the cover off it.

The little motor purred briskly. The plastic rods turned against fur brushes, while a wiper cleared off any dust they picked up. There was no dust he could see; the traps had done their work.

Some plant irritant, like poison ivy? No, he'd always worn his suit—Mars had an atmosphere, but it wasn't anything a man could breathe long. The suit was put on and off with automatic machine grapples, so he couldn't have touched it.

The rash seemed to get worse on his body as he looked at it.

This time, he tore one of the tissues in quarters as he sneezed. The little supply was almost gone; there was never space enough for much beyond essentials in a spaceship, even with the new atomic drive. As he looked for spots, the burning in his nose seemed to increase.

He dropped back to the pilot seat, cursing. Two months of being cramped up in this cubicle, sweating out the trip to Mars without knowing how the new engine would last; three weeks on Mars, mapping frantically to cover all the territory he could, and planting little flags a hundred miles apart; now a week on the trip back at high acceleration most of the way—and this! He'd expected adventure of some kind. Mars, though, had proved as interesting as a sandpile, and even the "canals" had proved to be only mineral striations, invisible from the ground.

He looked for something to do, but found nothing. He'd developed his films the day before, after carefully cleaning the static traps and making sure the air was dust-free. He'd written up the accounts. And he'd been coasting along on the hope of getting home to a bath, a beer, and a few bull sessions, before he began to capitalize on being the first man to reach another planet beyond the Moon.

He cut on full acceleration again, more certain of his motors than of himself. He'd begun to notice the itching yesterday; today he was breaking out in the rash. How long would whatever was coming take? Good God, he might die—from something as humiliating and undramatic as this!

It hadn't hit him before, fully. There was no knowing about diseases from other planets. Men had developed immunity to the germs found on Earth; but just as smallpox had proved so fatal to the Indians and syphilis to Europe when they first hit, there was no telling how wildly this might progress. It might go away in a day, or it might kill him just as quickly.

He was figuring his new orbit on a tiny calculator. In two days at this acceleration, he could reach radar-distance of Earth; in four, he could land. The tubes might burn out in continuous firing. But the other way, he'd be two weeks making a landing, and most diseases he could remember seemed faster than that.

Bill wiped the sweat off his forehead, scratched at other places that were itching, and stared down at the small disk of Earth. There were doctors there—

and, brother, he'd need them fast!

Things were a little worse when the first squeals came from the radar two days later. He'd run out of tissues, and his nose was a continual drip, while breathing seemed almost impossible. He was running some fever, too, though he had no way of knowing how much.

He cut his receiver in, punched out the code on his key. The receiver pipped again at him, bits of message getting through, but unclearly. There was no response to his signals. He checked his chronometer and flipped over the micropages of his Ephemeris; the big radar at Washington was still out of line with him, and the signals had to cut through too much air to come clearly. It should be good in another hour.

But right now, an hour seemed longer than a normal year. He checked the dust tray again, tried figuring out other orbits, managed to locate the Moon, and scratched. Fifteen minutes. There was no room for pacing up and down. He pushed the back down from the pilot seat, lowered the table, and pulled out his bunk; he remade it, making sure all the corners were perfect. Then he folded it back and lifted the table and seat. That took less than five minutes.

His hands were shaking worse when the automatic radar signals began to come through more clearly. It wasn't an hour, but he could wait no longer. He opened the key and began to send. It would take fifteen seconds for the signal to reach Earth, and another quarter minute for an answer, even if an operator was on duty.

Half a minute later, he found one was. "Earth to Mars Rocket I. Thank God, you're ahead of schedule. If your tubes hold out, crowd them. Two other nations have ships out now. The U.N. has ruled that whoever comes back first with mapping surveys can claim the territory mapped. We're rushing the construction, but we need the ship for the second run if we're to claim our fair territory. Aw, hell—congratulations!"

He'd started hammering at his key before they finished, giving the facts on the tubes, which were standing up beyond all expectations. "And get a doctor ready—a bunch of them," he finished. "I seem to have picked up something like a disease."

There was a long delay before an answer came this time—more than five minutes. The hand on the key was obviously different, slower and not as steady. "What symptoms, Adams? Give all details!"

He began, giving all the information he had, from the first itching through the rash and the fever. Again, longer this time, the main station hesitated.

"Anything I can do about it now?" Bill asked, finally. "And how about having those doctors ready?"

"We're checking with Medical," the signals answered. "We're… Here's their report. Not enough data—could be anything. Dozens of diseases like that. Nothing you can do, except try salt water gargle and spray; you've got stuff for that. Wash off rash with soap and hot water, followed by some of your hypo. We'll get a medical kit up to the Moon for you."

He let that sink in, then clicked back: "The Moon?"

"You think you can land here with whatever you've got, man? There's no way of knowing how contagious it is. And keep an hourly check with us. If you pass out, we'll try to get someone out in a Moon rocket to pick you up. But we can't risk danger of infecting the whole planet. You're quarantined on the Moon—we'll send up landing instructions later—not even for Luna Base, but where there will be no chance of contamination for others. You didn't really expect to come back here, did you, Adams?"

He should have thought of it. He knew that. And he knew that the words from Earth weren't as callous as they sounded. Down there, men would be sweating with him, going crazy trying to do something. But they were right. Earth had to be protected first; Bill Adams was only one out of two and a half billions, even if he had reached a planet before any other man.

Yeah, it was fine to be a hero. But heroes shouldn't menace the rest of the world.

Logically, he knew they were right. That helped him get his emotions under control. "Where do you want me to put down?"

"Tycho. It isn't hard to spot for radar-controlled delivery of supplies to you, but it's a good seven hundred miles from Lunar Base. And look—we'll try to get a doctor to you. But keep us informed if anything slips. We need those maps, if we can find a way to sterilize 'em."

"Okay," he acknowledged. "And tell the cartographers there are no craters, no intelligence, and only plants about half an inch high. Mars stinks."

They'd already been busy, he saw, as he teetered down on his jets for a landing on Tycho. Holding control was the hardest job he'd ever done. A series of itchings cropped out just as the work got tricky, when he could no longer see the surface, and had to go by feel. But somehow he made it. Then he relaxed and began an orgy of scratching.

And he'd thought there was something romantic about being a hero!

The supplies that had already been sent up by the superfast unmanned missiles would give him something to do, at least. He moved back the two feet needed to reach his developing tanks and went through the process of spraying and gargling. It was soothing enough while it went on, but it offered only momentary help.

Then his stomach began showing distress signs. He fought against it, tightening up. It did no good. His hasty breakfast of just black coffee wanted to come up—and did, giving him barely time to make the little booth. He washed his mouth out and grabbed for the radar key, banging out a report on this. The doctors must have been standing by down at the big station, because there was only a slight delay before the answering signal came: "Any blood?"

Another knot added itself to his intestines. "I don't know—don't think so, but I didn't look."

"Look, next time. We're trying to get this related to some of the familiar diseases. It must have some relation—there are only so many ways a man can be sick. We've got a doctor coming over, Adams. None on the Moon, but we're shipping him through. He'll set down in about nine hours. And there's some stuff to take on the supply missiles. May not help, but we're trying a mixture of the antibiotics. Also some ACS and anodynes for the itching and rash. Hope they work. Let us know any reaction."

Bill cut off. He'd have to try. They were as much in the dark about this as he was, but they had a better background for guessing and trial and error. And if the bugs in him happened to like tachiomycetin, he wouldn't be too much worse off. Damn it, had there been blood?

He forced his mind off it, climbed into his clothes and then into the spacesuit that hung from the grapples. It moved automatically into position, the two halves sliding shut and sealing from outside. The big gloves on his hands were too clumsy for such operations.

Then he went bounding across the Moon. Halfway to the supplies he felt the itching come back, and he slithered and wriggled around, trying to scratch his skin against his clothing. It didn't help much. He was sweating harder, and his eyes were watering. He manipulated the little visor-cleaning gadget, trying to poke his face forward to brush the frustration tears from his eyes. He couldn't quite reach it.

There were three supply missiles, each holding about two hundred pounds, Earth weight. He tied them together and slung them over his back, heading toward his ship. Here they weighed only a hundred pounds, and with his own weight and the suit added, the whole load came to little more than his normal weight on Earth.

He tried shifting the supplies around on his back, getting them to press against the spots of torment as he walked. It simply unbalanced him, without really relieving the itching. Fortunately, though, his eyes were clearing a little. He gritted his teeth and fought back through the powdery pumice surface, kicking up clouds of dust that settled slowly but completely—though the gravity was low, there was no air to hold them up.

Nothing had ever looked better than the airlock of the ship. He let the grapples hook the suit off him as soon as the outer seal was shut and went into a whirling dervish act. Aches and pains could be stood—but *itching*!

Apparently, though, the spray and gargle had helped a little, since his nose felt somewhat clearer and his eyes were definitely better. He repeated them, and then found the medical supplies, with a long list of instructions.

They were really shooting the pharmacy at him. He injected himself, swallowed things, rubbed himself down with others. and waited. Whatever they'd given him didn't offer any immediate help. He began to feel worse. But on contacting Earth by radar, he was assured that that might be expected.

"We've got another missile coming, with metal foil for the maps and photos—plus a small copying camera. You can print them right on the metal, seal that in a can, and leave it for the rocket that's bringing the doctor. The pilot will blast over it—that should sterilize it—and pick it up when it cools."

Bill swore, but he was in his suit when the missile landed, heading out across the pumice-covered wastes toward it. The salves had helped the itching a little, but not much. And his nose had grown worse again.

He jockeyed the big supply can out of the torpedo-shaped missile, packed it on his back, and headed for his ship. The itching was acting up as he sweated—this made a real load, about like packing a hundred bulky pounds over his normal Earth weight through the soft drift of the pumice. But his nose was clearing again; it was apparently becoming cyclic. He'd have to relay that information back to the medics. And where were they getting a doctor crazy enough to take a chance with him?

He climbed out of the suit and went through the ritual of scratching, noticing that his fever had gone up, and that his muscles were shaking. His head seemed light, as if he were in for a spell of dizziness. They'd be interested in that, back on Earth, though it wouldn't do much good. He couldn't work up a clinical attitude about himself. All he wanted was a chance to get over this disease before it killed him. He dragged out the photo and copying equipment, under a red light. It filled what little space was left in his cubbyhole cabin. Then he swore, gulping down more of the pills where they were waiting for him. The metal sheets were fine. They were excellent. The only thing wrong was that they wouldn't fit his developing trays—and they were tough enough to give him no way of cutting them to size.

He stuffed them back in their container and shoved it into the airlock. Then his stomach kicked up again. He couldn't see any blood in the result, but he couldn't be sure—the color of the pills might hide traces. He flushed it down, his head turning in circles, and went to the radar. This time he didn't even wait for a reply; let them worry about their damned maps. They could send cutting equipment with the doctor and pick up the things later. They could pick up his corpse and cremate it at the same time, for all he cared right now.

He yanked out his bunk and slumped into it, curling up as much as the itching would permit. And finally, for the first time in over fifty hours, he managed to doze off, though his sleep was full of nightmares.

It was the sound of the bull-throated chemical rocket that brought him out of it—the sound traveling along the surface through the rocks and up through the metal ship, even without air to carry it.

He could feel the rumble of its takeoff later, but he waited long after that for the doctor. There was no knock on the port. Finally he pulled himself up from the bunk, sweating and shaken, and looked out.

The doctor was there—or at least a man in a spacesuit was. But somebody had been in a hurry for volunteers, and given the man no basic training at all. The figure would pull itself erect, make a few strides that were all bounce and no progress, and then slide down into the pumice. Moon-walking was tricky until you learned how.

Bill sighed, scratching unconsciously, and made his way somehow out to his suit, climbing into it. He paused for a final good scratch, and then the grapples took over. This time, he stumbled also as he made his way across the powdery rubble. But the other man was making no real progress at all.

Bill reached him, and touched helmets long enough to issue simple instructions through metal sound conduction. Then he managed to guide the other's steps; there had been accounts of the days of learning spent by the first men on the Moon, but it wasn't that bad with an instructor to help. The doctor picked up as they went along. Bill's legs were buckling under him by then, and the itches were past endurance. At the end, the doctor was helping him. But somehow they made the ship, and were getting out of the suits—Bill first, then the doctor, using the grapples under Bill's guidance.

The doctor was young, and obviously scared, but fighting his fear. He'd been picked for his smallness to lighten the load on the chemical rocket, and his little face was intent. But he managed a weak grin.

"Thanks, Adams. I'm Doctor Ames—Ted to you. Get onto that cot. You're about out on your feet."

The test he made didn't take long, but his head was shaking at the conclusion.

"Your symptoms make no sense," he summarized. "I've got a feeling some are due to one thing, some to another. Maybe we'll have to wait until I come down with it and compare notes."

His grin was wry, but Bill was vaguely glad that he wasn't trying any bedside manner. There wasn't much use in thanking the man for volunteering—Ames had known what he was up against, and he might be scared, but his courage was above thanks.

"What about the maps?" Bill asked. "They tell you?"

"They've left cutters outside. I started to bring them. Then the pumice got me—I couldn't stand upright in it. They'll pick up the maps later, but they're important. The competing ships will claim our territory if we don't file first."

He knocked the dust off his instrument, and wiped his hands. Bill looked down at the bed to see a fine film of Moon silt there. They'd been bringing in too much on the suits—it was too fine, and the traps weren't getting it fast enough.

He got up shakily, moving toward the dust trap that had been running steadily. But now it was out of order, obviously, with the fur brushes worn down until they could generate almost no static against the rod. He groped into the supplies, hoping there would be replacements.

Ames caught his arm. "Cut it out, Adams. You're in no shape for this. Hey, how long since you've eaten?"

Bill thought it over, his head thick. "I had coffee before I landed."

Doctor Ames nodded quickly. "Vomiting, dizziness, tremors, excess sweating—what did you expect, man? You put yourself under this strain, not knowing what comes next, having to land with an empty stomach, skipping meals and loading your stomach with pills—and probably no sleep! Those symptoms are perfectly normal."

He was at the tiny galley equipment, fixing quick food as he spoke. But his face was still sober. He was probably thinking of the same thing that worried Bill—an empty stomach didn't make the itching rash, the runny nose and eyes, and the general misery that had begun the whole thing.

He sorted through the stock of replacement parts, a few fieldsistors, suit wadding, spare gloves, cellophane-wrapped gadgets. Then he had it. Ames was over, urging him toward the cot, but he shook him off.

"Got to get the dust out of here—dust'll make the itching worse. Moon dust is sharp, Doc. Just install new brushes...Where are those instructions? Yeah, insert the cat's fur brushes under the...*Cat's* fur? Is *that* what they use, Doc?"

"Sure. It's cheap and generates static electricity. Do you expect sable?"

Bill took the can of soup and sipped it without tasting or thinking, his hand going toward a fresh place that itched. His nose began running, but he disregarded it. He still felt lousy, but strength was flowing through him, and life was almost good again.

He tossed the bunk back into its slot, lifted the pilot's stool, and motioned Ames forward. "You operate a key—hell, I am getting slow. You can contact Luna Base by phone, have them relay. There. Now tell 'em I'm blasting off pronto for Earth, and I'll be down in four hours with their plans."

"You're crazy." The words were flat, but there was desperation on the little doctor's face.

He glanced about hastily, taking the microphone woodenly, "Adams, they'll have an atomic bomb up to blast you out before you're near Earth. They've got to protect themselves. You can't…"

Bill scratched, but there was the beginning of a grin on his face. "Nope, I'm not delirious now, though I damn near cracked up. You figured out half the symptoms. Take a look at those brushes—cat's fur brushes—and figure what they'll do to a man who was breathing the air and who is allergic to cats! All I ever had was some jerk in Planning who didn't check my medical record with trip logistics! I never had these symptoms until I unzipped the traps and turned 'em on. It got better whenever I was in the suit, breathing canned air. We should have known a man can't catch a disease from plants."

The doctor looked at him, and at the fur pieces he'd thrown into a wastebin, and the whiteness ran from his face. He was seeing his own salvation, and the chuckle began weakly, gathering strength as he turned to the microphone.

"Cat asthma—simple allergy. Who'd figure you'd get that in deep space? But you're right, Bill. It figures."

Bill Adams nodded as he reached for the controls, and the tubes began firing, ready to take them back to Earth. Then he caught himself and swung to the doctor.

"Doc," he said quickly, "just be sure and tell them this isn't to get out. If they'll keep still about it, so will I."

He'd make a hell of a hero on Earth if people heard of it, and he could use a little of a hero's reward.

No catcalls, thanks.

Fool's Errand

In spite of the wind from the Mediterranean, six miles to the south, the university city of Montpellier reeked with the stench of people huddled together in careless filth; and the twilight softness could only partially conceal the dirt and lack of sanitation in the narrow, twisting streets. No one in this leading medical center of the sixteenth century had heard of germs, and no one cared.

But Roger Sidney, Professor of Paraphysics at a university that would not be built for another six centuries, both knew and cared. He shuddered, and his tall, thin figure wove carefully around some of the worst puddles, while his eyes were turned upward fearfully toward the windows above; one experience with a shower of slop from them had been more than enough. He pressed a kerchief to his nose, but his weary feet went on resolutely. Somewhere in this city was a man called Nostradamus, and Sidney had not dared seven centuries to give up the search because of even this degree of dirt and stench and inconvenience.

Nostradamus, the prophet, author of the cryptic *Centuries!* More important, though, was the original clear manuscript of prophecy from which the *Centuries* were distorted; sheer accident had led to the discovery of that in 1989, where Nostradamus had hidden it from too curious eyes, and it had long since proven accurate. If authentic, it was the only known conclusive proof of prophecy beyond the life-span of the prophet, and that was now important. The parapsychologists denied that authenticity, since their mathematics showed such prophecy to be impossible, and had even devised an elaborate theory of a joke by some far-future time-traveler to account for its accuracy. With equally sound proof of unlimited prophecy, the paraphysicists could not accept such a useless jest, though they had known for years that time travel was theoretically possible.

Now, if Nostradamus would accept the manuscript as being his, the controversy would be ended, and the paraphysicists could extend their mathematics with sureness that led on toward glorious, breathtaking possibilities. Somewhere, perhaps within a few feet, was the man who could settle the question conclusively, and somehow Sidney must find him—and soon!

But the little sign appeared at last, a faded blue rooster crowing over the legend: *Le Coq Bleu*. He turned down the steps into the tavern and felt momentary relief from the unpleasant world outside; mercifully, the straw on the floor had just been changed, and there was the smell of spitted fowls to remind him of his forgotten appetite. He let his eyes wander along the benches and tables, but they were filled, and he hesitated.

In a booth at the side, a slight young man had been eyeing his soiled finery carefully, and now he motioned with a careless hand. "Ho, stranger, I've room in this booth for another. And my stomach has room for a pot more of wine, if you'd ask it." The French was still strange to Sidney's ears, even after the years of preparations, but the somewhat impudent grin was common to all centuries of students.

He dropped onto the hard bench, feeling his legs shake with weariness from the long chase as he did so. The pressing urge for haste before his time ran out was still in him, but he tried to conceal it as he approached the single subject on his mind. By sheer willpower he mustered an answering smile and tossed a coin on the table. "And perhaps food to go with it, eh? You're a student at the university?"

"Your questions are as correct as the color of your money, stranger, and that is correct indeed." The youth was up with the coin in his fingers, to return in a few moments with two thick platters bearing roasted pullets and with a smiling, bowing landlord carrying a jug of red wine. Sidney grinned ruefully as his fingers made clutching motions at the table where there were no forks, then ripped off a leg and used his fingers as the other was doing. The wine was raw and a bit sour, though there was strength to it, and some relief.

But there was no time to be wasted, and he returned to the pressing questions uppermost in his mind. "As a student, then, perhaps you know one Michel de Notredame? After I located his lodgings, they told me he might be here…and I've come all the way from Paris to find him. If you can point him out or take me to him, I'll pay you well for your trouble."

"From Paris, eh?" Suspicion crept slowly into the eyes of the other. "Four hundred miles—a week to ten days of hard journey—to see an obscure student? Stranger, your speech is odd, your clothes are strange, but that is fantastic! His relatives are poor and he is poorer. If this is some strange manner of pressing for his debts, you but waste your time; I'll have none of it. If you have other reasons, name them, and I'll think on it."

"Then you do know him?"

"By sight, but you'll not find him here, so save your glances. Well?"

Sidney pulled his eyes back, and his fingers shook with the eagerness that had carried him through the torture of that frantic chase from Paris after he'd learned of his mistake. But he fought again for reason and coolness and for some approach that would quiet the suspicion of the student. The truth was unbelievable, but he could think of nothing else that would ring true, and he was not adept at lies.

"I care nothing for his past his debts, his sins, or his crimes. All I'm concerned with is his future, which will make your obscure friend the greatest man of this age. But it's a strange story, and you'd think me raving mad."

The other shrugged. "I've studied philosophy and medicine, and there's little left I can't believe. Your story interests me. Spin it well, and perhaps I'll take you to him, unless he should come here first—which I think most unlikely this evening. As to madness, I'm a bit mad myself... Landlord, more wine!"

The student was far more interested in the wine than the story, and Sidney felt his upsurge of hope fading again. He'd found already how faint were his chances of tracking down any particular person in the maze of this city. And in another hour perhaps, or even at any minute, he might feel the surge and pull of the great machine in his home century, to go spinning back with his mission unfulfilled. Already his time was overdue! He narrowed his thoughts down, trying to find some quicker proof that might suffice if he could have the other. "Tell me—honestly in the name of God—how well do you know Michel de Notredame?"

"We share lodgings. Well enough."

"Then if my time grows too short and he does not come, perhaps you'll do. Here." He flipped his purse out on the table, filled with coins that had been matchlessly counterfeited by minters of the twenty-third century, and with others genuine to the time, received in change. "Take it—all—it's yours. Only believe me. Michel de Notredame, under the name of Nostradamus, will be the greatest of all prophets in the years to come. His name will be greater even than that of her Majesty, Catherine de Medici. Can you believe that a man from the future might find a need to see him—and even find a way of coming back to do so? I did! I left the year of Grace 2211, intending to reach Paris in 1550. By error, it was 1528, and he was not there, but I knew he had been studying here, so here I am. Can you believe that, young man—for the contents of this purse?"

The other's hands had come up slowly to cross himself, then dropped, while his eyes turned from fear to distrust, and then to speculation. "For the money—why not? I've heard that warlocks could bring the long dead from the past by magic and the use of certain Names of Power; perchance a greater one might journey back himself. Black magic? And yet, your face has none of Satan's knowledge in it. How?"

"I can't tell you. There are no words yet. Call it science—or white magic. Not black." Sidney's fingers shook again in reaction from the disbelief he had expected; but he should have known that skepticism is a product of a science advanced enough to doubt, but not to accept what lies beyond its knowledge. He shook his head, remembering the long years of preparation and the work that had gone into his being here. He could never explain that, or the need behind it, when paraphysics and parapsychology would be meaningless words.

He could never tell of the immense, inconceivable power needed to bridge time from one of its loops to another, or of the struggle he and his colleagues had waged for three decades to be granted the use of such power. Now, it had surged out, carrying him in the tiny network of wires woven into these garments into the past; sometime soon, the return surge must flow back to return him. They had figured a week, and already ten desperate days were gone while he fled south on the fool's errand that must be made. Their calculations had erred as to the length of the time loop by twenty-two years, and he could not guess how that would affect the length of the power surge, but the return flow must surely have begun.

He caught himself up and went urgently on. "Notredame won fame in the court of Catherine for prophecy while living; when he died, he left verses called *Centuries*, with tantalizing hints which some believed; and when his original manuscript was found, he won an undisputed place in all history. Now, we must know without the doubts that exist whether that manuscript was his; we *must*. Even a little evidence might decide, but... Do you know his writing?"

"I've seen it often enough. Stranger, your story begins to interest me, whatever truth lies in it. But as to prophecy, anyone will tell you it's no uncommon thing; the greatest astrologers in the world are in France." The student filled his mug again and leaned back, shaking his head to clear it of wine fumes. "If this Nostradamus was an astrologer and you need astrologers, why not find others?"

Sidney shrugged it aside. "No matter, they would not help. He claimed to be an astrologer, of course, but...But could you swear to his writing if you saw it? Here!" He thrust his hand into his clothes and brought out a parchment manuscript, to spread it quickly on the table. "This is an exact copy, down to the very texture of the parchment and smudges of ink upon it. Don't mind the contents; they no longer concern us, since we've passed the final date of specific forecasts. Only study the writing. It's a young man's script, and all else we have of his is from his later years. But you know his younger hand. Swear to me honestly, *is it his?*"

The youth bent his head over it, tracing with his finger, and running his other hand across reddened eyes. Sidney cursed the wine and the slowness of the man, but at last the other looked up, and something in the frantic desperation of Sidney's face seemed to settle his doubts, for his own turned suddenly serious.

"I don't know, stranger; it looks like it—and yet I never wrote such words, nor ever planned to."

"You...*you*—Notredame!"

"I am Michel de Notredame, a drunken fool to admit the fact even now, when you might be here on any—"

But Roger Sidney from 2211 was laughing, a wracking that shook him in convulsions, harshly soundless. One trembling finger pointed to the manuscript, then to the student, and the convulsive shaking redoubled. "A cycle—a closed cycle! And we—and that—that—" But he could not finish. Notredame swung his eyes about to see if others were noticing, but the tavern was emptied and the landlord was busy at the far end. He turned back, and suddenly crossed himself.

There was a glow about the stranger, a network of shining threads in his garments that might have been frozen lightning. It spread, misted, and was gone, while the bench where he had been was suddenly empty. Notredame was alone, and with slowly whitening face, he began to cross himself again, only to stop and snatch the purse and coins from the table where they lay and tuck them into his clothes. For a second, he hesitated, his now-sober eyes narrowing thoughtfully.

"Nostradamus," he muttered. "Nostradamus, astrologer to the court of the Queen. I like the sound of that."

His fingers picked up the manuscript, and he slipped swiftly out into the night.

The Stars Look Down

I

Erin Morse came down the steps slowly without looking back, and his long fingers brushed through the gray hair that had been brown when he first entered the building. Four years is a long time to wait when a man has work to do and the stars look down every night, reminding him of his dreams. There were new lines in his face and little wrinkles had etched themselves around his dark eyes. But even four years had been too few to change his erect carriage or press down his wide shoulders. At sixty, he could still move with the lithe grace of a boy. The heavy gate opened as he neared it and he stepped out with a slow, even pace. He passed the big three-wheeled car parked there, then stopped and breathed deeply, letting his eyes roam over the green woods and plowed fields and take in the blue sweep of the horizon. Only the old can draw full sweetness from freedom, though the young may cry loudest for it. The first heady taste of it over, he turned his back on the prison and headed down the road.

There was a bugling from the car behind him, but he was barely conscious of it; it was only when it drove up beside him and stopped that he noticed. A heavily built man stuck out a face shaped like a bulldog's and yelled.

"Hey, Erin! Don't tell me you're blind as well as crazy?"

Morse swung his head and a momentary flash of surprise and annoyance crossed his face before he stepped over to the car. "You would be here, of course, Stewart."

"Sure. I knew your men wouldn't. Hop in and I'll ride you over to Hampton." At Erin's hesitation, he gestured impatiently. "I'm not going to kidnap you, if that's what you think. Federal laws still mean something to me, you know."

"I wouldn't know." Erin climbed in and the motor behind purred softly, its sound indicating a full atomic generator instead of the usual steam plant. "I suppose the warden kept you well informed of my actions."

The other chuckled. "He did; money has its uses when you know where to put it. I found out you weren't letting your men visit or write to you, and that's about all. Afraid I'd find out what was in the letters?"

"Precisely. And the boys could use the time better for work than useless visits to me. Thanks, I have tobacco." But at Stewart's impatient gesture, he put the "makings" back and accepted a cigarette. "It isn't poisoned, I suppose?"

"Nor loaded."

Erin let a half smile run over his lips and relaxed on the seat, watching the road flash by and letting his mind run over other times with Stewart. Probably the other was doing the same, since the silence was mutual. They had all too many common memories. Forty years of them, from the time they had first met at the institute as roommates, both filled with a hunger for knowledge that would let them cross space to other worlds.

Erin, from a family that traced itself back almost to Adam, and with a fortune equally old, had placed his faith in the newly commercialized atomic power. Gregory Stewart, who came from the wrong side of the tracks, where a full meal was a luxury, was more conservative; new and better explosives were his specialty. The fact that they were both aiming at the same goal made little difference in their arguments. Though they stuck together from stubbornness, black eyes flourished.

Then, to complicate matters further, Mara Devlin entered their lives to choose Erin after two years of indecision and to die while giving birth to his son. Erin took the boy and a few workers out to a small island off the coast and began soaking his fortune into workshops where he could train men in rocketry and gain some protection from Stewart's thugs.

Gregory Stewart had prospered with his explosives during the war of 1958, and was piling up fortune on fortune. Little by little, the key industries of the country were coming under his control, along with the toughest gangs of gunmen. When he could, he bought an island lying off the coast, a few miles from Erin's, stocked it with the best brains he could buy, and began his own research. The old feud settled down to a dull but constant series of defeats and partial victories that gained nothing for either.

Erin came to the crowning stroke of Stewart's offensive, grimaced, and tossed the cigarette away. "I forgot to thank you for railroading me up on that five-year sentence, Greg," he said quietly. "I suppose you were responsible for the failure of the blast that killed my son, as well."

Stewart looked at him in surprise which seemed genuine. "The failure was none of my doing, Erin. Anyway, you had no business sending the boy up on the crazy experimental model; any fool should have known he couldn't handle it. Maybe my legal staff framed things a little, but it was manslaughter. I could have wrung your neck when I heard Mara's son was dead, instead of letting you off lightly with five years—less one for good behavior."

"I didn't send him up." Erin's soft voice contrasted oddly with Stewart's bellow. "He slipped out one night on his own, against my orders. If the whole case hadn't been fixed with your money, I could have proved that at the trial. As it was, I couldn't get a decent hearing."

"All right, then, I framed you. But you've hit back at me without trying to, though you probably don't know it yet." He brushed Erin's protest aside quickly. "Never mind, you'll see what I mean soon enough. I didn't meet you to hash over past grievances."

"I wondered why you came to see me out."

They swung off the main highway into a smaller road where the speed limit was only sixty and went flashing past the other cars headed for Hampton. Stewart gunned the car savagely, unmindful of the curves. "We're almost at the wharf," he pointed out needlessly, "so I'll make it short and sweet. I'm about finished with plans for a rocket that will work—a few more months should do the trick—and I don't want competition now. In plain words, Erin, drop it or all rules are off between us."

"Haven't they been?" Erin asked.

"Only partly. Forget your crazy ion-blast idea, and I'll reserve a berth for you on my ship; keep on bucking me and I'll ruin you. Well?"

"No, Greg."

Stewart grunted and shrugged. "I was afraid you'd be a fool. We've always wanted the same things, and you've either had them to begin with or gotten them from under my nose. But this time it's not going to be that way. I'm declaring war. And for your information, my patents go through in a few days, so you'll have to figure on getting along without that steering assembly you worked out."

Erin gave no sign he had heard as the car came to a stop at the small wharf. "Thanks for picking me up," he said with grave courtesy. Stewart answered with a curt nod and swung the car around on its front wheels. Erin turned to a boy whose boat was tied up nearby. "How much to ferry me out to Kroll Island?"

"Two bucks." The boy looked up, and changed his smile quickly. "You one of them crazy guys who's been playing with skyrockets? Five bucks, I meant."

Erin grimaced slightly but held out the money.

II

There was nobody waiting to greet him on the island, nor had he expected anyone. He fed the right combination into the alarm system to keep it quiet and set off up the rough wooden walk toward the buildings that huddled together a few hundred yards from the dock. The warehouses, he noticed, needed a new coat of paint, and the dock would require repairs if the tramp freighter were to use it much longer.

There was a smell of smoke in the air, tangy and resinous at first, but growing stronger as he moved away from the ocean's crisp counteracting odor. As he passed the big machine shop, a stronger whiff of it reached him, unpleasant now. There was a thin wisp of smoke going up behind it, the faint gray of an almost exhausted fire. The men must be getting careless, burning their rubbish so close to the buildings. He cut around the corner and stopped.

The south wall of the laboratory was a black, charred scar, dripping dankly from a hose that was playing on it. Where the office building had stood, gaunt steel girders rose from a pile of smoking ashes and half-burned boards, with two blistered filing cabinets poking up like ghosts at a wake.

The three men standing by added nothing to the cheerfulness of the scene. Erin shivered slightly before advancing toward them. It was a foreboding omen for his homecoming, and for a moment the primitive fears mastered him. The little pain that had been scratching at his heart came back again, stronger this time.

Doug Wratten turned off the hose and shook a small arm at the sandy-haired young husky beside him. "All right," he yelled in a piping falsetto, "matter's particular and energy's discrete. But you chemists try and convince an atomic generator that it's dealing with building-block atoms instead of wave-motion."

Jimmy Shaw's homely, pleasant face still studied the smoldering ashes. "Roll wave-motion into a ball and give it valence, redhead," he suggested. "Do that and I'll send Stewart a sample—it might make a better bomb than the egg he laid on us. How about it, Dad?"

"Maybe. Anyhow, you kids drop the argument until you're through being mad at Stewart," the foreman ordered. "You'll carry your tempers over against each other." Tom Shaw was even more grizzled and stooped than Erin remembered, and his lanky frame seemed to have grown thinner.

"All right," he decided in his twangy, down-East voice. "I guess it's over, so we...Hey, it's Erin!"

He caught at Jimmy's arm and pulled him around, heading toward Erin with a loose-jointed trot. Doug forgot his arguments and moved his underdone figure on the double after them, shouting at the top of his thin voice. Erin found his arm aching and his ears ringing from their questions.

He broke free for a second and smiled. "All right, I got a year off, I sneaked in, I'm glad to be back, and you've done a good job, I gather. Where are Hank and Dutch?"

"Over in the machine shop, I guess. Haven't seen them since the fire was under control." Shaw jerked a long arm at the remains. "Had a little trouble, you see."

"I saw. Stewart's men?"

"Mm-hm. Came over in a plane and dropped an incendiary. Sort of ruined the office, but no real damage to the laboratory. If those filing cabinets are as good as they claimed, it didn't hurt our records."

Doug grinned beatifically. "Hurt their plane more. Tom here had one of our test models sent up for it, and the rocket striking against the propeller spoiled their plans." He gestured out toward the ocean. "They're drinking Neptune's health in hell right now."

"Bloodthirsty little physicist, isn't he?" Jimmy asked the air. "Hey, Kung, the boss is back. Better go tell the others."

The Chinese cook came hobbling up, jerking his bad leg over the ground and swearing at it as it slowed him down. "Kung, him see boss fella allee same time more quick long time," he intoned in the weird mixture of pidgin, bêche-de-mer, and perverted English that was his private property. "Very good, him come back. Mebbeso make suppee chop-chop same time night."

He gravely shook hands with himself before Erin, his smile saying more than the garbled English he insisted on using, then went hobbling off toward the machine shop. Shaw turned to the two young men.

"All right, you kids, get along. I've got business with Erin." As they left, his face lengthened. "I'm glad you're back, boss. Things haven't been looking any too good. Stewart's getting more active. Oh, the fire didn't do us any permanent damage, but we've been having trouble getting our supplies freighted in—had to buy an old tramp freighter when Stewart took over the regular one—and it looks like war brewing all along the line."

"I know it. Stewart brought me back and told me he was gunning for us." Erin dropped back onto a rock, realizing suddenly that he was tired; and he'd have to see a doctor about his heart—sometime. "And he's stolen our steering unit, or thinks he's getting it patented, at least."

"Hmmm. He can't have it; it's the only practical solution to the controls system there is. Erin, we'll... Skip it, here come Dutch and Hank."

But a sudden whistle from the rocket test tower cut in, indicating a test. The structural engineer and machinist swung sharply, and Doug and Jimmy popped out of the laboratory at a run. Shaw grabbed at Erin.

"Come on," he urged. "This is the biggest test yet, I hope. Good thing you're here to see it." Even Kung was hobbling toward the tower.

Erin followed, puzzling over who could have set off the whistle; he knew of no one not accounted for, yet a man had to be in the tower. Evidently there was an addition to the force, of whom he knew nothing. They reached the guardrail around the tower, and the whistle tooted again, three times in warning.

"Where is the rocket?" Erin yelled over the whistle. There was nothing on the takeoff cradle.

"Left two days ago; this is the return. Jack's been nursing it without sleep—wouldn't let anyone else have it," Shaw answered hurriedly. "Only took time off to send another up for the bomber."

Following their eyes, Erin finally located a tiny point of light that grew as he watched. From the point in the sky where it was, a thin shrilling reached their ears. A few seconds later, he made out the stubby shape of a ten-foot model, its tubes belching out blue flame in a long, tight jet. With a speed that made it difficult to follow, it shot over their heads at a flat angle, heading over the ocean, while its speed dropped. A rolling turn pointed it back over their heads, lower this time, and the ion-blast could be seen as a tight, unwavering track behind it.

Then it reversed again and came over the tower, slowed almost to a stop, turned up to vertical with a long blast from its steering tubes, and settled slowly into the space between the guide rails. It slid down with a wheeze, sneezed faintly, and decided to stop peacefully. Erin felt a tingle run up his back at his first sight of a completely successful radio-controlled flight.

The others were yelling crazily. Dutch Bauer, the fat structural engineer, was dancing with Hank Vlček, his bald pate shining red with excitement. "It worked, it worked," they were chanting.

Shaw grunted. "Luck," he said sourly, but his face belied the words. "Jack had no business sending our first model with the new helix on such a flight. Wonder the darn fool didn't lose it in space."

Erin's eyes were focused on the young man coming from the pit of the tower. There was something oddly familiar about those wide shoulder, and the mane of black hair that hugged his head. As the boy came nearer, the impression was heightened by the serious brown eyes, now red from lack of sleep, that were slightly too deep in the round face.

The boy scanned the group and moved directly toward Morse, a little hesitantly. "Well," he asked, "how did you like the test— Mr. Morse, I think? Notice how the new helix holds the jets steady?"

Erin nodded slowly. So this was what Stewart had meant by his statement that he had been hit twice as hard. "You resemble your father, Jack Stewart!"

Jack shifted on his feet, then decided there was no disapproval on Erin's face, and grinned. He held out a small package. "Then I'll give you this, sir. It's a reel of exposed film, shot from the rocket, and it should show the other side of the Moon!"

III

The secretary glided into the richly appointed room, sniffing at the pungent odor given off by the dirty old pipe in Stewart's mouth.

"Mr. Russell's here, sir," she announced, wondering whether his scowl was indicative of indigestion or directed at some particular person.

"Send him in, then." He bit at the stem of the pipe without looking at her, and she breathed a sigh of relief. It wasn't indigestion, which was the only thing that made him roar at the office force; at other times he was fair and just with them, if not given to kindliness. Looking at Russell as she sent him in, she guessed the object of his anger.

"Well?" Stewart asked curtly as his right-hand man entered.

"Now look," Russell began, "I admit I sent the plane over before you said, but was it my fault if they brought it down? How was I to know they had a torpedo they could control in the air?"

"Not torpedo, you fool; it was a rocket. And that's bad news, in itself, since it means they're making progress. But we'll skip that. I gave orders you were to wait until Morse refused my offer, and you didn't. furthermore, I told you to send it over at night, when they'd be unprepared, and drop it on the tower and laboratory, not on the office. I'm not trying to burn people to death."

"But the pilot didn't want—"

"You mean you had your own little ideas." He tossed the pipe into i ii.iy and began picking at his fingernails. "Next time I give you orders, Russell, I expect them to be followed. Understand? You'd better. Now get down to Washington and see what you can do about rushing our patent on the unified control; Erin Morse didn't look surprised or bothered enough to suit me. He's holding something, and I don't want it to show up as an ace. Okay, beat it."

Russell looked up in surprise, and made tracks toward the door. Either the old man was feeling unusually good, or he was worried. That had been easier than he expected.

Back on Kroll Island, Erin Morse settled back in his chair in the corner of the workshop that served as a temporary office. "Read this," he said, handing over a dog-eared magazine with a harshly colored cover to Shaw. "It's a copy of *Interplanetary Tales*, one of the two issues they printed. It's not well known, but it's still classed as literature. Page 108, where it's marked in red."

Shaw looked at him curiously, and reached for the magazine. He began reading in his overly precise manner, the exact opposite of his usual slow speech. "Jerry threw the stick over to the right, and the *Betsy* veered sharply, jarring his teeth. The controls were the newest type, arranged to be handled by one stick. Below the steering rod was a circular disk, and banked around it was a circle of pistons that varied the steering jet blasts according to the amount they were depressed. Moving the stick caused the disk to press against those pistons which would turn the ship in that direction, slowly with a little movement, sharply if it were depressed the limit."

He looked at Erin. "But that's a fair description of the system we use."

"Exactly. Do you remember whether the submarine periscope was patented?"

"Why, Jules Verne...Hmmm. Anything described reasonably accurately in literature can't be given a basic patent." Shaw thought it over slowly. "I take it we mail this to the attorneys and get Stewart's claim voided. So that's why you didn't try for a patent on it?"

"Naturally."

Morse picked up the records that had been saved from the fire by insulated cabinets, and ran back over the last few years' work. They showed the usual huge expenditures and small progress. Rockets aren't built on a shoestring nor in the backyard during the idle hours of a boy scientist. "Total cost, five-foot experimental radio-controlled rocket, $13,843.51," read one item. From another book he found that it had crashed into the sea on its first flight and been destroyed.

But there were advances. The third model had succeeded, though the flickering, erratic blast had made control difficult. A new lightweight converter had been tested successfully, throwing out power from the atoms with only a .002 percent heat loss. An ion-release had been discovered by General Electratomic Company that afforded a more than ample supply of ions, and Shaw had secured rights for its use. Toward the last there were outlays for some new helix to control the ion-blast on a tight line under constant force and a new alloy for the chamber. Those had always been the problems.

"Good work," Erin Morse nodded. "This last model, I gather, is the one Jack used to reach the Moon." Under it he penciled the word "success" in bright green. "The boys were quite excited over those pictures, even if they did show nothing spectacular. I'm glad he sent it."

"So am I. They need encouragement." Shaw kicked aside a broken bearing and moved his chair back against the wall. "I suppose you're wondering why Jack's working with us. I didn't know how you'd take it."

"I'm reserving my opinion for the facts." It had been a shock, seeing the boy there, but he had covered up as best he could and waited until information was vouchsafed.

Shaw began awkwardly, not sure yet whether Erin approved or not. "Jack came here about a year ago and—well, he simply told us he was looking for work. Had a blowup with his father over your being sent up for the accident, it seems, back then. Anyway, they'd been quarreling before because Jack wanted to specialize in atomics, and the old man wanted him to carry on with explosives.

"So Jack left home, took his degree with money his mother had left him, and came here. He's good, too, though I wouldn't tell him so. That new helix control is his work, and he's fixed up the ion-release so as to give optimum results. Since Doug and you studied atomics, they've made big progress, I reckon, and we needed someone with his training."

"Any experimental work needs new blood," Erin agreed. "So Greg succeeded in teaching his son that Mars was the last frontier, but not how to reach it."

"Seems that way. Anyway, his father's kicking up a worse fuss with us since he came. Somehow, there's a leak, and I can't locate the source—Jack has been watched, and he's not doing it. But Stewart's getting too much information on what we're doing—like that control. He managed to cut off freighter service and choke our source of supplies until I bought up a tramp and hired a no-good captain."

"He'll hit harder when we get his patent application killed. By the way, are the plans for that air-renewer of Jimmy's still around?"

Shaw nodded. "Sure, I guess so. He never found out what was wrong with it, though, so we've been planning on carrying oxygen flasks with us." Based on the idea of photosynthesis, the air-renewer had been designed to break down the carbon dioxide waste product of breathing by turning it into sugar and free oxygen, as a plant does, and permit the same air being used over and over.

"All it needs is saturated air around the catalyst." Erin had fished around in the papers from the burned office until he had the plans. Now he spread them before Shaw and indicated the changes. "A spray of water here, and remove the humidity afterward. Took me three years up there, working when I could, to figure out that fault, but it's ready for the patent attorneys now. Dutch can draw up the plans in the morning."

They stuck the papers and books away and passed out of the building into the night. "Stars look right good," Shaw observed. "Mars seems to be waiting until we can get there."

"That shouldn't be long now, with the rocket blast finally under control. What's that?" Erin pointed toward a sharp streak of light that rose suddenly over the horizon and arced up rapidly. As they watched, it straightened to vertical and went streaking up on greased wings until it faded into the heights beyond vision.

"Looks like Stewart's made a successful model." A faint, high whine reached their ears now. "If he has, we *will* have a fight on our hands."

Erin nodded. "Start the boys on the big rocket in the morning; we can't stop for more experimental work now."

IV

The big electric hammer came down with a monotonous thud and clank, jarring against the eardrums in its endless hunger for new material to work on. Hank Vlček's little bullet head looked like a hairy billiard ball stuck on an ape's body as he bobbed up and down in front of it, feeding in sheets of cuproberyl alloy. But the power in the machinist's arms seemed to match that of the motor.

Dutch Bauer looked up from a sheet of blueprints and nodded approvingly, then went back to the elaborate calculations required to complete the design he was working on. The two co-operated perfectly, Dutch creating structural patterns on paper, and Vlček turning them into solid metal.

On paper, the *Santa Maria* was shaping up handsomely, though the only beauty of the ship itself was to be that given by severe utility. Short and squat, with flaring blast tubes, she showed little resemblance to the classic cigar-hulls of a thousand speculative artists. The one great purpose was strength with a minimum of weight, and the locating of the center of gravity below the thrust points of the rockets. When completed, there would be no danger of her tipping her nose back to Earth on the takeoff.

Out on the ways that had been thrown up hastily, gaunt girders were shaping into position to form her skeleton, and some of the outer sheathing was in position. The stubby air fins that would support her in the air until speed was reached were lying beside her, ready to be attached, and a blower was already shooting in insulation where her double hull was completed. Space itself would be insulation against heat loss, but the rays of the unfiltered sunlight needed something to check them, or the men inside the ship would have been boiled long before Mars was reached. Hsi Kung was running the blower, babbling at it in singsong Peking dialect. At a time like this, they were all common laborers when there was work to be done.

Erin pulled on coveralls and reached for the induction welder, while Jimmy Shaw consulted his blueprints. "Wonder why Doug hasn't shown up?" the boy asked. "He usually gets back from the mainland before morning, but it's nine already. Hmm. Looks like Hank's machined enough hull plates to keep us busy until supper."

"It does, though where he finds time is a puzzle. He must work all night. We need other workers, if we're to compete with Stewart's force. Even counting Kung, eight men aren't enough for this job." Erin began climbing up the wooden framing that gave access to the hull, wondering whether his heart would bother him today. Sleep had been slow coming the night before, and he was tired. This work was too heavy for an old man, though he hadn't thought of himself as old before. Certainly he didn't look old.

"Wonder why Doug goes to town once a week?" he asked.

Jimmy chuckled. "Don't you know? He's found a girl friend there, believe it or not. Some woman has either taken pity on him, or he's found his nerve at last."

Doug wasn't exactly the sort that would appeal to women. His short, scrawny figure was all angles, and his face, topped by its thin mop of reddish hair, was vaguely like that of an eagle. Then, too, he usually stuttered around women.

Erin smiled faintly. "It's a shame, in a way, that Doug's so shy around girls. I hope he has better luck with this one than that other."

"So do I, though I wouldn't tell him so. He's been as cocky as a rooster since he found this Helen." Jimmy settled into position with a grunt and began moving a sheet into place as it came up on the magnetic grapple Jack was working below him. "Okay, fire away."

The welder was heavy, and the heat that poured up from the plates sapped at Morse's strength. He was conscious of sudden relief at noon when a shout came up to him. He released the welder slowly, rubbing tired muscles, and looked down at the weaving form of Doug Wratten. One of the physicist's thin arms was motioning him down erratically.

"Drunk!" Jimmy diagnosed in amazement. "Didn't know he touched the stuff."

There was no question of Doug's state. His words were thick and muffled as Erin reached him. "Go 'head 'n' fire me," he muttered thickly. "Fire me, Erin. Kick m' out 'thout a good word. I'm a low-down dirty dog, tha's what."

"For being drunk, Doug? That hardly justifies such extreme measures."

"Huh-uh. Who's drunk? It's tha' girl…I foun' the leak we been worr'n' about."

Erin got an arm around him and began moving toward the bunk-house, meaning to pay no attention to his mumbled words. But the last ones struck home. The leak of information to Stewart's camp had been troubling them all for the last two months. "Yes?" he encouraged.

" 'S the girl. She's a spy for Stewart." His voice stuck in his throat and he rumbled unhappily. "Use'a be his sec'tary; planted her on me. Jus' usin' me, tha's all. Saw a letter she was writin' him when I was waitin' for her to come down. Din't wait anymore…Jus' usin' me; tol' me she was in'rested in my work. Tol' me she loved me. Foun' out all I knew…Better fire me, Erin."

"I think not, Doug. It might have happened to any of us. Why don't you go to sleep?"

Wratten rolled over in the bed as he was released, gagging sickly, and moaning to himself. "I love…Helen…Damn Helen!" As Erin closed the door, his voice came out, pleading. "Don't tell Jimmy; he'd laugh."

Jimmy stood at the door as Erin came out. "Poor devil," he said. "I heard enough to know what happened. Anything I can do for him?"

"Let him sleep it off. I'll have a talk with him when he wakes up and see what I can do about bolstering his faith in himself."

"Okay," Jimmy agreed, "but it was a dirty, rotten trick of Stewart's, using him like that. Say, Dad's up at the shack swearing at something else Stewart's done, and yelling for you. I just went up there."

Erin grunted, and turned hastily toward the temporary office building they had erected. It was always something, except when it was more than one thing. First the fire, the trouble with the patent, now safely squelched, difficulty in obtaining tools, and one thing after another, all meant to wear down their morale. This was probably one of the master strokes that seemed to happen almost at regular intervals.

Sometimes he wondered whether either of them would ever succeed; forty years of rivalry had produced no results except enough to keep them trying. Now, when success for one of them seemed at hand, the feud was going on more bitterly than before, though it was mostly one-sided. And war was menacing the world again, as it would always threaten a world where there were no other escape valves for men's emotions. They needed a new frontier, free of national barriers, where the headstrong could fight nature instead of their brothers.

He had hoped to provide that escape valve in leading men to another planet, just as Stewart hoped. But would either of them succeed? Erin was sure of Stewart's ultimate failure—explosives couldn't do the trick; though he had enough of a sense of humor to realize that Stewart was saying the same thing about him and his method. If only there could be peace until he finished!

Shaw was waiting impatiently, swearing coldly in a voice Erin hadn't heard since the days when Tom was tricked out of a discovery by a company for which he'd worked as metallurgist, and he joined the men on the island. "The mail's in," he said, breaking off his flow of invectives. "Here's a present from Captain Hitchkins—says he can't get the cargo of beryllium alloy we ordered made up. And here's the letter from the Beryl Company."

Erin picked up the letter and read it slowly. It began with too profuse apologies, then cited legal outs: "—will realize that we are not breaking our contract by this action, since it contains a clause to the effect that our own needs shall come first. Mr. G. R. Stewart, who has controlling interest in our company, has requisitioned our entire supply, and we are advised by our legal department that this contingency is covered by the clause mentioned. Therefore we can no longer furnish the alloy you desire. We regret—"

He skimmed the passage of regret and polite lies, to center on a sentence at the end, which conveyed the real message, and revealed the source of the letter. "We doubt that you can secure beryllium alloy at any price, as we are advised that Mr. Stewart is using all that the market can supply. If such is not the case, we shall, of course, be glad to extend our best wishes in your enterprise."

"How about that?" he asked Shaw, pointing to the last sentence. "Have you investigated?"

"Don't need to. Hitchkins showed more brains than I gave him credit for. He scoured the market for us, on his own initiative, and beryllium just ain't." Shaw passed over the other letters that had come, reverting to his invectives. "Now what do we do?"

"Without beryllium, nothing. We'll have to get it, someway." But Erin wondered. Whatever else Stewart was, he was thorough, and his last stroke had been more than the expected major move.

V

The supper table had turned into a conference room, since news of that importance was impossible to keep. Even Doug Wratten had partially forgotten his own troubles, and was watching Erin. Kung stood unnoticed in the doorway, his moon face picturing the general gloom,

Dutch Bauer finished his explanation and concluded. "So, that is it. No beryllium, no *Santa Maria*. Even aluminum alloys are too heavy for good design. Aluminum—bah! Hopeless." He shrugged and spread his pudgy hands to show just how hopeless it was.

Jimmy grunted and considered. "How about magnesium alloys—something like magnalium?" he asked, but without much hope. "It's even lighter than beryllium—1.74 density instead of 1.8."

"Won't work." Their eyes had turned to Shaw, who was the metallurgist, and his answer was flat. "Alloys aren't high enough in melting point, aren't hard enough, and don't have the strength of the one we've been using. When the ship uses the air for braking, or when the sun shines on it in space, we'll need something that won't soften up at ordinary temperatures; and that means beryllium."

"Then how about the foreign markets?" Jack wanted to know. "My fa...Mr. Stewart can't control all of them."

Erin shook his head. "No luck. They're turning all they can get into bombing planes and air torpedoes. They're not interested in idealism."

"I liked that new helix, too." Jack tapped his fingers on the table, then snapped them out flat. "Well, there goes a nice piece of applied atomics. We should have bought our own beryllium plant, I guess."

"And have to close down because Stewart gained control of the new process for getting beryllium out of its ores." Shaw grunted. "We'd have had to fall back on the old process of extracting it by dissolving out in alkalis."

Erin looked up suddenly, staring at Shaw. "When I was first starting," he said thoughtfully, "I considered buying one of the old plants. It's still standing, all the machinery in place, but it's been closed down by the competition of the new process. The owner's hard up, and he can't sell the place for love or money."

Jimmy's face dropped its scowl and came forth with a fresh grin; even the mention of a faint hope was enough to send up his enthusiasm. "So we buy it or get him to open up, start using it, and go ahead in spite of Stewart. How much does the old system cost, Dad?"

"About fifteen hundred dollars a ton, using a couple of tricks I could show them. Going to try it, Erin?"

Erin nodded silently, but the frown was still on his face as he got up and went out to the new office where he could use the visiphone. The plant had a maximum capacity of four tons a week, which was hardly adequate, and there were other objections, but trying would do no harm. The frown was heavier when he came back.

"Sanders will open up," he reported, "but he'll need money to fix the plant up. He agrees to turn the plant over to us, and furnish the alloy at the price Tom mentioned, but we'll have to invest about sixty thousand in new equipment. Add that to the cost of the metal, and it runs to a rather steep figure."

"But—"

"I know. I'm not kicking about the money, or wouldn't be if I had it to spend." Erin hadn't meant to tell them of his own troubles, but there was no way to avoid it now. "Stewart left nothing to chance. The stocks and investments I had began to slip a month ago, and they kept slipping. My brokers advised me that they have liquidated everything, and I have about ten cents on a dollar left; today's mail brought their letter along with the other news."

Jack swore hotly. "Da—Stewart always could ruin a man on the market. Erin, I've got a decent legacy from my mother, and we're practically running a co-operative here, anyhow. It's all yours."

Erin saw suddenly just what the loss of the boy had meant to Stewart, and the last of numbness from his own son's death slipped away. His smile was as sweet as a woman's, but he shook his head. "Did you read your mail today?"

"No, why?"

"Because Stewart would know his own son well enough to take precautions. See if I'm not right."

They watched intently as the letters came out of Jack's pocket and were sorted. He selected one bulky one and ripped it open hastily, drawing out the paper where all could see, skimming over it until it formed a complete picture. " 'It almost seems that someone is deliberately trying to ruin you,'" he read. " 'Our best efforts have failed completely—' Damn! There's about enough left to pay for the new machinery needed, and that's all."

Doug came out of his trance. "I won't be needing my savings for the future now," he said grimly. "It's not much, but I'd appreciate your using it, Erin. And I don't think any of us will want the salary you've been paying us."

The others nodded. All of them had been paid more than well, and had had no chance to spend much of their salary. Their contributions were made as a matter of course, and Erin totaled them.

"It may be enough," he said. "Of course, we form a closed corporation, all profits—if there are any from this—being distributed. I'll have the legal papers drawn up. Perhaps it will be enough, perhaps not, but we can put it to the test. Our big trouble is that we need new workers, men to help Hank particularly. Most of the machining will have to be done here on the island now."

"Mebbeso you fella catchee plenty man." Kung hobbled forward to the table, a dirty leather sack in his hands. "You fella catchee li'l planet, fin' allee same time catchee time makee free." His jargon went on, growing too thick for them to understand.

Tom Shaw held up a protesting hand. "Talk chink," he ordered. "I spent five years there once, so I can get the lingo if you take your time."

Kung threw him a surprised and grateful glance, and broke into a rambling discourse, motioning toward the sky, the bag in his hand, and counting on his fingers.

Shaw turned back to the others.

"He says he wants to join up, putting in the money he's been saving for his funeral when they ship his body back to China. Wants to know if his race will be allowed on the other planets when we reach them?"

"Tell him the planets are big enough for all races, provided ships are built to carry them."

"Very good, boss fella, savvee plenty." Kung lapsed again into Peking dialect.

"He says he can get us workers then, who'll obey with no questions asked, and won't cost us more than enough to buy them cheap food. His tong will be glad to furnish them on his say-so. Since Japan conquered them and they digested the Japanese into their own nation again, it seems they need room to expand.

"Darn it, Erin, with even the Chinese cook behind you, we're bound to beat Stewart."

VI

Captain Hitchkins had left the unloading to the ruffian he called his mate and was examining the progress made on the island. His rough English face was a curious blend of awe and skepticism. "Naow was that 'ere a ship, mitey," he told Erin, "I'd s'y 'twas a maost seaworthy job, that I would, thaough she's lackin' a bit o' keel. 'N' I m'y allaow as she's not bad, not bad atawl."

Erin left him talking, paying as little attention to his speech as the captain would have to a landlubber's comments on the tub of a freighter. Hitchkins was entirely satisfied with that arrangement. The *Santa Maria* could speak for herself.

The hull was completed, except for a section deliberately left open for the admission of the main atomic generator, and a gleaming coat of silver lacquer had been applied, to give the necessary luster for the deflection of the sun's rays. In comparison to a seagoing ship, she was small, but here on the ways, seen by herself, she loomed up like some monster out of a fantasy book. Even with the motors installed and food for six years stocked, she still held a comfortable living space for the eight men who would go with her.

"I've heard as 'aow they've a new lawr passed, mikin' aout against the like o' such, thaough," Hitchkins went on. "Naow w'y would they do that?"

"People are always afraid of new things, Captain. I'm not worried about it, though." Erin turned over the bills of lading. "Have any trouble this trip?"

"Some o' the men were minded the p'y was a bit laow. But they chinged their minds w'en they come to, that they did." He chuckled. "I've a bit o' a w'y wi' the men, sir."

They were back at the dock now, watching the donkey engines laboring under the load of alloy plates that was being transferred in the machine shop. The Chinese laborers were sweating and struggling with the trucks on which these were hauled, but they grinned at him and nodded. He had no complaint with the labor Kung had obtained. If the money held out, things looked hopeful.

Jack Stewart located him, and yelled. "There's a Mr. Stewart at the office," he said flatly. "He came while you were showing Captain Hitchkins the ship, and is waiting for you. Shall I tell him to go on waiting?"

"No, I'll see him; might as well find out the worst." Stewart had visiphoned that he was coming under a temporary truce, so Erin was not surprised. "Carry on, Captain." He turned after Jack toward the shack, wishing the boy would treat his father a little less coldly. It wasn't good for a man to feel that way about his father, and he wished Stewart no personal problems.

Jack swung off toward the ship as they sighted Stewart, and the older man's eyes followed the retreating figure.

"He's a good boy, Greg," Erin said, not unkindly. "I didn't plan this, you know."

"Skip it. He's no concern of mine, the stubborn ass." Stewart held out a newspaper. "I thought you might be interested to know that the law has been passed against the use of atomic power in any spaceship. It just went through the state legislature and was signed by the governor."

"Don't you think it's a bit high-handed? I thought that interstate and international commerce was out of the hands of the state legislature."

Stewart tapped the paper. "But there's no provision against their ruling on interplanetary commerce, Erin. A few scare stories in the Sunday supplements, and a few dinners to the right men did the trick. They were sure the Martians might find the secret and turn atomic power back on us."

"So you had to come and bring me the news. I suppose you expect me to quit now and twiddle my thumbs."

"That offer of a berth on my ship—which will work—still stands. Of course, if I have to get out an injunction to stop you, it will make matters a little more difficult, but the result will be the same."

Erin smiled grimly. "That was the poorest move you've made, Greg," he said. "Your lawmakers bungled. I read the law, and it forbids the use of atomic power in the 'vacuum of space.' And good scientists will tell you that a vacuum is absolute nothing in space—but between the planets, at least, there are a few molecules of matter to the cubic inch. Your law and injunction won't work."

"You've seen a lawyer, I suppose?"

"I have, and he assures me there's nothing to stop me. Furthermore, until I reach space, the law doesn't apply, and when I'm in space, no Earth-made laws can govern me."

Stewart shrugged. "So you've put one over on me again. You always were persistent, Erin. The only man I haven't been able to beat—yet. Maybe I'll have to wait until your crazy ship fails, but I hope not."

"I'll walk down to the dock with you," Erin offered. "Drop in any time you want to, provided you come alone." He was feeling almost friendly now that success was in sight. Stewart fell in beside him, his eyes turned toward the group of laborers Jack was directing.

"I suppose—" he began, and stopped.

"He goes along, according to his own wishes."

Stewart grunted. "You realize, Erin, that one false attempt might set the possibility of the public's accepting rocket flight back fifty years. And the men in the ship would be—well, wouldn't be." He hesitated. "How much would you take to stop it?"

"You know better than that." But Erin realized that the question was more an automatic reaction than anything else. When Stewart asked that, he could see no other solution, and money had been his chief weapon since he made his first fortune.

As the man left in the little boat that had brought him, Erin wondered, though. Was Stewart licked, for once and for all? Or was it only the combination of seeing his son turned against him, and finding his carefully laid scheme hadn't made a decent fizzle? He shrugged and dismissed it. There seemed little more chance for trouble, but if it came, it would be the unexpected, and worry would do no good.

It was the unexpected, but they were not entirely unwarned. The first pale light of the false dawn showed when a commotion at the door awakened them. Doug got up grumpily and went groping toward the key. "Some darned Chinese in a fight, I suppose," he began.

Then he let out a sound that scarcely fitted a human throat and jerked back in. The others could see only two small, rounded arms that came up around his neck, and a head of hair that might have been brown in a clearer light. The voice was almost hysterical. "Doug! Oh, I was afraid I wouldn't get here in time."

"Helen!" Doug's words were frigid, but he trembled under the robe. "What are—don't start anything...I saw the letter." They could see her more clearly now, and Jimmy whistled. No wonder Doug had taken it so hard. She was almost crying, and her arms refused to let him go. "I knew you'd seen the first page—part of it. But yon didn't read it all."

"Well?" Only the faintest ghost of a doubt tinged his inflection.

"I wasn't just acting the Saturday before; I meant it. That's why I was writing the letter—to tell Mr. Stewart I was through with him." She groped into her purse and came out with a wrinkled sheet. "Here, you can see for yourself. And then you were gone and I found this in the wastebasket where you threw it, so I didn't quit. I thought you'd never speak to me. Believe me, Doug!"

His wizened little face wasn't funny now, though two red spots showed up ridiculously on his white skin. His long, tapering fingers groped toward her, touched, and then drew back. She caught them quickly. "Well—" he said. Then: "What are you doing here, anyhow, Helen...Helenya?"

She jerked guiltily. "Stewart. His lieutenant—Russell—wanted the combination to your alarm system again—forgot it."

"You gave it?"

"I had to. Then I came here to warn you. There are a bunch of them, every rat on his force, and they're coming here. I was afraid you'd be—"

There was something almost wonderful about Doug then. All the silly cockiness and self-consciousness were gone. "All right," he said quietly. "Go back to the cook shack and stay there; you'll know where to find it. No, do as I say. We'll talk it over later, Helen. I don't want you around when it happens. Go on. Erin, Tom, you'll know what to do. I'll wake the Chinese and get them in order." And he was gone at a run.

VII

They didn't stop to dress fully, but went out into the chill air as they were. Doug had the Chinese lined up and was handing out the few spare weapons grimly, explaining while he worked. A tall North Country yellow man asked a few questions in a careful Harvard accent, then turned back and began barking orders in staccato Mandarin. Whether they would be any good in a fight was a question, but the self-appointed leader seemed to know his business. They were no cowards, at least.

Tom Shaw passed Jimmy a dried plug of tobacco. "Better take it," he advised. "When you're fighting the first time, it takes something strong in your mouth to keep your stomach down, son. And shoot for their bellies—it's easier and just as sure."

There was no time to throw up embankments at the wharf, so they drew back to the higher ground, away from the buildings, which would have sheltered them, but covered any flanking movement by the gunmen. Jack stared incredulously at the gun in his hand, and wiped the sweat from his hands. "Better lend me some of that tobacco," he said wryly. "My stomach's already begun fighting. You using that heavy thing?"

"Sure." The gun was a sixty-pound machine rifle, equipped with homemade grips and shoulder and chest pads, set for single fire. It looked capable of crushing Shaw's lanky figure at the first recoil, but he carried it confidently. "It's been done before; grew up with a gun in my hand in the Green Mountains."

Erin rubbed a spot over his heart surreptitiously and waited. Stewart would be defeated only when he died, it seemed, and maybe not then.

Then they made out the figures in the tricky light of the dawn, long shadows that slunk silently over the dock and advanced up the hill toward the bunkhouse. Some movement must have betrayed the watchers, for one of the advancing figures let out a yell and pointed. "Come on, mugs," a hoarse voice yelled. "Here's our meat, begging to be caught. A bonus to the first man that gets one."

Whing! Shaw twitched and swore. "Only a crease," he whispered, "and an accident. They can't shoot." He raised the heavy gun, coming upright, and aimed casually. It spoke sharply, once, twice, then in a slow tattoo. The light made the shooting almost impossible, but two of the men yelled, and one dropped.

"Make it before sunup," he warned, as the thugs drew back nervously. "The light'll hit our eyes then and give them the advantage." Then the men below evidently decided it was only one man they had to fear and came boiling up, yelling to encourage themselves; experience had never taught them to expect resistance. Shaw dropped back onto his stomach, beside the others, shooting with even precision, while Erin and Jimmy followed suit. The rest were equipped only with automatics, which did little good.

"Huh!" Jack rubbed a shoulder where blood trickled out, his eyes still on the advance.

Erin felt the gun in his hand buck backward and realized suddenly that he was firing on the rushing men.

Jimmy's voice was surprised. "I hit a man—I think he's dead." He shivered and stuck his face back to the sights, trying to repeat it.

Shaw spat out a brown stream. "Three," he said quietly. "Out of practice, I guess."

The few Chinese with handarms attempted a cross fire as the men came abreast, but their marksmanship was hopeless. Then all were swept together, waves breaking against each other, and individual details were lost. Guns were no good at close range, and Erin dropped the rifle, grabbing quickly for the hatchet in his belt as a heavy-set man singled him out.

He saw the gun butt coming at him in the man's hand, ducked instinctively, and felt it hit somewhere. But the movement with the hatchet seemed to complete itself, and he saw the man drop. Something tingled up his spine, and the weapon came down again, viciously. Brains spattered. "Shouldn't hit a man who's down," a voice seemed to say, but the heat of fighting was on him, and he felt no regret at the broken rule.

A sharp stab struck at his back, and he swung to see a knife flashing for a second stroke. Pivoting on his heel, he dived, striking low, and heard the knife swish by over his head. Then he grabbed, caught, and twisted, and the mobsman dropped the metal blade from a broken arm. Most of the fighting had turned away down the hill, and he moved toward the others.

Jimmy spat out a stream of tobacco in the face of an opponent, just as another swung a knife from his side. Erin jumped forward, but Tom Shaw was before him, and the knife fell limply as Shaw fired an automatic from his hip. "Five," Erin heard his dispassionate voice. Beside Shaw, Hank Vlček was reducing heads with a short iron bar.

Erin moved into the fight again, swinging the hatchet toward a blood-covered face, not waiting to see its effects. Two of the Chinese lay quietly, and one was dragging himself away, but none of his other men seemed fatally injured. He scooped up a fallen knife, jumped for one man, and twisted suddenly to sink it in the side of Jack's opponent, then jerked toward the two who were driving Doug backward.

Doug stumbled momentarily, and something slashed down. Morse saw the little body sag limply, and threw the hatchet. Metal streaked through the air to bury itself in the throat of one of the men, and Erin's eyes flashed sideways.

Kung stood there, another kitchen knife poised for the throwing. The remaining one of Doug's assailants saw it, too, and the knife and gun seemed to work as one. Kung gasped and twisted over on his bad leg; the knife missed, but Erin's hatchet found its mark. Only a split second had elapsed, but time had telescoped out until a hundred things could be seen in one brief flash.

And then, without warning, it seemed, the battle was over and the gunmen drew back, running for the dock. Shaw grabbed for his gun and yelled, "Stop!" A whining bullet carried his message more strongly, and they halted. He spat the last of his tobacco out. "Pick up your dead and wounded, and get out! Tell Stewart he can have the bodies with our compliments!"

Russell lay a few yards off, and their leader had been the first to fall under Erin's hatchet. Lacking direction, they milled back, less than a third of the original number, and began dragging the bodies toward the dock. Shaw followed them grimly, the ugly barrel of the machine gun lending authority to his words, and Erin turned toward Doug.

The physicist was sitting up. "Shoulder," he said thickly. "Only stunned when I hit the ground. Better see about Kung over there." Then a rushing figure of a girl swooped down, taking possession of him and biting out choking cries at his wound. Erin left him in Helen's hands and turned to the cook.

It was too late. Kung had joined his ancestors, and the big Hill Country Chinese stood over him. "A regrettable circumstance, Mr. Morse," he enunciated. "Hsi Kung tendered you his compliments and requested that I carry on for him. I can assure you that our work will continue as before. In view of the fact that you are somewhat depleted as to funds, Hsi Kung has requested that his funeral be a simple one."

Erin looked at Kung's body in dull wonder; since he could remember, the man had apparently lived only that he might have a funeral whose display would impress the whole of his native village in China. "I guess we can ship him back," he said slowly. "How many others?"

"Two, sir. Three with injuries, but not fatal, I am sure. I must congratulate your men on the efficiency with which the battle was conducted. Most extraordinary."

"Thanks." Erin's throat felt dry, and his knees threatened to buckle under him, while his heart did irregular flip-flops. To him it seemed that it was more than extraordinary none of his friends were dead; all were battered up, but they had gotten off with miraculous ease. "Can some of your men cook?"

"I should feel honored, sir, if you would appoint your servant, Robert Wah, to Hsi Kung's former position."

"Good. Serve coffee to all, and the best you can find for any that want to eat—your men as well." Then, to Shaw who had come up: "Finished?"

Shaw nodded. "All gone, injured and wounded with them. Wonder if Stewart's fool enough to drag us into court over it? I didn't expect this of him."

"Neither did I, but it will be strictly private, I'm—sure." Erin's knees weakened finally, and Shaw eased him to a seat. He managed a smile at the foreman's worried face. "It's nothing—just getting old." He'd have to see a doctor about his heart soon. But there was still work to be done. With surprise, he noticed blood trickling down one arm. Stewart had done that; it was always Stewart.

VIII

The clerks in Gregory Stewart's outer office sat stiffly at their work, and the machines beat out a regular tattoo, without any of the usual interruptions for talk. Stewart's private secretary alone sat idle, biting her nails. In her thirteen years of work, she thought she had learned all the man's moods, but this was a new one.

He hadn't said anything, and there had been no blustering, but the tension in the office all came from the room in which he sat, sucking at his pipe and staring at a picture. That picture, signed "Mara," had always puzzled her. It had been there while his wife was still living, but it was not hers.

The buzzer on the PBX board broke in, and the girl operator forgot her other calls to plug in instantly. "Yes, sir," she said hastily. "Erin Morse, on Kroll Island. I have the number. Right away, sir."

She could have saved her unusual efforts; at the moment, Stewart was not even conscious of her existence. He stared at the blank visi-screen, his lips moving, but no sound came out. There was a set speech by his side, written carefully in the last hour, but now that he had made his decision, he crumpled it and tossed it in the waste-basket.

The screen snapped into life, and the face of his son was on it, a face that froze instantly. At least they were open for calls today, which was unusual; ordinarily, no one answered the buzzer. Stewart's eyes centered on the swelling under the shirt, where the boy's wound was bandaged. "Jack," he said quickly. "You all right?"

The boy's voice was not the one he knew. "Your business, sir?"

Humbleness came hard to Stewart, who had fought his way up from the raw beginnings only because he lacked it. Now it was the only means to his end. "I'd like to speak to Erin, please."

"Mr. Morse is busy." The boy reached for the switch, but the others quick motion stayed his hand.

"This is important. I'm not fighting this morning."

Jack shrugged, wincing at the dart of pain, and turned away. Stewart watched him fade from the screen's focus and waited patiently until Erin's face came into view. It was a tired face, and the erect shoulders were less erect this time. Morse stared into the viewer without a change of expression. "Well, Stewart?"

"The fight's over, Erin." It was the hardest sentence Stewart had ever spoken, but he was glad to get it over. "I hadn't meant things to work out the way they did, last night. That was Russell's idea, the dirty rat, and I'm not sorry he found his proper reward. When I do any killing, I'll attend to it myself."

Erin still stared at him with a set face, and he went on, digging out every word by sheer willpower. "I'd meant them to blow up your ship, I admit. Maybe that would have been worse, I don't know. But Russell must have had a killing streak in him somewhere, and took things into his own hands. Who was killed?"

"A Chinese cook and two others of the same race. Your men might have done more."

"Maybe. Men might have. Yellow river rats never could put up a decent fight against opposition of the caliber you've got!" Stewart checked off a point on a small list and asked, "Any relatives of the dead?"

"The cook had an uncle in China—he must have slipped over the border, since he's not American-born. I'm shipping him back with the best funeral I can afford. The others came from Chinatown."

"I'll have the cook picked up today and see that he gets a funeral with a thousand paid mourners. The same to the others, and ten thousand cash to the relatives of each. No, I'd rather; I'm asking it as a favor, Erin."

Erin smiled thinly. "If you wish. Your rules may be queer, from my standards, but it seems you do have a code of your own. I'm glad of that, even if it's a bit rough."

Stewart twitched his mouth jerkily; that hurt, somehow. Erin had a habit of making him seem inferior. Perhaps his code was not the sporting one, but it did include two general principles: mistakes aren't rectified by alibis, and a man who has proved himself your equal deserves respect.

"I don't fight a better man, anyway, Erin," he admitted slowly. "You took all I handed out and came up fighting. So you'll have no trouble getting supplies from now on, and we'll complete this race on equal footing. How did Jack take it?"

"Like a man, Greg." In all the years of their enmity, neither had quite dropped the use of first names, and Erin's resentment was melting. "He's a fine boy. You sired well."

"Thank God for that, at least. Erin, you hold a patent on an air-conditioning machine, and I need it. The government's building submarines, and I can get a nice bunch of contracts if I can supply that and assure them of good air for as long as they want to stay under." Stewart's voice had gone businesslike. "Would ten percent royalties and a hundred thousand down buy all but space rights? It's not charity, if that worries you."

"I didn't think it was." For himself, the price mattered little, but here was a chance to pay back some of the money the others had invested with him. He made his decision instantly. "Send over your contracts, and I'll sign them."

"Good. Now, with all threats gone, how about that berth on my ship I offered you? She'll be finished in a week, with a dependable fuel, and there's room for one more."

Erin smiled broadly now at Stewart's old skepticism of his methods. "Thanks, but the *Santa Maria* is practically done, too, using a dependable power source. Why not come with me?"

It was Stewart's turn to smile. And as he cut connections, it seemed to him that even the face in the picture was smiling for the first time in almost forty years.

Erin rubbed his wounded arm tenderly and wondered what it would feel like to go ahead without a constant, lurking fear. At the moment, the change was too radical for his comprehension. Things looked too easy.

IX

The *Santa Maria* was off the skids, and the ground swell on the ocean bobbed her up and down gently, like a horse champing at the bit. Not clipper built, Erin thought, but something they could be proud of. Now that she was finished, all the past trouble seemed unreal, like some disordered nightmare.

"Jack and I are making a test run at once," he announced. "It'll be dark in a few minutes, so you can follow our jets and keep account of our success or failure. No, just the two of us, this first time. We're going up four thousand miles and coming back down."

"How many of us go on the regular trip?" Jimmy wanted to know. "Dutch says he'll stay on the ground and design them. Since Doug's turned into a married man, he'll stay with his wife, I suppose, but how about the rest?"

They nodded in unison; though there had been no decision, it had always been understood that all were to go. Doug wrapped his arm possessively around Helen and faced Erin. "I'm staying with my wife, all light," he stated, "but she's coming along. Why should men hog all the glory?"

Erin glanced at the girl hastily. This had not been in the plans. "I'm going," she said simply, and he nodded. This thing was too great for distinction of sex—or race. He motioned to Robert Wah who stood in the background, looking on wistfully, and the tall Chinese bowed deeply.

"I should be honored, sir, by the privilege." Pleasure lighted his face quickly, and he moved forward unobtrusively, adding himself to their company. That made eight, the number the ship was designed for.

Jack was already climbing into the port, and Erin turned to follow him, motioning the others back. There was no need risking additional lives on this first test, though he felt confident of this gleaming monster he had dreamed and fought for.

"Ready?" he asked, strapping himself in. Jack nodded silently, and Erin's fingers reached for the firing keys. They were trembling a little. Here under them lay the work of a lifetime. Suppose Stewart was right, after all? He shook the sudden doubt from himself, and the keys came down under his fingers.

The great ship spun around in the water, pointing straight out toward Europe. The ground swell made the first few seconds rough tiding, but she gathered speed under her heels and began skimming the crests until her motion was perfectly even. All the years Erin had spent in training, in planning, and in imagining a hundred times every emergency and its answers rose in his mind, and the metal around him became almost an extension of his body.

Now she was barely touching the water, though there was a great wake behind her that seethed and boiled. Then the wake came to an end, and she rose in the air around her, the stubby fins supporting her at the speed she was making. Erin opened up the motors, tilting the stick delicately in his hand, and she leaped through the air like a soul torn free. He watched the hull pyrometers, but the tough alloy could stand an amazing amount of atmospheric friction.

"Climb!" he announced at last, and the nose began tilting up smoothly. The rear-viewer on the instrument board showed the waves running together and the ocean seemed to drop away from them and shrink. At half power she was rising rapidly in a vertical climb.

"Look!" Jack's voice cut through the heady intoxication Erin felt, and he took his eyes from the panel. Off to the side, and at some distance, a long streak of light climbed into the sky, reached their height, and went on. Even through the insulated hull, a faint booming sound reached them. "Stewart's ship! He's beat us to the start!"

"The fool!" The cry was impulsive, and he saw the boy wince under it slightly. "There might be some small chance, though. I hope he makes it. He'll follow an orbit that takes the least amount of fuel, and we'll be cutting through with at least a quarter gravity all the way for comfort. He can't beat us."

The course of the other ship, he could see, held true and steady. Stewart knew how to pilot; holding that top-heavy mass of metal on its tail was no small job.

Jack gripped the straps that held him to his seat, but said nothing, his eyes glued on the blast that mushroomed down from the other ship, until it passed out of sight. Behind the *Santa Maria*, the pale-blue jet looked insignificant after seeing the other. Something prickled oddly at Erin's skin, and he wondered whether it was the Heaviside layer, but it passed and there was only the press of acceleration.

He opened up again as the air dropped behind, and the smooth hum of the atomics answered sweetly. Jack released himself and hitched his way toward the rear observation room, then fought the acceleration back to Erin's side. "Jets are perfect," he reported. "Not a waver, and they're holding in line perfectly. No danger to the tubes. How high?"

"Two hundred miles, and we're making about twenty-five miles a minute now. Get back to your seat, son, I'm holding her up." He tapped the keys for more power, and grunted as the pull struck them. By the time they were a few thousand miles out, most of Earth's gravity would be behind them, and they wouldn't have that added pressure to contend with. Acceleration alone was bad enough.

At the two-thousand-mile limit, Morse twisted the wheel of the control stick and began spinning her over on her tail. Steering without the leverage of atmosphere was tricky, though part of his training had taken that into account, to the best of his ability. He completed the reversal finally, and set the keys for a deceleration that would stop them at the four-thousand-mile limit.

Jack was staring out at the brilliant points made by the stars against the black of space, but he gasped as Erin cut the motors. "How far?" he asked again. "There seems to be almost no gravity."

"Earth is still pulling us, but only a quarter strength. We've reached the four-thousand mark we planned—and proved again that Gravity obeys the laws of inverse squares." The novelty of the sensation appealed to him, but the relief from the crushing weight was his real reason for cutting power. Now his heart labored from weight and excitement, and he caught his breath, waiting for it to steady before turning back.

"Ready?" he asked finally, and power came on. They were already moving slowly back, drawn by the planet's pull. "Hold tight; I'm going to test my steering." Under his hands the stick moved this way and that, and the ship struggled to answer, sliding into great slow curves that would have been sudden twists and turns in the air. All his ingenuity in schooling himself hadn't fully compensated for the difficulties, but practice soon straightened out the few kinks left.

His breath was coming in short gasps as he finished; the varying stress of gravity and acceleration had hit hard at him, and there was a dull thumping in his chest. "Take over, Jack," he ordered, holding his words steady. "Do you good to learn. Half acceleration."

But the thumping went on, seeming to grow worse. Each breath came out with an effort. Jack was intent on the controls, though there was little to do for the moment, and did not notice; for that, Erin was grateful. He really had to see a doctor; only fear of the diagnosis had made him put it off this long.

"Reversal," Jack called. He began twisting the control, relying on pure mathematics and quick reactions to do the trick. They began to come around, but Erin could feel it was wrong. The turn went too far, was inaccurately balanced, and the ship picked up a lateral spin that would give rise to other difficulties. Here was one place where youth and youth's quick reflexes were useless. It took the steady hand of calculating judgment, and the head that had imagined this so often it all seemed old.

He fought his way forward, pressing back the heart that seemed to burst through his chest. Jack was doing his best, but he was not the ship's master. He welcomed Erin's hand that reached down for the stick. Experience had corrected the few mistakes of the previous reversal, and the ship began to come around in one long, accurate blast. When it stopped, her tail was steadily blasting against Earth.

"I'll carry on." Erin knew he had to, since descent, even in an atmosphere, was far trickier than it might seem. To balance the speed so that the air-fins supported her, without tearing them off under too much pressure required no small skill. He buckled himself back in, and let her fall rapidly. Time was more important, something told him, than the ease of a slower descent. He waited till the last moment before tapping on more power, heard the motors thrum solidly, and waited for the first signs of air. The pyrometer needles rose quickly, but not to their danger point. The tingling feeling lashed through him again, and was gone, and he began maneuvering her into a spiral that would set her down in the water where she could coast to the island.

He glanced back at the boy, whose face expressed complete trust, and bit at his lips, but his main concern was for the ship. Once destroyed, that might never be duplicated. Time, he prayed, only time enough. The ocean was coming into view through thin clouds below, but it still seemed too far.

"God!" Jack's cry cut into his worries. "To the left—it's the other ship."

Erin stole a quick glance at the window, and saw a ragged streak of fire in the distance. Stewart's ship must have failed. But there was no time for that. The ocean was near, now.

He cut into a long flat glide, striving for the delicate balance of speed and angle that would set her down without a rebound, and held her there. A drag from the friction of the water told him finally that she was down. More by luck than design, his landing was near the takeoff point, and the island began poking up dimly through the darkness. He threw on the weak forward jets, guessing at the distance, and juggled the controls.

There was a red knot of pain in his chest and a mist in front of his eyes that made seeing difficult, but he let her creep in until the wood limbers of the dock stood out clearly. Then the mist turned black, and he had only time to cut all controls. He couldn't feel the light crunch as she touched the shore.

Erin was in bed in the bunkhouse when consciousness returned, and his only desire was to rest and relax. The strange man bending over him seemed about to interfere, and he shoved him away weakly. Tom Shaw bent over him, putting his hands back and holding them until he desisted.

"The ship is perfect," Tom's voice assured him, oddly soft for the foreman. "We're all proud of you, Erin, and the doctor says there's no danger now."

"Stewart?" he asked weakly.

"His ship went out a few thousand miles, and the tubes couldn't stand the concentrated heat of his jets. Worked all right on small models, but the volume of explosives was cubed with the square of the tube diameter, and it was too much. We heard his radio after he cut through the Heaviside, and he was trying to bring her down at low power without burning them out completely. We haven't heard from the rescue squad, but they hope the men are safe."

The strange man clucked disapprovingly. "Not too much talk," he warned. "Let him rest."

Erin stirred again, plucking at the covers. So he finally was seeing a doctor, whether he wanted to or not. "Is there—" he asked. "Am I—grounded?"

Shaw's hand fell over his, and the grizzled head nodded. "Sorry, Erin."

X

Erin stood in the doorway of the bunkhouse, looking out over the buildings toward the first star to come out. Venus, of course, but Mars would soon show up. He had not yet told the men that the flight was off, and they were talking contentedly behind him, discussing what they would find on Mars.

A motorboat's drone across the water caught his attention and he turned his eyes to the ocean. "There's someone coming," he announced. "At least they seem to be headed this way."

Jimmy jumped up, scattering the cards he had been playing with his father. "Darn! Must be the reporters. I notified the press that tonight was supposed to be the takeoff and forgot to tell them it was postponed when you came back from the test. Shall I send them back?"

"Bring them up. There should be room enough for them here. Have Wah serve coffee." Erin moved back toward his bunk, being careful to take it easy, and sank down. "There's something I have to tell them—and you at the same time."

Helen brought him his medicine and he took it, wondering what reception his words would have with the newspapermen. Previous experience had made him expect the worst. But these men were quiet and orderly as they filed in, taking seats around the recreation tables. Even though it had failed, Stewart's flight had taught them that rocketry was a serious business. Also, they were picked men from the syndicates, not the young cubs he had dealt with before. Wah brought in coffee and brandy.

"Your man tells us the flight has been delayed," one of them began. He showed no resentment at the long ride by rail and boat for nothing. "Can you tell us, then, when you're planning to make it, and give us some idea of the principle of flight you use?"

"Jimmy can give you mimeographed sheets of the ship's design and power system," Erin answered. "But the flight is put off indefinitely. Probably it will be months before it occurs, and possibly years. It depends on how quickly I can transfer my knowledge to a younger man."

"But we understood a successful trial had been made, with no trouble."

"No mechanical trouble, that is. But, gentlemen, no matter how perfectly built a machine may be, the human element must always be considered. In this case, it failed. I've been ordered not to leave the ground."

There were gasps from his own men, and the tray in Wah's hands spilled to the floor, unnoticed. Shaw and Jack moved about among the others, speaking in low voices.

Among the newspapermen, bewilderment substituted for consternation. "I fail to see—" the spokesman said.

Erin found it difficult to explain to laymen, but he tried an example. "When the Wright brothers made their first power flights, they had already gotten practice from gliders. But suppose one of them had been given a plane without previous experience and told to fly it across the Atlantic? This, to a much greater extent, is like that.

"Perhaps later, if rocketry becomes established, men can be given flight training in a few weeks. Until then, only those who have spent years of ground work can hope to master the more difficult problems of astronautics. This may sound like boasting to you, but an immediate flight without myself as pilot is out of the question."

Jack struck in, silencing their questioning doubts. "I tried it, up there," he told them, "and I had some experience with radio-controlled models. But mathematics and intelligence, or even a good understanding of the principles involved, aren't enough. It's like skating on frictionless ice, trying to cut a figure eight against a strong head wind. Without Erin, I wouldn't be here." They accepted the fact, and Erin went on. "Two men, to my knowledge, spent the time and effort to acquire the basic ground work—Gregory Stewart and myself. Even though he crashed, killing two of his men, he demonstrated his ability to hold a top-heavy ship on its course under the most trying conditions. To some extent, I have proved my own ability. But Stewart has no ship and I have no pilot. Mars will have to wait until one of my own men can be given adequate preparation."

The spokesman tapped his pencil against a pad of paper and considered. "But, since each of you lacks what the other has, why not let Stewart pilot your ship? Apparently he's willing to give up his interests here and try for some other planet."

"Because he doesn't consider my ship safe." Erin knew that it might prove detrimental to their acceptance of his design, but that couldn't be helped. "Stewart and I have always been rivals, less even in fact than in ideas. Now that his own ship proved faulty, he'd hardly be willing to risk one in which he has no faith."

A broad man in the background stirred uneasily, drawing his hat farther down over his face, which was buried in his collar. "Have you asked him?" he demanded in a muffled voice.

"No." It had never occurred to Erin to do so. "If you insist, I'll call him but there can be only one answer."

The heavy man stood up, throwing back his hat and collar. "You might consult me before quoting my opinion, Erin," Gregory Stewart stated. "Even a fool sometimes has doubts of his own wisdom." The eyes of those in the room riveted on him, but he swung to his son, who was staring harder than the others. "Will the *Santa Maria* get to Mars?" he asked.

Jack nodded positively. "It will get there, and back. I'm more than willing to stake my own life on that. But you—"

"Good. I'll take your word for it, Jack, with the test flight to back it up. How about it, Erin?" He swung to his rival, some of the old allowance in his voice. "Maybe I'd be glory-hogging, but I understand you're in the market for a pilot. Like to see my letters of reference?"

Strength flowed back into Erin's legs, and he came to his feet with a smile, his hand outstretched. "I think you'll prove entirely satisfactory, Greg." It had been too sudden for any of them to realize fully, but one of the photographers sensed the dramatic, and his flashbulb flared whitely. The others were not slow in following suit.

"When?" a reporter asked. "Expect to be ready in the near future?"

"Why not now? The time's about right, and my affairs are in order. Is everything ready here?" Judging from their looks that it was, Stewart took over authority with the ease of old habit. "All right, who's coming? A woman? How about you, Jack?"

Jack's voice was brisk, but the cold had thawed from it. "Count me in, Dad. I'm amateur copilot."

"Me, I think I go too," Dutch Bauer decided. "Maybe then I can build better when I come back."

Erin counted them, and rechecked. "But that's nine," he demurred. "The ship is designed for eight."

Tom Shaw corrected him. "It's only eight, Erin. I've decided to let Jimmy carry on the family tradition. Shall we stay here and watch them take off?"

There was a mad rush for the few personal belongings that were to go, and a chorus of hasty good-byes. Then they were gone, the reporters with them, and the two men stood quietly studying each other. Erin smiled at his foreman, an unexpected mist in his eyes. "Thanks, Tom. You needn't have done that."

"One in the family's enough. Besides, Dutch wanted to go." His voice was gruff as he steadied Erin to the door and stood looking out at the mob around the spaceship. The reporters were busy, getting last words, taking pictures, and the Chinese laborers were clustered around Wah, saying their own adieus. Then Greg's heavy roar came up, and they tumbled back away from the ship, while the men who were to go filed in. The great port closed slowly and the first faint trial jets blasted out.

Confidence seemed to flow into the tubes, and they whistled and bellowed happily, twisting the ship and sending her out over the water in a moonsilvered path. Erin saw for the first time the fierce power that lay in her as she dropped all normal bounds and went forward in a headlong rush. Stewart was lifting her rather soon, but she took it and was off.

They followed the faint streak she made in the air until it was invisible, and a hum from the speaker sent Shaw to the radio. Greg's voice came through. "Sweet ship, Erin, if you hear me. I'll send you a copy of *Gunga Dhin* from Mars. Be seeing you."

Erin stayed in the doorway, watching the stars that looked down from the point where the *Santa Maria* had vanished. "Tom," he said at last, "I wish you'd take my Bible and turn to the last chapter of Deuteronomy. You'll know what I mean."

A minute later Shaw's precise reading voice reached him. " 'And the Lord said unto Moses, This is the land which I sware unto Abraham, unto Isaac, and unto Jacob, saying, I will give it unto thy seed: I have caused thee to see it with thine eyes, but thou shalt not go hither.' "

"At least I have seen it, Tom; the stars look different up there." Erin took one final look and turned back into the room. "Until the reporters come back here, how about a game of rummy?"

The Still Waters
[a.k.a. In the Still Waters]

Zeke watched the red light on the panel fade, then listened to the chatter of the relays as the ship searched its way back to its course. The pip on the screen had disappeared into the background of snow that the anti-noise circuits could no longer blank, even this far from the sun. He dropped his eyes to his hands that lay on the board, staring bitterly at the knuckles that were swollen with arthritis and covered with coarse hairs that had begun to turn gray.

Behind him, he heard Mary sigh softly. "Those blamed blowtorches," she said, but her voice was as tired as he felt, and the old anger at the smaller, direct drive ships was almost automatic. "He might look where he's going."

"He looked," Zeke told her. "There wasn't any danger, Mary."

She smiled at him, as if to indicate there could be none with him at the controls. But he could feel no lift in response. There really had been no danger. The blowtorch must have spotted the huge bulk of the *Midas* well in advance; its newer radar couldn't have missed.

He stared at his hands again. He'd known there was no need for an emergency blast and had been reaching for the controls when the automatics went on. But, like the screen, age had let too much noise creep into the messages along his nerves. His fingers had reacted too late, and had fumbled. Just as the *Midas* had fumbled in overblasting needlessly.

An old man, he thought, in an old ship. But lately it seemed that he was growing old faster than even the ship. Once, he'd liked it best when they were furthest from the planets. Now he'd found the trip in from Tethys almost too long and wearying. He was actually looking forward to berthing at Callisto where there could be no alarms to wake him from what fitful sleep he could get.

He heard the control room door close softly and knew without thinking that Mary had gone to make tea for them. Their habits were as automatic as those of the ship, he thought. But he reached for his pipe and began filling it, unconsciously muttering the words that had become a symbol of their needs: "A good smoke and a pot of tea never hurt anyone."

If their boy had lived, things might have been different. Zeke sighed, and got up, heading back for his regular tour of inspection before tea. He passed the three other empty seats in the control room. Bates had died on Venus, Levitchoffsky had sold out to join a blowtorch company, and Ngambu had gasped out his life from a sudden stroke only three years before, leaving the *Midas* entirely to Zeke. Somehow, it had been harder and harder to get younger men to replace the missing ones. Now he was resigned to doing everything himself.

He'd had years enough in which to learn since he'd first been taken into the group as head engineer.

He went back through the empty crew quarters, past the equally empty passenger rooms, and through the holds with their small load of freight, until he came to the great engine that drove the *Midas*. There, for the first time that day, he relaxed. Elsewhere, the brightwork had long since dulled, but the huge fusion converter was the one thing he never neglected. It purred on smoothly, turning a trickle of the hydrogen in ordinary water into huge floods of power, and it gleamed under his approving glance. They weren't building engines like that any more—not since the blowtorches had taken over. A complete blowtorch weighed less than the seven thousand tons of power equipment the *Midas* carried. It had been constructed when space ships were so tremendously expensive that their engines were designed to last almost forever. The ship could fall to pieces around it, or he could be forgotten for generations before it began to fail.

Then the satisfaction passed. Even the engine had one weakness—it needed someone to feed it and to give it the minimum care. Once he was gone, the engine would die with him. With the blowtorches controlling the space lanes, nobody would be interested in an old ship, no matter how well the engine could convert hydrogen to power for the great ion blasters to hurl out in driving force.

Reluctantly, Zeke turned from the engine room and on back toward the complexities of the driving tubes. He moved slowly now, putting it off as long as he could. The blast that had been wasted in trying to avoid the blowtorch had been too strong; somewhere, some part of the controls had misfunctioned. Now...

It could have been worse. The drivers were still functioning, at least. But the imbalance that had been creeping up was worse. The strain of the needless correction had crippled them more than a year of normal use could have done.

Zeke moved about, avoiding enormous bus bars and giant electronic parts in the huge but crowded section out of old habit. He could make up for the damage to some extent, by inhibiting the less worn sections. But it was only a temporary expedient. The *Midas* was long since overdue for drydocking and repairs. It could no longer be delayed.

Mary had the tea ready when he finally went back to their cabin. She started to pour his, then stopped as she saw his face. "Bad?" she asked.

He nodded. He'd never been one to talk much, and with Mary it hadn't been necessary. "Shot!" he told her. "How much is left?"

She pulled the bankbook out and handed it to him. He added the figure to the freight he'd collect for at Callisto. There was some insurance he could borrow against. But he knew it wasn't enough.

"Maybe Mr. Williams will give us an advance against next year's contract," Mary suggested. "You've never asked before." She stared at him, the worry in her voice less for the ship than for him. "Zeke, why don't you lie down for an hour? It'll do more good than the tea."

He shook his head, picking up his cup. "Can't," he answered. "Too much figuring to do."

The *Midas* would need babying for its landing, with the drivers so badly out of condition, which would mean finding just the right landing orbit. And while he needed pampering too because of his own condition, that would have to wait.

There'd be time for that, maybe, after he talked to Williams.

It had been five years since Zeke had dropped into Callisto to discuss the last contract renewal with Williams, head of the Saturanus Mineral Corporation. Now, after resting from the long, cautious landing, he found Zeus City changed, without being able to say what the change was at first. Then it began to register; the city was the same, but for the first time, he walked down Main without meeting a single man who recognized him. And there was a new look to the faces—the old, wild expression of the spaceman had given place to a businesslike air he hadn't seen beyond Mars before.

At Saturanus, there were more changes. The receptionist was a young chit of a girl who kept him waiting for nearly half an hour before sending him into the President's office. And then it wasn't Burt Williams who greeted him. The man was a complete stranger!

"Mr. Williams died three years ago, Captain Vaughn," he said. He hesitated a second, then stood up and held out his hand. "I'm Julian Hathaway, used to be treasurer here, if you remember."

Zeke had a dim memory of a younger man, and he nodded. Hathaway wasn't exactly fat, but he'd added a solidity usually called respectable. Now he seemed vaguely uncomfortable.

"I suppose you came to collect what is still due on your contract, Captain Vaughn?" he asked.

Zeke nodded slowly. "And to discuss renewal," he said. He was still adjusting to the change. He'd never been close enough to Williams to be hit by the man's death, but all his figuring had been done in terms of the former president. He had no idea of how to broach an advance. Williams had always made it easy to talk to him, but…

Hathaway fidgeted uncomfortably, biting at the end of a cigar. Then he reached into a drawer of his desk and drew out what was obviously the former contract. He compared it with a sheet in front of him. Finally he shrugged and cleared his throat. "According to my figures, you have eighty-four hundred dollars and thirty-one cents due you, plus three hundred dollars retainer to the end of this month. I've already had a check made out. And there's a separate check for five hundred, since Mr. Williams had you listed on the employee roll. That means you're entitled to that as automatic termination pay after fifteen years. Here."

He passed over an envelope. Zeke fingered it open, staring at the checks. Then his eyes snapped back to Hathaway. "Termination? But—"

Hathaway looked more uncomfortable, but he nodded. "Unfortunately, we can't renew the contract, Captain Vaughn."

"But Williams told me—"

"I know. And I'm sure he meant to keep you under contract as long as you were in business. I don't know whether he ever told you, but he served for a year on one of the old ion-drive passenger liners, and he was quite sentimental about all ion-drive ships. He had contracts with five, in fact, at one time—though the other four have all been retired. But he had a constant fight with the stockholders over it. As a new president of the company, Captain Vaughn, I don't have the authority that he had."

"I don't get it," Zeke said. The man was practically telling him he'd been a charity case. And that made no sense. "I charged less than the blowtorches! And freight rates went up last year, too."

Hathaway looked like a man caught beating a dog. His voice was unhappy, but there was no uncertainty in it. "That's part of the reason. When the rates went up, Hermes Freight offered us a contract at the old rate, in return for exclusive rights. And since that represents an annual saving of several million dollars to us, we couldn't turn it down. I'm sorry, Captain Vaughn, but it was out of my hands."

"Yeah." Zeke stood up slowly, putting the envelope with the checks into his pocket. He held out his hand, trying to smile normally. "Thanks, Mr. Hathaway. I'll get the *Midas* off the Saturanus section of the docks as soon as I can."

"No need to do that. Until the end of the month, your ship's technically entitled to berth there, and I'll see there's no trouble. Good luck, sir." He shook Zeke's hand almost gratefully, and saw the older man out through the office and to the entrance. He was still watching as Zeke turned a corner two blocks away.

He deposited the checks and checked his balance, hoping that Mary's records had been wrong. But he knew better, without the words of the young teller. Then he headed back to the rocket field, avoiding the hotel where he and Mary were staying.

The *Midas* loomed up huge among the smaller blowtorches there. They had never succeeded in building a blowtorch drive larger than the original, and the problem of phasing more than one such drive had kept them from multiple drive. Originally, the small ships had contained less than half the cargo space of the *Midas*, though they'd stepped up the efficiency until it was now about the same.

When the direct conversion of a tiny, intermittent fusion blast to propulsive drive had been invented, the spacemen had laughed at the ships designed for it. They had seemed little more than toys. And the inability to increase their power beyond certain limits had already been recognized. Obviously, with a few more improvements in the reliable, proven ion-drive and fusion motors, the tiny blowtorches would never have a chance.

Spacemen, Zeke now knew, had been right in everything but their knowledge of economics. The big power generating motors and the ion-drive could have been improved, and ships far better than the maximum for the blowtorches could have been built. But they never were. A ship like the *Midas* had cost over twenty million dollars to build. The huge motor alone had cost sixty percent of that. And for the same money, forty of the direct-drive ships could be completed.

In every way except one, the ion-drive was more efficient. But that one way was the determinant. It wasn't economically efficient to tie up twenty million dollars and its interest when two blowtorches would yield the same return for a single million! The ship companies stopped contracting for ion-blast ships, and the progress that could have been made still remained only a possibility.

For a while, during the brief trouble between Mars and Earth, when it seemed interplanetary war might occur, Earth had suddenly grown interested in the big ships again. The government had bought them up, planning to arm them. Then the scare had blown over, and they were dumped onto the surplus market, since no freight company was still equipped to use them. Bates and Levitchoffsky had scraped up the price of one, taking Zeke in as engineer and Ngambu as pilot with equal shares for their skills. A lot of spacemen had done the same.

But that had been forty years ago, and now apparently the *Midas* was the last of the old ships. Zeke had seen some of the others, scrapped on the outer planets, or blown up because the old engineers died or quit; they weren't training men now to service the big motors properly.

He reached the ship finally and climbed up the ramp. Forty years! He wondered how often he'd climbed it, and then tried to remember how it had felt when he was young enough so that he didn't wheeze asthmatically before the last step, even on the light planets.

Callisto had been an outpost then, the point beyond which the big companies and the blowtorches didn't go. Zeke and men like him had built the outplanet colonies; when the blowtorches quit, ships like the *Midas* had been the lifeline for all beyond Jupiter. Even now, there was a copy of a picture of the *Midas* on the planet seal of Neptune. And kids had wanted to grow up to handle such ships. They hadn't been able to land without a bunch of kids—and grown-up kids, too—streaming out to admire them, and to ask to go inside, to gasp in awe at the engines.

Now to greet him there was only the estimator from the repair company Zeke had consulted on landing. He was standing doubtfully in the main lock, and he swung quickly as Zeke came in.

"Oh, hi, Captain Vaughn. I was just coming to look you up. How soon would you want her rebuilt?"

Zeke frowned. It was a foolish question, but it apparently wasn't meant for a joke. "As soon as possible, naturally. But—well, how much—"

"Impossible!" Now the estimator seemed to think Zeke was being foolish. He grinned doubtfully. "We don't keep stuff here to fabricate all this. In fact, you're lucky we've got a man who can handle the job. No other company this side of Earth would touch it. We'll have to send to Mars for scrap parts for some of it, and maybe get other parts specially tooled at Detroit. Look, you sure you want her drydocked?"

"How much?" Zeke asked again.

The man shrugged. "I haven't the foggiest notion. It'd take three months to get estimates on the parts. In round numbers, maybe a million dollars for parts, plus shipping and labor, if you want a complete overhaul. A quarter of that just to work on what you've got wrong with the drivers, if we disregard minor defects. Your engine looks sound. And you might get by a few more years on the controls. You sick?"

Zeke shook his hand off. He'd been foolish to think it could be done for what he had. With a bitter grin at himself, he took out his bank book and passed it over.

The estimator whistled.

"That's it," Zeke told him.

"Umm." The other stared at the older man, and then shrugged. "All right, I'll level with you, Captain Vaughn. I was padding it—I like a fat commission as well as the next. But I wasn't padding it that much. Not by a tenth!" He pulled at one ear lobe, staring about at the ship. Then he shrugged.

"Maybe there's something we can do, though," he suggested at last. "We've got a few old parts, and we can jury-rig a little more. For twenty-five thousand, we can retune those drivers enough for you to pass take-off inspection here. Hell, since I'm one of the inspectors, I'll guarantee that. Take us maybe two weeks. Then you can take the ship across to Venus. They're short of metal and paying top scrap prices. You could probably get enough for this outfit to pick up a fairly good used blowtorch, or to retire on. They jury-rigged a couple of scrapped ion blasters on Earth and crawled across with them recently, so there must be a good price there. How's it sound?"

Zeke brought a trembling hand up to a big wrench on the wall. "Get off!" His voice was thick in his ears. "Get off my ship, damn you!"

"What the heck gives?" The inspector took a backward step, more as if humoring Zeke than in fear. "Look, I'm trying to help you. You crazy, Captain?"

The brief anger ebbed back into the general dullness, and Zeke let his arm drop limply. He nodded. "I don't know. Maybe I am. I must be, landing on Callisto without finding out ahead of time they had take-off inspection now. All right, fix her up."

There was nothing else he could do, of course. It would leave him enough to buy supplies, at least. And fuel was no problem—he'd learned places to find frozen water years before, and the fuel tanks were nearly full.

But with the contract with Saturanus ended, getting freight enough to keep going was going to be tough. If the *Midas* had been in top condition, he could probably get a fat contract for the new mines on Pluto, since it was hard to get blowtorch pilots who would stick to the long haul so far from any recreation. But the mines wouldn't risk their ultra-precious ores without a full inspection of the ship. They'd turned him down five years ago. Now it was out of the question.

He headed back toward his hotel, trying to figure out what to tell Mary. She'd know he was lying, of course, but she'd feel better, somehow. Then he'd have to go looking for work. There had to be something.

"The Lord is my shepherd, I shall not want," he quoted to himself, trying to believe it. Then he stopped. His mind found it too easy to twist what came next. Green pastures and still waters! He might be old, but he wasn't ready to be turned out to pasture; nor was the ship going to be becalmed in still waters, out of the current, to rot and decay uselessly!

The ship behaved slightly better on the take-off from Callisto. He'd been nervous about that, after watching the fumbling, sloppy work of the men. And Mary had her own worries probably inspired by her contempt of anyone who would foul up the passageways without cleaning them. It had taken her hours, while he inspected the work, to restore the *Midas* in livable condition. But once beyond the planetary limits, they both breathed easier.

"I'll fix the tea, Zeke," she said. Then she smiled faintly, "He was such a nice young man."

Zeke knew she was thinking of Hathaway, and nodded. He had to admit she was right. Hathaway couldn't get the contract renewed, but he'd done all he could, as it turned out. He'd come to their hotel to tell them he'd got them a small job for another minerals company, carrying an emergency inspector to Ceres. The payment had been ridiculously low, but it was something, at least; and Hathaway had suggested there might be work for them on Ceres for a few trips. With the last of their money gone, they'd needed it.

It had been their only chance, after Zeke had tried every office in Zeus City. There had been no other work for a wornout ion blaster.

Hathaway had been almost a different man, as if a big load had been lifted from his conscience. He'd been as nice as Mary thought. Too nice, Zeke reflected bitterly. They were carrying a passenger now and making enough to pay for the trip, but he knew it was only Hathaway's charity. He'd won the job only because the younger man had put on pressure to help him, not on his own merits. He wasn't used to that. Then he remembered that Williams had given him fifteen years of contracts, and that it had been almost charity on Williams' part!

He picked up his pipe and began filling it as he went on his routine tour of inspection. The door to the passenger cabin was closed, and he felt almost grateful, uncertain about how much the young engineer knew of the situation. He made his way back to the driver compartment, groaning again as he saw the shoddy workmanship that had been done. They hadn't even bothered removing the rust from salvaged parts. And he remembered that there had been no guarantee, beyond passing take-off inspection. Maybe the work would hold up for another year—beyond that, it would probably fail with complete finality. From ten feet away, he could detect heat still leaking from damaged insulation.

But there was nothing he could do. He'd been one of the best spaceship power engineers turned out in his day. He could control the big generator almost to perfection, and could have taught its operation at any school, or to any younger man who might have been willing to learn. But drivers were too complicated for one man to balance, and he had no repair parts.

He shrugged, and turned back toward the huge engine, where the smooth flow of unceasing power would soothe some of his worries. He was surprised to find Grundy, the engineer-passenger there, studying the bulk of the motor. The blond young man looked almost embarrassed at being caught snooping.

"I had to take a look at her," he explained hastily. "I've never seen a fusion motor before. I meant to, while I was still on Earth, but it was always too much trouble getting into the sections where they are."

Zeke nodded. He'd heard that the projected fission motors for general use hadn't been built, since the solar-energy converters had been developed to near perfection. There were plenty of the fusion generators in existence, but they were confined to places where sunlight was unreliable. When a layer of solar-batteries could be sprayed on cheap cloth like paint, capable of extracting nearly a hundred percent of the energy of sunlight and when the new capacity storage cells could handle several days' accumulation of power, why should men bother with gigantic machinery? Of course, on the planets beyond Mars, sunlight was too weak. But there, the expense of freighting had made all but the biggest installations choose the much simpler and smaller uranium-fission power units; it was cheaper to pay for uranium than to pay interest on a fission motor.

"Glad to show her to you," he told Grundy.

The engineer shook his head. "No, thanks. I just wanted to take a look. I already know the general theory. Too bad these things couldn't be built smaller and cheaper. With uranium getting scarcer and more expensive, it's making it tough on some of the settlements."

"You a power engineer?" Zeke asked.

"No, mining," the younger man answered. He gestured to the ship in general around him. "This *Midas*—wasn't that the same ship Levitchoffsky was on when they found the uranium lode on that asteroid—the one where he got his start in building up Solar Freighting?"

Zeke nodded. It wasn't exactly the truth, but it was close enough. Levitchoffsky had bought the claim from a passenger to Saturn who'd given up trying to live off it. Then when he and the others on the *Midas* had stopped there to see what he had, they'd accidentally taken samples at just the right place. Levitchoffsky had promptly sold it to a speculating firm. It had been two years later, after he'd lost his profits in other worthless claims before he sold his interest in the *Midas* and joined Solar Freighting.

The engineer stood around a few minutes longer, and then wandered back to his own cabin, more impressed with the fact that Zeke had known Levitchoffsky than with the *Midas*. Zeke started to follow him, and then stopped. Levitchoffsky! Zeke hadn't been in touch with him for years, but the other would still remember him. He might be president of Solar Freighting and respectable now. But he wouldn't have forgotten. If he knew that Zeke was in trouble, he'd do anything he could to help.

Zeke dropped onto the base of the huge motor, caressing it softly as he thought it over. There were still scrapped ion blasters on Earth, and men trained to work with almost anything of a technical nature. They could fix up the *Midas*—probably for a fraction of what it would cost on Callisto. Then, with a ship like new, there was almost certain work at good rates on the Pluto run. If Levitchoffsky would lend him the money, he could probably pay it back in five years—even paying some younger man a salary high enough to entice him to help.

It wasn't a thing he liked. It was trading on old friendship. But if he had to have help, he'd rather have it from Levitchoffsky than anyone. And it wouldn't really be charity. He was good for at least ten more years, with a repaired ship and some kind of help.

He was still considering this when the alarm sounded harshly. One look at the auxiliary control panel in the engine room sent him running painfully back toward the driver section.

But it was all over before he reached it. The insulation on the main steering driver section had finally blown. It must have been over within microseconds as the searing ions blasted out and then the lagging cut-off had deactivated that section. But the damage was beyond any hope of repair!

It was the section supposedly repaired on Callisto. Zeke couldn't tell whether it had blown because of defective work or because the greater relative strength of the newer parts had put too much strain on old sections. It didn't matter. Now he had only the emergency steering power left.

That was good for perhaps a couple of landings and take-offs, if he nursed it. After that, the *Midas* was through.

There was no longer any doubt. Once he reached Ceres, he'd have to cable Levitchoffsky. And now that it was settled beyond a doubt, he began to wonder. Thirty years is a long time. The young man he'd known would have done anything for him; but he'd seen others change with prosperity and time. He suddenly wondered whether Levitchoffsky would even accept the collect cable.

Zeke was lucky that the little planetoid had so low a gravity. He was able to conserve on his use of the auxiliaries, without too rough a landing. He sat recovering from it and watching the engineer go hastily down the ramp; the young man must have been angry at the jolting, from the way he walked. But if he'd known it, he was lucky to be in one piece.

The field looked bleak. Ceres had been a regular stopping place for the *Midas* once, but that was long ago. He had remembered it as a beehive of activity, bustling with the business of its great germanium mines. Now the field seemed deserted, and the great warehouses were dark in the faint light of the sun.

And it seemed even gloomier when Zeke stepped out of the *Midas* and headed toward the cable office. As he passed nearer the line of warehouses, he saw some activity, but nothing like what it had been. Behind them, the processing mills were busy, with the little trucks hard at work. But there was none of the gaiety he had associated with busy miners. And a glance at the loads they were carrying told the answer.

Low-grade ore! Even the fabulous mines here were wearing out. He'd heard a rumor that they'd suddenly come to the end of the rich stuff, but he'd hardly believed it. Now he saw it was true. Ceres probably had enough low-grade to last for generations, but she'd been built on nearly pure ore, and this must be a starvation diet for her.

It seemed even worse than it should, however. Few lights were on, and he saw men in one of the stores wearing heavy clothes, as if they were conserving on heat. If there were a smiling face among the fifty thousand inhabitants of the world, Zeke couldn't find it.

Even the air in the plastic bubble that covered the town seemed old and weary. Zeke shivered, realizing it was cold. But it was more than the coldness that increased the ache of his joints. Age had crept up on him and the *Midas*; now it seemed to be pressing down on even the worlds he had known, as if the whole universe was running down into the stagnation of senility.

Age should be a period of peace and contentment—the still waters the Psalm mentioned, where everything was calm and serene. But here, as on board the *Midas*, the stillness was stagnation and decay, like a pool left behind the flood, when the current has ceased.

His steps lagged as he neared the cable office, partly from the general gloom around and partly from something else. Damn it, it wasn't really charity he was asking of Levitchoffsky. He repeated it to himself, but he couldn't quite believe it.

Here and there he recognized a store, but he felt no desire to enter them. Even if the same men owned them, they would have changed too much since he'd known them, as Levitchoffsky might have changed.

Then a sudden call swung him slowly around.

"Zeke!" The man was grey and bearded. At first Zeke didn't recognize him. Then his memory turned up the face in younger form—doubtfully. Yet from the use of the first name, it must be Aaron Cowslick, who'd been Ceres' chief blacksheep and general hellraiser. They'd been on binges enough once, before Zeke had married and quieted down.

"Zeke!" The man caught his hand, and now he recognized the scar over one eye, and knew for sure it was Aaron. "I wondered, when the *Midas* dropped, whether you'd still be on her. Then Mary said you'd headed this way. I thought you'd died long ago. We missed you around here. How's tricks?"

Zeke tried to shake off his gloom, cursing himself for not thinking to look Aaron up before the man searched him out. "Well enough," he lied, feeling sure the other knew better. "How come you're not in jail?"

"Because I run the jail, Zeke. I'm mayor here!" At Zeke's expression, his grin widened. "Nothing stronger than coffee now, and the doc tells me to cut down on that. Speaking of which…"

He grabbed one of Zeke's arms and began leading him toward a little restaurant. Zeke felt almost grateful for the stop. And when the coffee arrived, it helped to cut through some of the cold. He sat sipping it, while Aaron ran through all the proper questions. He tried to answer them casually, but the truth must have been obvious. The mayor sighed, and pointed outside.

"It was a great time, when the *Midas* was still full of ginger and this town was booming." He stared out, his face losing all its expression. "Don't lie to me, Zeke, and I won't try to fool you. It's bad. Unless young Grundy sends back the right message to his company, we're in trouble."

"The mines?" Zeke asked.

"The mines. One of our men thinks he's found what may be a formation that would lead to a rich lode. I wish I believed it. We've about reached the end of the rope. We can't cut down on power much more, and uranium is going higher and higher. That last discovery on Neptune turned out to be a bust—just a freak pocket. Now they've raised the ante on U-235. We can't afford enough to keep going. And without sufficient power on a world like this, we can't do anything Food, water, air—it's all U-235 to us. Besides, the processing plants need more power for low-grade stuff than for the high-quality ore. Even if we could afford the uranium, we'd still have to run our power plant too hot, and it wouldn't last forever. Looks like you might have some business if you're cheap enough."

"Resettlement?" Zeke asked.

The other nodded soberly. "Exactly. Vesta Metals says we can be split up among the Trojans—they've got booming mines there. If we can pay passage for ourselves and what we have to take, they've offered work and housing. We may have to take it, too."

"I can't take you," Zeke told him. He sucked at the last bit of coffee, then put the cup down heavily. "Steering drivers are shot, Aaron. Even your young Grundy is going to have to get back to Callisto on the first blowtorch that comes along. Until I get repairs, I can't risk carrying passengers or freight."

The mayor seemed almost relieved, though his voice was sympathetic. It must be hell to face breaking up a world and migrating in pieces. "I guessed it might be like that when I saw Mary," he said. "Well, it'll all work out somehow. We'll have to get together for dinner at my place. My wife's a swell cook."

"Bring her out to the *Midas* for a return engagement and let Mary show you she can still cook, then," Zeke suggested. "We've still got some Martian turkey in the freezer. Bring the whole family, if you've got kids."

Aaron grinned. "One—a girl. Teaches school here. Which reminds me, when she heard there was an ion blaster landing here, she got all set to descend on you with her class. She's never had a chance to show them a ship like that. Okay?"

"Sure," Zeke said automatically. "What time does the cable office close, Aaron?"

It turned out he had just time enough. He shook hands with the mayor again, almost relieved to drop back into his own thoughts. Normally, a chance to relive the old days would have been a gift from the blue, but right now he didn't want to be reminded of all the years that had passed.

Inside the cable office, a girl took his cable slip and frowned when she saw the check in the collect square. She glanced over it, came to his signature, and stopped to look up quickly. "Captain Vaughn?" He nodded.

"There's a message here for you. It came two days ago and we've been holding it. From Mr. Levitchoffsky! Maybe you'd better read it first."

Zeke stared at the envelope in blank amazement for a second, before the answer came. Mary, of course! She must have sent a cable to Levitchoffsky as soon as she knew the contract was ended—probably warning the man not to let Zeke know she'd cabled. She'd known them all, of course, and thought of him long before Zeke had.

He ripped it open with trembling fingers. It was a long cable, obviously sent with no regard to cost. Zeke skimmed over the cover-up for Mary on how Levitchoffsky had been trying to get in touch with him and had finally heard of his landing and trouble on Callisto. It was enough to know that the man was obviously filled with the same friendship he'd had so long ago, and that the words carried a genuine delight at being in touch again. Then he came to the important part.

"I'd like nothing better," the message went on, "than to put the old *Midas* back in shape. What a ship she was! But aside from getting a pig-headed man like you to let me do it, there seems to be no way. The only place where the necessary shops and skilled work can be found is right here on Earth. And since one of those taped-together scrap jobs broke up on the way to Venus, inspection here won't let another ion blaster land. I've tried getting them to wink at the law, but it's no dice.

"Anyhow, I'm sending my private blowtorch to Ceres on the double. Get back here where the money grows on the trees, Zeke. I've got a top job wide open beside me—needed a good engineer I could trust for years and couldn't find one. It's all yours, and I can't wait to see you and Mary again."

Zeke dropped the cable onto the desk and stood gazing at it without seeing it. The girl waited inquiringly.

"Will there be any answer?" she asked. "It's to go collect, unlimited."

He shook his head and started for the door. Then he changed his mind. He had to answer, of course.

But it was hard work inventing the words to explain about the repairs being good enough for him to get the job on Pluto. Lying wasn't easy for him. And nothing could have stopped Levitchoffsky, obviously, if he'd known the truth.

Later he sat in the control room with Mary while she read and reread the message and his copy of the answer. At last, she put it down.

"It's good, Zeke," she assured him. "I think he'll believe it."

He ran his hands over the controls, cutting on the panel lights that seemed too dim, as if the bulbs were about to fail. Under them, the hair on the back of his hands seemed more grizzled than ever as he filled his pipe.

"Maybe he did need an engineer," he said at last.

"Maybe," she agreed. Then she reached a hand out for his. "It was a good cable you sent him, Zeke."

From below, there was the sound of Grundy getting his things. He'd been mad when Zeke had told him he couldn't carry him back, until Zeke had shown him the ruined drivers. Then he'd turned white and shut up. His steps started for the ladder to the control room, then hesitated.

Zeke went to the door. "Sorry, Mr. Grundy. Maybe you won't have to wait long. I hear there's a blowtorch coming here in a couple days. How were the mines?"

He'd meant to ask that before, but had forgotten.

Grundy grunted in disgust. "Rotten. The lode's completely shot. Not a thing there my company can make any advances against. Why?"

"Curious," Zeke answered. "Well, so long."

He shut the door and watched Grundy carrying his suitcase across the field, noticing that the pickup on the rear telescreen was growing weak. But that wouldn't matter now.

Forty years, he thought again. Forty years while he and the old *Midas* earned their way and helped to keep men moving out to new frontiers. Now they had grown old together, and some of those frontiers were old and ready to be abandoned.

"There's still Venus," he said slowly. "I guess we could retire on what she'd bring for scrap. And it wouldn't be charity."

Mary nodded, but said nothing. Then she shook her head, and he sighed in sudden relief.

Above them, the sky was the black of space, with the hot pinpoints of stars burning through it. Zeke had read stories long before about ships that would someday cross the immense distance to those stars. But so far, nobody had found a drive that would make it possible during the span of one lifetime.

He'd even imagined that he might be on such a ship, when he was young and foolish. And now, maybe, he was old and foolish. Maybe a man began to get crazy notions when he was old. But what was crazy about it? There was nothing else. "Mary," he told her quietly, not knowing how to discuss it, "you married a fool, I guess."

She followed his gaze upwards, and made a funny, choking sound in her throat. Then, surprisingly, he saw her smile. "As long as a couple of fools stick together, Zeke, I guess it doesn't much matter, does it?"

And somehow, it was settled. Zeke reached for the big power switch and cut it on. From below there was the instant soft murmur of the great engine, eager as always to go, unmindful of the weakness of the failing, aged drivers. He stretched out his hands toward the controls, and then stopped. Below, on the field, the failing screen showed a group of people coming up under the big ship and heading for the ramp that he hadn't yet lifted. He couldn't take off with them in the path of the blast.

His legs trembled slightly as he stood up, but he reached the lock before they were up the ramp. In the light he cut on, he saw a young, rather pretty woman with a group of perhaps thirty boys and girls from eight to twelve following her. And behind them all came Mayor Aaron Cowslick.

The Mayor heaved his way up, puffing a little. "Meet my daughter Ruth," he introduced them. "You heard about the mines, Zeke?"

Zeke nodded. "I heard. Rotten luck, Aaron."

"Yeah. Toughest on the kids. Word leaked out, and they heard about it this afternoon. It's always tough on kids who've grown up on one world to find they've got to get out. Ruth thought they might be cheered up if she could promise them you'd let them go through a genuine ion blaster. They've been excited as hell all the way here."

"Bring them in," Zeke told him. It had been a long time since he'd been a kid, aching for a chance to get into a real ship. But he could remember some of it. In their case though, he supposed it was like going into the pages of a historical novel—like a chance to investigate a real pirate ship. "Mary's up topside, if you'd like to join us. And don't worry—they won't hurt anything."

"I'll show them around—I've read up on these ships," Ruth told her father and Zeke. "Dad, you don't have to come."

Aaron breathed an obvious sigh of relief and followed. But from below, there came the sound of yells of excitement that couldn't be stilled. Zeke had a picture of the young woman filling their heads with nonsense and misunderstanding. How could she answer their questions from books?

At last he stood up and went down again, leaving Aaron with Mary. Once, other kids had swarmed around the ship, when everything except the children was younger. If this had to be the last time, the old *Midas* was going to be handled justly!

And it had to be the last time. He'd been working it out as the minutes slipped by. They could risk one more landing and take-off, out on the wastes of Pluto. There was ice there that could be used to fill the fuel tanks and the cargo holds—enough to power the *Midas* for two years of steady drive, or a year with power left to operate her equipment indefinitely.

And on board was food enough for a long time, if they used the products of the air-replenishing hydroponics tanks to supplement it. Enough to keep two old people until death found them naturally.

It wouldn't be suicide, after all. They'd go further out than my man before, and after they died, the *Midas* would coast on forever, or until she reached some system out there that could trap her. She'd go on and on, and there was no known limit to the frontiers she could reach. Her steering drivers were shot, but the main drivers were all she'd need to build up an unthinkable speed.

There would be no still waters. Instead, there'd be what Tennyson had called "such a tide as moving seems asleep, too deep for sound and foam…"

He had almost reached the great engine compartment then, but he stopped to collect himself, wondering what nonsense Ruth would be telling the children.

Then he blinked in surprise. Amazingly, she'd gotten her facts pretty much correct. She was trying to answer anything they asked, and doing a good job of it.

He stood listening, nodding with approval. Some of that didn't come from books—it was almost his own words, as Aaron must have repeated them to her.

"As much power as a uranium plant?" one of her pupils interrupted her.

"More," she told the boy. "More than two plants like the one we have. And a lot bigger, as you can see. Why, one of the ships the spacemen call blowtorches couldn't even lift a power plant like this. It has to be powerful, just to lift its own weight."

"Boy!" It was a piping masculine voice, filled with awe. Zeke could see the boy, staring up at the huge motor, touching it with an almost reverent finger. "Boy, I wish they still used this kind of ship. Then I'd be an engineer. I'd sure like that!"

Zeke watched him touch the motor again, and the great power plant seemed to purr under his fingers, as Zeke had fancied it purred in response to his own ministrations.

He turned softly toward the control cabin, no longer worried about what Ruth would tell them.

Aaron and Mary were still sitting in the semi-darkness, but they turned as he came in. He walked to the control board and cut off the panel lamps, turning on the main dome light. He didn't need darkness now as he swung to face them.

"Aaron," he asked quietly, "if I landed this ship wherever you figure is handy, do you reckon your engineers could help me hook your power lines to that big engine I've got going to waste? And do you think maybe you could use a good engineer to teach some of your youngsters how to handle fusion engines?"

It was the only answer, of course. He had a motor that would work for a thousand years at least, at almost no cost for fuel; and Ceres had everything except the power such a motor could give. It was economically inefficient, of course, to consider using such motors today. But sometimes, age was more important than economics, whether on worlds, or motors, or men.

He saw surprise give place to slow understanding. Mary beamed at him through the tears that were suddenly coursing down her cheeks, and Aaron came to his feet with hope and life brightening his face.

The mayor choked, and his hand was reaching for Zeke's "We'll always be able to find a use for good men, Zeke," he said.

They would be still waters, after all—settling into one place, on a quiet little world old enough to have lost its roughness. But not all waters had to be stagnant, once the current had passed.

The One-Eyed Man
[as by Philip St. John]

A blank-faced zombie moved aside as Jimmy Bard came out of the Dictator's office, but he did not notice it; and his own gesture of stepping out of the way of the worried, patrolling *adult* guards was purely automatic. His tall, well-muscled body went on doing all the things long habit had taught it, while his mind churned inside him, rebelling hopelessly at the inevitable.

For a moment, the halls were free of the countless guards, and Jimmy moved suddenly to one of the walls, making quick, automatic motions with his hands. There was no visible sign of change in the surface, but he drew a deep breath and stepped forward; it was like breasting a strong current, but then he was inside and in a narrow passageway, one of the thousands of secret corridors that honeycombed the whole monstrous castle.

Here there could be no *adults* to remind him of what he'd considered his deficiencies, nor of the fact that those deficiencies were soon to be eliminated. The first Dictator Bard had shared the secret of the castle with none save the murdered men who built it; and death had prevented his revealing it even to his own descendants. No tapping would ever reveal that the walls were not the thick, homogenous things they seemed, for tapping would set off alarms and raise stone segments where needed, to make them as solid as they appeared. It was Jimmy's private kingdom, and one where he could be bedeviled only by his own thoughts.

But today, those were trouble enough. Morbid fascination with them drove him forward through the twisting passages until he located a section of the wall that was familiar, and pressed his palm against it. For a second, it seemed cloudy, and then was transparent, as the energies worked on it, letting vibration through in one direction only. He did not notice the quiet sounds of those in the room beyond, but riveted his eyes on the queer headpieces worn by the two girls and single boy within.

Three who had reached their twelfth birthday today and were about to become adults—or zombies! Those odd headpieces were electronic devices that held all the knowledge of a complete, all-embracing education, and they were now working silently, impressing that knowledge onto the minds of their wearers at some two hundred million impulses a second, grooving it permanently into those minds. The children who had entered with brains filled only with the things of childhood would leave with all the information they could ever need, to go out into the world as full adults, if they had withstood the shock of education. Those who failed to withstand it would still leave with the same knowledge, but the character and personality would be gone, leaving them wooden-faced, soulless zombies.

Once Jimmy had sat in one of those chairs, filled with all the schemes and ambitions of a young rowdy about to become a man. But that time, nothing had happened! He could remember the conferences, the scientific attempts to explain his inability to absorb information from the compellor Aaron Bard had given the world, and his own tortured turmoil at finding himself something between an adult and a zombie, useless and unwanted in a world where only results counted. He had no way of knowing, then, that all the bitter years of adjusting to his fate and learning to survive in the contemptuous world were the result of a fake. It was only within the last hour that he had discovered that.

"Pure fake, carefully built up!" His Dictator father had seemed proud of that, even over the worry and desperation that had been on his face these last few days. "The other two before you who didn't take were just false leads, planted to make your case seem plausible; same with the half dozen later cases. You'd have burned—turned zombie, almost certainly. And you're a Bard, someday to dictate this country! I took the chance that if we waited until you grew older, you'd pass, and managed to use blank tapes... Now I can't wait any longer. Hell's due to pop, and I'm not ready for it, but if I can surprise them, present you as an adult... Be back here at six sharp, and I'll have everything ready for your education."

Ten years before, those words would have spelled pure heaven to him. But now the scowl deepened on his forehead as he slapped off the one-way transparency. He'd learned a lot about this world in those ten years, and had seen the savage ruthlessness of the adults. He'd seen no wisdom, but only cunning and cleverness come from the Bard psychicompellors.

"Damn Aaron Bard!"

"Amen!" The soft word came sighing out of the shadows beside the boy, swinging him around with a jerk. Another, in here! Then his eyes were readjusting to the pale, bluish glow of the passages, and he made out the crouched form of an elderly man, slumped into one of the corners. That thin, weary figure with the bitter mouth and eyes could never be a castle guard, however well disguised, and Jimmy breathed easier, though the thing that might be a weapon in the hands of the other centered squarely on him.

The old man's voice trembled faintly, and there were the last dregs of bitterness in it. "Aaron Bard's damned, all right... I thought the discovery of one-way transparency was lost, though, along with controlled interpenetrability of matter-stuff around which to build a whole new science! And yet, that's the answer; for three days, I've been trying to find a trapdoor or sliding panel, boy, and all the time the trick lay in matter that could be made interpenetrable.

Amusing to you?"

"No, sir." Jimmy held his voice level and quite normal. A grim ability to analyze any situation had been knocked into him during the years of his strangeness in a world that did not tolerate strangeness, and he saw that the man was close to cracking. He smiled quietly—and moved without facial warning, with the lightning reaction he had forced himself to learn, ripping the weapon out of weakened hands. His voice was still quiet. "I don't know how you know those things, nor care. The important thing is to keep you from letting others know, and…"

Sudden half-crazed laughter cut off his words. "Go back to the others and tell them? Go back and be tortured again? They'd love that. Aaron Bard's come back to tell us about some more of his nice discoveries! So sweet of you to call, my dear…I'm damned, all right, by my own reputation."

"But Aaron Bard's been dead eighty years! His corpse is preserved in a glass coffin on exhibition; I've seen it myself." And yet there was more than simple insanity here; the old man had known the two secrets which were discovered by Aaron Bard and which his son, the first Dictator, had somehow managed to find and conceal for his own ends after the inventor's death in an explosion. Those secrets had been built into the palace as part of the power of his Dictatorship, until they had been lost with his death. But the old man was speaking again, his voice weak and difficult.

"What does a mere eighty-year span mean, or a figure of wax in a public coffin? The real body they held in sterile refrigeration, filled with counter-enzymes…my own discovery, again! You know of it?"

Jimmy nodded. A Russian scientist had found safe revival of dogs possible even after fifteen minutes of death; with later development, men had been operated on in death, where it served better than anesthesia, and revived again. The only limit had been the time taken by the enzymes of the body to begin dissolving the tissues; and with the discovery by Aaron Bard of a counteracting agent, there had ceased to be any theoretical limit to safe revival. Dying soldiers in winter had injected ampules of it and been revived days or weeks later, where the cold had preserved them. "But—eighty years!"

"Why not—when my ideas were still needed, when my last experiment dealt with simple atomic power, rather than the huge, cumbersome U-235 method? Think what it would mean to an army! My son did—he was very clever at thinking of such things. Eighty years, until they could perfect their tissue regrowing methods and dare to revive my body." He laughed again, an almost noiseless wracking of his exhausted shoulders, and there was the hint of delirious raving in his voice now, though the words were still rational.

"I was so pathetically grateful and proud, when they revived me. I was always gratefully proud of my achievements, you know, and what they could do for humanity. But the time had been too long—my brain only seemed normal. It had deteriorated, and I couldn't remember all I should; when I tried too hard, there were strange nightmare periods of half insanity. And their psychological torture to rip the secret from me didn't help. Two months of that, boy! They told me my name was almost like a god's in this world, and then they stopped at nothing to get what they wanted from that god! And at last I must have gone mad for a time; I don't remember, but somehow I must have escaped—I think I remember something about an air shaft. And then I was here, lost in the maze, unable to get out. But I couldn't be here, could I, if the only entrance was through interpenetrable stone panels that I couldn't remember how to energize?"

"Easy, sir." Jimmy slipped an arm under the trembling body of Aaron Bard and lifted him gently. "You could, all right. There's one out of order, in constant interpenetrable condition in an old air shaft. That's how I first found all this, years ago... There's some soup I can heat in my rooms, and you won't have to go back to them."

He might as well do one decent and human thing, while his mind was still his own, untouched by the damnable education machine. And seeing this bitter, suffering old man, he could no longer hate Aaron Bard for inventing it. The man had possessed a mind of inconceivable scope and had brought forth inventions in all fields as a cat brings forth kittens, but their misuse was no fault of his.

And suddenly it occurred to him that here in his arms was the reason for the desperation his father felt. They couldn't know of the interpenetrable panel, and the search that had undoubtedly been made and failed could have only one answer to them; he must have received outside help from some of the parties constantly plotting treason. With the threat of simple atomic power in such hands, no wonder his Dictator father was pulling all his last desperate tricks to maintain the order of things! Jimmy shook his head; it seemed that everything connected with Aaron Bard led to the position he was in and the inevitable education he must face. For a brief moment he hesitated, swayed by purely personal desires; then his hand moved out to the panel, and he was walking through into his own room, the aged figure still in his arms.

Later, when the old scientist had satisfied some of the needs of his body and was sitting on the bed, smoking, his eyes wandered slowly over the rows of books on the shelves about the room, and his eyebrows lifted slightly. "*The Age of Reason*, even! The first books I've seen in this world, Jimmy!"

"Nobody reads much, anymore, so they don't miss them at the old library. People prefer 'vision for amusement and the compellor tapes if they need additional information. I started trying to learn things from them, and reading grew to be a habit."

"Umm. So you're another one-eyed man?"

"Eh?"

Bard shrugged, and the bitterness returned to his mouth. " 'In the country of the blind, the one-eyed man is—killed!' Wells wrote a story about it. Where—when—I came from, men had emotional eyes to their souls, and my guess is that you've been through enough hell to develop your own. But this world is blind to such things. They don't want people to see. It's the old rule of the pack: Thou shalt conform! Jimmy, how did all this come to be?"

Jimmy frowned, trying to put it into words. The start had probably been when Aaron Bard tried his newly invented psychicompellor on his son. The boy had liked that way of learning, and stolen other experimental tapes, building with his cold, calculating little brain toward the future already. Unerringly, he'd turned to the army, apparently sensing the coming war, and making the most of it when it came. Fifteen years of exhausting, technological warfare had let him introduce the educator to furnish the technical men needed, and had seen him bring forth stolen secret of his father after stolen secret, once the accidental death of Bard had left him alone in possession of Bard's files. With the war's end, the old education system was gone, and boys of twelve were serving as technicians at home until they could be replaced for active duty when old enough.

Those same boys, grown to men and desiring the same things he did, had made possible his move from General to President, and finally to Dictator. He'd even adopted the psychicompellor as his heraldic device. And the ever-increasing demands of technology made going back to old methods impossible and assured him a constant supply of young "realists." Bard interrupted. "Why? It would have been hard—getting an education was always difficult and becoming worse, which is why I tried to make the compellor—but it would have been worth it when they saw where it led. After all, without such help I managed to find a few things—even if they turned out to be Frankenstein monsters!"

"But you depended on some odd linkage of simple facts for results, and most men can't; they need a multitude of facts. And even then, we still follow you by rote in some things!"

"Too easy knowledge. They aren't using it—when they get facts, they don't have the habits of hard thinking needed to utilize them. I noticed the meager developments of new fields… But when they began making these—uh—zombies…"

Jimmy punched a button and nodded toward the creature that entered in answer. It began quietly clearing the room, removing the evidence of Bard's meal, while the scientist studied it. "There's one. He knows as much as any adult, but he has no soul, no emotions, you might say. Tell him to do something, and he will—but he won't even eat without orders."

"Permanent mechanical hypnosis," Bard muttered, and there was hell in his eyes. Then his mouth hardened, while the eyes grew even grimmer. "I never foresaw that, but—you're wrong, and it makes it even worse! You—uh—4719, answer my questions. Do you have emotions such as hatred, fear, or a sense of despair?"

Jimmy started to shake his head, but the zombie answered dully before him. "Yes, master, all those!"

"But you can't connect them with your actions—is that right? You're two people, one in hell and unable to reach the other?"

The affirmative answer was in the same dull tone again, and the zombie turned obediently and left at Bard's gesture. Jimmy wiped sudden sweat from his forehead. He'd been hoping before that he might fail the compellor education as a release, but this would be sheer, unadulterated hell! And the psychologists must know this, even though they never mentioned it.

"And ten percent of us are zombies! But only a very few at first, until the need for ever more knowledge made the shock of education greater. By then—the world had accepted such things; and some considered them a most useful by-product, since they made the best possible workers." His own voice grew more bitter as he forced it on with the history lesson, trying to forget the new and unwelcome knowledge.

Bard's son had built the monstrous castle with its secret means for spying, and had fled into the passages with his private papers to die when his son wrested control from him. It was those moldy papers that had shown Jimmy the secret of escape when he'd stumbled into the labyrinth first. After that, the passage of Dictatorship from father to son had been peaceful enough, and taken for granted. On the whole, there had been little of the deliberate cruelty of the ancient Nazi regime, and the dictatorial powers, while great, were not absolute. The people were used to it—after all, they were products of the compellor, and a ruthless people, best suited by dictatorial government.

Always the compellor! Jimmy hesitated for a moment, and then plunged into the tale of his own troubles. "So I'm to be made into a beast, whether I like it or not," he finished. "Oh, I could turn you in and save myself. If I were an adult, I would! That's why I hate it, even though I might like it then. It wouldn't be me—it'd be just another adult, carrying my name, doing all the things I've learned to hate. I can save myself from becoming one of them—by becoming one!"

"*Requiescat in pace*! Rest the dead in peace. If you wake them, they may learn they've made a ghastly mess of the world, and may even find themselves ruining the only person in all the world whom they like!" Aaron Bard shook his head, wrinkles of concentration cutting over the lines of pain. "The weapon you took from me isn't exactly harmless. Sometime, during my temporary insanity, I must have remembered the old secret, since I made it then, and it's atom-powered. Maybe, without a dictator—"

"No! He's weak, but he's no worse than the others; I couldn't let you kill my father!"

"No, I suppose you couldn't; anyhow, killing people isn't usually much of a solution. Jimmy, are you sure there's any danger of your being made like the others?"

"I've seen the results!"

"But have you? The children are given no education or discipline until they're twelve, and then suddenly filled with knowledge, for which they haven't been prepared, even if preadolescents can be prepared for all that—which I don't believe. Even in my day, in spite of some discipline and training, twelve-year-old boys were little hoodlums, choosing to group together into gangs; wild, savage barbarians, filled with only their own egotism; pack-hunting animals, not yet civilized. Not cruel, exactly, but thoughtless, ruthless as we've seen this world is. Maybe with the sudden new flood of knowledge for which they never worked, they make good technicians; but that spurious, forced adulthood might very well discourage any real maturity; when the whole world considers them automatic adults, what incentive have they to mature?"

Jimmy thought back over his early childhood, before the education fizzle, and it was true that he and the other boys had been the egocentric little animals Bard described; there had been no thought of anything beyond their immediate whims and wants, and no one to tell them that the jungle rule for survival of the fittest should be tempered with decency and consideration for others. But the books had taught him that there had been problem children and boy-gangs before the compellor—and they had mostly outgrown it. Here, after education, they never changed; and while the pressure of society now resisted any attempt on their part to change, that wasn't the explanation needed; other ages had developed stupid standards, but there had always been those who refused them before.

"Do you believe that, sir?"

The old man shrugged slightly. "I don't know. I can't be sure. Maybe I'm only trying to justify myself. Maybe the educator does do something to the mind, carefully as I designed it to carry no personal feelings to the subject. And while I've seen some of the people, I haven't seen enough of the private life to judge; you can't judge, because you never knew normal people... When I invented it, I had serious doubts about it, for that matter. They still use it as I designed it—exactly?"

"Except for the size of the tapes."

"Then there's a wave form that will cancel out the subject's sensitivity, blanket the impulse, if broadcast within a few miles. If I could remember it—if I had an electronics laboratory where I could try it—maybe your fake immunity to education could be made real."

Relief washed over the younger man, sending him to his feet and to the panel. "There is a laboratory. The first Dictator had everything installed for an emergency, deep underground in the passages. I don't know how well stocked it is, but I've been there."

He saw purpose and determination come into the tired face, and Aaron Bard was beside him as the panel became passable. Jimmy turned through a side way that led near the Senatorial section of the castle. On impulse he turned aside and motioned the other forward. "If you want an idea of our private life, take a look at our Senators and judge for yourself."

The wall became transparent to light and sound in one direction and they were looking out into one of the cloakrooms of the Senate Hall. One of the middle-aged men was telling a small audience of some personal triumph of his: "Their first kid—burned—just a damned zombie! I told her when she turned me down for that pimple-faced goon that I'd fix her and I did. I spent five weeks taking the kid around on the sly, winning his confidence. Just before education, I slipped him the dope in candy! You know what it does when they're full of that and the educator starts in."

Another grinned. "Better go easy telling about it; some of us might decide to turn you in for breaking the laws you helped write against using the stuff that way."

"Hell, you can't prove it. I'm not dumb enough to give you birds anything you could pin on me. Just to prove I'm the smartest man in this bunch, I'll let you in on something. I've been doing a little thinking on the Dictator's son..."

"Drop it, Pete, cold! I was with a bunch that hired some fellows to kill the monkey a couple years ago—and you can't prove that, either! We had keys to his door and everything; but he's still around, and the thugs never came back. I don't know what makes, but no other attempt has worked. The Dictator's got some tricks up his sleeve, there."

Jimmy shut the panel off and grinned. "I don't sleep anywhere near doors, and there's a section of the floor that can be made interpenetrable, with a ninety-foot shaft under it. That's why I wangled that particular suite out of my father."

"These are the Senators?" Bard asked.

"Some of the best ones." Jimmy went on, turning on a panel now and again, and Bard frowned more strongly after each new one. Some were plotting treason, others merely talking. Once something like sympathy for the zombies was expressed, but not too strongly. Jimmy started to shut the last panel off, when a new voice started.

"Blane's weakling son is dead. Puny little yap couldn't take the climate and working with all the zombies in the mines; committed suicide this morning."

"His old man couldn't save him from that, eh? Good. Put it into the papers, will you? I want to be sure the Dictator's monkey gets full details. They were thick for a while, you know."

Jimmy's lips twisted as he cut off suddenly. "The only partly human person I ever knew—the one who taught me to read. He was a sickly boy, but his father managed to save him from euthanasia, somehow. Probably he went around with me for physical protection, since the others wouldn't let him alone. Then they shipped him to some mines down in South America, to handle zombie labor."

"Euthanasia? Nice word for killing off the weak. Biologically, perhaps such times as these may serve a useful purpose, but I'd rather have the physically weak around than those who treat them that way. Jimmy, I think if my trick doesn't work and the educator does things to you it shouldn't, I'll kill you before I kill myself!"

Jimmy nodded tightly. Bard wasn't the killing type, but he hoped he'd do it, if such a thing occurred. Now he hurried, wasting no more time in convincing the other of the necessity to prevent such a change in him. He located the place he wanted and stepped in, pressed a switch on the floor, and set the lift to dropping smoothly downward.

"Power is stolen, but cleverly, and no one has suspected. There are auxiliary fuel-batteries, too. The laboratory power will be the same. And here we are."

He pointed to the room, filled with a maze of equipment of all kinds, neatly in order, but covered with dust and dirt from long disuse. Aaron Bard looked at it slowly, with a wry grin.

"Familiar, Jimmy. My son apparently copied it from my old laboratory, where he used to fiddle around sometimes, adapting my stuff to military use. With a little decency, he'd have been a good scientist; he was clever enough."

Jimmy watched, some measure of hope coming to him, as the old man began working. He cleared the tables of dust with casual flicks of a cloth and began, his hands now steady. Wires, small tubes, coils, and various other electronic equipment came from the little boxes and drawers, though some required careful search. Then his fingers began the job of assembling and soldering them into a plastic case about the size of a muskmelon, filled almost solidly as he went along.

"That boy who taught you how to read—was he educated at the age of twelve?"

"Of course—it's compulsory. Everyone has to be. Or—" Jimmy frowned, trying to remember more clearly; but he could only recall vague hints and phrases from bits of conversation among Blane's enemies. "There was something about falsified records during the euthanasia judgment proceedings, I think, but I don't know what records. Does it matter?"

Bard shrugged, scribbling bits of diagrams on a scrap of dirty paper before picking up the soldering iron again. "I wish I knew...Umm? In that fifteen-year war, when they first began intensive use of the compellor, they must have tried it on all types and ages. Did any scientist check on variations due to such factors? No, they wouldn't! No wonder they don't develop new fields. How about a book of memoirs by some soldier who deals with personalities?"

"Maybe, but I don't know. The diary of the first Dictator might, if it could be read, but when I tried after finding it, I only got hints of words here and there. It's in some horrible code—narrow strips of short, irregularly spaced letter groups, pasted in. I can't even figure what kind of a code it is, and there's no key."

"Key's in the library, Jimmy, if you'll look up Brak-O-Type—machine shorthand. He considered ordinary typing inefficient; one time when I thoroughly agreed with him. Damn!" Bard sucked on the thumb where a drop of solder had fallen and stared down at the tight-packed parts. He picked up a tiny electrolytic condenser, studied the apparatus, and put it down again doubtfully. Then he sat motionlessly, gazing down into the half-finished object.

The work, which had progressed rapidly at first, was now beginning to go more slowly, with long pauses while the older man thought. And the pauses lengthened. Jimmy slipped out and up the lift again, to walk rapidly down a corridor that would lead him to the rear of one of the restaurants of the castle. The rats had been blamed for a great deal at that place, and they were in for more blame as Jimmy slid his hands back into the corridors with coffee and food in them.

Bard gulped the coffee gratefully as he looked up to see the younger man holding out the food, but he only sampled that. His hands were less sure again. "Jimmy, I don't know—I can't think. I get so far, and everything seems clear; then—*pfft*! It's the same as when I first tried to remember the secret of atomic power; there are worn places in my mind—eroded by eighty years of death. And when I try to force my thoughts across them, they stagger and reel."

"Grandfather Bard, you've got to finish it! It's almost five, and I have to report back at six!"

Bard rubbed his wrinkled forehead with one hand, clenching and opening the other. For a time, then, he continued to work busily, but there were long quiet intervals. "It's all here, except this one little section. If I could put that in right, it'd work—but if I make a mistake, it'll probably blow out, unless it does nothing." Jimmy stared at his watch. "Try it."

"You solder it; my hands won't work anymore." Bard slipped off the stool, directing the boy's hands carefully. "If I could be sure of making it by going insane, as I did the atom-gun, I'd even force my mind through those nightmares again. But I might decide to do almost anything else, instead...No, that's the antenna—one end remains free."

The hands of the watch stood at ten minutes of six as the last connection was made and Bard plugged it into the socket near the floor. Then the tubes were warming up. There was no blowout, at least; the tubes continued to glow, and a tiny indicator showed radiation of some form coming from the antenna. Jimmy grinned, relief stronger in him, but the older man shook his head doubtfully as they went back to the lift again.

"I don't know whether it's working right, son. I put that last together by mental rule of thumb, and you shouldn't work that way in delicate electronic devices, where even two wires accidentally running beside each other can ruin things! But at least we can pray. And as a last resort—well, I still have the atom-pistol."

"Use it, if you need to! I'll take you to the back wall of my father's inner office, and you can stay there watching while I go around the long way. And use it quickly, because I'll know you're there!"

It took him three tries to find a hallway that was empty of the guards and slip out, but he was only seconds late as his father opened the door and let him in; the usual secretaries and guards were gone, and only the chief psychologist stood there, his small stock of equipment set up. But the Dictator hesitated.

"Jimmy, I want you to know I have to do this, even though I don't know whether you have any better chance of passing it now than when you were a kid—that's just my private hunch, and the psychologist here thinks I'm wrong. But—well, something I was counting on is probably stolen by conspiracy, and there's a helluva war brewing in Eurasia against us, which we're not ready for; the oligarchs have something secret that they figure will win. It's all on a private tape I'll give you. I don't know how much help you'll be, but seeing you suddenly normal will back up the bluff I'm planning, at least. We Bards have a historic destiny to maintain, and I'm counting on you to do your part. You *must* pass!"

Jimmy only half heard it. He was staring at the headpiece, looking something like a late-style woman's hat with wires leading to a little box on the table, and varicolored spools of special tape. For a second, as it clamped down over his face, he winced, but then stood it in stiff silence. In the back of his mind, something tried to make itself noticed—but as he groped for it, only a vague, uneasy feeling remained. Words and something about the psychologist's face...

He heard the snap of the switch, and then his mind seemed to freeze, though sounds and sights still registered. But he knew that the device in the room so far below had failed! The pressure on his brain was too familiar by description; the Bard psychicompellor was functioning. For a second, before full impact, he tried to tear it off, but something else seemed to control his mind, and he sat rigidly, breathing hard, but unable to stop it. His thoughts died down, became torpid, while the machine went on driving its two hundred million impulses into his brain every second, doing things that science still could not understand, but could use.

He watched stolidly as the spools were finished, one by one, until his father produced one from a safe and watched it used, then smashed it. The psychologist bent, picked up one last one, and attached it...The face of the man was familiar... "Like to have the brat in front of a burner like those we use in zombieing criminals..."

Then something in his head seemed to slither, like feet slipping on ice. Numbed and dull of mind, he still gripped at himself, and his formerly motionless hands were clenching at the arms of the chair. Something gnawing inside, a queer distortion, that... Was this what a zombie felt, while its mind failed under education?

The psychologist bent then, removing the headset. "Get up, James Bard!" But as Jim still sat, surprise came over his face, masked instantly by a look of delighted relief. "So you're no zombie?"

Jim arose then, rubbing his hands across his aching forehead, and managed to smile. "No," he said quietly. "No, I'm all right. *I'm perfectly all right!* Perfectly."

"Praise be, Jimmy." The Dictator relaxed slowly into his chair. "And now you know... What's the matter?"

Jim couldn't tell him of the assurance necessary to keep Aaron Bard from firing, but he held his face into a pleasant smile in spite of the pain in his head as he turned to face his father. He knew now—everything. Quietly, unobtrusively, all the things he hadn't known before were there, waiting for his mind to use, along with all the things he had seen and all the conversations he had spied upon in secret.

He had knowledge—and a mind trained to make the most of it. The habits of thinking he had forced upon himself were already busy with the new information; even the savage, throbbing pain couldn't stop that. Now he passed his hand across his head deliberately, and nodded to the outer office. "My head's killing me, Father. Can't I use the couch out there?"

"For a few minutes, I guess. Doctor, can't you give the boy something?"

"Maybe. I'm not a medical doctor, but I can fix the pain, I think." The psychologist was abstract, but he turned out. The Dictator came last, and they were out of the little room, into the larger one where no passages pierced the walls and no shot could reach him.

The smile whipped from the boy's face then, and one of his hands snapped out, lifting a small flame gun from his father's hip with almost invisible speed. It came up before the psychologist could register the emotions that might not yet have begun, and the flame washed out, blackening clothes and flesh and leaving only a limp, charred body on the floor.

Jim kicked it aside. "Treason. He had a nice little tape in there, made out by two people of totally opposite views, in spite of the law against it. Supposed to burn me into a zombie. It would have, except that I'd already studied both sides pretty well, and it raised Ned for a while, even then. Here's your gun, Father."

"Keep it!" The first real emotion Jim had ever seen on his father's face was there now, and it was fierce pride. "I never saw such beautiful gun work, boy! Or such a smooth job of handling a snake! Thanks be, you aren't soft and weak, as I thought. No more emotional nonsense, eh?"

"No more. I'm cured. And at the meeting of the Senators you've called, maybe we'll have a surprise for them. You go on down, and I'll catch up as soon as I can get some amidopyrene for this headache. Somehow, I'll think of something to stop the impeachment they're planning."

"Impeachment! That bad? But how—why didn't you—"

"I did try to tell you, years ago. But though I knew every little treason plot they were cooking then, you were too busy to listen to a nonadult, and I didn't try again. Now, though, it'll be useful. See you outside assembly, unless I'm late."

He grinned mirthlessly as his father went down the hall and away from him. The look of pride in his too-heavy face wouldn't have stayed there if he'd known just how deep in treason some of the fine Senator friends were. It would take a dozen miracles to pull them through. Jim found the panel he wanted, looked to be sure of privacy, and slipped through, tracing quickly down the corridor.

But Aaron Bard wasn't to be found. For a second he debated more searching, but gave it up; there was no time, and he could locate the old man later. It wasn't important that he be found at the moment. Jim shrugged and slipped into one of the passages that would serve as a shortcut to the great assembly room. The headache was already disappearing, and he had no time to bother with it.

They were already beginning session when he arrived, even so, and he slipped quietly through the Dictator's private entrance, making his way unnoticed to the huge desk, behind a jade screen that would hide him from the Senators and yet permit him to watch. He had seen other sessions before, but they had been noisy, bickering affairs, with the rival groups squabbling and shouting names. Today there was none of that. They were going through the motions, quite plainly stalling for time, and without interest in the routine. This meeting was a concerted conspiracy to depose the Dictator, though only the few leaders of the groups knew that Eurasian bribery and treason were the real reasons behind it.

It had been in the making for years, while those leaders carefully built up the ever-present little hatreds and discontents. Jim's status had been used to discredit his father, though the man's own weaknesses had been more popular in distorted versions. As Jim looked, he saw that the twelve cunning men lured to treason by promises of being made American Oligarchs, though supposedly heading rival groups, were all still absent; that explained the stalling. Something was astir, and Jim had a hunch that the psychologist's corpse would have been of no little interest to them. The two honest group leaders were in session, grim and quiet; then, as he looked, the twelve came in, one by one, from different entrances. Their faces showed no great sense of defeat.

Naturally. The Dictator had no chance; he had tried to rule by dividing the now-united groups and by family prestige, and had kept afloat so long as they were not ready to strike; the methods would not stand any strain, much less this attack. He had already muffed one attack opportunity while the leaders were out. A strong man would have cut through the stalling and taken the initiative; a clever orator, schooled in the dramatics and emotions of a Webster or a Borah might even have controlled them. But the Dictator was weak, and the compellor did not produce great oratory; that was incompatible with such emotional immaturity.

But the Dictator had finally been permitted to speak, now. He should have begun with the shock of Jim's adulthood to snap them out of their routine thoughts, built up the revival of Aaron Bard and his old atomic power work, to make them wonder, and then swept his accusations over them in short, hard blows. Instead, he was tracing the old accomplishments of the Bard Family, stock, familiar phrases with no meaning left in them.

Jim sat quietly; it was best that his father should learn his own weakness, here and now. He peered down to watch the leading traitor, and the expression on the man's face snapped his head around, even as his father saw the same thing and stopped talking.

An arm projected from the left wall, waving a dirty scrap of paper at them, and Jim recognized the sheet Bard had used for his diagrams. Now the arm suddenly withdrew, to be replaced by the grinning head of Aaron Bard—but not the face Jim had seen; this one contained sheer lunacy, the teeth bared, the eyes protruding, and the muscles of the neck bunched in mad tension! As Jim watched, the old man emerged fully into the room and began stalking steadily down the aisles toward the Dictator's desk, the atom-gun in one hand centered squarely on Jim's father.

He had full attention, and no one moved to touch him as his feet marched steadily forward, while the scrap of paper in his hand waved and fluttered. Now his voice chopped out words and seemed to hurl them outward with physical force. "Treason! Barbarism! Heathen idolatry!"

For a second, Jim took his eyes from Bard to study his father, then to spring from the chair in a frantic leap as he saw the Dictator's nerve crack and his finger slip onto one of the secret tiny buttons on the desk. But the concealed weapon acted too quickly, though there was no visible blast from it. Aaron Bard uttered a single strangled sound and crumpled to the floor!

"Get back!" Jim wasted no gentleness on his father as he twisted around the desk to present the crowding Senators with the shock of his presence at assembly on top of their other surprise. He had to dominate now, while there was a power hiatus. He bent for a quick look. "Coagulator! Who carries an illegal coagulator here? Some one of you, because this man is paralyzed by one."

Mysteriously, a doctor appeared and nodded after a brief examination. "Coagulator, all right. His nerves are cooked from chest down, and it's spreading. Death certain in an hour or so."

"Will he regain consciousness?"

"Hard to say. Nothing I can do, but I'll try, if someone will move him to the rest room."

Jim nodded and stooped to pick up the scrawled bit of paper and the atom-gun. He had been waiting for a chance, and now fate had given it to him. The words he must say were already planned, brief and simple to produce the impact he must achieve, while the assembly was still disorganized and uncertain; if oratory could win them, now was the time for it. With a carefully stern and accusing face, he mounted the platform behind the desk. His father started to speak, then stopped in shock as Jim took the gavel, rapped for order, and began, pacing with words in a slow rhythm while measuring the intensity for his voice by the faces before him.

"Gentlemen, eighty years ago, Aaron Bard died on the eve of a great war, trying to perfect a simple atomic release that would have shortened that war immeasurably. Tomorrow you will read in your newspapers how that man's own genius preserved his body and enabled us to revive him on this, the eve of an even grimmer war.

"Now, a few moments ago, that same man gave his life again in the service of this country, killed by the illegal coagulator of some cowardly traitor. But he did not die in vain, or before he could leave us safely to find his well-earned rest. He has left his mark on many of us; on me, by giving me the adulthood that all our scientists could not; on some of you, in this piece of paper, he has left a grimmer mark...

"You saw him emerge from a solid wall, and it was no illusion, however much he chose to dramatize his entrance; the genius that was his enabled him to discover a means to search out your treason and your conspiracy in your most secret places. You heard his cry of treason! And one among you tried to silence that cry, forgetting that written notes cannot be silenced with a coagulator.

"Nor can you silence his last and greatest discovery, here in this weapon you saw him carry—*portable* atomic power...

"Now there will be no war; no power would commit such suicide against a nation whose men shall be equipped as ours shall be. You may be sure that the traitors among you will find no reward for their treason, now. But from them, we shall have gained. We shall know the folly of our petty, foreign-inspired hatreds. We shall know the need of cleansing ourselves of the taint of such men's leadership. We shall cease trying to weaken our government and shall unite to forge new bonds of strength, instead.

"And because of that unintended good they have done us, we shall be merciful! Those who leave our shores before the stroke of midnight shall be permitted to escape; those who prefer to choose their own death by their own hands shall not be denied that right. And for the others, we shall demand and receive the fullest measure of justice!

"In that, gentlemen, I think we can all agree."

He paused then for a brief moment, seeming to study the paper in his hand, and when he resumed, his voice was the brusque one of a man performing a distasteful task. "Twelve men—men who dealt directly with our enemies. I shall read them in the order of their importance: First, Robert Sweinend! Two days ago, at three o'clock in his secretary's office, he met a self-termed businessman named Yamimoto Tung, though he calls himself—"

Jim went on, methodically reciting the course of the meeting, tensing inside as the seconds stretched on; much more and they would know it couldn't all come from one small sheet of paper!

But Sweinend's hand moved then, and Jim's seemed to blur over the desk top. Where the Senator had been, a shaft of fire—atomic fire—seemed to hang for a second before fading into nothing. Jim put the gun back gently and watched eleven men get up from their seats and dart hastily away through the exits. Beside him, his father's face now shone with great relief and greater pride, mixed with unbelieving wonder as he stood up awkwardly to take the place the boy was relinquishing. The job had been done, and Jim had the right to follow his own inclinations.

Surprisingly to him, the still figure on the couch was both conscious and sane, as the boy shut the door of the little room, leaving the doctor outside. Aaron Bard could not move his body, but his lips smiled. "Hello, Jimmy. That was the prettiest bundle of lies I've heard in a lot more than eighty years! I'm changing my saying; from now on, the one-eyed man is king—so long as he taps the ground with a cane!"

Jimmy nodded soberly, though most of the strain of the last hour was suddenly gone, torn away by the warm understanding of the older man and relief at not having to convince him that he was still normal, in spite of his actions since education. "You were right about the compellor; it can't change character. But I thought...after I shot the psychiatrist... How did you know?"

"I had at least twenty minutes in which to slip back and examine my son's diary, before your education would be complete." His smile deepened, as he sucked in on the cigarette that Jimmy held to his lips, and he let the smoke eddy out gently. "It took perhaps ten minutes to learn what I wanted to know. During the war, his notes are one long paean of triumph over the results on the preadolescents, dissatisfaction at those who were educated past twenty! And he knew the reason, as well as he always knew what he wanted to. Too much information on a young mind mires it down by sheer weight on untrained thoughts, even though it gives a false self-confidence. But the mature man, with his trained mind, can never be bowed down by mere information; he can use it... No, let me go on. Vindication of my compellor doesn't matter; but this is going to be your responsibility, Jimmy, and the doctor told me I'm short of time. I want to be sure... In twenty years—but that doesn't matter.

"The compellor is poison to a twelve-year-old mind, and a blessing to the adult. You can't change that overnight; but you can try, and perhaps accomplish a little. Move the age up, but carefully. By rights I should repair the damage I helped cause, but I'll have to leave it to you. Be ruthless, as you were now—more ruthless than any of them. A man who fights for right and principle should be. Tap the ground with your cane! And sometimes, when none of the blind are around, you can look up and still see the stars! Now—"

"Grandfather Bard—you never were insane in there!"

The old man smiled again. "Naturally. I couldn't look on and see the only one of my offspring that amounted to anything needing help without doing something, could I? I threw in everything I could, knowing you'd make something out of it. You did. And I'm not sorry, even though I wasn't exactly expecting—this... How long after my heart begins missing?"

"A minute or two!" Aaron Bard obviously wanted no sympathy, and the boy sensed it and held back the words, hard though he found it now. Emotions were better expressed by their hands locked together than by words.

"Good. It's a clean, painless death, and I'm grateful for it. But no more revivals! Cremate me, Jimmy, and put up a simple marker—no name, just A One-Eyed Man!"

"*Requiescat in Pace*—A One-Eyed Man! I promise!" The old head nodded faintly and relaxed, the smile still lingering. Jimmy swallowed a lump in his throat and stood up slowly with bowed head, while a tumult of sound came in from the great assembly hall. His father was finally abdicating and they were naming him Dictator, of course. But he still stood there, motionless.

"Two such stones," he muttered finally. "And maybe someday I'll deserve the other."

Habit

Habit is a wonderful thing. Back in the days of apelike men, one of them invented a piece of flint that made life a little easier; then another found something else. Labor-saving ideas were nice, and it got to be a habit, figuring them out, until the result was what we call civilization, as exemplified by rocket racing.

Only, sometimes, habits backfire in the darnedest way. Look at what happened to the eight-day rocket race out of Kor on Mars.

I was down there, entered in the open-class main event, with a little five-ton soup can of rare vintage, equipped with quartz tube linings and an inch of rust all over. How I'd ever sneaked it past the examiners was a miracle in four dimensions, to begin with.

Anyway, I was down in the engine well, welding a new brace between the rocket stanchion and the main thrust girder when I heard steps on the tilly ladder outside. I tumbled out of the dog port to find a little, shriveled fellow with streaked hair and sharp gray eyes giving the *Umatila* the once-over.

"Hi, Len," he said casually, around his cigarette. "Been making repairs, eh? Well, not meaning any offense, son, she looks to me like she needs it. Darned if I'd risk my neck in her, not in the opens. Kind of a habit with me, being fond of my neck."

I mopped the sweat and grease off the available parts of my anatomy. "Would if you had to. Since you seem to know me, how about furnishing your handle?"

"Sure. Name's Jimmy Shark—used to be thick as thieves with your father, Brad Masters. I saw by the bulletin you'd sneaked in just before they closed the entries, so I came down to look you over."

Dad had told me plenty about Jimmy Shark. As a matter of fact, my father had been staked to the *Umatila* by this man, when racing was still new. "Glad to meet you." I stuck out my hand and dug up my best grin.

"Call me Jimmy when you get around to it—it's a habit." His smile was as easy and casual as an old acquaintance. "I'da known you anywhere; look just like your father. Never thought I'd see you in this game, though. Brad told me he was fixing you up in style."

"He was, only—" I shrugged. "Well, he figured one more race would sweeten the pot, so he blew the bankroll on himself in the *Runabout*. You heard what happened."

"Um-hm. Blew up rounding Ceres. I was sorry to hear it. Didn't leave you anything but the old *Umatila*, eh?"

"Engineering ticket that won't draw a job, and some debts. Since I couldn't get scrap-iron prices for the old soup can, I made a dicker for the soup on credit. Back at the beginning, starting all over—and going to win this race."

Jimmy nodded. "Um-hm. Racing kind of gets to be a habit. Still quartz tubes on her, eh? Well, they're faster, when they hold up. Since you aren't using duratherm, I suppose your soup is straight Dynatomic IV?"

I had to admit he knew his tubes and fuels. They haven't used quartz tube linings for ten years, so only a few people know that Dynatomic can be used in them straight to give a 40 percent efficient drive, if the refractory holds up. In the new models, duratherm lining is used, and the danger of blowing a tube is nil. But the metal in duratherm acts as an anticatalyst on the soup and cuts the power way down. To get around that, they add a little powdered platinum and acid, which brings the efficiency up to about 35 percent, but still isn't the perfect fuel it should be.

Jimmy ran his hand up a tube, tapped it, and listened to the coyote howl it gave off. "A nice job, son. You put that lining in yourself, I take it. Well, Brad won a lot of races in the old shell using home-lined quartz tubes. Must have learned the technique from him."

"I did," I agreed, "with a couple of little tricks of my own thrown in for good measure."

"How about looking at the cockpit, Len?"

I hoisted him and helped him through the port. There wasn't room for two in there, so I stood on the tilly ladder while he looked her over.

"Um-hm. Nice and cozy, some ways. Still using Brad's old baby autopilot, I see, and the old calculator. Only that brace there—it's too low. The springs on your shock hammock might give enough to throw you against it when you reverse, and you'd be minus backbone. By the way, you can't win races by sleeping ahead of time in your shock hammock—you ought to know that." He held up my duffel and half a can of beans. "And that isn't grub for preparing a meteor dodger, either."

"Heck, Jimmy, I'm tough." I knew he was right, of course, but I also knew how far a ten-spot went on Mars.

"Um-hm. Be like old times with a Masters in the running. Got to be a habit, seeing that name on the list." He crawled out of the port and succeeded in lighting a cigarette that stung acridly in the dry air. "You know, Len, I just happened to think; I was supposed to have a partner this trip, but he backed down. There's room and board paid for two over at Mom Doughan's place, and only me to use it. We'd better go over there before her other boarders clean the table and leave us without supper. Eating's sort of a habit with me."

He had me by the arm and was dragging me across the rocket pit before I could open my mouth. "Now, Jimmy, I'm used—"

"Shut up. You're used to decent living, same as anyone else, so you might as well take it and like it. I told you I'd paid for them already, didn't I? All right. Anyhow, I'm not used to staying alone; sort of a habit, having somebody to talk to."

I was beginning to gather that he had a few habits scattered around at odd places.

Jimmy was right; shock cushions and beans don't make winners. With a decent meal inside me, and an air-conditioned room around me, my chances looked a lot rosier. Some of the old cocksureness came back.

"Jimmy," I said, lying back and letting the bed ease my back lazily, "I'm going to win that race. That hundred-thousand first looks mighty good."

"Um-hm." Jimmy was opening a can of cigarettes and he finished before answering. "Better stick to the second, kid. This race is fixed."

"I'll change that, then. Who told you it was fixed?"

He grinned sourly. "Nobody. I fixed it myself." He watched my mouth run around and end up in an open circle. "Maybe Brad forgot to tell you, and it's not common news, but I'm a professional bettor."

It was news to me. "But I thought Dad—did he know?"

"Sure, he knew. Oh, he wasn't connected with it, if that's what you're wondering. When he switched from jockeying to dodging, I left the ponies to handicap the soup cans. Learned the gambling end from my father, the best handicapper in the business. It's a habit in the family."

There was pride in his voice. Maybe I was screwy; after all, some people have a pretty low opinion of rocket dodgers. I decided to let Jimmy spill his side without foolish questions.

"Um-hm. Natural-born handicapper, I am. I won twice every time I lost. Never cheated a man, welshed on a bet, or bribed a dodger to throw a race. Anything wrong with that?"

I had to admit there wasn't. After all, Dad used to do some betting himself, as I should know. "How about the race being crooked?"

Jimmy snorted. "Not crooked—fixed. Don't go twisting my words, Len." He stretched out on the bed and took the cigarette out of his mouth. "Always wanted to be famous, son. You know, big philanthropist, endow libraries and schools. Got to be a habit, planning on that; and you can't make that kind of money just handicapping. Your dad ever tell you about that fuel he was working on?"

I began to see light. "We knew he'd been doing something of that sort, though the formula couldn't be found. Matter of fact, he was using it in the *Runabout* when it went out."

"That's it." Jimmy nodded. "A little bit of the compound in the fuel boosts the speed way up. There was a couple of kinks in the original formula, but I got them straightened out. I pick the winner—the fellow who needs to win most, if that's any comfort to you—and sell him on the new fuel. Only the thing won't work in quartz tubes—burns 'em out."

"I won't need it. I'll win this race fair and square." All the same, that did mess things up; I knew Dad had thought a lot of that fuel.

"No rules against better fuels. A man can pick the fuel he wants, the same as he can travel any course he wants to, no matter how long, if he goes past the markers." He grunted. "Brad didn't want you racing, so he sent me the formula. Had a hunch about going out, I guess; dodgers get a habit of hunches."

"And we Masterses have a habit of winning. Better change your bets, Jimmy."

"It's all fixed, too late to change, and the odds are long. After this race, I'm going back and get the habit of being a big philanthropist. Look, kid, you're not sore about my using Brad's formula?"

"If he gave it to you, that was his business." I pulled the sheet up and reached for the light switch. "Only don't blame me when you lose your bets."

But the morning of the start, I had to confess I wasn't feeling so cocky, in spite of living high on Jimmy for a week. I'd seen the favorite—*Bouncing Betty*—and Jimmy's fix, the *Tar Baby*, and both looked mighty good to me.

"What's the *Tar Baby* pulling?" I asked Jimmy. "Or do you know?"

"Olsen says he's driving her at better than two G's all the way. The *Bouncing Betty*'s pulling straight two, which is tough enough, but Olsen thinks he can stand the strain at two and a quarter."

I looked them over again. An extra quarter gravity of acceleration, even if it is only an extra eight feet per second, uses a lot of additional fuel, even for a sixteen-ton soup can. "How about that mixture, Jimmy? Does it pep up the efficiency, or just the speed-combustion rate and exhaust velocity?"

"She'll throw out a fifty percent, mixture I gave Olsen; optimum is good for eighty." Something began to click in my head then, but his next words sidetracked it. "You'd better draw out, kid. An eight-day race is bad, even if you can hold two G's. How's your supplies?"

I was worried a little myself, but I wouldn't admit it. "They'll last. I've stocked enough soup to carry me to Jupiter and back at two G's, if I had to, and the marker station is forty million miles this side of the big fellow, on a direct line from here. I've got plenty of oxygen, water, and concentrates."

They'd given out the course that morning. We were to head out from Kor, point straight at Jupiter with a climb out of the plane of the ecliptic, drive down and hit a beacon rocket they were holding on a direct line with the big planet, forty million miles this side of him; that made about an even three-hundred-million-mile course from Mars, out and back, figured for eight days at a constant acceleration and deceleration of two gravities. It had been advertised as the longest and toughest race in rocket history, and they were certainly living up to the publicity.

"That's a tough haul on a youngster, Len," Jimmy grumbled. "And with quartz lining, it's worse."

"I've had plenty of practice at high acceleration, and the tubes are practically safe for six days' firing. I think they'll last the other two."

"Then you're matching the *Bouncing Betty*'s speed?"

I nodded grimly. "I'll have to. The *Tar Baby*'ll probably run into trouble at the speed she's meaning to make, but the *Betty*'s built to stand two."

The starter was singing out his orders, and the field was being cleared. Jimmy grabbed my hand. "Good luck, Len. Don't ride her harder'n she'll carry. You Masterses make too much of a habit of being crazy."

Then they forced him off the field and I was climbing into the cockpit, tightening the anchor straps of the shock hammock about the straitjacket I wore.

And I expected to need them. Two gravities mean double weight, during eight days, fighting your lungs and heart. If you take it lengthwise, it can't be done, but by lying stretched out on the hammock at right angles to the flight line, it's just possible.

The *Betty* roared up first, foaming out without a falter. Olsen took the *Tar Baby* up a little uncertainly, but straightened sharply and headed up. Finally, I got the signal and gave her the gun, leaving Mars dangling in space while I tried to keep my stomach off my backbone. The first ten minutes are always the toughest.

When that passed, I began feeding the tape into the baby autopilot that would take over when I had to sleep, which was about three quarters of the time, under the gravity drag. There wasn't anything exciting to the takeoff, and I was out in space before I knew it, with the automatic guiding her. I might have to make a correction or two, but she'd hold at the two-G mark on course for days at a stretch.

I'd been fool enough to dream about excitement, but I knew already I wasn't going to get it. By the time I was half an hour out, I was bored stiff, or felt that way. The automat ran the ship, space looked all alike, and the only sensation was weight pressing against me. I looked around for the *Betty*, and spotted her blast some fifty miles away, holding evenly abreast of me. The others were strung out behind in little clusters, except for Olsen. His blast was way up ahead, forging along at a good quarter gravity more than I could use. At the end of an hour, he was a full ten thousand miles away from me; there was no mistaking the harsh white glare of his jets. Olsen had decided to duck over the ecliptic, as I was doing, but the *Bouncing Betty* had headed below it, so it was drawing out of sight. That left me out of touch with what I hoped was my leading competitor.

Of course, the radio signals came through on the ultrawave every so often, but the pep-talk description of the thrilling contest for endurance racing didn't mean much when I put it up against the facts.

A racing ship in space on a long haul is the loneliest, most Godforsaken spot under the stars. For excitement, I'll take marbles.

Having nothing better to do, I turned over and went to sleep on my stomach. You can kill a lot of time sleeping, and I meant to do it.

The howler was banging in my ear when I woke up. I reached over and cut on, noting that the chronometer said sixteen hours out of Kor.

"Special bulletin to all pilots," said the ultrawave set. "The *Bouncing Betty*, piloted by James MacIntyre, is now out of the race. MacIntyre reports that, in cutting too close to the ecliptic, he was struck by a small meteoroid, and has suffered the loss of three main tubes. While out of the running, he feels confident of reaching Kor safely on his own power.

"This leaves Olsen of the *Tar Baby* and Masters of the *Umatila* in the lead by a long margin. Come in, Olsen."

Olsen's voice held a note of unholy glee that the obvious fatigue he was feeling couldn't hide. "Still holding two and a quarter, heart good, breathing only slightly labored; no head pains. Position at approximately twenty-two and a half million miles from Kor; speed, two million eight hundred thousand per hour. Confident of winning."

"Report acknowledged, Olsen. Come in, Masters."

I tried to sound carefree, but I guess I failed. "Acceleration at two, holding course beautifully on autopilot, rising over ecliptic. Body and ship standing up okay. Pyrometer indication of tube lining very satisfactory. Position, twenty million miles out, speed, two and a half million. No signs of meteoroids up here. Can you give next highest acceleration below me?"

Already it took time for the messages to reach Kor and return, and I tried to locate Olsen with his two-and-a-half-million-mile lead. Even if he cut down to two now, the race seemed a certainty for him—unless something happened. Finally the report came back.

"Burkes, on the *Salvador*, reports one and three quarters, refuses to try higher. No others above that except yourself and Olsen. Are you going to match the *Tar Baby*?"

Match the *Tar Baby*, indeed, and ran short of fuel or blow up! "No chance. Still expect to win, though."

Well, at least it would sound nice back home, and it might worry Olsen a little.

He was too conceited about his speed. But I couldn't see myself making good. Even if I cut closer to the ecliptic, it wouldn't save enough time to count, and the risk wasn't worthwhile. I dug into my store of concentrates and satisfied a raving hunger—double weight takes double energy, just as it does sleep. The only thing I could think of was to wish I could maintain acceleration all the way, instead of just half.

That's the trouble with racing. You accelerate with all you've got half the way, then turn around and decelerate just as hard until you reach your goal; then you repeat the whole thing in getting back. The result is that as soon as you reach top speed, you have to check it, and you average only a part of what you can do. If there were just something a man could get a grip on in space to slew around, instead of stopping dead, every record made would go to pieces the next day.

I checked over the automat, found it ticking cheerfully, and fiddled around with the calculator. But the results were the same as they'd been back in Kor. It still said I'd have to decelerate after about forty-four hours. Then I messed around with imaginary courses to kill time, listened to the thrilling reports of the race—it must have been nice to listen to—and gave up. Setting the alarm, I went back to sleep with the announcer's voice concluding some laudatory remarks about the "fearless young man out there giving his ship everything he's got in a frantic effort to win."

But I was awake when the next bulletin came in from Kor at the end of the forty-hour mark. "Special bulletin! We've just received word from Dynatomic fuels that there's a prize of fifty thousand additional to any and every man who makes the course in less than eight full days! Olsen and Masters are now way ahead in the field, and about to do their reversing. Come on, Masters, we're pulling for you; make it a close race! All right, Olsen, come in."

"Tell Dynatomic the prize is due me already, and give 'em my thanks. Holding up fine here, fuel running better than I expected. Hundred and forty million out; speed, seven million. Reversing in two hours."

By a tight margin, I might make it, since it applied to as many as came in within the time period. "I'll be in the special field, Kor. Everything like clockwork here, standing it fine. Pyrometer still says tubes okay. Position, one-twenty-five millions; speed, six and a quarter. Reversing in four hours."

"Okay, Masters; hope you make it. Watch out for Jupiter, both of you. Even at forty million miles, he'll play tricks with your steering when you hit the beacon. Signing off at Kor."

Jupiter! Right then a thought I'd been trying to nurse into consciousness came up and knocked on my dome. I dug my fingers into the calculator; the more the tape said, the better things looked.

Finally I hit the halfway. Olsen had reversed a couple of hours before with no bad effects from the change. But I was busy dialing Mars. They came in, after a good long wait. "Acknowledging Masters. Trouble?"

"Clear sailing, here and ahead, Kor." It's nice to feel confident after staring second prize in the face all the trip. "Is there any rule about the course, provided a man passes the beacon inside of a hundred thousand miles? Otherwise, do I have free course?"

"Absolutely free course, Masters. Anything you do after the beacon is okay, if you get back. Advise you don't cut into asteroids, however."

"No danger of that. Thanks, Kor."

I'd already passed the reversing point, but that wasn't worrying me. I snapped off the power, leaving only the automat cut into the steering tubes, and gazed straight ahead. Sure enough, there was Jupiter, with his markings and all; the fellow that was going to let me maintain full speed over halfway, and make the long course the faster one. I was remembering Jimmy's remark that put the idea into my head: "A man can pick the fuel he wants, the same as he can travel any course he wants, no matter how long."

With power off, I was still ticking off about seven million miles an hour, but I couldn't feel it. Instead, I felt plenty sick, without any feeling of weight at all. But I couldn't bother about that. Kor was calling again, but I shut them off with a few words. If I was crazy, that was my business, and the ship was doing okay.

I set the buzzer to wake me when I figured I'd be near Olsen. Looking out, when the thing went off, I could see his jets shooting out away off side, and a little ahead. But he was cutting his speed sharply, while I was riding free, and I began sliding past him.

I was all set to gloat when his voice barked in over the ultraset: "Masters! Calling Masters!"

"Okay, Olsen."

"Man, decelerate! You'll crack up on Jupiter at that rate. If something's wrong, say so. We're way out ahead, and there's plenty of time. Give me the word and I'll try to cut in on you. The *Tar Baby*'s strong enough to hold back your soup can. How about it, Masters?"

That was the guy I'd been hating for a glory hound, figuring him as out for himself only. "No need, Olsen, but a load of thanks. I'm trying out a hunch to steal first place from you."

The relief in his voice was as unquestionable as his bewilderment. "It's okay if you can do it, mister. I'll still make the special. Why not let me in on the hunch? I won't crib your idea."

"Okay, but I don't know how it'll work, for sure. I'm going around Jupiter at full speed instead of cutting to the beacon."

"You're crazy, Masters." The idea didn't appeal to him at all. "Hope your tubes hold up under the extra eighty million miles. So long!"

Sixty-seven hours out of Kor I passed the beacon at the required hundred thousand miles—which isn't as wide a margin at full speed as it sounds—and headed out. Olsen must have called ahead to tell them what I was doing, because the beacon acknowledged my call, verified my distance, and signed off without questions.

I caught an hour's sleep again, and then Jupiter was growing uncomfortably close. I'd already been over my calculations twenty times, but so darned much depended on them that I wasn't taking chances. I ran them through again. The big fellow was coming up alongside like a mountain rolling toward an ant, and I was already closer than anyone I'd ever heard of.

But it worked out all right, at first. I grazed around the side, was caught in his gravity, and began to swing in an orbit. That's what I'd been looking for, something to catch hold of out in space to swing me around without loss of momentum, and that's what I'd found; Jupiter's gravity pulled me around like a lead weight on a swung rope.

Which was fine—if I had enough speed to make him let go again, as close as I was to his surface. Fortunately, he hasn't any extensive atmosphere to speak of—beyond that which creates his apparent surface—in proportion to his diameter, or I'd have been warmed up entirely too much for pleasant living. In no time I was coming around and facing back in the general direction of Mars; and then two things happened at once.

Jupiter wasn't letting me go on schedule; he seemed to think he needed a little more time for observation of this queer satellite he'd just caught. And Io swung up right where it shouldn't have been. I'd forgotten the moons!

That's when I began counting heartbeats. Either Jupiter pulled me too far, or he threw me square into Io, and I didn't like either prospect. The steering tubes were worthless in the short space I had at that speed. I waited, and Jupiter began to let go—with Io coming up!

Whishh! I could hear—or imagine, I don't know which—the outer edges of the moon's atmosphere whistle briefly past the sides of my soup can, and then silence. When I opened my eyes, Io lay behind, with Jupiter, and I was headed straight for the beacon. Dear old Io!

Light as its gravity was, it had still been enough to correct the slight error in my calculations and set me back on my course, even if I did come too close for my peace of mind.

I was asleep when I passed the beacon again, so I don't know what they had to say. It was Olsen's call that woke me up. "Congratulations, Masters! When you reach Mars, tell them to hold the special and second prizes for me. And I'll remember the trick. Clear dodging!" He was still heading in toward the beacon on deceleration, and less than eighty hours had passed.

Well, there wasn't much more to it, except for the sleeping and the ravings of that fool announcer back on Kor. I reversed without any trouble at about the point where I'd stopped accelerating and began braking down for Mars. Then the monotony of the trip began again, with the automat doing all the work. The tubes, safe for six days, would be used for only about three and a half, thanks to all that time with power off, and I had soup to spare.

Miraculously, they had the landing pit cleared when I settled down over Kor, and the sweetest-looking white ambulance was waiting. I set her down without a jolt, slipped out, and was inside the car before the crowds could get to me. They've finally learned to protect the winning dodger that way.

Jimmy was inside, chewing on an unlit cigarette. "Okay," he told the ambulance driver, "take us to Mom Doughan's. Hi, kid. Made it in a hundred and forty-five hours. That gives you first and special, so you're out of the red. Nice work!"

I couldn't help rubbing it in a little. "Next time, Jimmy, bet on a Masters if you want to go through with those endowments of yours."

Jimmy's face was glum, and the cigarette bobbed up and down in his mouth in a dull rhythm, but his eyes crinkled up and he showed no rancor at the crack. "There won't be any endowments, kid. Should have stuck to the old handicapping, instead of trying to start something new. I'm cleaned, lock, stock, and barrel. Anyway, those endowment dreams were just sort of a habit."

"You've still got your formula."

"Um-hm. Your fuel formula; I'm sticking to the old habits and letting the newfangled ideas go hang."

I stopped playing with him then. "That's where you're wrong, Jimmy. I did a lot of thinking out there, and I've decided some habits are things to get rid of."

"Maybe." He didn't sound very convinced. "How'd you mean?"

"Well, take the old idea that the shortest time is made on the shortest possible course; that's a habit with pilots, and one I had a hard time breaking. But look what happened. And Dad had one habit, you another, and you'd both have been better off without those fixations."

"Um-hm. Go on."

"Dad thought a fuel was good only in racing, because he was used to thinking in terms of the perambulating soup cans," I explained. I'd done plenty of thinking on the way in, when I was awake, so I knew what I was talking about. "You had a habit of thinking of everything in terms of betting. Take that fuel. You say it gives eighty percent efficiency. Did you ever stop to think there'd be a fortune in it for sale to the commercials? The less load they carry in fuel, the more pay cargo."

"Well, I'll be—" He mulled it over slowly, letting the idea seep in. Then he noticed the cigarette in his mouth and started to light it.

I amplified the scheme. "We'll market it fifty-fifty. You put up the fuel and salesmanship; I'll put up the prize money and technical knowledge. And if you're looking for fame, there ought to be some of that mixed up in there, too."

"Um-hm." Jimmy stuck out his hand. "Shake on the partnership, Len. But, if you don't mind, I'll use the money like I said. Those endowment ideas sort of got to be a habit with me."

Nerves

I

The graveled walks between the sprawling, utilitarian structures of the National Atomic Products Co., Inc., were crowded with the usual five o'clock mass of young huskies just off work or going on the extra shift, and the company cafeteria was jammed to capacity and overflowing. But they made good-natured way for Doc Ferrel as he came out, not bothering to stop their horseplay as they would have done with any of the other half hundred officials of the company. He'd been just Doc to them too long for any need of formality.

He nodded back at them easily, pushed through, and went down the walk toward the Infirmary Building, taking his own time; when a man has turned fifty, with gray hairs and enlarged waistline to show for it, he begins to realize that comfort and relaxation are worth cultivating. Besides, Doc could see no good reason for filling his stomach with food and then rushing around in a flurry that gave him no chance to digest it. He let himself in the side entrance, palming his cigar out of long habit, and passed through the surgery to the door marked:

PRIVATE
ROGER T. FERREL
PHYSICIAN IN CHARGE

As always, the little room was heavy with the odor of stale smoke and littered with scraps of this and that. His assistant was already there, rummaging busily through the desk with the brass nerve that was typical of him; Ferrel had no objections to it, though, since Blake's rock-steady hands and unruffled brain were always dependable in a pinch of any sort.

Blake looked up and grinned confidently. "Hi, Doc. Where the deuce do you keep your cigarettes, anyway? Never mind, got 'em... Ah, that's better! Good thing there's one room in this darned building where the 'No Smoking' signs don't count. You and the wife coming out this evening?"

"Not a chance, Blake." Ferrel struck the cigar back in his mouth and settled down into the old leather chair, shaking his head. "Palmer phoned down half an hour ago to ask me if I'd stick through the graveyard shift. Seems the plant's got a rush order for some particular batch of dust that takes about twelve hours to cook, so they'll be running No. 3 and 4 till midnight or later."

"Hm-m-m. So you're hooked again. I don't see why any of us has to stick here—nothing serious ever pops up now. Look what I had today; three cases of athlete's foot—better send a memo down to the showers for extra disinfection—a guy with dandruff, four running noses, and the office boy with a sliver in his thumb! They bring everything to us except their babies—and they'd have them here if they could—but nothing that couldn't wait a week or a month. Anne's been counting on you and the missus, Doc; she'll be disappointed if you aren't there to celebrate her sticking ten years with me. Why don't you let the kid stick it out alone tonight?"

"I wish I could, but this happens to be my job. As a matter of fact, though, Jenkins worked up an acute case of duty and decided to stay on with me tonight." Ferrel twitched his lips in a stiff smile, remembering back to the time when his waistline had been smaller than his chest and he'd gone through the same feeling that destiny had singled him out to save the world. "The kid had his first real case today, and he's all puffed up. Handled it all by himself, so he's now Dr. Jenkins, if you please."

Blake had his own memories. "Yeah? Wonder when he'll realize that everything he did by himself came from your hints? What was it, anyway?"

"Same old story—simple radiation burns. No matter how much we tell the men when they first come in, most of them can't see why they should wear three ninety-five percent efficient shields when the main converter shield cuts off all but one-tenth percent of the radiation. Somehow, this fellow managed to leave off his two inner shields and pick up a year's burn in six hours. Now he's probably back on No. 1, still running through the hundred liturgies I gave him to say and hoping we won't get him sacked."

No. 1 was the first converter around which National Atomic had built its present monopoly in artificial radioactives, back in the days when shields were still inefficient to one part in a thousand and the materials handled were milder than the modern ones. They still used it for the gentler reactions, prices of converters being what they were; anyhow, if reasonable precautions were taken, there was no serious danger.

"A tenth percent will kill; five percent thereof is one two-hundredth; five percent of that is one four-thousandth; and five percent again leaves one eighty-thousandth, safe for all but fools." Blake sing-songed the liturgy solemnly, then chuckled. "You're getting old, Doc; you used to give them a thousand times. Well, if you get the chance, you and Mrs. Ferrel drop out and say hello, even if it's after midnight. Anne's gonna be disappointed, but she ought to know how it goes. So long."

"'Night." Ferrel watched him leave, still smiling faintly. Some day his own son would be out of medical school, and Blake would make a good man for him to start under and begin the same old grind upward. First, like young Jenkins, he'd be filled with his mission to humanity, tense and uncertain, but somehow things would roll along through Blake's stage and up, probably to Doc's own level, where the same old problems were solved in the same old way, and life settled down into a comfortable, mellow dullness.

There were worse lives, certainly, even though it wasn't like the mass of murders, kidnappings and applied miracles played up in the current movie series about Dr. Hoozis. Come to think of it, Hoozis was supposed to be working in an atomic products plant right now—but one where chrome-plated converters covered with pretty neon tubes were mysteriously blowing up every second day, and men were brought in with blue flames all over them to be cured instantly in time to utter the magic words so the hero could dash in and put out the atomic flame barehanded. Ferrel grunted and reached back for his old copy of the *Decameron*.

Then he heard Jenkins out in the surgery, puttering around with quick, nervous little sounds. Never do to let the boy find him loafing back here, when the possible fate of the world so obviously hung on his alertness. Young doctors had to be disillusioned slowly, or they became bitter and their work suffered. Yet, in spite of his amusement at Jenkins' nervousness, he couldn't help envying the thin-faced young man's erect shoulders and flat stomach. Years crept by, it seemed.

Jenkins straightened out a wrinkle in his white jacket fussily and looked up. "I've been getting the surgery ready for instant use, Dr. Ferrel. Do you think it's safe to keep only Miss Dodd and one male attendant here—shouldn't we have more than the bare legally sanctioned staff?"

"Dodd's a one-man staff," Ferrel assured him. "Expecting accidents tonight?"

"No, sir, not exactly. But do you know what they're running off?"

"No." Ferrel hadn't asked Palmer; he'd learned long before that he couldn't keep up with the atomic engineering developments, and had stopped trying. "Some new type of atomic tank fuel for the army to use in its war games?"

"Worse than that, sir. They're making their first commercial run of Natomic I-713 in both No. 3 and 4 converters at once."

"So? Seems to me I did hear something about that. Had to do with killing off boll weevils, didn't it?" Ferrel was vaguely familiar with the process of sowing radioactive dust in a circle outside the weevil area, to isolate the pest, then gradually moving inward from the border. Used with proper precautions, it had slowly killed off the weevil and driven it back into half the territory once occupied.

Jenkins managed to look disappointed, surprised and slightly superior without a visible change of expression. "There was an article on it in the *Natomic*

Weekly Ray of last issue, Dr. Ferrel. You probably know that the trouble with Natomic I-344, which they've been using, was its half life of over four months; that made the land sowed useless for planting the next year, so they had to move very slowly. I-713 has a half life of less than a week and reaches safe limits in about two months, so they'll be able to isolate whole strips of hundreds of miles during the winter and still have the land usable by spring. Field tests have been highly successful, and we've just gotten a huge order from two states that want immediate delivery."

"After their legislatures waited six months debating whether to use it or not," Ferrel hazarded out of long experience. "Hm-m-m, sounds good if they can sow enough earthworms after them to keep the ground in good condition. But what's the worry?"

Jenkins shook his head indignantly. "I'm not worried. I simply think we should take every possible precaution and be ready for any accident; after all, they're working on something new, and a half life of a week is rather strong, don't you think? Besides, I looked over some of the reaction charts in the article, and—What was that?"

From somewhere to the left of the Infirmary, a muffled growl was being accompanied by ground tremors; then it gave place to a steady hissing, barely audible through the insulated walls of the building. Ferrel listened a moment and shrugged. "Nothing to worry about, Jenkins; you'll hear it a dozen times a year. Ever since the Great War when he tried to commit hara-kiri over the treachery of his people, Hokusai's been bugs about getting an atomic explosive bomb which will let us wipe out the rest of the world. Some day you'll probably see the little guy brought in here minus his head, but so far he hasn't found anything with short enough a half life that can be controlled until needed. What about the reaction charts on I-713?"

"Nothing definite, I suppose." Jenkins turned reluctantly away from the sound, still frowning. "I know it worked in small lots, but there's something about one of the intermediate steps I distrust, sir. I thought I recognized…I tried to ask one of the engineers about it. He practically told me to shut up until I'd studied atomic engineering myself."

Seeing the boy's face whiten over tensed jaw muscles, Ferrel held back his smile and nodded slowly. Something funny there; of course, Jenkins' pride had been wounded, but hardly that much. Some day, he'd have to find out what was behind it; little things like that could ruin a man's steadiness with the instruments, if he kept it to himself. Meantime, the subject was best dropped.

The telephone girl's heavily syllabized voice cut into his thoughts from the annunciator. "Dr. Ferrel. Dr. Ferrel wanted on the telephone. Dr. Ferrel, please!"

Jenkins' face blanched still further, and his eyes darted to his superior sharply.

Doc grunted casually. "Probably Palmer's bored and wants to tell me all about his grandson again. He thinks that child's an all time genius because it says two words at eighteen months." But inside the office, he stopped to wipe his hands free of perspiration before answering; there was something contagious about Jenkins' suppressed fears. And Palmer's face on the little television screen didn't help any, though the director was wearing his usual set smile. Ferrel knew it wasn't about the baby this time, and he was right.

"'Lo, Ferrel." Palmer's heartily confident voice was quite normal, but the use of the last name was a clear sign of some trouble. "There's been a little accident in the plant, they tell me. They're bringing a few men over to the Infirmary for treatment—probably not right away, though. Has Blake gone yet?"

"He's been gone fifteen minutes or more. Think it's serious enough to call him back, or are Jenkins and myself enough?"

"Jenkins? Oh, the new doctor." Palmer hesitated, and his arms showed quite clearly the doodling operations of his hands, out of sight of the vision cell. "No, of course, no need to call Blake back, I suppose—not yet, anyhow. Just worry anyone who saw him coming in. Probably nothing serious."

"What is it—radiation burns, or straight accident?"

"Oh—radiation mostly—maybe accident, too. Someone got a little careless—you know how it is. Nothing to worry about, though. You've been through it before when they opened a port too soon."

Doc knew enough about that—if that's what it was. "Sure, we can handle that, Palmer. But I thought No. 1 was closing down at five thirty tonight. Anyhow, how come they haven't installed the safety ports on it? You told me they had, six months ago."

"I didn't say it was No. 1, or that it was a manual port. You know, new equipment for new products." Palmer looked up at someone else, and his upper arms made a slight movement before he looked down at the vision cell again. "I can't go into it now, Dr. Ferrel; accident's throwing us off schedule, you see—details piling up on me. We can talk it over later, and you probably have to make arrangements now. Call me if you want anything."

The screen darkened and the phone clicked off abruptly, just as a muffled word started. The voice hadn't been Palmer's. Ferrel pulled his stomach in, wiped the sweat off his hands again, and went out into the surgery with careful casualness. Damn Palmer, why couldn't the fool give enough information to make decent preparations possible? He was sure 3 and 4 alone were operating, and they were supposed to be foolproof. Just what had happened?

Jenkins jerked up from a bench as he came out, face muscles tense and eyes filled with a nameless fear. Where he had been sitting, a copy of the *Weekly Ray* was lying open at a chart of symbols which meant nothing to Ferrel, except for the penciled line under one of the reactions. The boy picked it up and stuck it back on a table.

"Routine accident," Ferrel reported as naturally as he could, cursing himself for having to force his voice. Thank the Lord, the boy's hands hadn't trembled visibly when he was moving the paper; he'd still be useful if surgery were necessary. Palmer had said nothing of that, of course—he'd said nothing about entirely too much. "They're bringing a few men over for radiation burns, according to Palmer. Everything ready?"

Jenkins nodded tightly. "Quite ready, sir, as much as we can be for routine accidents at 3 and 4!...Isotope R... Sorry, Dr. Ferrel, I didn't mean that. Should we call in Dr. Blake and the other nurses and attendants?"

"Eh? Oh, probably we can't reach Blake, and Palmer doesn't think we need him. You might have Nurse Dodd locate Meyers—the others are out on dates by now if I know them, and the two nurses should be enough, with Jones; they're better than a flock of the others, anyway." Isotope R? Ferrel remembered the name, but nothing else. Something an engineer had said once—but he couldn't recall in what connection—or had Hokusai mentioned it? He watched Jenkins leave and turned on an impulse to his office where he could phone in reasonable privacy.

"Get me Matsuura Hokusai." He stood drumming on the table impatiently until the screen finally lighted and the little Japanese looked out of it. "Hoke, do you know what they were turning out over at 3 and 4?"

The scientist nodded slowly, his wrinkled face as expressionless as his unaccented English. "Yess, they are make I-713 for the weevil. Why you assk?"

"Nothing; just curious. I heard rumors about an Isotope R and wondered if there was any connection. Seems they had a little accident over there, and I want to be ready for whatever comes of it."

For a fraction of a second, the heavy lids on Hokusai's eyes seemed lo lift, but his voice remained neutral, only slightly faster. "No connection. Dr. Ferrel, they are not make Issotope R, very much assure you. Besst you forget Issotope R. Very ssorry. Dr. Ferrel, I musst now ssee accident. Thank you for call. Goodby." The screen was blank again, along with Ferrel's mind.

Jenkins was standing in the door, but had either heard nothing or seemed not to know about it. "Nurse Meyers is coming back," he said "Shall I get ready for curare injections?"

"Uh—might be a good idea." Ferrel had no intention of being surprised again, no matter what the implication of the words. Curare, one of the greatest poisons, known to South American primitives for centuries and only recently synthesized by modern chemistry, was the final resort for use in cases of radiation injury that was utterly beyond control. While the Infirmary stocked it for such emergencies, in the four years of Doc's practice it had been used only twice; neither experiment had been pleasant. Jenkins was either thoroughly frightened or overzealous—unless he knew something he had no business knowing.

"Seems to take them long enough to get the men here—can't be too serious, Jenkins, or they'd move faster."

"Maybe." Jenkins went on with his preparations, dissolving dried plasma in distilled, de-aerated water, without looking up. "There's the litter siren now. You'd better get washed up while I take care of the patients."

Doc listened to the sound that came in as a faint drone from outside, and grinned slightly. "Must be Beel driving; he's the only man fool enough to run the siren when the runways are empty. Anyhow, if you'll listen, it's the out trip he's making. Be at least five minutes before he gets back." But he turned into the washroom, kicked on the hot water and began scrubbing vigorously with the strong soap.

Damn Jenkins! Here he was preparing for surgery before he had any reason to suspect the need, and the boy was running things to suit himself, pretty much, as if armed with superior knowledge. Well, maybe he was. Either that, or he was simply half crazy with old wives' fears of anything relating to atomic reactions, and that didn't seem to fit the case. He rinsed off as Jenkins came in, kicked on the hot-air blast, and let his arms dry, then bumped against a rod that brought out rubber gloves on little holders. "Jenkins, what's all this Isotope R business, anyway? I've heard about it somewhere—probably from Hokusai. But I can't remember anything definite."

"Naturally—there isn't anything definite. That's the trouble." The young doctor tackled the area under his fingernails before looking up; then he saw Ferrel was slipping into his surgeon's whites that had come out on a hanger, and waited until the other was finished. "R's one of the big maybe problems of atomics. Purely theoretical, and none's been made yet—it's either impossible or can't be done in small control batches, safe for testing. That's the trouble, as I said; nobody knows anything about it, except that—if it can exist—it'll break down in a fairly short time into Mahler's Isotope. You've heard of that?"

Doc had—twice. The first had been when Mahler and half his laboratory had disappeared with accompanying noise; he'd been making a comparatively small amount of the new product designed to act as a starter for other reactions. Later, Maicewicz had tackled it on a smaller scale, and that time only two rooms and three men had gone up in dust particles. Five or six years later, atomic theory had been extended to the point where any study could find why the apparently safe product decided to become pure helium and energy in approximately one-billionth of a second.

"How long a time?"

"Half a dozen theories, and no real idea." They'd come out of the washrooms, finished except for their masks. Jenkins ran his elbow into a switch that turned on the ultraviolets that were supposed to sterilize the entire surgery, then looked around questioningly. "What about the supersonics?"

Ferrel kicked them on, shuddering as the bone-shaking harmonic indicated their activity. He couldn't complain about the equipment, at least. Ever since the last accident, when the State Congress developed ideas, there'd been enough gadgets lying around to stock up several small hospitals. The supersonics were intended to penetrate through all solids in the room, sterilizing where the UV light couldn't. A whistling note in the harmonics reminded him of something that had been tickling around in the back of his mind for minutes.

"There was no emergency whistle, Jenkins. Hardly seems to me they'd neglect that if it were so important."

Jenkins grunted skeptically and eloquently. "I read in the papers a few days ago where Congress was thinking of moving all atomic plants—meaning National, of course—out into the Mojave Desert. Palmer wouldn't like that… There's the siren again."

Jones, the male attendant, had heard it, and was already running out the fresh stretcher for the litter into the back receiving room. Half a minute later, Beel came trundling in the detachable part of the litter. "Two," he announced. "More coming up as soon as they can get to 'em, Doc."

There was blood spilled over the canvas, and a closer inspection indicated its source in a severed jugular vein, now held in place with a small safety pin that had fastened the two sides of the cut with a series of little pricks around which the blood had clotted enough to stop further loss.

Doc kicked off the supersonics with relief and indicated the man's throat. "Why wasn't I called out instead of having him brought here?"

"Hell, Doc, Palmer said bring 'em in and I brought 'em—I dunno. Guess some guy pinned up this fellow so they figured he could wait. Anything wrong?"

Ferrel grimaced. "With a split jugular, nothing that stops the bleeding's wrong, orthodox or not. How many more, and what's wrong out there?"

"Lord knows, Doc. I only drive 'em, I don't ask questions. So long!" He pushed the new stretcher up on the carriage, went wheeling it out to the small two-wheeled tractor that completed the litter. Ferrel dropped his curiosity back to its proper place and turned to the jugular case, while Dodd adjusted her mask. Jones had their clothes off, swabbed them down hastily, and wheeled them out on operating tables into the center of the surgery.

"Plasma!" A quick examination had shown Doc nothing else wrong with the jugular case, and he made the injection quickly. Apparently the man was only unconscious from shock induced by loss of blood, and the breathing and heart action resumed a more normal course as the liquid filled out the depleted blood vessels. He treated the wound with a sulphonamide derivative in routine procedure, cleaned and sterilized the edges gently, applied clamps carefully, removed the pin, and began stitching with the complicated little motor needle—one of the few gadgets for which he had any real appreciation. A few more drops of blood had spilled, but not seriously, and the wound was now permanently sealed. "Save the pin, Dodd. Goes in the collection. That's all for this. How's the other, Jenkins?"

Jenkins pointed to the back of the man's neck, indicating a tiny bluish object sticking out. "Fragment of steel, clear into the medulla oblongata. No blood loss, but he's been dead since it touched him. Want me to remove it?"

"No need—mortician can do it if they want… If these are a sample, I'd guess it as a plain industrial accident, instead of anything connected with radiation."

"You'll get that, too, Doc." It was the jugular case, apparently conscious and normal except for pallor. "We weren't in the converter house. Hey, I'm all right!… I'll be—"

Ferrel smiled at the surprise on the fellow's face. "Thought you were dead, eh? Sure, you're all right, if you'll take it easy. A torn jugular either kills you or else it's nothing to worry about. Just pipe down and let the nurse put you to sleep, and you'll never know you got it."

"Lord! Stuff came flying out of the air-intake like bullets out of a machine gun. Just a scratch, I thought; then Jake was bawling like a baby and yelling for a pin. Blood all over the place—then here I am, good as new."

"Uh-huh." Dodd was already wheeling him off to a ward room, her grim face wrinkled into a half-quizzical expression over the mask. "Doctor said to pipe down, didn't he? Well!"

As soon as Dodd vanished, Jenkins sat down, running his hand over his cap; there were little beads of sweat showing where the goggles and mask didn't entirely cover his face. " 'Stuff came flying out of the air-intake like bullets out of a machine gun,' " he repeated softly. "Dr. Ferrel, these two cases were outside the converter—just by-product accidents. Inside—"

"Yeah." Ferrel was picturing things himself, and it wasn't pleasant. Outside, matter tossed through the air ducts; inside—He left it hanging, as Jenkins had. "I'm going to call Blake. We'll probably need him."

II

"Give me Dr. Blake's residence—Maple 2337," Ferrel said quickly into the phone. The operator looked blank for a second, starting and then checking a purely automatic gesture toward the plugs. "Maple 2337, I said."

"I'm sorry, Dr. Ferrel, I can't give you an outside line. All trunk lines are out of order." There was constant buzz from the board, but nothing showed in the panel to indicate whether from white inside lights or the red trunk indicators.

"But—this is an emergency, operator. I've got to get in touch with Blake!"

"Sorry, Dr. Ferrel. All trunk lines are out of order." She started to reach for the plug, but Ferrel stopped her.

"Give me Palmer, then—and no nonsense! If his line's busy, cut me in, and I'll take the responsibility."

"Very good." She snapped at her switches. "I'm sorry, emergency call from Dr. Ferrel. Hold the line and I'll reconnect you." Then Palmer's face was on the panel, and this time the man was making no attempt to conceal his expression of worry.

"What is it, Ferrel?"

"I want Blake here—I'm going to need him. The operator says—"

"Yeah." Palmer nodded tightly, cutting in. "I've been trying to get him myself, but his house doesn't answer. Any idea of where to reach him?"

"You might try the Bluebird or any of the other night clubs around there." Damn, why did this have to be Blake's celebration night? No telling where he could be found by this time.

Palmer was speaking again. "I've already had all the night clubs and restaurants called, and he doesn't answer. We're paging the movie houses and theaters now—just a second... Nope, he isn't there, Ferrel. Last reports, no response."

"How about sending out a general call over the radio?"

"I'd...I'd like to, Ferrel, but it can't be done." The manager had hesitated for a fraction of a second, but his reply was positive. "Oh, by the way, we'll notify your wife you won't be home. Operator! You there? Good, reconnect the Governor!"

There was no sense in arguing into a blank screen, Doc realized. If Palmer wouldn't put through a radio call, he wouldn't, though it had been done once before. "All trunk lines are out of order... We'll notify your wife... Reconnect the Governor!" They weren't even being careful to cover up. He must have repeated the words aloud as he backed out of the office, still staring at the screen, for Jenkins' face twitched into a maladjusted grin.

"So we're cut off. I knew it already; Meyers just got in with more details." He nodded toward the nurse, just coming out of the dressing room and trying to smooth out her uniform. Her almost pretty face was more confused than worried.

"I was just leaving the plant, Dr. Ferrel, when my name came up on the outside speaker, but I had trouble getting here. We're locked in! I saw them at the gate—guards with sticks. They were turning back everyone that tried to leave, and wouldn't tell why, even. Just general orders that no one was to leave until Mr. Palmer gave his permission. And they weren't going to let me back in at first. Do you suppose…do you know what it's all about? I heard little things that didn't mean anything, really, but—"

"I know just about as much as you do, Meyers, though Palmer said something about carelessness with one of the ports on No. 3 or 4," Ferrel answered her. "Probably just precautionary measures. Anyway, I wouldn't worry about it yet."

"Yes, Dr. Ferrel." She nodded and turned back to the front office, there was no assurance in her look. Doc realized that neither Jenkins nor himself were pictures of confidence at the moment.

"Jenkins," he said, when she was gone, "if you know anything I don't, for the love of Mike, out with it! I've never seen anything like this around here."

Jenkins shook himself, and for the first time since he'd been there, used Ferrel's nickname. "Doc, I don't—that's why I'm in a blue funk. I know just enough to be less sure than you can be, and I'm scared as hell!"

"Let's see your hands." The subject was almost a monomania with Ferrel, and he knew it, but he also knew it wasn't unjustified. Jenkins' hands came out promptly, and there was no tremble to them. The boy threw up his arm so the sleeve slid beyond the elbow, and Ferrel nodded; there was no sweat trickling down from the armpits to reveal a worse case of nerves than showed on the surface. "Good enough, son; I don't care how scared you are—I'm getting that way myself—but with Blake out of the picture, and the other nurses and attendants sure to be out of reach, I'll need everything you've got."

"Doc?"

"Well?"

"If you'll take my word for it, I can get another nurse here—and a good one, too. They don't come any better, or any steadier, and she's not working now. I didn't expect her—well, anyhow, she'd skin me if I didn't call when we need one. Want her?"

"No trunk lines for outside calls," Doc reminded him. It was the first time he'd seen any real enthusiasm on the boy's face, and however good of bad the nurse was, she'd obviously be of value in bucking up Jenkins' spirits. "Go to it, though; right now we can probably use any nurse. Sweetheart?"

"Wife." Jenkins went toward the dressing room. "And I don't need the phone;

we used to carry ultra-short-wave personal radios to keep in touch, and I've still got mine here. And if you're worried about her qualifications, she handed instruments to Bayard at Mayo's for five years—that's how I managed to get through medical school!"

The siren was approaching again when Jenkins came back, the little tense lines about his lips still there, but his whole bearing somehow steadier. He nodded. "I called Palmer, too, and he O.K.'d her coming inside on the phone without wondering how I'd contacted her. The switchboard girl has standing orders to route all calls from us through before anything else, it seems."

Doc nodded, his ear cocked toward the drone of the siren that drew up and finally ended on a sour wheeze. There was a feeling of relief from tension about him as he saw Jones appear and go toward the rear entrance; work, even under the pressure of an emergency, was always easier than sitting around waiting for it. He saw two stretchers come in, both bearing double loads, and noted that Beel was babbling at the attendant, the driver's usually phlegmatic manner completely gone.

"I'm quitting; I'm through tomorrow! No more watching 'em drag out stiffs for me—not that way. Dunno why I gotta go back, anyhow; it won't do 'em any good to get in further, even if they can. From now on, I'm driving a truck, so help me I am!"

Ferrel let him rave on, only vaguely aware that the man was close to hysteria. He had no time to give to Beel now as he saw the raw red flesh through the visor of one of the armor suits. "Cut off what clothes you can, Jones," he directed. "At least get the shield suits off them. Tannic acid ready, nurse?"

"Ready." Meyers answered together with Jenkins, who was busily helping Jones strip off the heavily armored suits and helmets.

Ferrel kicked on the supersonics again, letting them sterilize the metal suits—there was going to be no chance to be finicky about asepsis; the supersonics and ultra-violet tubes were supposed to take care of that, and they'd have to do it, to a large extent, little as he liked it. Jenkins finished his part, dived back for fresh gloves, with a mere cursory dipping of his hands into antiseptic and rinse. Dodd followed him, while Jones wheeled three of the cases into the middle of the surgery, ready for work; the other had died on the way in.

It was going to be messy work, obviously. Where metal from the suits had touched, or come near touching, the flesh was burned—crisped, rather. And that was merely a minor part of it, as was the more than ample evidence of major radiation burns, which had probably not stopped at the surface, but penetrated through the flesh and bones into the vital interior organs. Much worse, the writhing and spasmodic muscular contractions indicated radioactive matter that had been forced into the flesh and was acting directly on the nerves controlling the motor impulses. Jenkins looked hastily at the twisting body of his case and his face blanched to a yellowish white; it was the first real example of the full possibilities of an atomic accident he'd seen.

"Curare," he said finally, the word forced out, but level. Meyers handed him the hypodermic and he inserted it, his hand still steady—more than normally steady, in fact, with that absolute lack of movement that can come to a living organism only under the stress of emergency. Ferrel dropped his eyes back to his own case, both relieved and worried.

From the spread of the muscular convulsions, there could be only one explanation—somehow, radioactives had not only worked their way through the air grills, but had been forced through the almost air-tight joints and sputtered directly into the flesh of the men. Now they were sending out radiations into every nerve, throwing aside the normal orders from the brain and spinal column, setting up anarchic orders of their own that left the muscles to writhe and jerk, one against the other, without order or reason, or any of the normal restraints the body places upon itself. The closest parallel was that of a man undergoing metrozol shock for schizophrenia, or a severe case of strychnine poisoning. He injected curare carefully, metering out the dosage according to the best estimate he could make, but Jenkins had been acting under a pressure that finished the second injection as Doc looked up from his first. Still, in spite of the rapid spread of the drug, some of the twitching went on.

"Curare," Jenkins repeated, and Doc tensed mentally; he'd still been debating whether to risk the extra dosage. But he made no counter-order, feeling slightly relieved this time at having the matter taken out of his hands; Jenkins went back to work, pushing up the injections to the absolute limit of safety, and slightly beyond. One of the cases had started a weird minor moan that hacked on and off as his lungs and vocal cords went in and out of synchronization, but it quieted under the drug, and in a matter of minutes the three lay still, breathing with the shallow flaccidity common to curare treatment. They were still moving slightly, but where before they were perfectly capable of breaking their own bones in uncontrolled efforts, now there was only motion similar to a man with a chill.

"God bless the man who synthesized curare," Jenkins muttered as he began cleaning away damaged flesh, Meyers assisting.

Doc could repeat that; with the older, natural product, true standardization and exact dosage had been next to impossible. Too much, and its action on the body was fatal; the patient died from "exhaustion" of his chest muscles in a matter of minutes. Too little was practically useless. Now that the danger of self-injury and fatal exhaustion from wild exertion was over, he could attend to such relatively unimportant things as the agony still going on—curare had no particular effect on the sensory nerves. He injected neo-heroin and began cleaning the burned areas and treating them with the standard tannic-acid routine, first with a sulphonamide to eliminate possible infection, glancing up occasionally at Jenkins.

He had no need to worry, though; the boy's nerves were frozen into an unnatural calm that still pressed through with a speed Ferrel made no attempt to equal, knowing his work would suffer for it. At a gesture, Dodd handed him the little radiation detector, and he began hunting over the skin, inch by inch, for the almost microscopic bits of matter; there was no hope of finding all now, but the worst deposits could be found and removed; later, with more time, a final probing could be made.

"Jenkins," he asked, "how about I-713's chemical action? Is it basically poisonous to the system?"

"No. Perfectly safe except for radiation. Eight in the outer electron ring, chemically inert."

That, at least, was a relief. Radiations were bad enough in and of themselves, but when coupled with metallic poisoning, like the old radium or mercury poisoning, it was even worse. The small colloidially fine particles of I-713 in the flesh would set up their own danger signal, and could be scraped away in the worst cases; otherwise, they'd probably have to stay until the isotope exhausted itself. Mercifully, its half life was short, which would decrease the long hospitalization and suffering of the men.

Jenkins joined Ferrel on the last patient, replacing Dodd at handing instruments. Doc would have preferred the nurse, who was used to his little signals, but he said nothing, and was surprised to note the efficiency of the boy's cooperation. "How about the breakdown products?" he asked.

"I-713? Harmless enough, mostly, and what isn't harmless isn't concentrated enough to worry about. That is, if it's still I-713. Otherwise—"

Otherwise, Doc finished mentally, the boy meant there'd be no danger from poisoning, at least. Isotope R, with an uncertain degeneration period, turned into Mahler's Isotope, with a complete breakdown in a billionth of a second. He had a fleeting vision of men, filled with a fine dispersion of that, suddenly erupting over their body with a violence that could never be described; Jenkins must have been thinking the same thing. For a few seconds, they stood there, looking at each other silently, but neither chose to speak of it. Ferrel reached for the probe, Jenkins shrugged, and they went on with their work and their thoughts.

It was a picture impossible to imagine, which they might or might not see; if such an atomic blow-up occurred, what would happen to the laboratory was problematical. No one knew the exact amount Maicewicz had worked on, except that it was the smallest amount he could make, so there could be no good estimate of the damage. The bodies on the operating tables, the little scraps of removed flesh containing the minute globules of radioactive, even the instruments that had come in contact with them, were bombs waiting to explode. Ferrel's own fingers took on some of the steadiness that was frozen in Jenkins as he went about his work, forcing his mind onto the difficult labor at hand.

It might have been minutes or hours later when the last dressing was in place and the three broken bones of the worst case were set. Meyers and Dodd, along with Jones, were taking care of the men, putting them into the little wards, and the two physicians were alone, carefully avoiding each other's eyes, waiting without knowing exactly what they expected.

Outside, a droning chug came to their ears, and the thump of something heavy moving over the runways. By common impulse they slipped to the side door and looked out, to see the rear end of one of the electric tanks moving away from them. Night had fallen some time before, but the gleaming lights from the big towers around the fence made the plant stand out in glaring detail. Except for the tank moving away, though, other buildings cut off their view.

Then, from the direction of the main gate, a shrill whistle cut the air, and there was a sound of men's voices, though the words were indistinguishable. Sharp, crisp syllables followed, and Jenkins nodded slowly to himself. "Ten'll get you a hundred," he began, "that— Uh, no use betting. It is."

Around the corner a squad of men in State militia uniform marched briskly, bayoneted rifles on their arms. With efficient precision, they spread out under a sergeant's direction, each taking a post before the door of one of the buildings, one approaching the place where Ferrel and Jenkins stood.

"So that's what Palmer was talking to the Governor about," Ferrel muttered. "No use asking them questions, I suppose; they know less than we do. Come on inside where we can sit down and rest. Wonder what good the militia can do here—unless Palmer's afraid someone inside's going to crack and cause trouble."

Jenkins followed him back to the office and accepted a cigarette automatically as he flopped back into a chair. Doc was discovering just how good it felt to give his muscles and nerves a chance to relax, and realizing that they must have been far longer in the surgery than he had thought. "Care for a drink?"

"Uh—is it safe, Doc? We're apt to be back in there any minute."

Ferrel pulled a grin onto his face and nodded. "It won't hurt you—we're just enough on edge and tired for it to be burned up inside for fuel instead of reaching our nerves. Here." It was a generous slug of rye he poured for each, enough to send an almost immediate warmth through them, and to relax their overtensed nerves. "Wonder why Beel hasn't been back long ago?"

"That tank we saw probably explains it; it got too tough for the men to work in just their suits, and they've had to start excavating through the converters with the tanks. Electric, wasn't it, battery powered?... So there's enough radiation loose out there to interfere with atomic-powered machines, then. That means whatever they're doing is tough and slow work. Anyhow, it's more important that they damp the action than get the men out, if they only realize it—Sue!"

Ferrel looked up quickly to see the girl standing there, already dressed for surgery, and he was not too old for a little glow of appreciation to creep over him. No wonder Jenkins' face lighted up. She was small, but her figure was shaped like that of a taller girl, not in the cute or pert lines usually associated with shorter women, and the serious competence of her expression hid none of the loveliness of her face. Obviously she was several years older than Jenkins, but as he stood up to greet her, her face softened and seemed somehow youthful beside the boy's as she looked up.

"You're Dr. Ferrel?" she asked, turning to the older man. "I was a little late—there was some trouble at first about letting me in—so I went directly to prepare before bothering you. And just so you won't be afraid to use me, my credentials are all here."

She put the little bundle on the table, and Ferrel ran through them briefly; it was better than he'd expected. Technically she wasn't a nurse at all, but a doctor of medicine, a so-called nursing doctor; there'd been the need for assistants midway between doctor and nurse for years, having the general training and abilities of both, but only in the last decade had the actual course been created, and the graduates were still limited to a few.

He nodded and handed them back. "We can use you, Dr.—"

"Brown—professional name, Dr. Ferrel. And I'm used to being called just Nurse Brown."

Jenkins cut in on the formalities. "Sue, is there any news outside about what's going on here?"

"Rumors, but they're wild, and I didn't have a chance to hear many. All I know is that they're talking about evacuating the city and everything within fifty miles of here, but it isn't official. And some people were saying the Governor was sending in troops to declare martial law over the whole section, but I didn't see any except here."

***

Jenkins took her off, then, to show her the Infirmary and introduce her to Jones and the two other nurses, leaving Ferrel to wait for the sound of the siren again, and to try putting two and two together to get sixteen. He attempted to make sense out of the article in the *Weekly Ray,* but gave it up finally; atomic theory had advanced too far since the sketchy studies he'd made, and the symbols were largely without meaning to him. He'd have to rely on Jenkins, it seemed. In the meantime, what was holding up the litter? He should have heard the warning siren long before.

It wasn't the litter that came in next, though, but a group of five men, two carrying a third, and a fourth supporting the fifth. Jenkins took the carried man over, Brown helping him; it was similar to the former cases, but without the actual burns from contact with hot metal. Ferrel turned to the men.

"Where's Beel and the litter?" He was inspecting the supported man's leg as he asked, and began work on it without moving the fellow to a table. Apparently a lump of radioactive matter the size of a small pea had been driven half an inch into the flesh below the thigh, and the broken bone was the result of the violent contractions of the man's own muscles under the stimulus of the radiation. It wasn't pretty. Now, however, the strength of the action had apparently burned out the nerves around, so the leg was comparatively limp and without feeling; the man lay watching, relaxed on the bench in a half-comatose condition, his eyes popping out and his lips twisted into a sick grimace, but he did not flinch as the wound was scraped out. Ferrel was working around a small leaden shield, his arms covered with heavily leaded gloves, and he dropped the scraps of flesh and isotope into a box of the same metal.

"Beel—he's out of this world, Doc," one of the others answered when he could tear his eyes off the probing. "He got himself blotto, somehow, and wrecked the litter before he got back. Couldn't take it, watching us grapple 'em out—and we hadda go in after 'em without a drop of hootch!"

Ferrel glanced at him quickly, noticing Jenkins' head jerk around as he did so. "You were getting them out? You mean you didn't come from in there?"

"Heck, no, Doc. Do we look that bad? Them two got it when the stuff decided to spit on 'em clean through their armor. Me, I got me some nice burns, but I ain't complaining—I got a look at a couple of stiffs, so I'm kicking about nothing!"

Ferrel hadn't noticed the three who had traveled under their own power, but he looked now, carefully. They were burned, and badly, by radiations, but the burns were still new enough not to give them too much trouble, and probably what they'd just been through had temporarily deadened their awareness of pain, just as a soldier on the battlefield may be wounded and not realize it until the action stops. Anyway, atomjacks were not noted for sissiness.

"There's almost a quart in the office there on the table," he told them. "One good drink apiece—no more. Then go up front and I'll send Nurse Brown in to fix up your burns as well as can be for now." Brown could apply the unguents developed to heal radiation burns as well as he could, and some division of work that would relieve Jenkins and himself seemed necessary. "Any chance of finding any more living men in the converter housings?"

"Maybe. Somebody said the thing let out a groan half a minute before it popped, so most of 'em had a chance to duck into the two safety chambers. Figure on going back there and pushing tanks ourselves unless you say no; about half an hour's work left before we can crack the chambers, I guess, then we'll know."

"Good. And there's no sense in sending in every man with a burn, or we'll be flooded here; they can wait, and it looks as if we'll have plenty of serious stuff to care for. Dr. Brown, I guess you're elected to go out with the men—have one of them drive the spare litter Jones will show you. Salve down all the burn cases, put the worst ones off duty, and just send in the ones with the jerks. You'll find my emergency kit in the office, there. Someone has to be out there to give first aid and sort them out—we haven't room for the whole plant in here."

"Right, Dr. Ferrel." She let Meyers replace her in assisting Jenkins, and was gone briefly to come out with his bag. "Come on, you men. I'll hop the litter and dress down your burns on the way. You're appointed driver, mister. Somebody should have reported that Beel person before. The litter would be out there now."

The spokesman for the others upended the glass he'd filled, swallowed, gulped, and grinned down at her. "O.K., doctor, only out there you ain't got time to think—you gotta do. Thanks for the shot, Doc, and I'll tell Hoke you're appointing her out there."

They filed out behind Brown as Jones went out to get the second litter, and Doc went ahead with the quick-setting plastic cast for the broken leg. Too bad there weren't more of those nursing doctors; he'd have to see Palmer about it after this was over—if Palmer and he were still around. Wonder how the men in the safety chambers, about which he'd completely forgotten, would make out? There were two in each converter housing, designed as an escape for the men in case of accident, and supposed to be proof against almost anything. If the men had reached them, maybe they were all right; he wouldn't have taken a bet though. With a slight shrug, he finished his work and went over to help Jenkins.

The boy nodded down at the body on the table, already showing extensive scraping and probing. "Quite a bit of spitting clean through the armor," he commented. "Those words were just a little too graphic for me. I-713 couldn't do that."

"Hm-m-m." Doc was in no mood to quibble on the subject. He caught himself looking at the little box in which the stuff was put after they worked what they could out of the flesh, and jerked his eyes away quickly. Whenever the lid was being dropped, a glow could be seen inside. Jenkins always managed to keep his eyes on something else.

They were almost finished when the switchboard girl announced a call, and they waited to make the few last touches before answering, then filed into the office together. Brown's face was on the screen, smudged and with a spot of rouge standing out on each cheek. Another smudge appeared as she brushed the auburn hair out of her eyes with the back of her wrist.

"They've cracked the converter safety chambers, Dr. Ferrel. The north one held up perfectly, except for the heat and a little burn, but something happened in the other; oxygen valve stuck, and all are unconscious, but alive. Magma must have sprayed through the door, because sixteen or seventeen have the jerks, and about a dozen are dead. Some others need more care than I can give—I'm having Hokusai delegate men to carry those the stretchers won't hold, and they're all piling up on you in a bunch right now!"

Ferrel grunted and nodded. "Could have been worse, I guess. Don't kill yourself out there, Brown."

"Same to you." She blew Jenkins a kiss and snapped off, just as the whine of the litter siren reached their ears.

In the surgery again, they could see a truck showing behind it, and men lifting out bodies in apparently endless succession.

"Get their armor off, somehow, Jones—grab anyone else to help you that you can. Curare, Dodd, and keep handing it to me. We'll worry about everything else after Jenkins and I quiet them." This was obviously going to be a mass-production sort of business, not for efficiency, but through sheer necessity. And again, Jenkins with his queer taut steadiness was doing two for one that Doc could do, his face pale and his eyes almost glazed, but his hands moving endlessly and nervelessly on with his work.

Sometime during the night Jenkins looked up at Meyers, and motioned her back. "Go get some sleep, nurse; Miss Dodd can take care of both Dr. Ferrel and myself when we work close together. Your nerves are shot, and you need the rest. Dodd, you can call her back in two hours and rest yourself."

"What about you, doctor?"

"Me—" He grinned out of the corner of his mouth, crookedly. "I've got an imagination that won't sleep, and I'm needed here." The sentence ended on a rising inflection that was false to Ferrel's ear, and the older doctor looked at the boy thoughtfully.

Jenkins caught his look. "It's O.K., Doc; I'll let you know when I'm going to crack. It was O.K. to send Meyers back, wasn't it?"

"You were closer to her than I was, so you should know better than I." Technically, the nurses were all directly under his control, but they'd dropped such technicalities long before. Ferrel rubbed the small of his back briefly, then picked up his scalpel again.

A faint gray light was showing in the east, and the wards had overflowed into the waiting room when the last case from the chambers was finished as best he could be. During the night, the converter had continued to spit occasionally, even through the tank armor twice, but now there was a temporary lull in the arrival of workers for treatment. Doc sent Jones after breakfast from the cafeteria, then headed into the office where Jenkins was already slumped down in the old leather chair.

The boy was exhausted almost to the limit from the combined strain of the work and his own suppressed jitters, but he looked up in mild surprise as he felt the prick of the needle. Ferrel finished it, and used it on himself before explaining. "Morphine, of course. What else can we do? Just enough to keep us going, but without it we'll both be useless out there in a few more hours. Anyhow, there isn't as much reason not to use it as there was when I was younger, before the counter-agent was discovered to kill most of its habit-forming tendency. Even five years ago, before they had that, there were times when morphine was useful, Lord knows, though anyone who used it except as a last resort deserved all the hell he got. A real substitute for sleep would be better, though; wish they'd finish up the work they're doing on that fatigue eliminator at Harvard. Here, eat that!"

Jenkins grimaced at the breakfast Jones laid out in front of him, but he knew as well as Doc that the food was necessary, and he pulled the plate back to him. "What I'd give an eye tooth for, Doc, wouldn't be a substitute—just half an hour of good old-fashioned sleep. Only, damn it, if I knew I had time, I couldn't do it—not with R out there bubbling away."

The telephone annunciator clipped in before Doc could answer. "Telephone for Dr. Ferrel; emergency! Dr. Brown calling Dr. Ferrel!"

"Ferrel answering!" The phone girl's face popped off the screen, and a tired-faced Sue Brown looked out at them. "What is it?"

"It's that little Japanese fellow—Hokusai—who's been running things out here, Dr. Ferrel. I'm bringing him in with an acute case of appendicitis. Prepare surgery!"

Jenkins gagged over the coffee he was trying to swallow, and his choking voice was halfway between disgust and hysterical laughter. "Appendicitis, Doc! My God, what comes next?"

III

It might have been worse. Brown had coupled in the little freezing unit on the litter and lowered the temperature around the abdomen, both preparing Hokusai for surgery and slowing down the progress of the infection so that the appendix was still unbroken when he was wheeled into the surgery. His seamed Oriental face had a grayish cast under the olive, but he managed a faint grin.

"Verry ssorry, Dr. Ferrel, to bother you. Verry ssorry. No ether, pleasse!"

Ferrel grunted. "No need of it, Hoke; we'll use hypothermy, since it's already begun. Over here, Jones... And you might as well go back and sit down, Jenkins."

Brown was washing, and popped out again, ready to assist with the operation. "He had to be tied down, practically, Dr. Ferrel. Insisted that he only needed a little mineral oil and some peppermint for his stomach-ache! Why are intelligent people always the most stupid?"

It was a mystery to Ferrel, too, but seemingly the case. He tested the temperature quickly while the surgery hypothermy equipment began functioning, found it low enough, and began. Hoke flinched with his eyes as the scalpel touched him, then opened them in mild surprise at feeling no appreciable pain. The complete absence of nerve response with its accompanying freedom from post-operative shock was one of the great advantages of low-temperature work in surgery. Ferrel laid back the flesh, severed the appendix quickly, and removed it through the tiny incision. Then, with one of the numerous attachments, he made use of the ingenious mechanical stitcher and stepped back.

"All finished, Hoke, and you're lucky you didn't rupture—peritonitis isn't funny, even though we can cut down on it with the sulphonamides. The ward's full, so's the waiting room, so you'll have to stay on the table for a few hours until we can find a place for you; no pretty nurse, either—until the two other girls get here some time this morning. I dunno what we'll do about the patients."

"But, Dr. Ferrel, I am hear that now ssurgery—I sshould be up, already. There iss work I am do."

"You've been hearing that appendectomy patients aren't confined now, eh? Well, that's partly true, Johns Hopkins began it quite awhile ago. But for the next hour, while the temperature comes back to normal, you stay put. After that, if you want to move around a little, you can; but no going out to the converter. A little exercise probably helps more than it harms, but any strain wouldn't be good."

"But, the danger—"

"Be hanged, Hoke. You couldn't help now, long enough to do any good. Until the stuff in those stitches dissolves away completely in the body fluids, you're to take it easy—and that's two weeks, about."

The little man gave in, reluctantly. "Then I think I ssleep now. But best you should call Mr. Palmer at once, pleasse! He musst know I am not there!"

Palmer took the news the hard way, with an unfair but natural tendency to blame Hokusai and Ferrel. "Damn it, Doc, I was hoping he'd get things straightened out somehow—I practically promised the Governor that Hoke could take care of it; he's got one of the best brains in the business. Now this! Well, no help, I guess. He certainly can't do it unless he's in condition to get right into things. Maybe Jorgenson, though, knows enough about it to handle it from a wheel chair, or something. How's he coming along—in shape to be taken out where he can give directions to the foremen?"

"Wait a minute." Ferrel stopped him as quickly as he could. "Jorgenson isn't here. We've got thirty-one men lying around, and he isn't one of them; and if he'd been one of the seventeen dead, you'd know it. I didn't know Jorgenson was working, even."

"He has to be—it was his process! Look, Ferrel, I was distinctly told that he was taken to you—foreman dumped him on the litter himself and reported at once! Better check up, and quick—with Hoke only half able, I've got to have Jorgenson!"

"He isn't here—I know Jorgenson. The foreman must have mistaken the big fellow from the south safety for him, but that man had black hair inside his helmet. What about the three hundred-odd that were only unconscious, or the fifteen-sixteen hundred men outside the converter when it happened?"

Palmer wiggled his jaw muscles tensely. "Jorgenson would have reported or been reported fifty times. Every man out there wants him around to boss things. He's gotta be in your ward."

"He isn't, I tell you! And how about moving some of the fellows here into the city hospitals?"

"Tried—hospitals must have been tipped off somehow about the radioactives in the flesh, and they refuse to let a man from here be brought in." Palmer was talking with only the surface of his mind, his cheek muscles bobbing as if he were chewing his thoughts and finding them tough. "Jorgenson—Hoke—and Kellar's been dead for years. Not another man in the whole country that understands this field enough to make a decent guess, even; I get lost on Page 6 myself. Ferrel, could a man in a Tomlin five-shield armor suit make the safety in twenty seconds, do you think, from—say beside the converter?"

Ferrel considered it rapidly. A Tomlin weighed about four hundred pounds, and Jorgenson was an ox of a man, but only human. "Under the stress of an emergency, it's impossible to guess what a man can do, Palmer, but I don't see how he could work his way half that distance."

"Hm-m-m, I figured. Could he live, then, supposing he wasn't squashed? Those suits carry their own air for twenty-four hours, you know, to avoid any air cracks, pumping the carbon-dioxide back under pressure and condensing the moisture out—no openings of any kind. They've got the best insulation of all kinds we know, too."

"One chance in a billion, I'd guess; but again, it's darned hard to put any exact limit on what can be done—miracles keep happening, every day. Going to try it?"

"What else can I do? There's no alternative. I'll meet you outside No. 4 just as soon as you can make it, and bring everything you need to start working at once. Seconds may count!" Palmer's face slid sideways and up as he was reaching for the button, and Ferrel wasted no time in imitating the motion.

By all logic, there wasn't a chance, even in a Tomlin. But, until they knew, the effort would have to be made; chances couldn't be taken when a complicated process had gone out of control, with now almost certainty that Isotope R was the result— Palmer was concealing nothing, even though he had stated nothing specifically. And obviously, if Hoke couldn't handle it, none of the men at other branches of National Atomic or at the smaller partially independent plants could make even a half-hearted stab at the job.

It all rested on Jorgenson, then. And Jorgenson must be somewhere under that semimolten hell that could drive through the tank armor and send men back into the Infirmary with bones broken from their own muscular anarchy!

Ferrel's face must have shown his thoughts, judging by Jenkins' startled expression. "Jorgenson's still in there somewhere," he said quickly.

"Jorgenson! But he's the man who—Good Lord!"

"Exactly. You'll stay here and take care of the jerk cases that may come in. Brown, I'll want you out there again. Bring everything portable we have, in case we can't move him in fast enough; get one of the trucks and fit it out; and be out with it about twice as fast as you can! I'm grabbing the litter now." He accepted the emergency kit Brown thrust into his hands, dumped a caffeine tablet into his mouth without bothering to wash it down, then was out toward the litter. "No. 4, and hurry!"

Palmer was just jumping off a scooter as they cut around No. 3 and in front of the rough fence of rope strung out quite a distance beyond 4. He glanced at Doc, nodded, and dived in through the men grouped around, yelling orders to right and left as he went, and was back at Ferrel's side by the time the litter had stopped.

"O.K., Ferrel, go over there and get into armor as quickly as possible. We're going in there with the tanks, whether we can or not, and be damned to the quenching for the moment. Briggs, get those things out there, clean out a roadway as best you can, throw in the big crane again, and we'll need all the men in armor we can get—give them steel rods and get them to probing in there for anything solid and big or small enough to be a man—five minutes at a stretch; they should be able to stand that. I'll be back pronto!"

Doc noted the confused mixture of tanks and machines of all descriptions clustered around the walls—or what was left of them—of the converter housing, and saw them yanking out everything along one side leaving an opening where the main housing gate had stood, now ripped out to expose a crane boom rooting out the worst obstructions, Obviously they'd been busy at some kind of attempt at quenching the action, but his knowledge of atomics was too little even to guess at what it was. The equipment set up was being pushed aside by tanks without dismantling, and men were running up into the roped-in section, some already armored, others dragging on part of their armor as they went. With the help of one of the atomjacks, he climbed into a suit himself, wondering what he could do in such a casing if anything needed doing.

Palmer had a suit on before him, though, and was waiting beside one of the tanks, squat and heavily armored, its front equipped with both a shovel and a grapple swinging from movable beams. "In here, Doc." Ferrel followed him into the housing of the machine and Palmer grabbed the controls as he pulled on a short-wave headset and began shouting orders through it toward the other tanks that were moving in on their heavy treads. The dull drone of the motor picked up, and the tank began lumbering forward under the manager's direction.

"Haven't run one of these since that show-off at a picnic seven years ago," he complained, as he kicked at the controls and straightened out a developing list to left. "Though I used to be pretty handy when I was plain engineer. Damned static around here almost chokes off the radio, but I guess enough gets through. By the best guess I can make, Jorgenson should have been near the main control panel when it started, and have headed for the south chamber. Half the distance, you figure?"

"Possibly, probably slightly less."

"Yeah! And then the stuff may have tossed him around. But we'll have to try to get there." He barked into the radio again. "Briggs, get those men in suits as close as you can and have them fish with their rods about thirty feet to the left of the pillar that's still up—can they get closer?"

The answer was blurred and pieces missing, but the general idea went across.

Palmer frowned. "O.K., if they can't make it, they can't; draw them back out of the reach of the stuff and hold them ready to go in...No, call for volunteers! I'm offering a thousand dollars a minute to every man that gets a stick in there, double to his family if the stuff gets him, and ten times that—fifty thousand—if he locates Jorgenson!... Look out, you blamed fool!" The last was to one of the men who'd started forward, toward the place, jumping from one piece of broken building to grab at a pillar and swing off in his suit toward something that looked like a standing position; it toppled, but he managed a leap that carried him to another lump, steadied himself, and began probing through the mess. "Oof! You with the crane—stick it in where you can grab any of the men that pass out, if it'll reach—good! Doc, I know as well as you that the men have no business in there, even five minutes; but I'll send in a hundred more if it'll find Jorgenson!"

Doc said nothing—he knew there'd probably be a hundred or more fools willing to try, and he knew the need of them. The tanks couldn't work their way close enough for any careful investigation of the mixed mass of radioactives, machinery, building debris, and destruction, aside from which they were much too slow in such delicate probing; only men equipped with the long steel poles could do that. As he watched, some of the activity of the magma suddenly caused an eruption, and one of the men tossed up his pole and doubled back into a half circle before falling. The crane operator shoved the big boom over and made a grab, missed, brought it down again, and came out with the heaving body held by one arm, to run it back along its track and twist it outward beyond Doc's vision.

Even through the tank and the suit, heat was pouring in, and there was a faint itching in those parts where the armor was thinnest that indicated the start of a burn—though not as yet dangerous. He had no desire to think what was happening to the men who were trying to worm into the heart of it in nothing but armor; nor did he care to watch what was happening to them. Palmer was trying to inch the machine ahead, but the stuff underneath made any progress difficult. Twice something spat against the tank, but did not penetrate.

"Five minutes are up," he told Palmer. "They'd all better go directly to Dr. Brown, who should be out with the truck now for immediate treatment."

Palmer nodded and relayed the instructions. "Pick up all you can with the crane and carry them back! Send in a new bunch, Briggs, and credit them with their bonus in advance. Damn it, Doc, this can go on all day; it'll take an hour to pry around through this mess right here, and then he's probably somewhere else. The stuff seems to be getting worse in this neighborhood, too, from what accounts I've had before. Wonder if that steel plate could be pushed down?"

He threw in the clutch engaging the motor to the treads and managed to twist through toward it. There was a slight slipping of the lugs, then the tractors caught, and the nose of the tank thrust forward; almost without effort, the fragment of housing toppled from its leaning position and slid forward. The tank growled, fumbled, and slowly climbed up onto it and ran forward another twenty feet to its end; the support settled slowly, but something underneath checked it, and they were still again. Palmer worked the grapple forward, nosing a big piece of masonry out of the way, and two men reached out with the ends of their poles to begin probing, futilely. Another change of men came out, then another.

Briggs' voice crackled erratically through the speaker again, "Palmer, I got a fool here who wants to go out on the end of your beam, if you can swing around so the crane can lift him out to it."

"Start him coming!" Again he began jerking the levers, and the tank bucked and heaved, backed and turned, ran forward, and repeated it all, while the plate that was holding them flopped up and down on its precarious balance.

Doc held his breath and began praying to himself; his admiration for the men who'd go out in that stuff was increasing by leaps and bounds, along with his respect for Palmer's ability.

The crane boom bobbed toward them, and the scoop came running out, but wouldn't quite reach; their own tank was relatively light and mobile compared to the bigger machine, but Palmer already had that pushed out to the limit, and hanging over the edge of the plate. It still lacked three feet of reaching.

"Damn!" Palmer slapped open the door of the tank, jumped forward on the tread, and looked down briefly before coming back inside. "No chance to get closer! Wheeoo! Those men earn their money."

But the crane operator had his own tricks, and was bobbing the boom of his machine up and down slowly with a motion that set the scoop swinging like a huge pendulum, bringing it gradually closer to the grapple beam. The man had an arm out, and finally caught the beam, swinging out instantly from the scoop that drew backward behind him. He hung suspended for a second, pitching his body around to a better position, then somehow wiggled up onto the end and braced himself with his legs. Doc let his breath out and Palmer inched the tank around to a forward position again. Now the pole of the atomjack could cover the wide territory before them, and he began using it rapidly.

"Win or lose, that man gets a triple bonus," Palmer muttered. "Uh!"

The pole had located something, and was feeling around to determine size; the man glanced at them and pointed frantically. Doc jumped forward to the windows as Palmer ran down the grapple and began pushing it down into the semimolten stuff under the pole; there was resistance there, but finally the prong of the grapple broke under and struck on something that refused to come up. The manager's hands moved the controls gently, making it tug from side to side; reluctantly, it gave and moved forward toward them, coming upward until they could make out the general shape. It was definitely no Tomlin suit!

"Lead hopper box! Damn—Wait, Jorgenson wasn't anybody's fool; when he saw he couldn't make the safety, he might…maybe—Palmer slapped the grapple down again, against the closed lid of the chest, but the hook was too large. Then the man clinging there caught the idea and slid down to the hopper chest, his armored hands grabbing at the lid. He managed to lift a corner of it until the grapple could catch and lift it the rest of the way, and his hands started down to jerk upward again.

The manager watched his motions, then flipped the box over with the grapple, and pulled it closer to the tank body; magma was running out, but there was a gleam of something else inside.

"Start praying, Doc!" Palmer worked it to the side of the tank and was out through the door again, letting the merciless heat and radiation stream in.

But Ferrel wasn't bothering with that now; he followed, reaching down into the chest to help the other two lift out the body of a huge man in a Five-shield Tomlin! Somehow, they wangled the six-hundred-odd pounds out and up on the treads, then into the housing, barely big enough for all of them. The atomjack pulled himself inside, shut the door, and flopped forward on his face, out cold.

"Never mind him—check Jorgenson!" Palmer's voice was heavy with the reaction from the hunt, but he turned the tank and sent it outward at top speed, regardless of risk. Contrarily, it bucked through the mass more readily than it had crawled in through the cleared section.

Ferrel unscrewed the front plate of the armor on Jorgenson as rapidly as he could, though he knew already that the man was still miraculously alive—corpses don't jerk with force enough to move a four-hundred-pound suit appreciably. A side glance, as they drew beyond the wreck of the converter housing, showed the men already beginning to set up equipment to quell the atomic reaction again, but the armor front plate came loose at last, and he dropped his eyes back without in details, to cut out a section of clothing and make the needed injections; curare first, then neo-heroin, and curare again, though he did not dare inject the quantity that seemed necessary. There was nothing more he could do until they could get the man out of his armor. He turned to the atomjack, who was already sitting up, propped against the driving seat's back.

" 'Snothing much, Doc," the fellow managed. "No jerks, just burn and that damned heat! Jorgenson?"

"Alive at least," Palmer answered, with some relief. The tank stopped, and Ferrel could see Brown running forward from beside a truck. "Get that suit off you, get yourself treated for the burn, then go up to the office where the check will be ready for you!"

"Fifty-thousand check?" The doubt in the voice registered over the weakness.

"Fifty thousand plus triple your minute time, and cheap; maybe we'll toss in a medal or a bottle of Scotch, too. Here, you fellows give a hand."

Farrel had the suit ripped off with Brown's assistance, and paused only long enough for one grateful breath of clean, cool air before leading the way toward the truck. As he neared it, Jenkins popped out, directing a group of men to move two loaded stretchers onto the litter, and nodding jerkily at Ferrel. "With the truck all equipped, we decided to move out here and take care of the damage as it came up—Sue and I rushed them through enough to do until we can find more time, so we could give full attention to Jorgenson. He's still living!"

"By a miracle. Stay out here, Brown, until you've finished with the men from inside, then we'll try to find some rest for you."

The three huskies carrying Jorgenson placed the body on the table set up, and began ripping off the bulky armor as the truck got under way. Fresh gloves came out of a small sterilizer, and the two doctors fell to work at once, treating the badly burned flesh and trying to locate and remove the worst of the radioactive matter.

"No use." Doc stepped back and shook his head. "It's all over him, probably clear into his bones in places. We'd have to put him through a filter to get it all out!"

Palmer was looking down at the raw mass of flesh, with all the layman's sickness at such a sight. "Can you fix him up, Ferrel?"

"We can try, that's all. Only explanation I can give for his being alive at all is that the hopper box must have been pretty well above the stuff until a short time ago—very short—and this stuff didn't work in until it sank. He's practically dehydrated now, apparently, but he couldn't have perspired enough to keep from dying of heat if he'd been under all that for even an hour—insulation or no insulation." There was admiration in Doc's eyes as he looked down at the immense figure of the man. "And he's tough; if he weren't, he'd have killed himself by exhaustion, even confined inside that suit and box, after the jerks set in. He's close to having done so, anyway. Until we can find some way of getting that stuff out of him, we don't dare risk getting rid of the curare's effect—that's a time-consuming job, in itself. Better give him another water and sugar intravenous, Jenkins. Then, if we do fix him up, Palmer, I'd say it's a fifty-fifty chance whether or not all this hasn't driven him stark crazy."

The truck had stopped, and the men lifted the stretcher off and carried it inside as Jenkins finished the injection. He went ahead of them, but Doc stopped outside to take Palmer's cigarette for a long drag, and let them go ahead. "Cheerful!" The manager lighted another from the butt, his shoulders sagging. "I've been trying to think of one man who might possibly be of some help to us, Doc, and there isn't such a person—anywhere. I'm sure now, after being in there, that Hoke couldn't do it. Kellar, if he were still alive, could probably pull the answer out of a hat after three looks—he had an instinct and genius for it; the best man the business ever had, even if his tricks did threaten to steal our work out from under us and give him the lead. But—well, now there's Jorgenson—either he gets in shape, or else!"

Jenkins' frantic yell reached them suddenly. "Doc! Jorgenson's dead! He's stopped breathing entirely!"

Doc jerked forward into a full run, a white-faced Palmer at his heels.

IV

Dodd was working artificial respiration and Jenkins had the oxygen mask in his hands, adjusting it over Jorgenson's face, before Ferrel reached the table. He made a grab for the pulse that had been fluttering weakly enough before, felt it flicker feebly once, pause for about three times normal period, lift feebly again, and then stop completely. "Adrenalin!"

"Already shot it into his heart, Doc! Cardiacine, too!" The boy's voice was bordering on hysteria, but Palmer was obviously closer to it than Jenkins.

"Doc, you gotta—"

"Get the hell out of here!" Ferrel's hands suddenly had a life of their own as he grabbed frantically for instruments, ripped bandages off the man's chest, and began working against time, when time had all the advantages. It wasn't surgery—hardly good butchery; the bones that he cut through so ruthlessly with savage strokes of an instrument could never heal smoothly after being so mangled. But he couldn't worry about minor details now.

He tossed back the flap of flesh and ribs that he'd hacked out. "Stop the bleeding, Jenkins!" Then his hands plunged into the chest cavity, somehow finding room around Dodd's and Jenkins', and were suddenly incredible gentle as they located the heart itself and began working on it, the skilled, exact massage of a man who knew every function of the vital organ. Pressure here, there, relax, pressure again; take it easy, don't rush things! It would do no good to try to set it going as feverishly as his emotions demanded. Pure oxygen was feeding into the lungs, and the heart could safely do less work. Hold it steady, one beat a second, sixty a minute.

It had been perhaps half a minute from the time the heart stopped before his massage was circulating blood again; too little time to worry about damage to the brain, the first part to be permanently affected by stoppage of the circulation. Now, if the heart could start again by itself within any reasonable time, death would be cheated again. How long? He had no idea. They'd taught him ten minutes when he was studying medicine, then there'd been a case of twenty minutes once, and while he was interning it had been pushed up to a record of slightly over an hour, which still stood; but that was an exceptional case. Jorgenson, praise be, was a normally healthy and vigorous specimen, and his system had been in first-class condition, but with the torture of those long hours, the radioactive, narcotic and curare all fighting against him, still one more miracle was needed to keep his life going.

Press, massage, relax, don't hurry it too much. There! For a second, his fingers felt a faint flutter, then again; but it stopped. Still, as long as the organ could show such signs, there was hope, unless his fingers grew too tired and he muffed the job before the moment when the heart could be safely trusted by itself.

"Jenkins!"

"Yes, sir!"

"Ever do any heart massage?"

"Practiced it in school, sir, on a model, but never actually. Oh, a dog in dissection class, for five minutes. I...I don't think you'd better trust me, Doc."

"I may have to. If you did it on a dog for five minutes, you can do it on a man, probably. You know what hangs on it—you saw the converter and know what's going on."

Jenkins nodded, the tense nod he'd used earlier. "I know—that's why you can't trust me. I told you I'd let you know when I was going to crack—well, it's damned near here!"

Could a man tell his weakness, if he were about finished? Doc didn't know; he suspected that the boy's own awareness of his nerves would speed up such a break, if anything, but Jenkins was a queer case, having taut nerves sticking out all over him, yet a steadiness under fire that few older men could have equaled. If he had to use him, he would; there was no other answer.

Doc's fingers were already feeling stiff—not yet tired, but showing signs of becoming so. Another few minutes, and he'd have to stop. There was the flutter again, one—two—three! Then it stopped. There had to be some other solution to this; it was impossible to keep it up for the length of time probably needed, even if he and Jenkins spelled each other. Only Michel at Mayo's could—Mayo's! If they could get it here in time, that wrinkle he'd seen demonstrated at their last medical convention was the answer.

"Jenkins, call Mayo's—you'll have to get Palmer's O.K., I guess—ask for Kubelik, and bring the extension where I can talk to him!"

He could hear Jenkins' voice, level enough at first, then with a depth of feeling he'd have thought impossible in the boy. Dodd looked at him quickly and managed a grim smile, even as she continued with the respiration; nothing could make her blush, though it should have done so.

The boy jumped back. "No soap, Doc! Palmer can't be located—and that post-mortem misconception at the board won't listen."

Doc studied his hands in silence, wondering, then gave it up; there'd be no hope of his lasting while he sent out the boy. "O.K., Jenkins, you'll have to take over here, then. Steady does it, come on in slowly, get your fingers over mine. Now, catch the motion? Easy, don't rush things. You'll hold out—you'll have to! You've done better than I had any right to ask for so far, and you don't need to distrust yourself. There, got it?"

"Got it, Doc. I'll try, but for Pete's sake, whatever you're planning, get back here quick! I'm not lying about cracking! You'd better let Meyers replace Dodd and have Sue called back in here; she's the best nerve tonic I know."

"Call her in then, Dodd." Doc picked up a hypodermic syringe, filled it quickly with water to which a drop of another liquid added a brownish-yellow color, and forced his tired old legs into a reasonably rapid trot out of the side door and toward Communications. Maybe the switchboard operator was stubborn, but there were ways of handling people.

He hadn't counted on the guard outside the Communications Building, though. "Halt!"

"Life or death; I'm a physician."

"Not in here—I got orders." The bayonet's menace apparently wasn't enough; the rifle went up to the man's shoulder, and his chin jutted out with the stubbornness of petty authority and reliance on orders. "Nobody sick here. There's plenty of phones elsewhere. You get back—and fast!"

Doc started forward and there was a faint click from the rifle as the safety went off; the darned fool meant what he said. Shrugging, Ferrel stepped back—and brought the hypodermic needle up inconspicuously in line with the guard's face. "Ever see one of these things squirt curare? It can reach before your bullet hits!"

"Curare?" The guard's eyes flicked to the needle, and doubt came into them. The man frowned. "That's the stuff that kills people on arrows, ain't it?"

"It is—cobra venom, you know. One drop on the outside of your skin and you're dead in ten seconds." Both statements were out-and-out lies, but Doc was counting on the superstitious ignorance of the average man in connection with poisons. "This little needle can spray you with it very nicely, and it may be a fast death, but not a pleasant one. Want to put down the rifle?"

A regular might have shot; but the militiaman was taking no chances. He lowered the rifle gingerly, his eyes on the needle, then kicked the weapon aside at Doc's motion. Ferrel approached, holding the needle out, and the man shrank backward and away, letting him pick up the rifle as he went past to avoid being shot in the back. Lost time! But he knew his way around this little building, at least, and went straight toward the girl at the board.

"Get up!" His voice came from behind her shoulder and she turned to see the rifle in one of his hands, the needle in the other, almost touching her throat. "This is loaded with curare, deadly poison, and too much hangs on getting a call through to bother with physician's oaths right now, young lady. Up! No plugs! That's right; now get over there, out of the cell—there, on your face, cross your hands behind your back, and grab your ankles—right! Now if you move, you won't move long!"

Those gangster pictures he'd seen were handy, at that. She was thoroughly frightened and docile. But, perhaps, not so much so she might not have bungled his call deliberately. He had to do that himself. Darn it, the red lights were trunk lines, but which plug—try the inside one, it looked more logical; he'd seen it done, but couldn't remember. Now, you flip back one of these switches—uh-uh, the other way. The tone came in assuring him he had it right, and he dialed operator rapidly, his eyes flickering toward the girl lying on the floor, his thoughts on Jenkins and the wasted time running on.

"Operator, this is an emergency. I'm Walnut 7654; I want to put in a long-distance call to Dr. Kubelik, Mayo's Hospital, Rochester, Minnesota. If Kubelik isn't there, I'll take anyone else who answers from his department. Speed is urgent."

"Very good, sir." Long-distance operators, mercifully, were usually efficient. There was the repeated signals and clicks of relays as she put it through, the answer from the hospital board, more wasted time, and then a face appeared on the screen; but not that of Kubelik. It was a much younger man.

Ferrel wasted no time in introduction. "I've got an emergency case here where all Hades depends on saving a man, and it can't be done without that machine of Dr. Kubelik's; he knows me, if he's there—I'm Ferrel, met him at the convention, got him to show me how the thing worked."

"Kubelik hasn't come in yet, Dr. Ferrel; I'm his assistant. But, if you mean the heart and lung exciter, it's already boxed and supposed to leave for Harvard this morning. They've got a rush case out there, and many need it—"

"Not as much as I do."

"I'll have to call— Wait a minute, Dr. Ferrel, seems I remember your name now. Aren't you the chap with National Atomic?"

Doc nodded. "The same. Now, about that machine, if you'll stop the formalities—"

The face on the screen nodded, instant determination showing, with an underlying expression of something else. "We'll ship it down to you instantly, Ferrel. Got a field for a plane?"

"Not within three miles, but I'll have a truck sent out for it. How long?"

"Take too long by truck if you need it down there, Ferrel; I'll arrange to transship in air from our special speedster to a helicopter, have it delivered wherever you want. About—um, loading plane, flying a couple hundred miles, transshipping—about half an hour's the best we can do."

"Make it the square of land south of the Infirmary, which is crossed visibly from the air. Thanks!"

"Wait, Dr. Ferrel!" The younger man checked Doc's cut-off. "Can you use it when you get it? It's tricky work."

"Kubelik gave quite a demonstration and I'm used to tricky work. I'll chance it—have to. Too long to rouse Kubelik himself, isn't it?"

"Probably. O.K., I've got the telescript reply from the shipping office, it's starting for the plane. I wish you luck!"

Ferrel nodded his thanks, wondering. Service like that was welcome, but it wasn't the most comforting thing, mentally, to know that the mere mention of National Atomic would cause such an about-face. Rumors, it seemed, were spreading, and in a hurry, in spite of Palmer's best attempts. Good Lord, what was going on here? He'd been too busy for any serious worrying or to realize, but—well, it had gotten him the exciter, and for that he should be thankful.

The guard was starting uncertainly off for reinforcements when Doc came out, and he realized that the seemingly endless call must have been over in short order. He tossed the rifle well out of the man's reach and headed back toward the Infirmary at a run, wondering how Jenkins had made out—it had to be all right!

Jenkins wasn't standing over the body of Jorgenson; Brown was there instead, her eyes moist and her face pinched in and white around the nostrils that stood out at full width. She looked up, shook her head at him as he started forward, and went on working at Jorgenson's heart.

"Jenkins cracked?"

"Nonsense! This is woman's work, Dr. Ferrel, and I took over for him, that's all. You men try to use brute force all your life and then wonder why a woman can do twice as much delicate work where strong muscles are a nuisance. I chased him out and took over, that's all." But there was a catch in her voice as she said it, and Meyers was looking down entirely too intently at the work of artificial respiration.

"Hi, Doc!" It was Blake's voice that broke in. "Get away from there; when this Dr. Brown needs help, I'll be right in there. I've been sleeping like a darned fool all night, from four this morning on. Didn't hear the phone, or something, didn't know what was going on until I got to the gate out there. You go rest."

Ferrel grunted in relief; Blake might have been dead drunk when he finally reached home, which would explain his not hearing the phone, but his animal virility had soaked it out with no visible sign. The only change was the absence of the usual cocky grin on his face as he moved over beside Brown to test Jorgenson. "Thank the Lord you're here, Blake. How's Jorgenson doing?"

Brown's voice answered in a monotone, words coming in time to the motions of her fingers. "His heart shows signs of coming around once in a while, but it doesn't last. He isn't getting worse from what I can tell, though."

"Good. If we can keep him going half an hour more, we can turn all this over to a machine. Where's Jenkins?"

"A machine? Oh, the Kubelik exciter, of course. He was working on it when I was there. We'll keep Jorgenson alive until then, anyway, Dr. Ferrel."

"Where's Jenkins?" he repeated sharply, when she stopped with no intention of answering the former question.

Blake pointed toward Ferrel's office, the door of which was now closed. "In there. But lay off him, Doc. I saw the whole thing, and he feels like the deuce about it. He's a good kid, but only a kid, and this kind of hell could get any of us."

"I know all that." Doc headed toward the office, as much for a smoke as anything else. The sight of Blake's rested face was somehow an island of reassurance in this sea of fatigue and nerves. "Don't worry, Brown, I'm not planning on lacing him down, so you needn't defend your man so carefully. It was my fault for not listening to him."

Brown's eyes were pathetically grateful in the brief flash she threw him, and he felt like a heel for the gruffness that had been his first reaction toward Jenkins' absence. If this kept on much longer, though, they'd all be in worse shape than the boy, whose back was toward him as he opened the door. The still, huddled shape did not raise its head from its arms as Ferrel put his hand onto one shoulder, and the voice was muffled and distant.

"I cracked, Doc—high, wide and handsome, all over the place. I couldn't take it! Standing there, Jorgenson maybe dying because I couldn't control myself right, the whole plant blowing up, all my fault. I kept telling myself I was O.K., I'd go on, then I cracked. Screamed like a baby! Dr. Jenkins—*nerve* specialist!"

"Yeah... Here, are you going to drink this, or do I have to hold your blasted nose and pour it down your throat?" It was crude psychology but it worked, and Doc handed over the drink, waited for the other to down it, and passed a cigarette across before sinking into his own chair. "You warned me, Jenkins, and I risked it on my own responsibility, so nobody's kicking. But I'd like to ask a couple of questions."

"Go ahead—what's the difference?" Jenkins had recovered a little, obviously, from the note of defiance that managed to creep into his voice.

"Did you know Brown could handle that kind of work? And did you pull your hands out before she could get hers in to replace them?"

"She told me she could. I didn't know before. I dunno about the other; I think...yeah, Doc, she had her hands over mine. But—"

Ferrel nodded, satisfied with his own guess. "I thought so. You didn't crack, as you put it, until your mind knew it was safe to do so—and then you simply passed the work on. By that definition, I'm cracking, too. I'm sitting in here, smoking, talking to you, when out there a man needs attention. The fact that he's getting it from two others, one practically fresh, the other at a least a lot better off than we are, doesn't have a thing to do with it, does it?"

"But it wasn't that way, Doc. I'm not asking for grandstand stuff from anybody."

"Nobody's giving it to you, son. All right, you screamed—why not? It didn't hurt anything. I growled at Brown when I came in for the same reason—exhausted, overstrained nerves. If I went out there and had to take over from them, I'd probably scream myself, or start biting my tongue—nerves have to have an outlet; physically, it does them no good, but there's a psychological need for it." The boy wasn't convinced, and Doc sat back in the chair, staring at him thoughtfully, "Ever wonder why I'm here?"

"No, sir."

"Well, you might. Twenty-seven years ago, when I was about your age, there wasn't a surgeon in this country—or the world, for that matter—who had the reputation I had; any kind of surgery, brain, what have you. They're still using some of my techniques...uh-hum, thought you'd remember when the association of names hit you. I had a different wife then, Jenkins, and there was a baby coming. Brain tumor—I had to do it, no one else could. I did it, somehow, but I went out of that operating room in a haze, and it was three days later when they'd tell me she'd died; not my fault—I know that now—but I couldn't realize it then.

"So, I tried setting up as a general practitioner. No more surgery for me! And because I was a fair diagnostician, which most surgeons aren't, I made a living, at least. Then, when this company was set up, I applied for the job, and got it; I still had a reputation of sorts. It was a new field, something requiring study and research, and damned near every ability of most specialists plus a general practitioner's, so it kept me busy enough to get over my phobia of surgery. Compared to me, you don't know what nerves or cracking means. That little scream was a minor incident."

Jenkins made no comment, but lighted the cigarette he'd been holding. Ferrel relaxed farther into the chair, knowing that he'd be called if there was any need for his work, and glad to get his mind at least partially off Jorgenson. "It's hard to find a man for this work, Jenkins. It takes too much ability at too many fields, even though it pays well. We went through plenty of applicants before we decided on you, and I'm not regretting our choice. As a matter of fact, you're better equipped for the job than Blake was—your record looked as if you'd deliberately tried for this kind of work."

"I did."

"Hm-m-m." That was the one answer Doc had least expected; so far as he knew, no one deliberately tried for a job at Atomics—they usually wound up trying for it after comparing their receipts for a year or so with the salary paid by National. "Then you knew what was needed and picked it up in toto. Mind if I ask why?"

Jenkins shrugged. "Why not? Turnabout's fair play. It's kind of complicated, but the gist of it doesn't take much telling. Dad had an atomic plant of his own—and a darned good one, too, Doc, even if it wasn't as big as National. I was working in it when I was fifteen, and I went through two years of university work in atomics with the best intentions of carrying on the business. Sue—well, she was the neighbor girl I followed around, and we had money at the time; that wasn't why she married me, though. I never did figure that out—she'd had a hard enough life, but she was already holding down a job at Mayo's, and I was just a raw kid. Anyway—

"The day we came home from our honeymoon, Dad got a big contract on a new process we'd worked out. It took some swinging, but he got the equipment and started it... My guess is that one of the controls broke through faulty construction; the process was right! We'd been over it too often not to know what it would do. But, when the estate was cleared up, I had to give up the idea of a degree in atomics, and Sue was back working at the hospital. Atomic courses cost real money. Then one of Sue's medical acquaintances fixed it for me to get a scholarship in medicine that almost took care of it, so I chose the next best thing to what I wanted."

"National and one of the biggest competitors—if you can call it that—are permitted to give degrees in atomics," Doc reminded the boy. The field was still too new to be a standing university course, and there were no better teachers in the business than such men as Palmer, Hokusai and Jorgenson. "They pay a salary while you're learning, too."

"Hm-m-m. Takes ten years that way, and the salary's just enough for a single man. No, I'd married Sue with the intention she wouldn't have to work again; well, she did until I finished internship, but I knew if I got the job here I could support her. As an atomjack, working up to an engineer, the prospects weren't so good. We're saving a little money now, and some day maybe I'll get a crack at it yet... Doc, what's this all about? You babying me out of my fit?"

Ferrel grinned at the boy. "Nothing else, son, though I was curious, And it worked. Feel all right now, don't you?"

"Mostly, except for what's going on out there—I got too much of a look at it from the truck. Oh, I could use some sleep, I guess, but I'm O.K. again."

"Good." Doc had profited almost as much as Jenkins from the rambling off-trail talk, and had managed more rest from it than from nursing his own thoughts. "Suppose we go out and see how they're making out with Jorgenson? Um, what happened to Hoke, come to think of it?"

"Hoke? Oh, he's in my office now, figuring out things with a pencil and paper since we wouldn't let him go back out there. I was wondering—"

"Atomics?... Then suppose you go in and talk to him; he's a good guy, and he won't give you the brush-off. Nobody else around here apparently suspected this Isotope R business, and you might offer a fresh lead for him. With Blake and the nurses here and the men out of the mess except for the tanks, there's not much you can do to help on my end."

Ferrel felt better at peace with the world than he had since the call from Palmer as he watched Jenkins head off across the surgery toward his office; and the glance that Brown threw, first toward the boy, then back at Doc, didn't make him feel worse. That girl could say more with her eyes than most women could with their mouths! He went over toward the operating table where Blake was now working the heart message with one of the fresh nurses attending to respiration and casting longing glances toward the mechanical lung apparatus; it couldn't be used in this case, since Jorgenson's chest had to be free for heart attention.

Blake looked up, his expression worried. "This isn't so good, Doc. He's been sinking in the last few minutes. I was just going to call you. I—"

The last words were drowned out by the bull-throated drone that came dropping down from above them, a sound peculiarly characteristic of the heavy Sikorsky freighters with their modified blades to gain lift. Ferrel nodded at Brown's questioning glance, but he didn't choose to shout as his hands went over those of Blake and took over the delicate work of simulating the natural heart action. As Blake withdrew, the sound stopped, and Doc motioned him out with his head.

"You'd better go to them and oversee bringing in the apparatus—and grab up any of the men you see to act as porters—or send Jones for them. The machine is an experimental model, and pretty cumbersome; must weigh seven-eight hundred pounds."

"I'll get them myself—Jones is sleeping."

There was no flutter to Jorgenson's heart under Doc's deft manipulations, though he was exerting every bit of skill he possessed. "How long since there was a sign?"

"About four minutes, now. Doc, is there still a chance?"

"Hard to say. Get the machine, though, and we'll hope."

But still the heart refused to respond, though the pressure and manipulation kept the blood circulating and would at least prevent any starving or asphyxiation of the body cells. Carefully, delicately, he brought his mind into his fingers, trying to woo a faint quiver. Perhaps he did, once, but he couldn't be sure. It all depended on how quickly they could get the machine working now, and how long a man could live by manipulation alone. That point was still unsettled.

But there was no question about the fact that the spark of life burned faintly and steadily lower in Jorgenson, while outside the man-made hell went on ticking off the minutes that separated it from becoming Mahler's Isotope. Normally, Doc was an agnostic, but now, unconsciously, his mind slipped back into the simple faith of his childhood, and he heard Brown echoing the prayer that was on his lips. The second hand of the watch before him swung around and around and around again before he heard the sound of men's feet at the back entrance, and still there was no definite quiver from the heart under his fingers. How much time did he have left, if any, for the difficult and unfamiliar operation required?

His side glance showed the seemingly innumerable filaments of platinum that had to be connected into the nerves governing Jorgenson's heart and lungs, all carefully coded, yet almost terrifying in their complexity. If he made a mistake anywhere, it was at least certain there would be no time for a second trial; if his fingers shook or his tired eyes clouded at the wrong instant, there would be no help from Jorgenson. Jorgenson would be dead!

V

"Take over massage, Brown," he ordered. "And keep it up no matter what happens. Good. Dodd, assist me, and hang onto my signals. If it works, we can all rest afterward."

Ferrel wondered grimly with that part of his mind that was off by itself whether he could justify his boast to Jenkins of having been the world's greatest surgeon; it had been true once, he knew with no need for false modesty, but that was long ago, and this was at best a devilish job. He'd hung on with a surge of the old fascination as Kubelik had performed it on a dog at the convention, and his memory for such details was still good, as were his hands. But something else goes into the making of a great surgeon, and he wondered if that were still with him.

Then, as his fingers made the microscopic little motions needed and Dodd became another pair of hands, he ceased wondering. Whatever it was, he could feel it surging through him, and there was a pure joy to it somewhere, over and above the urgency of the work. This was probably the last time he'd ever feel it, and if the operation succeeded, probably it was a thing he could put with the few mental treasures that were still left from his former success. The man on the table ceased to be Jorgenson, the excessively gadgety Infirmary became again the main operating theater of that same Mayo's which had produced Brown and this strange new machine, and his fingers were again those of the Great Ferrel, the miracle boy from Mayo's, who could do the impossible twice before breakfast without turning a hair.

Some of his feeling was devoted to the machine itself. Massive, ugly, with parts sticking out in haphazard order, it was more like something from an inquisition chamber than a scientist's achievement, but it worked—he'd seen it functioning. In that ugly mass of assorted pieces, little currents were generated and modulated to feed out to the heart and lungs and replace the orders given by a brain that no longer worked or could not get through, to co-ordinate breathing and beating according to the need. It was a product of the combined genius of surgery and electronics, but wonderful as the exciter was, it was distinctly secondary to the technique Kubelik had evolved for selecting and connecting only those nerves and nerve bundles necessary, and bringing the almost impossible into the limits of surgical possibility.

Brown interrupted, and that interruption in the midst of such an operation indicated clearly the strain she was under. "The heart fluttered a little then, Dr. Ferrel."

Ferrel nodded, untroubled by the interruption. Talk, which bothered most surgeons, was habitual in his own little staff, and he always managed to have one part of his mind reserved for that while the rest went on without noticing. "Good. That gives us at least double the leeway I expected."

His hands went on, first with the heart which was the more pressing danger. Would the machine work, he wondered, in this case? Curare and radioactives, fighting each other, were an odd combination. Yet, the machine controlled the nerves close to the vital organ, pounding its message through into the muscles, where the curare had a complicated action that paralyzed the whole nerve, establishing a long block to the control impulses from the brain. Could the nerve impulses from the machine be forced through the short paralyzed passages? Probably—the strength of its signals was controllable. The only proof was in trying.

Brown drew back her hands and stared down uncomprehendingly. "It's beating, Dr. Ferrel! By itself…it's beating!"

He nodded again, though the mask concealed his smile. His technique was still not faulty, and he had performed the operation correctly after seeing it once on a dog! He was still the Great Ferrel! Then, the ego in him fell back to normal, though the lift remained, and his exultation centered around the more important problem of Jorgenson's living. And, later, when the lungs began moving of themselves as the nurse stopped working them, he had been expecting it. The detail work remaining was soon over, and he stepped back, dropping the mask from his face and pulling off his gloves.

"Congratulations, Dr. Ferrel!" The voice was guttural, strange. "A truly great operation—truly great. I almost stopped you, but now I am glad I did not; it was a pleasure to observe you, sir." Ferrel looked up in amazement at the bearded smiling face of Kubelik, and he found no words as he accepted the other's hand. But Kubelik apparently expected none.

"I, Kubelik, came, you see; I could not trust another with the machine, and fortunately I made the plane. Then you seemed so sure, so confident—so when you did not notice me, I remained in the background, cursing myself. Now, I shall return, since you have no need of me—the wiser for having watched you… No, not a word; not a word from you, sir. Don't destroy your miracle with words. The copter waits me, I go; but my admiration for you remains forever!"

Ferrel still stood looking down at his hand as the roar of the copter cut in, then at the breathing body with the artery on the neck now pulsing regularly. That was all that was needed; he had been admired by Kubelik, the man who thought all other surgeons were fools and nincompoops. For a second or so longer he treasured it, then shrugged it off.

"Now," he said to the others, as the troubles of the plant fell back on his shoulders, "all we have to do is hope that Jorgenson's brain wasn't injured by the session out there, or by this continued artificially maintained life, and try to get him in condition so he can talk before it's too late. God grant us time! Blake, you know the detail work as well as I do, and we can't both work on it. You and the fresh nurses take over, doing the bare minimum needed for the patients scattered around the wards and waiting room. Any new ones?"

"None for some time; I think they've reached a stage where that's over with," Brown answered.

"I hope so. Then go round up Jenkins and lie down somewhere. That goes for you and Meyers, too, Dodd. Blake, give us three hours if you can, and get us up. There won't be any new developments before then, and we'll save time in the long run by resting. Jorgenson's to get first attention!"

The old leather chair made a fair sort of bed, and Ferrel was too exhausted physically and mentally to be choosy—too exhausted to benefit as much as he should from sleep of three hours' duration, for that matter, though it was almost imperative he try. Idly, he wondered what Palmer would think of all his safeguards had he known that Kubelik had come into the place so easily and out again. Not that it mattered; it was doubtful whether anyone else would want to come near, let alone inside the plant.

In that, apparently, he was wrong. It was considerably less than the three hours when he was awakened to hear the bull-roar of a helicopter outside. But sleep clouded his mind too much for curiosity and he started to drop back into his slumber. Then another sound cut in, jerking him out of his drowsiness. It was the sharp sputter of a machine gun from the direction of the gate, a pause and another burst; an eddy of sleep-memory indicated that it had begun before the helicopter's arrival, so it could not be that they were gunning. More trouble, and while it was none of his business, he could not go back to sleep. He got up and went out into the surgery, just as a gnomish little man hopped out from the rear entrance.

The fellow scooted toward Ferrel after one birdlike glance at Blake, his words spilling out with a jerky self-importance that should have been funny, but missed it by a small margin; under the surface, sincerity still managed to show. "Dr. Ferrel? Uh. Dr. Kubelik—Mayo's, you know—he reported you were short-handed; stacking patients in the other rooms. We volunteered for duty—me, four other doctors, nine nurses. Probably should have checked with you, but couldn't get a phone through. Took the liberty of coming through directly, fast as we could push our copters."

Ferrel glanced through the back, and saw that there were three of the machines instead of the one he'd thought, with men and equipment piling out of them. Mentally he kicked himself for not asking help when he'd put through the call; but he'd been used to working with his own little staff for so long that the ready response of his profession to emergencies had been almost forgotten. "You know you're taking chances coming here, naturally? Then, in that case, I'm grateful to you and Kubelik. We've got about forty patients here, all of whom should have considerable attention, though I frankly doubt whether there's room for you to work."

The man hitched his thumb backward jerkily. "Don't worry about that. Kubelik goes the limit when he arranges things. Everything we need with us, practically all the hospital's atomic equipment; though maybe you'll have to piece us out there. Even a field hospital tent, portable wards for every patient you have. Want relief in here or would you rather have us simply move out the patients to the tent, leave this end to you? Oh, Kubelik sent his regards. Amazing of him!"

Kubelik, it seemed, had a tangible idea of regards, however dramatically he was inclined to express them; with him directing the volunteer force, the wonder was that the whole staff and equipment hadn't been moved down. "Better leave this end," Ferrel decided. "Those in the wards will probably be better off in your tent as well as the men now in the waiting room; we're equipped beautifully for all emergency work, but not used to keeping the patients here any length of time, so our accommodations that way are rough. Dr. Blake will show you around and help you get organized in the routine we use here. He'll get help for you in erecting the tent, too. By the way, did you hear the commotion by the entrance as you were landing?"

"We did, indeed. We saw it, too—bunch of men in some kind of uniform shooting a machine gun; hitting the ground, though. Bunch of other people running back away from it, shaking their fists, looked like. We were expecting a dose of the same, maybe; didn't notice us, though."

Blake snorted in half amusement. "You probably would have gotten it if our manager hadn't forgotten to give orders covering the air approach; they must figure that's an official route. I saw a bunch from the city arguing about their relatives in here when I came in this morning, so it must have been that." He motioned the little doctor after him, then turned his neck back to address Brown. "Show him the results while I'm gone, honey."

Ferrel forgot his new recruits and swung back to the girl. "Bad?" She made no comment, but picked up a lead shield and placed it over Jorgenson's chest so that it cut off all radiation from the lower part of his body, then placed the radiation indicator close to the man's throat. Doc looked once; no more was needed. It was obvious that Blake had already done his best to remove the radioactive from all parts of the body needed for speech, in the hope that they might strap down the others and block them off with local anaesthetics; then the curare could have been counteracted long enough for such information as was needed. Equally obviously, he'd failed. There was no sense in going through the job of neutralizing the drug's block only to have him under the control of the radioactive still present. The stuff was too finely dispersed for surgical removal. Now what? He had no answer.

Jenkins' lean-sinewed hand took the indicator from him for inspection. The boy was already frowning as Doc looked up in faint surprise, and his face made no change. He nodded slowly, "Yeah. I figured as much. That was a beautiful piece of work you did, too. Too bad. I was watching from the door and you almost convinced me he'd be all right, the way you handled it. But—So we have to make out without him; and Hoke and Palmer haven't even cooked up a lead that's worth a good test. Want to come into my office, Doc? There's nothing we can do here."

Ferrel followed Jenkins into the little office off the now emptied waiting room; the men from the hospital had worked rapidly, it seemed. "So you haven't been sleeping, I take it? Where's Hokusai now?"

"Out there with Palmer; he promised to behave, if that'll comfort you...Nice guy, Hoke; I'd forgotten what it felt like to talk to—an atomic engineer without being laughed at. Palmer, too. I wish—" There was a brief lightening to the boy's face and the first glow of normal human pride Doc had seen in him. Then he shrugged, and it vanished back into his taut cheeks and reddened eyes. "We cooked up the wildest kind of a scheme, but it isn't so hot."

Hoke's voice came out of the doorway, as the little man came in and sat down carefully in one of the three chairs. "No, not sso hot! It iss faily, already. Jorgensson?"

"Out, no hope there! What happened?"

Hoke spread his arms, his eyes almost closing. "Nothing. We knew it could never work, not sso? Misster Palmer, he iss come ssoon here, then we make planss again. I am think now, besst we sshould move from here. Palmer, I—mosstly we are theoreticianss; and, excusse, you alsso, doctor. Jorgensson wass the production man. No Jorgensson, no—ah—ssoap!"

Mentally, Ferrel agreed about the moving—and soon! But he could see Palmer's point of view; to give up the fight was against the grain, somehow. And besides, once the blow-up happened, with the resultant damage to an unknown area, the pressure groups in Congress would be in, shouting for the final abolition of all atomic work; now they were reasonably quiet, only waiting an opportunity—or, more probably, at the moment were already seizing on the rumors spreading to turn this into their coup. If, by some streak of luck, Palmer could save the plant with no greater loss of life and property than already existed, their words would soon be forgotten, and the benefits from the products of National would again outweigh all risks.

"Just what will happen if it all goes off?" he asked.

Jenkins shrugged, biting at his inner lip as he went over a sheaf of papers on the desk, covered with the scrawling symbols of atomics, "Anybody's guess. Suppose three tons of the army's new explosives were to explode in a billionth—or at least, a millionth—of a second? Normally, you know, compared to atomics, that stuff burns like any fire, slowly and quietly, giving its gases plenty of time to get out of the way in an orderly fashion. Figure it one way, with this all going off together, and the stuff could drill a hole that'd split open the whole continent from Hudson Bay to the Gulf of Mexico, and leave a lovely sea where the Middle West is now. Figure it another, and it might only kill off everything within fifty miles of here. Somewhere in between is the chance we count on. This isn't U-235, you know."

Doc winced. He'd been picturing the plant going up in the air violently, with maybe a few buildings somewhere near it, but nothing like this. It had been purely a local affair to him, but this didn't sound like one. No wonder Jenkins was in that state of suppressed jitters; it wasn't too much imagination, but too much cold, hard knowledge that was worrying him. Ferrel looked at their faces as they bent over the symbols once more, tracing out point by point their calculations in the hope of finding one overlooked loophole, then decided to leave them alone.

The whole problem was hopeless without Jorgenson, it seemed, and Jorgenson was his responsibility; if the plant went, it was squarely on the senior physician's shoulders. But there was no apparent solution. If it would help, he could cut it down to a direct path from brain to speaking organs, strap down the body and block off all nerves below the neck, using an artificial larynx instead of the normal breathing through vocal cords. But the indicator showed the futility of it; the orders could never get through from the brain with the amount of radioactive still present throwing them off track—even granting that the brain itself was not affected, which was doubtful.

Fortunately for Jorgenson, the stuff was all finely dispersed around the head, with no concentration at any one place that was unquestionably destructive to his mind; but the good fortune was also the trouble, since it could not be removed by any means known to medical practice. Even so simple a thing as letting the man read the questions and spell out the answers by winking an eyelid as they pointed to the alphabet was hopeless.

Nerves! Jorgenson had his blocked out, but Ferrel wondered if the rest of them weren't in as bad a state. Probably, somewhere well within their grasp, there was a solution that was being held back because the nerves of everyone in the plant were blocked by fear and pressure that defeated its own purpose. Jenkins, Palmer, Hokusai—under purely theoretical conditions, any one of them might spot the answer to the problem, but sheer necessity of finding it could be the thing that hid it. The same might be true with the problem of Jorgenson's treatment. Yet, though he tried to relax and let his mind stray idly around the loose ends and seemingly disconnected knowledge he had, it returned incessantly to the necessity of doing something, and doing it now!

Ferrel heard weary footsteps behind him and turned to see Palmer coming from the front entrance. The man had no business walking into the surgery, but such minor rules had gone by the board hours before.

"Jorgenson?" Palmer's conversation began with the same old question in the usual tone, and he read the answer from Doc's face with a look that indicated it was no news. "Hoke and that Jenkins kid still in there?"

Doc nodded, and plodded behind him toward Jenkins' office; he was useless to them, but there was still the idea that in filling his mind with other things, some little factor he had overlooked might have a chance to come forth. Also, curiosity still worked on him, demanding to know what was happening. He flopped into the third chair, and Palmer squatted down on the edge of the table.

"Know a good spiritualist, Jenkins?" the manager asked. "Because if you do, I'm about ready to try calling back Kellar's ghost. The Steinmetz of atomics—so he had to die before this Isotope R came up, and leave us without even a good guess at how long we've got to crack the problem. Hey, what's the matter?"

Jenkins' face had tensed and his body straightened back tensely in the chair, but he shook his head, the corner of his mouth twitching wryly. "Nothing. Nerves, I guess. Hoke and I dug out some things that give an indication on how long this runs, though. We still don't know exactly, but from observations out there and the general theory before, it looks like something between six and thirty hours left; probably ten's closer to being correct!"

"Can't be much longer. It's driving the men back right now! Even the tanks can't get in where they can do the most good, and we're using the shielding around No. 3 as a headquarters for the men; in another half hour, maybe they won't be able to stay that near the thing. Radiation indicators won't register any more, and it's spitting all over the place, almost constantly. Heat's terrific; it's gone up to around three hundred centigrade and sticks right there now, but that's enough to warm up 3, even."

Doc looked up. "No. 3?"

"Yeah. Nothing happened to that batch—it ran through and came out I-713 right on schedule, hours ago." Palmer reached for a cigarette, realized he had one in his mouth, and slammed the package back on the table. "Significant data, Doc; if we get out of this, we'll figure out just what caused the change in No. 4—if we get out! Any chance of making those variable factors work, Hoke?"

Hoke shook his head, and again Jenkins answered from the notes. "Not a chance; sure, theoretically, at least, R should have a period varying between twelve and sixty hours before turning into Mahler's Isotope, depending on what chains of reactions or subchains it goes through; they all look equally good, and probably are all going on in there now, depending on what's around to soak up neutrons or let them roam, the concentration and amount of R together, and even high or low temperatures that change their activity somewhat. It's one of the variables, no question about that."

"The sspitting iss prove that," Hoke supplemented.

"Sure. But there's too much of it together, and we can't break it down fine enough to reach any safety point where it won't toss energy around like rain. The minute one particle manages to make itself into Mahler's, it'll crash through with energy enough to blast the next over the hump and into the same thing instantly, and that passes it on to the next, at about light speed! If we *could* get it juggled around so some would go off first, other atoms a little later, and so on, fine—only we can't do it unless we can be sure of isolating every blob bigger than a tenth of a gram from every other one! And if we start breaking it down into reasonably small pieces, we're likely to have one decide on the short transformation subchain and go off at any time; pure chance gave us a concentration to begin with that eliminated the shorter chains, but we can't break it down into small lots and those into smaller lots, and so on. Too much risk!"

Ferrel had known vaguely that there were such things as variables, but the theory behind them was too new and too complex for him; he'd learned what little he knew when the simpler radioactives proceeded normally from radium to lead, as an example, with a definite, fixed half life, instead of the super-heavy atoms they now used that could jump through several different paths, yet end up the same. It was over his head, and he started to get up and go back to Jorgenson.

Palmer's words stopped him. "I knew it, of course, but I hoped maybe I was wrong. Then—we evacuate! No use fooling ourselves any longer. I'll call the Governor and try to get him to clear the country around; Hoke, you can tell the men to get the hell out of here! All we ever had was the counteracting isotope to hope on, and no chance of getting enough of that. There was no sense in making I-231 in thousand-pound batches before. Well—"

V

He reached for the phone, but Ferrel cut in. "What about the men in the wards? They're loaded with the stuff, most of them with more than a gram apiece dispersed through them. They're in the same class with the converter, maybe, but we can't just pull out and leave them!"

Silence hit them, to be broken by Jenkins' hushed whisper. "My God! What damned fools we are. I-231 under discussion for hours, and I never thought of it. Now you two throw the connection in my face, and I still almost miss it!"

"I-231? But there iss not enough. Maybe twenty-five pound, maybe less. Three and a half days to make more. The little we have would be no good, Dr. Jenkinss. We forget that already." Hoke struck a match to a piece of paper, shook one drop of ink onto it, and watched it continue burning for a second before putting it out. "Sso. A drop of water for sstop a foresst fire. No."

"Wrong, Hoke. A drop to short a switch that'll turn on the real stream—maybe. Look, Doc, I-231's an isotope that reacts atomically with R—we've checked on that already. It simply gets together with the stuff and the two break down into non-radioactive elements and a little heat, like a lot of other such atomic reactions; but it isn't the violent kind. They simply swap parts in a friendly way and open up to simpler atoms that are stable. We have a few pounds on hand, can't make enough in time to help with No. 4, but we do have enough to treat every man in the wards, *including Jorgenson!*"

"How much heat?" Doc snapped out of his lethargy into the detailed thought of a good physician. "In atomics you may call it a little; but would it be small enough in the human body?"

Hokusai and Palmer were practically riding the pencil as Jenkins figured. "Say five grams of the stuff in Jorgenson, to be on the safe side, less in the others. Time for reaction…hm-m-m. Here's the total heat produced and the time taken by the reaction, probably, in the body. The stuff's water-soluble in the chloride we have of it, so there's no trouble dispersing it. What do you make of it, Doc?"

"Fifteen to eighteen degrees temperature rise at a rough estimate. Uh!"

"Too much! Jorgenson couldn't stand ten degrees right now!" Jenkins frowned down at his figures, tapping nervously with his hand.

Doc shook his head. "Not too much! We can drop his whole body temperature first in the hypothermy bath down to eighty degrees, then let it rise to a hundred, if necessary, and still be safe. Thank the Lord, there's equipment enough. If they'll rip out the refrigerating units in the cafeteria and improvise baths, the volunteers out in the tent can start on the other men while we handle Jorgenson. At least that way we can get the men all out, even if we don't save the plant."

Palmer stared at them in confusion before his face galvanized into resolution. "Refrigerating units—volunteers—tent? What—O.K., Doc, what do you want?" He reached for the telephone and begun giving orders for the available I-231 to be sent to the surgery, for men to rip out the cafeteria cooling equipment, and for such other things as Doc requested. Jenkins had already gone to instruct the medical staff in the field tent without asking how they'd gotten there, but was back in the surgery before Doc reached it with Palmer and Hokusai at his heels.

"Blake's taking over out there," Jenkins announced. "Says if you want Dodd, Meyers, Jones or Sue, they're sleeping."

"No need. Get over there out of the way, if you must watch," Ferrel ordered the two engineers, as he and Jenkins began attaching the freezing units and bath to the sling on the exciter. "Prepare his blood for it, Jenkins; we'll force it down as low as we can to be on the safe side. And we'll have to keep tabs on the temperature fall and regulate his heart and breathing to what it would be normally in that condition; they're both out of his normal control, now."

"And pray," Jenkins added. He grabbed the small box out of the messenger's hand before the man was fully inside the door and began preparing a solution, weighing out the whitish powder and measuring water carefully, but with the speed that was automatic to him under tension. "Doc, if this doesn't work—if Jorgenson's crazy or something—you'll have another case of insanity on your hands. One more false hope would finish me."

"Not one more case; four! We're all in the same boat. Temperature's falling nicely—I'm rushing it a little, but it's safe enough. Down to ninety-six now." The thermometer under Jorgenson's tongue was one intended for hypothermy work, capable of rapid response, instead of the normal fever thermometer. Slowly, with agonizing reluctance, the little needle on the dial moved over, down to ninety, then on. Doc kept his eyes glued to it, slowing the pulse and breath to the proper speed. He lost track of the number of times he sent Palmer back out of the way, and finally gave up.

Waiting, he wondered how those outside in the field hospital were doing? Still, they had ample time to arrange their makeshift cooling apparatus and treat the men in groups—ten hours probably; and hypothermy was a standard thing, now. Jorgenson was the only real rush case. Almost imperceptibly to Doc, but speedily by normal standards, the temperature continued to fall. Finally it reached seventy-eight. "Ready, Jenkins, make the injection. That enough?"

"No. I figure it's almost enough, but we'll have to go slow to balance out properly. Too much of this stuff would be almost as bad as the other Gauge going up, Doc?"

It was, much more rapidly than Ferrel liked. As the injection coursed through the blood vessels and dispersed out to the fine deposits of radioactive, the needle began climbing past eighty, to ninety, and up. It stopped at ninety-four and slowly began falling as the cooling bath absorbed heat from the cells of the body. The radioactivity meter still registered the presence of Isotope R, though much more faintly.

The next shot was small, and a smaller one followed. "Almost," Ferrel Commented. "Next one should about do the trick."

Using partial injections, there had been need for less drop in temperature than they had given Jorgenson, but there was small loss to that. Finally, when the last minute bit of the I-231 solution had entered the man's veins and done its work, Doc nodded. "No sign of activity left. He's up to ninety-five, now that I've cut off the refrigeration, and he'll pick up the little extra temperature in a hurry. By the time we can counteract the curare, he'll be ready. That'll take about fifteen minutes, Palmer."

The manager nodded, watching them dismantling the hypothermy equipment and going through the routine of canceling out the curare. It was always a slower job than treatment with the drug, but part of the work had been done already by the normal body processes, and the rest was a simple, standard procedure. Fortunately, the neo-heroin would be nearly worn off, or that would have been a longer and much harder problem to eliminate.

"Telephone for Mr. Palmer. Calling Mr. Palmer. Send Mr. Palmer to the telephone." The operator's words lacked the usual artificial exactness, and were only a nervous sing-song. It was getting her, and she wasn't bothered by excess imagination, normally. "Mr. Palmer is wanted on the telephone."

"Palmer." The manager picked up an instrument at hand, not equipped with vision, and there was no indication of the caller. But Ferrel could see what little hope had appeared at the prospect of Jorgenson's revival disappearing. "Check! Move out of there, and prepare to evacuate, but keep quiet about that until you hear further orders! Tell the men Jorgenson's about out of it, so they won't lack for something to talk about."

He swung back to them. "No use, Doc, I'm afraid. We're already too late. The stuff's stepped it up again, and they're having to move out of No. 3 now. I'll wait on Jorgenson, but even if he's all right and knows the answer, we can't get in to use it!"

VI

"Healing's going to be a long, slow process, but they should at least grow back better than silver ribs; never take a pretty X-ray photo, though." Doc held the instrument in his hand, staring down at the flap opened in Jorgenson's chest, and his shoulders came up in a faint shrug. The little platinum filaments had been removed from around the nerves to heart and lungs, and the man's normal impulses were operating again, less steadily than under the exciter, but with no danger signals. "Well, it won't much matter if he's still sane."

Jenkins watched him begin stitching the flap back, his eyes centered over the table out toward the converter. "Doc, he's got to be sane! If Hoke and Palmer find it's what it sounds like out there, we'll have to count on Jorgenson. There's an answer somewhere, has to be! But we won't find it without him."

"Hm-m-m. Seems to me you've been having ideas yourself, son. You've been right so far, and if Jorgenson's out—" He shut off the stitcher, finished the dressings, and flopped down on a bench, knowing that all they could do was wait for the drugs to work on Jorgenson and bring him around. Now that he relaxed the control over himself, exhaustion hit down with full force; his fingers were uncertain as he pulled off the gloves. "Anyhow, we'll know in another five minutes or so."

"And Heaven help us, Doc, if it's up to me. I've always had a flair for atomic theory; I grew up on it. But he's the production man who's been working at it week in and week out, and it's his process, to boot… There they are now! All right for them to come back here?"

But Hokusai and Palmer were waiting for no permission. At the moment, Jorgenson was the nerve center of the plant, drawing them back, and they stalked over to stare down at him, then sat where they could be sure of missing no sign of returning consciousness. Palmer picked up the conversation where he'd dropped it, addressing his remarks to both Hokusai and Jenkins.

"Damn that Link-Stevens postulate! Time after time it fails, until you figure there's nothing to it; then, this! It's black magic, not science, and if I get out, I'll find some fool with more courage than sense to discovery why. Hoke, are you positive it's the theta chain? There isn't once chance in ten thousand of that happening, you know; it's unstable, hard to stop, tends to revert to the simpler ones at the first chance."

Hokusai spread his hands, lifted one heavy eyelid at Jenkins questioningly, then nodded. The boy's voice was dull, almost uninterested. "That's what I thought it had to be, Palmer. None of the others throws off that much energy at this stage, the way you described conditions out there. Probably the last thing we tried to quench set it up in that pattern, and it's in a concentration just right to keep it going. We figured ten hours was the best chance, so it had to pick the six-hour short chain."

"Yeah." Palmer was pacing up and down nervously again, his eyes swinging toward Jorgenson from whatever direction he moved. "And in six hours, maybe all the population around here can be evacuated, maybe not, but we'll have to try it. Doc, I can't even wait for Jorgenson now! I've got to get the Governor started at once!"

"They've been known to practice lynch law, even in recent years," Ferrel reminded him grimly. He'd seen the result of one such case of mob violence when he was practicing privately, and he knew that people remain pretty much the same year after year; they'd move, but first they'd demand a sacrifice. "Better get the men out of here first, Palmer, and my advice is to get yourself a good long distance off; I heard some of the trouble at the gate, and that won't be anything compared to what an evacuation order will do."

Palmer grunted. "Doc, you might not believe it, but I don't give a continental about what happens to me or the plant right now."

"Or the men? Put a mob in here, hunting your blood, and the men will be on your side, because they know it wasn't your fault, and they've seen you out there taking chances yourself. That mob won't be too choosy about its targets, either, once it gets worked up, and you'll have a nice vicious brawl all over the place. Besides, Jorgenson's practically ready."

A few minutes would make no difference in the evacuation, and Doc had no desire to think of his partially crippled wife going through the hell evacuation would be; she'd probably refuse, until he returned. His eyes fell on the box Jenkins was playing with nervously, and he stalled for time. "I thought you said it was risky to break the stuff down into small particles, Jenkins. But that box contains the stuff in various sizes, including one big piece we scraped out, along with the contaminated instruments. Why hasn't it exploded?"

Jenkins' hand jerked up from it as if burned, and he backed away a step before checking himself. Then he was across the room toward the I-231 and back, pouring the white powder over everything in the box in a jerky frenzy. Hokusai's eyes had snapped fully open, and he was slopping water in to fill up the remaining space and keep the I-231 in contact with everything else. Almost at once, in spite of the low relative energy release, it sent up a white cloud of steam faster than the air conditioner could clear the room; but that soon faded down and disappeared.

Hokusai wiped his forehead slowly. "The ssuits—armor of the men?"

"Sent 'em back to the converter and had them dumped into the stuff to be safe long ago," Jenkins answered. "But I forgot the box, like a fool. Ugh! Either blind chance saved us or else the stuff spit out was all one kind, some reasonably long chain. I don't know nor care right—"

"S'ot! Nnnuh…Whmah nahh?"

"Jorgenson!" They swung from the end of the room like one man, but Jenkins was the first to reach the table. Jorgenson's eyes were open and rolling in a semiorderly manner, his hands moving sluggishly. The boy hovered over his face, his own practically glowing with the intensity behind it. "Jorgenson, can you understand what I'm saying?"

"Uh." The eyes ceased moving and centered on Jenkins. One hand came up to his throat, clutching at it, and he tried unsuccessfully to lift himself with the other, but the aftereffects of what he'd been through seemed to have left him in a state of partial paralysis.

Ferrel had hardly dared hope that the man could be rational, and his relief was tinged with doubt. He pushed Palmer back, and shook his head. "No, stay back. Let the boy handle it; he knows enough not to shock the man now, and you don't. This can't be rushed too much."

"I—uh…Young Jenkins? Whasha doin' here? Tell y'ur dad to ge' busy ou' there!" Somewhere in Jorgenson's huge frame, an untapped reserve of energy and will sprang up, and he forced himself into a sitting position, his eyes on Jenkins, his hand still catching at the reluctant throat that refused to co-operate. His words were blurry and uncertain, but sheer determination overcame the obstacles and made the words understandable.

"Dad's dead now, Jorgenson. Now—"

" 'Sright. 'N' you're grown up—'bout twelve years old, y' were… The plant!"

"Easy, Jorgenson." Jenkins' own voice managed to sound casual, though his hands under the table were white where they clenched together. "Listen, and don't try to say anything until I finish. The plant's still all right, but we've got to have your help. Here's what happened."

Ferrel could make little sense of the cryptic sentences that followed, though he gathered that they were some form of engineering short-hand; apparently, from Hokusai's approving nod, they summed up the situation briefly, and Jorgenson sat rigidly still until it was finished, his eyes fastened on the boy.

"Helluva mess! Gotta think…yuh tried—" He made an attempt to lower himself back, and Jenkins assisted him, hanging on feverishly to each awkward, uncertain change of expression on the man's face. "Uh…da' sroat! Yuh…uh…urrgh!"

"Got it?"

"Uh!" The tone was affirmative, unquestionably, but the clutching hands around his neck told their own story. The temporary burst of energy he'd forced was exhausted, and he couldn't get through with it. He lay there, breathing heavily and struggling, then relaxed after a few more half-whispered words, none intelligently articulated.

Palmer clutched at Ferrel's sleeve. "Doc, isn't there anything you can do?"

"Try." He metered out a minute quantity of drug doubtfully, felt Jorgenson's pulse, and decided on half that amount. "Not much hope, though; that man's been through hell, and it wasn't good for him to be forced around in the first place. Carry it too far, and he'll be delirious if he does talk. Anyway, I suspect it's partly his speech centers as well as the throat."

But Jorgenson began a slight rally almost instantly, trying again, then apparently drawing himself together for a final attempt. When they came, the words spilled out harshly in forced clearness, but without inflection. "First...variable...at...twelve...water...stop." His eyes, centered on Jenkins, closed, and he relaxed again, this time no longer fighting off the inevitable unconsciousness.

Houksai, Palmer, and Jenkins were staring back and forth at one another questioningly. The little Japanese shook his head negatively at first, frowned, and repeated it, to be imitated almost exactly by the manager. "Delirious ravings!"

"The great white hope Jorgenson!" Jenkins' shoulders drooped and the blood drained from his face, leaving it ghastly with fatigue and despair. "Oh, damn it, Doc, stop staring at me! I can't pull a miracle out of a hat!"

Doc hadn't realized that he was staring, but he made no effort to change it. "Maybe not, but you happen to have the most active imagination here, when you stop abusing it to scare yourself. Well, you're on the spot now, and I'm still giving odds on you. Want to bet, Hoke?"

It was an utterly stupid thing, and Doc knew it; but somewhere during the long hours together, he'd picked up a queer respect for the boy and a dependence on the nervousness that wasn't fear but closer akin to the reaction of a rear-running thoroughbred on the home stretch. Hoke was too slow and methodical, and Palmer had been too concerned with outside worries to give anywhere nearly full attention to the single most urgent phase of the problem; that left only Jenkins, hampered by his lack of self-confidence.

Hoke gave no sign that he caught the meaning of Doc's heavy wink, but he lifted his eyebrows faintly. "No, I think I am not bet. Dr. Jenkins, I am to be command!"

Palmer looked briefly at the boy, whose face mirrored incredulous confusion, but he had neither Ferrel's ignorance of atomic technique nor Hokusai's fatalism. With a final glance at the unconscious Jorgenson, he started across the room toward the phone. "You men play, if you like. I'm starting evacuation immediately!"

"Wait!" Jenkins was shaking himself, physically as well as mentally. "Hold it, Palmer! Thanks, Doc. You knocked me out of the rut, and bounced my memory back to something I picked up somewhere; I think it's the answer! It has to work—nothing else can at this stage of the game!"

"Give me the Governor, operator." Palmer had heard, but he went on with the phone call. "This is no time to play crazy hunches until after we get the people out, kid. I'll admit you're a darned clever amateur, but you're no atomicist!"

"And if we get the men out, it's too late—there'll be no one left in here to do the work!" Jenkins' hand snapped out and jerked the receiver of the plug-in telephone from Palmer's hand. "Cancel the call, operator; it won't be necessary. Palmer, you've got to listen to me; you can't clear the whole middle of the continent, and you can't depend on the explosion to limit itself to less ground. It's a gamble, but you're risking fifty million people against a mere hundred thousand. Give me a chance!"

"I'll give you exactly one minute to convince me, Jenkins, and it had better be good! Maybe the blow-up won't hit beyond the fifty-mile limit!"

"Maybe. And I can't explain in a minute." The boy scowled tensely, "O.K., you've been bellyaching about a man named Kellar being dead. If he were here, would you take a chance on him? Or on a man who'd worked under him on everything he tried?"

"Absolutely, but you're not Kellar. And I happen to know he was a lone wolf; didn't hire outside engineers after Jorgenson had a squabble with him and came here." Palmer reached for the phone. "It won't wash, Jenkins."

Jenkins' hand clamped down on the instrument, jerking it out of reach. "I wasn't outside help, Palmer. When Jorgenson was afraid to run one of the things off and quit, I was twelve; three years later, things got too tight for him to handle alone, but he decided he might as well keep it in the family, so he started me in. I'm Kellar's stepson!"

Pieces clicked together in Doc's head then, and he kicked himself mentally for not having seen the obvious before. "That why Jorgenson knew you, then? I thought that was funny. It checks, Palmer."

For a split second, the manager hesitated uncertainly. Then he shrugged and gave in. "O.K., I'm a fool to trust you, Jenkins, but it's too late for anything else, I guess. I never forgot that I was gambling the locality against half the continent. What do you want?"

"Men—construction men, mostly, and a few volunteers for dirty work. I want all the blowers, exhaust equipment, tubing, booster blowers, and everything ripped from the other three converters and connected as close to No. 4 as you can get. Put them up some way so they can be shoved in over the stuff by crane—I don't care how; the shop men will know better than I do. You've got sort of a river running off behind the plant; get everyone within a few miles of it out of there, and connect the blower outlets down to it. Where does it end, anyway—some kind of a swamp, or morass?"

"About ten miles farther down, yes; we didn't bother keeping the drainage system going, since the land meant nothing to us, and the swamps made as good a dumping ground as anything else." When the plant had first used the little river as an outlet for their waste products, there'd been so much trouble that National had been forced to take over all adjacent land and quiet the owners' fears of the atomic activity in cold cash. Since then, it had gone to weeds and rabbits, mostly, "Everyone within a few miles is out, anyway, except a few fishers or tramps that don't know we use it. I'll have militia sent in to scare them out."

"Good. Ideal, in fact, since the swamps will hold stuff in there where the current's slow longer. Now, what about that superthermite stuff you were producing last year. Any around?"

"Not in the plant. But we've got tons of it at the warehouse, still waiting for the army's requisition. That's pretty hot stuff to handle though. Know much about it?"

"Enough to know it's what I want." Jenkins indicated the copy of the *Weekly Ray* still lying where he'd dropped it, and Doc remembered skimming through the nontechnical part of the description. It was made up of two superheavy atoms, kept separate. By itself, neither was particularly important or active, but together they reacted with each other atomically to release a tremendous amount of raw heat and comparatively little unwanted radiation. "Goes up around twenty thousand centigrade, doesn't it? How's it stored?"

"In ten-pound bombs that have a fragile partition; it breaks with shock, starting the action. Hoke can explain it—it's his baby." Palmer reached for the phone. "Anything else? Then, get out and get busy! The men will be ready for you when you get there! I'll be out myself as soon as I can put through your orders."

Doc watched them go out, to be followed in short order by the manager, and was alone in the Infirmary with Jorgenson and his thoughts. They weren't pleasant; he was both too far outside the inner circle to know what was going on and too much mixed up in it not to know the dangers. Now he could have used some work of any nature to take his mind off useless speculations, but aside from a needless check of the foreman's condition, there was nothing for him to do.

He wriggled down in the leather chair, making the mistake of trying to force sleep, while his mind chased out after the sounds that came in from outside. There were the drones of crane and tank motors coming to life, the shouts of hurried orders, and above all, the jarring rhythm of pneumatic hammers on metal, each sound suggesting some possibility to him without adding to his knowledge. The *Decameron* was boring, the whiskey tasted raw and rancid, and solitaire wasn't worth the trouble of cheating.

Finally, he gave up and turned out to the field hospital tent. Jorgenson would be better off out there, under the care of the staff from Mayo's, and perhaps he could make himself useful. As he passed through the rear entrance, he heard the sound of a number of helicopters coming over with heavy loads, and looked up as they began settling over the edge of the buildings. From somewhere, a group of men came running forward, and disappeared in the direction of the freighters. He wondered whether any of those men would be forced back into the stuff out there to return filled with radioactive; though it didn't matter so much, now that the isotope could be eliminated without surgery.

Blake met him at the entrance of the field tent, obviously well satisfied with his duty of bossing and instructing the others. "Scram, Doc. You aren't necessary here, and you need some rest. Don't want you added to the casualties. What's the latest dope from the powwow front?"

"Jorgenson didn't come through, but the kid had an idea, and they're out there working on it." Doc tried to sound more hopeful than he felt. "I was thinking you might as well bring Jorgenson in here; he's conscious, but there doesn't seem to be anything to worry about. Where's Brown? She'll probably want to know what's up, if she isn't asleep."

"Asleep when the kid isn't? Uh-huh. Mother complex, has to worry about him." Blake grinned. "She got a look at him running out with Hoke tagging at his heels, and hiked out after him, so she probably knows everything now. Wish Anne'd chase me that way, just once—Jenkins, the wonder boy! Well, it's out of my line; I don't intend to start worrying until they pass out the order. O.K., Doc, I'll have Jorgenson out here in a couple of minutes, so you grab yourself a cot and get some shut-eye."

Doc grunted, looking curiously at the refinements and well-equipped interior of the field tent. "I've already prescribed that, Blake, but the patient can't seem to take it. I think I'll hunt up Brown, so give me a call over the public speaker if anything turns up."

He headed toward the center of action, knowing that he'd been wanting to do it all along, but hadn't been sure of not being a nuisance. Well, if Brown could look on, there was no reason why he couldn't. He passed the machine shop, noting the excited flurry of activity going on, and went past No. 2, where other men were busily ripping out long sections of big piping and various other devices. There was a rope fence barring his way, well beyond No. 3, and he followed along the edge, looking for Palmer or Brown.

She saw him first. "Hi, Dr. Ferrel, over here in the truck. I thought you'd be coming soon. From up here we can get a look over the heads of all these other people, and we won't be tramped on." She stuck down a hand to help him up, smiled faintly as he disregarded it and mounted more briskly than his muscles wanted to. He wasn't so old that a girl had to help him yet.

"Know what's going on?" he asked, sinking down onto the plank across the truck body, facing out across the men below toward the converter. There seemed to be a dozen different centers of activity, all crossing each other in complete confusion, and the general pattern was meaningless.

"No more than you do. I haven't seen my husband, though Mr. Palmer took time enough to chase me here out of the way."

Doc centered his attention on the copters, unloading, rising, and coming in with more loads, and he guessed that those boxes must contain the little thermodyne bombs. It was the one thing he could understand, and consequently the least interesting. Other men were assembling the big sections of piping he'd seen before, connecting them up in almost endless order, while some of the tanks hooked on and snaked them off in the direction of the small river that ran off beyond the plant.

"Those must be the exhaust blowers, I guess," he told Brown, pointing them out. "Though I don't know what any of the rest of the stuff hooked on is."

"I know—I've been inside the plant Bob's father had." She lifted an inquiring eyebrow at him, went on as he nodded. "The pipes are for exhaust gases, all right, and those big square things are the motors and fans—they put in one at each five hundred feet or less of piping. The things they're wrapping around the pipe must be the heaters to keep the gases hot. Are they going to try to suck all that out?"

Doc didn't know, though it was the only thing he could see. But he wondered how they'd get around the problem of moving in close enough to do any good. "I heard your husband order some thermodyne bombs, so they'll probably try to gassify the magma; then they're pumping it down the river."

As he spoke, there was a flurry of motion at one side, and his eyes swung over instantly, to see one of the cranes laboring with a long framework stuck from its front, holding up a section of pipe with a nozzle on the end. It tilted precariously, even though heavy bags were well piled everywhere to add weight, but an inch at a time it lifted its load and began forcing its way forward, carrying the nozzle out in front and rather high.

Below the main exhaust pipe was another smaller one. As it drew near the outskirts of the danger zone, a small object ejaculated from the little pipe, hit the ground, and was a sudden blazing inferno of glaring blue-white light, far brighter than it seemed, judging by the effect on the eyes. Doc shielded his, just as someone below put something into his hands.

"Put 'em on. Palmer says the light's actinic."

He heard Brown fussing beside him, then his vision cleared, and he looked back through the goggles again to see a glowing cloud spring up from the magma, spread out near the ground, narrowing down higher up, until it sucked into the nozzle above, and disappeared. Another bomb slid from the tube, and erupted with blazing heat. A sideways glance followed another crane being fitted, and a group of men near it wrapping what might have been oiled rags around the small bombs; probably no tubing fitted them exactly, and they were padding them so pressure could blow them forward and out. Three more dropped from the tube one at a time, and the fans roared and groaned, pulling the cloud that rose into the pipe and feeding it down toward the river.

Then the crane inched back out carefully as men uncoupled its piping from the main line, and a second went in to replace it. The heat generated must be too great for the machine to stand steadily without the pipe fusing, Doc decided; though they couldn't have kept a man inside the heavily armored cab for any length of time, if the metal had been impervious. Now another crane was ready, and went in from another place; it settled down to a routine of ingoing and outcoming cranes, and men feeding materials in, coupling and uncoupling the pipes and replacing the others who came from the cabs. Doc began to feel like a man at a tennis match, watching the ball without knowing the rules.

Brown must have had the same idea, for she caught Ferrel's arm and indicated a little leather case that came from her handbag. "Doc, do you play chess? We might as well fill our time with that as sitting here on the edge, just watching. It's supposed to be good for nerves."

He seized on it gratefully, without explaining that he'd been city champion three years running; he'd take it easy, watch her game, handicap himself just enough to make it interesting by the deliberate loss of a rook, bishop, or knight, as was needed to even the odds—Suppose they got all the magma out and into the river; how did that solve the problem? It removed it from the plant, but far less than the fifty-mile minimum danger limit.

"Check," Brown announced. He castled, and looked up at the half-dozen cranes that were now operating. "Check! Checkmate!"

He looked back again hastily, then, to see her queen guarding all possible moves, a bishop checking him. Then his eye followed down toward her end. "Umm. Did you know you've been in check for the last half-dozen moves? Because I didn't."

She frowned, shook her head, and began setting the men up again, Doc moved out the queen's pawn, looked out at the workers, and then brought out the king's bishop, to see her take it with her king's pawn. He hadn't watched her move it out, and had counted on her queen's to block his. Things would require more careful watching on this little portable set. The men were moving steadily and there was a growing clear space, but as they went forward, the violent action of the thermodyne had pitted the ground, carefully as it had been used, and going become more uncertain. Time was slipping by rapidly now.

"Checkmate!" He found himself in a hole, started to nod; but she caught herself this time. "Sorry, I've been playing my king for a queen, Doctor, let's see if we can play at least one game right."

Before it was half finished, it became obvious that they couldn't. Neither had chess very much on the mind, and the pawns and men did fearful and wonderful things, while the knights were as likely to jump six squares as their normal L. They gave it up, just as one of the cranes lost its precarious balance and toppled forward, dropping the long extended pipe into the bubbling mass below. Tanks were in instantly, hitching on and tugging backward until it came down with a thump as the pipe fused, releasing the extreme forward load. It backed out on its own power, while another went in. The driver, by sheer good luck, hobbled from the cab, waving an armored hand to indicate he was all right. Things settled back to an excited routine again that seemed to go on endlessly, though seconds were dropping off too rapidly, turning into minutes that threatened to be hours far too soon.

"Uh!" Brown had been staring for some time, but her little feet suddenly came down with a bang and she straightened up, her hand to her mouth. "Doctor, I just thought; it won't do any good—all this!"

"Why?" She couldn't know anything, but he felt the faint hopes he had go downward sharply. His nerves were dulled, but still ready to jump at the slightest warning.

"The stuff they were making was a superheavy—it'll sink as soon as it hits the water, and all pile up right there! It won't float down river!"

Obvious, Ferrel thought; too obvious. Maybe that was why the engineers hadn't thought of it. He started from the plank, just as Palmer stepped up, but the manager's hand on his shoulder forced him back.

"Easy Doc, it's O.K. Umm, so they teach women some science nowadays, Mrs. Jenkins...Sue...Dr. Brown, whatever your name is? Don't worry about it, though—the old principle of Brownian movement will keep any colloid suspended, if it's fine enough to be a real colloid. We're sucking it out and keeping it pretty hot until it reaches the water—then it cools off so fast it hasn't time to collect in particles big enough to sink. Some of the dust that floats around in the air is heavier than water, too. I'm joining the bystanders, if you don't mind; the men have everything under control, and I can see better here than I could down there, if anything does come up."

Doc's momentary despair reacted to leave him feeling more sure of things than was justified. He pushed over on the plank, making room for Palmer to drop down beside him. "What's to keep it from blowing up anyway, Palmer?"

"Nothing! Got a match?" He sucked in on the cigarette heavily, relaxing as much as he could. "No use trying to fool you, Doc, at this stage of the game. We're gambling, and I'd say the odds are even; Jenkins thinks they're ninety to ten in his favor, but he has to think so. What we're hoping is that by lifting it out in a gas, thus breaking it down at once from full concentration to the finest possible form, and letting it settle in the water in colloidal particles, there won't be a concentration at any one place sufficient to set it all off at once. The big problem is making sure we get every bit of it cleaned out here, or there may be enough left to take care of us and the nearby city! At least, since the last change, it's stopped spitting, so all the man have to worry about is burn!"

"How much damage, even if it doesn't go off all at once?"

"Possibly none. If you can keep it burning slowly, a million tons of dynamite wouldn't be any worse than the same amount of wood, but a stick going off at once will kill you. Why the dickens didn't Jenkins tell me he wanted to go into atomics? We could have fixed all that—it's hard enough to get good men as it is!"

Brown perked up, forgetting the whole trouble beyond them, and went into the story with enthusiasm, while Ferrel only partly listened. He could see the spot of magma growing steadily smaller, but the watch on his wrist went on ticking off minutes remorselessly, and the time was growing limited. He hadn't realized before how long he'd been sitting there. Now three of the crane nozzles were almost touching, and around them stretched the burned-out ground, with no sign of converter, masonry, or anything else; the heat from the thermodyne had gassified everything, indiscriminately.

"Palmer!" The portable ultrawave set around the manager's neck came to life suddenly. "Hey, Palmer, these blowers are about shot; the pipe's pitting already. We've been doing everything we can to replace them, but that stuff eats faster than we can fix. Can't hold up more'n fifteen minutes more."

"Check, Briggs. Keep 'em going the best you can." Palmer flipped the switch and looked out toward the tank standing by behind the cranes. "Jenkins, you get that?"

"Yeah. Surprised they held out this long. How much time till deadline?" The boy's voice was completely toneless, neither hope nor nerves showing up, only the complete weariness of a man almost at his limit.

Palmer looked and whistled. "Twelve minutes, according to the minimum estimate Hoke made! How much left?"

"We're just burning around now, trying to make sure there's no pocket left; I hope we've got the whole works, but I'm not promising. Might as well send out all the I-231 you have and we'll boil it down the pipes to clear out any deposits on them. All the old treads and parts that contacted the R gone into the pile?"

"You melted the last, and your cranes haven't touched the stuff directly. Nice pile of money's gone down that pipe—converter, machinery, everything!"

Jenkins made a sound that was expressive of his worry about that. "I'm coming in now and starting the clearing of the pipe. What've you been paying insurance for?"

"At a lovely rate, too! O.K., come on in, kid; and if you're interested, you can start sticking A.E. after the M.D., any time you want. Your wife's been giving me your qualifications, and I think you've passed the final test, so you're now an atomic engineer, duly graduated from National!"

Brown's breath caught, and her eyes seemed to glow, even through the goggles, but Jenkins' voice was flat. "O.K., I expected you to give me one if we don't blow up. But you'll have to see Dr. Ferrel about it; he's got a contract with me for medical practice. Be there shortly."

Nine of the estimated twelve minutes had ticked by when he climbed up beside them, mopping off some of the sweat that covered him, and Palmer was hugging the watch. More minutes ticked off slowly, while the last sound faded out in the plant, and the men stood around, staring down toward the river or at the hole that had been No. 4. Silence. Jenkins stirred, and grunted.

"Palmer, I know where I got the idea, now. Jorgenson was trying to remind me of it, instead of raving, only I didn't get it, at least consciously. It was one of dad's, the one he told Jorgenson was a last resort, in case the thing they broke up about went haywire. It was the first variable dad tried. I was twelve, and he insisted water would break it up into all its chains and kill the danger. Only dad didn't really expect it to work!"

Palmer didn't look up from the watch, but he caught his breath and swore. "Fine time to tell me that!"

"He didn't have your isotopes to heat it up with, either," Jenkins answered mildly. "Suppose you look up from that watch of yours for a minute, down the river."

As Doc raised his eyes, he was aware suddenly of a roar from the men. Over to the south, stretching out in a huge mass, was a cloud of steam that spread upward and out as he watched, and the beginnings of a mighty hissing sound came in. Then Palmer was hugging Jenkins and yelling until Brown could pry him away and replace him.

"Ten miles or more of river, plus the swamps, Doc!" Palmer was shouting in Ferrel's ear. "All that dispersion, while it cooks slowly from now until the last chain is finished, atom by atom! The theta chain broke, unstable, and now there's everything there, too scattered to set itself off! It'll cook the river bed up and dry it, but that's all!"

Doc was still dazed, unsure of how to take the relief. He wanted to lie down and cry or to stand up with the men and shout his head off. Instead, he sat loosely, gazing at the cloud. "So I lose the best assistant I ever had! Jenkins, I won't hold you; you're free for whatever Palmer wants."

"Hoke wants him to work on R—he's got the stuff for his bomb now!" Palmer was clapping his hands together slowly, like an excited child watching a steam shovel. "Heck, Doc, pick out anyone you want until your own boy gets out next year. You wanted a chance to work him in here, now you've got it. Right now I'll give you anything you want."

"You might see what you can do about hospitalizing the injured and fixing things up with the men in the tent behind the Infirmary. And I think I'll take Brown in Jenkins' place, with the right to grab him in all emergency, until that year's up."

"Done." Palmer slapped the boy's back, stopping the protest, while Brown winked at him. "Your wife likes working, kid; she told me that herself. Besides, a lot of the women work here where they can keep an eye on their men; my own wife does, usually. Doc, take these two kids and head for home, where I'm going myself. Don't come back until you get good and ready, and don't let them start fighting about it!"

Doc pulled himself from the truck and started off with Brown and Jenkins following, through the yelling, relief-crazed men. The three were too thoroughly worn out for any exhibition themselves, but they could feel it. Happy ending! Jenkins and Brown where they wanted to be, Hoke with his bomb, Palmer with proof that atomic plants were safe where they were, and he—well, his boy would start out right, with himself and the widely differing but competent Blake and Jenkins to guide him. It wasn't a bad life, after all.

Then he stopped and chuckled. "You two wait for me, will you? If I leave here without making out that order of extra disinfection at the showers, Blake'll swear I'm growing old and feeble-minded. I can't have that."

Old? Maybe a little tired, but he'd been that before, and with luck would be again. He wasn't worried. His nerves were good for twenty years and fifty accidents more, and by that time Blake would be due for a little ribbing himself.

The New England Science Fiction Association (NESFA) and NESFA Press

Select books from NESFA Press

Brothers in Arms by Lois McMaster Bujold $25
Works of Art by James Blish $29
Years in the Making: The Time Travel Stories of L. Sprague de Camp ... $25
The Mathematics of Magic: The Enchanter Stories of de Camp and Pratt .. $26
Transfinite by A.E. van Vogt $29
Silverlock by John Myers Myers $26
Threshold: Vol 1 of the Collected Stories of Roger Zelazny $29
Power and Light: Vol 2 of the Collected Stories of Roger Zelazny .. $29
Once Upon a Time (She Said) by Jane Yolen $26
From Other Shores: An Omnibus by Chad Oliver $26
Call Me Joe: Vol 1 of the Short Fiction of Poul Anderson $29
The Queen of Air and Darkness: Vol. 2 of Poul Anderson $29
Expecting Beowulf by Tom Holt (trade paper) $16
Adventures in the Dream Trade by Neil Gaiman (trade paper) $16
A New Dawn: The Don A. Stuart Stories of John W. Campbell, Jr. .. $29
Ingathering: The Complete People Stories of Zenna Henderson $25
The Rediscovery of Man: The Complete Short SF of Cordwainer Smith ... $25

Details on these and many more books are online at: www.nesfa.org/press/
Books may be ordered online or by writing to:

NESFA Press, PO Box 809, Framingham, MA 01701

We accept checks (in U.S$), Visa, or MasterCard. Add $4 P&H for one book, $8 for an order of two to five books, $2 per book for orders of six or more. (For addresses outside the U.S., please add $12 for one or two books, $36 for an order of three to five books, and $6 per book for six or more.) Please allow 3-4 weeks for delivery. (Overseas, allow 2 months or more.)

The New England Science Fiction Association

NESFA is an all-volunteer, non-profit organization of science fiction and fantasy fans. Besides publishing, our activities include running Boskone (New England's oldest SF convention) in February each year, producing a semi-monthly newsletter, holding discussion groups relating to the field, and hosting a variety of social events. If you are interested in learning more about us, we'd like to hear from you. Contact us at info@nesfa.org, or at the address above. Visit our web site at www.nesfa.org.

Editor's Acknowledgements

All NESFA Press publications are a communal effort. Although every project needs a chief (or two) to honcho, a great deal of work is done by people for whom written Science Fiction is a passion, and all strive to disseminate outstanding works of extremely talented and often neglected authors. We wish to thank our proofreaders: David Grubbs, Mark Olson, and Pat Sayre McCoy; the cover artist, John Picacio, with whom I've wanted to work for years; David Grubbs and Mark Olson, again, for guiding me through the intricacies of InDesign layout and offering sound and sage editorial advice, and John Picacio and Alice Lewis for cover design and layout. I'd also like to thank Elizabeth Ann Hull and Frederik Pohl for making sure I received the introductory material; and Barry Malzberg for agreeing to to project.

-SHS